100
Fiendish
Little
Frightmares

100 Fiendish Little Frightmares

Selected by

Stefan Dziemianowicz
Robert Weinberg
Martin H. Greenberg

BARNES
&NOBLE
BOOKS
NEW YORK

1997 Barnes & Noble Books

ISBN 0-7607-0144-X

Printed and bound in the United States of America

97 98 99 00 01   M   9 8 7 6 5 4 3 2 1

BVG

Contents

Introduction

Frightmare.

You won't find the word in any dictionary. According to standard usage, it doesn't exist. Nevertheless, its meaning is obvious.

Fright. A scare or fright.

Mare. An abridgment of "nightmare." A bad dream. The downside of the sleep cycle which, we are told, lasts for mere seconds although it may seem to go on forever.

Frightmare. A nightmare with the power to frighten. A frightening experience so powerful that it leaves one as distraught and disoriented as a nightmare.

Why break the rules of language and invent a new word to describe the stories you are about to read? Because sometimes the old words are not adequate to do the job. They outline the periphery but don't cut to the heart. They catalog the bones and vital organs but fail to capture the soul. They smugly assure you that the tally on the bill of goods is correct, but when you unwrap the package at home you discover you've been sold something other than what you thought you paid for.

The stories in *100 Fiendish Little Frightmares* tax the descriptive powers of standard usage. They abound with horrors so novel and unpredictable that they can't be encompassed by the usual words. Don D'Ammassa will introduce you to the creepiest narrator it will ever be your misfortune to meet in "Misadventures in the Skin Trade." H. P. Lovecraft will take you on a trip beneath the streets of New England that stretches back in time itself in "The Festival." Ramsey Campbell will show you things from a train window that will make you never want to take public transportation again in "Missed Connection." Lisa Tuttle will explore the dark corridors of childish fancy in "Dollburger," and Joe R. Lansdale the claustrophobic interior of a dwelling that is worse than haunted in "The Shaggy House." Elizabeth Engstrom will seat you at the table of a kindly woman with an unsavory pastime in "Grandma's Hobby." William F. Nolan will show how you can go home again but why you shouldn't in "Dark Winner." How better to grasp the far corners of fear these tales stretch to and hem in their horrors than with a word designed specifically for them.

Frightmares.

Of course, there's another reason why we broke the rules when titling this book. And that's because horror doesn't play by the rules. It tackles you from behind when you're not expecting it. It trips you in the dark. It takes you gently by the hand and slowly turns a skeleton's face toward you. It assures you "this won't hurt" before it bares fangs. It shows you that "the rules" are nothing but wishful thinking for the faint of heart, a whistling in the dark that they make with their last gasp.

Frightmares.

Stories that don't play by the rules. Stories whose only assurance is that they will come upon you swiftly, and work their dark magic in the shortest time possible.

Pleasant dreams.

May your frightmares last for only as long as you can endure them.

—*Stefan Dziemianowicz*
New York, 1997

3.47 AM

David Langford

Dekker was dreaming. There had been a scattering of bright misty colours, a curve of soft grass, a woman whose eyes and smile were the most wonderful thing in all the world . . . and then the dream went sour. It was as though swirls of ink were blending with clear water, as the dark familiar tints spread their stain over Dekker's private landscape. Without any special feeling of transition, Dekker was standing suddenly alone, fuzzily peering at the something odd which was happening to his bare arm. Without pain a round black hole opened in the flesh, and tiny hairs sprouted; tiny hairs that were insect feelers probing out into the air. He was ready with a Band-Aid, but they wriggled underneath it, and now more of the small dark holes were opening in him. He gritted his teeth, and felt the teeth crumbling with a ghastly painlessness like stubs of chalk or like the clay pipe-stems which still came to light when he dug the garden. With a sort of dreamy double-vision he seemed to be watching the next step from both inside and outside as his eyes, his eyes, the eyeballs themselves—

'No . . . !'

Suddenly the far-off corner of Dekker's mind which knew it was all a dream was in full command, and his private hell collapsed into a black stuffy bedroom, cramped arms and legs, a taste in the mouth as though some small furry animal had been nesting there—an animal of revoltingly unclean habits. He rubbed at his crusted eyes and painfully rolled over in bed towards the lurid glow of his bedside clock.

3.47 AM. Again.

His heart was beating like a disco drum, and messages of terror were squirting up and down his bloodstream. Gentle signals from his bladder suggested that a downstairs trip would be a clever idea: but Brian Dekker had been through all that before. Following these dreams there always came an afterwash of horror in which the darkness waited most terribly on the stairs, so for all their soft carpet they were about as inviting as the crumbled and slimy steps leading down into a graveyard vault. To turn on the light did not happen to be the answer; that simply pushed the dark into the blind doorways opening on the hall downstairs, and in those doorways it would wait coiled and compressed, ready somehow to leap out on you. Easier to stay in bed.

3.47 AM. Still trembling, he watched the red neon figures until (after what seemed like the best part of a week) they flickered to 3.48. Was this the fourth time or the fifth?

There wasn't anything miraculous about the figure 3.47. It just happened that when you turned on this smart digital clock, some inner kink set it to that time at once; you had to fiddle with the little buttons at the back to reset it correctly, and whenever there was a power cut it would jump straight back at 3.47 AM afterwards. Just one of those things. Dekker had bought the new clock because he'd found the remorseless ticking of clockwork often kept him awake unless he hid the old alarm-clock in a drawer or under the bed—in which case the alarm was too muffled to wake him next morning. Now the electronic clock had a banshee scream which sliced clean through all the layers of sleep and bedding Dekker could wrap himself in: the only small problem was its red glow, faint by day but glaring in the dark, just visible even through closed eyelids. He'd solved *that* problem by sleeping on his other side—a triumph of original thinking, a victory of a man over machine. Now all he had to worry about was this tendency to wake up in the small hours with a strangled breathless grunt—a grunt which would be something more except that he was usually fully awake before he could gulp enough air to power a scream.

Five nights, then. Five in a row. Five times, the things he hated most in all the world: insect feelers against the skin, teeth crumbling and splitting because he hated dentists, and, because the worst things he could imagine happening to anybody were blindness and deformity, his eyes would—

No. Not to think about that, here in the stifling dark. Concentrate on real things, Dekker told himself, safe sharp-edged events, true facts, like in detective fiction.

Very well, Inspector, he thought. I'll tell you all I know. I dream the same dream every night—every night now for a week. That makes five times. This dream is, is . . . the way I've already described it. Each night I wake up terrified at just 3.47 AM. Yes, too scared to get out of bed—ridiculous isn't it? Of course I've tried sleeping pills. I'm not a fool, you know, I can feel them sucking me back down again now as I lie here, but every night for the last five nights there's been this hammerblow of fear, a million times stronger than the pills, five nights in a row . . .

Every night since I bought the clock? Why, yes. That's very significant, I'm sure.

Then the pills grabbed him and hauled him back down into a safe warm darkness where there were no dreams, no thoughts, nothing but the momentary glimpse of a pale brown woman whose features were not quite those of the Indians or Pakistanis he met in town or at work . . .

In the morning the clock shrieked efficiently, and Dekker fumbled his way downstairs in a stale reek of sweat, groaning under a headache which he reckoned was in the brain-haemorrhage class. One, two, three paracetamol tablets with his breakfast coffee, and the third stuck on his tongue to leave a foul-tasting track as though slugs had been crawling down his throat. The slight psychological uplift of vigorous washing, shaving and brushing of teeth left him feeling no better: he thought about work, about checking balance sheets and preparing VAT statements, shuddered slightly, and went to the telephone.

'Hello—Jenkins and Grey? That's right, luv, Brian Dekker . . . Can you tell Mr Grey I'll be off sick today? Thanks . . . Bye.'

The doctor agreed.

'You need a rest, I expect. Been working too hard.'

'I get these bad dreams,' Dekker began to tell him.

'Working far too hard. Your card says you haven't taken sick-leave for three years. Ridiculous. We all need a rest sometime.'

'I sort of wake up every night, about the same time—'

'Prescribing you a tonic: here. Chit for a week off work: here. Come and see me again if you don't feel better in a week. Next!'

'Yes, but about these nightmares—'

'Take it easy, take the tonic. Next!'

Dekker hadn't very much faith in the bottle of gooey liquid into which the chemist translated his prescription. He decided to take a few extra safety precautions of his own, and on the way home he paused at the supermarket to pick up a bottle of medium-cheap scotch whisky. For the rest of the day he loafed about, reading detective stories ('But surely, Inspector—') and the newspapers (NEW STRIKE THREAT, MIDDLE EAST CRISIS, MALAY SWEATSHOP SCANDAL) while upstairs the clock counted off its silent, red-glowing minutes.

At eight in the evening Dekker warmed a dubiously Cornish pasty in the oven, and ate it with baked beans.

At nine, the washing-up cleared away, he opened the whisky bottle and poured himself a large glass, neat. He didn't much like whisky . . . but he thought he might as well try it in style. Cheers! And he raised his glass to the half-opened hall door, and to the gathering, lurking darkness out there.

At ten he was trying to remember the words of a song, which were right on the tip of his tongue, just a matter of fitting them to the tune, how did it go, *Tum tummity tum* . . . that was funny, he couldn't quite remember the tune, but all the time there was a gentle singing in his head. Somehow the level in the scotch bottle had gone down rather a long way. With a feeling of immense devotion to duty, he fumbled after the doctor's tonic-bottle and—after some unsuccessful attempts to balance a five-millilitre teaspoon—took a generous swig. The taste sent him staggering hastily back to the whisky.

At eleven he had the sudden, terrible feeling of being absolutely cold sober with chilly winds whistling through his brain—except that his arms and legs wouldn't move properly. But as he sat there, the pictures lit up in his brain with a dreadful clarity. He remembered how the insect feelers would come writhing from his flesh with a tiny wink and gleam of chitin. He remembered the painless horror of teeth which crumbled and sheared like soft shale. He remembered, he tried not to remember, the feeling of his head being blown up like a balloon, the eyeballs which bulged until the lids wouldn't close no matter how hard he screwed them shut, his eyes bulging until—

'No, no, nooooo,' he moaned, trying to stand up and falling.

—until they burst in small wet explosions of jelly, like squeezed pimples or boils, the stuff running down his cheeks in enormous slow tears while tattered remnants of eyeball dangled from the sockets . . .

He managed to pour more whisky, more of it into his lap than into the glass. He tilted the glass against numb lips, and spilt more. The whole room was humming and swaying. The glass slithered from his fingers.

At midnight he was unconscious.

At 3.47 AM he was unconscious.

At 10.45 next morning, he stirred.

Later, having emptied his stomach a few times and dosed his massive new headache, Dekker thought again about his sleeping problem.

'That wasn't a whatsit, a controlled experiment,' he said aloud. 'Maybe being drunk keeps off the nightmares all right . . . but if that damned clock has anything to do with it, I might just have missed the dream because I never went upstairs to sleep at all . . .'

'Maybe I should just get rid of the clock. But that's *silly*. It's just *superstition*. It's not a hanged man's skull or an evil talisman from Transylvania. It's just a blasted clock and only a few months old at that—only a few weeks, maybe . . .'

He spent another quiet, aching afternoon. A photograph in *The*

Times—more about electronic-component sweatshops in Malaya—caught his eye. The women who put together radios for a few pence a day because there was nowhere else to work . . . the women in the picture looked familiar for a moment, and then not familiar at all when he peered at them more closely. That was the only odd moment in the whole long day.

That evening he still wasn't feeling a hundred-per-cent fit, but a night without the dream had given him more confidence. He thumbed his nose at the clock as he clambered into bed; he pulled up the blankets and let the friendly dark snuggle round him; he drifted into sleep.

And after many adventures in strange glowing countries, he was caught again in the evil dream. Helplessly he wandered into the dark, into the stained dream-place where things with legs erupted from his skin, where teeth met grittily and gave way, where eyes ballooned hideously . . .

Dekker woke gasping from the old hammerblow of dread, to see the figures 3.47 glowing in the night. He clicked on the bedside light to push the dark a little further away, and lay trembling and sweating, his mind an empty map of horror into which, from nowhere that he could tell, there drifted the memory that the longest and most complicated dreams are supposed to take only a few seconds of real time. One could cram a lot of frightfulness into those seconds, he thought as he lay there with a small child's fear of the dark and resisted the urge to pull sheets and blankets up over his head. Like colours in a slowly turning prism, his fear shifted into exhaustion and the exhaustion to drowsiness; adrift from body and bed and 3.47 AM, Dekker sank into the cloudy shapes of almost-sleep. There, for a moment, a pale brown woman's face peered at him with an uncomfortable smile. *It's nothing personal, but*—Or had she said something else, wordlessly? Her hands were busy with a dismantled digital clock.

It was as if a switch had been thrown in Dekker's head. The connection was made in showers of brilliant sparks, shocking him into rigidity. The night became neutral, empty of evil and of sleep, as he connected the familiar dream-face (*so* familiar, surely he'd glimpsed it each night of the dream) with that photo in *The Times*. Women at an assembly line. MALAY SWEATSHOP SCANDAL. He sat up and reached for the clock, which now showed a safe 3.50. It hummed in his hand as he lifted it, like some warm living thing stiff with fear, whose heart beat so desperately as to make a low buzz. It had come from one of those mail-order discount firms whose goods carried no trademarks or brand names, familiar or not. On the back though, he saw as he turned it over . . . on the back, stamped into the thin plastic casing, it said: MALAYA.

He almost smiled as he put down the clock, turned off the light, prepared for another attempt at the unclimbable north face of sleep. Imagine that.

Imagine some ill-treated Malayan lady in an electronic sweatshop, taking her own little bit of industrial action by building an occasional curse into the circuits she put together all day long for so little money. He wanted to chuckle at the silliness of the idea, but the chuckle was lost in a sourceless feeling that to let it out might be unsafe.

It's hardly fair, he thought. What did I ever do to her?

Well, he replied, I suppose you did buy this cheapo-cheapo clock and helped keep her rotten employers in business.

But . . . ridiculous. I mean, how can you believe in a politically motivated curse? The right to work, the right to strike, the right to stick pins in wax images?

But . . . well, then, why *not*?

In the morning, nursing yet another headache, Dekker looked through the newspapers and found two photos of oppressed Malayan women. He was disturbed to find that even though the faces there had a kind of family resemblance to the dull-golden face of his dreams, none of them looked quite like it. You might say that proved the dream-face wasn't just a figment smuggled into his mind by study of *The Times*. You might say that proved, even, that it was real.

He ate his bacon (greasy) and eggs (burst, like . . . never mind that), and went upstairs for the battered copy of the book on magic and religion which he'd bought years back. Frazer's *The Golden Bough*, that was it. It came to light amid piles of old science fiction magazines in what estate agents called the second bedroom and Dekker called the junk room.

The abridged *Golden Bough* (good grief, the full version ran to twelve volumes) mentioned Malays quite a few times in the index. Dekker went through them all. The very first dealt with wax images and cheerfully mentioned: *'pierce the eye of the image, and your enemy is blind'*. He closed the book convulsively. He didn't want to hear about eyes.

Well, if he dismantled the clock, was he going to find some wax model of a corpse lurking in between the integrated circuits? Unfortunately the thing was a sealed unit: to take it apart was to destroy it. Which mightn't be a bad idea, at that; certainly it was something to keep in reserve. He opened the book again, and on page 105 found: *'The Malays think that a bright glow at sunset may throw a weak person into a fever.'* So what, then, would they think of neon figures glaring red all night long? Onward . . . *'Nowhere perhaps is the art of abducting human souls more carefully culti-vated or carried to higher perfection than in the Malay Peninsula.'*

There was nothing specific, nothing about feelers or teeth, nothing suggesting how a charm could worm its way into electronic circuitry. Well, what could you expect from a book written in 1922? And nothing, nothing, on the mystical significance of 3.47 AM . . . All in the mind, Brian me lad. You're a weak person who's been thrown into a fever. The psychologists would mumble about compulsive neuroses or something. You wake up with a nightmare at 3.47 one morning and somehow it sets your own internal alarm-clock ticking away, screaming at you every twenty-four hours—but only when you sleep near that clock because the psycho-whatsit is all tied up with those glowing figures. Those figures that you can feel glowing in a dim red way, even with eyes tight shut.

Through the day Dekker swallowed his prescribed doses of tonic with great conscientiousness. And in the evening he had another idea, something to break the bad luck and finish all this silly business. Before going to bed, he cunningly set the alarm for 3.30 AM.

The banshee wail cut through his vague and innocuous dream, blasting him awake with the gentleness of a bucket of cold water in the stomach. The red figures 3.30 glared at him. There was no hint of menace or oppression in the surrounding dark. Dekker turned on the bedside light, and then got up to switch on the main room light as well.

Break the jinx, he thought cheerfully. Watch 3.47 flash up on that clock with no bad dream in sight, and that should deal with any worms lodged in my subconscious!—Or if my little Malayan dream-girl is responsible, a dose of cold hard facts in the small hours should help deal with her too, eh?

Though well-lit and warm, the room did contain a sort of bleakness, as though the walls were mere partitions in some enormous hall of damp concrete where echoes could scurry back and forth for hundreds of yards before dying of exhaustion. It's the small hours that do it, Dekker thought. The human spirit at its lowest ebb before dawn . . . didn't someone say that?

3.42.

The only sound was the faint hum of the clock. He sat on the bed in his old worn dressing-gown and wished the clock would get a move on.

3.44.

3.45.

3.46.

The last figure seemed to glow there for hours. Subjective time stretching out and out like plasticene, like the eternity of nightmare you could fit into a few seconds of dreaming. *'Between midnight and dawn, when the past is all deception . . .'* Where had he read that line?

He was thinking these thoughts when he felt the tickling and crawling on his arms, as of insect feelers writhing from the flesh. My God, he thought. Hysteria, I won't look under my sleeves, I won't, it's like those religious girls who sprout the marks of wounds in all the appropriate places, I'm expecting this and the teeth and the, the other thing, and so now I'm *imagining* —

But he was still almost sure he could feel motion under the loose sleeves of his pyjamas. He refused to look down. He clamped his jaws together, and with rotten snaps the teeth broke to powder. This time there wasn't the painlessness of the dream: he screamed aloud, and stinking fragments sprayed from his mouth. He wanted to screw up his eyes, but already they were swollen to the point where the lids would not close, were swelling painfully further.

Hysteria! Hallucination! DTs, anything! Please! Some part of his mind was whimpering that again and again. But somewhere, altogether elsewhere, was there a pale brown woman smiling bitterly?

The swelling of his eyes was incredible. His vision blurred and distorted. He flung himself prone on the bed as leggy creatures writhed from the backs of his hands and more teeth fell to chalky shards; he flung himself down, wanting desperately to take refuge in the safety of the dream before —

3.47 AM.

Angry Man

Darrell Schweitzer

Damn *them all.* His rage was an inexplicable knot within him, impenetrable, Gordian, never to be tangled or cut or understood.

Damn them all to Hell. He stood there on the train platform in the morning mist, hating. It was an active thing, something he *did* rather than merely felt, a task continuously carried out.

A young woman approached him, asking the time. He merely turned away. Her face went pale and slack, and she backed off, stuttering. A pack of school kids laughed and danced and shoved one another on the far end of the platform. *Damn them all. Radios the size of suitcases, but no damn books.* He glared, and they too backed away, silent.

He could project his anger through his eyes, like rays, like Superman's *damn-you-all* X-ray vision . . . and the thought was amusing, for all it didn't make him any less angry.

Gradually the platform filled with early morning commuters carrying briefcases, glancing at their wristwatches, rustling their newspapers, muttering among themselves: "Well, this *is* SEPTA after all . . . shoulda' brought camping gear . . . we're right on time, but this is yesterday's train . . ."

Damn them all.

As the sun rose higher, the mist thinned, revealing the long, silver box of a train car sitting no more than a hundred yards beyond the end of the platform. Even after several minutes, the car did not move. Sunlight glinted off the windows. The power gear on top touched the overhead wires like the arms of a metallic spider caressing its web.

After several minutes more a freight train went roaring by on the second track, buffeting everyone who stood on the platform, snatching newspapers and a couple of hats from the unwary, flattening the spiked hairdos of the school kids.

Damn them—

It gave him an opportunity for abstract thought. Somehow, inside his mind, he stepped away from his knotted rage and considered that if the outside track had a freight train on it, then any commuter train on *that* track had to be far behind, just leaving the Paoli yard *now.* Unless the other train, that single car sitting there, suddenly came to life, no one was going anywhere for a good long while.

Going where?

He realized, to his surprise, that he didn't know where he was going. The abstracted part of himself had placed the angry self into a kind of isolation ward, and now, in the corridor outside, it could rationally babble to itself: Name, *Albert Lovell,* age, *forty-three,* place of residence, *Six-seventy-two Croton Road,* occupation, *Senior Vice President, Fairfield-McDaniel Electronics*—and so on, like the responses to an interrogation, name, rank, serial number.

The angry *other* inside him was like an endless tape-loop, *damn-them-all-damn-them-all* and it wasn't going to tell him very much.

Are you married Mister Lovell?

There was a sharp pain at that, searing agony, a knife-blade twisted through his memory. He began to sob softly—still angry, the *other*, the someone-else still a throbbing mass of fury.

People are staring.

Damn them all.

Hit a nerve, eh?

Again he stood back from himself, opening another isolation ward, shoving the unclean *other* inside; and the grief, the pain were someone else's, along with the anger. He was reproducing like a cell in biology class, splitting off, and now there were three, one of them furious, one of them sorrowing, the third wondering when the damn train would start up, where Albert Lovell thought he was going this fine spring morning, and what Albert Lovell was so wrought up about.

Damn them all.

Oh, God, Janet! Oh, God—

So you *are* married, Mister Lovell. Is that it? A tiff with the wife?

He could not say. It was like a wiring diagram on tracing paper, all thin blue and red lines so faint they could hardly be made out. Whatever, it was something one of the *other* Albert Lovells had experienced. It was someone *else's* pain and mess, something he'd only vaguely overheard in the muttered conversation while standing among commuters.

". . . my appointment . . ."

". . . plane . . ."

Still the single car sat gleaming in the sun, completely revealed now. The mist had burned off completely. The car's windows were dark, like a row of staring eyes. Some distance behind, a dog trotted gingerly across the tracks.

". . . at least an hour since I got here," someone said.

". . . Jesus Christ, are they all *dead* in there?"

Damn them all. Albert Lovell, numbers one, two, three, all of him, started walking, no, marching toward the end of the platform, toward the stalled car.

Too short for a rush-hour train anyway. *One* damn car? By the time we get to Bryn Mawr there'll be people hanging from the luggage racks.

Damn them—

Walking. Onto the crunching gravel now. He hadn't walked along the edge of the tracks since he was a child, back when it was forbidden and therefore everybody did it—

People are staring.

As he neared the train car, he heard faint sounds from it, metal creaking, *ping*ing from heat stress and clutching brakes. He stared up at it, as if at a wall. He stood right in the middle of the tracks, daring the train to run him down. But the two-eyed metal face regarded him blankly.

Then, feeling a little foolish—but still angry, implacably angry, that *other's* anger like a fist of white-hot iron—he stepped down to the edge of the tracks again and walked along the stalled car. The door at the front, where the engineer would be, was closed, of course. He reached up and slapped his hand against the metal.

Back on the platform, one of the school kids shouted something.

He kept on going, to the far end, where passengers would board.

That door was closed too.

"Hey!"

He pounded on the metal with his fist, so hard his wedding ring left dents.

Damn them —

He wished he had a cane or a stick or an umbrella, something he could use to bang on the door higher up, or on one of the windows to get the attention of the crew inside. This car hadn't just materialized here. Someone drove it. No crewmen had debarked, so they still had to be on board. It only made sense.

Part of Albert Lovell, the part which felt no anger or pain, very reasonably came to that conclusion.

He reached into his coat pocket and felt something cold and hard, like a hammer. He drew it out and saw that it was a pistol, a big one, the size of a policeman's revolver.

And all of him felt pain then, as he clutched the vertical hand-hold by the side of the door and hung there, weeping, using his free hand to pound on the door with the butt of the pistol.

He could smell gunpowder. The pistol had been fired recently.

But that happened to someone else. He, Albert Lovell IV, stood apart from it all, merely cataloging the grief and rage and bewilderment of the others, quite insulated from pain.

It was merely an object of curiosity to him when the train door *did* open.

Still clutching the pistol by the barrel in his right hand, he caught the inner, curved hand-hold with his left and heaved himself up onto the steps, into the train.

Damn them all.

Janet. Oh, God —

o daddy we love you daddy please don't hurt mommy daddy please o—!

Do you have any children, Mister Lovell?

He knelt there on the steps, weeping once more, shaking uncontrollably, trying simultaneously to remember and to forget, to rip the wound open in a burst of pain and revelation, to cover it up, hide it, pretend it wasn't there; to untangle the screaming knot inside his head—until yet another Albert Lovell neatly filed it all away in a drawer.

Not me. That happened to someone else. Not me.

He put his shoulder against the inner door and pushed his way into the car.

"Hello—?"

The first thing he noticed was the smell, a dead smell, like the Augean Stables, like a dirty, old, possibly abandoned butcher shop, like garbage, like roadkill roasting in the sun—like all that, but fainter, far away, *dried* and forgotten for a very long time.

("... Jesus Christ, are they all *dead* in there?")

Damn.

For the first time he felt his anger beginning to unravel, blossoming like one of those Japanese paper flowers you drop into water. He remembered the screaming, Janet screaming every obscenity either of them knew while he stood there, facing her down, silent in cold rage, his hands on his hips.

Then he had laughed. "Are you *quite* finished?"

Back then. He *had*. That *other*, who remembered.

("... Jesus ... are they all ... ?")

Damn them, yes.

He took one step along the aisle. The old lady in the seat to the right was indeed dead, had been for a long time, for all she still clutched her pocketbook primly; her eyes were shut tight, her lips puckered as if she were about to kiss someone, her throat cut so wide that another, huge mouth gaped there and her head tilted at an impossible angle, about ready to fall off. She smelled like filthy straw.

The man in the seat with her was little more than a skeleton in a tattered, double-breasted suit with shiny silver buttons. He lay across the woman's lap like a sleeping child, staring up at her, one bony hand dangling down toward the floor.

The seat to the left was empty. But there was a boy in the one in front of it. About fourteen. He could have been one of the kids with the boom-boxes, save that he was neatly dressed in a jacket and tie, his red hair impeccably combed. He lay on his side as if he were asleep, but the whole downward half of his face was bruised where blood had pooled.

Albert Lovell could not weep now, of course, or even call out. He—all of his many selves—was beyond that now. He walked down the aisle in a state of flawless anesthesia. Yes, it was happening to someone else. Yes, *he* was only an observer, an outsider, peeking in at the world and all its strangeness, watching someone else's nightmare like an old flick on some Creature Feature, wondering all the while what that someone else was feeling and remembering.

He lurched slightly as the train began to slide forward, metal screeching. The pistol slipped out of his fingers, onto the floor.

Virtually every seat had a corpse in it, neat or messy, men, women, children. They could have been his neighbors, people he had seen on the platform every morning on his way to work. Some of them, absurdly, still covered their faces with newspapers where they sat or lay, but more than once the newspapers were brown—almost black—with old, dried blood.

One woman in her fifties lay naked in the seat, sideways, her feet drawn up, her body bloated and looking obscenely soft, her face a shriveled rictus of—what? Pain? Surprise? A hideous, all-*knowing* laughter?

Hello dearie, she seemed to say, not with words, just with her posture and expression and stench. Dearie, I know it all. I've been there. I've seen everything. You can't shock me. So give Mamma a little hug and tell me what's on your mind.

He turned away, covering his face, weeping again, nauseous, Albert Lovell V noting with amazement, *So this is what it's like.*

Damn them—

Yes, Albert. Damn them.

The train was moving steadily now. He made his way from one seat to the other, grabbing the hand-holds one by one to steady himself because it seemed, distinctly, the most horrible possibility of them all, the one thing which could make this unendurable, endlessly *real*, would be losing his balance and falling into the lap of one of *them*, those *others* whom he could still exclude from his life if he tried hard enough.

He was looking for a place to sit, an empty seat.

At the front of the car there was indeed an empty seat, reserved for him, he somehow knew.

No, for someone else. For *him*. That other.

The last two seats faced each other. The last forward-facing seat was empty. The one opposite, turned back toward the rest of the car, was occupied.

The train accelerated, heaving him backwards. He barely caught hold of the back of the empty seat. He sat down.

We must be far beyond the platform now, he told himself. Those people back there, they're all going to be late, alas.

It was almost funny. He took inventory of his various selves, couldn't find them, shouted after them into the empty caverns where they had once been: Wanna laugh? Anybody remember how to laugh?

Don't all answer at once.

Damn *you.*

"Hello, Albert—"

He looked around for the speaker. That had been a voice, external, not in his own mind.

"Albert."

The thing in the reversed seat lurched up, and, suddenly, the knot of his anger just dissolved, and he wasn't angry anymore. For a moment he was like a soldier in battle, who has just been hit so hard that the agony of his wound hasn't started to register yet. He can stagger on a few more steps, *abstractly* aware that he, no, someone else, has been shot. No, it could never happen to him. No, no, not me—

"Hello, Albert."

He recognized Janet, of course, for all that the bullets had blown out both her eyes and carried off the back of her head. He remembered the *other* reaching out, pointing the gun as she lay still thrashing across the dining room table while blood spouted from one eye socket as if from a broken hose. That *other* shot out her remaining eye in a split instant, at the very second of already certain death, just out of a sense of symmetry, like the final stroke in a well-drafted blueprint.

The whole scene replayed in his mind now, and he watched it like a movie, as the flat black-and-white characters screamed and repeated snatches of old arguments and threw things. It was a sordid, badly written melodrama which had been going on for years, strictly super-market tabloid stuff—I Chopped My Wife Up and Flushed Her Down the Toilet Piece by Piece—and now, inevitably, it ended, as he opened a drawer, *revealing* the gun. He did not touch it at first. That was to be *her* part. He was choreographing the whole thing, every move part of the plan, the *other* man's plan, a plan of self-defense, not in the legal sense but in his own mind, to justify his actions to himself.

(". . . daddy-daddy-daddy-don't—")

Sure enough, Janet reached for the gun. He caught her wrist. They wrestled over the table, shattering crystal.

(". . . daddy . . .")

That other man had done those things. It was too horrible for *him*, for Albert Lovell to have done. Yes.

He looked around. He thought he saw a figure exactly like himself leaning over the old woman, holding her hand. Another taking his place calmly in the seat behind the dead boy, still another standing in the aisle, clutching the seat-corners on either side in a desperate effort not to faint, yet another still in the doorway, hesitant.

Then they were gone. Somehow he couldn't manufacture an Albert VI. He was alone with . . . these. It was happening to *him* now, not someone else.

Damn them all.

To just *one* other then. Please? The other man who did these things.

". . . Daddy?"

He felt a hand touch his knee.

". . . Daddy, you hurt Mommy . . ."

Chrissy, aged four—yes, he could remember that, a checklist of birthdays and doctor's appointments and pre-school classes—her chest caved in, the whole front of her pink T-shirt a red-brown mass like a mud pie— yes, he knew her, that other man's daughter.

"Daddy. You hurt Mommy."

"No," he said gently, lifting her onto his lap.

"Daddy. You hurt me."

"No," he said again. "I didn't. *He* did. He had to. You saw. He wanted to kill his whole life, everything in it, just to finish it all. He even shot the dog and the cat and the goldfish. Everything. Gone. He should have burned the house down too. In the interests of completeness. That's what he wanted. Then he wanted to get on the train and just go, as he had every morning, and ride out of his world, away from guilt and memory and responsibility, away from everything, and just keep on going. Forever. Do you understand him at last?"

". . . no, daddy . . ."

"I don't either, Chrissy. I don't."

"You are the biggest goddamn liar—" his wife said, leaning toward him.

"I *am* the biggest goddamn liar," he said at last, sighing.

That was enough. He could say, could admit no more than that, weeping freely at last, as all memory of Albert Lovells Two through Five collapsed into a single, whole man who had just run out of lies.

The train was racing, shaking wildly from side to side, the outside dark now, as if they'd entered a tunnel.

He forced a feeble smile.

"At least we are together again."

He reached out and took his wife's cold, hard hand in his own. Chrissy clung to his side, sobbing gently.

Wait. Ride. Wait. With the others. He belonged here, with those others. It was complete, the last faint line traced on, the last "t" crossed, the envelope of his life neatly labeled and sealed and filed away.

At least we are together.

The train raced on, heaving, shuddering ever more violently, the roar of its motion louder and louder, plunging into the darkness without end.

Another House, Another Home

Bruce Boston

Once again it was happening to Richard Demens. He realized it over dinner, actually over the soup, which was an excellent homemade vichyssoise. He looked across the dining room table at his wife Jessica and he knew he didn't love her anymore. He hadn't loved her for some time. He couldn't pinpoint the exact failure of his affection, but he did recall a day last week when glancing up from a book he had caught her scowling out the window at the stunted azaleas. He had noticed how pinched and rigid the lines of her profile had become. At the time, there had been no clear emotion linked to the perception.

Now as he looked across the table at her—the way her spoon skimmed the surface of the soup, the way she swallowed with her head cocked to one side and dark eyes turned inward—he understood that the gestures and expressions he had once loved only bored him. And yes, soon they would begin to annoy. Richard sighed inwardly as he realized what he was going to do. Each time he swore it would be the last.

"Is everything all right?" Jessica asked.

"Just fine. Delicious," Richard answered, returning to his bowl.

After only a few mouthfuls he found himself staring down the table at their two daughters: Kimberly, thirteen, and Sonya, eleven. Having informed their mother earlier that they thought cold soup was "yucky," they were merely toying with their spoons while they whispered back and forth and giggled at one another. Catching their father's eyes upon them and taking it as a reprimand, they both fell silent. In the last several months, just as Richard was expecting to see them blossom into womanhood, they had become pudgy and hesitant children. The hesitant part puzzled him. The pudgy, he understood.

Even though he took time off from the office to play racquetball and spent a good part of every Sunday riding his ten-speed up and down Marin County, his own middle was steadily thickening. At home they never ate supper, they always dined, and they dined in style. Jessica was a gourmet cook. Beef bourguignon. Lamb curry. Sherried crab meat. This was the one thing about her he was going to miss. Tonight it was chicken with white wine and cream, wild rice, braised asparagus. Richard watched as Jessica loaded the girls' plates and then his own. She took a smaller portion for herself.

They ate for the most part in silence, as if any distraction from the food were out of place. As the girls were clearing, Jessica once again brought up the subject of their education.

"It wouldn't hurt them to attend public school for just one year," she insisted. "They could meet new friends, get a broader perspective on things. Wildwood is so small and narrow."

"All right," Richard answered.

Jessica looked at him strangely. "You mean it's all right? They can go?"

"Whatever you and the girls think is best."

"But you've always protested so much before."

"It doesn't really matter," Richard told her.

After dinner he retired to the living room couch and lit a cigaret. He could hear voices from the kitchen, Sonya and Kimberly helping their mother with the dishes. Now that his decision was made, Richard hoped to make this, their last evening together, special. But the pattern of their life was set. The evening progressed like so many others.

By eight o'clock the children dominated the living room and the TV, watching one mindless sitcom after another, all of which they laughed at earnestly. Jessica, amazingly enough, also seemed to enjoy these shows. Richard was suddenly acutely aware of the way his three women often excluded him, with their talk and laughter, with looks which seemed to imply that they shared some feminine secret he could never comprehend.

Since Jess had promised to take the girls to the city for a Saturday morning shopping spree, she sent them off to bed early. Richard was still on the couch when she returned to the room. He glanced up. She was wearing a nightgown, her robe belted loosely across it. Her eyes seemed too familiar, even in the shadows of the doorway.

"Is something wrong?" she asked.

He was hoping she wouldn't notice. Most often they didn't. "It's nothing," he told her, "just a bad week at work."

"Would you like a nightcap?"

"Yes," Richard sighed. "Make it a double."

After she mixed the drinks, Jessica came to sit by his side. She placed the palm of her hand against the back of his and leaned toward him. Her touch was warm and slightly damp. "If there's something troubling you, darling, I want you to tell me about it." She paused, searching his face. "Things always seem better if you can talk to someone."

"It's nothing, Jess, I'm just tired." It was very quiet outside. For some reason Richard expected to hear a clock ticking, but there was only the hum of the refrigerator. He smiled and hefted his drink. "Why don't we finish these upstairs?"

He wasn't sure if he wanted to be with Jessica one more time, but once they were beneath the covers and he felt her warmth against him, familiar desire stirred within. The inevitable followed. At the height of their lovemaking, her face below him, he remembered a day they'd spent at Stinson. The blue dome of the sky, the sand very white, the sea water beaded on Jessica's lean thighs and the girls playing somewhere down the beach. Life had seemed very complete.

Yet once they finished, side by side and the sweat drying upon them, reality asserted itself. Resolve hardened like a stone within his chest.

Richard waited, feeling the minutes pass in the even measures of his wife's breathing. Once he drifted off himself, to come awake suddenly, his mind startled by some instantly forgotten dream. When he was sure that Jessica was asleep, he sat up and lowered his feet into his slippers. He closed the bedroom door silently and made his way downstairs in his pajamas. Without turning on the light, he fumbled in the far back of the hall closet until he found the overcoat. He slipped it on and checked the pockets to see that nothing had been disturbed.

Outside it was warm, too warm for the coat. Richard left it hanging open. To the west the bulk of Mt. Tamalpais rose steeply to shadow the horizon. It was a clean starry night and a full moon hung high in the eastern sky. If he had been a more superstitious man, he might have attributed his decision to its pull.

Richard turned at the end of the front walk to survey his house for the last time.

A two story white frame with green forest trim, a wide front porch, a generous rectangle of neatly trimmed lawn. It was the kind of house one expected to find on the quiet back streets of some small Midwestern town. It resembled the house in which Richard had grown up, just as Jessica resembled his mother in her youth. Or at least she had at first.

Here the house stood alone, nestled in a hollow of the hills, with knee-high grasses and patches of scrub oak rising on every side. Except for the narrow dirt road on which he stood, which wended its way south to the highway and eventually San Rafael, they were completely cut off from the world.

Richard reached into one pocket of his coat and brought out a piece of chalk, not schoolroom chalk but the kind tailors used, a large irregular chunk, soft and crumbly enough so that it would adhere to any surface. He moved quickly now, afraid that Jessica might wake and find him missing. He knelt down on his haunches and began to draw a line in the dirt. Scooting along, supporting himself with one hand, he drew with the other. When he reached the driveway he continued across its smooth concrete. At the edge of the garage he turned, angling back along its length. Turning again past the azaleas, he encompassed the backyard in a wide V. He was breathing heavily and he could feel the dampness of his fingers sinking into the whiteness he held. At one point he stood momentarily, his knees trembling from the strain. Finally he angled in sharply to avoid the old oak which stood outside the living room windows. Back at his starting point, Richard stood again. The figure he had outlined was irregular, but it had the five points. That was all that mattered.

Richard reached into the other pocket of his overcoat and drew forth a sheet of paper. It was yellow with age and tattered at the edges; one creased corner fell away and tumbled to the ground as he unfolded it. He'd had the paper nearly twenty years, and suspected that the writing on it was far older than that. During his last year of graduate school the paper had been bequeathed to him, along with instructions for its use, by an uncle he'd barely known, a childless recluse of a man. It had changed Richard's life completely. As it no doubt had his uncle's.

The moon overhead illuminated the words he didn't understand, had never understood, didn't even know for sure in what language they were written. Yet he'd used the paper so many times in the past eighteen years, ever since he'd purchased this isolated plot of land, that by now he knew them perfectly.

At first his voice trembled as he began to read.

Soon the incantation took over and he centered his mind on the task before him. All at once the moon seemed to glow brighter and in the far distance a dog began to bark, faintly yet fiercely. Richard heard the strange foreign words upon the night air as if someone else were speaking them. It was over in minutes. He watched as his house rippled and grew insubstantial before him, as the moonlight began to penetrate its walls and ceilings. And then in a soundless rush of disintegrating tables and chairs, of couches and pictures and children's toys, it flew upward into the sky. All that remained within his awkward pentagram was a patch of rock strewn dirt and the gaping hole which had held the half basement.

Richard turned the paper over. Once more he began to read the words he knew by rote. And as always, he looked to the future with anticipation and hope.

This time he'd try something entirely different, he thought. Something more modern. A sprawling ranch style house. And perhaps a blonde. He hadn't had a blonde in nearly three years. He'd make her a modern emancipated woman, an artist and intellectual. And no more daughters for now. He'd go back to an only child, a teenage son, bright and athletic. There would be tennis courts out back and they could play together on Saturday mornings, tomorrow morning, while Marilyn, that would be her name, sketched their bodies in motion.

This time it began from the roof down. Redwood shingles. Dark brown stucco. Aluminum awnings. Richard folded the paper and slipped it back into his pocket. He still believed in his heart of hearts, in the farthest reaches of his soul, that if he kept trying, sooner or later he was bound to get it right.

The Back of the Mirror

Hugh B. Cave

You might call this a ghost story of sorts, although there aren't any ghosts in it. Not the ordinary kind that haunt old English mansions, at any rate.

It's about a man named Canaday—Montreal Canaday. He was five foot three and pushing sixty: a sweet, gentle, unassuming man with many friends and a lady cat named Spooky. The fact that his parents thought it smart to name him Montreal, and he never changed the name, has already told you something about his genes and amiability.

Monty Canaday was a ghost hunter. Any time he came across an item in a newspaper about something in that line, he'd make an effort to check it out. Provided, of course, it wasn't too far from the apartment in New York City's Greenwich Village where he and the cat dwelt together in quiet contentment.

When he had enough material, he would write a book and make a bucket of money, he said. After which he would probably buy Spooky a male cat to keep her company. Spooky was a silver-blue shorthair with big, glowy eyes that resembled pools of amber with black bubbles for pupils.

She loved him dearly—and he her—but after all, he was only a human being. A gorgeous creature like her deserved a boyfriend who could do more for her than he could.

Meanwhile, what kept the two of them in eating money and paid the rent on their modest apartment was the Monty Canaday Wax Museum.

They might have fared better had the figures in the little backstreet museum been done with more artistry. But Monty did the best he could with a limited talent, and luckily there are always a few visitors to Greenwich Village—from foreign countries and places like Wigby, Montana—who will try things like wax museums out of curiosity if the price of admission is low enough.

In his billfold Monty carried cards that said "M. Canaday, Ghost Hunter" on them. And in his museum he had wax figures of some of the ghosts he had investigated. Like the one in Paterson, New Jersey, who'd had his throat cut by an intruder and every year, on the anniversary of his demise, spent a whole night walking around his house with blood dribbling down his shirt.

A good maker of wax figures might have done much with a subject such as that. Poor Monty's ghost looked like Washington Irving's Headless Horseman without a horse.

But enough of that. If you have the picture pretty clear now—including the lady cat, of course—you're ready for the time Monty heard about the ghost of Professor Gribsby.

The newspaper item this time was headlined COLLEGE PROFESSOR HAUNTED BY OWN GHOST, and the story told of a man who claimed that a ghost of himself—himself, mind you—had moved in with him and was giving him all kinds of problems. He hadn't had any decent sleep in weeks because the creature prowled about the house all night. His health was failing. He felt he was on the edge of insanity.

Fortunately for Monty, the paper printed the professor's name and the name of the small town he lived in.

This was in the *Sunday Times*, which Monty read about nine o'clock that Sunday morning with Spooky in his lap. She always read the paper with him. She took her meals with him, too, being served not under the table but on it, where they could talk to each other while they ate. Monty was quite sure she understood everything he said.

This morning he told her about the professor. "Paper says he lives just over the state line in Connecticut, love. You want to come along?"

"You bet," she said, though to anyone else but Monty it probably would have come out a mere "Meow".

By twelve-thirty Monty's old wreck of a car pulled up at their destination, the address supplied by a phone book at a drugstore pay station. Surprisingly, it was not the hundred-year-old structure Monty had half anticipated, the sort you would normally expect to be haunted, but a small, new cottage. It was, however, suitably isolated, standing all by itself on a two-lane blacktop country road.

When Monty went up the walk with Spooky on his shoulder and pressed the bell button, the front door was opened almost at once by a tall, terribly thin man with glasses and near-white hair. Wearing dark trousers and a white open-necked shirt and leather slippers, he even looked like a college professor. Tipping his head to one side a little, he peered at his caller—and at his caller's amber-eyed cat, of course—and said not very hospitably, "Yes?"

"Professor Gribsby?"

"Yes, I am Professor Gribsby."

"My card, sir." Monty produced one from his billfold. "I have come all the way from New York to talk to you, if I may. Ghosts are my business."

"Your business?"

"Perhaps I can help you."

The professor peered at Monty's card and frowned again at the silver-blue creature on Monty's shoulder before making up his mind. Then he shrugged. "Very well. Please come in," he said, and led Monty into a small but neat living room, where he motioned his caller to a chair.

When Monty sat, Spooky leaped lightly to the shades-of-green carpet and sat there beside his left leg, rather like a bookend expecting some books.

"What kind of cat is that, Mr. Canaday?" the professor asked.

"She's a Korat, Professor. And lovely, isn't she? Even in Thailand, where they come from, they're quite special—almost never sold, but given as gifts. A dear friend who lived there for a time brought her to me as a gift."

"I see. Well, I don't really care for cats, myself, but she seems inoffensive." The professor stopped looking at Spooky. "So, Mr. Canaday—just how do you propose to help me?"

"First," said Monty, "suppose you tell me what's been going on here. All I know is what I read in the *Times* this morning."

"It's this house."

"House?"

"I'm convinced of it." Gribsby leaned forward on his chair in a state of agitation. His mouth twitched, his eyes blinked rapidly, his long-fingered hands gripped his knees so fiercely the knuckles turned white. "This house, yes! I never should have built it here!"

"Why, Professor? Is there something unusual about this site?"

"There was a house here before. An old farmhouse."

"And?"

"It was said to be haunted."

"Old farmhouses are rather often said to be haunted."

"But that specter, too, was the alter ego of the man who lived here. Just as *mine* is my alter ego."

"A second self?" Monty's eyebrows went up.

"Precisely. The man who wrote the story you read this morning in the paper should not have used the word 'ghost'. I do not believe in ghosts. What we have here is my alter ego. Or, as you put it, my second self."

"Is this a nocturnal thing?" Monty asked. The sooner he got to the crux of this, the better, for he had never heard of a haunting by a person's alter ego and felt he might be in some new kind of jeopardy. Like an explorer venturing onto quicksand, say, with something unknown lurking beneath the sand. It would make a really different story for his book, though, if he could get to the bottom of it.

"Nocturnal?" the professor echoed. "Heavens, no."

"The *Times* story said it was depriving you of sleep."

"True. But I never know when the thing will appear."

"Describe it, please." Sensing a movement beside his leg, Monty looked down. Spooky was leaning forward just as he was, and staring at the professor as he was, as though those invisible books she was holding up had tipped and pushed her off balance.

"What is there to describe? He, my alter ego, is me. Is I. Looks like me. Wears what I am wearing."

"He tries to harm you?"

"Well, he hasn't yet. But the mere fact that he's here in the house—that I never know when I might bump into him or find him watching me—is completely unnerving. It keeps me on edge."

"And you say," Monty pressed, "that this same thing happened to the farmer who lived here before."

"The very same. He wrote it all down in a notebook. I found the notebook when I tore the old house down."

"Had he any explanation?"

"None, Mr. Canaday."

"And do you?"

"I believe there is something in the earth here. Or under the earth." The professor's hands were making his knees shake now, and if he leaned forward any farther he would fall off his chair. By the same token, Monty's cat if *she* leaned any farther forward would fall on her silver whiskers.

Someone less concerned than Monty might well have thought, at this point, that the professor was pulling his caller's leg. Yet the man's voice literally trembled as he continued.

"I read once, Mr. Canaday—I don't recall, but it must have been in some very old book—I read once that there was devil worship in this part of Connecticut many years ago. Certain dark ceremonies were held at night in the forest hereabouts. At this very minute you and I, sir, may be sitting over one of the sites where such rituals took place."

Peering around the room, Monty felt that little things with lots of legs were creeping over his scalp. "I do get strange vibrations," he admitted. "The door may still be ajar."

"Door?"

"The one they open when they worshipped Lucifer. That would explain why I have become two persons, one good and the other wicked. For my alter ego *is* wicked, Mr. Canaday. He sneaks about with a sneer on his face, as though daring me to challenge his presence here. One of these nights, I'm sure, he will attempt to dispose of me, say turning the gas stove on unlit while I sleep."

"When did you last see him?"

"This morning, just at daybreak. He came into my bedroom and stood beside the bed, grinning down at me. A fiend, without question."

"I forgot to ask you—are you married, Professor Gribsby?"

"No."

"You live here quite alone?"

"Except for him."

"Would you mind very much if I stayed with you for a few days? Perhaps if I could see this alter ego of yours—confront him, as it were— I might think of some way to exorcise him."

"I'll tidy up the guest room," said the professor. "Excuse me for a few minutes, please."

Monty sat and waited, and a strange thing happened. With the professor gone from the room, the vibrations seemed to depart as well. It was as though they had left the room in pursuit of him. The silver-blue Korat resumed her normal bookend position, then looked up at him and me-owed as if to say, "Hey, this is better, don't you think?" Monty's scalp stopped tingling, and he reached down to rub Spooky behind her ears.

He was beginning to feel almost relaxed again when he heard the front door open. Rising, he turned to the living-room door and saw his host standing there.

"Did you go outside?" Monty asked. "I thought you said—"

"I have just arrived from the village," said Gribsby. "I live there now, sir. Have for the past week. Who, please, are you, and what are you and this cat doing here?"

Monty's apprehensions came rushing back. "What *is* this, Professor? You and I have been sitting here talking for nearly an hour!"

"Oh." The professor came toward him and peered into his face. "I believe I understand. You've been talking to *him*."

"Him?"

"My other self. It's just the sort of game he would enjoy playing. I'm the real Professor Gribsby." He offered his hand. Then when Monty glanced in near panic at the doorway, Gribsby added with a shrug, "Don't be alarmed. In the ten months he's been here he has never been violent. He just wants the place to himself."

"But you've come back," Monty said weakly, offering one of the cards from his billfold.

"M'm. 'Ghost hunter', eh? Well, yes, I've come back, Mr. Canaday. But only to get a notebook I left here."

"*The* notebook? The one in which the old farmer wrote down what happened to him?"

"That's right. The other Professor Gribsby told you about it, did he? Well, I want it. Some of my students have volunteered to look into this whole business in depth. The farmhouse. The old tales of devil worship. Everything. And then—"

A snicker from the doorway silenced the man, and both he and Monty turned swiftly to look in that direction. So, for that matter, did the cat at Monty's feet, and her silver-blue coat all but crackled as she did so.

The other Professor Gribsby leaned against the doorframe, grinning at them in a way that caused Monty's scalp to tingle worse than before. "You won't find that notebook," he said. "I burned it."

"You burned it?" demanded the good Professor Gribsby. "Why?"

"Oh, no special reason. Just because I knew you wanted it."

"Damn you!"

"I'm that already," said the other, still grinning. "But I don't mind. It's much more fun than teaching religion the way you do."

Waving a hand in farewell, he departed. So did the tingle in Monty's scalp. And so, apparently, did whatever had caused the hackles of the cat to rise, for she resumed her bookend stance and her eyes stopped looking like exploding stars.

The good Professor Gribsby gazed in silence at the empty doorway for a time, as though half expecting his alter ego to reappear. Then he turned to Monty. "If I were you, Mr. Canaday, I think I'd get out of here. Whatever influence is at work here doesn't need a whole lot of time to accomplish its purpose. I mean to say, it happened to me the very first day I moved in." He frowned and rubbed his nose. "How long have you been here, actually?"

"An hour or so," Monty said uneasily.

"Feel any different, do you?"

"I don't know how I feel. A little of this, a little of that."

"M'm." The professor's frown deepened. "I hope I didn't get here too late. Of course, I don't suppose everyone is vulnerable. I am because I teach religious history. You might be because of your research. Well, I don't suppose there's much we can do about it . . ."

As they left the house together, with the cat back on Monty's shoulder, one last thing happened to make the creepies crawl over Monty's scalp again. A sound of laughter followed them. Not loud laughter—it was cut off when the door closed—but definitely nasty and, worse, triumphant.

It certainly affected Spooky. She dug her claws into her master's shoulder, arched her back like a feline drawbridge, and let out a snarl that would have done credit to a cornered bobcat. Never before had Monty heard her snarl.

Before getting into his car, with the cat now protectively cradled in his arms, Monty said to the professor, "Tell me, sir—what will you do about this house?"

"I'll know better after my students and I have finished our in-depth study."

"And in the meantime?"

"Put up a lot of NO TRESPASSING signs to keep people like you away. And, of course, stay away myself."

Monty Canaday arrived back at his apartment without incident. He carefully typed up pages of notes on his investigation of the Gribsby "ghost" and put them away with other material for his forthcoming book.

A few days later a new wax figure appeared in the museum.

This one was a likeness of Monty, himself, sitting on a stool under a placard that read M. CANADAY, OUR FOUNDER, and his Greenwich Village friends insisted it was far and away the best piece of work he had ever done.

This was not the usual amateurish Canaday creation, they pointed out, but a genuine artistic masterpiece. It *was* Monty Canaday. You could see the gentleness in the face, the innocence in the eyes. Here was the mild little man who loved to investigate things supernatural and would one day write an amusing, unfrightening book about his findings.

It was so real, someone suggested, that you could almost believe it was really Monty there on the stool, sprayed with wax.

But the friends talked about something else, too. About Monty himself. For he was *not* the gentle, innocent, mild little man he had been before his adventure in Connecticut.

The new Monty Canaday wore a sly, sardonic smile they had never seen before. He slunk. He swaggered. His eyes harbored a shifty glint. He had somewhere acquired a loud voice and a shameful vocabulary.

The maker of wax figures had changed so much, so swiftly, that his friends felt they no longer knew him. Another thing that puzzled them was that his beloved cat, Spooky, had walked out on him. Soon after his return from Connecticut she disappeared, to be seen again in the Village only once.

That one and only sighting took place on a Sunday morning when some of Monty's old friends, homeward bound from church, stopped at the museum for another look at the new figure. They found the silver-blue Korat sitting there like a bookend, sadly gazing up at the waxen Monty's face.

Disturbed by their intrusion, she took one wide-eyed look at them and fled like a wisp of smoke out the open door.

Blood Ghost

John Helfers

Stop kid!" The man's voice behind me caused me to brake without thinking. The old car stopped in front of the intersection just before a tractor trailer went roaring through.

Sitting back from where I had been thrown against the steering wheel, my body concentrated very hard on just breathing for a while. Then the realization of where that voice had come from hit me. I slowly looked at my rearview mirror. The reflection showed the cavernous back seat of the Cadillac, empty. Then the voice spoke again.

"Turn around, kid."

I had just bought this car and driven it away from the very pretty female owner not more than five minutes ago.

Alone.

Slowly, I turned around. Resting very comfortably on my back seat was a lean man in a dark gray tailored suit. His hair was styled, and his neatly folded hands were manicured, fairly recently, too. His gaze fell upon me as I examined him and I looked up. He could have passed for anybody's favorite uncle except for his eyes, empty black voids that made my stomach lurch and my gaze drop. He saw me look away and smiled.

"Oh, sorry." He took a pair of designer sunglasses out of his inside jacket pocket and put them on, "Haven't gotten used to that yet."

"Get out of my car," I said. It was amazing how calm my voice sounded, especially after the two shocks I had suffered.

The man smiled again, a normal looking smile that chilled my spine, "I'd like to, kid, but I can't. Watch."

He leaned over and reached for the door handle. A puff of blue-gray mist rolled off his arm as his hand pushed right through the car door. He pulled his hand back and looked at me again, shrugging his shoulders.

I snorted and reached over, careful not to come anywhere near him, "Please, let me help you." The rear driver's side door swung open, letting a shaft of sunlight enter the car.

He smiled again, "All right, here goes, but it won't help." He moved over to the open door and tried to move past it, my eyes on him all the while. As soon as his hand got past the boundaries of the car, it started to fade into that white mist again. This time, however, he jerked it back with a grunt, "Shit, that hurts."

I would have stared at him for the rest of my life if the car behind mine hadn't blared its horn. Turning around and checking the intersection, I started driving again, not saying a word.

"In case you haven't figured it out by now, kid, I'm a ghost."

At that moment, it was the only thing that made sense, "And you're stuck in my car?"

"Well, apparently it's still *my* car just as much as it is yours, isn't it?"

I looked in the rearview mirror again. He still wasn't there. That was really annoying. Then I remembered the woman who sold me the car saying something about how her father always drove Cadillacs. I took a guess, "Wait a minute. You mean you're Mr. Capestan?"

"Yes, I am. Or at least I was. Do you think Jan would have driven a car like this? No, she goes for those foreign jobs, the ones with a back shelf instead of a seat and a hundred miles to the gallon. This beauty and I go way back."

I smiled as I thought of my internal wince at seeing the Nissan parked next to the Caddy. "So, how long are you going to be here?"

"I don't know," he said, wafting through the back of the seat and sitting next to me. The car swerved violently as I fought not to lose control at seeing this. Mr. Capestan shook his head, "Jesus, what are you trying to do, kill me twice? If I wasn't already dead, you would have given me a heart attack that time."

"Wait, wait, wait, just hold on here." I pulled the car off the street into a grocery store parking lot, driving around to the side of the building. Killing the engine, I turned to face him, "All right, I'm a rational guy. And what I see is, for lack of a better term, an entity in my front seat who won't or can't leave, for whatever reason. Let's just say, for whatever other reason, you do exist, and I am talking to a ghost, or apparition, or whatever the hell you are, and not hallucinating from too much time on the Net. Does this mean you'll be here forever?"

He chuckled, a sound I thought should have been a little more humorous and less ominous, "Of course not, kid, I—"

"And stop calling me kid. I'm twenty-five." Now that he hadn't disappeared into mist or revealed himself to be one of my dopey college friends playing a trick on me, I wanted to regain some control of the conversation.

"Sorry. Well, as I was saying, I chose you. My daughter, Jan, whom you've met, held the car until I could signal her as to whom to sell it to. That person is you."

I dreaded the next question, "Why me?"

"Because you can see and hear me," he said with what sounded suspiciously like a sigh of annoyance.

"How did you know I was the one?" I asked, although the answer was becoming painfully obvious.

"Because when I touched you, you noticed," he said.

I thought back to the test drive before buying the car. Jan had insisted on coming with, not that it bothered me. About halfway through the trip, I had felt an unbelievable chill settle on my shoulder and neck, causing me to start suddenly. Then, as quickly as it had come, the sensation was gone. Jan had noticed and asked if anything was wrong. I had shaken my head and passed it off, saying something about the air-conditioning. She watched me with a strange expression on her face the rest of the way back to her house.

"So you were the 'feeling' I got in the car," I said. He nodded.

I held up a finger, "So what? Whatever you need me for, you can just tell Jan to do. After all, you told her who to sell the car to, right?"

He smiled again, "I knew I found a sharp one. Good idea, ki—it's a good idea, but it doesn't work that way. The way I figure it, the only reason I could tell Jan what to do with the car was because of the strong ties both her and I had to it, with her growing up with it, and me owning it. Kind of a triangle-relationship, understand?"

I nodded, then interrupted as another question struck me, "Sure, but if that's true, where do I fit in?"

"I don't know, I'm just as new to this as you are. Maybe it was your love for the car. Maybe you're just different. Maybe you're crazy, I don't know. But you're the one."

"Insanity would be a welcome break right now," I said.

"Anyway, what I need you for, I can't tell her. All I was able to do was give her a feeling about you, that you were the one to sell my baby to." His hand caressed the leather of the front seat, or would have, if his fingers hadn't melted through the top of it. "Christ, that's enough to piss a man off. Twenty-nine years I drove this car, kept it in perfect condition, cherry, you understand? Now I can't even touch it."

I looked at him, "But how are you able to sit there?"

His shoulders rolled in what I assumed was a shrug, "I don't know. I saw an old movie where the hero, who was a ghost, was held up here by a locket he gave his wife before he died. Maybe that's what the car is, a, what-do-you-call it . . . ?"

"A focus?" I supplied.

He nodded, "Sounds good. Anyway, I have to take care of something for Jan, but, as you saw, I'm stuck in here."

"And you need me for that, right?"

He smiled again, "You got it."

"And I suppose you're going to sit here forever until I do, right?" I asked.

"What choice do I have? I'm not going anywhere," he said.

"What if I sell the car?" I said.

"I'll find another . . . associate. Of course, if you want to pass up the chance to make a little money . . ." his voice trailed off meaningfully.

"How much?" I asked.

"A good piece of half a million," he said.

I gulped. Was he kidding? Another look at his face dispelled that thought. Even though my job made life comfortable, there was always room for improvement. I thought of what could be done with the kind of money he was talking about. Finish paying off my college loans—and my parents, for that matter. Take a very well-earned vacation. Quit my job and look for something with a future, more than factory work at least. Get the hell out of this city, even. But something in the way he said it made me wonder. . . .

"What do you want?" I asked.

He said nothing for a long time, but just leaned back into the seat (which was odd because the seat didn't move, even though he did). When he spoke, his voice was quiet, almost wistful.

"First off, you gotta understand . . ." He looked at me hard, and then laughed quietly, long and low, "Jesus, where are my manners? Jack Capestan. You'll forgive me if I don't shake hands.

I smiled again. "Alec Ryerson."

"Anyway, Alec, you gotta understand that I wasn't a very nice man in my life. I was a Family man, you understand that?"

I had seen enough movies to know exactly what he meant. I nodded.

"Well, I did well enough, but I was careful to keep Jan out of it. Back then, there was honor in the Family, not like today, but that's beside the point. What matters is, I was pulling a job when I got double-crossed and whacked by my partner. He hid the money—of course I know where, the bastard used my own car to drop it off—then got himself busted for a speeding ticket that turned into 25-to-life up at Rikers Island. Charlie always was an asshole. Anyway, I want to provide for my daughter, and that's where you come in."

"So, all I have to do is get the money, give it to her, and your soul is at eternal peace, huh?"

"Something like that."

"What's my cut?" I asked.

"You watch too many movies. Your *share* is ten percent."

I shook my head, "Not good enough. Twenty-five."

His jaw dropped. "I don't think I quite heard you. This money is dropping into your lap and you have the nerve to ask for more?"

I nodded, "Look, call it negotiation, call it compensation for scaring the hell out of me a few minutes ago, call it whatever you want. The fact is, I've got you. If I keep the car, you're screwed, and Jan never sees the money. Of course, I got to put up with you for however long I own it, but I think that's manageable. Now, I'm sure we can come to an amicable agreement, aren't you?"

He stared at me so long and silently that I started to wonder if I had pushed him too far. Then I realized, what could he do to me? As far as he was concerned, I was holding all the cards, so to speak.

"Fifteen."

"Twenty."

"Done."

"All right. Now, where do you want to go?"

He shook his head and smiled. "Maybe you should have worked for us. You want to go to the Square Street Gym."

I drove the car out of the parking lot and plotted the fastest way there, then suddenly had a thought, "What if he's had the money moved?"

That sibilant laugh came from his mouth again, "No way. I know Charlie too well. He doesn't trust anybody. Until a few months ago, I thought I was different. Shit happens. Anyway, there's no way he'd move the money. Poor bastard thinks he's going to make parole one of these years."

I shivered at his implication.

Square Street was in a part of town that was slowly going to seed, although it wore it well. The gym was a three-story brick building that smelled like sweat from across the street. I turned to him, "Now what?"

"Now, you go inside and talk to the manager. Tell him you're getting a package for the Breezer that's in the locker room. He'll give you shit, but don't take it, tell him only you can get that package. New runners come and go all the time, it won't matter. The locker is number 653, the combination is 52–6–42. Got that?"

"Package for Breezer, 653, 52–6–42," I repeated.

"Attaboy, you'll do fine. Now get going."

I left the car and walked over to the cracked double doors. A dark staircase led upward, along with the strong smell of sweat and leather. Climbing to the top, I entered the gym.

Everybody, whether they were sparring in the boxing ring, working out, or just shooting the shit, turned and looked at me, then went back to their business.

There was a fat man sitting behind a window set in the wall. I walked over to him. After several seconds, he looked at me again. "Yeah?"

"I need to get a package for the Breezer," I said.

"What locker, I'll get it for ya," he said, starting to walk toward another door. He hadn't been sitting.

"No." He stopped, then turned around. "Breezer said only I could get it."

He snickered. "Look, kid, quit fuckin' with me, I ain't in the mood. Everybody knows that no one goes to the locker room but members, that's the rules."

I smiled and said, "Well, you'll just have to change the rules."

His face grew hard faster than I thought possible. "Get the fuck outta here, kid, before I have a couple of the boys throw you out the window."

"Wait a minute, I'm not looking for trouble." My brow furrowed in thought. "How much is a membership?"

He thought for a minute, taking considerably longer than me. "Fifty bucks a month." I checked my wallet and found what was left of my last paycheck there, sixty dollars. I sighed and forked the money over.

The fat man smiled. "Right this way, son."

A few minutes later, I was looking at the kind of money you usually only see in the movies. Picking up one of the top bundles of bills, I noticed brown stains dotting it. I put it back and carefully closed the lid. Then something Capestan said came back to me. Double-crossed and whacked by his partner . . . what if he was going to try the same thing? I sat down and thought it over, then dismissed the idea. Why? What could he possibly accomplish by killing me? And how would he get the money to Jan if the courier, me, was dead? I shook my head at my suspicions.

Then another idea came to me. What if I pulled the same scam on him? This money could set me up for years, and what could he do? Jack shit, that's what. But I shook my head again, realizing exactly what I was thinking. Even though Capestan was a dead mobster, he was still a mobster. If I could see him, then maybe someone else could. Maybe one of his Mob buddies. That would be bad, very bad. Besides, Jan was waiting for this back at her house. Maybe she would be grateful. *Very* grateful . . .

Seconds later, the heavy suitcase was in my hand and I was trotting down the stairs and out the door. I crossed the street and threw the suitcase in the trunk and myself in the front seat. He was still there.

"How'd it go?"

"Fine."

"That's good. Now we can go to Jan's and then your part of this will be almost over."

"Fine," I said, beginning to realize that I didn't have the stomach for Mob life.

The long drive to Jan's house passed in silence. Finally I pulled the car back into the driveway where I had purchased it, seemingly only an hour ago. That was before I believed in ghosts.

I got out and walked to the front door, the suitcase a reassuring weight under my hand. Ringing the doorbell, I was greeted by the pretty young woman who had taken my check that morning.

"Can I help you? Is something wrong with the car?"

"Not in the way you think," I replied. "May I come in?"

"You look very pale. Would you like something to drink?" she asked, backing up and motioning me inside.

A cup of coffee later, I was sitting at her kitchen table, telling her the story, which ended with the suitcase beside me. Hefting it up on the table, I watched her open it and riffle through the bills inside. Curiously, she was examining the same stack I had grabbed earlier, the one with the brown stains on it.

"I can't believe he did it. Finally, his soul will be at peace."

"Great, well, I'll just take my share and leave." I started to get up, but was overcome with a wave of weariness, causing me to collapse into the chair.

"I'm afraid your part in this is not over yet, Alec. When I said his soul would be at peace, I meant in your body. The money was never important, it was this," she said, pointing to the brown stains on the portrait of Benjamin Franklin. "His blood."

A creeping numbness was spreading from the pit of my stomach into my limbs.

"Poisoned . . ."

"Oh, no, my dear Alec, that would kill you. I need you alive for the transfer."

My last memory was of her looking up at the doorway. With effort, I raised my head before it locked in position. A shadowy form stood there.

"Hello, Father."

So now here I am, stuck. Once the "transfer" was complete, I learned a lot of interesting things about the Capestan family. I had all the time in the world to watch them. I also learned some of the tricks Jack pulled on me to fool me into taking that job. The turning into mist bit, among others. I look forward to using them on him, soon.

Well, I was right about one thing. Jan was grateful, all right. At least, that's what she kept telling me during the ceremony. Funny, all the feeling was gone in my body, but not pain. . . .

What really irritates me is seeing my body being used like this, while I'm trapped outside, in the void. But someday, somehow, I'll get it back. That's just one more interesting thing about ghosts. One doesn't always need a focus to come back to the world of the living.

Revenge works just as well.

The Burned House

Vincent O'Sullivan

One night at the end of dinner, the last time I crossed the Atlantic, somebody in our group remarked that we were just passing over the spot where the *Lusitania* had gone down. Whether this were the case or not, the thought of it was enough to make us rather grave, and we dropped into some more or less serious discussion about the emotions of men and women who see all hope gone, and realise that they are going to sink with the vessel.

From that the talk wandered to the fate of the drowned. Was not theirs, after all, a fortunate end? Somebody related details from the narratives of those who had been all-but drowned in the accident of the war. A Scotch lady inquired fancifully if the ghosts of those who are lost at sea ever appear above the waters and come aboard ships. Would there be danger of seeing one when the light was turned out in her cabin? This put an end to all seriousness, and most of us laughed. But a little, tight-faced man, bleak and iron-grey, who had been listening attentively, did not laugh. The lady noticed his decorum, and appealed to him for support.

"You are like me—you believe in ghosts?" she asked lightly.

He hesitated, thinking it over.

"In ghosts!" he repeated slowly. "N-no, I don't know as I do. I've never had any personal experience that way. I've never seen the ghost of anyone I knew. Has anybody here?"

No one replied. Instead, most of us laughed again—a little uneasily, perhaps.

"All the same, strange enough things happen in life," resumed the man, "even if you leave out ghosts, that you can't clear up by laughing. You laugh till you've had some experience big enough to shock you, and then you don't laugh any more. It's like being thrown out of a car—"

At this moment there was a blast on the whistle, and everybody rushed up on deck. As it turned out, we had only entered into a belt of fog. On the upper deck I fell in again with the little man, smoking a cigar and walking up and down. We took a few turns together, and he referred to the conversation at dinner. Our laughter evidently rankled in his mind.

"So many damn strange things happen in life that you can't account for," he protested. "You go on laughing at faith-healing, and at dreams, and this and that, and then something comes along that you just can't explain. You have got to throw up your hands and allow that it doesn't answer to any test our experience has provided us with. Now, I'm as matter-of-fact a man as any of those folks down there; but once I had an experience which I had to conclude was out of the ordinary. Whether other people believe it or not, or whether they think they can explain it, don't matter. It happened to me, and I could no more doubt it than I could doubt having had a tooth pulled after the dentist had done it. If you will sit down here with me in the corner, out of the wind, I'll tell you how it was.

"Some years ago I had to be for several months in the North of England. I was before the courts; it does not signify now what for, and it is all forgotten by this time. But it was a long and worrying case, and it aged me by twenty years. Well, sir, all through the trial, in that grimy Manchester court-room, I kept thinking and thinking of a fresh little place I knew in the Lake district, and I helped to get through the hours by thinking that if all went well with me I'd go there at once. And so it was that on the very next morning after I was acquitted I boarded the north-bound train.

"It was the early autumn; the days were closing in, and it was night and cold when I arrived. The village was very dark and deserted; they don't go out much after dark in those parts, anyhow, and the keen mountain wind was enough to quell any lingering desire. The hotel was not one of those modern places which are equipped and upholstered like the great city hotels. It was one of the real old-fashioned taverns, about as uncomfortable places as there are on earth, where the idea is to show the traveller that travelling is a penitential state, and that, morally and physically, the best place for him is home. The landlord brought me a kind of supper, with his hat on and a pipe in his mouth. The room was chilly, but when I asked for a fire, he guessed he couldn't go out to the wood-shed till morning. There was nothing else to do, when I had eaten my supper, but to go outside, both to get the smell of the lamp out of my nose and to warm myself by a short walk.

"As I did not know the country well, I did not mean to go far. But although it was an overcast night, with a high north-east wind and an occasional flurry of rain, the moon was up, and, even concealed by the clouds as it was, it yet lit the night with a kind of twilight grey—not vivid, like the open moonlight, but good enough to see some distance. On account of this, I prolonged my stroll, and kept walking on and on till I was a considerable way from the village, and in a region as lonely as anywhere in the country. Great trees and shrubs bordered the road, and many feet below was a mountain stream. What with the passion of the wind pouring through the high trees and the shout of the water racing among the boulders, it seemed to me sometimes like the noise of a crowd of people. Sometimes the branches of the trees became so thick that I was walking as if in a black pit, unable to see my hand close to my face. Then, coming out from the tunnel of branches, I would step once more into a grey clearness which opened the road and surrounding country a good way on all sides.

"I suppose it might be some three-quarters of an hour I had been walking when I came to a fork of the road. One branch ran downward, getting almost on a level with the bed of the torrent; the other mounted in a steep hill, and this, after a little idle debating, I decided to follow. After I had climbed for more than half a mile, thinking that if I should happen to lose track of one of the landmarks I should be very badly lost, the path—for it was now no more than that—curved, and I came out on a broad plateau. There, to my astonishment, I saw a house. It was a good-sized house, three storeys high, with a verandah round two sides of it, and from the elevation on which it stood it commanded a far stretch of country.

"There were a few great trees at a little distance from the house, and behind it, a stone's-throw away, was a clump of bushes. Still, it looked lonely and stark, offering its four sides unprotected to the winds. For all that, I was very glad to see it. 'It does not matter now,' I thought, 'whether I have lost my way or not. The people in the house will set me right.'

"But when I came up to it I found that it was, to all appearance, uninhabited. The shutters were closed on all the windows; there was not a spark of light anywhere. There was something about it, something sinister and barren, that gave me the kind of shiver you have at the door of a room where you know a dead man lies inside, or if you get thinking hard about dropping over the rail into that black waste of waters out there. This feeling, you know, isn't altogether unpleasant; you relish all the better your present security. It was the same with me standing before that house. I was not *really* frightened. I was alone up there, miles from any kind of help, at the mercy of whoever might be lurking behind the shutters of that sullen house; but I felt that by all the chances I was perfectly alone and safe. My sensation of the uncanny was due to the effect on the nerves produced by wild scenery and the unexpected sight of a house in such a very lonely situation. Thus I reasoned, and, instead of following the road farther, I walked over the grass till I came to a stone wall, perhaps two hundred and fifty yards in front of the house, and rested my arms on it, looking forth at the scene.

"On the crests of the hills far away a strange light lingered, like the first touch of dawn in the sky on a rainy morning or the last glimpse of twilight before night comes. Between me and the hills was a wide stretch of open country. On my right hand was an apple orchard, and I observed that a stile had been made in the wall of piled stone to enable the house people to go back and forth.

"Now, after I had been there leaning on the wall some considerable time, I saw a man coming towards me through the orchard. He was walking with a good, free stride, and as he drew nearer I could see that he was a tall, sinewy fellow between twenty-five and thirty, with a shaven face, wearing a slouch hat, a dark woollen shirt, and gaiters. When he reached the stile and began climbing over it I bade him good-night in neighbourly fashion. He made no reply, but looked me straight in the face, and the look gave me a qualm. Not that it was an evil face, mind you—it was a handsome, serious face—but it was ravaged by some terrible passion: stealth was on it, ruthlessness, and a deadly resolution, and at the same time such a look as a man driven by some uncontrollable power might throw on surrounding things, asking for comprehension and mercy. It was impossible for me to resent his churlishness, his thoughts were so certainly elsewhere. I doubt if he even saw me.

"He could not have gone by more than a quarter of a minute when I turned to look after him. He had disappeared. The plateau lay bare before me, and it seemed impossible that, even if he had sprinted like an athlete, he could have got inside the house in so little time. But I have always made it a rule to attribute what I cannot understand to natural causes that I have failed to observe. I said to myself that no doubt the man had gone back into the orchard by some other opening in the wall lower down, or there might be some flaw in my vision owing to the uncertain and distorting light.

"But even as I continued to look towards the house, leaning my back now against the wall, I noticed that there were lights springing up in the windows behind the shutters. They were flickering lights, now bright—now dim, and had a ruddy glow like firelight. Before I had looked long I became convinced that it was indeed firelight—the house was on fire. Black smoke began to pour from the roof; the red sparks flew in the wind. Then at a window above the roof of the verandah the shutters were thrown open, and I heard a woman shriek. I ran towards the house as hard as I could, and when I drew near I could see her plainly.

"She was a young woman; her hair fell in disorder over her white nightgown. She stretched out her bare arms, screaming. I saw a man come behind and seize her. But they were caught in a trap. The flames were licking round the windows, and the smoke was killing them. Even now the part of the house where they stood was caving in.

"Appalled by this horrible tragedy which had thus suddenly risen before me, I made my way still nearer the house, thinking that if the two should struggle to the side of the house not bounded by the verandah they might jump, and I might break the fall. I was shouting this at them;

I was right up close to the fire; and then I was struck by—I noticed for the first time an astonishing thing—the flames had no heat in them!

"I was standing near enough to the fire to be singed by it, and yet I felt no heat. The sparks were flying about my head; some fell on my hands, and they did not burn. And now I perceived that, although the smoke was rolling in columns, I was not choked by the smoke, and that there had been no smell of smoke since the fire broke out. Neither was there any glare against the sky.

"As I stood there stupefied, wondering how these things could be, the whole house was swept away by a very tornado of flame, and crashed down in a red ruin.

"Stricken to the heart by this abominable catastrophe, I made my way uncertainly down the hill, shouting for help. As I came to a little wooden bridge spanning the torrent, just beyond where the roads forked, I saw what appeared to be a rope in loose coils lying there. I saw that part of it was fastened to the railing of the bridge and hung outside, and I looked over. There was a man's body swinging by the neck between the road and the stream. I leaned over still farther, and then I recognised him as the man I had seen coming out of the orchard. His hat had fallen off, and the toes of his boots just touched the water.

"It seemed hardly possible, and yet it was certain. That was the man, and he was hanging there. I scrambled down at the side of the bridge, and put out my hand to seize the body, so that I might lift it up and relieve the weight on the rope. I succeeded in clutching hold of his loose shirt, and for a second I thought that it had come away in my hand. Then I found that my hand had closed on nothing, I had clutched nothing but air. And yet the figure swung by the neck before my eyes!

"I was suffocated with such horror that I feared for a moment I must lose consciousness. The next minute I was running and stumbling along the dark road in mortal anxiety, my one idea to rouse the town, and bring men to the bridge. That, I say, was my intention; but the fact is that when I came at last in sight of the village I slowed down instinctively and began to reflect. After all, I was unknown there; I had just gone through a disagreeable trial in Manchester, and rural people were notoriously given to groundless suspicion. I had had enough of the law, and of arrests without sufficient evidence. The wisest thing would be to drop a hint or two before the landlord, and judge by his demeanour whether to proceed.

"I found him sitting where I had left him, smoking, in his shirt-sleeves, with his hat on.

" 'Well,' he said slowly, 'I didn't know where you had got to.'

"I told him I had been taking a walk. I went on to mention casually the fork in the road, the hill, and the plateau.

" 'And who lives in that house?' I asked with a good show of indifference, 'on top of the hill?'

"He stared.

" 'House? There ain't no house up there,' he said positively. 'Old Joe Snedeker, who owns the land, says he's going to build a house up there for his son to live in when he gets married; but he ain't begun yet, and some folks reckon he never will.'

" 'I feel sure I *saw* a house,' I protested feebly. But I was thinking—no heat in the fire, no substance in the body. I had not the courage to dispute.

"The landlord looked at me not unkindly. 'You seem sort of done up,' he remarked. 'What you want is to go to bed.' "

The man who was telling me the story paused, and for a moment we sat silent, listening to the pant of the machinery, the thrumming of the wind in the wire stays, and the lash of the sea. Some voices were singing on the deck below. I considered him with the shade of contemptuous superiority we feel, as a rule, towards those who tell us their dreams of what some fortune-teller has predicted.

"Hallucinations," I said at last, with reassuring indulgence. "Trick of the vision, toxic ophthalmia. After the long strain of your trial your nerves were shattered."

"That's what I thought myself," he replied shortly, "especially after I had been out to the plateau the next morning, and saw no sign that a house had ever stood there."

"And no corpse at the bridge?" I said; and laughed.

"And no corpse at the bridge."

He tried to get a light for another cigar. This took him some little time, and when at last he managed it, he got out of his chair and stood looking down at me.

"Now listen. I told you that the thing happened several years ago. I'd got almost to forget it; if you can only persuade yourself that a thing is a freak of imagination, it pretty soon gets dim inside your head. Delusions have no staying power once it is realised that they are delusions. Whenever it did come back to me, I used to think how near I had once been to going out of my mind. That was all.

"Well, last year, being up north, I went up to that village again. I went to the same hotel, and found the same landlord. He remembered me at once as 'the feller who stayed with him and thought he saw a house,'—'I believe you had the jim-jams,' he said.

"We laughed, and the landlord went on:

" 'There's been a house there since, though.'

" 'Has there?'

" 'Yes; an' it ha' been as well if there never had been. Old Snedeker built it for his son, a fine big house with a verandah on two sides. The son, young Joe, got courting Mabel Elting from Windermere. She'd gone down to work in a shop somewhere in Liverpool. Well, sir, she used to get carrying on with another young feller 'bout here, Jim Travers, and Jim was wild about her; used to save up his wages to go down to see her. But she chucked him in the end, and married Joe; I suppose because Joe had the house, and the old man's money to expect. Well, poor Jim must ha' gone quite mad. What do you think he did? The very first night the new-wed pair spent in that house he burned it down. Burned the two of them in their bed, and he was as nice and quiet a feller as you want to see. He may ha' been full of whiskey at the time.'

" 'No, he wasn't,' I said.

"The landlord looked surprised.

" 'You've heard about it?'

" 'No; go on.'

" 'Yes, sir, he burned them in their bed. And then what do you think he did? He hung himself at the little bridge half a mile below. Do you remember where the road divides? Well, it was there. I saw his body hanging there myself the next morning. The toes of his boots were just touching the water.' "

The Cage

Ray Russell

T hey say," said the Countess, absently fondling the brooch at her young throat, "that he's the devil."

Her husband snorted. "Who says that? Fools and gossips. That boy is a good overseer. He manages my lands well. He may be a little—ruthless? cold?—but I doubt very much that he is the Enemy Incarnate."

"Ruthless, yes," said the Countess, gazing at the departing black-cowled, black-hosed, black-gloved figure. "But cold? He seems to be a favorite with the women. His conquests, they say, are legion."

" 'They' say. Gossips again. But there you are—would the angel Lucifer bed women?" The Count snorted again, pleased at his logical triumph.

"He might," replied his wife. "To walk the earth, he must take the shape of a man. Might not the appetites of a man go with it?"

"I am sure I do not know. These are delicate points of theology. I suggest you discuss them with a holy father."

The Countess smiled. "What did he want?"

"Nothing. Business. Shall we go in to dinner?"

"Yes." The Count proffered his arm and they walked slowly through the tapestried halls of the castle. "He seemed most insistent about something," the Countess said after a moment.

"Who did?"

"Your efficient overseer."

"He was urging more stringent measures with the serfs. He said his authority had no teeth if he could not back it up with the threat of severe punishment. In my father's day, he said, the thought of the castle's torture chamber kept them in line."

"Your father's day? But does he know of your father?"

"My father's harshness, my dear, has ever been a blight on our family's escutcheon. It has created enemies on many sides. That is why I am especially careful to be lenient. History shall not call us tyrants if I can help it."

"I still believe he is the devil."

"You are a goose," said the Count, chuckling. "A beautiful goose."

"That makes you a gander, my lord."

"An old gander."

They sat at table. "My lord—" said the Countess.

"Yes?"

"That old torture chamber. How strange I've never seen it."

"In a mere three months," said the Count, "you could not possibly have seen the entire castle. Besides, it can be reached only by descending a hidden stairwell with a disguised door. We'll go down after dinner, if you like, although there's really nothing there to interest a sweet young goose."

"Three months . . ." said the Countess, almost inaudibly, fingering the brooch again.

"Does it seem longer since our marriage?" asked the Count.

"Longer?" She smiled, too brightly. "My lord, it seems like yesterday."

"They say," said the Countess, brushing her hair, "that you're the devil."

"Do you mind?"

"Should I mind? Will you drag me down to the Pit?"

"In one way or another."

"You speak in metaphor?"

"Perhaps."

"You are equivocal."

"Like the devil."

"And, like him, very naughty."

"Why? Because I am here in your boudoir and you are dressed in hardly anything at all?"

"Because of that, yes; and because you counsel my dear husband to be a tyrant, like his father."

"Did he tell you that?"

"Yes. And he showed me the torture chamber you advised him to reopen. How wicked of you! It is a terrible place. So dark and damp, and so deep underground—why, a poor wretch could split his lungs screaming and never be heard in the castle proper."

"Your eyes are shining. I assume you found it fascinating."

"Fascinating! Of course not! It was disgusting. That horrible rack . . . ugh! to think of the limbs stretching, the tendons tearing! . . ."

"You shudder deliciously. It becomes you."

"And that dreadful wheel, and the iron boot . . . I have a pretty foot, don't you think?"

"Perfect."

"Such a high arch; and the toes so short and even. I hate long toes. You don't have long toes, do you?"

"You forget—I have no toes at all. Only hooves."

"Careful, I may believe you. And where are your horns?"

"They are invisible. Like those your husband will be wearing very soon."

"Indeed. You think highly of your charms."

"As do you. Of yours."

"Do you know what struck me as most horrible?"

"Eh? Horrible about what?"

"The torture chamber, of course."

"Oh, of course. What struck you as most horrible?"

"There was a cage. A little cage. It looked like something you might keep a monkey in. It was too small for anything larger. And do you know what my husband said they kept in it?"

"What?"

"People!"

"No!"

"They kept people in it, he said. They could not stand up straight, or lie down; they could not even sit, for there were only spikes to sit on. And they kept them crouching there for days. Sometimes weeks. Until they screamed to be let out. Until they went mad. I would rather be torn apart on the rack . . ."

"Or have that pretty foot crushed in the boot?"

"Don't. That tickles . . ."

"It was meant to."

"You must leave. The Count might walk in at any moment."

"Until tomorrow then, my lady . . ."

Alone, smiling to herself, the Countess abstractedly rubbed the tops of her toes where he had kissed them. She had heard of burning kisses, they were a commonplace of bad troubadours, but until this evening she had thought the term a poetic extravagance. He wanted her—oh, how he wanted her! And he would have her. But not right away. Let him wait. Let him smoulder. Let him gaze at her in her diaphanous nightdress; let him, as she lifted her arms to brush her hair, admire the high beauty of her breasts. Allow him a kiss now and then. Oh, not on the mouth, not yet—on the feet, the fingertips, the forehead. Those burning kisses of his. Let him plead and groan. Let him suffer. She sighed happily as she turned down her bed. It was fine to be a woman and to be beautiful, to dole out little favors like little crumbs and to watch men lick them up and pant and beg for more and then to laugh in their faces and let them starve. This one was already panting. Soon he would beg. And he would starve for a long, long time. Then, some night when she thought he had suffered long enough, she would allow him to feast. What a glutton he would make of himself! He would try to make up for lost time, for all the weeks of starvation, and he would feast too rapidly and it would all be over too soon and she would have to make him hungry again very quickly so he could gorge himself again. It would all be very amusing . . .

"If I *am* the devil, as you say they say, then why do I not overwhelm you with my infernal magic? Why do I grovel here at your feet, sick and stiff with love?"

"Perhaps it entertains you, my Dark Prince. Here: Kiss."

"No. I want your lips."

"Oh? You grow presumptuous. Perhaps you would rather leave."

"No . . . no . . ."

"That's better. I may yet grant you a promotion."

"Ah! my love! Then—"

"Oh, sit down. Not what you call my 'favor.' Just a *little* promotion. Though I don't know if you deserve even that. You want everything but you give nothing."

"Anything. Anything."

"What a large word! But perhaps *you* could indeed give me anything . . ."

"Anything."

"But they say you demand fearful things in return. I would suffer

43

torment without end, through eternity . . . Ah, I see you do not deny this. I do believe you *are* the devil."

"I'll give you anything you desire. You have but to ask."

"I am young. Men tell me—and so does my mirror—that I am beautiful, a delight from head to toe. Do you want all this?"

"Yes! Yes!"

"Then make this beauty never fade. Make it withstand the onslaught of time and violence. Make me—no matter what may befall—*live forever.*"

"Forever . . ."

"Haha! I've got you haven't I? If I never die, then what of that eternal torment? Do you grant me this boon, Evil One?"

"I cannot."

"Wonderful! Oh, what an actor you are! I begin to admire you! Other men, impersonating the Adversary, would have said Yes. But you . . . how clever you are."

"I cannot grant that."

"Stop—I'm weak with laughing! This game amuses me *so* much! It lends such spice to this dalliance! I would play it to the end. Satan, look here: you really cannot grant my wish, even if I give you in return—*all this*?"

"Tormentress!"

"All this, my demon? In return for that one thing I desire? All this?"

"The Powers of Night will swirl and seethe, but—yes, yes, anything!"

"Ah! You disarming rogue, come take these lips, come take it all!"

"You said he was the devil and now I am inclined to believe you. The treacherous whelp! To bed my own wife in my own castle!"

"My lord, how can you think that *I—*"

"Silence! Stupid goose, do you still dissemble? He left without a word, under cover of night. Why? And your brooch—the brooch of my mother!—was found in his empty room; in your bedchamber, one of his black gloves. Wretched woman!"

"Indeed, indeed I am wretched . . ."

"Tears will avail you nothing. You must be humbled and you will be humbled. Give thanks that I am not my father. *He* would have left you crammed naked in this little cage until your mind rotted and your body after it. But I am no tyrant. All night long, without your supper, you will shiver and squirm down here in repentance, but in the morning I will release you. I hope with sincerity you will have learned your lesson by then. Now I am going. In a few hours, you will probably start screaming to be let out. Save your breath. I will not be able to hear you. Think on your sins! Repent!"

❋   ❋   ❋

"They said he was the devil, but I place no stock in such talk. All I know is that he came to me directly from the old Count's castle where he had been overseer or something, and gave me complete plans for the storming of the battlements: information about the placement of the cannon, the least securely barricaded doors, the weakest walls, measurements, location of rooms, the exact strength of the castle guard and a schedule of its watch . . . everything I needed. My forces had been on a one-hour alert for months. I attacked that very night. Thanks to my informant, the battle was over before dawn."

"You are to be congratulated, Duke. And where is he now?"

"Gone. Vanished. I paid him handsomely, and just between the two of us, Baron, I was beginning to make plans for his disposal. A dangerous man to have near one. But the rascal was smart. He disappeared soon after my victory."

"And that head on the pike up there, with the gray beard fluttering in the wind—it belonged to the late Count?"

"Yes. To this end may *all* enemies of my family come."

"I'll drink to that. And what disposition was made of the old fool's wife?"

"The Countess? Ah. That is the only sourness in my triumph. I'd have enjoyed invading that pretty body before severing it from its pretty head. But she must have been warned. We searched and searched the castle that night. She was nowhere to be seen. She had escaped. Well . . . wherever she may be, I hope she gets wind of what I'm doing to her husband's castle."

"Razing it, aren't you?"

"Down to its foundation blocks—leaving only enough to identify it—and building on that foundation an edifice of solid stone that will be a monument to its downfall and to my victory. *Forever.*"

"Where do you suppose the Countess is now?"

"The devil only knows. May the wench scream in torment for eternity."

The Case of Lady Sannox

Sir Arthur Conan Doyle

The relations between Douglas Stone and the notorious Lady Sannox were very well known both among the fashionable circles of which she was a brilliant member, and the scientific bodies which numbered him among their most illustrious *confrères*. There was naturally, therefore, a very widespread interest when it was announced one morning that the lady had absolutely and for ever taken the veil, and that the world would see her no more. When, at the very tail of this rumour, there came the assurance that the celebrated operating surgeon, the man of steel nerves, had been found in the morning by his valet, seated on one side of his bed, smiling pleasantly upon the universe, with both legs jammed into one side of his breeches and his great brain about as valuable as a cap full of porridge, the matter was strong enough to give quite a little thrill of interest to folk who had never hoped that their jaded nerves were capable of such a sensation.

Douglas Stone in his prime was one of the most remarkable men in England. Indeed, he could hardly be said to have ever reached his prime, for he was but nine-and-thirty at the time of this little incident. Those who knew him best were aware that famous as he was as a surgeon, he might have succeeded with even greater rapidity in any of a dozen lines of life. He could have cut his way to fame as a soldier, struggled to it as an explorer, bullied for it in the courts, or built it out of stone and iron as an engineer. He was born to be great, for he could plan what another man dare not do, and he could do what another man dare not plan. In surgery none could follow him. His nerve, his judgement, his intuition, were things apart. Again and again his knife cut away death, but grazed the very springs of life in doing it, until his assistants were as white as the patient. His energy, his audacity, his full-blooded self-confidence—does not the memory of them still linger to the south of Marylebone Road and the north of Oxford Street?

His vices were as magnificent as his virtues, and infinitely more picturesque. Large as was his income, and it was the third largest of all professional men in London, it was far beneath the luxury of his living. Deep in his complex nature lay a rich vein of sensualism, at the sport of which he placed all the prizes of his life. The eye, the ear, the touch, the palate, all were his masters. The bouquet of old vintages, the scent of rare exotics, the curves and tints of the daintiest potteries of Europe, it was to these that the quick-running stream of gold was transformed.

And then there came his sudden mad passion for Lady Sannox, when a single interview with two challenging glances and a whispered word set him ablaze. She was the loveliest woman in London and the only one to him. He was one of the handsomest men in London, but not the only one to her. She had a liking for new experiences, and was gracious to most men who wooed her. It may have been cause or it may have been effect that Lord Sannox looked fifty, though he was but six-and-thirty.

He was a quiet, silent, neutral-tinted man, this lord, with thin lips and heavy eyelids, much given to gardening, and full of home-like habits. He had at one time been fond of acting, had even rented a theatre in London, and on its boards had first seen Miss Marion Dawson, to whom he had offered his hand, his title, and the third of a county. Since his marriage his early hobby had become distasteful to him. Even in private theatricals it was no longer possible to persuade him to exercise the talent which he had often showed that he possessed. He was happier with a spud and a watering-can among his orchids and chrysanthemums.

It was quite an interesting problem whether he was absolutely devoid of sense, or miserably wanting in spirit. Did he know his lady's ways and condone them, or was he a mere blind, doting fool? It was a point to be discussed over the teacups in snug little drawing-rooms, or with the aid of a cigar in the bow windows of clubs. Bitter and plain were the comments among men upon his conduct. There was but one who had a good word to say for him, and he was the most silent member in the smoking-room. He had seen him break in a horse at the University, and it seemed to have left an impression upon his mind.

But when Douglas Stone became the favourite all doubts as to Lord Sannox's knowledge or ignorance were set for ever at rest. There was no subterfuge about Stone. In his high-handed, impetuous fashion, he set all caution and discretion at defiance. The scandal became notorious. A learned body intimated that his name had been struck from the list of its vice-presidents. Two friends implored him to consider his professional credit. He cursed them all three, and spent forty guineas on a bangle to take with him to the lady. He was at her house every evening, and she drove in his carriage in the afternoons. There was not an attempt on either side to conceal their relations; but there came at last a little incident to interrupt them.

It was a dismal winter's night, very cold and gusty, with the wind whooping in the chimneys and blustering against the window-panes. A thin spatter of rain tinkled on the glass with each fresh sough of the gale, drowning for the instant the dull gurgle and drip from the eaves. Douglas Stone had finished his dinner, and sat by his fire in the study, a glass of rich port upon the malachite table at his elbow. As he raised it to his lips, he held it up against the lamplight, and watched with the eye of a connoisseur the tiny scales of beeswing which floated in its rich ruby depths. The fire, as it spurted up, threw fitful lights upon his bold, clear-cut face, with its widely-opened grey eyes, its thick and yet firm lips, and the deep, square jaw, which had something Roman in its strength and its animalism. He smiled from time to time as he nestled back in his luxurious chair. Indeed, he had a right to feel well pleased, for, against the advice of six colleagues, he had performed an operation that day of which only two cases were on record, and the result had been brilliant beyond all expectation. No other man in London would have had the daring to plan, or the skill to execute, such a heroic measure.

But he had promised Lady Sannox to see her that evening and it was already half-past eight. His hand was outstretched to the bell to order the carriage when he heard the dull thud of the knocker. An instant later there was the shuffling of feet in the hall, and the sharp closing of a door.

"A patient to see you, sir, in the consulting room," said the butler.

"About himself?"

"No, sir; I think he wants you to go out."

"It is too late," cried Douglas Stone peevishly. "I won't go."

"This is his card, sir."

The butler presented it upon the gold salver which had been given to his master by the wife of a Prime Minister.

" 'Hamil Ali, Smyrna.' Hum! The fellow is a Turk, I suppose."

"Yes, sir. He seems as if he came from abroad, sir. And he's in a terrible way."

"Tut, tut! I have an engagement. I must go somewhere else. But I'll see him. Show him in here, Pim."

A few moments later the butler swung open the door and ushered in a small and decrepit man, who walked with a bent back and with the forward push of the face and blink of the eyes which goes with extreme short sight. His face was swarthy, and his hair and beard of the deepest black. In one hand he held a turban of white muslin striped with red, in the other a small chamois-leather bag.

"Good evening," said Douglas Stone, when the butler had closed the door. "You speak English, I presume?"

"Yes, sir. I am from Asia Minor, but I speak English when I speak slow."

"You wanted me to go out, I understand?"

"Yes, sir. I wanted very much that you should see my wife."

"I could come in the morning, but I have an engagement which prevents me from seeing your wife tonight."

The Turk's answer was a singular one. He pulled the string which closed the mouth of the chamois-leather bag, and poured a flood of gold on to the table.

48

"There are one hundred pounds there," said he, "and I promise you that it will not take you an hour. I have a cab ready at the door."

Douglas Stone glanced at his watch. An hour would not make it too late to visit Lady Sannox. He had been there later. And the fee was an extraordinarily high one. He had been pressed by his creditors lately, and he could not afford to let such a chance pass. He would go.

"What is the case?" he asked.

"Oh, it is so sad a one! So sad a one! You have not, perhaps, heard of the daggers of the Almohades?"

"Never."

"Ah, they are Eastern daggers of a great age and of a singular shape, with the hilt like what you call a stirrup. I am a curiosity dealer, you understand, and that is why I have come to England from Smyrna, but next week I go back once more. Many things I brought with me, and I have a few things left, but among them, to my sorrow, is one of these daggers."

"You will remember that I have an appointment, sir," said the surgeon, with some irritation; "pray confine yourself to the necessary details."

"You will see that it is necessary. Today my wife fell down in a faint in the room in which I keep my wares, and she cut her lower lip upon this cursed dagger of Almohades."

"I see," said Douglas Stone, rising. "And you wish me to dress the wound?"

"No, no, it is worse than that."

"What then?"

"These daggers are poisoned."

"Poisoned!"

"Yes, and there is no man, East or West, who can tell now what is the poison or what the cure. But all that is known I know, for my father was in this trade before me, and we have had much to do with these poisoned weapons."

"What are the symptoms?"

"Deep sleep, and death in thirty hours."

"And you say there is no cure. Why then should you pay me this considerable fee?"

"No drug can cure, but the knife may."

"And how?"

"The poison is slow of absorption. It remains for hours in the wound."

"Washing, then, might cleanse it?"

"No more than in a snake bite. It is too subtle and too deadly."

"Excision of the wound, then?"

"That is it. If it be on the finger, take the finger off. So said my father always. But think of where this wound is, and that it is my wife. It is dreadful!"

But familiarity with such grim matters may take the finer edge from a man's sympathy. To Douglas Stone this was already an interesting case, and he brushed aside as irrelevant the feeble objections of the husband.

"It appears to be that or nothing," said he brusquely. "It is better to lose a lip than a life."

"Ah, yes, I know that you are right. Well, well, it is kismet, and it must be faced. I have the cab, and you will come with me and do this thing."

Douglas Stone took his case of bistouries from a drawer, and placed it with a roll of bandage and a compress of lint in his pocket. He must waste no more time if he were to see Lady Sannox.

"I am ready," said he, pulling on his overcoat. "Will you take a glass of wine before you go out into this cold air?"

His visitor shrank away, with a protesting hand upraised.

"You forget that I am a Mussulman, and a true follower of the Prophet," said he. "But tell me what is the bottle of green glass which you have placed in your pocket?"

"It is chloroform."

"Ah, that also is forbidden to us. It is a spirit, and we make no use of such things."

"What! You would allow your wife to go through an operation without an anæsthetic?"

"Ah! she will feel nothing, poor soul. The deep sleep has already come on, which is the first working of the poison. And then I have given her of our Smyrna opium. Come, sir, for already an hour has passed."

As they stepped out into the darkness, a sheet of rain was driven in upon their faces, and the hall lamp, which dangled from the arm of a marble Caryatid, went out with a fluff. Pim, the butler, pushed the heavy door to, straining hard with his shoulder against the wind, while the two men groped their way towards the yellow glare which showed where the cab was waiting. An instant later they were rattling upon their journey.

"Is it far?" asked Douglas Stone.

"Oh, no. We have a very little quiet place off the Euston Road."

The surgeon pressed the spring of his repeater and listened to the little tings which told him the hour. It was a quarter past nine. He calculated the distances, and the short time which it would take him to perform so trivial an operation. He ought to reach Lady Sannox by ten o'clock. Through the fogged windows he saw the blurred gas lamps dancing past, with occasionally the broader glare of a shop front. The rain was pelting and rattling upon the leathern top of the carriage, and the wheels swashed as they rolled through puddle and mud. Opposite to him the white headgear of his companion gleamed faintly through the obscurity. The surgeon felt in his pockets and arranged his needles, his ligatures and his safety-pins, that no time might be wasted when they arrived. He chafed with impatience and drummed his foot upon the floor.

But the cab slowed down at last and pulled up. In an instant Douglas Stone was out, and the Smyrna merchant's toe was at his very heel.

"You can wait," said he to the driver.

It was a mean-looking house in a narrow and sordid street. The surgeon, who knew his London well, cast a swift glance into the shadows, but there was nothing distinctive—no shop, no movement, nothing but a double line of dull, flat-faced houses, a double stretch of wet flagstones which gleamed in the lamplight, and a double rush of water in the gutters which swirled and gurgled towards the sewer gratings. The door which faced them was blotched and discoloured, and a faint light in the fan pane above it served to show the dust and the grime which covered it. Above in one of the bedroom windows, there was a dull yellow glimmer. The merchant knocked loudly, and, as he turned his dark face towards the light, Douglas Stone could see that it was contracted with anxiety. A bolt was drawn, and an elderly woman with a taper stood in the doorway, shielding the thin flame with her gnarled hand.

"Is all well?" gasped the merchant.

"She is as you left her, sir."

"She has not spoken?"

"No, she is in a deep sleep."

The merchant closed the door, and Douglas Stone walked down the narrow passage, glancing about him in some surprise as he did so. There was no oil-cloth, no mat, no hat-rack. Deep grey dust and heavy festoons of cobwebs met his eyes everywhere. Following the old woman up the winding stair, his firm footfall echoed harshly through the silent house. There was no carpet.

The bedroom was on the second landing. Douglas Stone followed the old nurse into it, with the merchant at his heels. Here, at least, there was furniture and to spare. The floor was littered and the corners piled with Turkish cabinets, inlaid tables, coats of chain mail, strange pipes, and grotesque weapons. A single small lamp stood upon a bracket on the wall. Douglas Stone took it down, and picking his way among the lumber, walked over to a couch in the corner, on which lay a woman dressed in the Turkish fashion, with yashmak and veil. The lower part of the face was exposed, and the surgeon saw a jagged cut which zig-zagged along the border of the under lip.

"You will forgive the yashmak," said the Turk. "You know our views about women in the East."

But the surgeon was not thinking about the yashmak. This was no longer a woman to him. It was a case. He stooped and examined the wound carefully.

"There are no signs of irritation," said he. "We might delay the operation until local symptoms develop."

The husband wrung his hands in uncontrollable agitation.

"Oh! sir, sir," he cried. "Do not trifle. You do not know. It is deadly. I know, and I give you my assurance that an operation is absolutely necessary. Only the knife can save her."

"And yet I am inclined to wait," said Douglas Stone.

"That is enough," the Turk cried, angrily. "Every minute is of importance, and I cannot stand here and see my wife allowed to sink. It only remains for me to give you my thanks for having come, and to call in some other surgeon before it is too late."

Douglas Stone hesitated. To refund that hundred pounds was no pleasant matter. But of course if he left the case he must return the money. And if the Turk were right and the woman died, his position before a coroner might be an embarrassing one.

"You have had personal experience of this poison?" he asked.

"I have."

"And you assure me that an operation is needful."

"I swear it by all that I hold sacred."

"The disfigurement will be frightful."

"I can understand that the mouth will not be a pretty one to kiss."

Douglas Stone turned fiercely upon the man. The speech was a brutal one. But the Turk has his own fashion of talk and of thought, and there was no time for wrangling. Douglas Stone drew a bistoury from his case, opened it and felt the keen straight edge with his forefinger. Then he held the lamp closer to the bed. Two dark eyes were gazing up at him through the slit in the yashmak. They were all iris, and the pupil was hardly to be seen.

"You have given her a very heavy dose of opium."

"Yes, she has had a good dose."

He glanced again at the dark eyes which looked straight at his own. They were dull and lustreless, but, even as he gazed, a little shifting sparkle came into them, and the lips quivered.

"She is not absolutely unconscious," said he.

"Would it not be well to use the knife while it will be painless?"

The same thought had crossed the surgeon's mind. He grasped the wounded lip with his forceps, and with two swift cuts he took out a broad V-shaped piece. The woman sprang up on the couch with a dreadful gurgling scream. Her covering was torn from her face. It was a face that he knew. In spite of that protruding upper lip and that slobber of blood, it was a face that he knew. She kept on putting her hand up to the gap and screaming. Douglas Stone sat down at the foot of the couch with his knife and his forceps. The room was whirling round, and he had felt something go like a ripping seam behind his ear. A bystander would have said that his face was the more ghastly of the two. As in a dream, or as if he had been looking at something at the play, he was conscious that the Turk's hair and beard lay upon the table, and that Lord Sannox was leaning against the wall with his hand to his side, laughing silently. The screams had died away now, and the dreadful head had dropped back again upon the pillow, but Douglas Stone still sat motionless, and Lord Sannox still chuckled quietly to himself.

"It was really very necessary for Marion, this operation," said he, "not physically, but morally, you know, morally."

Douglas Stone stooped forwards and began to play with the fringe of the coverlet. His knife tinkled down upon the ground, but he still held the forceps and something more.

"I had long intended to make a little example," said Lord Sannox, suavely. "Your note of Wednesday miscarried, and I have it here in my pocket-book. I took some pains in carrying out my idea. The wound, by the way, was from nothing more dangerous than my signet ring."

He glanced keenly at his silent companion, and cocked the small revolver which he held in his coat pocket. But Douglas Stone was still picking at the coverlet.

"You see, you have kept your appointment after all," said Lord Sannox.

And at that Douglas Stone began to laugh. He laughed long and loudly. But Lord Sannox did not laugh now. Something like fear sharpened and hardened his features. He walked from the room, and he walked on tiptoe. The old woman was waiting outside.

"Attend to your mistress when she awakes," said Lord Sannox.

Then he went down to the street. The cab was at the door, and the driver raised his hand to his hat.

"John," said Lord Sannox, "you will take the doctor home first. He will want leading downstairs, I think. Tell his butler that he has been taken ill at a case."

"Very good, sir."

"Then you can take Lady Sannox home."

"And how about yourself, sir?"

"Oh, my address for the next few months will be Hotel di Roma, Venice. Just see that the letters are sent on. And tell Stevens to exhibit all the purple chrysanthemums next Monday, and to wire me the result."

The Cat-Woman

M. E. Counselman

The first I heard of the strange Mademoiselle Chatte-Blanche (I shall call her this as I can not remember her real name) was that incoherent, absurd tale told me by the landlady.

"She ain't like us," the old lady insisted, glancing fearfully over her shoulder and speaking in a low tone. "A furriner, she is, and a quare one! I don't like the looks of 'er. Them eyes of hers are full of evil!"

I suppressed a smile. "Oh now, Mrs. Bates—not that bad, is she?" I said soothingly. "And you say she lives right across the hall from me, huh? I'm looking forward to meeting the lady."

"You'll come to no good, Mr. Harper, if you have any truck with the likes o' her!" the old lady warned, and waddled off, shaking her head slowly.

It was not until the second night after moving into Bates Boarding House that I really saw the lady. I had come in rather late from a show and was fumbling with my door-key, when a slight noise behind me caused me to turn quickly and straighten up.

A woman, a tall and beautifully formed woman, stood in the half-open doorway across from mine. She was very fair, with a straight ash-blond bob that fitted close to her head. There was something about her—I could not place it, unless it was her perfectly round green eyes—that reminded me immediately of a cat.

I swept off my hat with an unwonted nervousness, and murmured some sort of apology for disturbing her. She did not answer me at all, but merely stood there staring at me in the dimly lighted hall with those large cat-like eyes. I opened my mouth to speak again, closed it foolishly, and turned, red with discomfiture, to fumble again with my lock.

Suddenly behind me I heard a gentle but quite audible "pr-rrr" like the whir of an electric fan, though not as loud. Glancing over my shoulder I noticed that the strange woman had gone back into her room, although she must have moved very quietly for me not to have heard her.

In her half-open door stood a large white cat, and it was its purring which I had noticed.

"Hello, kitty!" I murmured, holding out a hand.

The animal seemed very friendly, for it came to me at once and rubbed against my legs, still purring loudly. I petted it a moment, then unlocking my door at last, I stepped inside, closed the door, and switched on my light. Glancing down I found that the cat had slipped in while I was not looking.

Scratching its head in a way cats love, I carried it across the hall and knocked timidly. There was no answer. I knocked again, then twice more, loudly. Still there was no answer. The lady must be out, or perhaps asleep, I told myself; and opening the door slightly I put the cat inside and shut it within. Then I returned to my room and went to bed.

I was wakened some hours later by something heavy on my feet. Sitting up and feeling about the covers, I touched something warm and furry. I switched on the bed lamp quickly, to find the white cat curled up contentedly on my feet. It must have come in through the window. Smiling slightly I went back to sleep, promising myself to return it to my queer neighbor in the morning.

Early the next day I knocked at the door, and receiving no answer put the cat inside as on the previous night. It was not until I was leaving for the office that I noticed with a start that all my windows were closed, as they must have been all night. I was sure, too, that my door had been locked against a chance thief. How, then, had the white cat gained admittance?

I was still wondering about this when I came home from the office. Mrs. Bates was dusting the stairs, and I paused a moment to speak to her. She mentioned again my queer neighbor, warning me to "keep shy" of her.

I smiled. "I saw her last night coming out of her door. Good-looking, isn't she?" The landlady shook her head ominously and cast her eyes toward heaven. "And she has a beautiful white cat," I added.

Mrs. Bates stiffened. "Cat?" she snapped. "I don't allow no pets kept in the boarders' rooms! I'll have to speak to her about that."

The front door opened just at this point and my strange neighbor came in. I was impressed once more with her odd beauty, the *feline* grace in her every motion. The word came inevitably to my mind—she reminded me so much of a sleek, well-fed cat.

"I'm told you keep a cat in your room, miss," began the landlady unpleasantly. "I thought you knew the rule —— "

Mademoiselle Chatte-Blanche turned her round green eyes upon Mrs. Bates in that disturbing unwinking stare of hers. "I haf no cat," she said.

Her voice was a purring, throaty contralto, very pleasant, with a slight accent—not French, not anything I had ever heard.

The landlady scowled. "But Mr. Harper here just tells me —— "

"I'm sorry," I broke in hastily. "It must have been a stray cat. I saw it in your doorway, and naturally I thought —— " I floundered help-lessly. That fixed green stare made me forget what I was trying to say.

"It iss all r-right," she murmured, and went upstairs to her room without another word. I followed suit in a moment; and there in the open door she stood as if waiting for me, motionless, silent, fixing me with her unwinking eyes.

"I'm terribly sorry," I began again, trying not to meet that disconcert-ing cat-like gaze. "You see, I put the cat —— "

Suddenly she moved toward me, closing her eyes slightly like a pleased cat—and to my utter consternation, rubbed her head gently against my shoulder!

My first thought was that this was merely an amusing trick of a clever street-woman, the advances of a *fille de joie* a little less blatant than those of her boldly dressed, loud-voiced sisters.

Then suddenly the feeling swept over me like a cold draft that she was not a woman at all, that she was not even a mortal—*that she was a cat!*

Moreover, as I drew myself away from her and entered my room queerly shaken, I could have sworn I heard, from the depths of that pale throat, the purring of a cat!

I strode across the room and stood a moment staring out the window, trying to collect my scattered wits, when I felt something rubbing against my ankle. It was the white cat, arching its furry back and purring loudly.

I was in no mood just then for anything resembling a cat, but its gentle wiles won me in spite of myself and I began playing with it. I rolled a ball of cord across the room and the animal bounded after it, tapping it playfully. Soon I had forgotten my upsetting encounter with Mademoiselle Chatte-Blanche and was having quite a time with my furry visitor, when our romp was interrupted by a rap on my door and a familiar call, announcing Mrs. Bates.

As she came in, her smile vanished. "Oh, this is your white cat, eh? I never liked the critters. . . . Scat!"

As the animal crouched motionless with fear, the old lady seized it quickly by the scruff of its neck and dropped it from my window into the muddy alley below. "There! Maybe it'll go away now."

She talked for a moment, collected her rent, and was standing in my open door for a parting word, when beyond her in the hall I saw Made-moiselle Chatte-Blanche.

She was strangely disheveled and spattered with mud; and she was directing upon the landlady's back such a look of concentrated hate that I shivered. Only a moment she stood thus; then she had disappeared into her room.

Next morning at breakfast (I ate alone, as I had to leave earlier than the other boarders) I noticed that Mrs. Bates' face was all but hidden behind a network of adhesive plaster, and bright red spots of mercuro-chrome.

"Why . . . why, what's the matter with your face?" I asked with concern as she served my breakfast.

"A cat got in my room last night," she wailed. "That big white one, it was! It jumped on me in bed and scratched me up terrible afore I could chase it out. I tried to kill it with the broom, but it got away. I never did like a cat . . . mean critters, they are! . . ." She prattled on until I left for the office.

It was two days later that I saw Mademoiselle Chatte-Blanche again. I confess I had avoided her in the hall; and as our meal hours were different, we had no occasion to meet. But on this afternoon she was standing in her door as usual, watching me as I came down the hall. Sensing that she was likely to repeat her disconcerting cat-caress, I nodded curtly and went straight into my room, stumbling over some-thing soft as I did so.

There was the white cat again, purring and rubbing against my legs affectionately. Something impelled me to glance back where the woman across the hall had been standing, with an uncanny knowledge that she was there no longer.

She was gone.

I shut my door with a creepy feeling, which the pranks of the white cat soon dispelled, however. We played together for a while, when our romp was again interrupted by the voice and knock of Mrs. Bates.

The cat seemed to know it was she, for it fluffed up its long fur and hissed angrily. Then it turned as if frightened and leaped out of the open window. It was a second-story window—not a pleasant jump, even for a cat. I glanced down to see if the animal had landed safely—just in time to see a huge mongrel dash down the alley and pounce upon my unfortu-nate pet.

The cat fought furiously, but it had not a chance against the big dog. I saw the mongrel snap twice at my little friend, heard the kitten give an odd cry of anguish—a cry that sounded far more human than feline. A moment later, Mrs. Bates and I saw the limp, blood-spattered form of the white cat lying very still in the muddy alley.

And somehow, it has always seemed to me something more than a mere coincidence that on that very day Mademoiselle Chatte-Blanche disappeared mysteriously as smoke, without a word of farewell—and, as Mrs. Bates reiterated plaintively, without even paying her rent. And strangely, she left behind all her personal belongings (from which Mrs. Bates managed to collect slightly more than her rent, though she would never have admitted it). All her clothes, hats, shoes, toilet articles, every little personal belonging, our lady left behind her . . . and an absurd thing the landlady remarked upon at length curiously: a foolish plaything fond old maids fashion for their cats—a small worsted mouse stuffed with catnip.

The Champion

Richard Laymon

Y ou're not going anywhere," said the man blocking the door.
He was smaller than Harry Barlow, with neither the bulk nor the muscle to make his words good. But he had a friend on each side. Though Harry figured he could take the trio, he didn't want to try. Like most big men, he'd been pestered all his life by people wanting to prove their toughness. He was tired of it. He wanted never to fight again.

"Please move," he said to the man.

"Not on your life, bud. You're staying right here. This is your big night."

The entire restaurant erupted with cheers. Harry turned slowly, studying the faces around him. Most belonged to men. Funny, he hadn't noticed that during the meal. He hadn't noticed much of anything, really, except his dinner of top sirloin.

When he first saw Roy's Bar and Steak House, he'd been surprised by the crowd of cars in its parking lot. The town, hidden in a valley deep in northern California's timber country, seemed too small to have so many cars. Once he tasted the rich, charcoal broiled steak, however, he realized that folks had probably driven miles for supper at Roy's. He was glad he'd stopped in.

Until now.

Now, he only wanted to leave. He took a step toward the three men barring his way.

"Hold up," someone called from behind.

Harry turned around. He'd seen this man before. During supper, the fellow had wandered from table to table, chatting and laughing with the customers; he'd even exchanged a few words with Harry. "I'm Roy," he'd said. "This your first time here? Whereabouts are you from? How's your beef?" He'd seemed like a pleasant, amiable man.

Now he had a shotgun aimed at Harry's midsection.

"What's that for?" Harry asked.

"Can't have you leave," Roy told him.

"Why's that?"

Except for a few scattered clinks of silverware, there was silence in the restaurant.

"You're the challenger," Roy said.

"What am I challenging?" Harry asked. He waited, feeling a tremor of fear.

"It's not a what, it's a who."

Harry heard a few quiet laughs. Looking around, he saw that every face was turned toward him. He rubbed his hands along the soft corduroy of his pants legs. "Okay," he said, "*who* am I challenging?"

"The champion."

"Am I?"

More laughter.

"You sure are. You ever hear of the Saturday Night Fights? Well, here at Roy's Bar and Steak House, we have our own version."

Cheers and applause roared through the restaurant. Roy held up his hands for silence. "The first man through the door after nine on Saturday night, he's the challenger. You walked in at nine-o-three."

Harry remembered the group of seven or eight men who had been standing just outside the door, talking in quiet, eager voices. A few had looked at him oddly as he stepped by. Now he knew why they were here: they'd arrived at nine, and had to wait until a chump went inside.

"Look," Harry said, "I don't want to fight anyone."

"They never do."

"Well, I'm not *going* to."

"We had a guy about two years back," Roy said. "Some kind of chicken pacifist. He wouldn't fight the champion. Just wouldn't do it. Made a run for the door." Roy grinned and waved the barrel of his shotgun. "I cut him down. I'll cut you down, if you make a run."

"This is crazy," Harry muttered.

"Just our way of having a good time." Roy turned his attention to the crowd. "All right, folks. For any newcomers to the Saturday Night Fight, I'll tell how she works." A waitress stepped up to his side, holding a fish bowl stuffed with red tickets. "We got a hundred tickets in the bowl. Each ticket has a three-second time period on it, going up to five minutes. Never had a fight go more than that. You pay five bucks for each chance. Winner gets the pot. Any tickets aren't sold by fight time, they belong to the house." He patted the arm of the woman holding the fish bowl. "Julie here, she's timekeeper. I'm referee. The fight's over when one or the other contestant's dead. Any questions?"

No questions.

"Buy your tickets at the counter. Fight starts in ten minutes."

During the next ten minutes, as customers filed past the cash register and drew their tickets from the bowl, Roy stood guard. Harry considered running for the door. He decided, however, that he would rather face the champion than Roy's shotgun. To pass the time, he counted the number of tickets sold.

Seventy-two.

At five dollars each, that came to $360.

Somebody'd be going home with a tidy prize.

"Fight starts in one minute," Roy announced. "Last call for tickets."

"Elmer?"

A thin, bald old man nodded and went out the rear door.

"The champion will be right in, folks. If a couple of you could help move these tables out of the way . . ."

Six tables from the center of the room were moved toward the sides, leaving a clear area that seemed awfully small to Harry.

The crowd suddenly cheered and whistled. Looking toward the rear door, Harry saw Elmer enter. A tall, lean man walked behind him.

"Ladies and gentlemen!" Roy called. "The champion!"

The champion scowled at the crowd as he hobbled toward the clear space. From his looks, he'd fought many times before. His broad forehead was creased with a scar. He wore a patch over his left eye. The tip of one ear was missing. So was the forefinger of his left hand.

Looking down, Harry saw the cause of the champion's strange, awkward walk: a three-foot length of chain dragged between his shackled feet.

"I'm not fighting this man," Harry said.

"Sure you are," Roy told him. "Elmer?"

The skinny old man knelt down. Opening a padlock, he removed the shackle from the right ankle of the champion.

Harry took a step backwards.

"Stand still," Roy ordered.

"There's no way you can make me fight this man."

"The fellas with low numbers'll be glad to hear that."

"Right!" someone yelled from the crowd.

"Just stand there," called another.

Others joined the shouting, some urging him to wait passively for death, some demanding that he fight.

Elmer locked the iron onto Harry's left ankle. The yard-long chain now connected the two adversaries.

"Time?" Roy called.

The yelling stopped.

"Ten seconds to starting," Julie said.

"Elmer?"

The old man scurried away. From behind the counter, he took a pair of matching knives.

"Five seconds," Julie said.

The knives had wooden handles, brass cross-guards, and eight-inch blades of polished steel.

"We won't do it," Harry said to the champion. "They can't make us."

The champion sneered.

Elmer handed one knife to the champion, one to Harry.

"Two seconds."

"Go!" said Julie.

Harry flung down his knife. Its point thunked the hardwood floor, biting deep. Its handle was still vibrating as the champion jabbed at Harry's stomach. Harry jumped away. The chain stopped his foot, and he fell backwards. The champion stomped on his knee. Harry cried out as his leg exploded with pain.

With a demented shriek, the champion threw himself down on Harry. Using both hands, Harry held back the knife that the champion was driving toward his face. The blade pressed closer. He blinked, and felt his right eyelashes brush the steel point. Turning his head, he shoved sideways. The blade ripped his ear, and stabbed the floor beside his head.

He smashed a fist upward into the champion's nose. Rolling, he got out from under the stunned man. He crawled away from the grasping hands, and stood.

"Enough!" he shouted. "That's enough! It has to stop!"

The crowd booed and hissed.

The champion, tearing his knife from the floor, leaped to his feet and swung at Harry. The blade sliced the front of Harry's plaid shirt.

"Stop it!"

The champion lunged, growling. He punched the knife toward Harry's belly. Harry chopped down, knocking the hand away. The champion stabbed again. This time, the blade slashed Harry's blocking hand. It struck at his stomach. Spinning aside, Harry dodged the steel.

He gripped the champion's right arm at the wrist and elbow, and pumped his knee upward, breaking the champion's forearm with a popping sound like snapped kindling. Screaming, the champion dropped his knife.

But he caught it with his left hand, and thrust it wildly at Harry, who ducked out of the way.

Dropping to one knee, Harry grabbed the chain and tugged upward. The champion's leg flew high, and he tumbled backwards. Harry sprang onto him. With both hands, he clutched the champion's left hand, and pinned it to the floor.

"Give up!" he shouted into the champion's blood-smeared face.

The champion nodded. The knife dropped from his hand.

"That's it!" Harry raised his eyes to the crowd. "He gave up! He quit!"

Abruptly, the man sat up and clamped his teeth on Harry's throat. Blind with pain and enraged by the deception, Harry slapped the floor. He found the knife. He plunged it four times into the champion's side before the jaws loosened their grip on his neck. The champion flopped backwards. His head hit the floor with a solid thunk.

Harry crawled aside, feeling his wounded neck. He wasn't bleeding as badly as he'd feared.

Sitting on the floor, he watched Roy kneel at the champion's side.

"Is he dead?" someone shouted from the crowd.

Roy felt the pulse in the champion's neck. "Not yet," he announced.

"Come on!" someone yelled.

"Hang on, champ!" shouted another.

"Give it up!" called a woman's voice.

The crowd roared for a few seconds. Then silence fell. Complete silence. All eyes were fixed on Roy kneeling beside the fallen champion.

"Gone!" Roy announced.

Julie clicked her stopwatch. "Two minutes, twenty-eight seconds."

"That's me!" a man yelled, waving his red ticket. "That's me! I got it!"

"Come on up and get your money," Roy said. Then he turned to his skinny old assistant. "Elmer?"

Elmer knelt between Harry and the body. He unlatched a shackle. Before Harry could move to prevent it, the metal cuff clamped shut around his right ankle. Elmer shut the padlock.

"Hey!" Harry cried. "Take 'em off! I won! You've got to let me go!"

"Can't do that," Roy said, smiling down at him. "You're the champion."

The Closed Window

A. C. Benson

The Tower of Nort stood in a deep angle of the downs; formerly an old road led over the hill, but it is now a green track covered with turf; the later highway choosing rather to cross a low saddle of the ridge, for the sake of the beasts of burden. The tower, originally built to guard the great road, was a plain, strong, thick-walled fortress. To the tower had been added a plain and seemly house, where the young Sir Mark de Nort lived very easily and plentifully. To the south stretched the great wood of Nort, but the Tower stood high on an elbow of the down, sheltered from the north by the great green hills. The villagers had an odd ugly name for the Tower, which they called the Tower of Fear; but the name was falling into disuse, and was only spoken, and that heedlessly, by ancient men, because Sir Mark was vexed to hear it so called. Sir Mark was not yet thirty, and had begun to say that he must marry a wife; but he seemed in no great haste to do so, and loved his easy, lonely life, with plenty of hunting and hawking on the down. With him lived his cousin and heir, Roland Ellice, a heedless good-tempered man, a few years older than Sir Mark; he had come on a visit to Sir Mark, when he first took possession of the Tower; and there had seemed no reason why he should go away; the two suited each other; Sir Mark was sparing of speech, fond of books and of rhymes. Roland was different, loving ease and wine and talk, and finding in Mark a good listener. Mark loved his cousin, and thought it praiseworthy of him to stay and help to cheer so sequestered a house, since there were few neighbours within reach.

And yet Mark was not wholly content with his easy life; there were many days when he asked himself why he should go thus quietly on, day by day, like a stalled ox; still, there appeared no reason why he should do otherwise; there were but few folk on his land, and they were content; yet he sometimes envied them their bondage and their round of daily duties. The only place where he could else have been was with the army, or even with the Court; but Sir Mark was no soldier, and even less of a courtier; he hated tedious gaiety, and it was a time of peace. So because he loved solitude and quiet he lived at home, and sometimes thought himself but half a man; yet was he happy after a sort, but for a kind of little hunger of the heart.

What gave the Tower so dark a name was the memory of old Sir James de Nort, Mark's grandfather, an evil and secret man, who had dwelt at Nort under some strange shadow; he had driven his son from his doors, and lived at the end of his life with his books and his own close thoughts, spying upon the stars and tracing strange figures in books; since his death the old room in the turret top, where he came by his end in a dreadful way, had been closed; it was entered by a turret-door, with a flight of steps from the chamber below. It had four windows, one to each of the winds; but the window which looked upon the down was fastened up, and secured with a great shutter of oak.

One day of heavy rain, Roland, being wearied of doing nothing, and vexed because Mark sate so still in a great chair, reading in a book, said to his cousin at last that he must go and visit the old room, in which he had never set foot. Mark closed his book, and smiling indulgently at Roland's restlessness, rose, stretching himself, and got the key; and together they went up the turret stairs. The key groaned loudly in the lock, and, when the door was thrown back, there appeared a high faded room, with a timbered roof, and with a close, dull smell. Round the walls were presses, with the doors fast; a large oak table, with a chair beside it, stood in the middle. The walls were otherwise bare and rough; the spiders had spun busily over the windows and in the angles. Roland was full of questions, and Mark told him all he had heard of old Sir James and his silent ways, but said that he knew nothing of the disgrace that had seemed to envelop him, or of the reasons why he had so evil a name. Roland said that he thought it a shame that so fair a room should lie so nastily, and pulled one of the casements open, when a sharp gust broke into the room, with so angry a burst of rain, that he closed it again in haste; little by little, as they talked, a shadow began to fall upon their spirits, till Roland declared that there was still a blight upon the place; and Mark told him of the death of old Sir James, who had been found after a day of silence, when he had not set foot outside his chamber, lying on the floor of the room, strangely bedabbled with wet and mud, as though he had come off a difficult journey, speechless, and with a look of anguish on his face; and that he had died soon after they had found him, muttering words that no one understood. Then the two young men drew near to the closed window; the shutters were tightly barred, and across the panels was scrawled in red, in an uncertain hand, the words CLAUDIT ET NEMO APERIT, which Mark explained was the Latin for the text, *He shutteth and none openeth.* And then Mark said that the story went that it was ill for the man that opened the window, and shut it should remain for him. But Roland girded at him for his want of curiosity, and had laid a hand upon the bar as though to open it, but Mark forbade him urgently. 'Nay,' said he, 'let it remain so — we must not meddle with the will of the dead!' and as he said the word, there came so furious a gust upon the windows that it seemed as though some stormy thing would beat them open; so they left the room together, and presently descending, found the sun struggling through the rain.

But both Mark and Roland were sad and silent all that day; for though they spake not of it, there was a desire in their minds to open the closed window, and to see what would befall; in Roland's mind it was like the desire of a child to peep into what is forbidden; but in Mark's mind a sort of shame to be so bound by an old and weak tale of superstition.

Now it seemed to Mark, for many days, that the visit to the turret-room had brought a kind of shadow down between them. Roland was peevish and ill-at-ease; and ever the longing grew upon Mark, so strongly that it seemed to him that something drew him to the room, some beckoning of a hand or calling of a voice.

Now one bright and sunshiny morning it happened that Mark was left alone within the house. Roland had ridden out early, not saying where he was bound. And Mark sate, more listlessly than was his wont, and played with the ears of his great dog, that sate with his head upon his master's knee, looking at him with liquid eyes, and doubtless wondering why Mark went not abroad.

Suddenly Sir Mark's eye fell upon the key of the upper room, which lay on the window-ledge where he had thrown it; and the desire to go up and pluck the heart from the little mystery came upon him with a strength that he could not resist; he rose twice and took up the key, and fingering it doubtfully, laid it down again; then suddenly he took it up, and went swiftly into the turret-stair, and up, turning, turning, till his head was dizzy with the bright peeps of the world through the loophole windows. Now all was green, where a window gave on the down; and now it was all clear air and sun, the warm breeze coming pleasantly into the cold stairway; presently Mark heard the pattering of feet on the stair below, and knew that the old hound had determined to follow him; and he waited a moment at the door, half pleased, in his strange mood, to have the company of a living thing. So when the dog was at his side, he stayed no longer, but opened the door and stepped within the room.

The room, for all its faded look, had a strange air about it, and though he could not say why, Mark felt that he was surely expected. He did not hesitate, but walked to the shutter and considered it for a moment; he heard a sound behind him. It was the old hound who sate with his head aloft, sniffing the air uneasily; Mark called him and held out his hand, but the hound would not move; he wagged his tail as though to acknowledge that he was called, and then he returned to his uneasy quest. Mark watched him for a moment, and saw that the old dog had made up his mind that all was not well in the room, for he lay down, gathering his legs under him, on the threshold, and watched his master with frightened eyes, quivering visibly. Mark, no lighter of heart, and in a kind of fearful haste, pulled the great staple off the shutter and set it on the ground, and then wrenched the shutters back; the space revealed was largely filled by old and dusty webs of spiders, which Mark lightly tore down, using the staple of the shutters to do this; it was with a strange shock of surprise that he saw that the window was dark, or nearly so; it seemed as though there were some further obstacle outside; yet Mark knew that from below the leaded panes of the window were visible. He drew back for a moment, but unable to restrain his curiosity, wrenched the rusted casement open. But still all was dark without; and there came in a gust of icy wind from outside; it was as though something had passed him swiftly, and he heard the old hound utter a strangled howl; then turning, he saw him spring to his feet with his hair bristling and his teeth bare, and next moment the dog turned and leapt out of the room.

Mark, left alone, tried to curb a tide of horror that swept through his veins; he looked round at the room, flooded with the southerly sunlight, and then he turned again to the dark window, and putting a strong constraint upon himself, leaned out, and saw a thing which bewildered him so strangely that he thought for a moment his senses had deserted him. He looked out on a lonely dim hillside, covered with rocks and stones; the hill came up close to the window, so that he could have jumped down upon it, the wall below seeming to be built into the rocks. It was all dark and silent, like a clouded night, with a faint light coming from whence he could not see. The hill sloped away very steeply from the tower, and he seemed to see a plain beyond, where at the same time he knew that the down ought to lie. In the plain there was a light, like the firelit window of a house; a little below him some shape like a crouching man seemed to run and slip among the stones, as though suddenly surprised, and seeking to escape. Side by side with a deadly fear which began to invade his heart, came an uncontrollable desire to leap down among the rocks; and then it seemed to him that the figure below stood upright and began to beckon him. There came over him a sense that he was in deadly peril; and, like a man on the edge of a precipice, who has just enough will left to try to escape, he drew himself by main force away from the window, closed it, put the shutters back, replaced the staple, and, his limbs all trembling, crept out of the room, feeling along the walls like a palsied man. He locked the door, and then, his terror overpowering him, he fled down the turret-stairs. Hardly thinking what he did, he came out on the court, and going to the great well that stood in the centre of the yard, he went to it and flung the key down, hearing it clink on the sides as it fell. Even then he dared not re-enter the house, but glanced up and down, gazing about him, while the cloud of fear and horror by insensible degrees dispersed, leaving him weak and melancholy.

Presently Roland returned, full of talk, but broke off to ask if Mark were ill. Mark, with a kind of surliness, an unusual mood for him, denied it somewhat sharply. Roland raised his eyebrows, and said no more, but prattled on. Presently after a silence he said to Mark, 'What did you do all the morning?' and it seemed to Mark as though this were accompanied with a spying look. An unreasonable anger seized him. 'What does it matter to you what I did?' he said. 'May not I do what I like in my own house?'

'Doubtless,' said Roland, and sate silent with uplifted brows; then he hummed a tune, and presently went out.

They sate at dinner that evening with long silences, contrary to their wont, though Mark bestirred himself to ask questions. When they were left alone, Mark stretched out his hand to Roland, saying, 'Roland, forgive me! I spoke to you this morning in a way of which I am ashamed; we have lived so long together—and yet we came nearer to quarrelling today than we have ever done before; and it was my fault.'

Roland smiled, and held Mark's hand for a moment. 'Oh, I had not given it another thought,' he said; 'the wonder is that you can bear with an idle fellow as you do.' Then they talked for a while with the pleasant glow of friendliness that two good comrades feel when they have been reconciled. But late in the evening Roland said, 'Was there any story, Mark, about your grandfather's leaving any treasure of money behind him?'

The question grated somewhat unpleasantly upon Mark's mood; but he controlled himself and said, 'No, none that I know of—except that he found the estate rich and left it poor—and what he did with his revenues no one knows—you had better ask the old men of the village; they know more about the house than I do. But, Roland, forgive me once more if I say that I do not desire Sir James's name to be mentioned between us. I wish we had not entered his room; I do not know how to express it, but it seems to me as though he had sate there, waiting quietly to be summoned, and as though we had troubled him, and—as though he had joined us. I think he was an evil man, close and evil. And there hangs in my mind a verse of Scripture, where Samuel said to the witch, "Why has thou disquieted me to bring me up?" Oh,' he went on, 'I do not know why I talk wildly thus'; for he saw that Roland was looking at him with astonishment, with parted lips; 'but a shadow has fallen upon me, and there seems evil abroad.'

From that day forward a heaviness lay on the spirit of Mark that could not be scattered. He felt, he said to himself, as though he had meddled light-heartedly with something far deeper and more dangerous than he had supposed—like a child that has aroused some evil beast that slept. He had dark dreams too. The figure that he had seen among the rocks seemed to peep and beckon him, with a mocking smile, over perilous places, where he followed unwilling. But the heavier he grew the lighter-hearted Roland became; he seemed to walk in some bright vision of his own, intent upon a large and gracious design.

One day he came into the hall in the morning, looking so radiant that Mark asked him half enviously what he had to make him so glad. 'Glad,' said Roland, 'oh, I know it! Merry dreams, perhaps. What do you think of a good grave fellow who beckons me on with a brisk smile, and shows me places, wonderful places, under banks and in woodland pits, where riches lie piled together? I am sure that some good fortune is preparing for me, Mark — but you shall share it.' Then Mark, seeing in his words a certain likeness, with a difference, to his own dark visions, pressed his lips together and sate looking stonily before him.

At last, one still evening of spring, when the air was intolerably languid and heavy for mankind, but full of sweet promises for trees and hidden peeping things, though a lurid redness of secret thunder had lain all day among the heavy clouds in the plain, the two dined together. Mark had walked alone that day, and had lain upon the turf of the down, fighting against a weariness that seemed to be poisoning the very springs of life within him. But Roland had been brisk and alert, coming and going upon some secret and busy errand, with a fragment of a song upon his lips, like a man preparing to set off for a far country, who is glad to be gone. In the evening, after they had dined, Roland had let his fancy rove in talk. 'If we were rich,' he said, 'how we would transform this old place!'

'It is fair enough for me,' said Mark heavily; and Roland had chidden him lightly for his sombre ways, and sketched new plans of life.

Mark, wearied and yet excited, with an intolerable heaviness of spirit, went early to bed, leaving Roland in the hall. After a short and broken sleep, he awoke, and lighting a candle, read idly and gloomily to pass the heavy hours. The house seemed full of strange noises that night. Once or twice came a scraping and a faint hammering in the wall; light footsteps seemed to pass in the turret — but the tower was always full of noises, and Mark heeded them not; at last he fell asleep again, to be suddenly awakened by a strange and desolate crying, that came he knew not whence, but seemed to wail upon the air. The old dog, who slept in Mark's room, heard it too; he was sitting up in a fearful expectancy. Mark rose in haste, and taking the candle, went into the passage that led to Roland's room. It was empty, but a light burned there and showed that the room had not been slept in. Full of a horrible fear, Mark returned, and went in hot haste up the turret steps, fear and anxiety struggling together in his mind. When he reached the top, he found the little door broken forcibly open, and a light within. He cast a haggard look round the room, and then the crying came again, this time very faint and desolate.

Mark cast a shuddering glance at the window; it was wide open and showed a horrible liquid blackness; round the bar in the centre that divided the casements, there was something knotted. He hastened to the window, and saw that it was a rope, which hung heavily. Leaning out he saw that something dangled from the rope below him—and then came the crying again out of the darkness, like the crying of a lost spirit.

He could see as in a bitter dream the outline of the hateful hillside; but there seemed to his disordered fancy to be a tumult of some kind below; pale lights moved about, and he saw a group of forms which scattered like a shoal of fish when he leaned out. He knew that he was looking upon a scene that no mortal eye ought to behold, and it seemed to him at the moment as though he was staring straight into hell.

The rope went down among the rocks and disappeared; but Mark clenched it firmly and using all his strength, which was great, drew it up hand over hand; as he drew it up he secured it in loops round the great oak table; he began to be afraid that his strength would not hold out, and once when he returned to the window after securing a loop, a great hooded thing like a bird flew noiselessly at the window and beat its wings.

Presently he saw that the form which dangled on the rope was clear of the rocks below; it had come up through them, as though they were but smoke; and then his task seemed to him more sore than ever. Inch by painful inch he drew it up, working fiercely and silently; his muscles were tense, and drops stood on his brow, and the veins hammered in his ears; his breath came and went in sharp sobs. At last the form was near enough for him to seize it; he grasped it by the middle and drew Roland, for it was Roland, over the window-sill. His head dangled and drooped from side to side; his face was dark with strangled blood and his limbs hung helpless. Mark drew his knife and cut the rope that was tied under his arms; the helpless limbs sank huddling on the foor; then Mark looked up; at the window a few feet from him was a face, more horrible than he had supposed a human face, if it was human indeed, could be. It was deadly white, and hatred, baffled rage, and a sort of devilish malignity glared from the white set eyes, and the drawn mouth. There was a rush from behind him; the old hound, who had crept up unawares into the room, with a fierce outcry of rage sprang on to the window-sill; Mark heard the scraping of his claws upon the stone. Then the hound leapt through the window, and in a moment there was the sound of a heavy fall outside. At the same instant the darkness seemed to lift and draw up like a cloud; a bank of blackness rose past the window, and left the dark outline of the down, with a sky sown with tranquil stars.

The cloud of fear and horror that hung over Mark lifted too; he felt in some dim way that his adversary was vanquished; he carried Roland down the stairs and laid him on his bed; he roused the household, who looked fearfully at him, and then his own strength failed; he sank upon the floor of his room, and the dark tide of unconsciousness closed over him.

Mark's return to health was slow. One who has looked into the Unknown finds it hard to believe again in the outward shows of life. His first conscious speech was to ask for his hound; they told him that the body of the dog had been found, horribly mangled as though by the teeth of some fierce animal, at the foot of the tower. The dog was buried in the garden, with a slab above him, in which are the words:

EUGE SERVE BONE ET FIDELIS

A silly priest once said to Mark that it was not meet to write Scripture over the grave of a beast. But Mark said warily that an inscription was for those who read it, to make them humble, and not to increase the pride of what lay below.

When Mark could leave his bed, his first care was to send for builders, and the old tower of Nort was taken down, stone by stone, to the ground, and a fair chapel built on the site; in the wall there was a secret stairway, which led from the top chamber, and came out among the elder-bushes that grew below the tower, and here was found a coffer of gold, which paid for the church; because, until it was found, it was Mark's design to leave the place desolate. Mark is wedded since, and has his children about his knee; those who come to the house see a strange and wan man, who sits at Mark's board, and whom he uses very tenderly; sometimes this man is merry, and tells a long tale of his being beckoned and led by a tall and handsome person, smiling, down a hillside to fetch gold; though he can never remember the end of the matter; but about the springtime he is silent or mutters to himself; and this is Roland; his spirit seems shut up within him in some close cell, and Mark prays for his release, but till God call him, he treats him like a dear brother, and with the reverence due to one who has looked out on the other side of Death, and who may not say what his eyes beheld.

The Clown

Jessica Amanda Salmonson

for Ray Bradbury

How can he do it?" Tina wondered aloud, she herself exhausted from the high-wire act which closed the night's show. "He's still out there, still full of energy!" She was gazing out from behind the curtain into the bigtop's one ring, from whence she had just departed, and where a single clown cavorted.

A quick sideways glance assured her that Jacob (billed tritely as Hercules) was watching *her*, not the antics in the ring. He watched the sweat trickle down her neck. She was hot despite the coldness of the evening and the skimpiness of her costume. She shivered merely to give Jacob the excuse to enfold her in his jacket, putting his strong arms around her in the process.

She encouraged him from instinct or habit, but her mind was elsewhere. Her eyes witnessed Tobo. He was jumping and running and falling down like a crazy mouse, scurrying from one end of the tent to the other with boundless, bounding energy. He squeezed one extra roar of laughter out of the departing audience, by faking a kick to the buttocks of the ringmaster.

Closing the show, the ringmaster shouted his thanks over and over, implying the necessity of everyone returning on the morrow to see, again, "the greatest 'little bigtop' west of the Mississippi." Half the crowd had already leaked through the front flaps, heading toward the gaudily lit concessions and amusement rides. Most of the performers had already retired to their wagons, done with another day's laborious entertainment. But Tobo always stayed until there was not even one more person left to be amused by his fool's act.

Departing children tried to touch the energetic clown; some of them succeeded. Children loved Tobo and he had a natural affinity for the youngsters, was even like them in his amiable fashion.

"He loves the sound of laughter," Jacob replied, his huge hands still resting on the slender woman's shoulders. "The audience feeds him energy."

"They feed me mine, too," she said. "But there's a limit for everyone. I've never seen Tobo reach his."

Jacob bit gently at the back of the distracted woman's sweat-slimed neck. He whispered, "Will I see you tonight? My wagon? Yours?"

Unexpectedly (for Tina), she shook loose his grasp and answered abruptly, "Not tonight, Jake. I've got to start getting some sleep for a change."

It was a good excuse, but only an excuse, and it annoyed Jacob. He stomped out the back flap of the bigtop, pouting the whole way.

Tina waited for Tobo. There were only a few stragglers left. Tobo was handing them deflated advertising balloons as they went out, squeaking horns at the youngest ones and wiggling bushy eyebrows at the kids who thought themselves mature. None could help but laugh. As the last man, with his tiny daughter, went out from the tent, the ringmaster had already brushed past Tina and cut the lights.

Tobo stood alone in the center of the ring. Despite the raucous sounds in the arcade, there was a sort of silence in the bigtop, magnified by Tobo's sudden stillness. For the first time all day, the clown looked a bit bedraggled. He didn't move for a long time, and did not know Tina watched him from the darkness.

A real smile shined out from the center of his painted one. It seemed as though he was never sad, although a subtle melancholy fell over him whenever a day was done, unlike every other performer, glad the work was over.

Fifteen hours a day or longer, Tobo cartwheeled and hopped about the tent, or, between shows, took to the crowded arcade, drumming up interest in the bigtop. He performed simple magic tricks when even kids could do better, delighting everyone with his ineptitude; he twisted skinny balloons into halos and hats, setting them on the heads of tots; he made silly noises with the conglomeration of whistles and horns dangling and clattering about his hobo clown costume; and he spread general joy to as many people as he could reach in a day.

Now, in the shadows of the lightless tent, he trudged slowly toward a curtain, eyes twinkling for all his weariness. It was time for him to bed down in his terrible little Ford canopy truck *cum* circus wagon; but he'd be up before any other performer, eager to greet the morning's visitors.

"You were really funny tonight," said Tina as the clown came through the curtain. She gave him her best smile and reached out her small, white hand to take his gloved one.

"Thank you," he said simply. He smiled back, and cocked his colorful face, his happy face which didn't know how to frown.

"You're always funny," she said, flattering him more. "You're really a very remarkable man."

If Tobo blushed, it didn't show under the colors of his face. He looked down at his oversized shoes and moved one leg from side to side in exaggerated shyness, his baggy trousers flapping.

"Won't you come to my wagon?" she asked in a careful tone, remembering how she had frightened him before. "Or perhaps we can find room to sit and talk in your little truck."

"You need to talk?" he asked, looking up again, like a cocker spaniel eager to please a friend.

"Yeah. Yeah."

Tobo nodded innocently. They went out into the chilly evening, Tina clutching Jacob's coat around her neck. Carnival rides were still twirling; recorded music blared; bright lights in twenty colors tried to push back the night. The clown and the tightrope walker sauntered toward the furthest edge of the grounds, where the noise and lights were less a nuisance, where wagons and trucks were parked in haphazard rows.

In the beat-up Ford which served as Tobo's home, there was only room for two to sit, and that was on the bed. Tina used the tightness of the quarters as an excuse to sit as close to Tobo as was possible without actually being in his lap. He didn't seem to notice.

Her seductive postures completely missed their mark, but Tina had a healthy ego, and did know other tricks. She'd found his weak spot earlier, and proceeded once again to flatter him as regards his comical routines. She praised his ceaseless vigor and empathy for the crowd, his easy rapport with children. "Some clowns scare the shit out of kids, you know? I've never seen a kid not want to shake your hand!"

Sweet Tobo nearly swooned. He had never been flattered so much.

"Really," she continued. "From first to final act and every moment in between, it seems you're always on the go, always performing, able to warm up even the most irascible crowd. Even while we're on the road, you're in full clown get-up, full of routines to cheer us on our journey. You're really something, Tobo, you really are."

He was so tongue-tied and embarrassed, his head just bobbed from one side to the other, as though he could hide behind himself. She'd reduced him to putty. Tobo loved his role in life, and nothing could more easily win his confidence than someone appreciating the finer points of his art. When Tina was convinced she had him in her power, her tone changed to a more seductive level.

"You know, Tobo," she began, "you work from dawn to dusk, so I've never seen what you look like out of costume." She slipped her arm around his waist. He didn't act as though he minded. "In fact, I don't know anyone who has ever seen you without the whistles and baggy stuff. Even travelling between towns. You always seem to be in the ring, always kidding around, always in costume."

She was practically breathing in his ear, and was whispering by the time she got around to her main point:

"Why don't you wash all that stuff off your face and slip out of those huge coveralls, huh? We'll, well, we'll have a little fun together. It would make me feel better. You, too, I bet."

"Wash it off?" he said innocently, gently pushing her away from his ear, then drying it out with a gloved finger. "Wash what off?"

"The clown make-up, silly! I want to see what you look like while we make love!" She grinned at him sweetly.

"I can't do that," he said. "You're teasing me; I can tell."

"What's so bad about washing it off?" she asked petulantly, realizing she was losing the thread of the web she had woven about him.

"I can't," he said, startled that she could ask him such a thing.

"Why not?" she demanded sulkily.

"Because," he informed her with all the dignity he could muster, "it doesn't come off. *I'm a clown.*"

He stared at her as though she were stupid. Tina grabbed Jacob's coat and backed out of the Ford canopy. She hurried from the uncomfortable confines, trying not to hear what Tobo was muttering. She was on the verge of an uncertain fear. She looked back once. She saw the face of the clown watching her from the Ford's smudgy window. As she ran for Jacob's wagon, her mind replayed what Tobo mumbled to himself: "Wash it off . . . indeed . . . how could anyone be so silly. . . ."

The Cocomacaque

Carl Jacobi

"There is no door open to the transgressor save the door to beyond."
Death of a Regiment
B. W. *Sykes*

They drove into Victoria at three in the afternoon. Right away Billings sensed he had a setup. The Farmers & Merchants Bank occupied a red brick building on the last intersection of the town's main street. Across from it was the lumber yard, empty at this hour, and farther down, the abandoned creamery. The bank had an alarm bell over the front entrance but the connecting cables weren't even concealed.

Down the street were a barber shop, two taverns, a hardware and a lunch counter, and at the far end the General Store—the sign read: "Supermarket." That was all. Billings parked the car and turned to the girl at his side.

"Back in five minutes," he said.

He walked to the bank, climbed the steps and pushed through the glass doors. The place smelled of ink and old paper. A man of fifty sat at a desk behind the half wall, visible through the grillwork. A woman in a blue dress stood at the counter. The only patron, a farmer, went out as Billings came in.

At the far wall the vault door stood open and with his 20-20 vision Billings saw what it was at a glance. It was a Simpson, Model XXV, double-tumbler, 14 or 15 pinion key, semi-time lock. Circa 1950. A trained ear should make opening it not too great a problem. But he still hadn't decided on a day or night operation.

"I'd like to see the manager," he said to the woman at the counter.

She nodded and turned. "Mr. Davis."

The man at the desk got up and came forward.

"My name is Parker," Billings said. "Clement Parker. I just bought a year-round cottage over on Lake Waconia. I'd like to see about getting insurance."

The man nodded and said what Billings expected him to say. "Our Miss Evans handles all our insurance matters. She just stepped out. Could you come back in half an hour?"

Over the banker's shoulder Billings took another appraising look at the Simpson. He directed a swift glance at the rear door which was sealed with steel bars. The only other modern preventative visible was an electric eye near the center of the enclosed area, low down on the baseboard.

A half hour would be fine, he told the banker, and went out with all the information he needed.

He walked back down the street to the parked car and nodded to the girl waiting for him. She got out and together they crossed the street and entered the larger of the two taverns. Inside were cool semidarkness with a yeasty smell and a half dozen men in work clothes lined up at the bar. Billings and the girl chose a booth midway down the aisle where they could watch the street through the glare of autumn sunlight on the plate-glass windows.

"How's it look?" the girl asked. She was an ash blonde with large, dark arachnid-like eyes.

He smiled. "Like candy from a baby. Are you sure, Spider, you don't want to wait till it's done and let me pick you up later?"

The girl he called Spider shook her head. "No," she said. "I want to be with you."

Billings lit a cigarette and tried to relax. In spite of the fact that things had been going well for him in recent weeks—that last job in Pine City had been a pushover—he was on edge. For one thing, there was something . . . well, sad about this place. Maybe it was just the way the building shadows fell across the sidewalks, with alternate patches of light where a structure had been torn down or none had ever been built. Victoria was an old town.

As he sat there he found himself looking at a man walking down the opposite side of the street—a big man with a thatch of copper-colored hair, streaked with grey. He was smoking a cigar and emitting great puffs of smoke at each step. The glare of sunlight was directly in Billings' eyes, blurring the man's features, but what was odd about him was the club he carried. The thing had a huge head and was fastened to his wrist by a leather thong.

"Who's the cave man?" Billings asked the tavernwaiter who had come to their booth.

"Cave man?" The waiter looked puzzled.

"The guy across the street with the club."

Something like a tremor passed through the tavernman. "Are you sure you saw him?"

Billings glanced back out the window. "He's gone now," he said. "But he carried the biggest shillelagh I've ever seen. Who is he, the local police force?"

"He was." The waiter turned away, an odd glint in his eyes. Presently he came back, polishing a glass. "As it happens," he said, "that's not an ordinary club. It's a *cocomacaque*. And you really didn't see him."

"A coco—what?"

"A kind of war club they used in Haiti before the French invasion. The guy carrying it was old Charlie Yarboro. He used to be village marshall."

"What do you mean, I really didn't see him?"

"Well the way Doc explains it—that's Doc Marple, our local G. P.— you don't really see nothin' but a personality-residue brought into your mind by what you were told to expect."

"That's hogwash," Billings said. "I saw him. And nobody told me anything until I came in here."

"Well, all of us don't agree with Doc," the tavern man admitted. "But it must be something like that, seeing as how Old Charlie's been dead and gone these five years. Malaria did him in; picked it up in the Haiti lowlands where he lived several years. Also got into a scrap with a filling-station bandit and that didn't help any."

"You mean someone robbed the filling-station?" Billings kept his face blank.

"Tried to. Old Charlie surprised 'em and waded in with that *cocoma-caque* he allus carried. Old Charlie claimed that club had mystic powers and I really think he believed it. Some queer dottle about the club being made from a growth that shaded a *mamaloi's* grave on the 'black island'."

Billings paid the man, left the booth and led the way outside. Things were looking up. A bank just waiting to be taken, in spite of the fact that a filling-station had been unsuccessfully hit a few years before. And a town with a ghost-legend that spoke eloquently for the courage of its citizens in the event of an emergency.

But there wasn't going to be any emergency—at least not until Billings was far removed from the scene, for he had now definitely decided on a night operation. Heisting a money-factory in the open may be quick and simple but it's just as likely to go wrong.

"I forgot cigarettes," he said to the girl. "Meet you at the car."

Walking across the street, he saw again ahead of him that big man with the copper-colored hair and the club but when the man seemed to pause in the darker shade of an overhead store awning and Billings came up to that spot, he was no longer there.

If it was to be a night operation he would need tools, he told himself, and he knew where to get them. He headed the car down the Chanhassen road toward 169 and Minneapolis. Several times before they reached Chanhassen the '67 Buick faltered—it seemed to be the distributor—and Billings thought he'd better pick up a newer model before he came back. Besides, there was always the chance of this one being recognized.

"I'll leave you at a motel," he said to the girl at his side.

"No," she said again. "I want to be with you."

They came by the Oak Ridge Cemetery and, as he always did when he passed a graveyard, he idly fell to noticing the tombstones that stood close to the road. Billings had an odd interest in names; it seemed to him that men with high-sounding handles were the most successful. Of course, he told himself, the owners of the names on the stones could hardly be called successful. Not any more, they couldn't. He read the markers: Alonzo Palquin, Frank Jessleton, Charles Yarboro . . .

Charles Yarboro! The grave was separated a little from the others, the grass had grown to weeds around it, and the stone was tilted. Billings had but a fleeting glimpse as the car sped by but he saw that he was wrong in his first observation that the plot was uncared for. A red-headed man was down on his hands and knees, working at the grass.

Billings spent six hours in Minneapolis where, among other things, he picked up tools and another car. He headed back for Victoria. The main street was a melancholy lane of light and shadow as he and Spider re-entered the town from the east; only three widely-spaced arc lights gave illumination. He drove to the last intersection, turned into it, made a U-turn and parked on the side opposite from the bank building, about fifty yards from the entrance in the shadow of an elm. He turned off the motor and sat in silence for several minutes, looking out the windshield. Then he turned to the girl. "Get out of the car and stand in the street next to it. If anyone comes tell them we had car trouble and I've gone to look up a garage man. Then tap the horn twice. If you do I won't come back here. I'll meet you at the highway. Don't panic. Just take it easy."

Spider bit her lip nervously. She was taut with fear. "How about the . . . marshall . . . the man with the club?"

He stared. "You mean the guy the fellow in the tavern called Charlie Yarboro?"

"Yes."

"For Pete's sake!" he said. "You heard the man. He's been dead five years."

"But you saw him. And I did, too. At least . . . I think I did."

"Think you did!" His voice was harsh. "When?"

"When we passed the cemetery. He was kneeling by his grave."

For an instant the contagion of the girl's fear sent an icy worm crawling up Billings' spine. Then he laughed unpleasantly.

"Don't go spiritualist on me. Just get out of the car and do as you're told."

He took up his bag of tools, crossed the street and walked slowly past the bank entrance until he reached the end of the building. He stopped there a moment, then turned into a narrow alleyway. The alley was L-shaped and led directly to the rear of the bank. Here two building lights, high up on the wall, shone on the rear door.

From his bag Billings took a small air pistol and inserted two pellets in the magazine. He took quick aim and fired twice. There were two soft implosions and the alleyway was plunged in darkness. He smiled in satisfaction. But then, in that moment before his eyes accustomed to the change of light, he threw himself to the ground and jerked out his Webley revolver. He thought he had seen a man crouching in the shadow of a refuse barrel. A man with a big something in his hand. He shook his head as the shadow resolved itself into a crumpled paper box. Nerves! He mustn't let them get the best of him at this stage. He exchanged the air pistol for an unframed soloid saw blade, strode to the door and fell to work.

It was tougher than he'd thought. First he had to locate the conduits and deactivate the alarm. Then he had to drill admission holes within cutting range of the bars holding the door. But the bars must have been a new alloy with glass insertions which played hob with the saw teeth. The better part of an hour elapsed before Billings stood in the bank interior. Here there was no sound save the hum of the electric clock on the near wall.

Billings advanced to the vault door and took two objects from his bag. One, a headphone, he clamped to his ear; the other, a magnetic sensor, he thrust against the panel just below the combination dial; he began to turn the dial very slowly.

From far off sounded the bull-throated Diesel horn as the night-freight approached the Victoria station. Twice as he worked he glanced over his shoulder. Somehow he had the inner feeling of being secretly watched. The room was lit with melancholy dimness by a night light and as he looked he fancied he saw a *cocomacaque*, or whatever they called such a club, depending from the ceiling without apparent support.

From Haiti, the tavern man had said. Billings had never been to Haiti and probably wouldn't have believed the voodoo tales told about the island if he had. But he did remember one story he had heard from a grizzled old codger in the Louisiana swamps where Billings had spent his rat-like younger years. The oldster claimed to have fled from Haiti after killing the Indies-famous *mamaloi*, Rosa Nagusta, while she was in the midst of her black ritual. "I was stone drunk," the old man said, "and I shot her just for the hell of it." That was in 1943 and her zombie-spirit had been searching for him ever since. In his shack in the swamp the old man with a macabre pride had showed Billings a newspaper clipping— dateline: Port-au-Prince 1944—But in the spring of '45 the old man had disappeared, utterly and completely.

Billings swore at his random thought and brought his mind back to the task at hand.

"Twelve . . . eighteen . . . stroke at four . . . eleven . . . nine . . . stroke at three . . ." he turned the dial. But he lost the tumblers. He moved the sensor slightly and tried again. Again he failed. A thin bead of perspiration began to ooze out onto his forehead. Eleven . . . nine . . . stroke at . . . stroke at . . .

The freight's klaxon sounded close by now as the train came into the station.

It was no go. Much as he disliked, he would have to "soup" it.

He got the nitro out of the bag and his hands trembled a little as he prepared it. When he had finished he retreated to the far end of the enclosed area and crouched behind a desk. The sound would wake the whole town of course. He wondered how long it would be before Marshall Charlie Yarboro reached the bank.

There he went again. Not Yarboro . . . !

The explosion came. A hollow thumping roar vibrated the windows, shook the floor and the furniture. Through the smoke and dust he saw the vault door yawning partially open.

He ran forward into the narrow chamber and began scooping up bundles of bills, throwing them into his tool bag. He was working against time now and he hoped Spider, hearing the explosion, was back inside the car with the motor running for a fast getaway.

He filled the tool bag, began cramming currency in an empty canvas sack he found on the vault floor. Far away a voice, pitched in authority, shouted something. A distant alarm bell sounded.

He hadn't figured it would be this close. He seized a last bundle of twenties and stuffed it in the bulging sack. Then he swung the sack toward the door, gained the alleyway and sprinted for the sidewalk.

As he emerged from the shadows he saw the girl, Spider, standing motionless in the street.

"In the car!" he yelled. "In the car . . . !"

But it wasn't Spider. It was Charlie Yarboro . . . Old Charlie there by the car . . . silently holding the *cocomacaque* . . . It was Charlie . . . waiting for him . . .

Rage at the sardonic aplomb of the man washed over Billings. He jerked up his Webley and fired twice in quick succession, but the slugs, impossible as it seemed, missed their mark. All in one motion he hurled the two bags in the car's open window and grappled with the red-haired figure, bearing him to earth. The ease of the action surprised him and for an instant he fancied he was fighting a shadow. Then the *cocomacaque* caught him an evil blow on the shoulder. In a fury he wrenched the club free and brought the heavy butt-end down upon the other's head. Again and again he struck until the prostrate form lay motionless beneath him.

Cruising down Blacktop 3 without destination, the Carver County Deputy Sheriff sighted a black sedan traveling toward the highway at excessive speed. The Deputy turned about, gave chase and after a mile flagged the car down. He checked the driver's license, the unlocked trunk and was about to end the matter with a routine ticket when something prompted him to look beneath the out-of-place rear seat. A moment later he was staring at bundles of currency. Billings realized the game was up and gave in without a struggle. He was taken to Chaska, the county seat, and lodged in the courthouse jail and the forces of law were swiftly marshalled against him.

"I don't understand it," the Deputy said. "We didn't find the weapon he used but it must have been something big and heavy. My guess is that Billings went momentarily crazy at the sight of all that easy money. Why else would he turn on his lookout girl friend and club her to death?"

Cold Heart

Peter D. Pautz

The one thing that made Jeremy Ludlow happiest was that the house had never sold. Each time he drove up the wide curving private road, passed the discreet For Sale sign on the front gate, he tried to imagine having to go somewhere else and a sharp pang bit into his stomach, for he was not sure if Noreen would have chosen another place. She may have just left him altogether. Somehow only in this place was she right; were they right, he corrected himself. No demands, no clinging. Here they engaged in not a mutual give-and-take but indulged in a taking, a permitted selflessness, one from the other.

It was late fall, the trees having already shed almost every crippled leaf that they would part with. The sun shot bright streams against the smooth white stone, reflecting a rippling pattern that looked like stucco from the boulevard but that became a moiré of gloss when you stood right next to the front wall of the house. And only when you actually touched it could you tell that it was glass-smooth. The only thing Jeremy had ever seen like it was an altar stone in an old Catholic church. The marble seemed glazed with a layer of frozen air that kept common flesh at a respectable distance from the holy structure.

Again, Jeremy parked his car directly in front of the columned portico, quietly shutting the door as he stood looking up at the peaked roof, three stories above. Anywhere else it would have been a brazen act, a défiance to peering eyes. But here no one ever saw.

He walked slowly around the car and stood as if naked before the house. He rolled back his head, stretched his neck tightly, closed his eyes, and let the warmth of its loving presence caress him. With the wave of blessed emotion his mind drifted back. He could feel Noreen waiting patiently within, just as he'd felt her through his office door the minute before she had entered.

It was just less than a year before. Jeremy was carefully going over the final reports on the appraisals from the Whitney. No less than a half-dozen works by Frampton and DeMott had been sold in the last month by the prestigious Madison Avenue museum, and Concord-Ludlow had been called upon to provide fair-market values for tax purposes. It was a late Saturday afternoon and Jeremy Ludlow was alone in the office, his door closed. There had not been a sound, not even a smooth wind-shift of the tall building, yet something suddenly tightened the skin along the small of his back. In an instant he was sitting bolt upright, staring at his door. Crazy, he thought. I'm alone. Still, he watched the door for several breaths, never coming close to returning to his work, until the handle revolved and she stepped into the room.

She was tall, powerful in the manner of a long-distance runner. Her shoulder-length hair flicked lightly in a breeze he did not feel as she crossed the room and sat in the plush client's chair by his desk. He'd never remember her clothes. In his mind only the turquoise of her eyes enwrapped her.

In that handful of seconds he was hers, heart and soul. And body, he thought later.

"Mr. Ludlow." Her voice melded them, stripping away all his past. "Can you come to my house?"

He had to shake himself before he found the strength to answer. "I beg your pardon."

"Can you come to my house?"

I'd be delighted to, he wanted to say, but could only stare, his strength suddenly gone.

"I've some lovely old pieces I want to have cleaned," she continued. "And I want to insure them first. The bondsman requires an appraisal."

"Oh. Oh, of course," he stammered. "Would that be in Manhattan?"

"Goodness, no," she said. "Bergen County, just north of Woodcliff."

"And how soon would you be requiring the appraisal, Mrs. . . ." Even the discussion of business details could not bring him back safely to earth. His breath came in sharp, ecstatic gasps.

"Bradley. Noreen Bradley."

"Noreen Bradley," he said softly, intending to write it down, but he did not move. For she leaned gently forward and slid her hand lightly over his.

"Call me Noreen," she said, "please."

"Noreen," he whispered.

Then his phone rang. She took her hand back, and he wanted to cry. Heat flashed through him, and after a moment he snatched it from its cradle.

"What?" He was furious.

A pause at the other end of the line. "Honey, what's the matter?"

He forced a deep, calming shot of air into his lungs and spun his chair. He turned his back on the lovely creature before him and gazed out the window at the smoked granite across the street.

"Nothing," he said, "nothing. I'm sorry, Jan. What is it?"

"I just wanted to check and see if you'd be home by five o'clock. We've got that dance at the club tonight and you promised to take the kids shopping for their skis tonight, too."

"Oh, Christ. I'd completely forgotten." He frowned. How could he even care? "Look, I guess I'll be home by then. I've got a lot of work."

"Honey." She paused again, then went on sincerely to say, "I'm sorry if I've bothered you."

"No, I'm the one who's sorry." He smiled. Even after twelve years of marriage, her concern was as touching as ever. It was one of the reasons he knew they would last together. "I'll make sure I'm home by 5:30 at the latest, okay?"

"Sure."

"Okay, see you then. Love you."

"Love you, too."

He sighed heavily and turned back to his desk to hang up the telephone.

The magnificent lady—Noreen—was gone. His office door was wide open.

"Damn," he said sharply and slumped deeply into his chair.

Jeremy Ludlow did no more work that day. He arrived home at 8 P.M.

Two weeks later he had at least the blessing of hearing her voice again.

"Come to me," was all she said.

"Noreen?"

"Come to my house."

"When?" he said.

She did not answer.

"Where?"

She told him.

Then she was gone. The phone dead in his hand. He held it to his ear for a long time afterward, waiting for a sound of her gentle breathing, her strong, commanding heartbeat, but heard nothing.

Laying the phone carefully on his desk, he rolled down his sleeves, stood, and grabbed his coat.

In the outer office he quickly told his secretary, "Cancel all my appointments; I'll be gone the rest of the day," and ran to his car.

The drive out of Manhattan was infuriating. Every hunk of steel on the streets seemed to die in front of him, daring him to get out of his own car and rant and scream, delaying him all the more. Once out of the city he drove maniacally, dodging from one lane to the next around buses and tractor-trailers. The mass of entrance ramps in the Meadowlands fed further obstacles in front of him, but he bored his way through them, cursing, crying, fighting his way to a slower, gentler place. By the end there was more grass than asphalt, hundreds of trees for every building.

The house itself was set far back from the road. There was no brick wall surrounding the grounds, just an ironwork gate, but its sense of isolation bled the rest of the world away from him. The same way *her* voice robbed all others of their presence.

She was standing in the doorway when he pulled up. Her hair rustled in a breeze he could feel this time, though the two seemed out of sync somehow. He halted before climbing the stairs, waiting for a welcome, an invitation. Then he was close enough to look into her eyes and he came to her, followed her through a large vaulted foyer and into a sitting parlor.

Sunlight coursed through tall, glistening windows. To his mind the furnishings were as indistinct as her garb. Only she was real, touchable, he told himself as she once again took his hand in hers. Her hair was the only source of movement.

"You have a cold heart," her voice said in his heart.

"Not the way you make me feel." His was barely a whisper.

"Yes, cold." She hesitated and stared into his eyes again. "Not calculating, not unfeeling. Strong, stable."

He would have laughed had he been able.

"It takes much. It will take whatever is offered."

"Whatever is offered." His words sounded soft and leadened to his own ears.

"Take me," she said.

And he did. As she took him.

They'd gone on for months. Taking, one from the other. Every few days she would call and he would come, leaving business or family, and take from her.

But as the spring came their lovemaking had stopped. He still came when she called. In the front parlor where she'd first taken him, they would sit and talk as she prepared him for responsibilities and for love. Then they would walk the house, particularly on cloudy days, wandering the halls, never staying long near or in any room, returning always to the parlor. Even here he began to notice her discomfort, and slowly he began to insist that they continue their strolls.

When the lovemaking stopped, he tried for the first time to remember her body, to recall the ecstasy of their entwining, but could not. A few nights as they lay together, Jan noticed the wistful joy in his face and offered her own loving—didn't he used to call it that?—smile and beseeching hands, but he could only close his eyes and turn from her. She would stroke his back then and try to talk with him, but he remained cold and unresponsive. Sometimes she had cried herself to sleep against his back while he tried in vain to recapture those precious moments with Noreen. He could no more describe her breasts than he could envision her walk or how her clothes draped. Indeed, in the interminable days and nights without her, he could not bring to his mind's eye anything about her except his craving need of her, of her presence. It did not surprise or distress him, however. For he had taken of her, as had she of him, and the desire was implicit.

Neither did it surprise or distress him when she vanished.

She had been calling him almost daily. Summer was trailing on, burning the city with great gasps of August.

His body blazed with the need of her, and for the first time he did not wait for her call. On a Saturday afternoon he had simply stepped from the deck chair by the club's pool, where Jan splashed happily with their children, collected his clothes but not bothering to change, and drove his car to her.

Unannounced, he followed the roads, the driveway, and climbed the stairs to the wide doorway where she was waiting for him. As always, she'd taken his hand and led him to their settee in the front parlor. Even their long tours of the house started this way.

This time, though, she remained seated. She did not meet his eyes for a long time, and he worried terribly that he'd done something wrong, that she'd not take from him, this time or ever again.

She said nothing. She did not move. Yet after a while she vanished, simply faded away while she held his hand, until she was finally and completely gone, then she let go.

Jeremy did not scream or move. He gazed blankly into the empty space that she had been. An hour later he drove back to his wife and children.

Jan was sitting on the couch when he entered. She was about to say something, but when he stepped into the light she ran to the front closet, pulled an afghan from its shelf, and threw it around him. It was only then that he realized that he was still dressed solely in his bathing trunks. He was shivering, a light shade of blue. And it was still 72 degrees out.

The next morning had been horrid. Jan wore an exhausted expression, the kind usually reserved for long-suffering widows. This time she did not even have the strength to ask him where he had been. The red glazing around her eyes evinced that she had been awake all night.

Try as he might, Jeremy could not bring himself to talk to her. He doubted he would get a response anyway and cared not at all enough to try. She merely sat in the wicker chair in the corner of their bedroom, unmoving, until her children came in an hour later and climbed into her lap. Eventually her arms closed around them and she cried without a sound.

For three months now the situation had gotten worse, although Jeremy rarely noticed anything beyond his time with Noreen. She'd called him two days after she had vanished and their meetings had regained their usual glorifying vagueness. For a while Jan asked him for explanations, wept when he tried some obvious lie, and finally withdrew altogether from him and the world around her. Her only solace seemed to be the children. For long hours every day and evening she held them, cuddling and stroking them like she had not done since they were infants.

In those brief moments of emotional awareness of her that came over Jeremy, he was immensely pleased. Children always seemed to give new life to the old and the lonely. As things now stood, a new baby would be their only hope if Noreen left him. The thought pained him terribly, for somehow he could sense her increasing distance, as if she had taken what she truly needed from him long ago, at the beginning, and now only waited with him for some final outcome.

He felt as if soon she would be ready to give him back to Jan.

The feeling had grown until that morning. Noreen had called him again, for the first time in over a week.

"Come to me," she'd said. "Come, these are my last moments."

He'd fled his office in a panic, but the fear slowly ebbed away as he approached the house. She was not waiting for him this time; the door was shut, yet he could feel her inside, stronger, more full of life than ever before. As he climbed the stairs to the entrance, he noticed that the stonework seemed duller, its shine somewhat muted even in the bright sunlight. He had to press his shoulder against the door to pry it from the jamb. It opened stiffly.

The moment he entered, Noreen's voice came to him, hurrying him to the parlor. He raced to the settee, though she was not there. A sheet covered it. Whether it was new or not, he could not say. In the year he'd been coming to her he could not remember the color or design or texture of the settee. It could have been covered, he realized; until now it had never mattered. In a second the panic was back, squeezing his heart.

Then he heard her voice again.

"Jeremy, it's over," she said. He spun around, searching the room for her. She was not there.

"Noreen," he pleaded to the empty air. He crumpled to the settee, his face twitching in his hands, and wept. It felt as if his entire chest were being forced through his throat.

"I love you, Jeremy." It was the first time she had ever said it.

His voice was weak, muffled by his sobbing. "Stay with me," he begged.

"I can't, Jeremy," she said softly. "I must rejoin my family. I've been away too long."

He looked up imploringly at the deserted room but he could not speak.

"I'll always be with you, Jeremy." Her voice was fading, spreading thin and distant toward the walls. A moment later, as she vanished from him forever, she added, "I've left something for you, my love. Take it, and remember me."

She was gone.

The sun set before he could bring himself to rise, and when he did, incongruously, he sneezed. He wiped at his face, leaving a dark smudge of dust across his cheeks, and stared down at the settee. It was no longer empty. Lying before him on the dirty sheet was a bundle. He bent and inspected it carefully. Even through the pain he smiled. It would be all right now, he knew.

Delicately carrying the gift from Noreen, Jeremy left the house and drove home; to Jan, to reunite their family.

With a little love from him and a little acceptance from Jan, he knew it would all be perfect again. He could have the best of both worlds.

Except that when he gave Jan the package, she stared at him blankly. Gazing back at the empty blanket in her hands she started to ask him something, but when the light, gentle crying came, she dropped the precious bundle and began screaming.

The Dancer in the Flames

David Drake

The flames writhing out of the ashtray were an eyeball-licking orange. For an instant Lt Schaydin was sure that the image dancing in them was that of the girl he had burned alive in Cambodia, six months before. But no, not quite; though the other's face had been of Gallic cast too.

The two enlisted men had turned at the sound of the officer brushing back the poncho curtain which divided his tent from the rear compartment of the command track. Radios were built into the right wall of the vehicle above a narrow counter. On that counter rested the CQ's clipboard and a cheap glass ashtray, full of flame. The men within—Skip Sloane, who drove the command track and was now Charge of Quarters, and the medic Evens—had been watching the fire when Schaydin looked in. It was to that ten-inch flame which the lieutenant's eyes were drawn as well.

He stared at her calves and up the swell of the hips which tucked in at a waist that thrust toward him. She looked straight at Schaydin then and her mouth pursed to call. Above the image hung the black ripples of smoke which were her hair. Abruptly the flame shrank to a wavering needle and blinked out. The compartment was lighted only by the instrument dials, pitch dark after the orange glare. The air was sharp with the residue of the flame; but more than that caused Schaydin's chest to constrict. He remembered he had called out some joke as he touched the flame-thrower's trigger and sent a loop of napalm through the window of the hooch they were supposed to destroy. The Cambodian girl must have been hiding in the thatch or among the bags of rice. She had been all ablaze as she leaped into the open, shrieking and twisting like a dervish until she died. But this tiny image had not screamed, it had really spoken. It/She had said—

"How did you do that?" Schaydin gasped.

The enlisted men glanced at each other, but their commander did not seem angry, only—strange. Sloane held up a 20-ounce block of C-4, plastic explosive. Sweat rolled down the driver's chest and beer gut. He wore no shirt since the radios heated the command vehicle even in the relative coolness of the Vietnamese night. "You take a bit of C-4, sir," Sloane said. His hairy thumb and forefinger gouged out an acorn-sized chunk of the white explosive. Another piece had already been removed. "It takes a shock to make it blow up. If you just touch a match to it in the open, it burns. Like that."

Sloane handed the pellet to Schaydin, who stood with a dazed look on his face. The C-4 had the consistency of nougat, but it was much denser. "We ought 'a air the place out, though," the driver continued. "The fumes don't do anybody much good."

"But how did you get it to look like a woman?" Schaydin demanded. "I could see her right there, her face, her eyes . . . and she was saying. . . ."

Evens reached past the lieutenant and flapped the poncho curtain to stir the dissipating tendrils of smoke. "C-4 makes a pretty flame," the stocky medic said, "but you don't want to get the stuff in your system. We used to have a mascot, a little puppy. She ate part of a block and went pure-ass crazy. Seeing things. She'd back into a corner and snap and bark like a bear was after her. . . . Middle of that afternoon she went haring out over the berm, yapping to beat Hell. We never did see her again."

The medic looked away from his CO, then added, "Don't think you ought to breathe the fumes, either. Hard to tell what it might make you see. Don't think I want to burn any more C-4, even if it does make the damnedest shadows I ever hope to see."

The lieutenant opened his mouth to protest, to insist that he had seen the image the instant he pushed the curtain aside; but he caught his men's expressions. His mind seemed to be working normally again. "You guys just saw a—fire?"

"That's all there was to see," said Evens. "Look, it's late, I better go rack out." Sloane nodded, tossing him the part block of explosive. The medic edged past Schaydin, into the tent and the still night beyond.

"Time for a guard check," Sloane said awkwardly and reseated himself before the microphone. One by one the heavy-set man began calling the vehicles sited around the circular berm. The tracks replied with the quiet negative reports that showed someone was awake in each turret. The CQ did not look up at his commander, but when Schaydin stepped back from the compartment and turned away, he heard a rustle. Sloane had pulled the poncho closed.

Schaydin sat down on the edge of his bunk, staring at the morsel of explosive. He saw instead the girl he had glimpsed in the flame. She had danced with her body, writhing sinuously like a belly dancer as her breasts heaved against the fire's translucence. Schaydin couldn't have been mistaken, the girl had been as real as—the Cambodian girl he had burned. And this girl's expression was so alive, her fire-bright eyes glinting with arrogant demand. *What had the Cambodian girl been crying? But her eyes were dulled by the clinging napalm. . . .*

The pellet of C-4 came into focus as Schaydin's fingers rotated it. All right, there was a simple way to see whether his mind had been playing tricks on him.

Schaydin set the ball of explosive on top of a minican, the sealed steel ammunition box prized as luggage by men in armored units. C-4 burned at over 1000 degrees, the lieutenant remembered, but it would burn briefly enough that only the paint would scorch. The flame of Schaydin's cigarette lighter wavered away from the white pellet and heated the case in his hand. Then a tiny spark and a flicker of orange winked through the yellow naphtha flare. Schaydin jerked his lighter away and shut it. Fire loomed up from the *plastique*. Its hissing filled the tent just as the roar of an incoming rocket does an encampment.

And the dancer was there again.

The engineer platoon ran a generator which powered lights all over the firebase through makeshift lines of commo wire. Left-handed and without looking at it, Schaydin jerked away the wire to his tent's lightbulb. The sputtering fire brightened in the darkness, and in it the girl's features were as sharp as if a cameo carven in ruddy stone. But the mouth moved and the dancer called to Schaydin over the fire-noise,

"Viens ici! Viens à Marie!" Schaydin had studied French as an under-graduate in divinity school, enough to recognize that the tones were not quite those of modern French; but it was clear that the dancer was calling him to her. His body tensed with the impossible desire to obey. Sweat rimmed all the stark lines of his muscles.

Then the flame and the girl were gone together, though afterimages of both danced across Schaydin's eyes. The lieutenant sat in the dark for some time, oblivious to the half-movement he might have glimpsed through a chink in the poncho. The CQ turned back to his microphone, frowning at what he had watched.

Schaydin was more withdrawn than usual in the morning, but if any of his fellow officers noticed it, they put it down to the lieutenant's natural anxiety about his position. The next days would determine whether Schaydin would be promoted to captain and take on for the rest of his tour the slot he now held in place of the wounded Capt Fuller. Other-wise, Schaydin would have to give up the company to another officer and return to Third Platoon. Schaydin had thought of little else during his previous week of command, but today it barely occurred to him. His mind had been drifting in the unreality of South-East Asia; now it had found an anchorage somewhere else in time and space.

The thin lieutenant spent most of the day in his tent, with the orange sidewalls rolled up to make its roof an awning. The First Sergeant was stationed permanently in the Regiment's base camp at Di An, running an establishment with almost as many troops as there were in the field. In Viet Nam, even in a combat unit, a majority of the troops were non-combatants. Bellew, the Field First, was on R&R in Taiwan, so an unusual amount of the company's day-to-day affairs should have fallen on the commander himself.

Today Schaydin sloughed them, answering the most pressing ques-tions distractedly and without particular interest. His eyes strayed often to his minican, where the paint had bubbled and cracked away in a circle the size of a fifty-cent piece.

She had seemed short, though he could not be sure, since the image had been less than a foot tall when the flames leapt their highest. Not plump, exactly, for that implied fat and the dancer had been all rippling muscularity; but she had been a stocky girl, an athlete rather than a houri. And yet Schaydin had never before seen a woman so seductively passionate, so radiant with desire. Every time Schaydin thought of the dancer's eyes, his groin tightened; and he thought of her eyes almost constantly.

Come to me. . . . Come to Marie. . . .

❖　❖　❖

The activities of the firebase went on as usual, ignoring Schaydin just as he did them. Second Platoon and some vehicles from Headquarters Company bellowed off on a Medcap to a village ten kilometers down Route 13. There the medics would dispense antibiotics and bandages to the mildly ill. The troops would also goggle at ravaged figures whom not even Johns Hopkins could have aided: a child whose legs had been amputated three years past by a directional mine; a thirty-year-old man with elephantiasis of the scrotum, walking bowlegged because of the bulk of his cantaloupe-sized testicles. . . .

Chinook helicopters brought in fuel and ammunition resupply in cargo nets swinging beneath their bellies. Schaydin did not notice their howling approach; the syncopated chop of their twin rotors as they hovered; the bustle of men and vehicles heading toward the steel-plank pad to pick up the goods. The lieutenant sat impassively in his tent even when the howitzer battery fired, though the hogs were lofting some of their shells to maximum range. The muzzle blasts raised doughnuts of dust that enveloped the whole base. Schaydin's mind's eye was on a dancing girl, not men in baggy green fatigues; the roar he heard was that of a crowd far away, watching the dancer . . . and even the dust in Schaydin's nostrils did not smell like the pulverized laterite of Tay Ninh Province.

"Time for the officers' meeting, sir," Sloane murmured.

Schaydin continued to sit like a thin, nervous Buddha in a lawn chair.

"Sir," the driver repeated loudly, "they just buzzed from the TOC. It's already 1500 hours."

"Oh, right," muttered the lieutenant dizzily. He shook his head and stood, then ran his fingertips abstractedly over the blackened minican. "Right."

The Tactical Operations Center was merely a trio of command vehicles around a large tent in the middle of the firebase. Schaydin had forgotten to carry his lawn chair with him. He pulled up a box which had held mortar shells and sat facing the acetate-covered map with its crayoned unit symbols. The afternoon rain started, plunging sheets of water that made the canvas jounce like a drumhead. It sounded like an angry crowd.

The Civil Affairs Officer and the lieutenant from the military intelligence detachment shared a presentation on the results of the Medcap. They proved that zero could be divided in half to fill twenty minutes. Then the Operations Officer described F Troop's morning sweep. It had turned up two old bunkers and some cartridge cases, but no signs of recent occupation. The sector was quiet.

The balding S-3 switched to discussing the operation planned in two days. When he directed a question to Schaydin, the lieutenant continued to rock silently on his box, his eyes open but fixed on nothing in the tent.

"Schaydin!" the squadron commander snarled. "Stop sitting there with your finger up your butt and pay attention!"

"Yes, sir!" Schaydin's face flushed hot and his whole body tingled, as if he had just been roused from a dead faint. "Would you please repeat the question, sir?"

The meeting lasted another ten minutes, until the rain stopped. Schaydin absorbed every pointless detail with febrile acuteness. His flesh still tingled.

After Col Brookings dismissed his officers into the clearing skies, Schaydin wandered toward the far side of the defensive berm instead of going directly to his tent. He followed the path behind one of the self-propelled howitzers, avoiding the pile of white cloth bags stuffed with propellant powder. The charges were packed in segments. For short range shelling, some of the segments were torn off and thrown away as these had been. Soon the powder would be carried outside the perimeter and burned.

Burned. A roaring, sparking column of orange flame, and in it —

Schaydin cursed. He was sweating again.

Three ringing explosions sounded near at hand. The noise had been a facet of the background before the rain as well, Schaydin remembered. He walked toward the source of the sounds, one of First Platoon's tanks. It had been backed carefully away from the berm, shedding its right tread onto the ground, straight as a tow line between the vehicle and the earthen wall. Four men hunched behind a trailer some yards from the tank. One of them, naked to the waist, held a detonator in his hand. The trooper saw Schaydin approaching and called, "Stand back, sir. We're blowing out torsion bars."

The lieutenant stopped, watching. The trooper nodded and slapped closed the scissors handle of the detonator. Smoke and another clanging explosion sprang from among the tank's road wheels. The enlisted men straightened. "That's got it," one of them murmured. Schaydin walked to them, trying to remember the name of the tall man with the detonator, the tank commander of this vehicle.

"What's going on, Emmett?" Schaydin asked.

None of the enlisted men saluted. "Emery, sir," the TC corrected. "Our tank had six torsion bars broke, so she steered and rode like a truck with square wheels. Back in the World they've got machines to drift out torsion bars, but here we're just using a couple ounces of C-4 to crack each one loose." The tall non-com pointed at the block of explosive dropped on the ground beside him. Its green sandwich backing had been peeled away from both sides, and half the doughy white *plastique* had been pinched off. Several copper blasting caps lay on the ground beside the C-4.

Emery ignored the lieutenant's sudden pallor. He stopped paying attention to Schaydin entirely since it was obvious that the officer was not about to help with the job. "Come on, snakes," Emery said, "we got a lot to do before sundown."

The crewmen scrambled to their fifty-ton mount, hulking and rusted and more temperamentally fragile than any but the men responsible for such monsters will ever know. Schaydin's staring eyes followed them as he himself bent at the knees and touched the block of C-4. Its smooth outer wrapper was cool to his fingers. Without looking at the explosive, Schaydin slid it into a side pocket of his fatigue trousers. He walked swiftly back to his tent.

Tropic sunset is as swift as it is brilliant. It crams all the reds and ochres and magentas of the temperate zones into a few minutes which the night then swallows. But the darkness, though it would be sudden, was hours away; and Schaydin's pulsing memory would not let him wait hours.

Sloane was radio watch this afternoon. The driver sat on the tailgate of the command vehicle with his feet on the frame of his cot. He was talking to the staff sergeant who would take over as CQ at 2000 hours. They fell silent when Schaydin appeared.

"Go ahead, Skip, get yourself some supper," the lieutenant said stiffly. "I'll take the radio for a while."

"S'okay, sire, Walsh here spelled me," Sloane said. He pointed at the paper plate with remnants of beef and creamed potatoes, sitting on his footlocker. "Go ahead and eat yourself."

"I said I'd take the radio!" Schaydin snapped. He was trembling, though he did not realize it. Sloane glanced very quickly at his commander, then to the startled sergeant. The driver lowered his feet from the cot and squeezed back so that Schaydin could enter the track. The two enlisted men were whispering together at the open end of the tent when their lieutenant drew the poncho shut, closing off the rest of the world.

It was dim in the solid-walled vehicle, dimmer yet when Schaydin unplugged the desk lamp. Radio dials gleamed and reflected from the formica counter, chinks of light seeped in past the curtain. But it would serve, would serve. . . .

The texture of the C-4 steadied Schaydin's fingers as he molded it. The high sides of the ashtray made it difficult to ignite the pellet. The hot steel of the lighter seared his fingers and he cursed in teary frustration;

but just before Schaydin would have had to pull away winked the spark and the orange flare—

—and in it, the girl dancing.

Her head was flung back, the black, rippling, smokey hair flying out behind her. Schaydin heard the words again, "À Marie! Ici! Viens ici!" The radio was babbling, too, on the command frequency; but whatever it demanded was lost in the roar of the crowd. Passion, as fiercely hot as the explosive that gave it form, flashed from the girl's eyes. "Come to me!"

The flame sputtered out. Schaydin was blind to all but its afterimage.

The compartment was hot and reeking. Sweat beaded at Schaydin's hairline and on his short, black moustache. He stripped the backing away from the rest of the explosive and began to knead the whole chunk, half a pound, into a single ball.

"Battle Six to Battle One-Six," the radio repeated angrily in Col Brookings' voice. "Goddammit, Schaydin, report!"

The ashtray had shattered in the heat. Schaydin swept the fragments nervously to the floor, then set the lump of explosive on the blood-marked formica. A shard of clear glass winked unnoticed in the heel of his hand. He snapped his lighter to flame and it mounted, and she mounted—

—and she called. Her hands could not reach out for him but her soul did and her Hell-bright eyes. "Viens ici! Viens!"

The dancer's smooth flesh writhed with no cloak but the flame. Higher, the radio dials melting, the lizard-tongue forks of the blaze beading the aluminum roof—Schaydin stood, his ankles close together like hers. He did not reach for her, not because of the heat but because the motion would be—*wrong.* Instead he put his hands behind his back and crossed his wrists. Outside the curtain, voices snarled but the dragon-hiss of the C-4 would have drowned even a sane man's senses. She twisted, her eyes beckoning, her mouth opening to speak. Schaydin arched, bending his body just so and—

"Come!"

—and he went.

The poncho tore from Col Brookings' fingers and a girl plunged out of the fiery radio compartment. She was swarthy but not Vietnamese, naked except for smouldering scraps of a woolen shift. Neither Brookings nor the enlisted men could understand the French she was babbling; but her joy, despite severe burns on her feet and legs, was unmistakable.

No one else was in the vehicle.

❀   ❀   ❀

On October 14, 1429, the assembled villagers of Briançon, Province of Dauphine, Kingdom of France, roared in wonderment. The witch Marie de la Barthè, being burned alive at the stake, suddenly took the form of a demon with baggy green skin. The change did not aid the witch, however, for the bonds still held. Despite its writhing and unintelligible cries, the demon-shape burned as well in the fire as a girl would have.

The Dark Beasts

Frank Belknap Long

Peter bent and examined the frog. It was dead. It lay amongst the pebbles at the edge of the stream, and its long legs were rigidly outthrust. "Who would want to hurt a poor little thing like that?" muttered Peter. "The poor little thing!"

Peter was not very bright. He was eighteen, but he had the mind of a child. Yet he knew that the frog had been cruelly and maliciously strangled by person or persons unknown. Shivering, he laid a cautious finger on the tight, gleaming wire which encircled the amphibian's neck. The cold flesh sent shivers up his wrist almost as far as his elbow. "Who would want to hurt a poor little thing like that?" he reiterated, in perplexity and amazement.

He did not linger over the small, pathetic corpse. It was growing dark, and he was afraid of the rapidly lengthening shadows and the black, spidery branches that met in the air high above his head. The wood was an unfriendly place when the sun ceased to shine upon it. Unfriendly, and very dismal and full of voices.

When Peter arrived home his mother was setting the table for supper, and his stepfather was sitting by the window with a week old newspaper across his knee, and a corn-cob pipe between his decayed and discolored teeth. Peter shut the door and advanced awkwardly into the room.

"Hello," said his stepfather. "Where've you been?"

"Just fishin' some over by the creek," replied Peter nervously. "I was hopin' a trout might come up and swallow the worm, and then I'd have him. I was just over there fishin'. That's all I was doin' ever since I went over there. I been there and nowheres else. I was just hopin' a trout would come up so I could get him."

Peter's stepfather frowned. He was a tall, gaunt man, well past middle age, with dark, ill-humored eyes and a grim mouth.

"Look here, boy," he rasped. "Didn't I tell you not to go snoopin' around in them woods? Ain't you got no sense at all?"

"I didn't mean no harm, pa," whimpered Peter. "I was just fishin' in the creek. I was hopin' a trout would come up so I could get him. I wasn't over there for nothin' else."

"Yeah? Well, don't you let me catch you goin' into them woods again. If I catch you so much as puttin' a foot in them woods I'll give you a hidin' you'll remember as long as there's a breath of life in you."

"Now, now, Henry," said Peter's mother from beside the stove.

Peter was silent and contrite all during supper. But as soon as the last morsel of food was disposed of, he excused himself awkwardly, and retired to his room. He was horribly frightened. In his sensitive, untutored mind the savage moodiness of his stepfather was obscurely linked with the way he felt deep down inside when the sun ceased to shine upon the wood and the still, dark waters of the creek. He wanted to run when his stepfather threatened to give him a hiding, not because he dreaded the sting of the lash, but because—well, because he was afraid of something that lay concealed behind the cruel inhuman mask of his stepfather's face.

"You shouldn't have spoken so harshly to him," said Peter's mother, as she gathered up the supper dishes and carried them wearily to the sink. "He's a good boy, and he didn't mean harm."

"Oh, didn't he?" said Henry. "Didn't he, though? What about his goin' into the woods against my orders? What about his snoopin' around where them things are waitin' and watchin'? Maybe he's talked with 'em. For all I know he may be on their side. He ain't bright, and you got to watch out for that kind, Mary. You got to watch 'em mighty close. You can't tell what they'll be doin' and sayin'."

Peter's mother sighed. "He's got to have *some* fun."

"Yeah? Well, he'd better stay out of them woods. I can take care of the beasts they set against us, but the law wouldn't let me harm a hair of his stupid head. If they set him against us there ain't nothin' I could do. He's your son, not mine. If they set him against us I'd just have to clear out. How'd you like that, woman?"

Peter's mother moistened her lips with her tongue. "Have you been doin' anything—anything cruel again, Henry?"

Peter's stepfather arose from the table, and sent his chair spinning against the wall. "It ain't none of your business, woman," he cried. "I got to protect myself, ain't I? If the crops all dry up, and the cows won't give no milk, I got to fight back." He cleared his throat. "It's them croakin' frogs they set against us that's causin' all the trouble. You can't tell me it wasn't them croakin' frogs. Night after night we been hearin' 'em croakin'. Well, I stopped it. You won't hear no croakin' tonight."

Mary's face went ashen. She set down the platter she was holding, and faced him. "The frogs were our friends," she moaned. "I've been hopin' and praying that you'd never do anything so cruel. You said you'd do it, but I was hopin'—"

"What good does hopin' and prayin' do when we've got worse than the Devil against us? When God made the Devil, Mary, he made him good, but them things were made bad in the first place. They didn't have to fall. I reckon they was no part of creation at all. They got in somehow by mistake."

"The frogs were our friends," reiterated Mary, despairingly. "Yesterday when I was walkin' in the woods they warned me. One of the things was in the tree, waitin'. If I hadn't got the warnin' it would have dropped on me. I could see its wicked, cruel eyes glarin' down at me through the leaves. But when the frogs started croakin' I turned and ran. They're gettin' bolder and bolder, Henry. They know that Jim's father ain't comin' back, I guess. They're gettin' ready to—to get us, I guess. I'll have to go to them when they really want me, I guess. I'll have to take Jim's father's place. I'm not of the same blood, but I married into the family, and the curse is on me."

"How about me, woman?" muttered Henry. "Don't think I ain't been thinkin' about what's goin' happen to me if we don't fight 'em. When I married you I took you for better or worse. Well, it's been for worse, but I'll stick to you if you'll stick to me. You got no right criticizin' me. I've been mighty good to you. When you told me about your dead husband and the curse on his family, I said it didn't matter, because I reckoned you'd make me a good wife. But when I said that, I hadn't seen them things. I didn't know what they was like. I didn't know they'd set every beast in the woods against us."

"They didn't set the frogs against us, Henry. The frogs liked us. The frogs were warnin' us."

"Don't you believe it. Them croakin' frogs was against us. They was against us from the very start." He laughed mirthlessly. *"I did just what I said I'd do.* I said I'd put the heads of every one of them croakin' frogs into a noose, and I did. I been over there all day. There ain't a croakin' frog left in them woods."

Mary sank into a chair by the window, and plucked nervously with her fingers at the loose, wrinkled flesh of her face. "It was a cruel, evil thing to do," she murmured. "No good can come of it. The frogs were our friends. They were the only friends we had."

"They was set against us. They put a blight on the crops and kept the hens from layin' and the cows from givin' milk. I'm glad I put their croakin' heads into a noose. It will be a warnin' to them things that I ain't standin' for no nonsense."

"You are goin' to be sorry, Henry. The frogs were our friends; they were only tryin' to warn us. Those things are gettin' restless and impatient. They'll be wantin' me and Peter before long. They'll be wantin' you, too. They'll come for all of us before long. So long as we had the frogs to warn us there was hope, but now there ain't no hope for none of us. We got no friends even in the woods. The things got claws, Henry. They'll tear—tear us. There ain't nothin' we can do. I felt kind of safe, with the frogs there to warn us. Maybe they weren't much help, but I felt as though they were watchin' out for us. The things know now that Jim's father ain't comin' back to his grave. He ain't goin' to keep the bargain he made with them. But with the frogs there, there was always hope. They seemed to keep the curse from workin'. They sorta made me feel safe."

It was past midnight when Peter awoke. He sat up, rubbed his eyes and stared bewilderedly about him. *Something was tapping on the window pane.* Peter didn't want to get out of bed. It was a chilly night, and he felt warm and comfortable beneath the heavy blankets.

But something was tapping on the heavy window, insistently, monotonously. Tap, tap—tap, tap, tap—tap, tap.

Slowly, reluctantly, Peter threw back the covers and slipped to the floor. "I'm comin'," he muttered. "I'll open the window for you. I'll do what you want. I'll open it wide."

Tremulously he advanced across the floor. His heart was beating wildly, and fright and horror looked out of his eyes. Yet when he reached the window his gaze encountered merely a dark, amorphous blotch beyond the moon-silvered pane. To his dazed and sleep-befuddled consciousness it seemed to be moving slowly and awkwardly about, like a great helpless June bug. Only it was much larger than a June bug.

Peter raised the window till the wind blew full upon his frightened, vacuous-looking countenance, and ruffled his unruly reddish hair. Ordinarily he would have feared the consequence of so rash an act, but a curious and powerful compulsion was upon him, and he acted instinctively and without thought. For several seconds he stared into the wavering, earth-scented darkness. Then, shaking his head, he turned about and shambled back into the room. "Ain't nothin' there," he muttered. "I thought there was somethin', but I must've been wrong about that."

Frowning perplexedly, he climbed into bed. "I was afeared it might have been somethin' out of the woods," he murmured, as he pulled the covers up over his chest. "Something alive. Like—like them things I seen when I was eight years old."

For a moment he lay staring up at the ceiling. His childish, untutored mind was teeming with images, memories, impressions of a dim and shadow-haunted past. "It is not good to ask what's in where they put grandfather," he uttered. "It is not good to ask where grandfather went when it came in. I was not there when it came in, but I heard mother say it was awful, and grandfather was a very wicked man for all his goodness. He made a bargain with it that came in.

"Once, many years ago, when I was eight years old, I saw grandfather talkin' with what looked like one of them. Only the room was dark, and I could not see very plain. It was standin' in the corner by the chimney, and grandfather was talkin' to it. It was not as tall as grandfather, and it was bent like as if it had a hump on its back. Its head I could not see very well, but as good as I could make out it was like a snake's head when you look at it from its back. A bear with a snake's head, that's what it looked like, and it was enough for me. I couldn't have stayed in that room much more, as the smell made me sick, but I didn't stay as much as I could've stayed if I had wanted. The head of what stood by the chimney was enough.

"When I told mother what I'd saw she nearly fainted. She said: 'It is what I feared. Your father too has talked to them. Oh, why did I marry in such a family?' Then she kissed me and said: 'Poor boy, oh, you poor boy! You will see them too. They will come for you!'

"'What was it, mother?' I asked. 'Tell me, please, what it was.'

"'When you are older,' she said. 'You would not understand if I told you now.'

"I never saw one of them again, but before grandfather died he told me about them. 'They only want to rest,' he said, 'but they can only do that when somebody dies. They are from far away, and they only want to rest in new graves.'

"The trouble is, I guess, grandfather never came back. He never kept his bargain. They want to rest, but they can't rest forever and ever, and they was waitin' for grandfather to come back. But grandfather is out in the world somewhere right this minute. He's walkin' the earth now, and he ain't comin' back if he can help it. And all the while they was layin' in his place in his grave on the hill, waitin'. I guess they got tired of waitin' there in that deep, dark grave for grandfather to come back.

"Mother said I would see them some time. She said they would come for me. Maybe that's why I get feelin' so funny inside of me when I go into the woods. Maybe that's why pa doesn't want me to go into the woods. Maybe it's because when some one makes a bargain with them which he doesn't keep they comes back and takes someone who's related when they get tired of restin' and waitin'. That's the only way I can figure it. Mother knew that grandfather wasn't goin' ever to come back again. When somebody's got a chance to live forever and ever he ain't goin' to come back if he can help it. Who'd want to give up seein' the green grass and feelin' the cool wind on his face and smellin' the earth after it's been rainin' just because he's made a bargain he don't have to keep? I don't blame grandfather for not wantin' to come back.

"If I got a chance to live forever I wouldn't come back. I'd go walkin' on forever, just happy in the thought that I could see the green grass and smell the wet earth and have someone lovin' me all the time."

Drowsiness was creeping slowly over Peter's brain. For several minutes he continued to mumble, but his thoughts gradually ceased to dwell on the dim and shadow-haunted past. His eyes closed, and his lips parted in a peaceful smile. His conscious mind, purged of all imagery, was becoming once more an immobile instrument, vacuous and content. It drowsed in peace, cut off from the waking world and utterly unaware that an alien presence had entered the room.

The object that appeared in the open window was squat and wet. It stood for a moment swaying unsteadily on the silvery sill. Then, with a croak, it leaped swiftly downward.

For an instant thereafter the window remained empty. Then another shape emerged from the blackness and flopped to the floor with a raucous croak. It was followed by another—and another. Peter did not wake as the strange procession hopped and hobbled over the floor. He did not even stir in his sleep.

A few minutes later the window was again occupied. The new intruder was much larger than the croaking shapes. Larger and darker. It was covered with thick black hair, and its small, ill-proportioned head moved agilely about in the moonlight. For a moment it lingered on the sill. Then slowly, deliberately, and without uttering a sound it lowered itself to the floor, and ran rapidly across the room. As it ran it opened its mouth, and a low hiss came from between its white and gleaming teeth.

The false dawn crept like a wounded thing through the aisles of the forest, spilling a redness over the gaunt trees, and casting flickering shadows on the deep, dark waters of the creek.

In Eaton's Pond a lily pad turned into a gigantic scarlet hand and a spotted salamander broke water with a soggy plop, strewing air bubbles in all directions, and leaving in its wake a swirling trail of caddis houses miraculously aglow.

The lily-pad hand burned upon the water, and burning bright in all the illumed aisles of the forest were the keen, inquiring eyes of the forest, the moistly sniffing nostrils of the forest, and the scampering small feet of the forest.

The woodchuck is not a *too* curious animal. Nor are the red squirrel, the flat gray fieldmouse, and the sly and furtive ferret. Even the hoot owl with its wide, distended vision will not tarry to watch a haystack go up in flames.

But Ogelthorpe's neighbors collected at a safe distance to watch his cottage burn. The flames crackled and soared, and cast a weaving radiance on Ogelthorpe's gray-walled barn, and the manure pile which towered between the barn and the well by the ice-house, with its rusty pump, and water-logged bucket brimming with red Novembral leaves.

When the local fire company arrived, the intermittent flickering had given way to a blinding glare, and the entire landscape was illumed. In helpless despair the firemen joined the bystanders, and watched the flames subside to a dull red glow. Before morning the darkness covered everything like a heavy blanket.

At dawn the neighbors swarmed in. They poked about amongst the ruins and made a hideous and appalling discovery. The charred remains of three human bodies lay scattered gruesomely about admist the blackened brick and still smouldering embers. All that was mortal of Peter and his mother lay dispersed and unattached, but Peter's stepfather had suffered no disseverment. He lay upon his back, with his long legs outthrust. The flesh of his body had been charred to a crisp, and his features were blackened and distorted almost beyond recognition.

One of the bystanders bent and laid a tremulous finger on the tight and gleaming wire which encircled the dead man's neck. The still warm flesh sent shivers up his wrist almost as far as his elbow. "He's been strangled," he muttered. "Before ever the flames got to him he was a dead man."

"It's the queerest thing I ever laid eyes on," said Sheriff Simpson as he emerged from the tool-shed.

"Did you find somethin'?" asked Chief-Deputy Wilson. He was standing in the long, dew-drenched grass at the rear of the shed, gazing westward in contemplative detachment at the blackened ruins of the ill-fated farmhouse.

"Frogs, Jim," said the Sheriff.

"Frogs?"

"Yeah. About twenty of 'em. All strangled with a brass wire. Just like Ogelthorpe was strangled. Only—the wire Ogelthorpe was strangled with was made of copper and was about ten times as heavy."

"But what about the frogs?"

"They're all layin' in the shed there. All dead—strangled. But the funny part of it is that they're layin' beside a big spool of copper wire, the same kind that Ogelthorpe was strangled with."

The Chief-Deputy shook his head. "It looks to me like there's more to this than appears on the surface."

The Sheriff nodded. "One of the neighbors was watchin' the house burn, and he said that just before the fire company got there he saw somethin' run right out the front door. He said it was smaller than a man, but that it had a human look. It was dark, he said, and as good as he could make out, it had a human look. He couldn't see it very plain because of the glare, but it seemed to be all covered with heavy black hair, and the mere sight of it, he said, made him want to vomit. Queer, ain't it? He said the thing was carrying a *lighted torch!*"

Dark Winner

William F. Nolan

NOTE: The following is an edited transcript of a taped conversation between Mrs. Franklin Evans, resident of Woodland Hills, California, and Lt. Harry W. Lyle of the Kansas City Police Department. Transcript is dated 12 July 1984. K.C. Missouri.

LYLE: . . . and if you want us to help you we'll have to know everything. When did you arrive here, Mrs. Evans?

MRS. EVANS: We just got in this morning. A stopover on our trip from New York back to California. We were at the airport when Frank suddenly got this idea about his past.

LYLE: What idea?

MRS. E: About visiting his old neighborhood . . . the school he went to . . . the house where he grew up . . . He hadn't been back here in twenty-five years.

LYLE: So you and your husband planned this . . . nostalgic tour?

MRS. E: Not *planned*. It was very abrupt . . . Frank seemed . . . suddenly . . . *possessed* by the idea.

LYLE: So what happened?

MRS. E: We took a cab out to Flora Avenue . . . to 31st . . . and we visited his old grade school. St. Vincent's Academy. The neighborhood is . . . well, I guess you know it's a slum area now . . . and the school is closed down, locked. But Frank found an open window . . . climbed inside . . .

LYLE: While you waited?

MRS. E: Yes—in the cab. When Frank came out he was all . . . upset . . . Said that he . . . Well, this sounds . . .

LYLE: Go on, please.

MRS. E: He said he felt . . . very *close* to his childhood while he was in there. He was ashen-faced . . . his hands were trembling.

LYLE: What did you do then?

MRS. E: We had the cab take us up 31st to the Isis Theatre. The movie house at 31st and Troost where Frank used to attend those Saturday horror shows they had for kids. Each week a new one . . . *Frankenstein* . . . *Dracula* . . . you know the kind I mean.

LYLE: I know.

MRS. E: It's a porno place now . . . but Frank bought a ticket anyway . . . went inside alone. Said he wanted to go into the balcony, find his old seat . . . see if things had changed . . .

LYLE: And?

MRS. E: He came out looking very shaken . . . saying it had happened again.

LYLE: *What* had happened again?

MRS. E: The feeling about being close to his past . . . to his childhood . . . As if he could—

LYLE: Could what, Mrs. Evans?

MRS. E: . . . step over the line dividing past and present . . . step back into his childhood. That's the feeling he said he had.

LYLE: Where did you go from the Isis?

MRS. E: Frank paid off the cab . . . said he wanted to walk to his old block . . . the one he grew up on . . . 33rd and Forest. So we walked down Troost to 33rd . . . past strip joints and hamburger stands . . . I was nervous . . . we didn't . . . belong here . . . Anyway, we got to 33rd and walked down the hill from Troost to Forest . . . and on the way Frank told me how much he'd hated being small, being a child . . . that he could hardly wait to grow up . . . that to him childhood was a nightmare . . .

LYLE: Then why all the nostalgia?

MRS. E: It wasn't that . . . it was . . . like an *exorcism* . . . Frank said he'd been haunted by his childhood all the years we'd lived in California . . . This was an attempt to get rid of it . . . by facing it . . . seeing that it was really gone . . . that it no longer had any reality . . .

LYLE: What happened on Forest?

MRS. E: We walked down the street to his old address . . . which was just past the middle of the block . . . 3337 it was . . . a small, sagging wooden house . . . in terrible condition . . . but then, *all* the houses were . . . their screens full of holes . . . windows broken, trash in the yards . . . Frank stood in front of his house staring at it for a long time . . . and then he began repeating something . . . over and over.

LYLE: And what was that?

MRS. E: He said it . . . like a litany . . . over and over . . . "I hate you! . . . I hate you!"

LYLE: You mean, he was saying that to *you*?

MRS. E: Oh, no. Not to *me* . . . I asked him what he meant . . . and . . . he said he hated the child he once was, the child who had lived in that house.

LYLE: I see. Go on, Mrs. Evans.

MRS. E: Then he said he was going inside . . . that he *had* to go inside the house . . . but that he was afraid.

LYLE: Of what?

MRS. E: He didn't say of what. He just told me to wait out there on the walk. Then he went up on to the small wooden porch . . . knocked on the door. No one answered. Then Frank tried the knob . . . The door was unlocked . . .

LYLE: House was deserted?

MRS. E: That's right. I guess no one had lived there for a long while . . . All the windows were boarded up . . . and the driveway was filled with weeds . . . I started to move towards the porch, but Frank waved me back. Then he kicked the door all the way open with his foot, took a half-step inside, turned . . . and looked around at me . . . There was . . . a terrible fear in his eyes. I got a cold, chilled feeling all through my body—and I started towards him again . . . but he suddenly turned his back and went inside . . . the door closed.

LYLE: What then?

MRS. E: Then I waited. For fifteen . . . twenty minutes . . . a half hour . . . Frank didn't come out. So I went up to the porch and opened the door . . . called to him . . .

LYLE: Any answer?

MRS. E: No. The house was like . . . a hollow cave . . . there were echoes . . . but no answer . . . I went inside . . . walked all through the place . . . into every room . . . but he wasn't there . . . Frank was gone.

LYLE: Out the back, maybe.

MRS. E: No. The back door was nailed shut. Rusted. It hadn't been opened for years.

LYLE: A window then.

MRS. E: They were all boarded over. With thick dust on the sills.

LYLE: Did you check the basement?

MRS. E: Yes, I checked the basement door leading down. It was locked, and the dust hadn't been disturbed around it.

LYLE: Then . . . just where the hell did he *go*?

MRS. E: I don't *know*, Lieutenant! . . . That's why I called you . . . why I came here . . . You've got to find Frank!

NOTE: Lt. Lyle did not find Franklin Evans. The case was turned over to Missing Persons—and, a week later, Mrs. Evans returned to her home in California. The first night back she had a dream, a nightmare. It disturbed her severely. She could not eat, could not sleep properly; her nerves were shattered. Mrs. Evans then sought psychiatric help. What follows is an excerpt from a taped session with Dr. Lawrence Redding, a licensed psychiatrist with offices in Beverly Hills, California.

Transcript is dated 3 August 1984. Beverly Hills.

REDDING: And where were you . . . ? In the dream, I mean.

MRS. E: My bedroom. In bed, at home. It was as if I'd just been awakened . . . I looked around me—and everything was normal . . . the room exactly as it always is . . . Except for *him* . . . the boy standing next to me.

REDDING: Did you recognize this boy?

MRS. E: No.

REDDING: Describe him to me.

MRS. E: He was . . . nine or ten . . . a *horrible* child . . . with a cold hate in his face, in his eyes . . . He had on a black sweater with holes in each elbow. And knickers . . . the kind that boys used to wear . . . and he had on black tennis shoes . . .

REDDING: Did he speak to you?

MRS. E: Not at first. He just . . . smiled at me . . . and that smile was so . . . so *evil*! . . . And then he said . . . that he wanted me to know he'd won at last . . .

REDDING: Won what?

MRS. E: That's what I asked him . . . calmly, in the dream . . . I asked him what he'd won. And he said . . . oh, my God . . . he said . . .

REDDING: Go on, Mrs. Evans.

MRS. E: . . . that he'd won Frank! . . . that my husband would *never* be coming back . . . that he, the boy, had him now . . . forever! . . . I screamed—and woke up. And, instantly, I remembered something.

REDDING: What did you remember?

MRS. E: Before she died . . . Frank's mother . . . sent us an album she'd saved . . . of his childhood . . . photos . . . old report cards . . . He never wanted to look at it, stuck the album away in a closet . . . After the dream, I got it out, looked through it until I found . . .

REDDING: Yes . . . ?

MRS. E: A photo I'd remembered. Of Frank . . . at the age of ten . . . standing in the front yard on Forest . . . He was smiling . . . that same, awful smile . . . and . . . he wore a dark sweater with holes in each elbow . . . and knickers . . . black tennis shoes. It was . . . the *same* boy exactly—the younger self Frank had always hated . . . I *know* what happened in that house now.

REDDING: Then tell me.

MRS. E: The boy was . . . waiting there . . . inside that awful, rotting dead house . . . waiting for Frank to come back . . . all those years . . . waiting there to claim him—because . . . *he* hated the man that Frank had become as much as Frank hated the child he'd once been . . . and the boy was *right*.

REDDING: Right about what, Mrs. Evans?

MRS. E: About winning . . . He took all those years, but . . . He won . . . and . . . Frank lost.

Daylight Shadows

Arthur J. Burks

I had been told by a more experienced officer than myself that only a fool would attempt the passage of Neiba Desert after ten o'clock in the morning. No white man, afoot, could bear up under the terrible heat, and there are few Dominican mules that can carry with ease a bulk as great as mine. Neiba Desert, in the heart of the tropics, is a hundred feet below the level of the sea.

But what youngster ever listened to the advice of his elders? I never had, and because I did not in this instance, I qualified for the first rank among fools.

We, a tenderfoot pharmacist's mate and myself, left Barahona at five o'clock in the morning, intent on reaching Las Salinas in time to make the crossing in the cool of the morning. We rode a pair of Dominican mules that were too small for us. But, even so, we should have made it, had we not tarried overlong in Cabral to listen to the raucous cries of the natives in the marketplace—until it was eight o'clock by the sun.

We pulled out finally, after breakfasting on Dominican coffee, which is nectar fit for the gods after one has acquired the taste for it. We reached the branching of the road at about nine, and it was ten o'clock exactly when we gave the mules their last chance at water just Neibaward from Las Salinas. We filled our canteens there, after which we gave our mounts a breathing space ere we struck out through the thorn-tree studded waste of sand.

I shall never forget that momentous first glance toward Neiba. Just behind us to the south were the broad reaches of the Bahoruco mountains, while away ahead we could see the blue outline of the distant Cordilleras. We could not see the town of Neiba because of the fringe of palm-trees which hide her from view, even as they disclose her whereabouts. Even at that distance, which must have been very great, we could see that the palm-trees bowed and beckoned to us, as if they urged us ahead with promises of hospitality upon arrival.

We started blithely on our way. My companion was a pharmacist's mate in Uncle Sam's navy, and we talked of some of his queer experiences in hospital wards during the war, I remember. This was during the first hour, only, of the crossing. There was a dim trail through the sand, and the dust came up in clouds, filling our eyes and nostrils with fine layers of the stuff. The heat was almost unbearable. It must have been one hundred four degrees Fahrenheit even then. And we had just started. The palm-trees looked no nearer. The Cordilleras were just as blue as at first. Our talking died away to oppressive silence. We drank often from our canteens, and we did not try to spare the water. Those palm-trees looked much closer than they really were, although we had been warned that their beckoning was treacherous—like that of *Die Lorelei*. Our water was gone before we had half completed the passage.

Two hours more.

Half an hour after the water gave out we were slumped low in our saddles, our shirts pulled up about our necks to keep the heat from frying our brains, and our mules were creeping along with their heads hanging almost into the trail. They were very tired, and the dust had built gray coats on their sweat-drenched hides.

My companion, who had been but a few weeks out of the States, rode along without a glance to right or left. He was feeling the heat more than I was. It was tough on him. Another hour passed, with the palm-trees seemingly no nearer. I saw that his gaze was fixed steadfastly upon them. Once when their fronded heads bowed and beckoned to us, he raised his hand and waved, as if he answered their silent greeting. He listened. Then he laughed—a laugh that was as dry as footfalls in the leaves of autumn. I knew without looking that his lips had begun to crack and that his tongue was swelling in his mouth.

I began to see queer things. A lizard scrambled from beneath a thorn-tree and stopped in the trail ahead, his yellow throat moving in the heat like a bellows. Before my eyes, as we approached, he swelled in size until

107

he was not a lizard, but an iguana—not an iguana, but a dinosaur—a monster. He did not move as my mule approached, but ducked his serpentine head as if he would hide it in the sand. He kept on swelling until, just as the mule's hoof must strike him, he covered the entire road, and his body stretched away in the desert on either side. But the mule never noticed. Nor did my companion. The mule's foot struck without a jar. In a flash the monster vanished. I looked back after we had passed. There was only a greenish smear in the footprint, which was rapidly filling with dust. I laughed, loud and long, but my companion did not turn around.

When I had looked back, I had lowered my head so that my gaze was upon the ground beneath. I noticed a strange thing. Neither myself, my companion, nor the mules, cast a sign of a shadow upon the sand beneath us! I pinched myself and it hurt. I struck spurs to the mule and he grunted dismally. Real enough. But why were there no shadows? I bent over to look beneath the animal I rode. Still no shadow! The pharmacist's mate looked at me then. We laughed in each other's faces and neither knew why the other laughed.

My mule stopped. His sides were moving rapidly out and in—out and in, as if he could not stop them. His breath came groaning from drooling lips; slobbers made cakes of sand and dried at once, leaving little hills like the workings of certain kinds of yellowjackets. I knew at once that the mule could proceed no farther. I alighted and attempted to pull the creature along. Not to be done.

My lips were cracked and bleeding. My tongue protruded from between sand-gritted teeth. I addressed the pharmacist's mate in a weird kind of croak:

"Go on to Neiba, and tell the *guardia* to come back out for me. Your mule can make it. You never could do it afoot if I took your mule. I don't know that I can do it myself, but my chances are better than yours. Beat it!"

"Just so, sir. Certainly! It was to me that they beckoned, anyway. They have no welcome for you in Neiba. The greeting was for me."

What was the fool talking about? And why did he laugh like a croaking raven as he set spurs to his mule and moved on up the trail? I stood and watched him until he mingled with the heat waves, vanishing into the shimmering stuff like a creature from the pit.

Once more I tried to pull the mule along. It was no use, but my knees were knocking together and I was as weak as a cat before I gave it up and tied my mule in the dubious shade of a thorn-tree, where it was hotter even than out in the sunlight.

I started on afoot. I came to myself at the end of a hundred yards or so, to see that I was heading toward Las Salinas. That would never do!

Two hundred yards of needless walking when I needed every ounce of my strength!

The mate would never reach Neiba, I felt sure. He was already crazy from the heat. He'd be bound to try a short cut and leave his bones to bleach in the sun. I had to make it on in. I need not look for the arrival of *guardia* soldiers. The pharmacist's mate would never get in to tell them. He was too crazy.

I had to laugh when I thought about it. Then I looked down and turned clear around once, looking for my shadow. Not a shade of a shadow! Pretty good, that, I thought. Shade of a shadow. Carefully, solemnly, I raised one foot at a time, looking under each one. No shadow.

I started on again, saying "Eeny, meeny, miny, mo" to be sure I got started in the right direction this time. Queer how I had got turned around while turning around looking for the shade of my shadow!

I stumbled along, cursing to myself because my scuffling feet stirred up dust which flew into my nostrils. I didn't hear myself curse. My tongue was so big now that no sound could get out. But I should be all right in a brace of minutes. There was a sparkling stream crossing the trail right up ahead of me. Queer, too, that—the officer who had given me that crazy advice had told me that there were no streams between Las Salinas and Neiba. But I could see it, couldn't I? Sure! I stumbled along until I reached its very edge, flung myself down and pressed my lips to its cooling surface. They came away coated with burning sand, some of which worked past my lips, past my swollen tongue, and into my mouth. I had to stumble on with the gritty grains scratching me terribly. Somebody had placed the stream there as a kind of funny joke; but whoever had done it had hauled it away just when I would have slaked my thirst!

I looked back at the mule. He brayed at me with the note of a croaking raven. I turned and looked at the palm-trees that beckoned me on to Neiba. I could almost hear the whispering of the fronds. But the Cordilleras were as blue as ever. Where was that dratted pharmacist's mate? Damn him!

I looked once more for my shadow. No shadow. Then I knew that I was nearing the end. The thought brought me back to a semblance of reason for a few minutes. I was suffering the torments of the utterly damned. How many a poor fool had left his bones to bleach in this desert? There must have been many of them, surely. But not if they remained on the road. Someone would surely come along and find them. Only the poor fool who wandered off the trail left his bones to bleach. I had better sense. I would stick to the trail.

But where was the trail? I saw trails now which led to every point of the compass. Follow the beckoning of the palm-trees? There were palm-trees all around me. But some of them were thorn-trees! I couldn't for the life of me tell the difference. Eeny, meeny, miny, mo! Straight ahead. I looked for my shadow again and could not find it.

But all at once there were shadows all around me! But where were the bodies that caused the shadows? The substance which was the father of the shadows? I saw not a single upright creature. Only those shadows, flat on the ground, that danced and eddied around me. The shadows of human beings! But where were the human beings? I looked more closely at the shadows. Arms, legs, heads, bodies—all were there. But the substance which caused them? None to be seen. No solid bodies. The shadows were whole and perfectly formed. But stay! They weren't entirely whole. In each and every shadow there were three bright spots, marking two eyes and a gash of a mouth to each shadow, where the sun shone through the substance I could not see!

I stopped dead in my tracks as an idea came to me. The shadows, which were increasing at an alarming rate, paused, radiating out from me like the spokes of a wheel, and thumbed shadow noses at me with shadow thumbs. My idea was this: I, who was human and alive, cast no shadow. Therefore these shadows must be the shadows of those who had ceased to exist. It was perfectly reasonable, like a proposition in geometry. The living cast no shadow, therefore that which cast a shadow must be dead and gone! It followed, as a corollary, that I should cast a shadow only after I had died!

Queer about this desert. Lizards that were iguanas; iguanas that were dinosaurs; streams that did not exist; shadows of the desert dead! Why did the shadows gather about me? Were they inviting me to join the ranks of those who were able to cast shadows? Were the dead who had died in Neiba asking me to join them? Or were they taunting me because they knew I must join them whether I willed it or not?

"But you haven't got me yet!" I croaked to the shadows. "I am still of those who cast no shadows! See? Look about me and see if there be even the sign of a shadow!"

And I looked down to satisfy myself that I spoke truth.

My God! I didn't cast a shadow, no; but right where my shadow would have been had there been a shadow was a thin pencil mark of darkness, as if someone had drawn a black line about my shadow's outline and then jerked the shadow away! Like that practical joker who had jerked the stream away when I would have slaked my thirst.

I paused for a moment, studying that weird outline, while the real shadows kept thumbing their noses at me. There was a heavier shadow among those real shadows—the shadow of a fat man who had died. Fat men are said to be jolly. I looked at the fat man as I recalled this. The spot where the right eye would have been, had it been a person instead of a shadow, closed slowly and strangely, in a terrible and horrifying wink! The bright eye opened again and the bright gash of a mouth widened into a terrible, ghastly, silent grin!

I screamed and ran, closing my eyes to shut out the shadows. I fell to my knees and slumped forward on my stomach, crawling slowly ahead through the scorching sand. It burned my hands and body. Hellfire rushed into my nostrils from the desert floor. I dragged myself to my feet, then fell and lay still for a long time. I opened my eyes to see that the shadows were dancing in hellish glee upon my chest! All thumbed their noses except the fat man. He winked, and grinned with that bright gash of a mouth.

I arose and looked at my own shadow. I could call it that now, for there was only the bright outline of a miniature of myself, within that other outline of black. I was almost a shadow. I closed my eyes again and stumbled ahead.

Suddenly I met three Dominican women riding toward me on three burros piled high with gourds. Filled with water, I knew, for the gourds were dripping precious moisture upon the gray coats of the burros. I raised a hand beseechingly and pointed to my swollen tongue. The women crossed themselves and shied away from me. I tried to run toward them and the burros bolted. One of the women called back to me:

"Go back to Barahona, or on to Neiba, if you wish water! There is more than you can drink, ever, in either place!"

Surely, that was truth! Stupid of me! I would go on to Neiba. That's where I had started for, wasn't it?

I walked on, stumbling, falling, crawling forward on my stomach like a snake—rising and going forward with feet that were heavy as lead. Molten lead.

Where were the palm-trees? I could not see them. And this trail was not a trail at all. It was the snaky trace of a lizard! No, of an iguana! Or a dinosaur. I don't know. I'll follow it anyway. My shadow tells me that there isn't much time. The miniature within the outline isn't a miniature any more—just a weirdly shaped spray of blinding light, growing smaller. And there are other shadows all about me—countless numbers of them.

What is that up ahead there? Another stream? But I shan't be disappointed if it isn't; I'll have a look anyway. I'm going in that direction. I stumble into the stream. It is real! I feel its coolness creep up over my shoetops, creep into my shoes and harden the molten lead which composes my feet. I fall face downward in the stream and drink—drink—

drink! The water is green because the cattle use it overmuch, but it is nectar for all that—nectar superior to the best Dominican coffee.

I crawl out on the bank and look at my shadow. There is only a spot of light in its center now. To be cheated, after I have reached water at last!

But whence come these other shadows? They are shadows of black soldiers, and they are upright instead of flat on the ground. I am not to be fooled. I'm all turned around, I know that, but I am not crazy yet. They look at me queerly, hesitantly, as they approach. One man, a sergeant, is in the lead, and he is running toward me with swift strides. He stops just before me and his shadow blots out the spray of light which is all that stands between me and the desert dead.

"Curse you! Curse you!" I cry, slashing out with my fist; "would you relegate me to the shadows after I have slaked my thirst and am able to go on! I don't want to be a shadow, I tell you!"

My fist takes him in the mouth, and I see the red blood start as total darkness closes around me, filling the world itself with shadow.

I came to myself in the *guardia* barracks at Neiba. The sergeant sat opposite me, wiping his lips with a soiled handkerchief.

"Where am I?" I asked feebly. "Did the pharmacist's mate get in all right? How did I get here?"

He smiled at me and answered in Spanish.

"You are in Neiba. Yes, he got in all right. We brought you in, after tracking you halfway to Lake Enriquillo, toward which, leaving the trail, you were wandering. You were unconscious, flat on the desert floor, and licking up sand with your swollen tongue, which, sticking through between your teeth, was so big that it wouldn't carry the sand into your mouth! It kept rolling off your tongue and you mumbled to yourself as if cursing. I caught the words 'cattle' and 'shadows.' Then you hit me in the mouth. That's all!"

It was enough.

The Devil and Simon Flagg

Arthur Porges

The Devil is a great one for riddle games. Sometimes he will appear and, without even making a decent offer for your soul, he will start asking you questions, and if you cannot answer them he will carry you off. One of the earliest British ballads is "The False Knight on the Road," which is a question-and-answer dialogue that begins:

> "O where are you going?"
> Quoth the false knight on the road.
> "I'm going to the school,"
> Quoth the wee boy, and still he stood.

Folk-lorists tell us that the false knight is the Devil, but the steadfast wee boy bests him. In many Scandinavian and Baltic legends the Devil buys a soul, but agrees to let him off if he can answer certain questions, for example, "How far is it from heaven to earth?" There are two answers given to that one, "You ought to know, for you fell the distance," a reply which apparently satisfies the Devil, and the other, "One step, for my grandfather has one foot in the grave and one in heaven." Another situation is the converse of this: the mortal is let off if he can ask the Devil a question he cannot answer, or set him a task he cannot perform.

After several months of the most arduous research, involving the study of countless faded manuscripts, Simon Flagg succeeded in summoning the devil. As a competent medievalist, his wife had proved invaluable. A mere mathematician himself, he was hardly equipped to decipher Latin holographs, particularly when complicated by rare terms from Tenth Century demonology, so it was fortunate that she had a flair for such documents.

The preliminary skirmishing over, Simon and the devil settled down to bargain in earnest. The devil was sulky, for Simon had scornfully declined several of his most dependable gambits, easily spotting the deadly barb concealed in each tempting bait.

"Suppose you listen to a proposition from me for a change," Simon suggested finally. "At least, it's a straightforward one."

The devil irritably twirled his tail-tip with one hand, much as a man might toy with his key chain. Obviously, he felt injured.

"All right," he agreed, in a grumpy voice. "It can't do any harm. Let's hear your proposal."

"I will pose a certain question," Simon began, and the devil brightened, "to be answered within twenty-four hours. If you cannot do so, you must pay me $100,000. That's a modest request compared to most you get. No billions, no Helen of Troy on a tiger skin. Naturally there must be no reprisals of any kind if I win."

"Indeed!" the devil snorted. "And what are *your* stakes?"

"If I lose, I will be your slave for any short period. No torment, no loss of soul—not for a mere $100,000. Neither will I harm relatives or friends. Although," he amended thoughtfully, "there are exceptions."

The devil scowled, pulling his forked tail petulantly. Finally, a savage tug having brought a grimace of pain, he desisted.

"Sorry," he said flatly. "I deal only in souls. There is no shortage of slaves. The amount of free, wholehearted service I receive from humans would amaze you. However, here's what I'll do. If I can't answer your question in the given time, you will receive not a paltry $100,000, but any sum within reason. In addition, I offer health and happiness as long as you live. If I do answer it—well, you know the consequences. That's the very best I can offer." He pulled a lighted cigar from the air and puffed in watchful silence.

Simon stared without seeing. Little moist patches sprang out upon his forehead. Deep in his heart he had known what the devil's only terms would be. Then his jaw muscles knotted. He would stake his soul that nobody—man, beast, or devil—could answer *this* question in twenty-four hours.

"Include my wife in that health and happiness provision, and it's a deal," he said. "Let's get on with it."

The devil nodded. He removed the cigar stub from his mouth, eyed it distastefully, and touched it with a taloned forefinger. Instantly it became a large pink mint, which he sucked with noisy relish.

"About your question," he said, "it must have an answer, or our contract becomes void. In the Middle Ages, people were fond of proposing riddles. A few came to me with paradoxes, such as that one about a village with one barber who shaves all those, and only those, who don't shave themselves. 'Who shaves the barber?' they asked. Now, as Russell has noted, the 'all' makes such a question meaningless and so unanswerable."

"My question is just that—not a paradox," Simon assured him.

"Very well. I'll answer it. What are you smirking about?"

"Nothing," Simon replied, composing his face.

"You have very good nerves," the devil said, grimly approving, as he pulled a parchment from the air. "If I had chosen to appear as a certain monster which combines the best features of your gorilla with those of the Venusian Greater Kleep, an animal—I suppose one could call it that—of unique eye appeal, I wonder if your aplomb—"

"You needn't make any tests," Simon said hastily. He took the proffered contract, and satisfied that all was in order, opened his pocketknife.

"Just a moment," the devil protested. "Let me sterilize that; you might get infected." He held the blade to his lips, blew gently, and the steel glowed cherry red. "There you are. Now a touch of the point to some—ah—ink, and we're all set. Second line from the bottom, please; the last one's mine."

Simon hesitated, staring at the moist red tip.

"Sign," urged the devil, and squaring his shoulders, Simon did so.

When his own signature had been added with a flourish, the devil rubbed his palms together, gave Simon a frankly proprietary glance, and said jovially: "Let's have the question. As soon as I answer it, we'll hurry off. I've just time for another client tonight."

"All right," said Simon. He took a deep breath. "My question is this: Is Fermat's Last Theorem correct?"

The devil gulped. For the first time his air of assurance weakened.

"Whose last what?" he asked in a hollow voice.

"Fermat's Last Theorem. It's a mathematical proposition which Fermat, a Seventeenth Century French mathematician, claimed to have proved. However, his proof was never written down, and to this day nobody knows if the theorem is true or false." His lips twitched briefly as he saw the devil's expression. "Well, there you are—go to it!"

"Mathematics!" the devil exclaimed, horrified. "Do you think I've had time to waste learning such stuff? I've studied the Trivium and Quadrivium, but as for algebra—say," he added resentfully, "what kind of a question is that to ask me?"

Simon's face was strangely wooden, but his eyes shone. "You'd rather run 75,000 miles and bring back some object the size of Boulder Dam, I suppose!" he jeered. "Time and space are easy for you, aren't they? Well, sorry. I prefer this. It's a simple matter," he added, in a bland voice. "Just a question of positive integers."

"What's a positive integer?" the devil flared. "Or an integer, for that matter?"

"To put it more formally," Simon said, ignoring the devil's question, "Fermat's Theorem states that there are no nontrivial, rational solutions of the equation $X^n + Y^n = Z^n$, for n a positive integer greater than two."

"What's the meaning of—"

"You supply the answers, remember."

"And who's to judge—you?"

"No," Simon replied sweetly. "I doubt if I'm qualified, even after studying the problem for years. If you come up with a solution, we'll submit it to any good mathematical journal, and their referee will decide. And you can't back out—the problem obviously is soluble: either the theorem is true, or it is false. No nonsense about multivalued logic, mind. Merely determine which, and *prove* it in twenty-four hours. After all, a man—excuse me—demon, of your intelligence and vast experience surely can pick up a little math in that time."

"I remember now what a bad time I had with Euclid when I studied at Cambridge," the devil said sadly. "My proofs were always wrong, and yet it was all obvious anyway. You could see just by the diagrams." He set his jaw. "But I can do it. I've done harder things before. Once I went to a distant star and brought back a quart of neutronium in just sixteen—"

"I know," Simon broke in. "You're very good at such tricks."

"Trick, nothing!" was the angry retort. "It's a technique so difficult—but never mind, I'm off to the library. By this time tomorrow—"

"No," Simon corrected him. "We signed half an hour ago. Be back in exactly twenty-three point five hours! Don't let me rush you," he added ironically, as the devil gave the clock a startled glance. "Have a drink and meet my wife before you go."

"I never drink on duty. Nor have I time to make the acquaintance of your wife . . . now." He vanished.

The moment he left, Simon's wife entered.

"Listening at the door again?" Simon chided her, without resentment.

"Naturally," she said in her throaty voice. "And darling—I want to know—that question—is it really difficult? Because if it's not—Simon, I'm so worried."

"It's difficult, all right." Simon was almost jaunty. "But most people don't realize that at first. You see," he went on, falling automatically into his stance for Senior Math II, "anybody can find two whole numbers whose squares add up to a square. For example, $3^2 + 4^2 = 5^2$; that is, $9 + 16 = 25$. See?"

"Uh huh." She adjusted his tie.

"But when you try to find two cubes that add up to a cube, or higher powers that work similarly, there don't seem to be any. Yet," he concluded dramatically, "nobody has been able to prove that no such numbers exist. Understand now?"

"Of course." Simon's wife always understood mathematical statements, however abstruse. Otherwise, the explanation was repeated until she did, which left little time for other activities.

"I'll make us some coffee," she said, and escaped.

✻   ✻   ✻

Four hours later as they sat together listening to Brahm's Third, the devil reappeared.

"I've already learned the fundamentals of algebra, trigonometry, and plane geometry!" he announced triumphantly.

"Quick work," Simon complimented him. "I'm sure you'll have no trouble at all with spherical, analytic, projective, descriptive, and non-Euclidean geometrics."

The devil winced. "Are there so many?" he inquired in a small voice.

"Oh, those are only a few." Simon had the cheerful air suited to a bearer of welcome tidings. "You'll like non-Euclidean," he said mendaciously. "There you don't have to worry about diagrams—they don't tell a thing! And since you hated Euclid anyway—"

With a groan the devil faded out like an old movie. Simon's wife giggled.

"Darling," she sang, "I'm beginning to think you've got him over a barrel."

"Sh," said Simon. "The last movement. Glorious!"

Six hours later, there was a smoky flash, and the devil was back. Simon noted the growing bags under his eyes. He suppressed a grin.

"I've learned all those geometrics," the devil said with grim satisfaction. "It's coming easier now. I'm about ready for your little puzzle."

Simon shook his head. "You're trying to go too fast. Apparently you've overlooked such basic techniques as calculus, differential equations, and finite differences. Then there's—"

"Will I need all those?" the devil moaned. He sat down and knuckled his puffy eyelids, smothering a yawn.

"I couldn't say," Simon replied, his voice expressionless. "But people have tried practically every kind of math there is on that 'little puzzle,' and it's still unsolved. Now, I suggest—" But the devil was in no mood for advice from Simon. This time he even made a sloppy disappearance while sitting down.

"I think he's tired," Mrs. Flagg said. "Poor devil." There was no discernible sympathy in her tones.

"So am I," said Simon. "Let's get to bed. He won't be back until tomorrow, I imagine."

"Maybe not," she agreed, adding demurely, "but I'll wear the black lace—just in case."

It was the following afternoon. Bach seemed appropriate somehow, so they had Landowska on.

"Ten more minutes," Simon said. "If he's not back with a solution by then, we've won. I'll give him credit; he could get a Ph.D. out of my school in one day—with honors! However—"

There was a hiss. Rosy clouds mushroomed sulphurously. The devil stood before them, steaming noisomely on the rug. His shoulders sagged; his eyes were bloodshot; and a taloned paw, still clutching a sheaf of papers, shook violently from fatigue or nerves.

Silently, with a kind of seething dignity, he flung the papers to the floor, where he trampled them viciously with his cloven hoofs. Gradually then, his tense figure relaxed, and a wry smile twisted his mouth.

"You win, Simon," he said, almost in a whisper, eyeing him with ungrudging respect. "Not even I can learn enough mathematics in such a short time for so difficult a problem. The more I got into it, the worse it became. Non-unique factoring, ideals—Baal! Do you know," he confided, "not even the best mathematicians on other planets—all far ahead of yours—have solved it? Why, there's a chap on Saturn—he looks something like a mushroom on stilts—who solves partial differential equations mentally; and even he's given up." The devil sighed. "Farewell." He dislimned with a kind of weary precision.

Simon kissed his wife—hard. A long while later she stirred in his arms.

"Darling," she pouted, peering into his abstracted face, "what's wrong now?"

"Nothing—except I'd like to see his work; to know how close he came. I've wrestled with that problem for—" He broke off amazed as the devil flashed back. Satan seemed oddly embarrassed.

"I forgot," he mumbled. "I need to—ah!" He stooped for the scattered papers, gathering and smoothing them tenderly. "It certainly gets you," he said, avoiding Simon's gaze. "Impossible to stop just now. Why, if I could only prove one simple little lemma—" He saw the blazing interest in Simon, and dropped his apologetic air. "Say," he grunted, "you've worked on this, I'm sure. Did you try continued fractions? Fermat must have used them, and—move over a minute, please—" This last to Mrs. Flagg. He sat down beside Simon, tucked his tail under, and pointed to a jungle of symbols.

Mrs. Flagg sighed. Suddenly the devil seemed a familiar figure, little different from old Professor Atkins, her husband's colleague at the university. Any time two mathematicians got together on a tantalizing problem . . . Resignedly she left the room, coffee pot in hand. There was certainly a long session in sight. She knew. After all, she was a professor's wife.

The Devilet

R. Chetwynd-Hayes

Roland Adams did not work, spin or toil. He had been mother-raised, cossetted, and ruined, and when the old lady died she left just enough money to ensure that necessity did not spoil her handiwork. If her ghost did not haunt the little house at 23 Paradise Road, at least her memory still drove Roland along the narrow path she had laid out. When he went shopping he carried the same old leather bag as in her lifetime, and his shopping list was written on the back of an envelope; his money, never more than was strictly necessary, nestled in a steel-jawed purse, and passersby turned their heads when he balanced his accounts in a low, but perfectly audible, voice.

To say he did not work is not strictly true; he worked hard at living. He swept, polished, scrubbed, washed the household linen, cooked his food, and kindly matrons remarked he would have made some woman a good husband, while those not so kindly disposed said he would have made some man a good wife. When not engaged in these domestic chores, he spent his time in mooching, shop-window gazing, and—collecting.

He was not an educated collector. That is to say, he did not collect china, stamps, books, or specialise in a selected period; in fact he was often totally unaware of the age of his purchases. No, Roland just collected. Any object that caught his eye in the numerous second-hand shops and stalls that lined, or were adjacent to, the Portobello Road, and most important, were cheap, he bought. Brass coal scuttles, old oil lamps, an occasional age-darkened picture, candlesticks, swords; by now the house was better stocked than most of the shops he patronised.

His latest acquisition was wrapped in newspaper, and his short, stumpy fingers tore impatiently at the layers, much like a housewife denuding a cabbage. The torn paper floated down to the faded carpet, and Roland's small black eyes glistened with satisfaction, for your true collector lives only to gloat. It was a black egg.

A little larger than a chicken egg, and black—as black as pitch, but deep shining black; not glass, Roland decided, or crystal, more like an oval shaped black diamond. He fondled the smooth blackness, and gloried in its beautiful uselessness. 'Make a good paper weight,' the man had said. Roland giggled when he imagined trying to keep papers intact with that oval object; why it could hardly weigh more than a few ounces. This thought opened up a line of enquiry. He tapped the egg gently; it sounded hollow. He placed it to his ear, and shook. Nothing. It was empty, or so packed with some light substance as to appear hollow. Next came the question that followed all of his finds. Where should he put it? His gaze flashed round the over-crowded room; a stuffed bear glared at him from one corner; the sideboard was crammed, the glass cabinet a miniature shop window; the mantelpiece—there was a gap by the marble clock. Rising swiftly, he transformed his thought into action. The egg looked lost; the clock towered above it, a Victorian napkin holder smothered it. Unless he looked very carefully, the egg could not be seen. Suddenly he gave a little titter of joy, and stumped his way across the room to the china cabinet. A few minutes sufficed for him to find what he was looking for. A small china eggcup decorated with minute pink roses. He sank back on to the sofa with a sigh of satisfaction. The black egg was in the eggcup, and the eggcup stood on top of the marble clock.

'A good find,' he spoke aloud, for such was his habit, 'a rarity, that's what it is. A rarity.'

Twenty-four hours later, and he'd almost forgotten its existence.

Friday was dusting day. Roland flicked, rubbed, and blew. The mantelpiece came in for its share of blowing; the weekly accumulated dust rose into the stale air, floated gently, before descending into a new position. Roland was quite red in the face when he reached the marble clock. There he stopped and allowed his breath to drift out as a deep sigh. The egg was out of its cup; it lay on the mantelpiece—broken.

'Dirty rotten swine,' he swore aloud.

He was of course cursing the fates that were, in his opinion, responsible for this catastrophe. The Little People, the Gremlins, those irresponsible beings who put banana skins under our feet and grit in the petrol tank. He gathered up the jagged halves, for the egg was split in two, and gazed at them in childish sorrow.

'Dirty, rotten swine,' he muttered again, then toyed with the idea of trying to join them together with Durafix, but somehow it seemed to be too much trouble for a poor return. The shell was much thinner than he had supposed, and on reflection he decided he had been cheated. A black egg, was, all said and done, an egg coloured black, so he tossed the fragments into the blazing log fire, and turned his attention to the glass cabinet.

Two days after the mysterious breaking of the egg he found that half a pound of ham and three doughnuts were missing. There was no question of blaming the 'beings' this time, for it is a well known fact that while these ill intentioned creatures may put banana skins under our feet. and possibly break black eggs, they are not partial to either ham or dough-

120

nuts. A terrible fear invaded Roland's mind, a fear that had haunted his late lamented mother all her days. Burglars.

He made a quick inventory of his collection; so far as he could see nothing was missing, at any rate there was no vacant space. He examined all doors and windows; none had been forced. Clearly if a burglar was involved he must be so constructed as to be able to crawl under locked doors, and be cursed with an addiction for ham and doughnuts. Roland pondered on the problem all day, then after screwing the window sashes together, and barricading both back and front doors with the wardrobe and kitchen table, retired to bed. During the night he was disturbed by a scratching sound, and another possible solution presented itself. Mice, or—heaven forbid—rats. Next morning he found that six rashers of streaky bacon had gone.

Roland, like many simple souls, had an affinity for animals. Mice might be a nuisance, rats he certainly loathed, but he recognised their inalienable right to life and the pursuit of happiness, so he bought two cage traps; one, a flimsy wood and wire affair, and the other, a formidable barred construction that looked as if it could house any number of rats. These he baited with cheese, and in the rat trap he placed the eggcup filled with water, in case the prisoner should get thirsty during the night. Next morning found the traps unsprung, the bait uneaten, but a pork pie had gone from the larder shelf.

Roland was more perturbed by the complete disappearance of the food, than the gradual denuding of his pantry. Surely mice, even rats, eat on the spot, and at least leave some crumbs behind; this thief (or thieves) seemed to be on a shop-lifting spree and, the possibility could not be ignored, building up an unsavoury store in some secluded spot, more than likely under the floor-boards.

That evening Roland baited his traps with pork pie, cleared the larder shelves of all eatables, and after turning out the lights, sat, not without considerable trepidation, to await results. The marble clock struck a quivering twelve; one o'clock followed and Roland nodded in his chair; he did not hear two or half past, but a sharp crack followed by a hissing scream made him sit upright.

'Wassat?' He was frightened by the sound of his own voice.

A rattle of iron bars being shaken, accompanied by a hissing squeak. Roland's answer was a whimper, and whatever was in the trap retorted with a shrill scream. For five minutes this indeterminate duet went on: squeak, whimper, scream, gasp, then a rattling of bars, once the cage was shaken and the unseen thing seemed to spit. It was the rattle of the locking bar that finally drove Roland to his feet, and sent him lurching across the room in a frantic search for the light switch.

The front room looked ridiculously the same as usual once the light was on, and his eyes drew comfort from the familiar scene, even if they were reluctant to look downwards. The rat trap was bouncing about in a most agitated manner, and was in fact bumping its way in the general direction of Roland's feet. He surrendered and looked down, first giving a sigh of relief, then a gasp of horror. Relief was caused by the tail; a long thin appendage such as a rat would not be ashamed of, but horror followed at once when he saw what was attached to the tail. The creature was bent almost double, but free from the cage it would have stood all of eight inches high. It had a black humanoid body, complete with miniature legs and arms, the perfect little fingers and toes were crowned with scarlet talons; the face was goat-shaped—Roland could think of no better description—the eyes bright red and slanting, the ears pointed, and out of a nest of tightly curling jet black hair grew two tiny horns. The beginnings of a beard covered the sharp chin, and when the thing rolled back its dark red lips in a snarl, Roland saw a set of even, white, tapered teeth.

'Crumbs!' he said, this being an expression denoting astonishment much in use when he was a schoolboy thirty odd years before. 'Crikey!'

The captive rolled over to crouch down on its haunches, careful to coil the long tail round its toes. The scarlet eyes looked Roland's shaking form up and down, then stopped when they reached his thick, short-fingered hand; a black tongue came out and licked red lips. The man retreated backwards, never once taking his eyes off this miniature horror; when he reached the door, he turned and ran, to spend the rest of the night shivering in his bedroom.

Next morning the marble clock had chimed nine before he found sufficient courage to re-enter the front room. He experienced a feeling of relief when he saw the cage was empty. The locking bar had been lifted up and placed on top of the trap; having performed this feat, it would have been an easy matter for the alien to push open the door and walk out. The sideboard door, behind which Roland had hidden the larder contents, was open, and on investigation, he found a pound of wrapped sausages, a box of figs, and a packet of assorted biscuits were missing. He said 'Rotten swine,' before bursting into tears.

The Station Sergeant was not impressed.

'A what?' he asked looking up from the record book.

'A kind of—devilet,' Roland tried to explain, 'with red eyes, and horns . . .'

'Take more water with it,' the sergeant advised.

'Pray for guidance,' the Vicar murmured, after he had been buttonholed outside his church, then added: 'Why not come to our Thursday evening Bible class?'

The milkman laughed, the butcher smirked, and the grocer nodded gravely before popping an extra egg into Roland's shopping basket. A cat he stopped to stroke swore at him, a dog tried to bite him, then the heavens wept and he was drenched by the time he got home. He went straight to his bedroom, and after jamming a chair under the door handle sat down on his bed to think things out. After a while his brain, a not very active organ, had come up with three solutions.

1. He leave the house.
2. The devilet leave the house.
3. Neither of them leave the house.

Number one was unthinkable. The house, its furniture, his collection, was an extension of himself; once removed from them and he would die. Of that he was certain. Number two was very desirable, but the devilet seemed well established; to make it leave meant seeking it out, and from that possibility he shrank, even as he would have shrunk from entering a snake pit. Number three was just possible if you did not think about it. Appeasement carried to the extreme, and a little beyond. The devilet wanted food, that was clear; so long as it got food, there was no reason why it should put in an appearance.

'Pork pies, sausages, ham, bacon and biscuits,' Roland nodded slowly, 'it shouldn't be too difficult to keep it satisfied.' Then he paused. 'I wonder if it likes liver?'

As the days passed and merged into months, Roland became horrified by the amount of food his hidden guest was consuming. Before retiring to bed he laid out what he considered to be its rightful ration on the kitchen floor. This was usually a pork pie, half a pound of best streaky bacon, a packet of biscuits, and half a pint of milk. Next morning all these items had disappeared plus half the contents of his larder as well. In consequence he doubled the devilet's share; for a few days his own stores were untouched, then the pilfering started again. An entire fruit cake he had bought for his Sunday tea went, so did a wrapped loaf and twelve eggs. Again he doubled the devilet's ration, and the tradesmen began to make remarks.

'That little devil of yours seems to eat well,' said the butcher with a knowing smile.

'Yes,' Roland sighed, 'he does.'

'Got a harem in there?' enquired the milkman when asked to increase his daily order to six pints.

'Oh, no.' Roland was shocked. 'Nothing like that.'

Presently he began to wonder where the devilet put it all, he was eating enough to feed three or four navvies; and Roland was pulled up by the sudden thought that all this nourishment must be resulting in growth, or. . . . He did not dare consider the other possibility.

It was three months before he found the other black egg. He was just about to sit down to breakfast when he saw it on the sofa, nestling between two cushions. He could not bring himself to touch it; was only able to stare down at the smooth gleaming blackness, and shiver. When he came back from shopping it had gone.

He appealed to the grocer.

'Do chickens lay eggs all the time?'

'Can they . . .' he hesitated, for his mother had always stressed this was a forbidden subject, 'can they hatch them—all?'

The grocer winked at his assistant.

'Not unless the cock has a hand in it, they can't.'

'My mum had a hen that did,' the assistant butted in. 'Funny looking chicks they were, but there was no cock, honest.'

'You sure?' The grocer scratched his head. 'I know some reptiles can, but I've never heard of a chicken before.'

Roland took longer and longer to reach home. There was a lot more pattering of taloned feet under the floor-boards, and latterly over the ceiling; nothing on earth would have tempted him to push open the trap-door leading to the loft. The demand for food was growing daily; he always knew when the offering was insufficient. Locked in his bedroom he could hear the crash of crockery being flung across the kitchen, the soul-wrenching clatter, the result of havoc wrecked among his collection. The cost was mounting, soon it would be more than his little annuity could support. And he knew all the locality was talking; looking at him with concern, even fear.

He might have continued for a little while longer if he had not fallen ill; to keep it—them—satisfied meant cutting down on his own food, and one cold day in early spring he caught a chill; within three days he had developed pneumonia and could not leave his bed.

He lay all through the daylight hours listening to his own rasping breathing, his eyes on the chair-barricaded bedroom door, every sense strained to detect the faintest sound in the rooms below. When the sun set he reached out and switched on his bedside lamp, causing the shadows to rush away, and as he did so tiny feet pattered over the ceiling, and he heard the sound of sliding bodies in the hollow walls.

It was not long before pandemonium reigned in the kitchen; plates, saucepans, dishes, all contributed to the general din; a crash told him the dresser had been overturned; the squeals became hissing screams; the kitchen door crashed open; the hall was invaded. Roland waited for the ultimate. He had fed the devilet, and in return it had hidden its ugliness, now it had multiplied; a dozen, a hundred, who knew, perhaps

124

a legion of mouths were demanding food. He had given of his all—almost his all.

Taloned feet were scampering up the stairs; pattering up over old Mrs Adams's stair carpet, swinging along the banisters; crowding over each other, rushing—tearing—gibbering, mouths watering, tongues protruding, hungry, thirsty, all converging on to the great provider, the fount of all nourishment. Only one last obstacle remained. The bedroom door.

To the end Roland spoke his thoughts aloud.

'Mother, let me out. I'm sick, mother, I want to get out. . . .'

The screams filled his ears; the entire world was a bedlam of crashing, slithering, and the door was bulging; the chair slid to the floor, and in the final fear-fed desperation he left his bed, and crawled to the window.

People were walking with callous unconcern along the dimly lit street, and he banged weakly upon the window panes he had so carefully cleaned but a few days ago.

'Why can't you hear?' The crash of splintered wood smothered his faint whisper, so he turned to face the inevitable.

They crowded into the room; some were minute, a scarce three inches tall, others reared up to a glorious foot—or more; as black as midnight, red eyes, long tails, two sharp little horns, white teeth, black tongues that licked dark red lips, pointed ears; they were packed three layers high on the bed; they covered the wardrobe, coated the dressing table; two swung on the ceiling lamp. The hissing screams died. Roland tasted the silence; it was bitter, like brimstone. The devilets waited: dinner was about to say grace.

'It was only a little egg,' Roland pleaded, 'one, crummy little egg.'

With a screech of triumph they rushed in.

The Devil's Debt

James Platt

Somewhere about the Middle Ages—somewhere in a mediæval town—there lived a man who walked always on the shady side of the way. None of his neighbours could have assigned a reason he should only tread where the lapse of time leaves no trace on the dial, yet so it was. None had ever seen him in sunshine.

This man was known by the name of Porphyro, though we may reasonably doubt if it was given to him in baptism. For he belonged to a class that baptised toads by night at their Sabbaths in mockery of the baptism of babes by day. In a word, Porphyro was a wizard, and for one circumstance (which will presently be mentioned) was perhaps better known among his like than any practiser of the Black Art before or since.

There was, and likely enough still is, in Europe a University of the occult sciences, buried underground, carved out of the roots of mountains, far from the hum of men. Here taught weird professors—eerie, eldritch, elflocked. Here came weird students to tread the intoxicating wine-press of magical study. Your true wizard is set apart from birth by some particularity which bespeaks his vocation. To the University came representatives of every class which felt this call. Here was the demoniac and the stigmatic: the abortion and the albino, the hermaphrodite and the changeling, the hag-ridden and the pixy-led, sleep-walker, Cesarean, Sunday-child, seventh son, and he that is born with the caul. This motley crew was of as many hues as there are ends of the earth. Many tongued as Mithridates, all wrote their notes by common consent in the *lingua angelorum*.

The University boasted a laboratory of at least a hundred paces in length and proportionately broad and high. A mock sun gave it cold light by day, and a mock moon by night. Here experiments in exorcism were conducted, of course under the strictest supervision of the principals. Here the students learned that the ghosts of dead men (having always some of the old Adam that was unpurged from them) are easier to call back to us than elemental spirits can be wrenched from their eternal spheres. The most trivial task (and therefore that of the junior classes), was to re-incarnate some suicide, set in four cross roads, whose soul still hovered like a noxious gas about the only body where it could hope to find toleration. The pupils were very properly forbidden to incur the danger of repeating these experiments in private. Nevertheless something of the kind went on under the rose. As a rule the novices (and these were after all the lucky ones) ignominiously failed in their attempts to storm the outworks of hell. They knew how to call spirits from the vasty deep, but the spirits refused to come when they did call them. One youth, however, boasted that he had raised the devil, or at any rate a devil. He described him to his bosom friends nearly as follows:—

"A great and full stature, soft and phlegmatic, of colour like a black obscure cloud, having a swollen countenance, with eyes red and full of water, a bald head, and teeth like a wild boar."

One of the listeners, doubtless jealous, attempted to cheapen this success of his companion, remarking that an exorcist, if worth his salt, should be able to make the spirit appear in what guises he chose.

"Then, by the belt of Venus," swore a third, "I would command it to appear as a lovely girl, with longer hair and smaller feet than any on this top which the Almighty set spinning and dubbed earth."

Another poor fellow appears to have been so inflamed with the suggestion of this rustler, that he tried to bring it into the sphere of practical politics. He was never seen alive again. Not answering to his name at the roll-call next morning, his bedroom was visited, and a thin trickle of blood found oozing under the door. One of the search party put a pistol to the lock and fired. The door flew open. A cry burst from all present, and some of the youngest, covering their faces with their hands, fled. The body of the devoted wretch who had played with unholy fire, was scattered piece meal about the room. The lopped limbs were twisted round into spirals as if boneless. One of stronger stomach than the rest of the onlookers, and who examined them more closely, declared that the bone had melted and run out under some incredible heat. One of the teachers opined that if the demon had only breathed upon the bone, it would have been enough to fuse it. There were no more experiments in students' rooms.

Apart from such accidental deaths, the Academy paid a regular yearly rent of one living soul to hell, and woe unto teachers and taught had they lapsed into arrear one day. The victim who was to suffer, that the rest might live and learn, was selected in the following traditional manner. The whole of the pupils toed a line at one extreme end of the hall, and, at a given signal, raced to the opposite door. There was, as may be imagined, a terrible struggle to pass through the hangings. The last to cross the threshold was hugged to hell by the awaiting fiend. It was on such an occasion that Porphyro earned the unique distinction, alluded to above, of having successfully cozened the Prince of Darkness himself. Strain as he might, he was the last to touch the winning post. His competitors, who now breathed themselves in safety in the lobby, had given him up for lost. But no piercing shriek of dissolution stabbed the air, no fiendish laughter made horrible the echoes. Instead, voices were heard, until presently their comrade rejoined those who had already mourned him. Amid a scene of the wildest excitement, he was dragged into the light. Something unprecedented must obviously have occurred. His hair had turned snowy white. Those fell back who looked first into his eyes, for they saw in them reflected the face of Hell himself.

The tale which Porphyro told them was in substance this, that when he arrived last at the curtains and already felt the breath of punishment upon his cheek, there occurred to him one loophole of escape. He turned desperately at bay, like hunted quarry, and roundly told the scrutineer that all he could claim by the letter of his bond was Porphyro's shadow. That was the last living thing which passed out of the lists; and not Porphyro, who preceded it. Strange as it may seem, after heated words, the justice of this quibble was acknowledged by the father of all such juggleries. He bore off the shadow with a sort of smile, that was more terrible than men's frown, and lo and behold! when the schoolfellows, with one accord, looked down at the feet of him who had so miraculously escaped the infernal maw, they saw that Porphyro was, as he ever after-wards remained, shadowless. And now our readers can guess why our hero walked always on the shady side of the way.

Nothing had ever been known (even in circles like this) so success-fully daring as this piece of evasion. Round and round the whole round globe, by means only known to wizards, the news sped fast to all the wizard world. It was proclaimed at every Sabbath, from Blockula to the Brocken. The Lapland witch whispered it to the Finland witch, as they sat tying up wind after wind in knots for their seafaring customers. The Druids of Carnac knew it, and the Persian devil worshippers. The Sha-mans of Siberia made a song of it and beat their magic drums thereto. The magicians of Egypt pictured it in their mirrors of ink. The African Obi men washed their great fetish in the blood of a thousand virgins, and sent it as a present, over the desert sands, to Porphyro. Even the medi-cine men heard of it, in the heart of an undiscovered continent, and emblazoned it upon the walls of their medical lodge. Everyone foresaw a brilliant career for Porphyro. They fully expected him to disembowel Hell. The reverse was what really happened. Instead of swinging himself at once to the top rung of the ladder, he showed no disposition to trouble himself at all. He opened a private office in the town referred to at the beginning of our story, and carried on a private business in magic of the whitest kind. For him no monster evocations, with a million demons at his beck and call, like the Sicilian whom Benvenuto Cellini employed to conjure for him in the Coliseum. Porphyro refused in the most stiff-necked manner to exorcise on any terms for anyone. He confined himself solely to pettifogging business, such as writing talismans, and reckoning magic squares, drawing horoscopes, and casting schemes of geomancy, poisoning rivals for lovers, or close-fisted relatives for spendthrift heirs.

Need we state in black and white the reason (concealed from every-one else) why he held his hand from higher things? Oh, the humiliation of it! He was afraid! Yes, Porphyro was afraid, even he, who had plucked a hair from the devil's beard; for that very reason he was afraid. He had saved his soul alive, losing only a shadow of little moment to him; but in return, he had incurred the eternal enmity of one whose grudge had once shaken the high heavens. The general adversary of all mankind was first and beyond all things, most ferociously, Porphyro's adversary. Unhappy Porphyro, who had already given seisin to hell, Porphyro with one half of him already in the living devil's clutch, who never slept but he dreamed of the tortures his poor shadow suffered at the hands of those that lovingly work evil! Tortures which were but foreshadowings of his own! No wonder Porphyro dared not invoke even the least of spirits. He knew too well that the mightiest of them would appear, with no greater calling than a word.

But, there was one antidote which wrestled with the nightshade in his cup, one star of the right colour appeared above his horizon. There was a woman in his town (one only for him), a princess and the ward of a king, an exquisite beauty. From the first time he saw her, he loved her with a passion which reproached his meaner self. She fed upon his sighs without knowing that the air she breathed was full of them. In any case, he would never have dared to speak to her. It was sufficient daily bread to him to see her move. He hung upon her footsteps. He kept pace with her in her rides, running ever in the shadow because he himself had no shadow to call his own. Yet he forgot while looking at her this one great fact of his life. Even in his dreams she presently held his hand while he suffered. And he dreamed of her thus till he set his teeth in his pillow. Gradually her little mouth sucked up all the breath of his body. He wrote poems about his princess and swallowed them. Often he took no other food for days. He made philtres which would infallibly have caused her to love him, had he not ruthlessly thrown them all away as soon as made. He constructed an image of her in wax, and worshipped it five times daily. It was this which wrought his downfall. Certain of his clients (they had not paid him) denounced him as a sorcerer. Without notice he received a domiciliary visit from the authorities. Apart from other evidence which the house contained, the wax image of the princess was discovered, and he was at once charged with intending to make away with her life. Oh, the irony of fate, he who would have cheerfully laid down his own for her! Being forcibly removed from his house, the secret he had so long kept was discovered, and this shadowlessness, though accounted for in a hundred ways, all wide of the truth, was added at once to the long list of crimes in his indictment. At the preliminary examination he would confess nothing. He was accordingly imprisoned pending the preparation of tortures to shake his resolution. With the aid of these refinements, he might be made to confess anything, even that he had attempted the life of his best beloved. The scaffold loomed before him. And oh, that her name should be bandied about in such context.

Meanwhile Porphyro sat, body and soul in darkness. He saw none but the jailer, who brought him food once daily, with a finger ever on his lips. Rats there were, and such small cheer, but with these he could hold no converse, although in his youth he had met with men who professed to teach their languages. Porphyro was fain to chatter constantly to himself that he might have no time to think. He played his school games over again, rehearsed his school tasks to imaginary masters, held imaginary conversations with clients and with his parents long dead, and with his princess who was more than parent, and more than dead to him. He wooed her in a thousand ways, now as an emperor, raising her to his level, now as the meanest of her grooms, to whom she sweetly condescended, now he was a soldier, better used to red lips of wounds than red lips which wound, now he was a scholar, who forgot all wisdom save hers, now he was a miser, who came like Jupiter in a shower of gold. Thus riotous reigned carnival before his coming Lent.

And now comes the strangest part of all this strange eventful history. He fancied once or twice that he was replied to as he spoke. Again and again he groped all over the blind prison, and felt no one. Yet there was of a surety a tongue which answered him. And the weirdness of it was that, turn though he might, it always spoke from behind him. Again he searched the litter of the dungeon, and again without result. The voice was at first unintelligible, like the murmur of the sea, yet with a cadence which soon struck his ear as strangely familiar. He had heard it only once before, but it had been in that cock-pit underground where he had fought a main which had coloured his whole life. He was bound up with the memory of it like a poor prisoner whom men fetter to a corpse. It was the still small voice which dominates the brawl of Hell.

His hair could grow no whiter, else it had done so. He listened with all his ears and began to catch syllables and afterwards words, till at last he made out that the Tempter was proposing terms of peace with him.

Right well knew Porphyro (none better) the price that must be paid for such a truce. His soul must feed the quick of Hell. It seemed hard to yield up at last to that immortal henchman which he had once so gloriously saved from these same talons. Yet what chance had he? On the one hand, if he maintained his feud with the Evil One, the halter was weaving which must strangle love and life. On the other part, if he surrendered his soul to the Exile, he could at any rate make what terms he pleased. And there were terms he pictured himself exacting which made ultimate payment of the highest price seem easy to the blood which had once stood face to face with Satan, and given him better than he gave. Porphyro still continued to argue *pro* and *con*, though his decision was a foregone conclusion. At last he formulated his demands to the spirit. He must marry the Princess. He must be her husband, were it but for a single night.

The walls of the dungeon suddenly became bright with a kind of phosphorescent glow. Porphyro (still alone, or, at any rate, he seemed so) saw a table standing in front of him, bearing a bond already drawn and the materials for signing it. The terms set forth were those he had himself proposed. He signed, sealed, and delivered it, and was plunged into darkness again as his finger left the parchment. A sense of infernal laughter pervaded the air, though nothing was to be heard. Porphyro fell full length to the ground in a fainting fit.

When he recovered his jailer was standing over him, come (as he thought) to bring him food, but he was soon disabused of any such notion by the man himself. He, who had refused on all prior occasions to hold converse with his prisoner, now spoke voluntarily to tell him the sands of his captivity had run out. At first the dazed cage bird (who had forgotten for the moment his compact) believed that he was on the point of expiating his crimes, real and imaginary, upon the scaffold. But the jailer, not without difficulty, made it clear to him that all captives received pardon on the joyous occasion of the marriage of their Princess, which was fixed for that day. Then Porphyro remembered all, and swooned again.

When he revived, our hero was sitting in the open air upon the steps which led from the jail. He caught the smell of oxen roasting whole in the market-place. The sky was red with the fires. The streets, as far as he could see them, were paved with flowers and decorated with triumphal arches. The citizens were bustling about in holiday attire. Music seemed to be playing everywhere. Occasionally some exuberant person fired off a gun. Porphyro rubbed his eyes and wondered whether this could really be his wedding day. He had faith in the boundless powers of the banner under which he had enrolled himself. And yet was it possible? But his faith was amply justified. An equerry suddenly rode up, parting the spectators to right and left, leading a spare horse magnificently caparisoned, and followed in the distance by a brilliant retinue.

He doffed his cap to Porphyro and sprang to the ground, and with a profound obeisance, said in tones of deep respect:—

"I trust your Highness has recovered from your indisposition. I have brought the horse as your Highness commanded."

Porphyro dimly understood that some potent influence was at work on his behalf. With the assistance of his squire he took to the saddle. The latter then, with another bow, remounted his own horse, scattered a handful of gold to each side to break up the crowd, and with the rest of the train (which had caught up with them) they galloped to the Cathedral. Porphyro noted with stupid surprise that all the fountains spouted wine, whereto certain of the citizens, judging by the hiccups which mingled with their cheers, had already applied themselves, not wisely but too well. But our hero was in a state of so great fog himself as to feel his heart warm more towards these than to the soberer ones, whose salutations he clumsily returned. By the time the Cathedral was reached, he was rolling in his saddle. He could not have dismounted without help. The incense made him dizzy. He could not get the ringing of the bells out of his ears. The candles danced before his eyes. Of all the service he heard one word, and that was uttered by one who stood beside him, and whom alone he saw (and that through a mist) of all that gay assembly. It was the Princess. He pressed her hand as if he would never part with it.

The service over, he had no idea how, or in what order they reached the castle, and the banquet which followed was more or less of a blank to him. The wines of which he partook liberally, could make him no more drunk, nor all the compliments of all the fulsome speeches (had he heard them) raise by one degree his pride. He soared empyrean high in the thought that he had won the right to crush into one moment, all the eternal delirium of all the heavens.

That moment of fruition had come at last. Porphyro stood in that holy of holies, his princess's chamber. A guard of soldiers was ranged along the four walls of this dainty nest. Each leaned with one arm upon a pike, while with the other hand he held aloft a blazing torch. Great personages were also present, both courtiers and noble dames, and at last the bride herself was brought in by her women.

While complimentary discourse passed from mouth to mouth, Porphyro longed with his whole bartered soul to be alone with her. He was burning with internal fire which he could hold in little longer. At last he approached one that appeared to act as master of the ceremonies.

"When is this rigmarole going to end?" he muttered between his teeth.

"Whenever your Highness pleases to draw your sword and lay it in the middle of the bed, the princess will take up her place upon one side of it, while you occupy the other," was the reply.

Porphyro started. He surely recognised that voice. The official kept his face averted, but it was undoubtedly the demon.

"What mean you by this gabble of naked swords between me and her?" thundered Porphyro, unheeding who might hear. "Damned posture master, is she not my wife?"

"Your wife, yes, but only by letters of procuration," and there was a note of triumph in that voice.

"God of the Judgment! What is that you say?"

"I say you must be dreaming not to remember that you are only temporarily united to the princess in your character of proxy for his Imperial Majesty, the Holy Roman Emperor."

"Alas the while! Then I am dreaming, indeed!"

"These soldiers," continued the demon, "will remain here all night. These ladies and gentlemen will also attend here till morning, to entertain you and your bride of an hour through your somewhat tedious spell of lying fully dressed together."

"Death and the Pit! Is this true?"

"True as death, assured as the pit. Tomorrow you will sheathe your sword and depart from her for ever."

Porphyro pressed his hands to his temples. He thought his brain would burst. He saw it all now. He was the dupe of the fiend who had once been his dupe. His place in this pageant had been contrived with infernal subtlety, only to wring the uttermost pang from his heart strings. He who sups with the devil (they say) must needs have a very long spoon. No help was possible. The Evil One was reaping his revenge. And now he was assured his victim had at last grasped the situation, he threw off the mask, and showed himself in his true colours. He raised his eyes for the first time from the ground: those brimming lakes of bottomless hate which Porphyro had confronted once before in the underground hall. It was his turn now to quail.

"Ha! ha!" laughed the fallen angel. "By mine ancient seat in heaven (and that is an oath I never lightly take as you may guess), confess, have I not bested you, friend Porphyro? He laughs best who laughs the last; is it not so?"

"But what about that bond registered between us in Hell's chancery?" cried Porphyro, in a voice which would have melted triple brass.

"Your bond," shrieked Beelzebub. "Do you remind me of your bond; you who once outfaced me that a bond should be read by the letter, and not by the spirit? I have come round to your views, and I now fling that word back in your teeth. You have had your bond to the letter, and now go and kill yourself, for there is nothing more for you to do."

Porphyro bent like a broken reed. He had found over-mastering fate. His hopes were ash. He breathed in gasps. He staggered to the window, and threw open the casement. A great pitiful star looked in, but to his eyes it appeared red and blood-shot. He turned round again to the room. He wished to see once more, before he died, that mistress of his soul for whose sake he had flung it away. But the figure of his master had swelled, and was swelling rapidly in size that it seemed to fill every available corner of the room. Porphyro raised his hands to heaven, and called upon his lady's name. Three times he called it, and then sprang out of the window.

The princess, who had grasped nothing of what had passed, ran to the shutter, and looked out just in time to hear the splash of his body as it fell into the moat.

It was the first sign of interest in him which she had shown.

The Diary of Mr Poynter

M. R. James

The sale-room of an old and famous firm of book auctioneers in London is, of course, a great meeting-place for collectors, librarians, and dealers: not only when an auction is in progress, but perhaps even more notably when books that are coming on for sale are upon view. It was in such a sale-room that the remarkable series of events began which were detailed to me not many months ago by the person whom they principally affected—namely, Mr James Denton, M.A., F.S.A., etc., etc., sometime of Trinity Hall, now, or lately, of Rendcomb Manor in the county of Warwick.

He, on a certain spring day in a recent year, was in London for a few days upon business connected principally with the furnishing of the house which he had just finished building at Rendcomb. It may be a disappointment to you to learn that Rendcomb Manor was new; that I cannot help. There had, no doubt, been an old house; but it was not remarkable for beauty or interest. Even had it been, neither beauty nor interest would have enabled it to resist the disastrous fire which about a couple of years before the date of my story had razed it to the ground. I am glad to say that all that was most valuable in it had been saved, and that it was fully insured. So that it was with a comparatively light heart that Mr Denton was able to face the task of building a new and considerably more convenient dwelling for himself and his aunt who constituted his whole *ménage*.

Being in London, with time on his hands, and not far from the sale-room at which I have obscurely hinted, Mr Denton thought that he would spend an hour there upon the chance of finding, among that portion of the famous Thomas collection of MSS., which he knew to be then on view, something bearing upon the history or topography of his part of Warwickshire.

He turned in accordingly, purchased a catalogue and ascended to the sale-room, where, as usual, the books were disposed in cases and some laid out upon the long tables. At the shelves, or sitting about at the tables, were figures, many of whom were familiar to him. He exchanged nods and greetings with several, and then settled down to examine his catalogue and note likely items. He had made good progress through about two hundred of the five hundred lots—every now and then rising to take a volume from the shelf and give it a cursory glance—when a hand was laid on his shoulder, and he looked up. His interrupter was one of those intelligent men with a pointed beard and a flannel shirt, of whom the last quarter of the nineteenth century was, it seems to me, very prolific.

It is no part of my plan to repeat the whole conversation which ensued between the two. I must content myself with stating that it largely referred to common acquaintances, e.g., to the nephew of Mr Denton's friend who had recently married and settled in Chelsea, to the sister-in-law of Mr Denton's friend who had been seriously indisposed, but was now better, and to a piece of china which Mr Denton's friend had purchased some months before at a price much below its true value. From which you will rightly infer that the conversation was rather in the nature of a monologue. In due time, however, the friend bethought himself that Mr Denton was there for a purpose, and said he, 'What are you looking out for in particular? I don't think there's much in this lot.' 'Why, I thought there might be some Warwickshire collections, but I don't see anything under Warwick in the catalogue.' 'No, apparently not,' said the friend. 'All the same, I believe I noticed something like a Warwickshire diary. What was the name again? Drayton? Potter? Painter—either a P or a D, I feel sure.' He turned over the leaves quickly. 'Yes, here it is. Poynter. Lot 486. That might interest you. There are the books, I think: out on the table. Someone has been looking at them. Well, I must be getting on. Good-bye—you'll look us up, won't you? Couldn't you come this afternoon? we've got a little music about four. Well, then, when you're next in town.' He went off. Mr Denton looked at his watch and found to his confusion that he could spare no more than a moment before retrieving his luggage and going for the train. The moment was just enough to show him that there were four largish volumes of the diary—that it concerned the years about 1710, and that there seemed to be a good many insertions in it of various kinds. It seemed quite worth while to leave a commission of five and twenty pounds for it, and this he was able to do, for his usual agent entered the room as he was on the point of leaving it.

That evening he rejoined his aunt at their temporary abode, which was a small dower-house not many hundred yards from the Manor. On the following morning the two resumed a discussion that had now lasted for some weeks as to the equipment of the new house. Mr Denton laid before his relative a statement of the results of his visit to town—particulars of carpets, of chairs, of wardrobes, and of bedroom china. 'Yes, dear,' said his aunt, 'but I don't see any chintzes here. Did you go to —— ?' Mr Denton stamped on the floor (where else, indeed, could he have stamped?). 'Oh dear, oh dear,' he said, 'the one thing I missed. I *am* sorry. The fact is I was on my way there and I happened to be passing Robins's.' His aunt threw up her hands. 'Robins's! Then the next thing will be another parcel of horrible old books at some outrageous price. I do think, James, when I am taking all this trouble for you, you might contrive to remember the one or two things which I specially begged you to see after. It's not as if I was asking it for myself. I don't know whether you think I get any pleasure out of it, but if so I can assure you it's very much the reverse. The thought and worry and trouble I have over it you have no idea of, and *you* have simply to go to the shops and order the things.' Mr Denton interposed a moan of penitence. 'Oh, aunt—' 'Yes, that's all very well, dear, and I don't want to speak sharply, but you *must* know how very annoying it is: particularly as it delays the whole of our business for I can't tell how long: here is Wednesday—the Simpsons come tomorrow, and you can't leave them. Then on Saturday we have friends, as you know, coming for tennis. Yes, indeed, you spoke of asking them yourself, but, of course, I had to write the notes, and it is ridiculous, James, to look like that. We must occasionally be civil to our neighbours: you wouldn't like to have it said we were perfect bears. What was I saying? Well, anyhow it comes to this, that it must be Thursday in next week at least, before you can go to town again, and until we have decided upon the chintzes it is impossible to settle upon one single other thing.'

Mr Denton ventured to suggest that as the paint and wallpapers had been dealt with, this was too severe a view: but this his aunt was not prepared to admit at the moment. Nor, indeed, was there any proposition he could have advanced which she would have found herself able to accept. However, as the day went on, she receded a little from this position: examined with lessening disfavour the samples and price lists submitted by her nephew, and even in some cases a qualified approval to his choice.

As for him, he was naturally somewhat dashed by the consciousness of duty unfulfilled, but more so by the prospect of a lawn-tennis party, which, though an inevitable evil in August, he had thought there was no occasion to fear in May. But he was to some extent cheered by the arrival on the Friday morning of an intimation that he had secured at the price of 12 10s. the four volumes of Poynter's manuscript diary, and still more by the arrival on the next morning of the diary itself.

The necessity of taking Mr and Mrs Simpson for a drive in the car on Saturday morning and of attending to his neighbours and guests that afternoon prevented him from doing more than open the parcel until the party had retired to bed on the Saturday night. It was then that he made certain of the fact, which he had before only suspected, that he had indeed acquired the diary of Mr William Poynter, Squire of Acrington (about four miles from his own parish)—that same Poynter who was for a time a member of the circle of Oxford antiquaries, the centre of which was Thomas Hearne, and with whom Hearne seems ultimately to have quarrelled—a not uncommon episode in the career of that excellent man. As is the case with Hearne's own collections, the diary of Poynter contained a good many notes from printed books, descriptions of coins and other antiquities that had been brought to his notice, and drafts of letters on these subjects, besides the chronicle of everyday events. The description in the sale-catalogue had given Mr Denton no idea of the amount of interest which seemed to lie in the book, and he sat up reading in the first of four volumes until a reprehensibly late hour.

On the Sunday morning, after church, his aunt came into the study and was diverted from what she had been going to say to him by the sight of the four brown leather quartos on the table. 'What are these?' she said suspiciously. 'New, aren't they? Oh! are these the things that made you forget my chintzes? I thought so. Disgusting. What did you give for them, I should like to know? Over Ten Pounds? James, it is really sinful. Well, if you have money to throw away on this kind of thing, there *can* be no reason why you should not subscribe—and subscribe handsomely—to my anti-Vivisection League. There is not, indeed, James, and I shall be very seriously annoyed if—Who did you say wrote them? Old Mr Poynter, of Acrington? Well, of course, there is some interest in getting together old papers about this neighbourhood. But Ten Pounds!' She picked up one of the volumes—not that which her nephew had been reading—and opened it at random, dashing it to the floor the next instant with a cry of disgust as an earwig fell from between the pages. Mr Denton picked it up with a smothered expletive and said, 'Poor book! I think you're rather hard on Mr Poynter.' 'Was I, my dear? I beg his pardon, but you know I cannot abide those horrid creatures. Let me see if I've done any mischief.' 'No, I think all's well: but look here what you've opened him on.' 'Dear me, yes, to be sure! how very interesting. Do unpin it, James, and let me look at it.'

It was a piece of patterned stuff about the size of the quarto page, to which it was fastened by an old-fashioned pin. James detached it and handed it to his aunt, carefully replacing the pin in the paper.

Now, I do not know exactly what the fabric was; but it had a design printed upon it, which completely fascinated Miss Denton. She went into raptures over it, held it against the wall, made James do the same, that she might retire to contemplate it from a distance: then pored over it at close quarters, and ended her examination by expressing in the warmest terms her appreciation of the taste of the ancient Mr Poynter who had had the happy idea of preserving this sample in his diary. 'It is a most charming pattern,' she said, 'and remarkable too. Look, James, how delightfully the lines ripple. It reminds one of hair, very much, doesn't it? And then these knots of ribbon at intervals. They give just the relief of colour that is wanted. I wonder—' 'I was going to say,' said James with deference, 'I wonder if it would cost much to have it copied for our curtains.' 'Copied? how could you have it copied, James?' 'Well, I don't know the details, but I suppose that is a printed pattern, and that you could have a block cut from it in wood or metal.' 'Now, really, that is a capital idea, James. I am almost inclined to be glad that you were so— that you forgot the chintzes on Wednesday. At any rate, I'll promise to forgive and forget if you get this *lovely* old thing copied. No one will have anything in the least like it, and mind, James, we won't allow it to be sold. Now I *must* go, and I've totally forgotten what it was I came in to say: never mind, it'll keep.'

After his aunt had gone James Denton devoted a few minutes to examining the pattern more closely than he had yet had a chance of doing. He was puzzled to think why it should have struck Miss Denton so forcibly. It seemed to him not specially remarkable or pretty. No doubt it was suitable enough for a curtain pattern: it ran in vertical bands, and there was some indication that these were intended to converge at the top. She was right, too, in thinking that these main bands resembled rippling—almost curling—tresses of hair. Well, the main thing was to find out by means of trade directories, or otherwise, what firm would undertake the reproduction of an old pattern of this kind. Not to delay the reader over this portion of the story, a list of likely names was made out, and Mr Denton fixed a day for calling on them, or some of them, with his sample.

The first two visits which he paid were unsuccessful: but there is luck in odd numbers. The firm in Bermondsey which was third on his list was accustomed to handling this line. The evidence they were able to produce justified their being entrusted with the job. 'Our Mr Cattell' took a fervent personal interest in it. 'It's 'eartrending, isn't it, sir,' he said, 'to picture the quantity of reelly lovely medeevial stuff of this kind that lays wellnigh unnoticed in many of our residential country 'ouses: much of it in peril, I take it, of being cast aside as so much rubbish. What is it Shakespeare says—unconsidered trifles. Ah, I often say he 'as a word for us all, sir. I say Shakespeare, but I'm well aware all don't 'old with me there—I 'ad something of an upset the other day when a gentleman came in—a titled man, too, he was, and I think he told me he'd wrote on the topic, and I 'appened to cite out something about 'Ercules and the painted cloth. Dear me, you never see such a pother. But as to this, what you've kindly confided to us, it's a piece of work we shall take a reel enthusiasm in achieving it out to the very best of our ability. What man 'as done, as I was observing only a few weeks back to another esteemed client, man can do, and in three to four weeks' time, all being well, we shall 'ope to lay before you evidence to that effect, sir. Take the address, Mr 'Iggins, if you please.'

Such was the general drift of Mr Cattell's observations on the occasion of his first interview with Mr Denton. About a month later, being advised that some samples were ready for his inspection, Mr Denton met him again, and had, it seems, reason to be satisfied with the faithfulness of the reproduction of the design. It had been finished off at the top in accordance with the indication I mentioned, so that the vertical bands joined. But something still needed to be done in the way of matching the colour of the original. Mr Cattell had suggestions of a technical kind to offer, with which I need not trouble you. He had also views as to the general desirability of the pattern which were vaguely adverse. 'You say you don't wish this to be supplied excepting to personal friends equipped with a authorization from yourself, sir. It shall be done. I quite understand your wish to keep it exclusive: lends a catchit, does it not, to the suite? What's every man's, it's been said, is no man's.'

'Do you think it would be popular if it were generally obtainable?' asked Mr Denton.

'I 'ardly think it, sir,' said Cattell, pensively clasping his beard. 'I 'ardly think it. Not popular: it wasn't popular with the man that cut the block, was it, Mr 'Iggins?'

'Did he find it a difficult job?'

'He'd no call to do so, sir; but the fact is that the artistic temperament—and our men are artists, sir, every one of them—true artists as much as many that the world styles by that term—it's apt to take some strange 'ardly accountable likes or dislikes, and here was an example. The twice or thrice that I went to inspect his progress: language I could understand, for that's 'abitual to him, but reel distaste for what I should call a dainty enough thing, I did not, nor am I now able to fathom. It seemed,' said Mr Cattell, looking narrowly upon Mr Denton, 'as if the man scented something almost Hevil in the design.'

'Indeed? did he tell you so? I can't say I see anything sinister in it myself.'

'Neether can I, sir. In fact I said as much. "Come, Gatwick," I said, "what's to do here? What's the reason of your prejudice—for I can call it no more than that?" But, no! no explanation was forthcoming. And I was merely reduced, as I am now, to a shrug of the shoulders, and a *cui bono*. However, here it is,' and with that the technical side of the question came to the front again.

The matching of the colours for the background, the hem, and the knots of ribbon was by far the longest part of the business, and necessitated many sendings to and fro of the original pattern and of new samples. During part of August and September, too, the Dentons were away from the Manor. So that it was not until October was well in that a sufficient quantity of the stuff had been manufactured to furnish curtains for the three or four bedrooms which were to be fitted up with it.

On the feast of Simon and Jude the aunt and nephew returned from a short visit to find all completed, and their satisfaction at the general effect was great. The new curtains, in particular, agreed to admiration with their surroundings. When Mr Denton was dressing for dinner, and took stock of his room, in which there was a large amount of the chintz displayed, he congratulated himself over and over again on the luck which had first made him forget his aunt's commission and had then put into his hands this extremely effective means of remedying his mistake. The pattern was, as he said at dinner, so restful and yet so far from being dull. And Miss Denton—who, by the way, had none of the stuff in her own room—was much disposed to agree with him.

At breakfast next morning he was induced to qualify his satisfaction to some extent—but very slightly. 'There is one thing I rather regret,' he said, 'that we allowed them to join up the vertical bands of the pattern at the top. I think it would have been better to leave that alone.'

'Oh?' said his aunt interrogatively.

'Yes: as I was reading in bed last night they kept catching my eye rather. That is, I found myself looking across at them every now and then. There was an effect as if someone kept peeping out between the curtains in one place or another, where there was no edge, and I think that was due to the joining up of the bands at the top. The only other thing that troubled me was the wind.'

'Why, I thought it was a perfectly still night.'

'Perhaps it was only on my side of the house, but there was enough to sway my curtains and rustle them more than I wanted.'

That night a bachelor friend of James Denton's came to stay, and was lodged in a room on the same floor as his host, but at the end of a long passage, half-way down which was a red baize door, put there to cut off the draught and intercept noise.

The party of three had separated. Miss Denton a good first, the two men at about eleven. James Denton, not yet inclined for bed, sat him down in an armchair and read for a time. Then he dozed, and then he woke, and bethought himself that his brown spaniel, which ordinarily slept in his room, had not come upstairs with him. Then he thought he was mistaken: for happening to move his hand which hung down over the arm of the chair within a few inches of the floor, he felt on the back of it just the slightest touch of a surface of hair, and stretching it out in that direction he stroked and patted a rounded something. But the feel of it, and still more the fact that instead of a responsive movement, absolute stillness greeted his touch, made him look over the arm. What he had

140

been touching rose to meet him. It was in the attitude of one that had crept along the floor on its belly, and it was, so far as could be recollected, a human figure. But of the face which was now rising to within a few inches of his own no feature was discernible, only hair. Shapeless as it was, there was about it so horrible an air of menace that as he bounded from his chair and rushed from the room he heard himself moaning with fear: and doubtless he did right to fly. As he dashed into the baize door that cut the passage in two, and—forgetting that it opened towards him—beat against it with all the force in him, he felt a soft ineffectual tearing at his back which, all the same, seemed to be growing in power, as if the hand, or whatever worse than a hand was there, were becoming more material as the pursuer's rage was more concentrated. Then he remembered the trick of the door—he got it open—he shut it behind him—he gained his friend's room, and that is all we need know.

It seems curious that, during all the time that had elapsed since the purchase of Poynter's diary, James Denton should not have sought an explanation of the presence of the pattern that had been pinned into it. Well, he had read the diary through without finding it mentioned, and had concluded that there was nothing to be said. But, on leaving Rendcomb Manor (he did not know whether for good), as he naturally insisted upon doing on the day after experiencing the horror I have tried to put into words, he took the diary with him. And at his seaside lodgings he examined more narrowly the portion whence the pattern had been taken. What he remembered having suspected about it turned out to be correct. Two or three leaves were pasted together, but written upon, as was patent when they were held up to the light. They yielded easily to steaming, for the paste had lost much of its strength and they contained something relevant to the pattern.

The entry was made in 1707.

'Old Mr Casbury, of Acrington, told me this day much of young Sir Everard Charlett, whom he remember'd Commoner of University College, and thought was of the same Family as Dr Arthur Charlett, now master of ye Coll. This Charlett was a personable young gent., but a loose atheistical companion, and a great Lifter, as they then call'd the hard drinkers, and for what I know do so now. He was noted, and subject to severall censures at different times for his extravagancies: and if the full history of his debaucheries had bin known, no doubt would have been expell'd ye Coll., supposing that no interest had been imploy'd on his behalf, of which Mr Casbury had some suspicion. He was a very beautiful person, and constantly wore his own Hair, which was very abundant, from which, and his loose way of living, the cant name for him was Absalom, and he was accustom'd to say that indeed he believ'd he had shortened old David's days, meaning his father, Sir Job Charlett, an old worthy cavalier.

'Note that Mr Casbury said that he remembers not the year of Sir Everard Charlett's death, but it was 1692 or 3. He died suddenly in October. [Several lines describing his unpleasant habits and reputed delinquencies are omitted.] Having seen him in such topping spirits the night before, Mr Casbury was amaz'd when he learn'd the death. He was found in the town ditch, the hair as was said pluck'd clean off his head. Most bells in Oxford rung out for him, being a nobleman, and he was buried next night in St Peter's in the East. But two years after, being to be moved to his country estate by his successor, it was said the coffin, breaking by mischance, proved quite full of Hair: which sounds fabulous, but yet I believe precedents are upon record, as in Dr Plot's *History of Staffordshire.*

'His chambers being afterwards stripp'd, Mr Casbury came by part of the hangings of it, which 'twas said this Charlett had design'd expressly for a memoriall of his Hair, giving the Fellow that drew it a lock to work by, and the piece which I have fasten'd in here was parcel of the same, which Mr Casbury gave to me. He said he believ'd there was a subtlety in the drawing, but had never discover'd it himself, nor much liked to pore upon it.'

The money spent upon the curtains might as well have been thrown into the fire, as they were. Mr Cattell's comment upon what he heard of the story took the form of a quotation from Shakespeare. You may guess it without difficulty. It began with the words 'There are more things'.

Dollburger

Lisa Tuttle

When she listened hard, Karen thought she could hear the men downstairs searching for dolls. Although she didn't know what they looked like, she thought of them as hairy troll-like men with the large square teeth of horses. She glanced at the attic door. All her dolls were safe in there. Surely the men would never come upstairs into her room?

The thought made her clutch the blankets to her chin, her body rigid with the effort of not breathing. The bed was safe, it had always been a sanctuary, but she didn't know the powers or limits of these doll thieves and could only guess at protection. She'd learned about them just that morning, from her father.

'Daddy, have you seen Kristina?'

'Let daddy read his paper, sweetie — he doesn't know which doll Kristina is,' her mother said, flipping pancakes.

Daddy dipped a piece of toast in his coffee and looked at it thoughtfully before biting. He replied with his mouth full.

'Did you leave her downstairs?'

'Yeah — I think.'

Daddy shook his head. 'Shouldn't have done that. Dangerous. Don't you know what happens to dolls that get left downstairs all night?'

Karen glanced quickly at her mother. Catching the half smile on her mother's face, Karen raised her eyebrows sceptically.

'No,' she said, in a tone that dared him.

Daddy shook his head again and consumed the last of the piece of toast.

'Well, if you leave your doll downstairs, you can just expect that when those men come looking —'

'What men?'

He looked surprised that she should need to ask. 'Why, the men who eat dollburgers, of course!'

'Dollburgers?'

'Just like hamburgers. Only, of course, made out of dolls.'

'No.'

'No?'

'People don't eat dolls, and dollburgers are just tiny hamburgers, like what mommy made on my last birthday, which you feed to dolls.'

'But dolls don't eat — people do.'

'You *pretend*,' Karen said, exasperated with him. He was shaking his head.

'I don't care what you call little hamburgers — but I happen to know about dollburgers. People eat them, and they're made out of dolls. There are people who just love them. Of course, they're illegal; so they have to sneak around, looking for houses where little girls have forgotten to put their dolls safely away. When they find abandoned dolls, they pop them into a sack until they collect enough to grind up into dollburgers.'

'That's a story,' Karen said.

Her father shrugged. 'I'm just trying to warn you so when you lose a doll you'll know what's happened to it and maybe you'll be more careful in the future.'

Her mother came to the table. 'No dollburgers in *this* house. Pancakes, though. Karen, get your plate if you want some.'

Karen suddenly remembered where she'd left Kristina. Of course —

last night before she went to bed, she and Kristina had been lost in the wilderness and had crawled into a cave to rest for the night—Kristina must still be in the cave.

'In a minute,' she said, and went purposefully into the living room.

The bridge table was the cave, but there was no doll underneath. Karen dropped to her hands and knees. Kristina was gone. Something gleamed in the corner by a table leg, and she picked it up.

A blue eye gazed impassively up from her hand. There were some shards of pink plastic on the carpet. Kristina?

'Karen, do you want pancakes or don't you?'

'In a minute,' she called, and carefully picked up each tiny piece and put it in her pocket. She looked at the eye again. Kristina's eyes were blue. She put the eye in her pocket.

'Daddy,' she asked over pancakes, 'do the people—the people who eat dollburgers—do they ever just, you know, eat dolls? I mean, right where they find them?'

Her father considered. 'I suppose sometimes they get so hungry that they might just crunch up a doll right there, with their teeth,' he said. 'You never know what they'll do.'

'I'm sure Kristina is perfectly safe,' said her mother. 'I'll help you find her after I do the dishes.'

After breakfast Karen went up to her room and examined the eye and the pieces of pink plastic, the last remains of Kristina. What daddy had said about the dollburger eaters was real, then, and not just a story like the grizzly bear in the cedarwood cupboard.

Karen had the attic room. Her closet was actually the attic itself—without wallpaper, beams bare overhead and decorated with bits of discarded furniture and boxes of old clothes. She kept her toys there, and it was home to all her dolls. She took Kristina's eye there, climbed onto a rickety chair and put it in a secret place atop a ceiling beam. It would do better than a funeral, she thought, since there was so little of poor Kristina left.

The dolls watched her steadily from their places. Karen looked around at all of them from her position atop the chair, feeling queen of all she surveyed, giant queen-mother to all these plastic, rag and rubber babies.

Hard-faced Barbie sat stonily beside doltish Ken in front of their dreamhouse. Her clothes spilled out of the upstairs bedroom; two nude teenagers (Barbie's friends) sprawled in the kitchen.

The bride doll sat next to Princess Katherine where she'd sat for months undisturbed. There was dust in her hair, and the shoulders of her white gown looked grimy. Princess Katherine's crown was bent, her green dress stained, and her lower right leg secured to the upper leg with Band-Aids and masking tape.

Raggedy Ann, Raggedy Andy, Aunt Jemima and Teddybear slouched together in the rocking chair. The talking dolls, Elizabeth, Jane and Tina, sat grimly silent. The babydolls had been tossed into one crib where they lay like lumps. Susan, bald and legless, had been wrapped tenderly and put in the blue plastic bassinet.

Karen looked at the top of the old dresser, where Kristina used to sit with Beverly. Now Beverly sat there alone. Karen felt tears in her eyes: Kristina had been her favourite. She suddenly felt uncomfortable standing above her dolls, felt that they were blaming her for Kristina's disappearance.

She felt guilt, a heaviness in her stomach, and thought she saw grim indictment on the still, staring faces.

'Poor Kristina,' she said. 'If only someone had warned me.' She stepped down from her perch, shaking her head sadly. 'If only daddy had told me before — then I could have protected her. When I think of all the times I've left some of you out — well, now that I know I'll be sure to take good care.'

She looked around at all the dolls, who had not changed expression, and suddenly the silence of the attic became oppressive.

Louisa, Karen's best friend, called that afternoon. 'Would you and Kristina care to join me and Isabella in having a tea party?' she asked in her best society-lady voice.

Karen assumed a similar voice to reply. 'Oh, my deah, I would love to, but Kristina has been kidnapped.'

'Oh, how dreadful, my deah.'

'Yes, it is, my deah, but I think I shall bring my other child, Elizabeth.'

'Very good, I shall see you in a few minutes. Ta-ta.'

'Ta-ta, my deah.'

Elizabeth was one of the talking dolls, always her favourite until golden-haired Kristina had come as a birthday gift.

Louisa's little sister Anne and her ragdoll Sallylou were the other guests at the tea party, treated with faint disdain by Louisa and Karen for their lack of society manners.

'Why don't you let Elizabeth eat her own biscuit?' Anne demanded as Karen took a dainty bite. Elizabeth had politely refused the biscuit.

'Be quiet, silly,' Louisa said, forgetting her role. 'Dolls don't eat biscuits.'

'Yes, they do.'

'No, they don't.'

'Uh-huh.'

'They do not.'

'Well, if they don't, then what *do* they eat?'

'Nothing.'

'Pretend food,' Karen amended. 'They have to eat pretend food because they only have pretend teeth and pretend stomachs.'

Anne shook her head. 'Sallylou has *real* teeth, and so she has to eat real food.'

'Oh, she does not,' Louisa said. 'All you do is mash biscuit in her face so she gets crumbs all over her. Show me her teeth if she has them.'

'I can't, 'cause her mouth is closed,' Anne said smugly.

'You're just stupid.'

Later, when they were alone, Karen told Louisa what had happened to Kristina and watched her friend's eyes grow wider. This was no story; it was real and immediate, and the proof was the blue eye now lying on a bed of dust and staring unceasingly at the attic roof.

Karen's ears ached from trying to hear movement downstairs. She always lay awake at the top of the house, feeling silence and sleep wrap the house from the bottom up until it finally reached her and she slept. But now every distant creak of board, every burp of pipe, made her tense and listen harder. She'd left no dolls downstairs, of course, but what if those men should not be deterred by stairs but were lured on by the scent of dolls up in the attic?

She thought of Louisa across the street and wondered if she too lay awake listening. Louisa, she knew, had put all her dolls under the bed, the safest place she could think of.

Karen suddenly thought of her own dolls, more frightened than she, sitting terrified in the dark attic, listening to the sounds as she did and wondering if the next creaking board would bring a dark sack over their heads, labelling them dollburger meat. It was her duty to protect them.

She went on bare feet to the attic door, the full moon through her window giving her light enough to find her way. She opened the attic door and thought as she did so that she heard a movement inside, as if perhaps a doll had been knocked over.

She had to go inside the attic several feet to reach the light cord. Her bare foot nudged something as she did, and when the light came on, she looked down to see what it was.

Poor, bald, legless Susan lay naked on the floor, and Karen noticed at once that Susan now was not only legless, but armless as well. When she picked her up, small shards of pink plastic fell from the arm sockets.

Karen felt an almost paralysing fear. They were up here, somehow in the attic without having come past her bed, and already they'd begun on her most helpless doll. Holding Susan to her, she began to gather all the other dolls into her arms. She lifted the skirt of her nightgown to make a bag and tumbled the dolls in there. They were scattered around as if they'd been thrown, none in their right places. Barbie on the floor, Ken in the rocking chair with Raggedy Andy and the bride. Every time she bent to pick up another doll, she was sure she could hear the muffled breathing of the hungry dollburger eaters and feel the pressure of their eyes against her back.

She began to pray, whispering and thinking, 'Oh, please, please, please, oh, please.'

Finally she had all the dolls together, and she stumbled to the door and closed it, leaving the light still burning in the attic. For safety she pushed her chair in front of the door.

Then she went to bed, arranging all the dolls around her, lying down, falling asleep sandwiched by their small hard bodies.

She may have dreamed, but she never woke as they began to move closer to her in the night, and she didn't see the crumbs of plastic that fell from Elizabeth's open, hungry mouth.

Down Home

Edward Bryant

Everybody in the house tonight was family, save for Kirk, and if I knew my big sister at all, he was going to be family real soon. 'Course I thought the same thing about the park ranger two years ago, but he went and took a transfer to Yellowstone up north, and that was that. April-Marie was desolate. For a while. But then she started taking classes at the junior college in Marricola, and that's where she met Kirk.

I figured he'd make an okay brother-in-law. No squinchy little close-set eyes, no vacant stare, no moron spells, none of the things we get accused of in magazines and books just 'cause we're a big family and we live in the mountains.

I mean, Mom's got her college degree. Daddy would have if it hadn't been for the war. Most of us are smart enough. Shoot, we've got a few dumb ones, but name a family that doesn't. Sure, there are a couple who wouldn't know to come in out of a pigeon flock doodoo storm, but we take care of them ourselves. No government help. That's Daddy's way. Actually we've been doing it like that for close to three hundred years now, ever since some of us came over on a boat as bond-servants from Scotland. Didn't take long before the ancestors moved inland and headed for the high ground. Each generation, one kid's got to learn to squeeze the bagpipes. I'm glad it wasn't me. I'd rather play electric guitar. I listen to Eric Clapton tapes all the time.

April-Marie was finishing up giving Kirk some MacKendree family history.

He smiled at her. "Pretty interesting stuff," he said.

I figured he was fibbing. April-Marie knew better than to give him any of the good stuff. That's for family to know, and family to find out. No secrets, you understand. Just . . . family.

"So'd you ever get captured by them Indians and taken to a teepee and be held against your will?" That was my cousin Frank. He wasn't one of the geniuses.

Kirk looked blank for a moment. "A teepee?" he said. An expression bloomed on his face. "You're putting me on, right?" April-Marie shook her head. No put-on. Honest injun.

His confusion settled into a look of concentration. "I think I see," Kirk said. "Before, when I was talking Indians, I meant like the subcontinent out there in the Pacific, not Sioux or Apaches or something. No cowboys."

"No cowboys?" said Frank.

Kirk shook his head again. "Just a lot of cows you can't shoot for food, and the beggars who're starving because they can't eat the cows."

Frank looked puzzled. "How come?"

"They're sacred."

"Like the stone rings, up to the pasture," said Frank.

It was Kirk's turn to look bewildered. "Huh?"

"Nothing," said April-Marie. She shook Frank by the shoulder and hustled him off to wash up for supper.

"So just what did you do in the Peace Corps?" said my big brother, William. About a head taller than Kirk, he grinned down at him. William's hair was curly and black. He had a bushy beard and long sideburns. Sometimes he looked like a bigfoot peering out of the brush of all that hair. William was the taxidermist in the family. The bear's head staring down from above the mantel in the living room was his work. Those ham hands and long, thick fingers were surprisingly delicate when it came to his work.

Before Kirk could answer, there was something of a stir at the front door. We were all standing in the end of the front room over by the entrance to the living room proper. Across the room, I saw Brenda and cousin Donald come in out of the early night. Brenda was carrying their little baby, all wrapped in a pink blanket. My aunts and mom crowded around, giving them the usual family welcome.

Brenda still moved a little slow, I noticed. She'd been hurting pretty bad after the baby was born. It was just one of those births, Mom had said. Brenda was lucky to be alive. It'd be a while before she was back to normal. But the family did its best to take care of her. We got all three of them over to Sunday dinner about every week.

"So," William repeated. "India?"

"Oh, right." Kirk had been staring off toward Brenda, Donald, and their baby. He refocused on us. "I spent the better part of a year teaching men how to dig wells and rig up paddle-generators."

"You teach 'em dowsing?" said Uncle Poplar, leaning into the conversation interestedly.

Kirk looked nonplused. "Nope, I stuck to hydrological surveys, seismic tests—" He smiled. "And an abundance of cheap labor for digging a lot of test holes."

"Where 'bouts was all this going on?" said William.

"In the south of India. Way out in the sticks." Kirk stopped a moment, looked a little sheepish like maybe he shouldn't say things like *out in the sticks* when he was visiting a place like ours. Then he went on. "Little village called Krishnavijayawadapore."

Uncle Pop laughed. "How you manage to remember names like that? They all six-dollar words?"

Kirk laughed too. "The endings are almost always either one sound or another. I had an Indian friend who said that all the towns in the whole country were either bad or poor."

William and Uncle Pop looked momentarily puzzled.

"Like Ranchipoor or Hyderabad," said Kirk. "Um, you know, a joke, but like one I couldn't ever tell over there." He shook his head. "You know, like a black guy calling another one a nigger."

Uncle Pop and William exchanged looks.

"Okay," said Kirk. "You don't get it. Let's say—"

"We get it," said William. He smiled indulgently at our guest. "We got some black in our family too."

"Uh," stammered Kirk. "Like I didn't mean to—"

William clapped him on the shoulder. It was a little like a twenty-pound mallet hitting a steer between the eyes. Kirk staggered. "No offense taken," said William. "Let's eat."

The rest of the family had been drifting past us toward the dining room. Daddy had wedged all the extra leaves in place in the big old oak table. Of course that wouldn't be enough. All the kids had to sit around card tables set up in one end of the room. That was okay, 'cause that put them right by the sideboard with all the food, but I was still glad that I could now sit at the big table as one of the grownups.

Daddy had already done the carving in the kitchen. He waited until all the women were seated, then sat in his chair at the far end and pretty much acted as a traffic cop, motioning at chairs and dishes and re-minding folks to pass something on when they got lost in all the good food that was set before them.

One thing about the food—there was plenty of it. Mom and the aunts, most of the girl cousins, a few of the boy cousins, had all been working during the morning. There was roast wild turkey, steam rising up from each freshly sliced breast. There was pink beef with brown gravy, some filleted trout with lemon and nuts, and, like a little cousin to the turkeys, a pheasant my cousin Angus had bagged with his .22 the day before. Lots of vegetables—Mom insisted on those—and fresh-baked bread with dishes of butter I'd churned last night. It was quite a spread, even not allowing for cheeses and pickles and the pies that would be brought out for dessert.

I looked at that spread of food, and all of a sudden I remembered Kirk talking about folks starving in India because they wouldn't eat the sacred cattle.

Cousin Frank was sitting right beside me and I guess he was recalling the same thing. "No McDonald's in Poorabad or Badapoor," I heard him mutter. Sometimes he wasn't so dumb. He didn't get to eat Big Macs much, except when his parents took him into town. Mostly he just ate the same stuff the rest of us did up here. Frank told me once that eating fast-food burgers and fries was like he imagined eating gold to be.

Kirk sat right beside April-Marie in a place of honor up close to the head of the table. Mom was down at the foot where she could keep an eye on the kids—and make sure their plates stayed full. Donald and Brenda were sitting right across from Frank and me. Brenda really didn't look at anyone else other than her baby; just kept rocking him back and forth, crooning a real old song in her low, sweet voice. Donald went ahead and served her food, as well as to his own plate, when the dishes were passed by.

Daddy waited until everybody was seated and then rapped on his water glass for quiet. "Just wanted to formally welcome Kirk here to our hospitality," he said in that deep rumble that always reminded me of the river when it got full to the top of the banks with spring runoff. He smiled. "April-Marie always does invite some mighty interesting folks to Sunday dinner."

April-Marie's never been what anyone would call wild, but she has had some interesting choices in men from time to time. It keeps things interesting.

Daddy made sure Kirk was introduced to anyone he might have missed before dinner. Then he stared right at me and said, "All right, Brook, we'd all be honored if you would deliver us grace."

Stopped me right short for a second. Suddenly I felt real shy. Then I remembered all those years of Sunday class and I mumbled out something about "thanks" and "good company" and "blessing." Everybody joined in with a hearty "Amen" and we all fell to.

Naturally most of the talk during the meal was directed up the table toward Kirk. Folks were curious about his family and schooling and all that. April-Marie's interest was the key that let everybody forget anything at all about his being a stranger and having privacy. Hadn't been for that, we could have treated him like a census taker or maybe someone from the Fish and Game.

It was getting along toward time for pies and fresh-cranked ice cream that Frank piped up with, "Mr. Kirk?"

Kirk looked down the table questioningly.

"What's the weirdest thing you ever saw over there? I mean, in India?"

Our guest looked thoughtful. "I saw lots of strange things," he said slowly. Then it was like a porch light going on behind his eyes. "Okay, there was one thing that happened right before I left to come back to the States. I'll tell you, it really told me something about what life was like over there." I guess he realized he had everybody's undivided attention. His voice rose a little and it was like he was on a stage.

I wiped my lips and set my napkin down. Across from me, Donald put Brenda's fork back on the plate.

"About the most valuable possession anyone can have over there is a bullock," said Kirk. "The natives use them for plowing and hauling and just about any other hard work you can think of. They don't eat them, but they sure do work 'em."

Frank poked me in the side. "Bullock?" he said.

"Like an ox," I answered.

My cousin nodded, satisfied.

"There was a guy I was working with on the wells," Kirk continued. "He had a female bullock. I swear, he loved that animal like it was family. Lavished care on it, affection, all the food he could spare. Anyhow, he'd got it bred from his neighbor's bull the season past. That cow was getting pretty close to term; it'd swollen up close to bursting." Kirk paused. "The thing was, my friend kept working that cow. He had to. Work needed to get done. There was no rest for anybody, man or beast."

He broke off for a second. "Can I have some more of that fine coffee, please? Thanks," he said when the cup was passed back to him from the head of the table. Kirk poured in some cream. "Okay, where was I? Oh, right. Anyhow, to make a really long story shorter, the cow lost the calf. She miscarried pretty close to when she was due."

I heard a small noise across the table. I looked away from Kirk and saw Brenda staring back at me with wide eyes. She was hugging her baby real tight.

"I'll tell you, something happened then I wouldn't have believed," said Kirk. "That cow mourned her calf something fierce. She wouldn't work, go to the field, do nothing. All she'd do was stand protective by that dead little calf. It was sad. I mean it."

I could detect a stirring among some of the kin at the table. Kirk paused, either recollecting, or maybe just trying to raise the drama. "The owner could not get that cow to do a blessed thing. And then finally he had a brilliant idea. He got some of his buddies to hogtie the cow while he took the calf away."

I think Kirk realized everybody's attention was again focused on him. He smiled a little.

"The owner had that calf skinned, and then put the hide over a frame that sort of looked like the original calf. Now here's the unbelievable part." Kirk paused, I guess for effect. "He stuck that dried, skinned calf on the end of a pole and took it back to the mama. He just hitched her up to a cart and put the shell of her calf out in front of her. Worked like a charm. That cow would go anywhere my pal wanted. Out to the fields. Back home. Man, I never saw anything like it."

Kirk smiled indulgently. "Pretty weird, huh? Those people over there just don't live like us." He looked startled when he heard the scream.

Brenda got up from the table. She looked around at us all, her eyes really wild. Donald's chair went over and hit the floor like a gunshot. "Darlin'," he said, reaching for her arm. She jerked away and headed for the door, still cradling her baby. She had that little tyke tucked tight into her neck, his tan cheek up against hers. Donald glared at Kirk, really angry, as he went past.

Kirk looked bewildered, like we were all crazy. "Something wrong?" he said. April-Marie reached over and grabbed his arm. I could see her nails digging in. She looked just plain sick. I figured maybe Kirk wouldn't be coming to many more Sunday dinners.

Donald got the front door for Brenda and slammed it after them both.

I couldn't help it—I felt tears leaking out of my eyes. I saw aunts and cousins and a few uncles begin to weep.

Brother William was on his feet, those big, sensitive hands opening and closing. He stared toward the door helplessly.

Kirk said, "What'd I say?"

From outside, I heard a commotion as my cousins went up to their truck. I could hear a great wailing that ripped at my heart. It might have been Donald or it might have been Brenda.

I knew it wasn't the baby.

Dwindling

David B. Silva

In the summer, just after school let out, the pastures were still green and there was a freshness in the air that wouldn't die until the raw August temperatures broiled it from memory. The wind was tender and breezy then. During the day, the sky was a faint blue. But near sundown it would open its throat and the blue would turn purple, thick and rich and friendly. It had always been a special time of year for Derrick.

As he scooted off the last bus, making its last stop of the school year, and gazed across the forever fields to the farmhouse, a vague and chilling premonition marched in gooseflesh up his arms. The sensation was too obscure to trouble him. But as he kicked stones at his younger brothers and slowly made his way home, he made note of the bitter feeling and how similar it tasted to the bitterness he had experienced the day before Grandma Sanders had died. Then Georgie hit him in the back with a dirt clod and the feeling was put aside.

Six-year-old Tammy folded her hands in front of her, bowed her head, and took a deep breath. "Thank you, Lord, for this food upon our table. Amen."

"Amen," said in chorus, then hands, small-medium-large, reached for corn on the cob and broth of chicken and fresh green salad made of lettuce and tomato, bell pepper and carrot, celery and onion. There was hot homemade bread and cold unpasteurized milk. Everything and everyone that was important in Derrick's life was all right there. Except for . . .

"Where's Sarah?" he asked as he buttered a slice of bread that warmed the palm of his hand. And when no one answered, he asked again, "Where's Sarah?" this time looking directly at his mother. Her eyes seemed tired, as if she were gone somewhere faraway in a daydream. A swirl of black hair, singed with lean flames of gray, fell across her forehead. She brushed it back, seeming never to have left the day-dream. "Mom?"

"Hmm?" she said, only half-there.

"I asked where Sarah was?"

"Who?"

"Sarah."

For a moment, there was an eerie pause in the meal. Forks stalled in mid-air. Mouths were closed, ears were opened, and a dozen questioning eyes turned to stare at him. *Who's Sarah?*

Then Tammy grinned, and with her mouth full of a thick, cheesy casserole, she said, "Betcha Derr's got a girlfriend."

Derrick felt himself blushing then, even though he had nothing at all to blush about. He was just curious about Sarah, that's all. No big deal. He was sure she was all right, someone would have told him if she weren't. So he smiled uncomfortably and turned back to his plate of vegetables, doing his best to divert the attention away from him.

His thoughts about Sarah would just have to wait.

Derrick didn't breathe another word of her until he was in bed that night. Brian was already asleep in the corner, one of his arms hanging off the edge of the bed, his hand brushing against the floor. Georgie was tossing in the bottom bunk, rocking himself back and forth as he did every night until he eventually fell asleep. From the upper bunk, Derrick whispered, "Georgie?"

"What?" The light sway of the bunk beds stopped.

"Where's Sarah?"

The rocking started up again.

"Georgie?"

"I don't know."

Derrick leaned over the edge of his bed. "If you don't stop that blessed rocking, I'm gonna slug you."

"I don't even know who she is," his brother whispered.

And for a moment, Derrick couldn't believe his ears. "She's your sister," he said. "Your sister! The one that tried to eat the tail right off your kite yesterday."

"That was Tammy." His brother quietly said before he rolled over, face to the wall, back to Derrick where he could see a luminescent iron-on patch of the Incredible Hulk glowing green in the dark. "Ain't one pesky sister bad enough for you?"

Derrick could have argued. He could have pointed out a handful of recent incidents when little Sarah had pestered both of them. Little sisters did things like that. And eventually he could have made Georgie admit that Sarah was missing. But he didn't. Somewhere inside, gnawing

154

at his gut, Derrick knew that there had never been a Sarah, that her four years of giggling and gurgling and crying—sometimes all night long—had been little more than an imaginative spasm, a bizarre tic on the face of his reality. And that's why they had all stared at him with eyes that asked, *Who's Sarah?* Because there was no Sarah. His imagination had been playing games in his head, as it must do with everyone, as it did when Tammy played tea party with playmates that weren't really there.

An imaginative spasm.

That's what it was.

The summer's first one-hundred-degree temperature arrived less than a week later, pushing the mercury above the red zone on the rusting Orange Crush thermometer that had been tacked to the big oak as long as Derrick could remember.

Pa had allowed them the day down at Miner's Pond. Clad in cut-offs made from an old pair of jeans he'd worn out during the winter, Derrick was busy cleaning the spring weeds out of the little patch of sand which covered the ground between the water and the cliff of rock they used as a diving platform. The others were already in the water, squirming and churning enough to make the pond look like a pot of boiling watercress soup.

Tammy let out a squeal just before Brian dunked her.

Sometimes, like now, when her hair was damp and it closely embraced her thin, almost-hollow cheeks, he would see Sarah looking out from Tammy's laughing eyes. Even though he realized that there had never been a Sarah. And when he remembered those special things she would do, those special things his imagination had made so real for him—like the time she tried to cut her own hair and Ma nearly had to shave her head to make it all even again—after times like those, he wished she had been more than just a daydream.

But she hadn't. He knew that now. She was gone, her dolls were gone, her clothes were gone. There had never been a real Sarah.

Derrick collapsed into the soft sand and sifted his strange emptiness from hand to hand in the form of a thousand gritty particles.

"Come on, Derr," one of the others called.

He smiled and shook his head, all of a sudden feeling too old to be splashing carelessly in Miner's Pond. And he felt a little sad just then, as if at age twelve he had suddenly realized the time was nearing when he would have to give up some of those cherished things that stood between being a boy and being a man. Perhaps the joy of Miner's Pond. Perhaps some other never-to-be-forgotten place or time or person.

That's what his parents had done. Over the years, they had somehow given up their happiness for something else, something he wasn't sure he understood. And maybe that was what growing up was all about. Giving away those things you liked most about yourself.

If so, it didn't seem fair.

"Derr, come on!"

It didn't seem fair at all.

Derrick wiped the sand from the butt of his cut-offs, and with a laughter he wasn't yet ready to give up, he did a painful belly flop into the circle of his brothers and sister.

It felt great.

They played away the afternoon, exploring creek rocks for crawdads, building a miniature dam to house minnows, diving off the cliff, playing tag up and down the creek's banks until their feet were sore and their bodies were bright pink from too much sun.

It was getting time to head back home again.

Derrick had gathered up the towels they had brought along, and the lunch bags which Ma would want returned for recycling. The others were down the creek a ways. He could hear their laughter whistling through the paw-like leaves of the oak trees.

"Gotta go!" he yelled as he shook the sand out of the towels. He liked being big brother, the one they looked up to and depended upon. Sometimes, he felt more like their father than their brother.

"Let's go!" he called again.

The boys came busting through the bushes. Brian collapsed in the sand. "Beat ya," he said, lying flat on his back.

"Did not," Georgie cried. His arms were braced on his legs as he collected a breath. His eyes kept looking to Brian, as if he knew he had been beaten and wondered if his younger brother might make too big a deal out of it.

"Where's Tammy?" Derrick asked. "Pa's gonna be real upset if we don't get ourselves back by supper time."

Brian dragged himself to his feet. "I beat ya," he said again, pushing Georgie up the side of the short bank. When they had made it to the top, they stopped and turned back to their older brother. "Thought you were in a hurry," Brian said.

"What about Tammy?"

Then there was a short pause that seemed to last forever, and his brothers exchanged a curious glance. Then a chill wound up Derrick's spine as he recognized their bewilderment. He didn't inquire a third time. The story was still fresh in his mind. *Who's Tammy?* Just another spasm, that's all. No need to ask further, just fill in the blanks. *There is no Tammy. There never has been. She was just a product of the same game, the same hiccup of imagination that birthed Sarah. And now they were both gone.* An imaginative quirk, that's all it was.

"Derr, it's getting late."

He glanced up at the voice and wondered, almost casually, if the two boys who had been his brothers for almost every minute of his life, if they too, were mere quirks. The thought scared him.

"Derr . . ."

"Yeah," he said, flipping the towels over his shoulders. "Coming."

Tammy never returned. He knew she wouldn't. And like his parents and his brothers, he never asked about her.

That night, Brian went off to sleep in his own room, the room that Derrick's imagination had lent to Sarah and Tammy. It seemed lonelier without Brian sleeping in the corner, without his arm hung over the edge of the bed, brushing a hand against the floor. At least he still felt the comfort of Georgie's rocking, the comfort of the bunk bed swaying back and forth as it had always done as long as he could remember. At least that hadn't been taken from him.

Summertime lost its magic after that. The days became too hot, Miner's Pond too cold. The beautiful yellows and greens around the farm shriveled, becoming deathly browns. The laughter that had so often swept around the dinner table, became a whisper, a cough of its past joy. Everything changed, and somewhere along the line, memories of yesterdays gradually became more and more difficult to call up again, as if pieces of his life were somehow being consumed. The magic of summertime had been lost and everything was suddenly different.

Even his parents seemed somehow different, somehow changed. He wasn't sure exactly what the difference was, and wondered if perhaps it was merely his imagination at play again.

"Remember before?" Derrick heard his mother ask his father one night. They were outside on the front porch, casually gliding back and forth on the porch swing, allowing themselves to be overheard by the evening stars and by Derrick himself. He was upstairs in the attic, poking through old boxes of toys, searching for a game of Cootie which he hadn't seen in years. Just a bored-night impulse, that was the only reason he was there.

"Before what?" Pa said.

The arthritic squeaking of metal to rusting metal filled the moment of silence and drew Derrick curiously closer to the window.

"Before we got married," she said. "Remember how we used to walk along Dogwood Creek at night and the breeze would rustle through the trees, sounding like God himself was trying to talk to us? And how we always knew we'd get married and live out the rest of our lives together? How it was never gonna change?"

Pa chuckled. "I remember."

"I miss those times," she told him.

"Guess I do, as well."

"They were *good* times."

"The best," his Pa agreed.

"I want to go back." The rhythmic squeaking paused for a breath, then started up again. "I want it to be like it was then, without the worries and the fears, without the kids and the farm to look after."

Pa didn't say so much as "Hmm."

"Mind ya, I'm not unhappy," she said. "But it's all slipping by so quickly. I want to do it all again. I want to court and marry and make babies all over again, like it was the first time."

"Been feeling this way all summer, have you?"

Derrick couldn't see them on the porch, they were sitting almost right underneath him, but he imagined her nodding her head. He stepped back from the window, suddenly feeling a strange sense of shame from his eavesdropping, realizing his ears had crossed the path of something they were never meant to hear. But they *had* heard, and Ma *had* been different all summer. Perhaps that was the only trick of his imagination that hadn't really been a trick. She *had* been different. The whole summer had been different.

He left the attic without ever finding the game of Cootie.

Brian blinked out of his life two days later. Derrick woke up to find the bottom bunk empty and when he went searching for Georgie, he found the ten-year-old in Brian's room where Brian should have been, rocking Brian's bed the way he used to rock the bunk beds.

"What are you doing in here?" he asked. "Where's Brian?"

Through sleepy eyes, Georgie expressed his puzzlement, that same puzzlement that had surfaced after each of Derrick's summer-long inquiries, after each loss that had seemingly slipped away unnoticed. And Derrick knew, he knew and he understood and he felt the emptiness devour another portion of his life. Georgie was all he had left, and what would happen after his last brother slipped away?

What would happen then?

It was early August all too soon. The fields were dry and dusty. Miner's Pond had dipped so low that a soul couldn't dive off the cliffs without meeting the bottom head first. His mom was looking different by the day. His father was too. Like the summer hadn't withered them like everything else it touched. Like they thrived somehow on the heat and the dirt and the peace that had shadowed the farm. That's what it was —

158

peace. Too much for Derrick's liking. The meals were too quiet, the days too empty.

He stayed close to Georgie whenever he could, whenever he wasn't off tending to chores or running errands or sleeping in his own bed, a wall away from his little brother. But it happened just the same.

He woke up one morning and he was the last, all his brothers and all his sisters were finally gone. He was all that remained. And he imagined his parents breathing a heavy sigh, relieved that at last the inevitable moment was near, the moment when their oldest child would finally slip away like the others.

There were days now, unlike past summers, when he wished he had never been the oldest, the last to go. How much easier it would have been to have simply slipped away like Sarah, right at the beginning, never having to watch as the others were taken one by one, never having to feel each loss. How much easier.

Each day thereafter painfully dwindled away, seconds feeling like minutes, minutes like hours, until his leave-taking finally arrived. It was nine-thirty. The sky was black on a moonless night. The window was open, inviting the slight breeze inside to chase away the godawful heat. It was like a thousand other summer nights, yet unlike any that had come his way before. From the top bunk, with his arms folded behind his neck, he gazed out the window to the darkness of the universe and wondered where it ended, wondered if he would float out there after . . .

. . . as he sometimes did in his dreams.

"Derr?" A shaft of hall light sectioned his darkness, and his mother's silhouette filled the doorway. "How you doing?"

"Okay." He didn't want to look at her, kept his watch on the universe instead. It would be easier that way. But she crept into the darkness, right up next to his bed, and she stood over him, a shaft of light falling across her face. It was the first time, as he forced himself to look at her, that he realized just how she had changed over the summer.

"Is it too hot for you?"

The singe of gray that had danced like a wind-blown scarf through her hair was no longer there.

"I'm comfortable."

And her eyes had come alive again, they had a sparkle in them that he hadn't noticed in years.

"You sure?" she brushed the hair away from his forehead, then held his hand in hers. "You know I love you," she said.

Derrick glanced out the bedroom window at the watching universe. He wanted to tell her he still loved her, but knew he wouldn't be able to find a way to say the words.

"Remember that," she said. "Remember I love you." Then all too quickly, she turned and started out of the room.

"Ma," he said, still moving away. "Are you sorry I'm your son? Are you and Pa sorry you ever had me?"

She paused, a wisp of shadow in the doorway. "Of course not. You're our son, our flesh and blood. You're a part of us. We'll always love you."

"Even if I have to go away?"

Her eyes were hidden in a checkerboard pattern of black and white, but the long silence answered his question for her. And he knew then that she didn't even understand what she had done, that it had all been done out of innocence, out of an ignorance of the consequences of her wishing. *I want to court and marry and make babies all over again, like it was the first time.*

"I still love you, Ma," he told her. "Even if I have to go away."

"There's nowhere to go," she said. "Nowhere at all."

The bedroom door closed.

Darkness rushed in through the open window.

Derrick rolled over, rolled away from his doorway to the windowed universe, until he was nestled safely in the wings of his blankets. Then a single tear tumbled down his cheek, a tear not for himself, but for his mother.

Echoes

Lawrence C. Connolly

Marie stood in the kitchen, staring at the magnetic birds on the refrigerator door, and after a while Billy yelled in from the living room to tell her that Paul wanted some milk. She didn't answer.

Paul had been dead for three months.

"Mom?"

She looked around, trying to remember what she had come to the kitchen for.

"Mom! Paul wants some milk. Can he have some?"

It wasn't a game anymore, and it was starting to worry her. Billy was old enough to understand death. He was old enough to know that Paul couldn't be there in the living room, watching television. Billy was six.

Paul, had he lived, would have been five.

She turned, walking from the kitchen and feeling the awful stabbing pains in her back that the doctor said she would have the rest of her life. Marie was twenty-nine; the rest of her life—if she died of old age and not another accident—would be a long time. She wondered if she would ever come to regard pain as a normal thing.

The living room was dark. She had tried opening the heavy blue drapes before breakfast, but Billy had wanted them closed. He had become an indoor child, preferring dark rooms to the world outside, preferring his dead brother's company to that of living children. He sat alone, leaning on the couch's arm, slouching with wonderful ease; it was amazing how his young body had recovered. His scars were gone. His broken bones were whole and straight. Looking at him, it was easy to forget that he, too, had been involved.

An uneaten doughnut sat on the coffee table. She pointed to it. "Don't you want that?"

He shook his head. "I'm leaving it for Paul, but he won't eat it without milk. He's mad because you wouldn't give him breakfast."

She looked at the television and asked, "What are you watching?"

"*Edge of Night*. Paul wants to know if—"

"Aren't there any kids' shows on?"

"Yeah, but you put this one on. Remember? You put it on, then you went to the kitchen. Paul says—"

"Well, let's at least turn it down. I have a headache, and—"

"Why are you doing that?"

"What?"

"Talking about other things when I talk about Paul."

"What would you like for lunch?"

"Mom?"

He looked near tears, and she almost gave in, almost turned to the empty spot beside Billy to say hello, almost went into the kitchen for milk. It would have been easy to play along. She knew. She had done it. And, sometimes, she had caught herself believing Paul was there . . .

"Mom?"

She turned away, knowing that if the discussion continued it would go Billy's way. And she couldn't allow that. Last night Roger had come home early and caught the two of them talking to Paul. Roger had laid down the law then; he had told her it was no good pretending, no good for anyone.

She looked back at the couch, back at her oldest child who was once again an only child, and she said, "Later I might want you to go to the store for me. We're nearly out of butter."

Billy stared at the uneaten doughnut.

Marie wondered if she was getting through.

❋   ❋   ❋

Later, when lunch was long gone and the empty afternoon became evening, Roger mixed a martini and asked about her day. She said it had been fine, and he took the chair across from her at the kitchen table. He no longer wore the neck brace, but she could see that his pain was no better. The doctor had been against his working full days, but Roger wasn't one for taking orders. He would probably have two more martinis before dinner.

The television was still on in the living room; Billy had spent the whole day in front of it, passively watching whatever Channel 4 threw at him. Now he was watching a *Leave It to Beaver* rerun. The sound was still too high. Roger looked over Marie's shoulder toward the noise, and something in his look roused her.

She realized dimly what was coming.

"Marie," he said, "why is the television on?"

Beaver and Wally laughed.

"Please, Roger, let the boy be." She had met the man halfway. Surely that was enough.

She looked away as he got up from the table. He moved into the living room. The television fell silent. "I don't like you doing that," he said, stepping back into the kitchen. "I don't like you playing that set to an empty room."

She cried after that. And after that she tried telling him about the talk she and Billy had had that morning. But every time she began he asked her about dinner, or about sewing, or about Mrs. Burke up the street.

After a while, when it seemed useless to insist, she put on her coat and went to the store for butter. It was five blocks. The walk was painful, but she didn't want to drive. She no longer felt safe in cars.

Roger stayed behind in the empty house. He mixed a second martini, wondering if he was getting through.

The Eerie Mr. Murphy

Howard Wandrei

No one knows where he came from, and no one knows where he is now, nor how he got there. He is a subtle man at getting about, and very dangerous in spite of his appearance. Like the Wandering Jew, he may be the next man that passes unobserved on the street, and though he is never mentioned by name, his dreadful talent may be seen at work almost daily in the newspapers. In the past tense, the reason why something ought to be done about Murphy is plain enough, eventually.

There was not more than one hundred and thirty pounds of Timothy Murphy. His height was approximately right for his weight, but he appeared shrunken because he was shrinking from the prodigious thing within himself, his own, unwanted, diabolical genius. His head, balanced on a slim neck like a woman's, was a few sizes too large for himself. His white forehead bulged, and his round black eyes always looked frightened, as though he had just found out that he had got leprosy somehow, and his straight black hair was always somewhat mussed. His blue suit fitted him all right, but he had made the last press do for some while.

To the best of anyone's knowledge, Murphy made his initial appearance at the age of twenty-five or -six years near the intersection of Fourth and Wisconsin Streets in the city of Groveland. It was a broiling August noonday, and he was engaged in the comparatively innocent pastime of stopping clocks and watches. His method was unique.

Accosting the large and perspiring figure of a banker named Beresford, Murphy said worriedly, "Pardon me, but I wonder if you could give me the right time."

Beresford paused long enough to fish a splendid platinum watch out of his vest and gave Murphy the correct time within a couple of dozen seconds. Not much thicker than a silver dollar, the watch was uncommonly accurate and one of the best pieces money could buy.

"Thank you," said Murphy. "But I think your watch has just stopped."

Automatically Beresford glanced up at the stained face of the courthouse clock a block away.

"I'm sorry," Murphy apologized in a reedy, melancholy voice, "but the courthouse clock has just stopped, too."

Beresford thought Murphy was trying to pull some kind of stunt, because the big clock in the tower had finished bonging off the noon hour only a few minutes previously. But he remembered the insidious Murphy when he returned to his bank, hot and flustered at finding himself late for the first time in his life. That princely watch of his had stopped, never to go again until the whole works, including the stem, were replaced by the manufacturer. The giant Belgian clock in the courthouse tower had stopped, likewise, and the chimes were jammed. Men who knew all about clocks worked whole days on the courthouse giant and quit, baffled. The only time the clock ever told after that was the time of Murphy's strange visit.

Murphy wasn't fooling.

Not far from the courthouse he stepped from the curb and walked up to the front seat of a fire truck which had rolled up behind a pair of passenger vehicles waiting for a change of lights. The truck was returning leisurely from a false alarm.

"Your motor has just quit," Murphy told one of the firemen, "and you won't be able to get it started again."

The driver looked at him, noting that he was a queer little guy somewhat green around the gills, then began jamming his heel down on the starter because the motor had just quit.

"And there is going to be a terrible traffic jam," Murphy added, walking away. After the lights changed there was considerable embarrassment; traffic jammed rapidly, and the jam held for hours.

Murphy stopped two more motors later on, but mostly he confined himself to stopping clocks. Most of the clocks in the business district stopped, including electric clocks and the chronometers in jewelry store windows. It wasn't necessary for him to tell anyone when a clock or watch was going to stop, or a car motor. When it was convenient he would just make his announcement out of courtesy.

Certainly his preoccupation with timekeepers and gasoline motors was doing no one any real harm. But then something horrible occurred.

At first it was a remote drone in his ears that he was scarcely aware of. Through some accident of the atmosphere the drone became a loud lunge of sound that drew Murphy's attention to the heights of the sky overhead. It was the exhaust of a tri-motored airlines transport that gleamed like a soaring silver hawk in the sun.

It was Flight Number Six for Salt Lake City; it was perfect flying weather and the plane was in perfect condition, but Murphy groaned, "Oh, God! It's going to crash!"

Shuddering, he wiped the sweat from his face. There was no sound in the sky as he continued on his way, keeping his eyes on the sidewalk as much as possible. The plane hadn't crashed yet, but it was going to, and Timothy Murphy knew that he was the murderer of all aboard. Innocent persons.

The announcement of the crash, in which fourteen were killed, interrupted a program of dance music coming over the radio of a taxi parked in front of a hotel as Murphy passed. The music was resumed.

"That radio is going to stop working," Murphy thought dismally, "and the meter in that hack won't work from now on, either."

Therewith the radio stopped working. The cab-driver was fiddling with it as Murphy looked wretchedly over his shoulder and saw the driver open the door for a couple who had just emerged from the hotel.

Murphy felt so foul that he proceeded to police headquarters and gave himself up; if he remained at large there was no limit to the heinous things he might do. Unconsciously. He had slain fourteen with a stroke of the eye.

He said to the desk-sergeant, "I am going to see the Chief of Police."

So he was escorted to the office of Chief of Police August Steinbecker with considerable courtesy. When they were alone, Murphy told Steinbecker that he was a wholesale murderer; Steinbecker clasped his hands behind his neck, leaned back in his swivel chair and told Murphy to go ahead.

In his reedy voice Murphy told his story in its essentials, straight-forwardly. Steinbecker didn't interrupt, but listened closely with his grayish-blue eyes fixed on Murphy's scared black ones.

When Murphy had finished, tight-lipped, Steinbecker asked sooth-ingly, "You don't really think you made that plane crash, Mr. Murphy, do you?" The swivel chair came back to level and he rested his elbows on the desk. He said carefully, "Of course, it's really quite a coincidence. You know it's nearly a hundred in the shade, don't you? Sometimes the heat gives me funny ideas, too."

Murphy shook his head. "You don't understand. I don't *do* anything. I just know when something's going to happen."

"Same thing, isn't it?" Steinbecker argued placatingly. "You don't stop a clock when you look at it, but when you look at it you know that it's going to stop. What's the difference?"

Murphy fluttered his hands. "That's just the trouble."

Steinbecker stretched his arm out for the telephone on his desk, saying, "Well, it won't do to let you go around stopping clocks and automobiles. You really want to get this kink ironed out of you, do you?"

"Yes! Oh, yes!" Murphy exclaimed fervently.

"There's a brainy psychiatrist I know, down the line in the Medical Arts Building. I'll just call him up and make an appointment for you," Steinbecker offered.

"Thank you," Murphy quavered as the chief lifted the handpiece from the telephone, "but the telephone has just stopped working."

Steinbecker smiled a skeptical little smile and started to check a call through the switchboard downstairs. But the phone was dead. It stayed dead while he jiggled the connection, and he carefully replaced the handpiece in its prongs.

"That's calling your shots," he muttered thoughtfully.

"You've got a pistol there in the middle drawer, haven't you?" Murphy proceeded forlornly. "Do you know that it isn't loaded?"

Steinbecker regarded Murphy steadfastly, suddenly yanked the drawer open and produced a .38 caliber revolver, broke it. He kept that gun loaded, knew it was loaded, and it took him ten or twelve seconds to get used to the idea that the chambers were empty.

"The bullets are in your coat pocket. The left one," Murphy announced timorously.

Steinbecker dug into his pocket, looked shocked, and brought out the six slugs with a few coins. If Murphy had performed this sorcery, he had done what no one in human form could do. Steinbecker swallowed, weighing the bullets in his sweating palm as though he had found a half-dozen .38 caliber maggots in his jacket. He asked quietly, "How did you work that, Murphy?"

"It isn't anything I do," Murphy protested anxiously in his E-string voice. There was a touch of hysteria. "It's—it's just that I know when. Things just occur to me, do you see? I just know when, and I can't stop it! Don't you understand?"

He didn't understand it himself. He knew when an object won't be found where it must be, when a foolproof instrument would cease to function, when the billionth chance in the law of averages would occur. It would be all right if the chances weren't occurring in wholesale lots. The frightening thing, the thing that frightened Murphy so profoundly, was that he was unable to control the outlaw power of which he was the feeble instrument. He did the best he could with it, confining it to odd jobs of the most harmless variety possible, like letting a license number on a car change, or stopping a man from casting a shadow in strong sunlight. Feeding peanuts to the tiger within him, as it were.

"I understand, all right," Steinbecker said grimly. "You just know when. Let's pay a visit to the Bertillon room downstairs, shall we? Do you think you can give the boys a demonstration?"

"A demonstration?" Murphy faltered. "I guess so." As they left the office and headed down the corridor to the elevator, "You're going to keep me here, aren't you?"

"We'll see," Steinbecker answered ambiguously. There wasn't a charge Murphy could be held on. For that matter, Steinbecker knew he was sticking his neck out by asking Murphy to perform. There was such a thing as a run of coincidences.

He punched the red button at the elevator, frowning. Both of them watched the indicator above the door inch through its half circle as the elevator came down from the penthouse, which contained the radio-telephone equipment. The tiger that had broken loose when Murphy looked up at the big monoplane got loose again now.

"No! No!" he protested frantically. "It's going to fall!"

It fell. The indicator jumped backward through its arc, and they glimpsed the operator's sick face as the car flashed past and down. Steinbecker pulled in his neck, anticipating the crash, but there wasn't any. It was a heavy, shuddering jar as the automatic safety brakes took hold and stopped the car in its fall with unexpected violence that nearly broke the operator's legs. They could hear him yelling into his telephone down there for a repair crew because the car was jammed fast in the shaft, yelling to cover the fact that he was scared.

"See? See?" Murphy screamed; terror closed his throat and thinned the scream to a high, tearing whisper.

Steinbecker's rate of breathing crept up a little with relief. He was a big man with not much fat on him in spite of his generally peaceful roost behind his desk, and not easily shaken, but he was shaken now. He had a family himself, and the veteran in the elevator had a wife and three children. Purposefully he escorted Murphy down six flights of stairs to the Bertillon room in the basement.

Tall, barred windows let in the afternoon sunlight. Under Steinbecker's supervision a dozen men, made up of sergeants, lieutenants, two Bertillon experts, a reporter and a photographer from the Groveland *Free Press*, gave Murphy the works.

First of all, they failed to fingerprint him. Except for a useless moisture-crease here and there, they got nothing for the files but two sets of black spots. Murphy had no prints. His fingertips were slick as glass.

Then it was mugging him.

For the benefit of the men from the *Free Press* Steinbecker asked, "You're submitting to this of your own free will, aren't you?"

"Yes, certainly," Murphy responded hopelessly. "But it's just a waste of plates. That camera won't work."

The police photographer growled something and snapped Murphy front and right profile, and standing up beside a perpendicular rule marked with inch and foot divisions.

"Well, go develop the plates and see," Murphy said. "You haven't got anything."

"If I haven't, it'll be the first time," the photographer said for Steinbecker's benefit.

While he was busy in the darkroom adjacent, the press photographer was getting shots with a "candid" camera loaded with a fresh roll of film. He and the reporter smelled a feature story in this thing.

"Mix the pictures," Murphy suggested resignedly. "The ones I'm supposed to be in won't come out."

The photographer grinned willingly. He got Steinbecker, Murphy, then Lieutenants Reisner and Hubbard, Murphy, Steinbecker, and so on. This was pretty good. If this little pop-eyed hoodoo was calling his shots, it would be even better.

The police photographer strolled out of the darkroom drying his hands and announced casually, "Them plates come out blank. They've been exposed, but there's nothing on them."

The press photographer asked permission to use the darkroom, and the two photographers went in together.

"What else have you got?" Lieutenant Hubbard asked. He had a metallic, hostile voice that he had cultivated to screen a heart as soft as an over-ripe tomato.

"Well, you're not wearing your badge, for example," Murphy said gloomily.

Hubbard made a pass at his breast. The holes made by the pin were there, but the shield was gone. The fact that the pin had been secured with a double-lock device was something to think about. The reporter made a sound of delight.

"It's over there under the fingerprint table," Murphy announced. Hubbard glanced in that direction, walked over to retrieve his shield. All the lieutenants and sergeants looked at each other with a kind of bewildered glee. Murphy stood with his head bowed.

"Go ahead, Murphy," Steinbecker prompted.

Murphy looked up, looked around timidly; picking out Lieutenant Reisner he said timidly, "Shoot me."

Reisner didn't understand, and looked at Steinbecker.

"Suppose I had just robbed the First National and was running with a satchel full of money," Murphy explained nervously. "You were shooting at me. You could shoot at me all day and the bullets would never get to me."

Murphy was Steinbecker's protégé, so all the cops laughed mildly. Steinbecker ordered one of them to go out and get a bullet-proof vest from one of the emergency trucks in the garage.

"It isn't necessary," Murphy protested.

"Do you think I'll take a chance on having a man murdered before my eyes?" Steinbecker snapped. "Lieutenant Reisner. Is your gun in perfect condition?"

Reisner flushed and reported that it was. It was. The gun had been cleaned less than an hour ago, after he had hung up another perfect score on the target range. He was a deadly marksman, the best in the department.

The bullet-proof vest was a yoke of laminated steel encased in black canvas. It weighed about thirty pounds. The front and rear panels were held snug against the body by means of tapes which were tied at the sides. They got Murphy inside it.

"Go ahead," Steinbecker ordered grimly.

At a dozen paces Reisner drew aim on Murphy's breast. "Get ready," he warned. "This is going to knock you down."

Deep in Murphy's brain the tiger purred; he smiled half-heartedly, standing relaxed. There was dead silence just before the heavy bark of the .38 caliber revolver. That would be a hell of a blow to take on the chest.

The slug, an alloy of copper and nickel that was guaranteed to sock through nine inches of pine, fizzled out of the muzzle of Reisner's gun and hopped along the floor. It rolled, coming to rest about a yard from Murphy's feet. Reisner ogled it, then emptied the five remaining slugs into Murphy's chest. But they all fizzled out and stopped hopping and rolling within a yard of the first one.

One of the men had a .45. Reisner borrowed it and emptied it in Murphy's direction as fast as he could pull the trigger. He borrowed another gun. And at the end there they lay, eighteen slugs in a cluster at Murphy's feet. Not one had got to him. Reisner wiped sweat from his forehead and grinned sheepishly at Steinbecker.

The press photographer emerged from the darkroom holding up a snake of wet film. He said, "All the shots came out fine except the ones Murphy was in. Take a look."

All the shots of Murphy were blank rectangles interrupting the sequence of good shots of Steinbecker and the others. All the men looked at each other, looked at Murphy.

Murphy hadn't been weighed. Steinbecker took him over to the scales, and a man took a slug of iron representing a hundred pounds off the balance. He shoved the brass weights back on the graduated bars, shoved them all the way back. At the end, the arm slowly oscillated as it was supposed to when there was nothing on the platform. Even with the steel vest on Murphy weighed less than an ounce, if anything. Seinbecker weighed his own hundred and eighty pounds, and he still had them. There was nothing wrong with the scales. There was something wrong with Murphy. Murphy's weight was going to look like a mistake in the records. "Weight: 0."

"I guess it isn't any use," Murphy decided in his melancholy, E-string voice. "I shouldn't have come here. What's the use of your locking me up in a cell when I could walk right out again?"

Steinbecker asked, "You mean you could get out of a cell if we locked you in? With a brake and all?"

"Oh, yes," Murphy said lugubriously. In the back of his mind the tiger was purring again. His head ached.

Seinbecker's eyes lighted on a heavy pine packing box in which some equipment had been delivered. It was empty, and the lid was in one piece. The box was pretty small, but Murphy could just about make it if he doubled up.

They crammed Murphy, unprotesting, into the box and they nailed the lid down fast all around. They nailed the lid down so tight that no living thing would be able to break out of that box.

"I always wanted to see how they do this trick," said one of the cops.

"Damned if that little guy doesn't give me the creeps," someone muttered.

"He sure has got something."

"Quiet." Steinbecker hauled the pine crate farther out on the floor so that they could all gather around, and said, "I think he's got his weight back. Try it, Reisner."

Reisner straddled the box, hefted it a few inches from the floor and agreed that it weighed a hundred and thirty pounds or so. When he had set it down, Murphy rapped on the wood inside. All the cops gathered round, and Steinbecker put his ear close to the wood. In a muffled, elfin voice Murphy announced, "I'm gone, now."

"What did he say?" Hubbard asked.

"He says he's gone, now," Steinbecker answered, quietly.

All of them watched. They waited, listened, but nothing happened. They grinned. Solemnly Steinbecker moved the box with his foot, and it moved as though Murphy had lost his weight again. The silence got pregnant. A man said uneasily, "I bet he can't breathe in there. Much."

Steinbecker ordered a man to yank the nails, and the man did it with pincers and a claw-hammer. When the lid was bent back they saw that Murphy had told the truth. He had been gone for about ten minutes.

There was no denying that Murphy had worked a very good dodge. He wasn't there. They waited expectantly for the rest of the trick, for Murphy's reappearance. He didn't show up; the crate was absolutely empty, and nothing happened.

The men shuffled their feet or cleared their throats, but nothing happened. They looked at each other, half expecting Murphy to stick his head out of someone's pocket. They all jumped when Steinbecker kicked the box irritably and bellowed, "Murphy!"

Immediately the echoes were swallowed in a hush; the heavy pine crate remained empty; Murphy wasn't in it. He wasn't anywhere; he was gone.

Though all the men were off duty now, they responded eagerly when Steinbecker barked an order to search the Bertillon room and darkroom. Murphy couldn't have got any further away, because the only exit door had been closed and guarded.

Long before the search ended in failure, Steinbecker had worked up a generous, clammy sweat. Through his unwilling mind sneaked the thought that trains would wreck, planes would crash, general hell would pop, and through a dirty stroke of fate it would be the fault of August Steinbecker.

For he had had that little nightmare of a Murphy nailed up securely in a box, and he had let him loose.

170

An Elegy for Mr. Danielson

August Derleth

It was not like Mr. Rufus Danielson to have died with such secrecy, nor was it like his sisters to have kept his death quiet for so long. Danielson's death occurred fully forty-eight hours before the papers got hold of the story and began to print obituary notices of the richest antiquary in London. "No one," said Miss Reba Danielson primly, "except the doctor and the undertaker and the lawyer knew of Rufus' death."

And yet Rufus Danielson had not been dead an hour when there appeared on the stoop of the Danielson home in Mayfair an elderly gentleman wearing peculiar octagonal spectacles, a long purple frock coat, a tall beaver hat, and carrying an umbrella which might have made even such a hardened antiquary as Rufus Danielson purr with delight. This personage rang the bell, and was in due time confronted by a butler who informed him that no one was at home to anybody. The visitor, however, explained that he had come a long way, and having learned only a short time before of Mr. Danielson's sudden death, desired a word or two with Miss Reba, the older of the two Danielson sisters.

He was shown with obvious reluctance into a prim parlor, where in a few moments Miss Reba Danielson faced him. He bowed. She bowed.

"May I ask—" she began.

"My name," he interrupted, "is Mortimer Flaccet, late of Idbury. I knew your brother very well—indeed, so well that I may with all modesty say that some details of his business which are unknown even to you are known to me." He smiled dryly, nodded somewhat stiffly, and caressed his umbrella jerkily with one brownish hand. "I do not wish to take up your time, Miss Danielson. I came, hearing of your brother's sudden death, to bring you an elegy which I had written especially for him; you see, I am by way of being a composer." Here he paused and smiled disquietingly, displaying a set of rather frightening teeth. "Indeed, this elegy was more or less asked for by Mr. Danielson himself—I might add that he asked me to make sure that it would be played for him on the occasion of his death, which has now taken place—not, perhaps, in so many words did he ask for the elegy, but indirectly he demanded it."

Miss Reba Danielson was astonished, and showed it. "My dear Mr. Flaccet," she murmured, "I am sure—"

He thrust a neat roll of age-yellowed paper at her. "Here is the manuscript," he said. "I trust that Mr. Danielson's wish will be carried

171

out." Whereupon he bowed again, clapped his hat on his head, and walked rapidly to the door, leaving Miss Reba with the manuscript held in one awkwardly outstretched hand.

At the threshold he turned. "Perhaps you remember," he said softly, "the Flaccet stones, which helped to make your late brother so wealthy. I am the man from whom he got them."

Then he was gone.

Miss Reba looked curiously at the manuscript and turned to face her sister, Esta, who had been listening from behind a heavy portière.

"What a strange man!" exclaimed Esta. And before her sister could reply, she continued, "Is that the music—the elegy for Rufus?"

They unfurled the roll and bent over the notes on the paper. They looked at each other, looked again at the notes, and once more at each other, bewildered.

"This was certainly not written for the piano," said Miss Reba. "It looks as if it had been written for some kind of reed instrument—or instruments, perhaps."

"I suppose the tune could be picked out, though, couldn't it?" asked Esta.

"I dare say it could."

They continued to study the odd notes until Miss Reba looked up, a sudden expression of annoyance on her face. "How did that man know Rufus had died?" she asked. "I was so careful in calling the doctor and the undertaker about Rufus and making them promise to say nothing about his death to any one."

Esta shrugged. "I don't think it matters," she murmured, "even though he was most odd and insistent about our keeping his death a secret until after he'd been buried."

The doorbell rang suddenly, and presently the undertaker came into the room. An assistant followed, and another. Miss Reba led them to the body and watched them leave the house with Rufus, hoping that the neighbors might not guess which of the three of them it was, should their inquisitive eyes penetrate the foliage about the house. Then for a few hours Mortimer Flaccet and his elegy for Rufus Danielson were forgotten.

When the undertaker had finished and returned with Rufus, and the corpse lay exposed in a coffin in the front room of the house, the elegy came to the fore again when Miss Reba began to wonder whether it ought to be played or not. She talked the matter out with Esta, and Esta thought it would do no harm to try picking out the tune at least. Accordingly, they went to the piano in the drawing-room, which adjoined the room in which the corpse lay. They propped up the awkward manuscript and prepared to play.

172

Miss Reba struck the first note, while Esta pressed hard upon the soft pedal, lest some one in the neighborhood hear and remember later when the news of Rufus' death came out. Both Reba and Esta struck the second note, an octave removed. They looked at each other graciously and smiled. They did the first two notes over again and ventured boldly on to the third. Within a few minutes they had struck and played the theme.

"How weird!" whispered Reba.

"Yes, isn't it?"

"Now let's do it over."

They did it over. Weird it was, certainly. It sounded like faint, far-away reed flutes playing, and for a fleeting moment it seemed to Miss Reba that there was an odd echo which did not seem to come from the piano. Esta recklessly released the soft pedal, and they played the melody again, making it sound through the quiet of the house. They felt a little guilty, and stopped playing suddenly. A faint echo lingered and whispered away. They looked at each other.

At that moment they heard a loud thump in the adjoining room.

"What was that?" whispered Reba.

"I don't know."

A soft sound broke. The sisters sat quite still, their hands catching together. A succession of soft, sinister noises followed rapidly, and stopped abruptly when the front door announced its opening by a faint creaking.

"My friend," said a cold and vaguely familiar voice, "I have waited many years for you."

Then the door closed.

Still a few moments the sisters waited. Then Reba rose cautiously and tiptoed toward the adjoining room. She looked in, her view of the coffin obstructed by a fern. She turned to Esta, smiling.

"Everything's all right," she said.

Esta came to her side, and together they went confidently into the room. Then, with one accord, as they rounded the fern and came upon the coffin, they caught at each other, their eyes opened wide with terror, little cries choked in their throats.

For Rufus Danielson had vanished from his coffin!

During the first half-hour after their disconcerting discovery, the sisters occupied themselves with attempts to convince themselves that something had happened to them, rather than to the corpse. But the coffin gaped empty.

Having finally convinced themselves that they, the doctor, and the undertaker had made the same regrettable error—namely, that Rufus

Danielson was not after all dead, but in a state of suspended animation — they thought of telephoning the doctor. Miss Reba called.

The doctor said that Rufus Danielson had unquestionably died of an apoplectic stroke.

They called the undertaker.

The undertaker said wryly that if Rufus Danielson hadn't been dead before, he had certainly been dead when the undertaker had finished with the body.

Then, in a panic, the sisters telephoned Mr. Grimesby, the family lawyer. Even Thaddeus Grimesby's lugubrious face would be a comfort in the circumstances. Besides, he must soon be told of Rufus Danielson's death.

Mr. Grimesby came, a tall, bent old man with a long, sad face made grim by a pince-nez on an endless black cord. He carried a brief-case bearing the marks of long usage, and containing at the moment a ponderous sheaf of papers neatly inscribed "Danielson." The sisters flew at him, each eager to relate what had happened. They told it together, though Reba, being older, had the most to say.

For a few moments after they had finished, Mr. Grimesby was somewhat put out. However, because he began immediately to rationalize what he had heard, he soon convinced himself that something had occurred to disturb the sisters to the point of insanity. He was, therefore, tactful enough to say nothing, and just sufficiently tactless to ignore the odd features of the occurrence.

"Let us consider this matter logically," he said. "You mentioned Flaccet's stones. These stones, I happen to know, are still in your brother's possession, and I think he intends to keep them to the end of his days. They're immensely valuable, you know."

Miss Reba interrupted. "Rufus has reached the end of his days, Mr. Grimesby," she said in some irritation. "He died this noon. The doctor certified his death and the undertaker made it sure. Somehow, however, his corpse has vanished."

Mr. Grimesby was nonplussed. He glanced severely at Reba, and presently he continued. "The Flaccet stones were obtained by trickery from this man Mortimer Flaccet, a very old and rather queer gentleman living in Idbury. This happened when your brother was but twenty. They are, as I said, of immense value, and are thought to have been Druidic jewels. Your brother practically built his fortune on them."

Mr. Grimesby had been taking in the room while he was talking, and his eyes came to rest presently upon the manuscript of Mortimer Flaccet's elegy for Rufus Danielson. He continued to look at the music unseeingly for some moments as he talked; then abruptly he came to his feet, strode over to the piano, and picked up the manuscript.

174

"Where did you get this?" he demanded in a hoarse, excited voice.

"Mr. Flaccet brought it," said Esta.

Mr. Grimesby looked from the sisters to the manuscript in his hand and back again. "Do you know what it is?" he asked breathlessly.

"An elegy for Rufus," said Reba.

"It's a chant, a magic chant for raising the dead," said Mr. Grimesby, "an ancient chant supposedly used in Druidic rites. What a find! What a find! This is valuable, very valuable. Haven't you noticed how old the manuscript is? And for what instruments it was written—pan-pipes?"

The sisters shook their heads.

"Very old. And a Mr. Flaccet brought it, you say?" Mr. Grimesby cocked his head oddly to one side and closed his eyes. "Very odd," he said presently. "I'm sure the original Mortimer Flaccet died without issue, indeed I am; but apparently some distant relative of the same name has since come forward. Was he a young man, or an old man?"

"Mr. Flaccet was an old man, dressed in a purple frock coat and beaver hat, wearing octagonal spectacles, and carrying an ancient umbrella," said Reba.

For the first time that afternoon Mr. Grimesby was palpably upset. "My dear Miss Danielson," he said in a shaky voice, "the man you describe has been dead over fifty years." He cleared his throat and added, "Something must indeed have disturbed you greatly today."

Fortunately for the sisters, who were rapidly losing patience with Mr. Grimesby, both the doctor and the undertaker arrived at that moment to inquire into the state of Rufus Danielson's corpse, and Mr. Grimesby, having the sisters' improbable tale thus confirmed, was seriously distressed.

But he recovered himself shortly, for it was he who, in a reluctant voice, pointed out that Rufus Danielson's corpse had vanished while the sisters were playing an elegy which was in reality an ancient magical chant for the raising of the dead. "And that music," he added in a halting voice, "was brought here by a dead man who always threatened to return for his stones—which Rufus, I regret to say, frankly stole from him."

Mr. Grimesby turned to take up the music from the piano bench where he had placed it. But his hand paused in mid-air. For where the music had lain, there now lay a thin mocking film of dust, an outline of the manuscript, nothing more.

Suddenly the telephone rang. Mr. Grimesby forced himself away from the piano bench in some agitation and went to answer it.

He returned to the silent room some minutes later and said, "Your brother's bank calling, asking what ailed Rufus. Apparently he was just down at the bank, opened his safety deposit box, took out the Flaccet stones and gave them to his companion—who gave the name of Mortimer Flaccet."

"Down at the bank!" exclaimed the doctor. "But he was dead—I know!"

Even as Mr. Grimesby was about to answer, there came the creaking sound of the front door opening. Reba half rose to go to the door, then sat down again. There was a noise as of feet shuffling across the floor—then a horrific grunting sound—and a terror-fraught silence.

Reba rose and went to the door of the adjoining room, her hand at her throat. With one accord the others followed at her heels. They went into the room, rounded the fern, and came upon the coffin.

The corpse of Rufus Danielson lay there, ungainly, sprawling—its feet still wet from rain fallen outside—and a terrible line of glistening footprints led across the rug from the outer door!

Empty Walls

Elizabeth Engstrom

Karen slammed the door shut behind her and listened to it echo through the barren apartment. She collapsed against the empty wall without energy, without motivation, without a future. At least now she was home and didn't have to act normal, or brave, or as if everything were fine.

A lick of flame in her guts flared up. Her white shoes squeaked on the tile foyer floor as she tried to take a deep breath. *Breathe*, she said to herself. *Breathe.*

The stomach cramp eased and she collected a long, ragged breath of stale, abandoned air. Without the distraction of work, the scenario began to run again, for the zillionth time, right from the beginning.

All the evidence laid out on the dining room table.

"Here it is. Look at this. You must have *wanted* to get caught."

"What is this," he said, "a fucking trial?"

"If you like. Exhibit a: Lipstick on the shoulder of your shirt. Not mine. Exhibit b: *Smell* this. I would never wear perfume like this."

"That's enough. A secretary's lipstick over a birthday hug. Sometimes

I come home smelling like cigarette smoke, too, but that doesn't mean I smoke."

"Exhibit c: Receipt for flowers. When did you ever send me flowers?"

When did you ever send me flowers? When did you ever send me flowers? When did you ever send ME flowers?

"I never sent anybody flowers. Let me see that."

"And you charged them to *our* goddamn Visa card. What the hell is the matter with you?"

"I swear to God—"

"Exhibit d."

"What is that?"

"My diary. Times you said you were going someplace and then didn't go there. Things you said you were going to do but didn't, because you were with *her.*"

"What did you do, follow me? Check up on me? Spy on me?"

"I built a file, is all. Here it is, all laid out. Pretty, isn't it? You're guilty as hell."

Guilty as hell. Guilty as hell. Guilty.

"You're nuts."

"And you're leaving."

"You're throwing me out?"

"On your ass, buddy. Your shit is already packed. But before you go, I have one question. Just one. What kind of woman does this? What kind of woman sleeps with another woman's husband, hammering an irreversible wedge between them? What could you possibly find attractive about a woman who would do that? What kind of woman does that?"

What kind of woman does that? What kind of woman? What kind?

Karen unbuttoned her white uniform with a tired hand and shrugged out of it, pulling the syringe out of the pocket before letting the fabric pool at her feet.

Even her presence echoed in the empty apartment.

In the kitchen, she opened the refrigerator and stared inside. She had no appetite, but her body needed fuel or she wouldn't be able to work tomorrow. She needed to work tomorrow. She needed to work. She needed to do something to take her mind off the despicable woman . . .

She set the syringe on the refrigerator shelf, grabbed a tub of yogurt and a spoon and wolfed down a couple of mouthfuls, then stuck the spoon in it and put it back on the shelf.

She could feel the yogurt echoing in the emptiness of her stomach. She closed her eyes and told it to stay there.

She closed the refrigerator door and made her way slowly through the empty living room to the bedroom. The worst thing about an empty apartment was the square marks on the walls where framed pictures, photographs, paintings and prints used to hang. Walls gave an apartment its personality. A completely empty room with art on the walls was still decorated. Fill the apartment with furniture, and if the walls aren't personalized, the apartment isn't finished yet.

This apartment had been personalized, had been finished, had been filled with family and fun and memories.

But not now.

Karen walked through the living room, and if she'd had a pencil in her hand, she would have drawn frames around those square dirt marks on the walls, and then she would have drawn people, happy people, inside the frames.

But she didn't have a pencil, and she didn't have any energy.

Her bed was a futon mattress on the floor in the corner of the bedroom. Her brother's sleeping bag was on top of it. It was all she had. All she had. It was all there was. That and dirt marks on the walls where pictures used to hang.

It shouldn't be like this, Karen thought to herself. It's not supposed to be like this. I shouldn't be alone, not at this stage of life. She felt like there were square dirt marks on the empty walls of her mind, the empty walls of her soul, where portraits of loved ones used to provide personality.

She pulled her slip off and let it fall to the floor. Panty hose followed. She shrugged into an oversized t-shirt and pair of cotton panties. As she passed a mirror, she glimpsed what looked like a hollow-eyed little boy. She didn't stop to investigate. She had no time.

The scenario continued.

"Don't you love me? Don't you respect me? How could you do something like this?"

"All right. You're right. I did have a fling. But she meant nothing to me."

"She meant nothing? How could you do something so serious, so seriously damaging to me, to our marriage, with someone who meant nothing to you?"

"I don't know, darling, I'm sorry. What would it take—"

"Does *she* know she means nothing to you?"

"I'm sure she does."

"I'm sure she does *not*. What kind of a woman would do this? A woman with no soul, that's what kind. A woman with no self esteem, a woman with no life of her own. A terrible, horrible, awful woman, that's who. And you carried on with her, for . . . how long?"

"Can we get beyond this?"

"I don't know. I don't think so. I don't think I know how."

"Please?"

"How long?"

How long? How long? How long?

Satisfied that the yogurt finally felt settled, Karen went back to the refrigerator, thinking about adding something to it.

The door opened and the light echoed in the cold emptiness. Even the refrigerator was cold and empty.

Yogurt. Grape jelly. Syringe.

She was going to do that home wrecker, that bitch, that . . . *woman* . . . some harm.

There were lots of things she could have picked up at the hospital. Karen could kill her easily with some drug or some infectious disease. She could have picked up a vial of blood that was HIV positive. She could have gone to the lab and gotten any one of a number of things, including herpes, or yellow fever. Those were her first choices, but she got a much better idea.

Oh yeah, a much better idea.

The woman was a slut. She had no moral fiber at all. She seduced husbands and ruined marriages all over town. She needed to be punished, but punished periodically for the rest of her life. She didn't need to be dead, and she didn't need to be giving herpes or AIDS to all the men around. No, Karen had a better plan than that.

She picked up the syringe and walked back to the bedroom, flopped down on the futon and held the syringe up to look at it.

Simple. Innocent. She handled a hundred, sometimes several hundred syringes a day, and they were nothing. A tool. A tool to heal.

But not this baby.

The aching, the longing, the pain wrenched her gut and she pulled her knees up to her stomach and turned on her side. The syringe fell from her fingers and rolled across the floor.

"How long?"

"I don't know. Three weeks. A month."

"A month?! You were seeing this bitch for a month? What, you . . . you'd fuck her, come home and sleep with me? You felt no remorse, no guilt?"

"Of course I did."

"You're an animal."

"Listen—"

"I no longer listen to you. Where did you meet her?"

"That's not important. She's gone now, she's out of my life, I'll never see her again."

"As of when? Just this minute? Just now, when you got caught? Is she expecting to see you tonight? Is she somewhere, right now, waiting for you?"

Waiting for you. Waiting. Wait.

Karen could have gotten a syringeful of instant death or slow death, but what she finally opted for was intermittent death.

Malaria. A new strain. An exotic. The worst yet.

The fever came on unexpectedly, like weakness. Like an affair. Like lust.

She'd seen the results of it, too: delirium, sweat, muscle spasms, helplessness. Like sex. Like heartbreak.

But this was severe. So severe, those stricken usually prayed for death. And it lasted two, three weeks, sometimes. Like a cheap affair. An affair that meant nothing.

Karen reached over a thin hand and picked up the syringe. She held it up to the light again and marveled at how calm it looked to her professional eye, yet she knew quite precisely the devastating chaos it would effect on a home wrecker.

She visualized the little microbes, like tiny lobsters with giant pincers jumping with glee into the bloodstream, headed for the brain, the eyes, the liver, the vagina.

It would sting, but the sting would be nothing. Comparatively speaking, the sting would be nothing. Compared to the anguish of the fever, compared to the anguish she caused . . .

"Where did you meet her?"

"Can we stop this?"

"At the hospital, right? What is she . . . a *nurse*?"

Before she could change her mind, Karen pulled off the pink needle guard, stabbed the needle deeply into her thigh and pushed the plunger.

It did sting. "Ow," she said, then plucked it out and threw it across the room.

She lay back on the futon. Her first round of punishment should begin well before morning.

Then maybe she could relax. Then maybe she could stop hating herself. Then maybe she could stop imagining the homewrecking scenes between her lovers and their wives. Then maybe she could stop acting on those impulses that hurt her, hurt them, hurt them all.

Karen lay there, imagining the fire in her veins as the microbes went to work.

To pass the time, she looked at those square dirty marks on the walls of her new apartment and tried to visualize what kind of pictures used to hang there.

A real boyfriend would paint them over for her.

An Eye for an Eye, a Tooth for a Tooth

Lawrence Schimel

The alarm clock went off and I rolled over to slam down on it, hard. It stopped buzzing. I wanted to roll over and go back to sleep, but I knew I shouldn't. I debated whether to get up or not, arm still outstretched to the clock since I was too tired to pull it back into bed. Finally, I opened my left eye to check the time. 6:47. I could snooze ten more minutes.

I rolled over and pulled the covers up close, but I couldn't fall asleep. There was something lumpy under my pillow. I tried to ignore it, but it wouldn't go away. I couldn't imagine what it was, and for an absurd moment I thought of the fairy tale, "The Princess and the Pea." I knew I hadn't been eating peas in bed; I hate vegetables.

When I couldn't stand it any more, I rolled onto my stomach and reached under my pillow, keeping my eyes shut so I could go back to sleep when I rolled over again. My fingers closed on something hard and cold and round. Coin? Quarter? No, more like one of those Susan B. Anthonys they pulled out of circulation because they were so much like quarters.

I rolled over onto my back again and settled my head into the now comfortable pillow, wondering what the silver dollar was doing there. I hadn't seen a Susan B. Anthony in years, not since I was a little kid. And even if I had accidentally gotten one with my change, what would it be doing under my pillow?

My parents used to give me them whenever I lost a tooth, back when I still believed in the tooth fairy. Nervously, I felt around my mouth with my tongue to make sure I hadn't lost a tooth during the night, just in case the tooth fairy really did exist and this was the exchange I'd gotten. But I couldn't feel any gaps in my teeth.

I wondered what the tooth fairy did with all those teeth, anyway. Or how it got a hold of the Susan B. Anthony dollars, and why that was how much it paid for teeth.

Stupid, I told myself. There's no such thing as the tooth fairy.

I nestled back into the pillow, ready to nap for a few more minutes, when I felt a weight land on my chest. Cracking my left eye open again I saw a little gnome-like creature sitting on my chest, with a million eyes all over its body. My heart pounding, I tried to sit up. I couldn't, though, because he was pretty heavy. Lifting my head to get a better look, I tried to open my other eye, but it refused to open.

I rubbed at my eyes with my hands. When my fingers pressed against the lid of my right eye I could feel that there wasn't anything inside the socket. I started screaming. Or at least I tried to. The guy was really heavy and having him sitting on my chest didn't make matters any easier. Not to mention the fact that he had clamped his hands over my mouth.

Wondering what he was doing there and what he wanted, I stared at the gnome-like creature again with my left eye. He had eyes all over his body, like that Greek god, whatever his name was. Only they weren't all human eyes. I could see a whole bunch of compound ones, like a fly's, as well as perfectly round ones, slit-pupiled ones, and other variations. I thought it was disgusting, so I closed my eye, then thought better of it; I'd rather know what he was doing so I could maybe have a few seconds warning if he tried anything.

When I reopened my eye I noticed he was wearing a T-shirt. There wasn't much of it left—he'd cut holes into it for all the eyes—but I still could make out a few letters. There was an "L" followed by an "X," then an "AL," and at the end was an "S." I had no idea what it meant.

I felt something moving around on the bed near my feet, and I risked looking away from the thing on my chest to see what it was. It was another gnome, like the one on my chest, but all teeth instead of eyes. He was wearing a T-shirt as well, and his was readable. It said: LEX TALIONIS.

"Hi!" the thing at the foot of the bed croaked. Its voice was really deep and scratchy. "I'm the tooth fairy. And this here's my brother."

I turned my head to look back at the thing on my chest, but it was too late; his hand was in my face. I could feel him pop my eye out of the

182

socket and was surprised that it didn't hurt. It felt hot, like a water bottle when you're sick, but that was it, no pain or anything.

I reached out to grab him, but he was suddenly off me. I kicked around, but couldn't feel the thing at the foot of the bed either.

"My brother's always jealous," the deep, scratchy voice said. "I mean, who ever loses an eye and leaves it for him under their pillow?"

So this was his revenge. I expected I would be angrier, but I merely wondered if they would at least leave me another Susan B. Anthony. A moment later, something cool was placed on the space my left eye had formerly occupied. I flailed around near my head, but aside from banging my hand against the bed boards couldn't grab whichever one of them had put it there.

As I was wondering why they had put the coin over my eye, I heard a thumping, like the pounding of blood in my ears. It's like the pennies to pay Charon, I realized, and my heart nearly froze. The pounding grew louder, *thump-thump, thump-thump,* and suddenly the deep, scratchy voice of the tooth fairy said from right beside my left ear, "And this is my other brother."

The Festival

H. P. Lovecraft

"Efficiunt Daemones, ut quae non sunt, sic
tamen quasi sint, conspicienda hominibus
exhibeant."

—Lactantius.

I was far from home, and the spell of the eastern sea was upon me. In the twilight I heard it pounding on the rocks, and I knew it lay just over the hill where the twisting willows writhed against the clearing sky and the first stars of evening. And because my fathers had called me to the old town beyond, I pushed on through the shallow, new-fallen snow along the road that soared lonely up to where Aldebraran twinkled among the trees; on toward the very ancient town I had never seen but often dreamed of.

It was the Yuletide, that men call Christmas though they know in their hearts it is older than Bethlehem and Babylon, older than Memphis and mankind. It was the Yuletide, and I had come at last to the ancient sea town where my people had dwelt and kept festival in the elder time when festival was forbidden; where also they had commanded their sons to keep festival once every century, that the memory of primal secrets might not be forgotten. Mine were an old people, and were old even when this land was settled three hundred years before. And they were strange, because they had come as dark furtive folk from opiate southern gardens of orchids, and spoken another tongue before they learnt the tongue of the blue-eyed fishers. And now they were scattered, and shared only the rituals of mysteries that none living could understand. I was the only one who came back that night to the old fishing town as legend bade, for only the poor and the lonely remember.

Then beyond the hill's crest I saw Kingsport outspread frostily in the gloaming; snowy Kingsport with its ancient vanes and steeples, ridge-poles and chimney-pots, wharves and small bridges, willow-trees and graveyards; endless labyrinths of steep, narrow, crooked streets, and dizzy church-crowned central peak that time durst not touch; ceaseless mazes of colonial houses piled and scattered at all angles and levels like a child's disordered blocks; antiquity hovering on grey wings over winter-whitened gables and gambrel roofs; fanlights and small-paned windows one by one gleaming out in the cold dusk to join Orion and the archaic stars. And against the rotting wharves the sea pounded; the secretive, immemorial sea out of which the people had come in the elder time.

Beside the road at its crest a still higher summit rose, bleak and windswept, and I saw that it was a burying-ground where black grave-stones stuck ghoulishly through the snow like the decayed fingernails of a gigantic corpse. The printless road was very lonely, and sometimes I thought I heard a distant horrible creaking as of a gibbet in the wind. They had hanged four kinsmen of mine for witchcraft in 1692, but I did not know just where.

As the road wound down the seaward slope I listened for the merry sounds of a village at evening, but did not hear them. Then I thought of the season, and felt that these old Puritan folk might well have Christmas customs strange to me, and full of silent hearthside prayer. So after that I did not listen for merriment or look for wayfarers, but kept on down past the hushed lighted farmhouses and shadowy stone walls to where the signs of ancient shops and sea-taverns creaked in the salt breeze, and the grotesque knockers of pillared doorways glistened along deserted, un-paved lanes in the light of little, curtained windows.

I had seen maps of the town, and knew where to find the home of my people. It was told that I should be known and welcomed, for village legend lives long; so I hastened through Back Street to Circle Court, and across the fresh snow on the one full flagstone pavement in the town, to where Green Lane leads off behind the Market House. The old maps still held good, and I had no trouble; though at Arkham they must have lied when they said the trolleys ran to this place, since I saw not a wire overhead. Snow would have hid the rails in any case. I was glad I had chosen to walk, for the white village had seemed very beautiful from the hill; and now I was eager to knock at the door of my people, the seventh house on the left in Green Lane, with an ancient peaked roof and jutting second story, all built before 1650.

There were lights inside the house when I came upon it, and I saw from the diamond window-panes that it must have been kept very close to its antique state. The upper part overhung the narrow grass-grown street and nearly met the overhanging part of the house opposite, so that I was almost in a tunnel, with the low stone doorstep wholly free from snow. There was no sidewalk, but many houses had high doors reached by double flights of steps with iron railings. It was an odd scene, and because I was strange to New England I had never known its like before. Though it pleased me, I would have relished it better if there had been footprints in the snow, and people in the streets, and a few windows without drawn curtains.

When I sounded the archaic iron knocker I was half afraid. Some fear had been gathering in me, perhaps because of the strangeness of my heritage, and the bleakness of the evening, and the queerness of the silence in that aged town of curious customs. And when my knock was answered I was fully afraid, because I had not heard any footsteps before the door creaked open. But I was not afraid long, for the gowned, slippered old man in the doorway had a bland face that reassured me; and though he made signs that he was dumb, he wrote a quaint and ancient welcome with the stylus and wax tablet he carried.

He beckoned me into a low, candle-lit room with massive exposed rafters and dark, stiff, sparse furniture of the seventeenth century. The past was vivid there, for not an attribute was missing. There was a cavernous fireplace and a spinning-wheel at which a bent old woman in loose wrapper and deep poke-bonnet sat back toward me, silently spinning despite the festive season. An indefinite dampness seemed upon the place, and I marvelled that no fire should be blazing. The high-backed settle faced the row of curtained windows at the left, and seemed to be occupied, though I was not sure. I did not like everything about what I saw, and felt again the fear I had had. This fear grew stronger from what had before lessened it, for the more I looked at the old man's bland face the more its very blandness terrified me. The eyes never moved, and the skin was too like wax. Finally I was sure it was not a face at all, but a fiendishly cunning mask. But the flabby hands, curiously gloved, wrote genially on the tablet and told me I must wait a while before I could be led to the place of festival.

Pointing to a chair, table, and pile of books, the old man now left the room; and when I sat down to read I saw that the books were hoary and mouldy, and that they included old Morryster's wild *Marvells of Science*, the terrible *Saducismus Triumphatus* of Joseph Glanvill, published in 1681, the shocking *Daemonolatreia* of Remigius, printed in 1595 at Lyons, and worst of all, the unmentionable *Necronomicon* of the mad Arab Abdul Alhazred, in Olaus Wormius' forbidden Latin translation; a book which I had never seen, but of which I had heard monstrous things whispered. No one spoke to me, but I could hear the creaking of signs in the wind outside, and the whir of the wheel as the bonneted old woman continued her silent spinning, spinning. I thought the room and the books and the people very morbid and disquieting, but because an old tradition of my fathers had summoned me to strange feastings, I resolved to expect queer things. So I tried to read, and soon became tremblingly absorbed by something I found in that accursed *Necronomicon*; a thought and a legend too hideous for sanity or consciousness. But I disliked it when I fancied I heard the closing of one of the windows that the settle faced, as if it had been stealthily opened. It had seemed to follow a whirring that was not of the old woman's spinning-wheel. This was not much, though, for the old woman was spinning very hard, and the aged clock had been striking. After that I lost the feeling that there were persons on the settle, and was reading intently and shudderingly when the old man came back booted and dressed in a loose antique costume, and sat down on that very bench, so that I could not see him. It was certainly nervous waiting, and the blasphemous book in my hands made it doubly so. When eleven struck, however, the old man stood up, glided to a massive carved chest in a corner, and got two hooded cloaks; one of which he donned, and the other of which he draped round the old woman, who was ceasing her monotonous spinning. Then they both started for the outer door; the woman lamely creeping, and the old man, after picking up the very book I had been reading, beckoning me as he drew his hood over that unmoving face or mask.

We went out into the moonless and tortuous network of that incredibly ancient town; went out as the lights in the curtained windows disappeared one by one, and the Dog Star leered at the throng of cowled, cloaked figures that poured silently from every doorway and formed monstrous processions up this street and that, past the creaking signs and antediluvian gables, the thatched roofs and diamond-paned windows; threading precipitous lanes where decaying houses overlapped and crumbled together, gliding across open courts and churchyards where the bobbing lanthorns made eldritch drunken constellations.

Amid these hushed throngs I followed my voiceless guides; jostled by elbows that seemed preternaturally soft, and pressed by chests and stomachs that seemed abnormally pulpy; but seeing never a face and hearing never a word. Up, up, up the eerie columns slithered, and I saw that all the travellers were converging as they flowed near a sort of focus of crazy alleys at the top of a high hill in the centre of the town, where perched a great white church. I had seen it from the road's crest when I looked at Kingsport in the new dusk, and it had made me shiver because Aldebaran had seemed to balance itself a moment on the ghostly spire.

There was an open space around the church; partly a churchyard with spectral shafts, and partly a half-paved square swept nearly bare of snow by the wind, and lined with unwholesomely archaic houses having peaked roofs and overhanging gables. Death-fires danced over the tombs, revealing gruesome vistas, though queerly failing to cast any shadows. Past the churchyard, where there were no houses, I could see over the hill's summit and watch the glimmer of stars on the harbour, though the town was invisible in the dark. Only once in a while a lanthorn bobbed horribly through serpentine alleys on its way to overtake the throng that was now slipping speechlessly into the church. I waited till the crowd had oozed into the black doorway, and till all the stragglers had followed. The old man was pulling at my sleeve, but I was determined to be the last. Then I finally went, the sinister man and the old spinning woman before me. Crossing the threshold into that swarming temple of unknown darkness, I turned once to look at the outside world as the churchyard phosphorescence cast a sickly glow on the hilltop pavement. And as I did so I shuddered. For though the wind had not left much snow, a few patches did remain on the path near the door; and in that fleeting backward look it seemed to my troubled eyes that they bore no mark of passing feet, not even mine.

The church was scarce lighted by all the lanthorns that had entered it, for most of the throng had already vanished. They had streamed up the aisle between the high white pews to the trap-door of the vaults which yawned loathsomely open just before the pulpit, and were now squirming noiselessly in. I followed dumbly down the footworn steps and into the dank, suffocating crypt. The tail of that sinuous line of night-marchers seemed very horrible, and as I saw them wriggling into a venerable tomb they seemed more horrible still. Then I noticed that the tomb's floor had an aperture down which the throng was sliding, and in a moment we were all descending an ominous staircase of rough-hewn stone; a narrow spiral staircase damp and peculiarly odorous, that wound endlessly down into the bowels of the hill past monotonous walls of dripping stone blocks and crumbling mortar. It was a silent, shocking descent, and I observed after a horrible interval that the walls and steps were changing in nature, as if chiselled out of the solid rock. What mainly troubled me was that the myriad footfalls made no sound and set up no echoes. After more aeons of descent I saw some side passages or burrows leading from unknown recesses of blackness to this shaft of nighted mystery. Soon they became excessively numerous, like impious catacombs of nameless menace; and their pungent odour of decay grew quite unbearable. I knew we must have passed down through the mountain and beneath the earth of Kingsport itself, and I shivered that a town should be so aged and maggoty with subterraneous evil.

Then I saw the lurid shimmering of pale light, and heard the insidious lapping of sunless waters. Again I shivered, for I did not like the things that the night had brought, and wished bitterly that no forefather had summoned me to this primal rite. As the steps and the passage grew broader, I heard another sound, the thin, whining mockery of a feeble flute; and suddenly there spread out before me the boundless vista of an inner world—a vast fungous shore litten by a belching column of sick greenish flame and washed by a wide oily river that flowed from abysses frightful and unsuspected to join the blackest gulfs of immemorial ocean.

Fainting and gasping, I looked at that unhallowed Erebus of titan toadstools, leprous fire, and slimy water, and saw the cloaked throngs forming a semicircle around the blazing pillar. It was the Yule-rite, older than man and fated to survive him; the primal rite of the solstice and of spring's promise beyond the snows; the rite of fire and evergreen, light and music. And in the Stygian grotto I saw them do the rite, and adore the sick pillar of flame, and throw into the water handfuls gouged out of the viscous vegetation which glittered green in the chlorotic glare. I saw this, and I saw something amorphously squatted far away from the light, piping noisomely on a flute; and as the thing piped I thought I heard noxious muffled flutterings in the foetid darkness where I could not see. But what frightened me most was that flaming column; spouting volcanically from depths profound and inconceivable, casting no shadows as healthy flame should, and coating the nitrous stone above with a nasty, venomous verdigris. For in all that seething combustion no warmth lay, but only the clamminess of death and corruption.

The man who had brought me now squirmed to a point directly beside the hideous flame, and made stiff ceremonial motions to the semicircle he faced. At certain stages of the ritual they did grovelling obeisance, especially when he held above his head that abhorrent *Necronomicon* he had taken with him; and I shared all the obeisances because I had been summoned to this festival by the writings of my forefathers. Then the old man made a signal to the half-seen flute-player in the darkness, which player thereupon changed its feeble drone to a scarce louder drone in another key; precipitating as it did so a horror unthinkable and unexpected. At this horror I sank nearly to the lichened earth, transfixed with a dread not of this nor any world, but only of the mad spaces between the stars.

Out of the unimaginable blackness beyond the gangrenous glare of that cold flame, out of the Tartarean leagues through which that oily river rolled uncanny, unheard, and unsuspected, there flopped rhythmically a horde of tame, trained, hybrid winged things that no sound eye could ever wholly grasp, or sound brain ever wholly remember. They were not altogether crows, nor moles, nor buzzards, nor ants, nor vampire bats, nor decomposed human beings; but something I cannot and must not recall. They flopped limply along, half with their webbed feet and half with their membraneous wings; and as they reached the throng of celebrants the cowled figures seized and mounted them, and rode off one by one along the reaches of that unlighted river, into pits and galleries of panic where poison springs feed frightful and undiscoverable cataracts.

The old spinning woman had gone with the throng, and the old man remained only because I had refused when he motioned me to seize an animal and ride like the rest. I saw when I staggered to my feet that the amorphous flute-player had rolled out of sight, but that two of the beasts were patiently standing by. As I hung back, the old man produced his stylus and tablet and wrote that he was the true deputy of my fathers who had founded the Yule worship in this ancient place; that it had been decreed I should come back, and that the most secret mysteries were yet to be performed. He wrote this in a very ancient hand, and when I still hesitated he pulled from his loose robe a seal ring and a watch, both with my family arms, to prove that he was what he said. But it was a hideous proof, because I knew from old papers that that watch had been buried with my great-great-great-great-grandfather in 1698.

Presently the old man drew back his hood and pointed to the family resemblance in his face, but I only shuddered, because I was sure that the face was merely a devilish waxen mask. The flopping animals were now scratching restlessly at the lichens, and I saw that the old man was nearly as restless himself. When one of the things began to waddle and edge away, he turned quickly to stop it; so that the suddenness of his motion dislodged the waxen mask from what should have been his head. And then, because that nightmare's position barred me from the stone staircase down which we had come, I flung myself into the oily underground river that bubbled somewhere to the caves of the sea; flung myself into that putrescent juice of earth's inner horrors before the madness of my screams could bring down upon me all the charnel legions these pest-gulfs might conceal.

At the hospital they told me I had been found half frozen in Kingsport Harbour at dawn, clinging to the drifting spar that accident sent to save me. They told me I had taken the wrong fork of the hill road the night before, and fallen over the cliffs at Orange Point; a thing they deduced from prints found in the snow. There was nothing I could say, because everything was wrong. Everything was wrong, with the broad window shewing a sea of roofs in which only about one in five was ancient, and the sound of trolleys and motors in the streets below. They insisted that this was Kingsport, and I could not deny it. When I went delirious at hearing that the hospital stood near the old churchyard on Central Hill, they sent me to St. Mary's Hospital in Arkham, where I could have better care. I liked it there, for the doctors were broad-minded, and even lent me their influence in obtaining the carefully sheltered copy of Alhazred's objectionable *Necronomicon* from the library of Miskatonic University. They said something about a "psychosis", and agreed I had better get any harassing obsessions off my mind.

So I read again that hideous chapter, and shuddered doubly because it was indeed not new to me. I had seen it before, let footprints tell what they might; and where it was I had seen it were best forgotten. There was no one—in waking hours—who could remind me of it; but my dreams are filled with terror, because of phrases I dare not quote. I dare quote only one paragraph, put into such English as I can make from the awkward Low Latin.

"The nethermost caverns," wrote the mad Arab, "are not for the fathoming of eyes that see; for their marvels are strange and terrific. Cursed the ground where dead thoughts live new and oddly bodied, and evil the mind that is held by no head. Wisely did Ibn Schacabao say, that happy is the tomb where no wizard hath lain, and happy the town at night whose wizards are all ashes. For it is of old rumour that the soul of the devil-bought hastes not from his charnel clay, but fats and instructs *the very worm that gnaws;* till out of corruption horrid life springs, and the dull scavengers of earth wax crafty to vex it and swell monstrous to plague it. Great holes secretly are digged where earth's pores ought to suffice, and things have learnt to walk that ought to crawl."

The Foghorn

Gertrude Atherton

What an absurd vanity to sleep on a hard pillow and forgo that last luxurious burrowing into the very depths of a mass of baby pillows! . . . her back was already as straight as—a chimney? . . . who was the Frenchman that said one must reject the worn counters? . . . but this morning she would have liked that sensuous burrowing, and the pillow had never seemed so hard, so flat . . . yet how difficult it was to wake up! She had had the same experience once before when the doctor had given her veronal for insomnia . . . could Ellen, good creature, have put a tablet in the cup of broth she took last thing at night: "as a wise precaution," the doctor had said genially. What a curse insomnia was! But she had a congenital fear of drugs and had told no one of this renewal of sleeplessness, knowing it would pass.

And, after all, she didn't mind lying awake in the dark; she could think, oh, pleasant lovely thoughts, despite this inner perturbation—so cleverly concealed. How thankful she was to be tall enough to carry off this new fashion in sleeves! If trains would only come in again, she would dress her hair high some night (just for fun) and look—not like her beloved Mary Stewart, for Mary was almost ugly if one analyzed her too critically. Charm? How much more charm counted than mere beauty, and she herself had it "full measure and running over," as that rather fresh admirer had announced when drinking her health at her coming-out party . . . what was his name? . . . six years ago. He was only a college boy . . . how could one remember? There had been so many since.

Ninon de l'Enclos? She was passable in her portraits, but famous mainly for keeping young . . . Diane de Poitiers? She must have needed charm double-distilled if she looked anything like an original portrait of her hung at a loan exhibition in Paris: flaxen hair, thin and straight, drawn severely from a bulging brow above insufferably sensual eyes—far too obvious and "easy" for the fastidious male of today—a flaxen complexion, no high lights: not very intelligent. Interesting contrast in taste centuries apart—perhaps.

Madame Récamier? Better-looking than most of the historic beauties: hair piled high—but then she wore a slip of an Empire gown . . . well, never mind.

She ranked as a beauty herself, although perhaps charm had something to do with it. Her mouth was rather wide, but her teeth were

191

exquisite. Something rather obscure was the matter in that region of brilliant enamel this morning. A toothache? She had never had a toothache. Well, there was no pain . . . what matter? . . . something wrong, though; she'd go to the dentist during the day. Her nose was a trifle tip-tilted, but very straight and thin, and anyhow the tilt suited the way she carried her head, "flung in the air." Her complexion and hair and eyes were beyond all cavil . . . she was nothing so common-place as a downright blonde or brunette . . . how she should hate being catalogued! The warm, bright waving masses of her hair had never been cut since her second birthday. They, too, were made for burrowing.

Her mother's wedding dress had a long train. But the delicate ivory of the satin had waxed with time to a sickly yellow. Her mother hadn't pressed the matter when she was engaged to John St. Rogers, but she had always expressed a wish that each of her daughters should wear the dress to the altar. Well, she had refused outright, but had consented to have her own gown trimmed with the lace: yards and yards of *point d'Alençon*— and a veil that reached halfway down the train. What a way to spend money! Who cared for lace now? Not the young, anyhow. But Mother was rather a dear, and she could afford to be quite unselfish for once, as it certainly would be becoming. When the engagement was broken, they told the poor old darling that she cried because she would have another long wait before watching all that lace move up the aisle on a long slender figure that made her think pridefully of the graceful skeleton hidden within one hundred and seventy resented pounds.

Well, she would never wear that lace—nor any wedding gown. If she were lucky enough to marry at all, the less publicity the better . . . a mere announcement (San Francisco papers please copy) . . . a quiet return from Europe . . . a year or two in one of those impersonal New York apartment-houses where no one knew the name of his next-door neighbor . . . no effacement in a smaller city for her!

How strange that she of all girls should have fallen in love with a married man—or, at all events, accepted the dire consequences. With a father that had taken to drugs and then run off with another woman— luckily before Mother had come in for Granddad's fortune—and . . . what was it Uncle Ben had once said, Queer twists in this family since "way back." It had made her more conventional than her natural instincts would have prompted; but, no, let her do herself justice: she had cultivated a high standard of character and planted her mind with flowers both sturdy and fair—that must have been the reason she had fallen in love at last, after so many futile attempts. No need for her to conceal from him the awful truth that she read the Greek and Latin classics in the original text, attended morning classes over at the University . . . odd, how men didn't mind if you "adored" music and pictures, but if they suspected you of being intellectual, they either despised or feared you, and faded away.

Fog on the Bay. Since childhood she had loved to hear that long-drawn-out, almost-human moan of the foghorn as she lay warm and sheltered in bed. It was on a night of fog they had spoken for the first time, although they had nodded at three or four formal dinners given to the newcomers who had brought letters to the elect. Bostonians were always popular in San Francisco; they had good manners and their formality was only skin-deep. The men were very smart; some of the women, too; but as a rule they lacked the meticulous grooming and well-set-up appearance of their men. She had been impressed the first time she had met him: six feet (she herself was five feet six), somewhere in the thirties, very spare, said to be a first-rate tennis player, and had ranked as an all-round athlete at Harvard; had inherited a piece of property in San Francisco which was involving him in litigation, but he was in no haste to leave, even before they met.

That had been at the Jeppers', and as the house commanded a fine view of the Bay, and she was tired of being torn from some man every time they had circled the ballroom, she had managed to slip away and had hidden behind the curtains of the deep bow window at the end of the hall. In a moment she was aware that someone had followed her, and oddly enough she knew who it was, although she didn't turn her head; and they stood in silence and gazed together at the sharp dark outlines of the mountains on the far side of the Bay; the gliding spheroids of golden light that were ferryboats, the islands with their firm, bold outlines, now almost visibly drooping in slumber . . . although there always seemed to her to be an atmosphere of unrest about Alcatraz, psychic emanation of imprisoned men under rigid military rule, and officials no doubt as resentful in that dull monotonous existence on a barren rock . . . A light flickered along a line of barred upper windows; doubtless a guard on his rounds.

The band of pulsing light on the eastern side of the Bay: music made visible . . . stars as yellow and bright above, defying the thin silver of the hebetic moon . . . lights twinkling on Sausalito opposite, standing out boldly from the black mass of Tamalpais high-flung above. Her roving eyes moved to the Golden Gate, narrow entrance between two crouching forts, separating that harbor of arrogant beauty from the gray waste of the Pacific—ponderous, rather stupid old ocean. . . .

For the first time he spoke: "The fog! Chief of San Francisco's many beauties."

She had nodded, making no other reply, watching that dense yet imponderable white mass push its way through the Golden Gate like a laboring ship . . . then riding the waters more lightly, rolling a little, writing, whiffs breaking from the bulk of that ghostly ship to explore the hollows of the hills, resting there like puffs of white smoke. Then, over the cliffs and heights on the northern side of the Bay, a swifter, more formless, but still lovely white visitant that swirled down and over the inland waters, enshrouding the islands, Sausalito, where so many Englishmen lived, the fulgent zone in the east; but a low fog—the moon and stars still visible . . . the foghorns, one after another, sending forth their long-drawn-out moans of utter desolation. . . .

With nothing more to look at, they had seated themselves on a small sofa, placed there for reticent couples, and talked for an hour—a desultory exploring conversation. She recalled none of it. A few mornings later they had met on the Berkeley ferryboat, accidentally no doubt, and he had gone on with her in the train and as far as the campus. . . . Once again. After that, when the lecture was over, in the Greek Theatre . . . wonderful hours . . . how easy to imagine themselves in Greece of the fifth century B.C., alone in that vast gray amphitheatre, the slim, straight tenebrous trees above quivering with the melody of birds!

Never a word of love—not for months. This novel and exciting companionship was enough . . . depths of personality to explore—in glimpses! Sometimes they roamed over the hills, gay and carefree. They never met anyone they knew.

Winter. Weeks of pouring rain. They met in picture galleries, remote corners of the Public Library, obscure restaurants of Little Italy under the shadow of Telegraph Hill. Again they were unseen, undiscovered.

He never came to the house. Since her mother's death and the early marriages of the girls, Uncle Ben had come to live with her in the old house on Russian Hill; the boys were East at school; she was free of all family restrictions, but her old servants were intimate with all the other servants on the Hill. She barely knew his wife. He never spoke of her.

Spring. A house-party in the country, warm and dry after the last of the rains. After dinner they had sat about on the terraces, smoking, drinking, listening to a group singing within, admiring the "ruins" of a Roman temple at the foot of the lawn lit by a blazing moon.

He and she had wandered off the terrace, and up an almost perpendicular flight of steps on the side of the mountain that rose behind the house . . . dim aisles of redwoods, born when the earth was young, whose long trunks never swayed, whose high branches rarely sang in the wind—unfriendly trees, but protective, sentinel-like, shutting out the modern world; reminiscent those closely planted aisles were of ancient races . . . forgotten races . . . god-like races, perhaps.

Well, they had felt like gods that night. How senseless to try to stave off a declaration of love . . . to fear . . . to wonder . . . to worry

. . . How inevitable . . . natural . . . when it came! Hour of hours. . . .

They had met the next day in a corner of their favorite little restaurant, over a dish of spaghetti, which she refused to eat as it had liver in it, and talked the matter out. No, she would not enter upon a secret intrigue; meeting him in some shady quarter of the town, where no questions were asked, in some horrible room which had sheltered thousands of furtive "lovers" before them . . . she would far rather never see him again. . . . He had smiled at the flight taken by an untrained imagination, but nodded. . . . No, but she knew the alternative. He had no intention of giving her up. No hope of a divorce. He had sounded his wife; tentatively at first, then told her outright he loved another woman. She had replied that he could expect no legal release from her. It was her chance for revenge and she would take it. . . . A week or two and his business in San Francisco would be settled . . . he had an independent fortune . . . would she run away with him? Elope in good old style? Could she stand the gaff? All Europe for a perpetual honeymoon— unless his wife were persuaded by her family later on to divorce him. Then he would return and work at something. He was not a born idler.

She had consented, of course, having made up her mind before they met. She had had six years of "the world." She knew what she wanted. One might "love" many times, but not more than once find completion, that solidarity which makes two as one against the malignant forces of life. She had no one to consider but herself. Her mother was dead. Her sisters, protected by husbands, wealth, position, would merely be "thrilled." The boys and Uncle Ben, of course, would be furious. Men were so hopelessly conservative.

For the rest of the world she cared exactly nothing.

That foghorn. What was it trying to tell her? A boat . . . fog . . . why was it so hard to remember? So hard to awaken? Ellen must have given her an overdose. Fragmentary pictures . . . slipping down the dark hill to the wharf . . . her low delighted laugh echoed back to her as he helped her into the boat . . . one more secret lark before they flung down the gage. . . . How magnificently he rowed . . . long, sweeping, easy strokes as he smiled possessively into her eyes and talked of the future. . . . No moon, but millions of stars that shed a misty golden light . . . rows of light on the steep hillsides of the city. The houses dark and silent . . . a burst of music from Fort Mason. . . .

Out through the Golden Gate, still daring . . . riding that oily swell . . . his chuckle as she had dared him to row straight across to China. Her sharp anxious cry as she half-rose from her seat and pointed to a racing mountain of snow-white mist.

He had swept about at once and made for the beach below Sutro

Heights. Too late. Almost as he turned, they were engulfed. Even an old fisherman would have lost his sense of direction.

And then the foghorns began their warnings. The low, menacing roar from Point Benito. The wailing siren on Alcatraz. Sausalito's throaty bass. The deep-toned bell on Angel Island. She knew them all, but they seemed to come from new directions.

A second . . . a moment . . . an hour . . . later . . . a foreign but unmistakable note. Ships—two of them . . . blast and counter-blast. . . . She could barely see his white rigid face through the mist as he thrust his head this way and that trying to locate those sounds. . . . Another abrupt swerve . . . crash . . . shouts . . . her own voice shrieking as she saw his head almost severed—the very fog turn red . . .

She could hear herself screaming yet. It seemed to her that she had been screaming since the beginning of time.

She sat up in bed, clasping her head between her hands, and rocked to and fro. This bare small room, just visible in the gray dawn. . . . She was in a hospital, of course. Was it last night or the night before they had brought her here? She wondered vaguely that she felt no inclination to scream any more, now that she had struggled to full consciousness. . . . Too tired, perhaps . . . the indifference of exhaustion. . . . Even her eyes felt singularly dry, as if they had been baked in a hot oven. She recalled a line, the only memorable line, in Edwin Arnold's *Light of Asia,* "Eyepits red with rust of ancient tears." Did her eyes look like that? But she did not remember crying . . . only screaming.

Odd that she should be left alone like this. Uncle Ben and the girls must have been summoned. If they had gone home, tired out, they should have left a nurse in constant attendance . . . and surely they might have found her a better room. . . . Or had she been carried into some emergency hospital? . . . Well, she could go home today.

Her hands were still clasping her head when another leaf of aware-ness turned over, rattling like parchment. Hair. Her lovely abundant hair. . . . She held her breath as her hands moved exploringly over her head. Harsh short bristles almost scratched them.

She had had brain fever, then. Ill a long time . . . weeks . . . months, perhaps. No wonder she felt weak and spent and indifferent! But she must be out of danger, or they would not leave her like this. . . . Would she suffer later, with renewed mocking strength? Or could love be burnt out, devoured by fever germs? A short time before, while not yet fully conscious, she had relived all the old hopes, fears, dreams, ecstasies; reached out triumphantly to a wondrous future, arrogantly sure of herself and the man, contemptuous of the world and its makeshift conventions. . . . And now she felt nothing. . . .

But when she was well again? Twenty-four! Forty, fifty years more; they were a long-lived family. Her mother had been killed at a railroad crossing. . . . Well, she had always prided herself on her strength. She would worry through the years somehow.

Had the town rung with the scandal when the newspapers flared forth next morning? No girl goes rowing at night with a married man unless there is something between them. Had his wife babbled? Were the self-righteous getting off the orthodoxies of their kind? Punished for their sin. Retributive justice meted out to a girl who would break up a home and take a married man for her lover.

Retributive justice! As if there were any such thing in life as justice. All helpless victims of the law of cause and effect. Futile, aspiring, stupidly confident links in the inexorable chain of circumstance. . . . Commonplace minds croaking, "Like father like daughter" . . .

How she hated, hated, *hated*, self-righteousness, smug hypocrisy . . . illogical minds—one sheep bleating like another sheep—not one of them with the imagination to guess that she never would have stopped to a low secret intrigue.

She had been pounding her knee with her fist in a sudden access of energy. As it sputtered out and she felt on the verge of collapse, her hand unfolded and lay palm down on the quilt. . . . She felt her eyes bulging. She uttered her first sound: a low almost inarticulate cry.

Her hand? That large-veined, skinny thing? She had beautiful long white hands, with skin as smooth as the breast of a dove. Of no one of her beauty's many parts had she been prouder, not even when she stood now and then before the cheval glass and looked critically, and admiringly, at the smooth, white, rounded perfection of her body. She had given them a golden manicure set on one of their birthdays, a just tribute; and they were exquisitely kept, although she hated conspicuous nails.

A delusion? A nightmare? She spread the other hand beside it . . . side by side the two on the dingy counterpane . . . old hands. . . . Shorn hair will grow again . . . but hands . . .

Mumbling. Why mumbling? She raised one of those withered yellow hands to her mouth. It was empty. Her shaking fingers unbuttoned the high night-gown, and she glanced within. Pendent dugs, brown and shrivelled.

Brain fever! The sun had risen. She looked up at the high barred window. She understood.

Voices at the door. She dropped back on the pillow and closed her eyes and lay still.

The door was unlocked, and a man and woman entered: doctor and nurse, as was immediately evident. The doctor's voice was brisk and business-like and deeply mature; the woman's, young and deferential.

"Do you think she'll wake again, doctor?"

"Probably not. I thought she would be gone by now, but she is still breathing." He clasped the emaciated wrist with his strong fingers. "Very feeble. It won't be long now."

"Is it true, doctor, that sometimes, just before death, reason is restored and they remember and talk quite rationally?"

"Sometimes. But not for this case. Too many years. Look in every hour, and when it is over, ring me up. There are relatives to be notified. Quite important people, I believe."

"What are they like?"

"Never seen them. The law firm in charge of her estate pays the bills. Why should they come here? Couldn't do her any good, and nothing is so depressing as these melancholia cases. It's a long time now since she was stark raving. That was before my time. Come along. Six wards after this one. Don't forget to look in. Good little girl. I know you never forget."

They went out and locked the door.

The Garrison

Donald A. Wollheim

You may recall reading of the discovery several years ago of an ancient temple of Mithra being uncovered strictly by accident in the business city of London during the excavations for a new building. It made a bit of a sensation for a while—not that it was any secret that there had been such a faith during the Roman days, but that somehow this temple, basically untouched—if you disregard having been filled with silt and many feet of dirt—had been there all the past seventeen centuries without anyone suspecting its existence.

It brought home to some of us just how many wonders and secrets are buried from sight beneath the busy everyday feet of men and women. Surely all the towns and cities, the farmers' fields, and the scenic mountains of old Europe and Asia must conceal beneath their folds innumerable fragments of human meanderings over the past thousands of years. The fact that there was once a major empire that rivaled Egypt and Babylon for power and size which had been very nearly totally forgotten until only the past dozen years is something that still staggers historians. I refer, of course, to the Hittites, mentioned once in the Bible and then forgotten.

Of course, for Americans like myself there is an extra marvel in this evidence of antiquities untold. We live in such a new country, inhabited before us only by nomadic savages, so that when a building is a mere hundred and fifty years old we put a plaque on it and visitors come to stand in the street and stare at it. I was driving along a road in New England when I saw one of those markers. It said something about somebody having erected a grist mill there in 1712. Big thing for us! But tell me, how many mills in Europe and Asia still standing and operating were already old when this American thing was first built?

That's what confounds me as an American. In Europe a house less than five hundred years old wouldn't get a second glance. Why, there must be slums all over the Old World whose dirty old hovels are a thousand years standing! But I'm getting away from what I started out to tell. About that temple in London having gone unnoticed. I can tell you now that there's something like that in New York, too.

I know it seems impossible, for after all there were no Romans here. That's true and I'm not going to claim otherwise. But still there was a structure uncovered in Manhattan Borough once that gave the archeologists a start. How is it that you've never heard of it? Well, that's my story.

I never heard of it either and I've lived here all my life. I've been a magazine feature writer for many years now and I've probed into a lot of odd places about this city for stories. But this is a part of one such story that I never did write up. I'm only putting it down now, just for the record, as it were.

Oh, the main story was written long ago and sold, and the magazine containing it will be found now only in secondhand stores, if anyone still wants it, which I doubt. It was about the subways of New York and mostly about the first subways and the old ones.

I covered the well-known subways, to be sure. The story of the IRT and the BMT and of the tunnels they dug and discarded—there are a couple such way down near the Battery—and the story of the original plans and the difficulties that were encountered—underground streams and suchlike. The subway management cooperated with me. I walked the rails under the East River and I poked through their old blueprints and files, talked with engineers, and took pictures of some old tunnels.

Then one old-timer, a dispatcher he was, mentioned that there was a private subway in New York practically nobody knew about. Not any of the big three. It ran—and still runs, as a matter of fact—from the Manhattan office of the gas works under the river to Randalls Island where the gas company maintains a pumping station and storage tank. That was news to me and sounded like just the ticket to round off my article.

I called up the gas company and after beating my way through a dozen officials finally found one who thought he could help me. I went up there to his office and told him what I had heard. He nodded, confirmed it. Yes, there really was a subway that had been built by the gas company about seventy years ago. They'd built it because there was no convenient ferry or bridge at that end of Manhattan to reach their works—Randalls Island being a small, uninhabited isle in the middle of the East River with Queensborough on the far side. Some company bigwig had money to burn and an idea. It wasn't such a hot idea.

The fact was, the man said, it was never officially put into use. It was a regular boring, a full-size single-track tunnel running underground and under the river bottom. But after it had been built and the track laid, it just turned out to be unnecessary.

Was it still passable? Could I get to see it?

The official scratched his head. He didn't know for sure. The matter had never come up. So he gave me a note to the superintendent of the works up at 135th Street and the riverfront and asked him to look into it with me.

I went up there and found the super. He knew about the private subway all right. Its Manhattan station, if you could call it that, was right here in this building, in the basement, he said. In fact, and what was more, the subway was clear and it was actually used. One man used it, once a day.

That man was the watchman of the Randalls Island installation. He lived in Manhattan in the neighborhood and each morning he would take his lunch box, go down to the basement, climb aboard a little hand-driven truck standing on the rails and go on down that long, dark tunnel under the river to Randalls Island. In the evening when his duties were done, he'd get aboard it and run it back again. Just one man, imagine! A whole subway line to serve one man!

Nothing would suffice but that I'd have to make that trip with him. Well, he was out at the island now, I'd have to wait until he returned. I did that, too. Went down to the basement, under the gas works, and found a little tiled room at one end of it. Sure enough, there were the end of tracks running out of a whopping big wide round hole in the wall. Look down into it—total darkness.

I sat down there on a small bench and looked down that hole around five o'clock and after a while I heard a faint humming in the tracks. Then I saw a tiny light way off down that huge rat hole and by and by it came closer and there was this little hand truck with an old guy standing on it pumping the handles up and down vigorously, the light coming from a battery lamp set on the truck.

When the truck pulled up and stopped, I asked the old fellow whether he'd take me along tomorrow morning. He was quite pleased, talked a good deal about the trip. Most of the men who worked in the plant were scared stiff at the thought of it. It didn't bother him, for he'd been doing it for thirty years already.

But I'm not going to tell you about this—I've already written about that weird trip down the pitch-black hole with nobody but the old man and the crazy shadows as he bobbed up and down on that pump and the single light pushing into that absolute darkness. It was damp and silent and spooky as all hell—and yet, in a way, fun.

I'd taken a big flashlight of my own along and searched the old walls, the grimy tiling, the ancient piping, and you know, it was in pretty good condition still. When we got to Randalls Island, I saw something interesting. There was a branch of the subway going off in a side direction, but no tracks.

Later on, I asked the old watchman about it. He frowned a bit, trying to recollect. "Oh, yes," he said finally, "I never pay no attention to it. When they first built this thing they was going to extend it across the island and connect it up with the Queens side. But that there section of side tunnel is as far as they got. They changed their minds fast after they'd got a little way along it."

"How's that? What made them stop?" I asked, sensing a story.

"They never rightly said. I've heard stories, of course. My father, who worked for the company in those days, once told me they'd run into some old diggings and decided not to bust them up."

"Old diggings? Dutch? Indian? I never heard of any discoveries having been made here," I said.

"Well, I wouldn't know. I never paid no attention to that sort of museum stuff. I supposed the professors had found what they wanted and put it in books and all that. Maybe they didn't, though. Maybe they didn't at that. My pa did say they was sort of quiet about it all." The old fellow was enjoying himself. He had visions of seeing himself in print. I pressed my luck.

"Could you stop at that side tunnel going back and wait for me to walk along it to where they stopped excavating?"

The old fellow thought awhile, then said he'd accommodate me. Sometimes I wish he hadn't been so helpful.

That evening we got back on the handcart and pumped our way a little bit down the track until we found the dark branch-off. We stopped the truck and I got down with my flashlight. The watchman said he'd stay on the truck and wait for my return.

So I walked down that pitch-black tunnel by myself, my steps echoing hollowly in that pipe, big enough for a subway car to fit through. The tunnel turned sharply and the light of the hand truck was cut off. I flashed my light ahead, saw where the diggers had stopped.

There was an abrupt end of the tiling and piping. Beyond was a stretch of several yards of raw stone cut through with pick and drill. Beyond that there were some black breaks and loose masses of small rocks and debris. I walked as far as I could, flashed my beam and saw that what had happened was that they'd broken into what was apparently an underground cavern or hole.

I started to climb over the piles of rock to reach the lip of the breakthrough and when I'd stretched out my body through the opening to look through, I noticed something. I wasn't lying on dirt and rock any more—I was lying, at least my chest and elbows, on smooth, chiseled rock, rock that had been squared off and joined to blocks of other rock by angles out like a jigsaw puzzle. This rock was different than the kind in the passage outside—it looked as if it were something that had been constructed, like part of a wall.

And that's what it was, a thick wall. An artificially constructed wall, several feet thick, beyond which was the dark expanse of a buried structure. The excavators had broken into a room of this structure, a room still standing, whose ceiling had not crumpled.

I flashed my light around. The walls were smooth and undecorated. I couldn't place the style, but it was old. It had to be old to have been under all that soil and so forgotten.

I climbed through, stood up in that damned lightless room and figured I'd made the find of the century. I'd be famous. I knew no Dutchman could have built that place, it was long before their time; they weren't building stone fortresses without cement. It reminded me of what I'd read of the Inca walls, but I was willing to bet this was older even than any Inca structure.

I crossed that empty room—a watchtower, I think now that it must have been, and at the end of it was a dark hole. It was probably meant for a ladder, but there was nothing there now. I knelt down beside that hole and looked down to see what was below.

It was vast down there. That much I knew. I realized that I was high up above the next landing. I felt it, I sensed it, that down below me was a drop of hundreds of feet. I flashed my light down and it barely shone on a smooth stone surface far, far below. I was beginning to get frightened then, and I don't scare easily. How big was this place, I thought to myself. If it was a fortress, who built it and when and against what enemy?

For it was a fortress, of that I'm convinced. It was made to stand age and siege and fire and sword. It was made to stand tons of rock piled on it; it was made impregnable to man and nature.

And then I wondered why the tunnel diggers had kept mum about it. I wondered that while staring down that hole into the unknown depths of the fortress below me. And by and by, I suspected something. I suspected the answer. And when I was sure of it, I got up, kept my flashlight away from that hole and made my way out. I got back to the watchman and we went back to Manhattan and I made my way home through the electric lights and the hurly-burly and the mobs in the streets and I was near crazy with wonder and the mystery of the universe. I looked up at the sky and I saw a million stars shining down and knew that to them and their mysteries all this clamor and bustle was tinsel and junk.

I knew why the excavators had shut up about the old fortress they'd dug into under the surface of the metropolis. The Temple of Mithra in London was ruined and abandoned. The catacombs of Rome have served their purpose and have been left to the curious. The great city of Angkor has been deserted by its citizens and left to the jungle.

But when I looked down that hole in the buried watchtower's floor, down into the keep of the fortress, into the darkness there, I saw a light appear. I saw a sentinel go his rounds. I saw a member of the garrison still keeping up the vigil against an enemy that would not be one of the insignificant cloth-covered biped scramblers of the surface, but something that would be coming some day from the place that fortress was built to oppose, something worthy of that monstrous trooper's steel.

There are still some things that it is necessary to conceal for the sake of human pride. One of them is that that fortress, which is older than our entire geological epoch, has never been abandoned.

Gavon's Eve

E. F. Benson

It is only the largest kind of ordnance map that records the existence of the village of Gavon, in the shire of Sutherland, and it is perhaps surprising that any map on whatever scale should mark so small and huddled a group of huts, set on a bare, bleak headland between moor and sea, and, so one would have thought, of no import at all to any who did not happen to live there. But the river Gavon, on the right bank of which stand this half-dozen of chimneyless and wind-swept habitations, is a geographical fact of far greater interest to outsiders, for the salmon there are heavy fish, the mouth of the river is clear of nets, and all the way up to Gavon Loch, some six miles inland, the coffee-coloured water lies in pool after deep pool, which verge, if the river is in order and the angler moderately sanguine, on a fishing probability amounting almost to a certainty. In any case, during the first fortnight of September last I had no blank day on those delectable waters, and up till the 15th of that month there was no day on which some one at the lodge in which I was stopping did not land a fish out of the famous Picts' pool. But after the 15th that pool was not fished again. The reason why is here set forward.

The river at this point, after some hundred yards of rapid, makes a sudden turn round a rocky angle, and plunges madly into the pool itself. Very deep water lies at the head of it, but deeper still further down on the east side, where a portion of the stream flicks back again in a swift dark backwater towards the top of the pool again. It is fishable only from the western bank, for to the east, above this backwater, a great wall of black and basaltic rock, heaved up no doubt by some fault in strata, rises sheer from the river to the height of some sixty feet. It is in fact nearly precipitous on both sides, heavily serrated at the top, and of so curious a thinness, that at about the middle of it where a fissure breaks its topmost edge, and some twenty feet from the top, there exists a long hole, a sort of lancet window, one would say, right through the rock, so that a slit of daylight can be seen through it. Since, therefore, no one would care to cast his line standing perched on that razor-edged eminence, the pool must needs be fished from the western bank. A decent fly, however, will cover it all.

It is on the western bank that there stand the remains of that which gave its title to the pool, namely, the ruins of a Pict castle, built out of rough and scarcely hewn masonry, unmortared but on a certain large and impressive scale, and in a very well-preserved condition considering its extreme antiquity. It is circular in shape and measures some twenty yards of diameter in its internal span. A staircase of large blocks with a rise of at least a foot leads up to the main gate, and opposite this on the side towards the river is another smaller postern through which down a rather hazardously steep slope a scrambling path, where progress demands both caution and activity, conducts to the head of the pool which lies immediately beneath it. A gate-chamber still roofed over exists in the solid wall: inside there are foundation indications of three rooms, and in the centre of all a very deep hole, probably a well. Finally, just outside the postern leading to the river is a small artificially levelled platform, some twenty feet across, as if made to support some super-incumbent edifice. Certain stone slabs and blocks are dispersed over it.

Brora, the post-town of Gavon, lies some six miles to the south-west, and from it a track over the moor leads to the rapids immediately above the Picts' pool, across which by somewhat extravagant striding from boulder to boulder a man can pass dry-foot when the river is low, and make his way up a steep path to the north of the basaltic rock, and so to the village. But this transit demands a steady head, and at the best is a somewhat giddy passage. Otherwise the road between it and Brora lies in a long detour higher up the moor, passing by the gates of Gavon Lodge, where I was stopping. For some vague and ill-defined reason the pool itself and the Picts' Castle had an uneasy reputation on the country-side, and several times trudging back from a day's fishing I have known my gillie take a longish circuit, though heavy with fish, rather than make this short cut in the dusk by the castle. On the first occasion when Sandy, a strapping yellow-bearded viking of twenty-five, did this he gave as a reason that the ground round about the castle was "mossy," though as a God-fearing man he must have known he lied. But on another occasion he was more frank, and said that the Picts' pool was "no canny" after sunset. I am now inclined to agree with him, though, when he lied about it, I think it was because as a God-fearing man he feared the devil also.

It was on the evening of September 14 that I was walking back with my host, Hugh Graham, from the forest beyond the lodge. It had been a day unseasonably hot for the time of year, and the hills were blanketed with soft, furry clouds. Sandy, the gillie of whom I have spoken, was behind with the ponies, and, idly enough, I told Hugh about this strange distaste for the Picts' pool after sunset. He listened, frowning a little.

"That's curious," he said. "I know there is some dim local superstition about the place, but last year certainly Sandy used to laugh at it. I remember asking him what ailed the place, and he said he thought nothing about the rubbish folk talked. But this year you say he avoids it."

"On several occasions with me he has done so."

Hugh smoked awhile in silence, striding noiselessly over the dusky fragrant heather.

"Poor chap," he said, "I don't know what to do about him. He's becoming useless."

"Drink?" I asked.

"Yes, drink in a secondary manner. But trouble led to drink, and trouble, I am afraid, is leading him to worse than drink."

"The only thing worse than drink is the devil," I remarked.

"Precisely. That's where he is going. He goes there often."

205

"What on earth do you mean?" I asked.

"Well, it's rather curious," said Hugh. "You know I dabble a bit in folklore and local superstition, and I believe I am on the track of something odder than odd. Just wait a moment."

We stood there in the gathering dusk till the ponies laboured up the hillside to us, Sandy with his six feet of lithe strength strolling easily beside them up the steep brae, as if his long day's trudging had but served to half awaken his dormant powers of limb.

"Going to see Mistress Macpherson again tonight?" asked Hugh.

"Aye, puir body," said Sandy. "She's auld, and she's lone."

"Very kind of you, Sandy," said Hugh, and we walked on.

"What then?" I asked when the ponies had fallen behind again.

"Why, superstition lingers here," said Hugh, "and it's supposed she's a witch. To be quite candid with you, the thing interests me a good deal. Supposing you asked me, on oath, whether I believed in witches, I should say 'No.' But if you asked me again, on oath, whether I suspected I believed in them, I should, I think, say 'Yes.' And the fifteenth of this month—to-morrow—is Gavon's Eve."

"And what in Heaven's name is that?" I asked. "And who is Gavon? And what's the trouble?"

"Well, Gavon is the person, I suppose, not saint, who is what we should call the eponymous hero of this district. And the trouble is Sandy's trouble. Rather a long story. But there's a long mile in front of us yet, if you care to be told."

During that mile I heard. Sandy had been engaged a year ago to a girl of Gavon who was in service at Inverness. In March last he had gone, without giving notice, to see her, and as he walked up the street in which her mistress's house stood, had met her suddenly face to face, in company with a man whose clipped speech betrayed him English, whose manner a kind of gentleman. He had a flourish of his hat for Sandy, pleasure to see him, and scarcely any need of explanation as to how he came to be walking with Catrine. It was the most natural thing possible, for a city like Inverness boasted its innocent urbanities, and a girl could stroll with a man. And for the time, since also Catrine was so frankly pleased to see him, Sandy was satisfied. But after his return to Gavon, suspicion, fungus-like, grew rank in his mind, with the result that a month ago he had, with infinite pains and blottings, written a letter to Catrine, urging her return and immediate marriage. Thereafter it was known that she had left Inverness; it was known that she had arrived by train at Brora. From Brora she had started to walk across the moor by the path leading just above the Picts' Castle, crossing the rapids to Gavon, leaving her box to be sent by the carrier. But at Gavon she had never arrived. Also it was said that, although it was hot afternoon, she wore a big cloak.

By this time we had come to the lodge, the lights of which showed dim and blurred through the thick hill-mists that had streamed sullenly down from the higher ground.

"And the rest," said Hugh, "which is as fantastic as this is sober fact, I will tell you later."

Now, a fruit-bearing determination to go to bed is, to my mind, as difficult to ripen as a fruit-bearing determination to get up, and in spite of our long day, I was glad when Hugh (the rest of the men having yawned themselves out of the smoking-room) came back from the hospitable dispensing of bedroom candlesticks with a briskness that denoted that, as far as he was concerned, the distressing determination was not imminent.

"As regards Sandy," I suggested.

"Ah, I also was thinking of that," he said. "Well, Catrine Gordon left Brora, and never arrived here. That is fact. Now for what remains. Have you any remembrance of a woman always alone walking about the moor by the loch? I think I once called your attention to her."

"Yes, I remember," I said. "Not Catrine, surely; a very old woman, awful to look at. Moustache, whiskers, and muttering to herself. Always looking at the ground, too."

"Yes, that is she—not Catrine. Catrine! My word, a May morning! But the other—it is Mrs. Macpherson, reputed witch. Well, Sandy trudges there, a mile and more away, every night to see her. You know Sandy: Adonis of the north. Now, can you account by any natural explanation for that fact? That he goes off after a long day to see an old hag in the hills?"

"It would seem unlikely," said I.

"Unlikely! Well, yes, unlikely."

Hugh got up from his chair and crossed the room to where a bookcase of rather fusty-looking volumes stood between windows. He took a small morocco-backed book from a top shelf.

"Superstitions of Sutherlandshire," he said, as he handed it to me. "Turn to page 128, and read."

"September 15 appears to have been the date of what we may call this devil festival. On the night of that day the powers of darkness held preeminent dominion, and over-rode for any who were abroad that night and invoked their aid, the protective Providence of Almighty God. Witches, therefore, above all, were peculiarly potent. On this night any witch could entice to herself the heart and the love of any young man who consulted her on matters of philtre or love charm, with the result that on any night in succeeding years of the same date, he, though he was lawfully affianced and wedded, would for that night be hers. If, however, he should call on the name of God through any sudden grace of the Spirit, her charm would be of no avail. On this night, too, all witches had the power by certain dreadful incantations and indescribable profanities, to raise from the dead those who had committed suicide."

"Top of the next page," said Hugh. "Leave out this next paragraph; it does not bear on this last."

"Near a small village in this country," I read, "called Gavon, the moon at midnight is said to shine through a certain gap or fissure in a wall of rock close beside the river on to the ruins of a Pict castle, so that the light of its beams falls on to a large flat stone erected there near the gate, and supposed by some to be an ancient and pagan altar. At that moment, so the superstition still lingers in the countryside, the evil and malignant spirits which hold sway on Gavon's Eve, are at the zenith of their powers, and those who invoke their aid at this moment and in this place, will, though with infinite peril to their immortal souls, get all that they desire of them."

The paragraph on the subject ended here, and I shut the book.

"Well?" I asked.

"Under favourable circumstances two and two make four," said Hugh.

"And four means—"

"This. Sandy is certainly in consultation with a woman who is supposed to be a witch, whose path no crofter will cross after nightfall. He wants to learn, at whatever cost, poor devil, what happened to Catrine. Thus I think it more than possible that to-morrow, at midnight, there will be folk by the Picts' pool. There is another curious thing. I was fishing yesterday, and just opposite the river gate of the castle, someone has set up a great flat stone, which has been dragged (for I noticed the crushed grass) from the débris at the bottom of the slope."

"You mean that the old hag is going to try to raise the body of Catrine, if she is dead?"

"Yes, and I mean to see myself what happens. Come too."

The next day Hugh and I fished down the river from the lodge, taking with us not Sandy, but another gillie, and ate our lunch on the slope of the Picts' Castle after landing a couple of fish there. Even as Hugh had said, a great flat slab of stone had been dragged on to the platform outside the river gate of the castle, where it rested on certain rude supports, which, now that it was in place, seemed certainly designed to receive it. It was also exactly opposite that lancet window in the basaltic rock across the pool, so that if the moon at midnight did shine through it, the light would fall on the stone. This, then, was the almost certain scene of the incantations.

Below the platform, as I have said, the ground fell rapidly away to the level of the pool, which owing to rain on the hills was running very high, and, streaked with lines of greyish bubbles, poured down in amazing and ear-filling volume. But directly underneath the steep escarpment of rock on the far side of the pool it lay foamless and black, a still backwater of great depth. Above the altar-like erection again the ground rose up seven rough-hewn steps to the gate itself, on each side of which, to the height of about four feet, ran the circular wall of the castle. Inside again were the remains of partition walls between the three chambers, and it was in the one nearest to the river gate that we determined to conceal ourselves that night. From there, should the witch and Sandy keep tryst at the altar, any sound of movement would reach us, and through the aperture of the gate itself we could see, concealed in the shadow of the wall, whatever took place at the altar or down below at the pool. The lodge, finally, was but a short ten minutes away, if one went in the direct line, so that by starting at a quarter to twelve that night, we could enter the Picts' Castle by the gate away from the river, thus not betraying our presence to those who might be waiting for the moment when the moon should shine through the lancet window in the wall of rock on to the altar in front of the river gate.

Night fell very still and windless, and when not long before midnight we let ourselves silently out of the lodge, though to the east the sky was clear, a black continent of cloud was creeping up from the west, and had now nearly reached the zenith. Out of the remote fringes of it occasional lightning winked, and the growl of very distant thunder sounded drowsily at long intervals after. But it seemed to me as if another storm hung over our heads, ready every moment to burst, for the oppression in the air was of a far heavier quality than so distant a disturbance could have accounted for.

To the east, however, the sky was still luminously clear; the curiously hard edges of the western cloud were star-embroidered, and by the dove-coloured light in the east it was evident that the moonrise over the moor was imminent. And though I did not in my heart believe that our expedition would end in anything but yawns, I was conscious of an extreme tension and rawness of nerves, which I set down to the thunder-charged air.

For noiselessness of footstep we had both put on india-rubber-soled shoes, and all the way down to the pool we heard nothing but the distant thunder and our own padded tread. Very silently and cautiously we ascended the steps of the gate away from the river, and keeping close to the wall inside, sidled round to the river gate and peered out. For the first moment I could see nothing, so black lay the shadow of the rock-wall opposite across the pool, but by degrees I made out the lumps and line of the glimmering foam which streaked the water. High as the river was running this morning it was infinitely more voluminous and turbulent now, and the sound of it filled and bewildered the ear with its sonorous roaring. Only under the very base of the rock opposite it ran quite black and unflecked by foam: there lay the deep still surface of the backwater. Then suddenly I saw something black move in the dimness in front of me, and against the grey foam rose up first the head, then the shoulders, and finally the whole figure of a woman coming towards us up the bank. Behind her walked another, a man, and the two came to where the altar of stone had been newly erected and stood there side by side silhouetted against the churned white of the stream. Hugh had seen too, and touched me on the arm to call my attention. So far then he was right: there was no mistaking the stalwart proportions of Sandy.

Suddenly across the gloom shot a tiny spear of light, and momentarily as we watched, it grew larger and longer, till a tall beam, as from some window cut in the rock opposite, was shed on the bank below us. It moved slowly, imperceptibly to the left till it struck full between the two black figures standing there, and shone with a curious bluish gleam on the flat stone in front of them. Then the roar of the river was suddenly overscored by a dreadful screaming voice, the voice of a woman, and from her side her arms shot up and out as if in invocation of some power. At first I could catch none of the words, but soon from repetition they began to convey an intelligible message to my brain, and I was listening as in paralytic horror of nightmare to a bellowing of the most hideous and un-nameable profanity. What I heard I cannot bring myself to record; suffice it to say that Satan was invoked by every adoring and reverent name, that cursing and unspeakable malediction was poured forth on Him whom we hold most holy. Then the yelling voice ceased as suddenly as it had begun, and for a moment there was silence again, but for the reverberating river.

Then once more that horror of sound was uplifted.

"So, Catrine Gordon," it cried, "I bid ye in the name of my master and yours to rise from where ye lie. Up with ye—up!"

Once more there was silence; then I heard Hugh at my elbow draw a quick sobbing breath, and his finger pointed unsteadily to the dead black water below the rock. And I too looked and saw.

Right under the rock there appeared a pale subaqueous light, which waved and quivered in the stream. At first it was very small and dim, but as we looked it seemed to swim upwards from remote depths and grew larger till I suppose the space of some square yard was illuminated by it. Then the surface of the water was broken, and a head, the head of a girl, dead-white and with long, flowing hair, appeared above the stream. Her eyes were shut, the corners of her mouth drooped as in sleep, and the

210

moving water stood in a frill round her neck. Higher and higher rose the figure out of the tide, till at last it stood, luminous in itself, so it appeared, up to the middle. The head was bend down over the breast, and the hands clasped together. As it emerged from the water it seemed to get nearer, and was by now half-way across the pool, moving quietly and steadily against the great flood of the hurrying river.

Then I heard a man's voice crying out in a sort of strangled agony.

"Catrine!" it cried; "Catrine! In God's name; in God's name!"

In two strides Sandy had rushed down the steep bank, and hurled himself out into that mad swirl of waters. For one moment I saw his arms flung up into the sky, the next he had altogether gone. And on the utterance of that name the unholy vision had vanished too, while simultaneously there burst in front of us a light so blinding, followed by a crack of thunder so appalling to the senses, that I know I just hid my face in my hands. At once, as if the flood-gates of the sky had been opened, the deluge was on us, not like rain, but like one sheet of solid water, so that we cowered under it. Any hope or attempt to rescue Sandy was out of the question; to dive into that whirlpool of mad water meant instant death, and even had it been possible for any swimmer to live there, in the blackness of the night there was absolutely no chance of finding him. Besides, even if it had been possible to save him, I doubt whether I was sufficiently master of my flesh and blood as to endure to plunge where that apparition had risen.

Then, as we lay there, another horror filled and possessed my mind. Somewhere close to us in the darkness was that woman whose yelling voice just now had made my blood run ice-cold, while it brought the streaming sweat to my forehead. At that moment I turned to Hugh.

"I cannot stop here," I said. "I must run, run right away. Where is She?"

"Did you not see?" he asked.

"No. What happened?"

"The lightning struck the stone within a few inches of where she was standing. We—we must go and look for her."

I followed him down the slope, shaking as if I had the palsy, and groping with my hands on the ground in front of me, in deadly terror of encountering something human. The thunderclouds had in the last few minutes spread over the moon, so that no ray from the window in the rock guided our search. But up and down the bank from the stone that lay shattered there to the edge of the pool we groped and stumbled, but found nothing. At length we gave it up: it seemed morally certain that she, too, had rolled down the bank after the lightning stroke, and lay somewhere deep in the pool from which she had called the dead.

None fished the pool next day, but men with drag-nets came from

Brora. Right under the rock in the backwater lay two bodies, close together, Sandy and the dead girl. Of the other they found nothing.

It would seem, then, that Catrine Gordon, in answer to Sandy's letter, left Inverness in heavy trouble. What happened afterwards can only be conjectured, but it seems likely she took the short cut to Gavon, meaning to cross the river on the boulders above the Picts' pool. But whether she slipped accidentally in her passage, and so was drawn down by the hungry water, or whether unable to face the future, she had thrown herself into the pool, we can only guess. In any case they sleep together now in the bleak, wind-swept graveyard at Brora, in obedience to the inscrutable designs of God.

The Ghastly Priest Doth Reign

Manly Wade Wellman

The jury found Jack Bowdry not guilty of murder. All anybody could testify was that he'd cursed and damned Kib Wordin for a witch-man and gave him twenty-four hours to leave the Sawback Mountain country, and twenty-five hours later Kib Wordin lay dead under the creepy tree in his cabin yard with a homemade silver bullet in his head. Come to think, a witch-man had died at that red-painted cabin thirty years back, and another witch-man years before that.

Anyway, Jack's neighbors helped him fetch his stuff from the county jail and rejoiced him up Walnut Creek to his home place next to Hosea's Hollow. They'd shucked his corn for him, handed and hung his tobacco in the curing barn. All vowed he'd done a good thing about Kib Wordin, whatever the jury couldn't decide, and at sundown that pretty fall day they good-byed him at his door.

Tolly Paradine, the schoolmaster's daughter, waited with him, making him feel almighty big because she was so little, with her pale-gold hair and rosy-gold cheeks. He stood a foot over her and near about a foot broader, with his brickbat jaw and big hands dangling from his blue shirtsleeves with gray-threaded black hair, with thirty-four years to Tolly's twenty.

"I redded your place up for you," she said. "Jack, I'm proud you'll neighbor us again. And glad Kib Wordin won't pester me no more to come live with him."

He stared up slope to the ridge. "Better haste to catch up you daddy yonder," he said. "I'll come visit tomorrow if you say I can."

"Well you know you can, Jack." She upped to kiss his rough cheek, then ran after her folks. Jack looked again at what he'd seen to make him hurry her off from there.

Against the soft evening sky at ridge top stood a squatty man, with a long, ashy-pale coat down to his ankles. As Jack looked, the fellow slid away into some brushy trees.

"Huh," said Jack Bowdry, deep in his deep chest, and faced toward his notch-logged cabin with its lime-painted clay chinking. He pushed the door open and set foot on the sill. Then he scowled down at what he'd near about stepped on. A gold coin, big as a half dollar, a double eagle such as was still round when Roosevelt started being President. It looked put there for him to pick up.

He glowered back to where that long-coated somebody had been. Then he toed the coin down into the yard and kicked it away in a twinkle of light into the bushes and went inside.

His cabin was just the one long room. The plank floor was swept. On the fireplace crane hung a kettle of stewed chicken, dumplings, carrots, the things Tolly knew he relished most. Jack built a fire under the kettle and put the match to the wick of his lamp. It let him see his bed at the far end, made up with a brown blanket and a white pillow, more of Tolly's doing. A smile creased the corners of Jack's wide mouth as he set the lamp on the fireboard, under his rifle and shotgun on the deer horns up there, and next to the row of books he'd read over and over.

Grandma Cutshaw's Bible; *Amateur Builder's Handbook;* Macaulay's poems that Jack almost knew by heart; *Guide to Rocks and Minerals; Jack Ranger's School Days; Robinson Crusoe;* Hill's *Manual of Social and Business Forms,* how to make a will, figure interest, all like that; and—

But he had only seven books. What was this one with the white paper cover at the end of the row?

He took it down. *Albertus Magnus, or White and Black Magic for Man and Beast.* Jack had heard tell of it, that you couldn't throw or give it away or burn it, you must bury it and say a funeral over it like for a dead man. Tolly had never left that here for him, nor either that gold eagle on the door log. The book flopped open in his hand:

. . . in the red forest there is a red church, and in the red church stands a red altar, and upon the red altar there lies a red knife; take the red knife and cut red bread.

Jack slammed it shut and put it back on the shelf. Tomorrow he'd show it to Tolly's educated father. He took down the Macaulay and opened it to wash away the taste of the other book. Here was "The Battle of Lake Regillus":

> *Those trees in whose dim shadow*
> *The ghastly priest doth reign,*
> *The priest who slew the slayer*
> *And shall himself be slain*

Now, what in hell might that mean? He shoved the Macaulay back, too, and spooned out a plateful of chicken stew and carried it to his table. Tasty, the stew was. He was glad to find himself enjoying to eat, proving to himself that he wasn't pestered by all these funny happenings. Even after two big helps, enough was left in the kettle to hot up for noon dinner tomorrow. Jack lighted his corncob pipe and went yet again for a book. Better be the Bible this time. He carried it and the lamp to the table.

Grandma used to cast signs, open the Bible anywhere and put a finger on whatever text is there. Do that three times and figure out the meaning. Jack opened the Bible midway and stabbed down his big finger.

. . . preparest a table before me in the presence of mine enemies.

The Twenty-third Psalm. Tolly had prepared Jack a mighty good table. But the presence of enemies, now. He opened farther along, pointed again.

. . . cried out, Great is Diana of the Ephesians.

Book of Acts that time, and Saint Paul getting hollered at, scolded. One more time, the very last page, a verse at the end of Revelation.

. . . Without are dogs, and sorcerers . . .

Just then, a scrabbling at the door.

Jack sailed out of his chair, dropping the Bible and snatching his double-bitted axe from beside the fireplace. He ran and grabbed the latch string and yanked the door inward. "What's going out here?" he roared.

A half-cowering shape backed off down the path toward the road. "Where did you come from?" Jack yelled at it.

It stood up then, in a drench of moonlight, in its long pale coat, lifting its hands toward him. Not a dog, after all. Jack charged, axe lifted, and the shape scuttled away among the trees. Jack stood alone in the moon-bright road. Something else hurried at him from down-slope. Again he whirled up the axe.

"Jack!" cried Tolly Paradine's voice.

He caught her wrist. "I thought you were that other one yonder."

"No, I came to tell you—"

"Inside, quick." He whirled her along the path and into the cabin and slammed the door behind them. Tolly looked at him with big scared eyes, and her golden skin was as pale as her hair.

"How come you to be out?" Jack demanded.

"Daddy was reading in a book he's got," she quavered. "It's *The Golden Bough*, somebody named Frazer wrote it."

"Ain't never heard tell of it." He cracked the door open, peered out, then shut them in again. "What's a book got to do with it?"

"Daddy says there's some kind of old worship." She dropped into his chair. "Long time ago, over the sea, somewhere near Rome. But longer ago than Rome." She trembled her lips. "Folks worshipped Diana."

"Just so happens I was reading in the Bible about Diana," Jack told her. "Wasn't she the hunting goddess, goddess of the moon? I recollect that from a book in school."

"Daddy says she was all kinds of goddess. They worshipped her with fire; sometimes they killed people for a sacrifice. Why, Daddy says some scholars think the whole witch business comes down from old worship of Diana. Like Kib Wordin's witch stuff."

"There's another tale about Diana," remembered Jack, leaning against the fireboard. "A man was out hunting and he seen her in swimming, naked as a jaybird. It was just a happen-so, but she flung water on him and turned him into a buck deer for his own dogs to pull down and kill. Ain't what sounds like a good goddess to worship."

"In those old days, the chief priest lived under a sacred tree," Tolly pattered on. "And when somebody killed him, that fellow got to be the priest, till another killed *him*, and—"

She fell quiet. Jack frowned.

"What sort of tree is it got to be?" he asked her.

"Daddy never said that." Her eyes got wider. "You're thinking on that tree at Kib Wordin's place. Maybe one like that. No telling what a tree can get to be, over thousands of years, no more than what worship can get to be."

"And before Kib Wordin, a witch-man died up there," Jack reminded. "And before him, another one."

"And now—" she began, but again she stopped.

"And now, you aim to say, it's me," he finished for her. He shook his

215

head, and his black hair stirred. "All right, what if old Jack Bowdry just ain't accepting the nomination? What if I just ain't having it, no way?"

"Daddy explained me about it," she stammered. "A branch from that old witch-tree could be planted and grow to a witch-tree itself, and be their worship place." She looked near about ready to cry. "You don't believe it's so," she half accused.

"Yes, I do. Stuff tonight makes me to believe."

He told her about the man in the long gray coat, the gold coin, the messages from the books.

"What man was it?" asked Tolly. "I don't call to mind anybody with a coat like that."

"I doubt if he wore it to be known," said Jack. "Anyway, it's like he was here to threaten me, and the money to buy me, and this here book to teach me."

He took down *Albertus Magnus*. "No, Tolly, don't touch it. Anyway, I've seen that tree at Wordin's place, far off. Maybe it's what's grown up to cause this witch business."

"Kib Wordin read to me out of that book one time," she said. "Told me he'd put a spell on me so I couldn't refuse him."

"But you refused him."

"It was just about then when you—" She broke off. "You know."

"Sure enough I know. I put that silver bullet right back of his ear."

"You killed the priest, and that makes you the new one," said Tolly. "It's in Daddy's books. If you say no, they'll kill you, whoever they are."

"Ain't I a sitting duck to be killed?" he cried out. "Whoever wants that priest job next, won't he kill me if he can?"

"But when you see what's happening—"

"Stop rooting against me, Tolly!" he yelled, and she shrank down in the chair. "Whatever happens, I still ain't their man."

He glared at the book in his hand and walked to the door.

"What are you going to do?" Tolly squeaked behind him.

"A couple things needing to be done. The first of them won't take but two—three minutes."

He dragged the door open and stepped out into the night. Scraps of moonlight flitted among the trees as he walked to the road. He knelt and groped with his free hand until he found soft earth. Powerfully he scooped out great clods. He pushed *Albertus Magnus* into the hole, dragged the loosened earth back over it and rammed it down hard.

Still kneeling, he tried to think of the burial service. "Ashes to ashes, dust to dust," he said aloud, and the night around him was as still as stone. "Until the day break and the shadows flee away," he recollected a few more words to say. Then he got up. There was Tolly standing beside him.

"Get back inside," he grumbled.

"Not with you out here."

He took her arm and pulled her to the door and inside. "Sit," he ordered her, pointing to the chair. "Don't you leave out of here till I get back."

"What you aiming to do Jack?"

"I've kindly got it in mind that that witch-tree up yonder's been growing long enough."

"If you don't come back—"

"Just start pestering about that when I don't."

He rolled his shirtsleeves back from his corded arms and took the double-bitted axe again. Out he tramped, slamming the door behind him.

Out to the road, past the grave where he'd buried *Albertus Magnus*, up slope. He moved between bunches of big trees he'd once reckoned he knew as friends, oaks and walnuts and tall watching pines, with sooty shadows amongst them. They stared at him from both sides; they seemed to hold their breath. He heard only his own dull footsteps until, before he knew it, he was where the path turned off to the red-painted cabin where once he'd sneaked up on Kib Wordin.

There was light through the trees there; not the moon glow on the road, but a dull red light. Jack stole along the path. Now he saw the slumpy-roofed cabin where three witch-men had lived and died, with its sneaky look like a hungry beast waiting, waiting. The red light soaked out through curtains at the windows. Who was inside there now? Doing what?

He decided not to knock and find out. He took careful steps into the yard, and he was right under the tree he'd come to find.

Never had he relished the look of that tree, even from far off, and he didn't relish its look now. It seemed to move or shiver in the dull red light. Its coaly black trunk might could be a foot and a half thick above roots that clutched deep down among rocks. Just above Jack's head the branches kinked this way and that way, like nothing so much as snakes. They wiggled, or maybe it was just the stir of lean, ugly leaves.

He walked all the way round, bending his head under the snaky branches, studying the trunk. Finally he set his booted feet just so on the damp-feeling earth. He shifted his grip on the axe helve and hiked it high. If whoever or whatever was in yonder with the red light heard him chop and came out, he'd be ready, axe in hand. Hard and deep he drove down the blade just above the roots.

Sound rose round him, soft to hear but scary to feel. It was like an echoed cry of pain, as if the wood he chopped was living flesh. He ripped the axe loose and raised it, and knew without looking up that those branches sure enough squirmed. A whisper sneaked in the air, like an angry voice. Again he swung the axe. A big chip sailed loose, showing white wood that glowed with its own pale, sick light.

Jack recollected the old Cherokee who'd said that trees felt when they were chopped, and it hadn't made him like to cut timber any right much. But this tree was different, it was an enemy tree. He looked toward the cabin. Not a stir from there. He slashed and slashed at the blackness of the trunk, every blow flinging white chips away. Sweat popped out on him. The murmur kept murmuring, but it didn't slow him up a hooter. Another six or seven chops at the right place, and that tree would fall. It would slap down right on the pulpy shingles of that red-lighted cabin. Once more he heaved up his axe.

And something grabbed onto it and held it on high.

At once he was fighting to get the axe back, but he couldn't. They crawled and struggled above him, those snaky branches, winding the axe helve, sliding twigs round his right arm like a basket weaving itself there. He let go the axe to fight that grip on him. His feet came clear of the ground with the effort, and the branches bent with his weight. Power-fully he fought his way round the trunk, the twigs still netting his arm. His hand and wrist tingled as if they were being bitten, sucked.

His free left hand hustled his great big clasp knife out of his pants pocket. He yanked the longest blade open with his teeth and slashed at those snaring twigs.

They parted under the edge that was as sharp as a whetrock could make it. As his right hand came free, more twigs scrambled down to spiral his left arm. His whipped the knife over to his right hand to hack and chop those new tethers. Free for a second, he tried to flounder away, but he slipped on soggy earth and fell to his knees. The branches grabbed and tied him again.

He started to curse, but saved his breath. He slashed with the knife, passing it from hand to hand. He cleared the twigs from wrists and arms, but a thicker branch wound him, tying his right arm to his side. It squeezed tighter than the strongest wrestler he'd ever tried holds with; he sawed at it, and it was hard to cut through. He got it whittled free of him, just as a bigger branch snapped a loop on his ankle and flung him full length.

"If I knew where your heart was," he panted as if the tree could hear, and maybe it did. Twenty twigs scraped and felt for new holds on him, wove and twisted round him, made it harder for him to cut at them. The cut ends kept crawling back, thicker, harder to slice away. He wished he had his axe, flung down yonder out of reach.

He turned himself over, and over again. He was as strong as any man in the Sawback Mountain country, and the surge of his turning broke some twigs, not all of them. Hacking at the ones still at him, he saw the cabin door open and somebody stepping out in the red light.

Hunched, wearing a long pale coat, it must be the one who'd spied at his homecoming. Close it came. A hand lifted a dark-shining blade, a big corn knife, just over him.

"Stay right there," said the quiet, cold voice of Tolly, from just beyond them.

The fellow froze, the corn knife drooped.

"Put that thing to Jack and I'll shoot you," Tolly said, as quiet as if she was saying the time of day. "I've got Jack's shotgun here, and a bunch of silver dimes wadded down both barrels on top of the buckshot."

The corn knife sank and pointed to the ground.

"You want to kill Jack and be the priest," Tolly said. "Then what if I killed you and got to be priestess? What if I used that witch book to witch your soul right down to the floor of hell?"

The fellow spun round and scurried off. Jack heard the long coat whip, heard a crash among dark trees. Tolly ran close.

"Look out," Jack wheezed.

But she stood right over him, laid the shotgun muzzles to that pallid wound he'd cut in the trunk, and slammed loose with both barrels. Flame flashed, the two shots howled like two claps of thunder, and something screamed a death scream. All those holds on Jack turned weak and fell away. With one floundering, scrambling try he ripped free of them and came to his feet beside Tolly.

The tree blazed up like fat meat where the blasts had driven into it. Jack pulled Tolly clear as the whole thing fell away from them, fell right on the roof of the cabin. The flames ran up into the branches and caught the shingles, burning blood red and sick white. Still holding to Tolly, Jack started her away at a run to the road and down the mountain.

Once they looked back. Flames jumped high and bright into the high darkness against the stars, gobbling that tree and that cabin, putting an end to both of them.

Tolly and Jack got married Thanksgiving week. Before that, the neighbor folks built a bedroom to Jack's cabin at the left, a lean-to kitchen at the right. Before that, too, half a dozen sorry men and women left out of the Sawback Mountain country. Nobody knew where they went, or even for dead sure which was the one who wore the long coat. All anybody was certain sure of was that you could live another sight better there without that half dozen people and whatever they'd been up to.

The Gorgon

Clark Ashton Smith

Yet it is less the horror than the grace
Which turns the gazer's spirit into stone.

–Shelley

I have no reason to expect that anyone will believe my story. If it were another's tale, probably I should not feel inclined to give it credence myself. I tell it herewith, hoping that the mere act of narration, the mere shaping of this macabre day-mare adventure into words will in some slight measure serve to relieve my mind of its execrable burden. There have been times when only a hair's-breadth has intervened betwixt myself and the seething, devil-ridden world of madness; for the hideous knowledge, the horror-blackened memories which I have carried so long, were never meant to be borne by the human intellect.

A singular confession, no doubt, for one who has always been a connoisseur of horrors. The deadly, the malign, and baleful things that lurk in the labyrinth of existence have held for me a fascination no less potent than unholy. I have sought them out and looked upon them as one who sees the fatal eyes of the basilisk in a mirror; or as a savant who handles corrosive poisons in his laboratory with mask and gloves. Never did they have for me the least hint of personal menace, since I viewed them with the most impersonal detachment. I have investigated many clues of the spectral, the ghastly, the bizarre, and many mazes of terror from which others would have recoiled with caution or trepidation. . . . But now I could wish that there were one lure which I had not followed, one labyrinth which my curiosity had not explored. . . .

More incredible than all else, perhaps, is the very fact that the thing occurred in Twentieth-century London. The sheer anachronism and fabulosity of the happening has made me doubt the verities of time and space; and ever since then I have been as one adrift on starless seas of confusion, or roaming through unmapped dimensions. Never have I been quite able to re-orient myself, to be altogether sure that I have not gone astray in other centuries, in other lands than those declared by the chronology and geography of the present. I have continual need of modern crowds, of glaring lights, of laughter and clangor and tumult to reassure me; and always I am afraid that such things are only an insubstantial barrier; that behind them lies the realm of ancient horror and immemorial malignity of which I have had this one abominable glimpse.

And always it seems to me that the veil will dissolve at any moment, and leave me face to face with an ultimate Fear.

There is no need to detail the events that brought me to London. It should be enough to say that I had endured a great grief, the death of the only woman whom I had loved. I traveled as others have done, to forget, to seek distraction among the novelties of foreign scenes; and I tarried long in London, because its gray and mist-enfolded vastness, its ever-varying throngs, its inexhaustible maze of thoroughfares and lanes and houses, were somehow akin to oblivion itself, and offered more of refuge from my sorrow than brighter cities had given.

I do not know how many weeks or months I lingered in London. Time meant little to me, except as an ordeal to be undergone; and I recked not of its disposal. It is hard to remember what I did or where I went; for all things were blurred in a negligible monotone.

However, my meeting with the old man is clear as any present impression—and perhaps clearer. Among the faint recollections of that period, it is etched as with some black acid. I can not recall the name of the street on which I saw him; but it was not far from the Strand, and was full of a late afternoon crowd, beneath a heaven of high fog through which the sun had not penetrated for days or weeks.

I was strolling idly along, amid hurrying faces and figures that meant no more to me than the featureless heavens or the uniform shops. My thoughts were idle, empty, immaterial; and in those days (since I had been brought face to face with an all-too-real horror) I had relinquished my search for the darker mysteries of existence. I was without forewarning, without anticipation of anything but the daily drabness of the London streets and people. Then, from that anonymous welter of humanity, the man stood before me with the terrifying suddenness of an apparition; and I could not have sworn from which direction he had come.

He was not unusual in frame or stature, apart from the erectness with which he carried himself notwithstanding his extreme and manifest age. Nor were his garments uncommon, aside from the fact that they too were excessively old, and seemed to exhale an air of greater antiquity than was warranted even by their cut and fabric. It was not these, but the man's visage, which electrified all my drowsy faculties into a fascinated and awe-struck attention. With the mortal pallor of his deeply wrinkled features, like graven ivory, with his long, curling hair and beard that were white as moon-touched vapor, with his eyes that glowed in their hollow sockets like the coals of demon fires in underworld caverns, he would have made a living model for Charon, the boatman who ferries the dead to Hades across the ebon silence of the Styx. He seemed to have stepped from an age and land of classic mythology, into the teeming turmoil of that London street; and the strange impression

221

which he made upon me was in no wise modified by his habiliments. I paid so little attention to these that I could not remember their details afterward; though I think that their predominant color was a black that had begun to assume the green of time, and suggested the plumage of some sinister bird. My astonishment at the appearance of this singular old man was increased when I saw that no one else in the throng seemed to notice anything unusual or peculiar about him; but that all were hastening on their way with no more, at most, than the off-hand scrutiny which one would give to some aged beggar.

As for me, I had paused in my strolling, petrified with an instant fascination, an immediate terror which I could not analyse or define. The old man, too, had paused; and I saw that we were both a little withdrawn from the current of the crowd, which passed so obviously, intent on its own fears and allurements. Evidently realizing that he had caught my attention, and perceiving the effect which he had upon me, the old man stepped nearer, smiling with a hint of some horrible malevolence, some nameless antique evil. I would have drawn back; but I was bereft of the power of movement. Standing at my very side, and searching me with the gaze of his coal-like orbs, he said to me in a low tone which could not have been overheard by any of the passers-by:

'I can see that you have a taste for horror. The dark and awful secrets of death, the equally dreadful mysteries of life, allure your interest. If you care to come with me, I will show you something which is the quintessence of all horror. You shall gaze on the head of Medusa with its serpent locks—that very head which was severed by the sword of Perseus.'

I was startled beyond measure by the strange words, uttered in accents which seemed to be heard by the mind rather than the ear. Somehow—unbelievable as this will seem—I have never been quite sure in what language he spoke: it may have been English, or it may have been Greek, which I know perfectly. The words penetrated my understanding without leaving any definite sense of their actual sound or linguistic nature. And of the voice itself, I know only that it was such as might issue from the very lips of Charon. It was guttural, deep, malign, with an echo of profound gulfs and sunless grottoes.

Of course, my reason strove to dismiss the unaccountable feelings and ideas that had surged upon me. I told myself that it was all imagination; that the man was probably some queer sort of madman, or else was a mere trickster, or a showman who took this method of drumming up custom. But his aspect and his words were of necromantic strangeness; they seemed to promise in a superlative degree the weirdness and bizarrerie which I had sought in former time, and of which, so far, I had found little hint in London. So I answered him quite seriously:

'Indeed, I should like to see the head of Medusa. But I have always understood that it was quite fatal to gaze upon her—that those who beheld her were turned immediately into stone.'

'That can be avoided,' returned my interlocutor. 'I will furnish you with a mirror; and if you are truly careful, and succeed in restraining your curiosity, you can see her even as Perseus did. But you will have to be very circumspect. And she is really so fascinating that few have been able to refrain from looking at her directly. Yes, you must be very cautious. He! he! he!' His laughter was more horrible even than his smile; and even as he laughed, he began to pluck my sleeve, with a knotted hand that was wholly in keeping with his face, and which might well have gripped through untold ages the dark oars of the Stygian barge.

'Come with me—it is not far,' he said. 'And you will never have a second opportunity. I am the owner of the Head; and I do not show it to many. But I can see that you are one of the few who are fitted to appreciate it.'

It is inexplicable to me that I should have accepted his invitation. The man's personality was highly abhorrent, the feeling he aroused in me was a mixture of irresistible fear and repugnance. In all likelihood he was a lunatic—perhaps a dangerous maniac; or, if not actually mad, was nurturing some ill design, some nefarious purpose to which I would lend myself by accompanying him. It was madness to go with him, it was folly even to listen to his words; and of course his wild claim concerning the ownership of the fabled Gorgon's head was too ridiculous even for the formality of disbelief. If such a thing had ever existed, even in mythic Greece, it was certainly not to be found in present-day London, in the possession of a doubtful-looking old man. The whole affair was more preposterous than a dream . . . but nevertheless I went with him. I was under a spell—the spell of unknown mystery, terror, absurdity; and I could no more have refused his offer than a dead man could have refused the conveyance of Charon to the realms of Hades.

'My house is not far away,' he assured me, repetitiously, as we left the crowded street and plunged into a narrow, lightless alley. Perhaps he was right; though I have no precise idea of the distance which we traversed. The lanes and thoroughfares to which he led me were such as I could hardly have believed to exist in that portion of London; and I was hopelessly confused and astray in less than a minute. The houses were foul tenements, obviously of much antiquity, interspersed with a few decaying mansions that were doubtless even older, like remnants of some earlier city. I was struck by the fact that we met no one, apart from rare and furtive stragglers who seemed to avoid us. The air had grown extremely chill, and was fraught with unwonted odors that somehow served to reinforce the sensations of coldness and utter age. Above all was a dead, unchanging sky, with its catafalque of oppressive and super-incumbent grayness. I could not remember the streets through which we passed, though I was sure that I must have traversed this section of the city before in my wanderings; and a queer perplexity was now mingled with my feeling of dismay and bemusement. It seemed to me that the old man was leading me into a clueless maze of unreality, of deception and dubiety, where nothing was normal or familiar or legitimate.

The air darkened a little, as with the first encroachment of twilight, though it still lacked an hour of sunset-time. In this premonitory dusk, which did not deepen, but became stationary in its degree of shadow, through which all things were oddly distorted and assumed illusory proportions, we reached the house which was our destination.

It was one of the dilapidated mansions, and belonged to a period which I was unable to name despite my extensive architectural knowl-edge. It stood a little apart from the surrounding tenements; and more than the dimness of the premature twilight seemed to adhere to its dark walls and lampless windows. It impressed me with a sense of vastness; yet I have never been quite sure concerning its exact dimensions; and I can not remember the details of its façade apart from the high and heavy door at the head of a flight of steps which were strangely worn as by the tread of incalculable generations.

The door swung open without sound beneath the gnarled fingers of the old man, who motioned me to precede him. I found myself in a long hall, illumed by silver lamps of an antique type such as I had never before seen in actual use. I think there were ancient tapestries and vases; and also a mosaic floor; but the lamps are the only things which I remember clearly. They burned with white flames that were preternatu-rally still and cold; and I thought that they had always burned in this manner, unflickering, unreplenished, throughout a frozen eternity whose days were in no wise different from its nights.

At the end of the hall, we entered a room that was similarly litten, and whose furniture was more than reminiscent of the classic. At the oppo-site side was an open door, giving on a second chamber, which appeared to be crowded with statuary; for I could see the outlines of still figures that were silhouetted or partly illumined by unseen lamps.

'Be seated,' said my host, indicating a luxurious couch. 'I will show you the Head in a few minutes; but haste is unseemly, when one is about to enter the very presence of Medusa.'

I obeyed; but my host remained standing. He was paler and older and more erect than ever in the chill lamplight; and I sensed a sinewy, unnatural vigor, a diabolic vitality, which was terrifyingly incongruous with his extreme age. I shivered with more than the cold of the evening air and the dank mansion. Of course, I still felt that the old man's invitation was some sort of preposterous foolery or trickery. But the circumstances among which I found myself were unexplainable and uncanny. However, I mustered enough courage to ask a few questions.

'I am naturally surprised,' I said, 'to learn that the Gorgon's head has survived into modern times. Unless the query is impertinent, will you not tell me how it came into your possession?'

'He! he!' laughed the old man, with a loathsome rictus. 'That is easily answered: I won the Head from Perseus at a game of dice, when he was in his dotage.'

'But how is that possible?' I countered. 'Perseus lived several thousand years ago.'

'Yes, according to your notation. But time is not altogether the simple matter which you believe it to be. There are short-cuts between the ages, there are deviations and overlappings among the epochs, of which you have no idea. . . . Also, I can see that you are surprised to learn that the Head is in London. . . . But London after all is only a name; and there are shiftings, abbreviations, and interchanges of space as well as of time.'

I was amazed by his reasoning, but was forced to admit internally that it did not lack a certain logic.

'I see your point,' I conceded. . . . 'And now, of course, you will show me the Gorgon's head?'

'In a moment. But I must warn you again to be supremely careful; and also, you must be prepared for its exceeding and overwhelming beauty no less than for its horror. The danger lies, as you may well imagine, in the former quality.'

He left the room, and soon returned, carrying in his hand a metal mirror of the same period as the lamps. The face was highly polished, with a reflecting surface, wellnigh equal to that of glass; but the back and handle, with their strange carvings of Laocoön-like figures that writhed in a nameless, frozen agony, were black with the tarnish of elder centuries. It might well have been the very mirror that was employed by Perseus.

The old man placed it in my hands.

'Come,' he said, and turned to the open door through which I had seen the crowded statuary.

'Keep your eyes on the mirror,' he added, 'and do not look beyond it. You will be in grave peril as soon as you enter this door.'

He preceded me, averting his face from the portal, and gazing back across his shoulder with watchful orbs of malignant fire. My own eyes intent on the mirror, I followed.

The room was unexpectedly large; and was lit by many lamps that depended from chains of wrought silver. At first sight, when I had crossed the sill, I thought that it was entirely filled with stone statues, some of them standing erect in postures of a painful rigor, and others lying on the floor in agonized eternal contortions. Then, moving the mirror a little, I saw that there was a clear space through which one could walk, and a vaster vacant space at the opposite end of the room, surrounding a sort of altar. I could not see the whole of this altar, because the old man was now in my line of mirrored vision. But the figures beside me, at which I now dared to peep without the mirror's intermediation, were enough to absorb my interest for the moment.

They were all life-size; and they offered a most singular medley of historic periods. Yet it would seem that all of them, by the sameness of their dark material, like a black marble, and the uniform realism and verisimilitude of their technique, might well have been sculptured by the same hand. There were boys and bearded men in the chitons of Greece, there were mediaeval monks, and knights in armor, there were soldiers and scholars and great ladies of the Renaissance, of the Restoration, there were people of the Eighteenth, the Nineteenth, the Twentieth centuries. And in every muscle, in every lineament of each, was stamped an incredible suffering, an unspeakable fear. And more and more as I studied them, a ghastly and hideous conjecture was formulated in my mind.

The old man was at my elbow, leering and peering into my face with a demoniac malice.

'You are admiring my collection of statuary,' he said. 'And I can see that you are impressed by its realism. . . . But perhaps you have already guessed that the statues are identical with their models. These people are the unfortunates who were not content to see Medusa only in a mirror. . . . I warned them . . . even as I have warned you. . . . But the temptation was too much for them.'

I could say nothing. My thoughts were full of terror, consternation, stupefaction. Had the old man told me the truth, did he really possess anything so impossible and mythical as the Gorgon's head? Those statues were *too* life-like, *too* veridical in all their features, in their poses that preserved a lethal fear, their faces marked with a deadly but undying torment. No human sculptor could have wrought them, could have reproduced the physiognomies and the costumes with a fidelity so consummate and so atrocious.

'Now,' said my host, 'having seen those who were overpowered by the beauty of Medusa, it is time for you to behold the Gorgon herself.' He stepped to one side, eyeing me intently; and I saw in the metal mirror the whole of that strange altar which his body had partially intercepted from my view. It was draped with some funereal black fabric; and lamps were burning on each side with their tall and frozen flames. In the center, on a broad paten of silver or electrum, there stood the veritable Head, even as the ancient myths have depicted it, with vipers crawling and lifting among its matted locks.

How can I delineate or even suggest that which is beyond the normal scope of human sensation or imagining? I saw in the mirror a face of unspeakably radiant pallor—a dead face from which there poured the luminous, blinding glory of celestial corruption, of superhuman bale and suffering. With lidless, intolerable eyes, with lips that were parted in an agonizing smile, she was lovely, she was dreadful beyond any vision ever vouchsafed to a mystic or an artist, and the light that emanated from her features was the light of worlds that lie too deep or too high for mortal perception. Hers was the dread that turns the marrow into ice, and the anguish that slays like a bolt of lightning.

Long did I gaze in the mirror with the shuddering awe of one who beholds the veilless countenance of a final mystery. I was terrified, appalled—and fascinated to the core of my being; for that which I saw was the ultimate death, the ultimate beauty. I desired, yet I did not dare, to turn and lift my eyes to the reality whose mere reflection was a fatal splendor.

The old man had stepped closer; he was peering into the mirror and watching me with furtive glances, by turns.

'Is she not beautiful?' he whispered. 'Could you not gaze upon her forever? And do you not long to behold her without the intermediation of the mirror, which hardly does her justice?'

I shivered at his words, and at something which I sensed behind them.

'No! no!' I cried, vehemently. 'I admit all that you say. But I will not gaze any longer; and I am not mad enough to let myself be turned into a stone image.'

I thrust the mirror into his hands as I spoke, and turned to leave, impelled by an access of overmastering fright. I feared the allurement of Medusa; and I loathed that evil ancient with a loathing that was beyond limit or utterance.

The mirror clattered on the floor, as the old man dropped it and sprang upon me with a tigerish agility. He seized me with his knotted hands, and though I had sensed their sinewy vigor, I was not prepared for the demoniacal strength with which he whirled me about and thrust me toward the altar.

'Look! Look!' he shrieked, and his voice was that of a fiend who urges the damned to some further pit of perdition.

I had closed my eyes instinctively, but even through my lids I felt the searing radiance. I knew, I believed implicitly the fate which would be mine if I beheld Medusa face to face. I struggled madly but impotently

227

against the grip that held me; and I concentrated all my will to keep my lids from lighting even by the breadth of an eyelash.

Suddenly my arms were freed, and I felt the diabolic fingers on my brow, groping swiftly to find my eyes. I knew their purpose, and knew also that the old man must have closed his own eyes to avoid the doom he had designed for me. I broke away, I turned, I grappled with him; and we fought insanely, frantically, as he strove to swing me about with one arm and tore at my shut eyelids with his other hand. Young as I am, and muscular, I was no match for him; and I swerved slowly toward the altar, with my head bent back till my neck was almost broken, in a vain effort to avoid the iron fumbling of his fingers. A moment more, and he would have conquered; but the space in which we fought was narrow, and he had now driven me back against a row of the stone figures, some of which were recumbent on the floor. He must have stumbled over one of these, for he fell suddenly with a wild, despairing cry, and released me as he went down. I heard him strike the floor with a crash that was singularly heavy—a crash as of something harder and more massive and more ponderous than a human body.

Still standing with shut eyes, I waited; but there was no sound and no movement from the old man. Bending toward the floor, I ventured to look between half-open lids. He was lying at my feet, beside the figure on which he had tripped; and I needed no second glance to recognize in all his limbs, in all his lineaments, the same rigidity and the same horror which characterized the other statues. Like them, he had been smitten instantaneously into an image of dark stone. In falling, he had seen the very face of Medusa, even as his victims had seen it. And now he would lie among them forever.

Somehow, with no backward glance, I fled from the room, I found my way from that horrible mansion, I sought to lose it from sight and memory in half-deserted, mysterious alleys that were no legitimate part of London. The chill of ancient death was upon me; it hung in the web of timeless twilight along those irrecognizable ways, around those innominable houses; and it followed me as I went. But at last, by what miracle I know not, I came to a familiar street, where people thronged in the lamplit dusk, and the air was no longer chill except with a falling fog.

Grandma's Hobby

Elizabeth Engstrom

I'd forgotten all about Grandma's hobby. But then, it had been years since I'd spent much time with her.

Daniel and I had moved in with her for a couple of weeks while our new house was being finished. Grandma, I was distressed to see, had become quite frail and slightly dotty, so to help earn our keep, we did a few badly-needed odd jobs around the place.

Daniel fixed the gutters, the sprinklers, pruned the apple tree, rehung the shed doors and that kind of thing. I relined the pantry shelves, cleaned the attic, reorganized the linen closet and then tackled the fruit cellar.

The fruit cellar.

My grandpa died in the fruit cellar when I was a little girl, and for years I wouldn't go near it. Grandma said it was a simple heart attack one morning when he was going down for a fresh jar of jelly, but the fruit cellar had always been too dark, too damp, too spooky for me, and knowing that my grandfather, my wonderful grandfather had given up his ghost in there—well, it was still too much for me to take.

So when I asked Grandma what the next job was to be, and she said, in her adorable, innocent, irresistible way, that the fruit cellar really needed the cobwebs swept, I swallowed, nodded and mentally scheduled it for a rainy Sunday.

The next Sunday it rained.

I snuggled up to Daniel's back in bed that morning, listening to the water run through the new gutters, and I whispered that he ought to take advantage of this good cuddling, because I was about to descend to no-man's-land. I might not return. He thought I'd probably return, but he took good advantage of the cuddling anyway.

Soon I was up and showered and into my old clothes, ready for anything. Or so I thought.

I had toast and coffee for breakfast, quietly, just the rain on the windows and me in the tiny breakfast nook, while Grandma took her Sunday morning soak with half the Sunday papers and Daniel went back to sleep.

And I thought about the fruit cellar.

And thought about the fruit cellar.

The more I thought about it, the farther away it became, the larger it grew, the deeper it sank, the ranker it smelled, the more *unreal* my chore began to be.

I chugged down the last of my cold coffee, grabbed broom, bucket and mop, basket of rags and bottle of ammonia and opened the cellar door. It was now or never.

No place in the world smelled as wonderful as Grandma's basement. It smelled like coal dust and aging apples. It smelled like little kids playing school. It smelled like old dresses stored in leather boxes and mothballs around Great-great-grandma's precious few things.

I clanked my way down the stairs, took a deep breath of that wonderfully perfumed air of my childhood and turned to face the fruit cellar door. It was like a barn door, slatted with one crosspiece. It was dark wood, with one knot punched out at five-year-old eye level from the time when Randy, my brother, wanted to see if Grandpa was still in there, dead, and he was too scared to open the door.

I wanted to bend down and look through the knothole first, too, but that was silly, that was silly, that was silly, and I lifted the latch and the door swung out.

What a relief! I almost laughed out loud. You nut, I thought, and stepped into the musty room and viewed it with the critical eye of the cleaner.

It was a mess. Grandma was right. It did need the cobwebs swept.

The one little window-well window was too thickly encrusted with webs and dust and dirt to let in much light, so I turned on the bare bulb overhead. The little room was maybe eight feet square, and ringed by wooden shelves. In the faint light, I could discern rows of canned fruits and vegetables, and then I remembered about Grandma's hobby.

There was a big box on the top shelf of the closet that was filled with hundreds of ribbons, red, white, gold, but mostly blue from the county and state fairs. Grandma took all the prizes for canned fruit, vegetables, relishes, jams and jellies and sauces. Grandma turned food preservation into an art; she grew most of her spices as well as her fruit and vegetables, and her reputation was as widespread as her recipes were secret.

I leaned against the dusty wall and crossed my arms over my chest. When Grandma was my age, she had a house, a husband, three little kids and was winning blue ribbons for food preservation during the depression. She was quite a woman in her youth. It was hard for me to imagine her in her thirties—vibrant, sharp, energetic, witty.

Look what time does to a person, I thought. All that energy, all that ambition, gone out into the atmosphere, leaving Grandma old, frail and not quite all there.

But at least she's had three children to hold her memory, and a lot of people that she's touched and helped, and secret recipes that must be around somewhere . . . What am *I* doing besides chasing the almighty dollar? What am I doing that's worthwhile?

Cleaning the fruit cellar, I thought, and grabbed the mop.

I looked again at the half-empty shelves of bottled fruit and vegetables and saw the rings of where the used ones had been, their rings in descending order of dustiness, according to when they were taken upstairs. Boxes of empty mason jars and wide-mouth lids were lined up along the bottom row of shelves.

Grandma hadn't canned anything in a long time. The most recent red-bordered gummed label read three years ago in Grandma's fine hand. And she still had a lot left to eat.

I put my hands on my hips and looked around, pleased with myself for once. I had faced a mindless fear and won. Not only that, but the fruit cellar was so terribly filthy, I'd be able to see real progress.

I wrapped a rag around the broom and began to dust away at the window.

Daniel brought me a sandwich and cold beer at noon. We sat together on the damp floor and ate. I began telling him about Grandma's fame, and while I did, a memory floated up, of Grandma holding two beautiful peaches, ripe to perfection. "These are wonderful," she said. "God meant for peaches this nice to be preserved." My throat filled with sadness for Grandma, and it crowded out my sandwich. Time caught up with a person, and I needed some silence to ponder that. I pushed away the tears of fear about my own aging, chugged the beer, wrapped the rest of the sandwich, and even though Daniel still had half a sandwich left, I stood up and brushed him gently out of my way. I had to get back to work.

Late in the afternoon, the rain clouds parted and shafts of light came in through the newly cleaned little window. I was wiping down the last of the shelves, had only the bottom shelf and the floor left to do, when a little jar caught the sunlight, caught my attention. It looked out of place, being smaller than the other jars on the shelf, and of a different color, and stashed way in the back, in the corner, next to the wall.

I dusted my way over to it, reached behind the jars of apricots and picked it up. It was small, maybe a half pint or so, of fancy cut glass, with a miniature rubber seal and a wire-snap top. Those wire-snap tops were so old that not even Grandma used them anymore. I held it up to the light, but as I did, the sun went behind a cloud. The bare light bulb in the ceiling showed through a clear, golden-green substance. It looked like jelly. I was intrigued—almost enough to open it, but not quite. It wasn't mine to open, and besides, maybe it was special to Grandma. I set it on the floor next to the door to remind myself to take it upstairs and ask.

But by the time I was finished, my muscles were howling. I was not

231

used to this kind of labor, and when I emptied the final load from the dustpan into the garbage, I barely had enough energy to look around the little room in satisfaction before hobbling up the stairs to the bath. I left the little jar next to the bucket of filthy water, the broom, the dustpan and the pile of rags. I'd fetch them all the next morning.

But the next morning, it wasn't there. I moved the mop around and the bucket, but that jar wasn't there. Then I looked on the shelf where I'd first found it, and there it was. Tucked back in the corner behind the apricots. Next to the wall.

A little chill ran through me.

I reached in and brought it out, wondering again at the strangely rich color.

By the time I'd finished cleaning up the cleaning tools, Grandma was having her toast and marmalade in the sunny breakfast nook.

"You did a beautiful job on the fruit cellar, Jan," she said.

So she'd been down to see. *She'd* put the jar back on the shelf. "Thanks, Grandma. It was a real challenge." I sat down next to her, thinking that I noticed something a little different in her manner, and I wished I'd left the jar on the shelf where she was telling me it belonged. Suddenly I felt a little shy, but I knew if I didn't ask her now, that curiosity would certainly torture me. I pulled the jar from my pocket. "Grandma. What's this?"

She looked at it without surprise, but with an indefinable look that seemed to be a little melancholy, a little misty. Then that passed, and she returned her look to the newspaper. "Jelly," she said.

"It looks so . . . so old."

Grandma smiled to herself.

"Can we try some? Or were you saving it for some special occasion?"

Grandma looked at me, looked at the jar, looked back at me. "Well, no," she said hesitantly, "not really. Sure. Let's have some."

I opened it and the fragrance was deep, pungent and spicy. It didn't smell like any kind of jelly or jam I'd ever smelled before, but it did smell sweet, and quite irresistible. I spooned out a gentle amount and put it on my toast, then passed the jar to Grandma. She smelled it first, too, then without comment she scooped a dollop out onto her toast.

She spread it around carefully, then lifted it up. A toast of toast, you might say, and she said, "To Grandpa."

And we both took a big bite.

It was delicious.

"He loved my homemade jelly so much," Grandma said around a mouthful. "I always said he'd someday turn into a jar of it."

The toast caught in my throat.

There was a glazed, slightly hysterical look in Grandma's eyes. She wiped a few toast crumbs with jelly from the corner of her mouth and then looked at her napkin. "And now look at him," she said.

Imperfect Strangers

Joel Lane

When the old man came into view, the doctor had the impression of having listened to his footsteps for some time; having recognised them, even. The old man was shuffling after him along the slick path to the front steps of the surgery. Dr Radley stopped and watched him pass through the veils of rain. He was wearing a grey raincoat that gleamed in the weak sunlight, and a cap whose shadow obscured his face. He paused, stooped and spat on the path; as he picked his way onward, a smaller figure mummified in a black coat and scarf clung to him like an image in double vision. The rain forced the doctor inside before they reached the door. That they did not go in before him gave Dr Radley an obscure sense of relief.

He was early, but already the waiting room was half filled with sleepy patients. The uncertain onset of spring always seemed to revive infection more effectively than any other kind of life. In spite of the surgery's airless warmth, few of those waiting had removed their humid coats or headgear; nursing umbrellas, blotched newspapers and not a few restless infants, they might as easily have been waiting to board or dismount from a bus. In the relative sanctuary of his consulting-room, Dr Radley took off his misted spectacles and polished them with a handkerchief. He listened; but there was only the gasping rattle of the rain at the window. The Venetian blind reminded him of a cage.

Bars kept him in, though they couldn't keep the stranger out. He rubbed at his damp hair, pulled the crooked knot of his tie. I need a cigarette, he thought, looking with distaste at his stained fingernails. He'd begun to smoke more heavily since Sarah's death. Her picture on his desk had become blurred with dust, he saw; it was a cheap black-and-white print, taken before their marriage. The dust was sticky; even when he rubbed it clean the face still looked damaged. He would have to replace the print with another. (But did he still have the negative?)

Through the morning, he played the unamusing game of counting his patients' defects. This too had become a habit. One had false teeth . . .

another squinted, her gaze simultaneously fixing the doctor and his shadow. He glanced behind him; but there was only the rain pulsing at the slitted window. Another patient walked with a stick. There was something wrong with everyone, wasn't there? But the man had not been ugly. He ought to have stooped, dragged his feet; his dark eyes should not have stared so directly. He had not worn a raincoat even though it was raining outside. Ha ha. Surely he had been pale and furtive, with burst veins under his peppered cheeks? But the doctor could not recall any detail of the man's appearance.

That was strange, when the whole incident was still so clear in his memory. (Dr Radley found himself seated behind his desk, alone; he must have omitted to call for the next patient.) He'd been fifteen years old, the man about forty; they were of similar height. The man stood aside, watching him, then blocked his way out toward daylight. "Like a cigarette?" The boy refused. He closed the crumpled, half empty box, like an illusionist folding a pack of cards. Pursued up the steps with more questions, the boy clung to his refusal. *No, I can't. Sorry.*

"Why not? We're all strangers, aren't we . . . until we get to know each other?" (There was a fumbled knock.) That remark had disturbed him, though he still wasn't sure why. ("Come in," he said.) This was what fear of the unknown meant: he had feared someone, and so he had *unknown* him . . . He reached for something opening in his mind; but a chill of panic, like a draught, slammed it shut. The thought lost its outline. *Those in darkness go unseen.*

At the same moment a door opened. The elderly man shuffled in, his damp-streaked raincoat still clinging to him. The other, shrunken figure was silent close behind.

"It's my wife," he said. "I come with her because she's deaf and dumb." The doctor noticed that he was wearing spectacles so strong as to make his eyes appear huge. He shifted aside, but the woman did not step forward. Her small, flat face resembled a fractured eggshell in a nest; her hair and the dripping black scarf were indistinguishable, until the thin hands reached up to disentangle them. She was registered with one of Dr Radley's colleagues; her name, Mrs Waite, headed the file presently on his desk. While her husband's gaze was steady and intense, hers floated, unfocussed. For a moment the doctor imagined that her eyes had no pupils.

At his gesture, they both sat, the wife in front of the desk, the husband to one side. "What can I do for you?"

Mr Waite ran a winglet of tawny fingers over his shining forehead. "Her face looks strange," he suggested. The doctor peered at her; she did not respond. He crossed the room to switch on the light. Mrs Waite's eyes followed his movements passively. Then she tilted her chin slightly upward, and the disfigurement was suddenly obvious. Starting around the cheekbones and extending almost to the creases of the throat, a slight oedemic swelling covered the lower portion of her face; it was faintly discoloured, like old newspaper. Perhaps because of its smoothness, the swollen skin appeared moister than that elsewhere.

"How recently has this appeared?"

"Yesterday and more this morning." He coughed into a grey handkerchief, without taking his eyes from the doctor. "There's no pain; it's numb. There was no injury to it." He spoke as though the condition were his. Dr Radley continued to ask questions as he examined the blemish; but he was uncertain of its cause or potential treatment. Mrs Waite's bland medical record offered no clues. He suppressed an unusual sense of repulsion at contact with the patient; perhaps it was because she appeared virtually empty, her will suspended in rapport with her watching husband, or perhaps because of the cool patch of flesh, like a translucent bruise, that seemed almost to absorb his fingertips. As he touched her throat, a sound trembled through it and dissolved without stirring the mouth. Her lips were unevenly smeared with some pale lipstick, and brown mascara had run below the wide eyes (like sepia in an old photograph), blurring their outlines. Her heavy clothes were imbued with rain and a stale perfume. The doctor felt her inertia somehow taking hold of him; the clockface gestured . . . but that was only circular, after all. The rain would patter out dots and dashes, while faces would appear like a sequence of photographs against a common background. The spirit medium who gave them voices was reliable, but had no imagination.

While the couple brooded in their chairs, Dr Radley telephoned to arrange an appointment with a specialist in the town's major hospital. When they had gone, it occurred to him that he had not observed the two to communicate in any way. He had complied, as well, by accepting Mr Waite's response to every question concerning his wife. He watched his hands resting on the desk, pale against the dark wood. Table turning . . . how could you turn the table? He glimpsed the image of a hand waving on the horizon, forming a fist that pulled the night down with it like a blind. The sun must have come out: the perspectives of the room shifted, releasing him. There was a gleam in the chair where Mrs Waite had sat: rainwater on the leather back.

By the end of the day his oppression seemed to have lifted; but the outside had become a gross projection of the consulting-room. Though the rain was diminished to a falling mist, a high sheet of nimbus trapped the remaining, oblique sunlight. The paving-stones and windows glittered; but it was false gold, momentarily reverting to lead. Feathers of light streaked the clouds. There was a gentle wind: a hiss like static. As he was nearing home, the streetlamps began to flicker: red dilating to a dense yellow glow. The houses were two-dimensional. Their colours too were unconvincing, as in a poorly made film.

The approach of a storm always induced in him a rather perverse desire for an open space. In spite of himself, Dr Radley could not unlock his front door and pass through the darkness in his hallway. It had gone in before him. Nor did he feel able to allow food into himself. As he had not eaten since morning, it may be that hunger as well as tiredness influenced what followed. Afterwards, he would wonder if autosuggestion could mimic externally induced suggestion; a dream not within a dream, but projected outward from it.

He was used to rain when out walking: once it began to rain in this region, it continued for several days. He took a familiar eastward route, somehow believing he could cover several miles' walk to the village before the weather took hold. Gradually the lamps thinned out; dusk curtained the windows framed by cloud. Houses gave way to tilted fields, between which factory buildings slumped like polymorphous monsters put out to graze. The invisible rain, irritated by the wind, swelled to a steady percussion. The tall trees lining the road held up fascinatingly intricate traceries of bare branches and twigs, clotted by badly-formed crows' nests. Cars ground past, creating images of crystal in the road ahead and of blood draining behind them.

Soon the doctor's head was aching with the pulse of rain. His hands itched; he wanted a cigarette. When he removed his useless spectacles, his vision cleared. Perhaps this enabled him to observe that peculiar illusion which, at the time, was so disturbing. The irregular dark that clung around the various sources of light (all brought to a similar apparent nearness, though some must have been miles away) thickened abruptly, and then redissolved, as though a hand had closed briefly over the shrunken horizons. The effect on him was as disorientating as a sudden faint. A few moments later it happened again; this time, he noticed that it was preceded by a general muting of the storm. By now the rain was intense as hail, pocking his skin, and forcing him into a hunched posture.

He was running, unable to hear his own breath, when he realised that he had seen a kind of negative lightning, accompanied by an absence of sound that corresponded to thunder. The effect re-occurred several times, and once he felt himself almost struck fully by the wave of nothing. The trees on either side were betraying him. The uneven surface clutched at his right heel and made him limp, but he ran faster, welcoming the pain.

He must have taken a wrong road: he found himself on a rough, unlit path and with no signpost in sight. His feet kicked at rags of grass. At that moment he felt that the earth had inverted, and he stared into the violence at its core—an irresistible machinery. He was as good as naked in his saturated clothing; his face, too, was a blank slate that might alter if he saw or was seen. Was the smell of mud mixed with that of water-logged flowers? He thought of rain combing the blossoms out of a fruit tree.

Defining the horizon, a single yellow light shone far ahead like a quarantine flag. It seemed to flicker and sink. Another, smaller light rose and fell. He recalled the image of a hand reaching above water—a boat passed over it and it did not reappear. He was unable to pursue it into the envelope of water: if he lost the sense of himself here, there would be no other place where he could recover it . . . Struggling to make his thoughts cohere, he managed to force the storm back outside himself.

Several bends further along the path he saw that the smaller light was a lamp at a crossroads, where the path intersected a wider road. Oppo-site was a signpost, not legible at any distance. Just beyond the lamppost was a bus shelter with plastered walls and slate roof, like a tiny house. Its back projected under overhanging trees: the interior was considerably larger than he had expected. Inside the shelter were two benches side by side, crowded with sitting people. Some of them looked up at him, the oblique lamplight catching their eyes. More people leant or slouched by the damp walls. The doctor slipped into a corner, out of the light's reach, and sank, suddenly confused by exhaustion, to a crouching position. He cupped his breath in his swollen hands.

Each bench was occupied, he could see, by three elderly women. On the nearer, the three were silently busy with knitting; they seemed all to be adding to a single long garment. On the farther bench, three still older-looking women were passing small photographs to one another, from a pile on the lap of the leftward woman, to the right and back again.

An old man by the door, half upright, appeared to be counting coins between his hands. A cigarette glowed crimson at his mouth; its smoke was invisible. The rest of the shelter's occupants were still, some drows-ing, one leaning on a walking-stick. He realised with some unease that all of them were elderly. The shelter was filled with a mild odour composed of soaked clothing, smoke, damp wood and plaster. Were they, perhaps, waiting for a special coach to collect them all?

He decided to ask someone which bus they were expecting. Turning his head, he realised that somebody was crouching at his side. The figure was small, its face hidden by a scarf. He started to rise. "Excuse me—" he began. Then, to his intense embarrassment, the figure slumped onto him and pressed its head against his chest. It was a woman; the untidy web of her dark hair stuck to his coat. She clutched at his upper arms sharply and began to whimper, a high-pitched gasping note.

"Are you ill? I'm a doctor . . . Excuse me, are you all right?" She did not move; he was reluctant to touch her. He looked around help-lessly. His eyes met those of the old man by the door, and were caught.

He coughed with a familiar movement into a handkerchief. Dr Radley realised who the woman at his side must be, and saw the futility of questioning her. He wasn't sure which was worse: to look at her face here, where it might have changed, or to endure it pressed into his chest. Slowly, the old man stubbed out his cigarette and started forward, straightening. His hands reached forward, the nails like tarnished coins. As he smiled, the corners of his mouth gleamed. He turned his hand over, presenting the empty palm, then turned it back: a stage magician's gesture. Nearly within reach, the old man held still.

The light must have altered, since the standing figure seemed to grow taller as Dr Radley watched. The face was less wrinkled than it had seemed in the consulting-room. Moonlight made his skin paler; but surely it could not thicken his dark hair? "Let me go," the doctor mut-tered; it was no use. The hand extended was as strong as his own; and the face above it was . . . not ugly, nor old. "Let me go," he repeated. "I don't belong to you."

The woman clung hard onto him and sobbed more loudly, making inarticulate sounds in her throat. Her perfume made him sleepy again. Passively, he watched the approach. The young man hesitated above him. He was very pale now, his skin almost translucent. His hand dropped. Even the eyes faltered: a step away, he glanced to either side; the others were watching, but gave no sign of encouragement. Losing interest, the old women returned to their occupations. Sheer weariness defeated him. For a moment he looked back to the doctor, and whis-pered something which sounded like ". . . to know each other"; then he stumbled back, coughing, shrunken again in an instant. His face relapsed into the expression of all the others: dull, nerveless acceptance.

After all, this was a bus shelter: a functional place, not intended as a stage for any kind of confrontation.

A minute or so passed before the woman let go of Dr Radley and turned her head away. He stood up, and blood rushed from his head, leaving him briefly caught in a grey funnel. He leaned on the wall, wondering if he were too tired to leave; surely he would not have to wait long. He was about to sit down when he felt the woman's small hand pushing at his back.

He stepped into the rain. She would not hear if he thanked her, and he did not want to turn around. The rain's violence was a relief: it distracted him from a twofold guilt. The signpost did not even appear to carry any words. There was no use in trying to retrace his steps. As he

238

began to follow the wider road uphill, he imagined that he could still hear the continuous, shrill sound of her voice, weeping back in the shelter.

In Case of Disaster Only

Henry S. Whitehead

It was not Sir Austin Fynes, who occupied Suite A with his stout wife, a trained nurse who had given up the training, who told us the story. Sir Austin Fynes uses affairs like thought-transference every day in that "mental-and-nervous" practice of his which had made him the light of Harley Street, that physician's paradise of London. No, it was a quiet big fellow who, as so often happens in such cases, had sat over to one side of the ship's smoking-room, at one of the separate, small tables beside a mug of beer which he had allowed to grow stale, listening to the rest of us. The big fellow as a native West Indian, with an accent you could cut with a knife, a Barbados brogue. He was "in sugar"; or, maybe—now that cane isn't so good any more what with the Tariff and Beetroot, and the German bounty, "in mules"; or perhaps "in" what is commercially known in the market as "Cuban beef."

That big fellow got off the ship early the next morning, and I, for one, never even learned his name. He got off at St. John, Antigua, where, I daresay, he lived, and bossed his plantation-hands, and rode around his plantation early mornings, and ate fresh-killed tough meat and drank too-strong tea after noon, alternated with swizzles of antique rum.

It had been the subject of telepathy on which our talk had turned towards midnight. It was about last-order time, when the smoking-room steward makes his final rounds to see what you'll take before he locks up his little cubby-hole of a bar with its swizzle-stick and its green limes, and its staple of *Prunier* for the French-Island passengers and the even more numerous British calls for "B. & S.'s."

Sir Austin had contributed his bit, about the therapeutic use of "suggestion" in mental-and-nervous and "borderline" cases. The whole field had been pretty thoroughly covered, in fact. Even I had put in a word or two. I'm no scientist but I had read my *Laws of Psychic Phenomena* by Thompson W. Hudson, Ph.D. Some book, that one! Gives you pretty much all the dope. Shows, incidentally, what's "Science" and what's just merely plain blah. Lot of people wouldn't know the difference, I daresay, me for a good example! The big fellow hitched around in his chair when that midnight lull came, and started in in his big beefy, British voice.

"Do any of you chaps by any chance know Reuter, in St. Thomas — Clinton Reuter? No? Sorry. An exceedingly good chap, Reuter. In 1926 he was in the States, and was rather hastily summoned back to St. Thomas. Took the first ship he could get — sailed that same afternoon in rather a rush. It was a tramp, carrying a few passengers — the *Bonaventure.*"

Then, the big fellow, having caught everybody's attention, went on to tell what happend to Clinton Reuter on that voyage from New York to St. Thomas, in the Virgin Islands. St. Thomas is the first port of call going "down the Islands" from New York. We had been there two days before. It's about the best looking town in the Lesser Antilles, way ahead of the rest of them, although Bridgetown, the capital of Barbados, and Port-of-Spain down on Trinidad ar a lot bigger and a lot busier.

It was some story, and the big fellow told it right: very simply. It was the only real story we had had that evening, although there had, of course, been a number of instances brought up, as there always are when people get together on a subject like telepathy.

I'm not reproducing the English-West Indian's yarn. It would be a dialect-story, for one thing, with that brogue of his, and besides, I didn't believe the big fellow's yarn for sour apples. I handed it to him for a well-told tale, coming in on that general conversation at precisely the right time to click and get a lot of plausibility in such a setting. It didn't, to tell the truth, impress me, otherwise.

And then, seven months afterwards, by a kind of dumb luck I came back on the *Bonaventure* myself.

Mr. Sills, who had been the Third Officer on Reuter's voyage, was still with the ship. He was Number One now. That company operated a number of vessels, it seemed, and followed a policy of shifting its men around, Captain Sills told me.

That wasn't all the genial young Captain told me, however, sitting evenings in his pleasant cabin over a jugful of mild Martinique rum swizzle with plenty of lime juice in it. Of course, I told him what the big West Indian had told us in that brogue of his, and Sills, one of the least superstitious seamen I have ever encountered, came back at me that the West Indian had not altered the facts in one single particular; had not stretched the plain truth; had not been pulling our leg that night in the smoking-room.

Here, then, is the story.

When Reuter stepped across the sill of his stateroom on the *Bonaventure* the first thing he saw was a sign, which read:

Alarm-Bell—To Be Used In Case of Disaster Only.
When This Bell Rings, Go On Deck At Once.

Just above the sign was a gong, painted white with ship's paint. Reuter had never seen just such an arrangement, and when the steward, just behind him with the hand-luggage, spoke, he had to repeat himself because Reuter had his eyes on the sign and had to pull them away, as it were!

He had a large stateroom to himself. He stowed his luggage, put on a cap, and went up on deck. He took an overcoat, too, it was late October and chilly. He stood up on deck and watched the last of the lading.

The stevedores, like bees, swarmed above and below the opened hatches. The winches creaked and groaned incessantly to the usual accompaniment of various bellowed directions, commands, and countercommands. Both the forward hatches had already been closed because the lading forward had been finished. Now the First Officer, a chap named Pollard, was driving the work aft. A cold wind blew up the Hudson River where the ship was docked.

Reuter looked on at all this, and, I daresay, anyone watching him might have supposed him immensely interested. But, as a matter of fact, he had been at sea a good bit and such affairs were an old story to him. His mind was really in St. Thomas. He looked at the maneuvers of two tugboats which hovered out in the river off the *Bonaventure*'s stern, flannel-shirted captains with peaked caps aslant over their eyes leaning nonchalantly out of their respective pilothouses, spinning the great wheels as though negligently, jockeying skillfully about among the thick and varied traffic of the river.

Only that morning he had received Morrison's letter from St. Thomas. Morrison was his partner. When he had grasped its purport he had dropped everything else abruptly, hurriedly telephoned to the steamship office, and cabled Morrison of his sailing at once. It was his singular good fortune that there happened to be this vessel sailing late that afternoon. Because of that stroke of luck he would be able to arrive in St. Thomas at the end of six days, even though the *Bonaventure* was no more than a slow tramp which carried passengers only incidentally. There had been no time to await a reply to his cabled message; cables had to be relayed through Puerto Rico. Morrison should, of course, have cabled him in the first place instead of writing. The mails were very slow. Perhaps, though, poor old Morrison had not realized the gravity of his own condition. Reuter had been obliged to use his instinct over that letter. The information it contained and his knowledge of the tropics and of Morrison all had conspired to make him realize the necessity for this hastily undertaken voyage.

Morrison had written that he was coming down again with another attack of pneumonia. His letter had been written in the Municipal Hospital. This attack, Reuter knew, would be likely to finish him. If he were to see Morrison alive—if their affairs were not to dissolve in sudden ruin, now that they were in their most critical state of development—he must go, and go at once; be standing by to see poor Morrison out if he should last until his arrival, and then immediately take over the control of affairs himself. One thing was certain; Morrison was still alive. Otherwise he would have had a cable. It was peculiarly unfortunate that Morrison had come down ill at this particular time. Their business required constant, personal attention, Morrison on one end, in St. Thomas; he on the other, in New York.

A sudden, general movement among the stevedores aroused Reuter out of his thoughts to watch what was going on below him on deck. The stevedores, their task finished, were collecting their coats, swarming over the ship's side onto the dock. Under the direction of a ship's officer the crew now turned to at getting the tarpaulins over the closed hatches; the wedges were already being driven home on one of them. Hawsers were being cast off. The two tugboats were no longer weaving in and out among the traffic out in the river. Both were attached, now, and hauling skillfully.

The ship was beginning to move. Reuter watched the careful process of backing out into the stream, but his mind was still on Morrison. Poor old Morrison! Well, if he passed out in the meantime, he would be getting a message, after three days at sea, at about the extreme range of the St. Thomas wireless station. He arranged for that in his cable. He could not keep his mind off Morrison, somehow. Well, that was natural enough. He sighed deeply, turned, and went forward to the boat-deck. The *Bonaventure* was well out in the river now, her bows swinging toward the open sea. The tugs dropped off. The breeze from the lower bay began to blow. The voyage had begun.

When Reuter went back to his stateroom afer the early dinner which the occasional passengers on his line took with the ship's officers, the alarm-bell and its accompanying sign again struck his eye. He read through the sign again, carefully, his mind still preoccupied with Morrison.

After a short evening spent arranging his cabin for the voyage, and tired out by the unusual exertions of that very busy day ashore, he turned in not long after eight bells. It was a comfort to settle down in the narrow berth and relax. Just before switching off the light he paused and read the sign through once more. Then he shut his eyes and slept like the dead until a smiling black steward carrying hot black coffee

242

awakened him at six bells in the morning, announcing: "Breakfast in half an hour, sir."

The voyage was entirely uneventful. For three days and nights the *Bonaventure* plowed along at a steady ten knots S.S.E. through the deepening blue of the ocean. Every day, at first as they traversed the Gulf Stream, then later, to the south'ard of it, the hue of the water became more intense until it took on that perfect indigo color which artists find easy to paint, and viewers of their pictures who have not seen the West Indian waters, find hard to credit. About the ship the trailing edge-weed of the Atlantic Sargasso wavered out in long strings, indicating the direction of the current wind to the least knowing landsman. Reuter noted the first of the flying fish in the late afternoon of the second day, and on the early morning of the third a few of the snouted porpoises which suggest to the beholder the dolphins of antique pictorial art.

Every evening, before retiring, he read through gravely the sign below the bell in his cabin. Every morning when he awakened it was always, somehow, the first object to catch his eye. It was as though some vague premonition, connected inexplicably with the alarm-bell, had laid its strong hold upon his imagination. Once, after he had switched off the light and slipped into his bunk, so strongly did this feeling persist, that he could not get asleep. Rather shamefacedly he rose, turned on the light, drew out and dusted a life-preserver, and tried it on. Rather grimly he smiled at his reflection, wearing it, in the small mirror before he replaced it and turned in again.

On the stroke of six bells—three o'clock in the early morning—of the fourth day at sea, he was abruptly wrenched into full wakefulness by a deep, insistent clanging beside him. *The alarm-bell!*

He rolled hastily out of his bunk and fumbled for the light. When he had found it and switched it on, and struggled to adjust his suddenly blinded eyes to its glare, he noted the bell had ceased ringing, though clearly in his mind still sounded its harsh note of clangorous, insistent warning.

He reached up and rapped the gong smartly with his seal ring. It answered with the note which had awakened him. Though that made it unmistakable, he wondered vaguely why it had ceased ringing. It should, he supposed, have continued automatically. He wondered what disaster could have overtaken the ship. As he tugged on his bathrobe and thrust his feet hurriedly into his slippers, and reached to the rack for a life-preserver, he heard, clearly, the steady throb of the engines. Disaster? What had happened? Well, the directions on the sign—(did he not know them by heart!)—were to go on deck at once. Out there, of course, he would find out in short order.

He opened his cabin door, expecting to meet he knew not what. He stepped carefully over the high iron door-sill, life-preserver hanging over his left arm. He turned aft at once and made his way, rapidly for the semi-darkness, along the covered-in passageway on which his door opened, towards the ladder leading to the deck above. It was there that the lifeboats stood in their chocks. As he mounted the ladder he remembered, inconsequently, that he had always wanted to see just how efficiently those new-fashioned leaning davits worked in the actual launching of a lifeboat. Now, probably, he was to find out!

He found the boat-deck deserted. A slight breeze, the very northernmost edge of the early-morning Trade, freshly blowing, was just beginning to make itself felt. Above, in a perfectly cloudless sky, the great stars flamed and glowed. There was no moon, but the reflection of Venus lay to starboard like a thin, unbroken bar of faint moonlight along the smooth sea. The *Bonaventure* forged steadily onward, her engines throbbing monotonously in their incessant, sustained beat.

Somewhat bewildered now, he walked farther forward along the boat-deck. He paused under a broad canvas awning just below the extension of the bridge on the port side. There was no motion except the slight, undulating pitch of the vessel as she responded to the long Atlantic swell of Latitude 28. In the soft and silent calm of this subtropic night the footfalls, regular and unhurried, of the slowly pacing officer on duty came delicately to his ears. It would be Mr. Sills, the Third Officer, at this hour.

Reuter spoke hesitantly up the bridge companionway.

"Good morning, Mr. Sills."

The officer on the bridge paused in his steady walk. Doubtless he would think it somewhat strange for a passenger to be up on the boat-deck at this unusual hour. That bell!

"Good morning, Mr. Reuter," came Sills's voice. "Very bright starlight this morning. Did you notice Venus?"

"Remarkably clear—yes! I was noticing Venus particularly. Shows up quite like a regular little moon, doesn't she?"

The officer remained to chat for a moment, then resumed his duty-tramp along the bridge, his tread leisurely—no indication here of anything out of the ordinary. Disaster!

Reuter glanced down at his life-preserver, dangling awkwardly from his arm. He hoped Mr. Sills had not noticed it. The life-preserver seemed an incongruity on this perfect night.

That bell!

Could this, perhaps, be one of those cases such as one read about occasionally—an assumed, reassuring calm on the part of the officers, a professionally false calm to keep the passengers from a stampede in the face of imminent danger? No! Hardly that, here, under these circumstances. There were only two or three passengers aboard the tramp besides himself, all men. He was alone on this deck where the lifeboats stood, still in their chocks, belted down, their rigging coiled as though no one ever expected to disturb it. This, of course, was no passenger ship. The ringing of the alarm-bell at this time of night could have no possible meaning except public and necessary announcement of disaster. Even on passenger vessles boat-drills always came daytimes at convenient hours. The wording of the sign was explicit and unmistakable.

To Reuter's now thoroughly alert mind only one explanation was possible. He must have dreamed, vividly, of the bell's ringing. Such an explanation seemed absurd, ridiculous. But that would at least account for its silence after he had switched on his light and noticed that it was ringing no longer. Perhaps, he reminded himself, the sign had made, in his state of preoccupation about poor Morrison, an absurdly strong impression on his mind. It was curious, though, that the *note* of the bell, as he had heard it—in his sleep, if that were the true explanation—had exactly corresponded to its actual note; the sound it had given out when he had rapped it with his ring. He had never tried ringing it before. He had no previous knowledge of the gong's note.

He remained there on the boat-deck a few minutes longer, greatly puzzled. He looked out at the slightly phosphorescent sea and upward at the serene stars. Disaster! Well—it had been a very queer experience for him, in his matter-of-fact existence; something to think about, surely—it would supply him with a story to tell. . . .

He went below, almost reluctantly, now, because of the charm of this warm night out here on deck, and the soft early-morning breeze, which was now coming in little puffs from the West, the land side—somewhere off Florida they would be now—back to his cabin. He looked first at the sign and the bell, half fascinated, his brows heavily puckered in his deep puzzlement. He did not tap the bell again before putting out the light and turning in. Contrary to his expectation, for he felt very completely awake, he fell asleep immediately. He slept straight through until the arrival of the steward with the morning coffee aroused him at seven.

After his shower and breakfast he settled himself in a deck chair on the shady starboard side of the boat-deck, away from the blazing morning sun. Idly he ran through the unread portions and even the advertisements of a magazine hastily purchased just before coming aboard four days before. It was here, about the middle of the morning, that the wireless operator found him and handed him a message just received. It was from St. Thomas, from the Chief Municipal Physician, at the hospital, Commander Joseph Carver of the Navy. The message was explicit and terse, Navy style.

Poor old Morrison! Always careful and considerate, Morrison. He, of course, had provided for the sending of this message in case he was called West before Reuter's ship arrived.

He would not even be able to get there in time for the funeral! Two full days, possibly a third, must necessarily intervene before the *Bonaventure* could tie up to the West India Docks in St. Thomas harbor. In the Islands they buried people, usually, the same day on which they died. Reuter looked at his watch. It was ten-thirty-three now. Morrison had been dead more than seven hours.

He had gone out at three o'clock! Abruptly it flashed into Reuter's mind—that was when he had heard the "disaster" bell. He could fell little chills now running up and down his spine. . . .

He pulled himself together. He stood up, thrust the wireless message into the pocket of his drill coat. There would be a tremendous lot for him to attend to when he arrived. Too bad he could not be at the funeral! That could not be helped. Thinking of the endless details that would be piled up for him on his arrival, an anxious frown on his forehead, he walked aft, descended the ladder, and entered his stateroom.

The sign took his first glance, held it. He stood there, just inside the stateroom door, looking at it fixedly, as though fascinated. Had it actually rung or not? Would he ever, really, know? He walked the length of the room and looked closely at the bell. It was, of course, no more than an inanimate thing, a mechanical device, glistening in its white ship's paint. He could recall, as though it were only a few moments ago, the precise tone of it, as it had sounded, recording itself in his sleep-ridden brain; that had been nearly eight hours ago, just at the time when Morrison had passed out, hundreds of miles away down there in St. Thomas.

Abruptly he reached up and inserted his index finger under the gong's heavy spehrical clapper. As he tried to raise it he encountered a stiff resistance. He thrust a little harder with a muscular finger. He saw that he was only bending the wire by which the globular copper ball was attached to the make-and-break electrical appliance which rang the gong. Then, very carefully, he straightened the bent wire. He took hold of the rectangular piece of metal to which the wire was attached at its other end. He tried to force this up. Again he encountered resistance. It would not budge. *The gong was not in working order!* He stepped on the metal railing of the lower bunk. He peered at the apparatus, his head bent close.

Successive coatings of the ship's paint had fastened down the gong's clapper rigidly. Reuter took out his knife and pried under the paint, hard now as cement. Flakes of it came away under the knife blade. He had the clapper entirely freed now. Probably it had not rung the gong since its original installation. It moved stiffly, grating back and forth reluctantly under his hand. He lifted it up forcibly, then let it fall back into place upon the gong's rim with a solid impact. . . .

The gong sounded in the very middle of the note that had been ringing in his mind; the note he had been expecting; the note that had been stamped into his mind at three o'clock that morning, when Morrison had died.

Disaster.

He stepped down slowly to the stateroom's deck, dusting off white flaked particles and chippings of ancient paint from his hands and the front of his coat. He stood in the middle of the room, his feet wide apart, and read the sign through once more. Unconscious of his own action, he shook his head, doubtfully. He remained standing there for a long time, balancing himself to the ship's slow roll, in a musing daze.

At last he lowered his eyes, turned, and walked slowly out of his stateroom, mounted to the deck, resumed his chair, and picked up the abandoned magazine.

But he did not open the magazine. Instead he laid it across his knees to serve as a writing desk. It had occurred to him that he ought to jot down as many things as he could think of—it would be wise to have them clearly in mind—the many things that would have to be attended to as soon as the *Bonaventure* had made fast alongside the West India Company's docks in St. Thomas.

In the Hour Before Dawn

Brad Strickland

Charles was unmistakably in the country of dreams. He stood alone in a shallow, bowl-like valley, scooped from fine-grained, silvery sand. Here and there boulders interrupted the gently curved surface, boulders that were themselves smooth and golden, like polished statues of sleeping elephants.

Charles' own body seemed indistinct. He could not say whether he wore a suit, shirt and trousers, or nothing at all. Otherwise his senses registered nothing unusual. The air smelled like air. When he stooped and thrust his hand into the sand, it was silky and cool to the touch. It tasted of nothing. Standing with head bowed, as if intent on prayer or thought, he heard no sound. And as for vision, except for the bowl-shaped valley and the boulders, all he could see was the sky, doomed like a lid badly put into place over him, a luminescent mother-of-pearl gray all around the horizon's edge, darkening in the concavity overhead to a red-purple, reminding him of the color of a bruise.

I am dreaming, Charles thought suddenly. How strange, to be dreaming, and to be aware that he was dreaming! As strange, he suspected, as to be fully awake and to be aware that one was fully awake. The notion struck him as in some sense profound, and to himself, he thought, *That is something I must remember. I must hold on to that idea for the time when I awake.*

"Excuse me." In that silence the voice boomed loud as an earthquake, startling as summer thunder. "Excuse me. I am dreaming of you, I know, but I don't know you."

Charles turned. The speaker had just come from behind one of the boulders. He was a man about Charles' age—thirty-one—but shorter, much darker of hair and eye, and more muscular. Oddly, Charles had less trouble seeing the stranger than he had seeing himself: the man wore tan trousers, no shirt, no shoes. Heat glistened in the perspiration underlying the dark mat of chest hair. "That's odd," Charles said. "I am dreaming you, and you believe yourself to be dreaming me. How very odd."

The other man had a one-sided smile, a quarter inch higher on the left side of his face than his right. "You're wrong. *I* am dreaming you. Don't confuse yourself by imagining you really exist."

Charles laughed. "Certainly I exist. I have a name and address. I am Charles Dayton, and I live on Revere Drive in Somerville. My students at the university would be very surprised to find that I *don't* exist. Maybe not unhappy, but definitely surprised."

The stranger shook his head, still smiling his one-sided smile. "I don't know how I came to dream of a teacher from Somerville. I don't even know where that is—if there is such a place. But I *know* I exist. I'm Paul Dupont. I'm a trial lawyer. And I live in Sierra Heights, outside of Santa Rosita, with my wife."

"I've got a wife, too," Charles blurted, feeling obscurely as if the other had scored a point. "Now look, I never dream of strangers. Always people I know, or sort of odd conglomerations of people I know. I don't know you—and I don't believe there's even a place named Santa Rosita."

Paul looked annoyed. "Come to think of it, I've never dreamed up a stranger, either. Not one with a phony name and address, anyhow. But there's always a first time."

248

"What am I wearing?" Charles asked.

Paul frowned. "What do you mean by that?"

"Come on," Charles said. "You call yourself a lawyer—you're supposed to have some intelligence, aren't you? Just tell me what you see. How am I dressed?"

"You're barefoot. You have on some white shorts; tennis shorts, I guess. That's all. So what?"

"What are you wearing?" Charles asked.

Paul frowned down at himself. "Something's keeping me from seeing it. I guess I haven't dreamed that part yet."

"You're not dreaming at all. Get it through your head that *you're* the imaginary one. I am real, and my home and family are real. There's no Paul, no wife, no Santa Rosita."

"Nonsense!" The lawyer paced back and forth on the silver sand, his head down. Then he paused and gazed sidelong at Charles. "Is it not true that you never know when you're dreaming?"

"No. I know I'm dreaming now."

"Have you ever done it before? Known you were dreaming while you were dreaming?"

"Not that I remember."

Paul turned to face Charles. "Then you would say that it's unusual for you to be aware of your own dreams, while you are actually dreaming?"

"Very unusual," Charles agreed, amused at how much like a real lawyer his imaginary lawyer sounded.

Paul's voice rang with triumph: "Then that indicates, wouldn't you say, that the probability is that you are not dreaming now—because you cannot dream, you are just a figment of my imagination?"

"That's idiotic. Look, Paul whatever-your-name-is, you may think you're real, but that's only because I dreamed you so well. I gave you the illusion of reality so strongly that you believe in yourself."

Paul wouldn't give up. "But isn't it at least as likely that I have given you the illusion of reality? That I have dreamed *you* so well that you believe you exist, when in fact you do not?" He stooped suddenly, snatched a handful of sand, and flung it at Charles.

Charles spun, lifting his arm to ward off the stinging particles. They hit forearm, shoulder, neck, but missed his eyes. "Hey!"

"Funny," Paul said. "I thought it'd go right through you. Maybe I ought to try a rock."

Charles rubbed a hand across his face and held up a dripping palm. "Look at that. I suppose you think that isn't real?"

"Imaginary sweat," scoffed Paul. "You fool. Even if you were right, you'd still be dreaming it, so even then it wouldn't be real. And if I dreamed of something as unpleasant as you, I could certainly dream of sweat."

Charles stalked over to Paul. He came so close he could feel the exhaled breath of the other man stirring the air, could hear the faint rush of it through the other's nose and sinuses. "See if this seems real," he said, and hit the other man in the mouth.

Paul reeled back, blood spurting from a cut lip. He shook his head, scattering drops that made pear-shaped red spatters on the sand, and then lunged head down at Charles. The two rolled over in the silver sand, and though Charles strained muscle and sinew, it was no use. They were too evenly matched and too inexpert for either to get a temporary advantage.

Charles' breath burned hot and harsh when at last both of them rested on hands and knees, a yard away from each other. Both were panting, sweating, and bleeding. "This is nonsense," Paul said. "Soon I'll wake up, and you will be gone."

"I agree," Charles said. "Except *I'll* wake up, and you will vanish."

"Then all we have to do is wait." Paul pushed up, grimacing as if weary and in pain. He backed away and sat on one of the golden boulders. His shoulders bowed and his chest heaved.

Charles sank onto another stone. He felt every ache in his muscles, every rip in his skin, every drop of sweat that crawled like a warm little snail down his face. *I am real,* Charles thought. *I will wake up, and it will all be as it has been before. He will vanish.* He looked into the other's haunted eyes. *He really believes that he is the dreamer,* Charles thought. *He really does — just as I do.* Panic fluttered light butterfly wings in his belly. *What if he is right?* Charles wondered for the first time.

Almost simultaneously, he read the exact thought in the other's eyes.

Exhausted, helpless beneath the bruised dome of the dreamed sky, the two sat staring at one another, hating one another, and waiting out the hour before dawn.

Waking came quickly, with an outrush of breath. He looked up at the familiar white ceiling. From the corner of his left eye, he could see the night table where he had carelessly thrown his trousers last night. Through the open bedroom door came kitchen sounds and smells. Meg making Monday's breakfast for the two of them.

He had not wept in ages, but he did now. He closed his eyes. "God," he said. "What did I do to deserve that?" Then he laughed silently, his chest bucking beneath the sheet.

"You awake?" Meg called.

He did not trust himself to speak.

250

After a moment she called again, closer, louder, "Honey, wake up. Time to get going. You have to be in court at nine."

He frowned. "Court? What in hell do you mean?"

A strange woman stood in the doorway. "Paul, get up. What's got into you this morning?"

Open-mouthed, she backed into the hallway as the man in the bed held out his dark-skinned arms, studied his compact hands, and started to scream.

Is This a Horror Story?

Scott Edelman

This is a horror story. Of that I am certain. Yet no ghosts are in it, nor werewolves, nor vampires. There are only people.

Sunday had been quiet. My wife and I were four months into a stay with my in-laws as we saved the money necessary to purchase our own home. We had been house-hunting all that morning and afternoon, and now we were resting while our son made trips back and forth from his room to proudly show us different toys. In the basement, my sister-in-law was talking to a family friend who was in the process of installing a ceiling lamp.

Balancing precariously atop a ladder, the friend came across a cache of photos hidden above a heating duct. Between two of the packages was a letter of license suspension from the Department of Motor Vehicles. While my sister-in-law continued overseeing the repair of the basement, my wife and I sat on the edge of our bed and began to examine the photographs.

The first package contained a series of photos of a naked man fucking a child-sized doll. Rough words, but these were rough pictures. The man, faceless in every photo, violated that doll in dozens of positions, exhibiting himself for a photographer who snapped him from every angle. Who was willing to take those photos? Who would? My wife and I nervously returned them to their envelope.

The next batch of photos were of neatly folded kids' underwear. On the floor. On a bed. I tried to decide whether they had been bought or stolen, whether they'd been worn or were fresh, but could not. Halfway through the subject changed to a panda doll stuffed into a kid's underwear, and then twisted into sexual positions. Ridiculous. And yet, to the former owner of these photos, they had surely been erotically charged with sexual power. What thoughts had gone through this man's head as he masturbated? That is surely what he did. I looked at the plush toy, and wondered how he could stop from laughing.

Children's lingerie ads from Sears catalogs made up most of the next envelope. There were also photos of children, school portraits and the like, and photos of groupings of other photos, dizzying us with their density. My wife and I flipped through these photos with a strange curiosity, intrigued at seeing into another's soul and yet fearful of the horrors that could come. We peeked through the fingers of our minds, trying to stay in an adult *"Chacun à son gout,"* even as each photo propelled us to an "Oh, come on!" It was then that we thought to look at the backs of the photos. They had all been taken five years before—before my mother-in-law had purchased the property.

It wasn't until the last batch that we came across the photos that had been taken of the children.

Snapshot number one:

A prepubescent girl in a short skirt, her hands held high over her head so that her underwear could be seen. Was her face full of fear? Did she realize what was happening? Or did she think she was playing some sort of game with a family friend? The photographer's bare knee was visible in the foreground. My curiosity suddenly turned to nausea.

"Oh, no," I said, my mind imposing a subtext on the photo. Our find had suddenly been pushed from a matter of personal and private kinkiness, in which case we would have simply trashed the photos, to something possibly far, far more. "Do you think we should call the police?"

We looked through the rest of the photos in the final packet. Nothing more explicit than the first, but still . . .

"I think we should call the police," I said.

I wanted those photos out of our house, but no one in authority could be reached that night. I went to sleep expecting nightmares, but none came.

Immediately upon awakening the next morning, I phoned the police. I was extremely nervous as I tried to explain exactly what it was we had found, for I was afraid they would think my wife and I were overreacting. I was at a loss for words. I couldn't quite claim we'd found evidence of child abuse, so I fell silent as I tried to give words to what we had found. After my voice had trailed off my wife prompted me, and I repeated what she'd said, that the photographs, though not in themselves criminal, "indicated an interest in children."

A detective from the Juvenile Sex Squad was over in less than twenty minutes to take possession of our discovery, and to take his own photos of the place where they had been found.

The officer raised an eyebrow as he examined the letter from the Department of Motor Vehicles.

"I can't tell you exactly why," he said softly. "But I'm already familiar with the name on that envelope."

The officer left, carrying his prize, and we returned to our lives. My wife took our son to his library playschool, and did a manuscript evaluation for an aspiring author. I went to my salaried daytime job, and later that evening tried to write.

Sometimes the pieces that I write are considered horror stories. At least, that is what the market chooses to call them, for they end up being printed in magazines published for a horror audience, magazines with titles such as *Deathrealm* and *Eldritch Tales*. That evening, as I contemplated the blank page, I did not think that anything I wrote could ever make anyone feel as uneasy as I felt turning that last photo and seeing that little girl's white underwear. Even attempting to fill that blank page somehow seemed pointless . . .

A question reverberated through me then. It echoes through me now, and I don't know if there is any answer to it.

If this is a horror story, is it one?

Or two?

The Journal of Edward Hargood

D. N. J.

Several years ago I happened to be in the Library of Downing College for the purpose of consulting some Register, and in my wanderings in search of the catalogue of books, I came upon an old dirty, long-neglected volume, bound in cardboard and dingy yellow leather, stamped on the back with the title "Journal of Edward Hargood, Surgeon, of Cambridge." Inside the cover was an inscription to the effect that this book, with many others, had been left to the College by one John Hamilton Craik, at the time of his death in 1852, and to judge from its outward appearance it had never been touched since the first day of its sojourn in the College. On turning over the pages, I was surprised to find, not some hundred odd pages of dull print, as I had expected, but a long manuscript journal, written in a firm, clear hand, bound up with a few letters and papers. This was, in itself, surprising enough, but on reading some way into the book, my eye fell upon a sentence which effectually roused my interest. It ran as follows: "Jan. 18. To-day at work all day with Dr Dunning who made a communication [to] me of greatest importance." A few pages further on I read again: "Dunning at work with me most of this day and a long conversation after."

I need hardly retail in full to Cambridge readers the strange story that centres round the name of Dunning, but in case there should be some who have not yet heard it, I will relate, without adornment, the main facts of his life. He was born in 1692 and came to Benét College, Cambridge, in 1710. From 1714 to 1720 he resided as a Fellow of his College, but in the last-mentioned year he seems to have inherited some considerable fortune, and for the next seventeen years he was never in Cambridge. But in 1737 he suddenly re-appeared, evidently a poor man once more, and for thirty years lived in his old rooms on the ground-floor of L staircase in Benét College, seeing hardly a soul outside his College, and devoting his energies to the translation of the works of several obscure German physicians. Towards the end of the year 1767 he disappeared as suddenly as he had re-appeared, and to this day, in spite of many theories, the mystery of his fate has never been solved.

Readers, therefore, will understand my excitement when I came across this name in the manuscript journal in Downing Library. I obtained leave to take it home with me, and at once looked up the dates of its commencement and ending; my interest was, if possible, redoubled on finding that the first entry was made on January 1st, 1761, and the last on November 9th, 1768, that is to say, about twelve months after Dunning's disappearance. At last, I thought, I shall find some clue to the Dunning Mystery. But on reading through the journal I was, at first, bitterly disappointed and then horribly fascinated. It is one of the most amazing productions that it has ever been my fate to read. Of life and thought in Cambridge in the eighteenth century it gives hardly a glimpse, and in all its three hundred and seventy-three pages there are only about twenty names mentioned, the most frequent of which is that of Dunning. The rest of the book is confined to a few domestic details of rather a sordid nature, a vast deal of outrageous and indecent blasphemy, and long-drawn descriptions of disease and of operations carried out with all the barbarity of surgery in the eighteenth century. These last descriptions fill nearly three-quarters of the book, and they shew a dark and perverted nature, absolutely heartless and devoid of any feeling for human weakness or human pain. Over all there reigns a spirit of grim and brutal humour that finds expression in comments that, at first, sound only naive and childish, until their lurking ferocity becomes manifest.

254

For instance, in describing the death of some unhappy victim under his hands, he writes: "never did I hear a boy give so much outcry; he died after a vast deal of it, as I was scraping the bone, more of the pain than his injuries I suppose." This is one of the more tolerable incidents recorded; others are too repulsive for print, and the kindest interpretation to put upon them is that Edward Hargood had lost all semblance of humanity in his love of his profession.

But, as regards Dunning, the journal is, at first sight, disappointing. In the beginning there are several records of him, such as "at work with old Mr Dunning again in Findsilver St.," "a long talk with old Dunning," and once or twice mention is made of "a conversation through his window with D. tonight till very late." But in the crucial year of 1767 Dunning is only mentioned by name five times, and at the supposed date of his disappearance from his rooms there is one of the frequent lacunae in the journal, of some seven weeks duration. Although all Cambridge was gossiping about the "strange story," Hargood, one of Dunning's few acquaintances outside his college, makes no mention of it until January 17th, 1768. On January 17th, he notes that "Mr Cowper came to see [me] to-day from the Master and Fellows of his college, and asked me of this alleged disappearance of Dr Dunning. I gave what information I could, and said I thought he was only gone from Cambridge a time." After this entry follows a diatribe against "Fellows and the like," with whom Hargood, to judge from one or two earlier passages, was not on good terms.

After this incursion of foreign interest, the journal continues on its bloodthirsty way, and the accounts of dissections and operations are given with greater regularity and almost more copiousness than usual, and Dunning's name is not mentioned again until November 7th. At this date the Diary assumes, of a sudden, a most dramatic form, which we must describe in detail.

On November 7th the entry is short and alarming, and runs as follows:

"Nov. 7. to-night had in Mr Morden of Catherine Hall, who talks of publishing Dunning's old papers, which worthless, when a most surprising Occurence. I was standing talking to M. seated before me, when he goes into a Fit, becoming first much suffused with Blood in the Face, and very red, his eyes shooting out, as he saw something which frightened [him]. Then he became very pale, his mouth dropping down in a Grin, and he waves, half rising from the Chair, his Hand at the Mirrour behind me, as if he saw something, and falls in a Swoon upon the Floor. I have in help and he was carried to his Rooms. I am curious to know what gave him such Terrour and what he thought to see behind me."

Under this startling entry there comes a black line, evidently drawn with a quill pen in some impatience. On close inspection, under this line, can be descried some faded handwriting, extraordinarily minute and spider-like and quite illegible. Two days later, Hargood notes that Morden has died "of the Fit he had in my House," and then the entry goes on to say

"being ill with a putrid sore throat, little work to-day, and I am much provoked to find th ———— "

The entry breaks off dramatically at this point, and then follows this strange exclamation, written in an agitated hand,

"God whom I have denied help me."

and again underneath,

"God whom I have denied help me."

But under this second wild appeal for help, once more there can be descried the faint, weird handwriting that appears under the black line on November 7th. After these two last entries there comes a sentence, written in quite a different hand,

"I have guessed   this is a terrible book,"

and so the journal ends.

So far, it may be said that this Journal throws no new light on the Dunning mystery, but I now must quote two MSS I found incorporated with the Journal. The first is short and runs as follows:

"This book came into the possession of my friend Charles Morrison from the Library of his uncle, Archdeacon Morrison. I have often heard him tell how he found it in his uncle's hands at the time of his sudden death." (signed) J. H. Craik.

The other document is a letter from Charles Morrison to John Craik, Esq (dated March 2nd, 1851) and copied out in Craik's handwriting. It runs as follows:

"Dear Craik. I have found out the mystery of that abominable book and I wish to Heaven I had not. All my suspicions of H. were true.

'The truth suddenly flashed through my mind as I was sitting by myself after dinner with the book on my knees, and before I knew what I was about, I was round at the side-board and had flung the book upside down before the glass, open at the last page, where that horrible little impish handwriting comes. After a few minutes poring, I made out in the reflection of the page, that the first sentence after Hargood's remark 'I am curious to know what he thought to see behind me,' ran as follows, with no capitals and repeated twice:

'it was i o mine enemy.'

"I was hurrying on in wild agitation to the next sentence under H's appeal for help, when suddenly an overpowering thought seized me. I remembered how my uncle had died with this book in his hand and *I felt I now knew why.* I did not dare to look up or take my eyes away from the reflected page, but stood staring at it stupidly. You may laugh at what I saw next, but I tell you in that moment I saw in the glass the hand of an old man, very thin and wrinkled and very cruel looking, with soiled ruffles at the wrist, glide over my sleeve and point with its fore-finger to the second sentence and slowly pass along the page. Fascinated I followed it and read 'i come to-morrow the end of one year for mine enemy.' At the end of the sentence the hand stopped. I did not dare to look up to see what might be at my back, but shut my eyes and turned round, opening them saw—nothing. I have not been able to abide the sight of a looking glass these last two days, and write to ask you to come quickly, yours, C. Morrison.

"Postscript. My poor friend died before I came to him, on March 5th, 1851.

"J. H. C."

Inspired by my interest in this book, some years ago, I made enquiries into Hargood's life. I met with disappointingly little success. All I could find was that he lived in Cambridge from 1759 to 1768 in a large house on the High Street, next door to the Dolphin Inn, with a small garden at the back, going up to the walls of Benét College. This house (which was once occupied by the famous Dr E. D. Clarke) was destroyed in 1817 to make room for the new buildings of Corpus Christi College. The other fact which I found of any interest is that he was buried in St Benét's Churchyard on November 12th, 1768.

Whether the terrible theory propounded in the letter I have quoted contains the right explanation of the mystery or whether it is a grim joke of Mr Craik's conception, I have not presumed to find out. I returned the book to the Library the day after I had taken it out, and there it is lying probably at the present moment, unknown and untouched by any hand since the day I placed it once more upon its obscure and dusty shelf.

Kisses from Auntie

Craig Shaw Gardner

It was the punch that did it.

We decided that afterward, of course. There wasn't time to think of anything else when it happened, which was funny. At Auntie's we usually had more time than we could ever use.

"Give us a kiss, loves," Auntie said, and she smiled with her big red lips. Both Bruce and I closed our eyes and waited. We knew what was coming. If you kept still and didn't squirm, you'd get it over with right away.

I mean, it was bad enough when I had to put on one of my smelly old dresses and then had to let Mom brush out my hair before we went to Auntie's party. And Auntie had parties *every* week! And then, first thing, right when we got there, Auntie always had to kiss us. A big wet one on the cheek. Absolutely blech!

Auntie had this smell—lavender water, Mom said when we asked her about it. Bruce and I decided that she had to pour it all over herself to smell that bad.

"Oh, you're my special children!" Auntie said when the kissing was over. "If only Uncle were here to see you now. You know, I've watched you grow since you were knee-high to a grasshopper. But you probably wouldn't remember that, would you?"

Bruce and I both shook our heads. "Be polite!" Mom and Daddy always said. For a while we tried.

But I was talking about the punch, half ginger ale and half cranberry juice. It tasted much worse than either one tasted by itself, I mean, absolutely blech. We got it when the grown-ups got their wine or liquor or whatever it was that grown-ups drink. Auntie would go around and ask, "What would you like to drink, Tom?" And Daddy would say, "I don't know, Alma. Maybe a Manhattan." And then Auntie would ask Mom the same question, and Mom would say, "Oh, whatever Tom's having is fine with me." And then she'd ask Gramma and Gramma's other sisters. But never, never did Auntie ask us what we wanted. She just brought us the punch.

Something had to be done about it. Bruce and I both stared at our glasses and frowned.

"Oh dear," Auntie said, bending close so that we could really smell the lavender. "It looks like poor Bruce and Laura have the fidgets. You don't have to stay here, dears, and be bored. Why don't you run upstairs and play until dinner?"

So we did.

Bruce and I decided that everything about Auntie couldn't be that bad, because upstairs was a special place, particularly the door right at the top of the stairs, the place Auntie called the back bedroom. It was full of all sorts of things; Daddy called it junk, but Bruce and I knew better. I mean, there were a lot of dusty green books with gold lettering that nobody would ever want to look at, but there were also three big brown photo albums with pictures of Auntie when she was my parents' age, standing in all sorts of places with some man Bruce and I figured must be "Uncle." And there were piles of old *National Geographics*, some of them with pictures of people without any clothes on. There was a big box of old toys that sat in front of the closet door with a lot of dolls and a red metal fire engine and a big bag of crayons, half of them black. When we could get away from the grown-ups, Auntie's back bedroom was all right.

But this time, when we reached the bedroom, the box of toys was gone. I frowned at Bruce. We'd have to look at the pictures again.

"Maybe," Bruce said, "Auntie put it behind the door." He walked over to the closet, with me close behind. Bruce turned to me and grinned. It was a door we had never opened!

He pulled the door open as quietly as he could. We were wrong. It wasn't a closet; there were stairs going up.

"Should we?" I whispered. Mom and Daddy might get mad if we didn't come down in time for supper, but I'd never seen a real attic!

Bruce hit my shoulder. "C'mon! It's better than going back downstairs to drink Auntie's punch!" The first stair creaked when he put his foot on it. He went up anyway.

I climbed right behind. I had to lift up my dress a little so that it wouldn't get dirty on the old steps. They were narrow and spaced wide apart, more like a ladder, almost. It was dark. Something brushed my forehead—a piece of string. I grabbed at it and pulled the light on.

We were in the attic, and we saw the skeleton.

I had turned on two light bulbs with the string somehow. We were under one of them, and the skeleton was under the other—a human skeleton. Bruce grabbed my arm. It got to me too, but I wanted to explore.

"Don't be a scaredy-cat!" I whispered. "Bones can't hurt you." I took a step toward the skeleton. Bruce stayed close behind. It was my turn to be brave.

The walls of the attic were full of shelves, and the shelves were full of jars, all sizes and shapes of jars, each one labeled with tiny handwriting that was hard to read. Bruce squinted inside a particularly big one.

"Aren't those eyeballs?" he whispered.

Honestly! My big brave brother. The first time we get into a strange place, he gets the creepies.

I thought the attic was great. We crept down a narrow path left between the jars on one side and the piles of old furniture and boxes on the other. Bruce started to slow down, but I pulled him after me. We were walking toward the skeleton. The bones hung from a hook in the ceiling, and there was an open space on the floor around them. It was the only open space in the whole attic. On the other side of the cleared place was a big desk, with the biggest book I'd ever seen on top of it. In between the desk and the bones, I could see something written on the floor.

I bent down to take a closer look. There was a big yellow circle painted on the floor, with some kind of black marks scribbled next to it. I tried to see whether the marks said something, but the floor was much too dusty. I rubbed the dirt off one with my thumb, but the shape underneath didn't look like any letter I'd ever seen.

I dared Bruce to step into the circle, but he wouldn't do it. He just froze in one spot and stared at the skeleton. What was he afraid of? Brother Bruce, always teasing me, daring me to go places?

I stepped into the circle.

I felt like I was going downhill in a roller coaster, swinging up in a swing, and flying through the air all at the same time. I giggled and danced. I could dance, or jump, or somersault, or fly, or do anything I wanted to. That's how I felt.

My hand hit the skeleton when I jumped.

"How dare you!" I jumped again, and all the happiness left me. Auntie stood on the stairs. "What are you children doing?"

Bruce and I looked at each other. Bruce blurted out something about looking for the box of toys.

"Well, come down from there right away. You could get hurt."

Mom and Daddy were waiting for us in the back bedroom. Daddy looked angry, like he was ready to yell.

"Now, Tom," Auntie said, as she led us both by the hand past our parents. "Don't be too harsh. They're still only children, and I never told them they couldn't go up there. If I move a couple things out of the way they might get hurt with, they can go up there every time you visit."

"Mommy!" Bruce blurted out. "There was a skeleton!"

Auntie laughed. "That's something I'll definitely move. Uncle was very fond of it, you know. Part of some research or other. I really never understood it." She steered Bruce and me down the staircase to dinner.

That night, after I got home, I wanted to go back to Auntie's again. I wanted to find out all about the attic and stand inside the circle again. Who cared about my uncle's old skeleton?

Anyway, we went to Auntie's almost every week for what Daddy called "family dinner parties." Daddy called them other things too, but Mom told us never to repeat those. And so we went back to Auntie's pretty soon, even though it seemed like forever to me.

I barely waited for Auntie to kiss us to run upstairs with Bruce before she even got to the punch.

"I don't know if I want to go!" Bruce said as I pulled him up the attic stairs. But he calmed down when we got to the top and he saw that the skeleton was gone. He still looked around nervously, as if he expected it to jump out from the shadows or something. But I told him that Auntie had probably locked it in one of the trunks in the back of the attic or hung it in a closet somewhere, and that seemed to make him feel better.

I dragged him straight to the circle and pushed him in. He looked afraid for a second, but then he smiled. I stepped in after him.

Things started to happen. I mean, first it was the same feeling I had had the last time, the flying and all that. Except this time Bruce was flying with me. But then . . .

Bruce and I looked at each other, really looked at each other so that I saw right inside Bruce's eyes and saw blue lightning deep down. Bruce told me that he saw orange fire deep in mine. And the lightning flashed from Bruce's eyes, the fire jumped from mine, and they hit each other halfway between us. And where they hit, something grew.

I couldn't see what was growing there, not exactly. But I knew that it was there just the same. It grew and rose toward the ceiling.

Then I had an idea. I looked around the room. Jars shook on their shelves; something rattled in an old crate pushed into a corner. Then I saw the book on the desk, that heavy, heavy book that looked like the biggest dictionary I'd ever seen. I pointed to it. Bruce nodded. We stared at it, lightning and fire. The book took off all of a sudden and flew just above our heads. We shrieked and ducked, and the book crashed to the ground.

Bruce and I looked at each other. The lightning and flame were gone. I was happy and scared at the same time.

We heard Auntie's voice calling us to dinner.

The trouble started just as we pulled into Auntie's driveway.

"Laura, darling," my mother said, "and you too, Bruce. Your father and I have been talking. We think you should stay downstairs and talk with the relatives tonight."

"What?" Bruce yelled. "But we have to go into the attic!"

"You don't have to do anything, young man," Daddy said with a frown. "A good part of the reason we come to these silly dinners is for your grandmother and her sisters to see you. So I think you can be polite enough to stay away from the attic for once and talk to everybody."

But we couldn't do that! We had to go to the attic and fly and make everything around us fly! We always went to the attic!

Bruce started to wail, but I shook him and shook my head. Wailing never did any good with our parents. I whispered in his ear.

We ran upstairs before Auntie could even kiss us. We ran into the circle. Jars shook. The crate rattled and bumped. We'd do what we wanted! We'd show our parents!

Bruce stopped and stared behind me. I turned my head. Auntie was there.

She smiled her big red smile.

"My special children. Your father's very angry at you, you know."

"So what?" Bruce demanded. We were in the circle. We could do anything.

"I told them you'd get tired of your game and come down to dinner eventually. You're both very special to me. I don't want to see anything happen to you."

She walked toward us on old, shaky legs. The smell of lavender filled the room.

"Give us a kiss," she said. For some reason, we let her.

"Now be careful," Auntie said as she walked away. "I don't want to worry your parents."

And she left us alone.

We were still in the circle, and I still felt the fire. It warmed my fingers and toes and ran hot along my spine. Cold lightning flashed in the dusty air, and the fire from my eyes mixed with it, and the thing that came from part of Bruce and part of me grew.

It wanted something. It wanted to be free. It would make us free. We'd never have to do anything we didn't want to again. No more being polite for our parents, no more kisses from Auntie, no more homework, no more early bedtime. We just had to let it grow, and it would show us how.

The cloud moved away. We heard Daddy's voice echo up from the back bedroom.

"Come on, kids! Time to go home!"

I looked at Bruce. He shook his head. We couldn't go home now, not now! Neither of us made a sound.

"Come on, you little devils! Don't be so stubborn! You've already missed your dinner! I'm not going to let you miss your bedtime, too!"

We heard Daddy's feet on the stairs.

"Go away!" I screamed. He couldn't come up!

"Nope! Time to go home!"

Blue light flashed in my head. I looked at Bruce. He was right. We couldn't let Daddy get us. Not until we knew.

I concentrated too and could feel the fire meet the lightning, and it grew again. It was stronger than ever this time. I could feel it throbbing in the air.

We pushed it down the stairs.

Daddy said a dirty word. Something fell, bumpity-bump-bump. "Tom!" Auntie screamed.

It was quiet after that. We were scared. What had we done? We only wanted to stay a little while and play.

Bruce went down the stairs first. I came down right behind him. There was no one in the back bedroom. We walked out onto the landing. Daddy lay there, very still. I could hear Mommy on the phone downstairs. She sounded upset.

We walked into the living room as the siren whirred outside. Mommy flung the door open to let in two men carrying some poles. They walked up to where Daddy lay. One of the men felt Daddy's body.

They undid the poles into some sort of stretcher while one of the men talked to Mommy. She nodded, and they put Daddy on the stretcher and carried him outside.

Mommy turned to us. I could tell that she'd been crying.

"Daddy's broken his leg and maybe something else. I've got to go to the hospital with him. Auntie's been good enough to volunteer to take care of you overnight. Don't give her any trouble."

Mommy grabbed her coat and ran out the door.

Auntie smiled her big red smile. "Now, Bruce and Laura, don't be frightened. Give us a kiss."

She put her big wet lips on my cheek and hugged me tight. I almost choked on the lavender smell. She went over and did the same to Bruce.

Blue flashed in my brain. I blinked. Maybe we could do it now anywhere in Auntie's house. Maybe we could do it anyplace we wanted.

We could do anything we wanted.

"You're Auntie's special children." She patted Bruce on the head. "Come into the kitchen. I'll give you some punch."

Bruce and I looked at each other. Absolutely blech.

"And then we can play some games. I imagine you children have lots of games you like to play. We'll have such a good time. And you can stay forever and ever."

Lightning flashed. I could feel the fire. We'd do what we wanted. Nobody—not Auntie, not our parents, nobody—would ever tell us what to do again.

"Come into the kitchen, children. Your punch is ready."

Bruce and I looked at each other. No more cranberry juice and ginger ale!

It grew.

No more kisses! No more boring games!

The cloud filled the room over our heads. I could really see it now. Spots of orange flame flashed in the darkness. Blue bolts of light stretched to the carpet. No more! No more!

"So soon?" It was Auntie's voice. She could see the cloud too.

The cloud moved toward her. Auntie stumbled against the refrigerator. "Bruce, Laura, you were always my special children. So gifted. When Uncle made his plans, I knew. . . ." Her voice trailed off as the first flashes of blue light snapped at her outstretched hands. She closed her eyes and let the cloud cover her.

The cloud vanished, and Auntie was gone too.

I felt like I hadn't slept in a month. It hit me just like that. The cloud had been too big; it had used up too much of us.

Bruce had fallen on the floor, his eyes closed.

What had we done? What would Mommy and Daddy say when they couldn't find Auntie?

"Bruce?" I whispered, even though there was no one around to hear. "What can we do?"

My brother opened his eyes and smiled. "It's a shame it had to happen so young."

"Bruce?" I asked. What was he talking about?

He rolled over and pushed himself up. He swayed when he stood.

"Still, Uncle will be here soon, and we'll be together forever and ever."

"Stop talking like that!" I backed up toward the kitchen door.

He walked toward me like he didn't quite know how to use his feet. He stretched out his arms to touch me. The smell of lavender was in the air.

"Give us a kiss, love," he said.

The Last Drop

Nicholas Royle

He pushed the man gently back on to the consultation chair and withdrew a gun from the pocket of his white coat. He pointed the muzzle at the man's forehead and squeezed the trigger. Then he had a better idea.

Dallman sat in his study until he heard Queenie get up and announce she was going to bed. She leaned against the study door, eyelids heavy with gin.

'Are you coming?' she asked, brushing hair out of her eyes.

'I have to finish this,' Dallman said, gesturing at the papers on his desk. They were scrap, old case notes he used for rough work. If she came and read over his shoulder she might realize, but she was unlikely to take the trouble.

She pouted and let fall the hand that was holding her unbuttoned blouse in place. He looked down and caught sight of her petticoat trailing below her skirt.

Dallman felt his ears redden. He knew that he would never stop wanting her. After she had gone he took a packet of photographs from a desk drawer. Taken a few months ago, they showed her as happy as when they had first met. Laughing and running in a city park on a Sunday afternoon. There was one of himself smiling broadly, his eyes clear and happy.

He later calculated that they were taken around the time she started seeing Kent.

For three months after he began to suspect, he did nothing. The signs became obvious to him. She started going out more often, to see French films and meet old friends in art galleries. 'I suppose you're busy,' she would say and he would collude with her, nodding miserably. He did nothing because she was happy and he didn't want to take that away from her. It made her glow.

Dallman pushed his chair back quietly and reached across the desk for his car keys.

He injected epinephrine into the scalp causing blood vessels to contract, so that when he cut into the shaved section of skin there would not be so much blood that his view was obscured. A retractor held the scalp apart, revealing a tiny rhomboid section of skull.

He took the craniotome, a stainless-steel drill with a bit that disengaged when the bone was penetrated, and pressed it against the skull. There was no nurse available to spray sterile water into the hole as he drilled. But in the circumstances it didn't matter.

He pierced the dura with the scalpel and used an electrical probe, wire-thin, to disable the motor cortex, the part of the brain controlling the voluntary muscles.

Dallman parked a couple of streets away and walked to the practice. His card permitted entry twenty-four hours a day. On the third floor he passed his own suite and proceeded to the door bearing Kent's name. In case of emergency, both senior partners had keys to the other's door. Dallman let himself in, still hoping he wouldn't find the evidence he was looking for.

He had seen the name of a restaurant in Queenie's address book when she left it by the phone one evening. La Cucina. It was not a place they had ever eaten in, nor had she mentioned it when he asked her where she went with her friends.

In the top drawer of Kent's desk Dallman found credit card receipts from La Cucina. He crumpled them in his fist and sat down heavily in a leather armchair, sighing. Regrets filled his mind. That Queenie was having an affair. And that she had chosen Kent, his partner for five years, a fine neurosurgeon and a friend.

Dallman leaned forward over the desk and jammed his knuckles into his eyes. But he couldn't stop the tears. They'd been building up since the signs first appeared and he'd been determined to contain them until he knew for certain one way or the other.

Shoulders heaving, his tears fell on to Kent's blotter. He opened his eyes and the office presented blurred forms of its angular furniture. He looked down at the blotter that was soaking up his hurt. Among the doodles he saw small concentrated groups of the letter Q.

He used a local anaesthetic the next time he opened up Kent's skull so that he could talk and his patient would be able to hear. The craniotome was required again to access another part of the brain. He located the occipital lobe and reached for his electrical probe.

'I imagine you know what I'm doing,' he said. 'Take a good look around while you still can.'

With a quick burst of volts, Dallman killed the visual centre of the brain.

Before the anaesthetic wore off he also removed Kent's power of speech, though he hadn't used it for some time, by disabling Broca's Area on the left side of the brain.

He said nothing, to Queenie or to Kent. Maybe it would run its course and she would tire of him. He was no great conversationalist, though it would not have occurred to Dallman to criticize him before in any respect. Although their liaison clearly consisted of more than talk he didn't imagine they ate in silence at La Cucina.

Weeks passed and Queenie continued to spend as many evenings out of the house as in. Dallman would go into their bedroom and smell her clothes—a scarf or petticoat—hoping in vain that her scent would bring him some pleasure.

In his study, work papers were scattered across the desk. He pored obsessively over the photographs taken in the park, as if searching for a way to alter the past.

He took out the auditory centre and a portion of the somatosensory cortex, which received and analysed sensory impulses coming from all parts of the body. He wielded his lethal probe in the fissure between the two hemispheres to block messages to the brain from the trunk, hip, leg, foot, and genitals.

Kent was sustained by a drip-feed and catheterized. A machine aided his breathing, but his condition was by no means vegetative.

Vegetables didn't think.

Dallman had so far left untouched the prefrontal area of the frontal lobe so that Kent could think about what was happening to him and why. Maybe he would look back on the affair and wish he had not been so foolish for the sake of a few Italian meals, a pile of credit card bills, and whatever secrets he and Queenie had shared. Dallman hoped so.

Revenge came unnaturally to him. Initially, the end of the affair had numbed him. But within hours, paralysis gave way to grief such as he had never known. It fell upon him with the force of a house collapsing. Even when he thought the pain had levelled out, lone bricks detached themselves from the ruins and thumped him in the head.

He had loved Queenie. But just how much he found out when it was too late.

Reluctantly, he burnt out the prefrontal area. If thoughts of Queenie had comforted Kent at all throughout his cranial decimation, they would do so no more.

Dallman reached a point where action had to be taken. Queenie was drinking herself to unhappiness. He couldn't bear to see her go into a decline.

He acquired the practice secretary's signature on a piece of letterhead, then typed a note from Kent to Queenie proposing dinner that

267

evening at La Cucina. He sent it by courier and told the secretary Kent was too busy to take calls.

He waited an hour at La Cucina and discovered later that the car crash had happened half an hour before he arrived at the restaurant. Kent had phoned Queenie and they had put two and two together. He picked her up to drive to La Cucina and confront Dallman. But they never got there.

Kent was badly shaken but unhurt. Queenie was dead.

Dallman regarded the man in the bed. Amidst all the technology and hardware of life-support he seemed barely human. Within his skull, however, were remnants of life, the premotor cortex, controlling muscular coordination, and that tiny part of the somatosensory cortex relating to the nose. The drip and the catheter continued to feed and empty him.

Dallman stared out of the window a few feet away. Dusk obscured the few people out on the streets, but he watched them pass and wondered what it must be like to *be* them. He took Queenie's petticoat from out of his pocket. The last pedestrian passed out of sight and he turned back towards Kent.

He held the petticoat under Kent's nose. Dallman could smell it himself from where he stood. Nothing changed. The drip fed him and the catheter emptied him. Dallman waited. He didn't take his eyes from Kent's.

Just when he thought it was hopeless and was about to take the petticoat away, he saw what he wanted to see.

A tear formed in the corner of Kent's eye, like dew on a rose and swelled until it overflowed and trickled slowly down his cheek. Dallman watched it for a moment, then wrapped it in the petticoat.

Left Hand Drive

Christopher Fowler

A messenger could have made the delivery just as easily. Packham, passing between the shadowed buildings of the business district, picked up the envelope and checked the address. As the heat of the day ebbed into evening, cool fingers of air ruffled his hair, and he set the envelope back on the seat beside him. Packham figured he'd save the cost of a messenger and detour past 5454 West

Plaza on his way home, nosing his big blue Oldsmobile between the cars parked in front of the area's many cocktail bars and restaurants.

The building turned out to be typical of so many of the new office buildings being constructed across Los Angeles, vast and characterless, the symmetry of its endless white walls broken by giant squares of bleak mirrored glass. He slowed the car as it approached the silent fountains in the plaza forecourt. Although the working day had ended over an hour ago, there were no parking spaces to be had on the street. Behind crackling neon signs, hidden beyond darkened glass, executives sat, presumably, theorizing on the office politics of the day. Perhaps he would stop for a beer before tackling the freeway tonight. As much as he resented having to pay a dollar fifty for a five-minute stop, Packham sighed and turned the vehicle along the west side of the building until he reached the underground parking facilities. Snatching a card from the striped yellow ticket meter, he barely waited for the metal arm to rise in front of him before pushing down on the accelerator.

He was in luck. The enormous concrete cavern below him yielded a parking space in the first underground level. Packham edged the Oldsmobile in between a Toyota truck and a Volkswagen. He opened the car door gingerly to prevent scratching his new paintwork, and looked about. Throughout the garage giant metal signs were set into the concrete support posts, their color-coded reflective messages aiming visitors at banks of elevators and escalators.

It always amazed Packham how these vast underground garages managed to remain as antiseptically clean as the buildings above them. And indeed, the tower above proved to be a model of its kind. The muted pastel carpeting in the foyer ended against tall, pale marble-faced walls. Lettered tables, gold on black, revealed the presence of hundreds of small companies. The obligatory "modern" metal sculpture towered over low purple seating arranged in the reception area. Packham patted the envelope in his jacket. It felt powerful and hard, as only a lawsuit could when slipped into smooth manila. Kimberly Inc. had repeatedly failed to pay on time, and now they would suffer the consequences of their bad business policy. Fair was fair. The same set of rules applied to everyone. Aside from that, it was the easiest way to make money that Packham was aware of.

After depositing the envelope with the night receptionist, his heels ticking on the glistening marble runway across the foyer, Packham returned to the elevators and touched the pressure-sensitive DOWN button. Colleagues thought that he spent too much money on lawyers, that he knew. The elevator arrived. He stepped in. Lawyers were worth spending money on. How else would he discover the little legal loopholes through which money poured into his business? Not a vast amount of

269

money, to be sure, but certainly enough to keep Packham's otherwise ailing company afloat. When the elevator arrived at P1, the doors slid open and Packham found himself facing his Oldsmobile. He congratulated himself on an energy-saving piece of parking. Seated behind the wheel once more, Packham decided to stop off on the way home for a cocktail or three, secure in the knowledge that his wife would be content if he even appeared at all that evening. Turning around in his seat with one hand on the wheel, Packham looked out through the back window in an attempt to locate the garage's exit teller. He assumed that, as in most places of this kind, the exit would be at the far end of a one-way system designed to keep traffic flowing in a circle around the garage. Outside he could see the sidewalk darkening to soft crimson as night began to fall.

Packham backed the car out into the lane ahead and followed the arrows painted on the floor as they led around to his left. Slowly guiding the big old car between columns of parked vehicles, he turned on the radio to catch the early evening traffic news.

"And there's a two-mile backup on the southbound lane of the Hollywood Freeway tonight at Gower exit, so try and avoid that route if you can. Now it's time for the latest weather. . . ."

Ahead, the floor arrows continued to point around to the left. Packham coasted the Olds in an arc, searching for the familiar yellow stripes of the exit booth. The arrows led down a narrow ramped tunnel to the floor below. That couldn't be right. Packham leaned forward and looked up through the windshield at the top of the tunnel. The sign was large, clear and straightforward. It read simply EXIT—and there was a reflective arrow below it pointing straight on. Irritated, he eased the car down the tunnel to the floor below. Here there were two signs, one repeating the message EXIT, and the other which read MONTHLY PARKING ONLY. Packham curved the car in the direction of the exit arrows.

On this level there were fewer cars, and the ones which were here looked as if they had been for quite a while. Overhead, the lighting had grown dimmer, the neon strips having been replaced with dusty, flickering panels recessed into the ceiling. Packham slowed the car down for a moment and rested his arms on the wheel. It seemed that he had made a complete circuit around the second floor of the garage but still no exit teller was visible. Anyway, how could there even be one on the second floor down? Weren't they always near the entrance? The building was of fairly new design. Perhaps this was a new system. Ahead, the arrowed lane continued for five hundred yards and then split into two directions. Above the split a sign hung from the ceiling, difficult to read at this distance. Packham gunned the accelerator in annoyance and pulled up to the painted forking of the ways. The sign read LONG TERM PARKING and

270

had an arrow beneath it pointing right. Below this it said, once again, EXIT, and this was joined with a similar arrow pointing left. *Finally,* thought Packham as he swung the car to the left only to reach the corner and discover to his amazement that the arrows were pointing downward once more to a ramp leading to the floors below. Packham was not an irrational man. He was sure that the architectural quirks of this particular building were merely an annoying development of the crazy new fire regulations. Even so, he felt a brief quiver in the pit of his stomach when the radio began crackling with static as he descended the ramp. Down here there were only a handful of cars filling the parking spaces in dusty clutches. Some looked as if they had been there for a very long time indeed. Old newspapers were plastered against the windshields and tires, and dust had left thick lines of gray along chrome trims and wipers. Cruising slowly along the arrowed lane, Packham leaned forward, searching the concrete columns for any further instructions for locating the exit ramps.

Some of the cars he was now passing looked as if they had not been disturbed for months. The Olds crawled past a rusting Chevy Vega, then a weather-beaten '59 Chevrolet, its vast tail fins caked with streaks of dirt. On the radio the static now overpowered the station announcer's voice. Packham clicked it off with annoyance. Obviously he had missed a turn somewhere. He must be near the basement of the garage down here.

Flickering panels of light slid over the windshield of the Oldsmobile as it passed each crusted metal hulk. In the distance glowed a two-way sign, too far away as yet to be deciphered in the gloom.

Packham pulled the car up beneath it and idled the engine. A leaking water pipe overhead had streaked the notice with rust. One side read: GARAGE CLOSES AT 9:00 P.M. The other side read EXIT. As on all the other floors, there were two lanes ahead, branching and curving off to the left and the right. Packham pulled his tie loose and unbuttoned his collar. He could feel the sweat dripping between his shoulder blades. The air was warm and heavy, and felt long undisturbed. Having had no luck following the exit signs, Packham decided to head in the opposite direction of the painted exit arrows, swinging the wheel of the Olds around to the right and accelerating once more. With growing horror he found the car descending a ramp again to the floor below.

Flicking on the main beam of his headlights, Packham hunched forward against the wheel, his forehead leaving condensation marks against the glass. The signs were fewer now, the lighting poor and sporadic. Several of the overhead light panels were missing, revealing tangles of dusty plastic wiring. Slowly the Oldsmobile wound downward into the dark, past a rusted Ford Pinto with four flat tires.

Ahead, he turned the wheel to avoid an abandoned Pontiac convertible, left at an angle across the center of the lane, its slashed seats exposing contusions of ragged foam rubber. At the next corner, a sign had fallen down and lay amid old rags and dust, its single word EXIT pointing straight down into the earth.

The oppressive heat forced beads of sweat into Packham's eyes. He pulled the car over, shifted it into PARK and applied the handbrake. As he extracted his keys from the ignition, the sudden silence was so disturbing that he quickly reapplied his key and turned over the engine of the Olds once more. He looked at his watch. How long had he been down here? The luminous dial glowed faintly in the warm gloom. It appeared to read 7:50—but that would mean he had been circling the garage for three quarters of an hour, and Packham knew that it couldn't have been more than ten minutes at the most. He ran his hand through his thinning brown hair, feeling the moisture that had gathered at the roots. It was stupid to continue following the signs. There was no way that the exit could be this far down. He had to go back the way he had come. Keeping in as tight a turning circle as possible, Packham drove across the empty parking spaces and headed back up the lane. He reached the foot of the ramp upward to the next floor, and gently applied the accelerator. Slowly the car rose back up the ramp until it reached the abandoned convertible it had passed minutes before. Packham accelerated once more as the Olds passed under the flickering signs which had urged him downward.

He passed the Pinto, passed another EXIT sign pointing back the way he had gone, and overhead the lighting grew stronger and less patchy. Hopefully he tried the radio, but the deafening static forced him to turn it back off. In another moment he reached the base of the next ramp upward. It seemed steeper than he remembered, and narrower. Surely it had to be the same one? Packham set his teeth and revved the engine. Ahead, at the top of the tunnel, he could see the cool brilliance of the neon ceiling paneling. Halfway up the ramp, the engine died and the car began to roll slowly backward.

Packham stared at the instrument panel in disbelief. He had plenty of gasoline. The battery was fully charged. Everything else read normal. Twisting in his seat, Packham guided the car back down the ramp and swung it in an arc at the bottom so that the vehicle faced forward once more. He turned off the ignition, waited a moment, and tried the engine again. On the fourth try, the car drummed into life once more. Relief flooded through him. He had been meaning to take the car in for service for two months now—he just hated shelling out to those bastards in the body shop for wiping the engine with a damp rag and charging him eighty dollars.

Edging the Oldsmobile around, Packham stepped on the gas and headed up the ramp again. As he reached the midway point of the tunnel, the engine coughed and failed. Only his previous experience kept Packham from running the trunk of the car into the concrete wall behind. Once more he parked at the bottom of the ramp and clicked off the ignition. This time the engine failed to turn over until the battery was nearly dead.

The choice facing him was a simple one. Either he had to leave the car here and walk up—which as far as he was concerned was out of the question—or go back down and continue to follow the signs to the exit. Packham reached into the backseat and pulled a Kleenex from the door pocket. Mopping his forehead, he coasted the Olds gently around and along the arrowed lane, back past the Pinto and down the narrow concrete ramp into the gloom of the floor below. As he passed his previous turning point, it occurred to Packham that he had been traversing the lanes of this underground crazy house for quite a while now, and as the car passed beneath a buzzing and spluttering light panel he peered once more at his watch. The face now read 8:35. That was impossible! He had looked at his watch in the foyer of the building above him at precisely 7:05, and again—just a few minutes ago, surely? He *couldn't* have been down here for an hour and a half!

The Oldsmobile passed a cluster of vehicles which looked as if they had not been moved for five years. An old Plymouth with a smashed front windshield, a small brown Fiat with its passenger door torn off, a burned-out Chevy Nova, a Toyota Celica with no hood or headlights. Veering away from the arrowed lane before him, Packham angled the car across the lot toward its farthest side. He must have been traveling faster than he realized, for the tires screamed in the tomblike emptiness of the building.

Set in the far wall was a dark square hole, and above yet another EXIT sign. By the light reflecting against the angled ceiling, Packham could tell that the ramp beyond the sign led downward once more. There had to be an end to the number of floors available for parking, even for an office building as large as the one overhead. Taking care to keep the car engine revving gently, he entered the ramp tunnel. This one was definitely smaller than any of the others. The walls seemed to be pressing in against the sides of the car. They were mere inches farther apart than the Olds. If he had wanted to open the doors of the car, he would not have been able to. As the floor leveled out once more, his headlights picked up the wreckage of destroyed and abandoned cars in the near pitch darkness. Above him flickered one single paneled light, its plastic cover shattered and dripping rusty water.

With a sudden shock, Packham realized that he was frightened. He was aware of a physical change in himself. His hands were oozing sweat, making the steering wheel slippery to hold. He wiped them on his slacks. His face was wet and cold, his heart beating way too fast. He could feel it pulsing through the dampness of his shirt. Looking at the speedometer he realized he was crossing the darkened floor at nearly forty miles an hour. The wheel slid in his hands. He shifted his gaze to the windshield just in time to see the light from his main beam reflected on the pale-blue roof of an upturned Chrysler before the Oldsmobile slammed into it.

It seemed to Packham that some time was lost before he remembered touching his bruised forehead and climbing out of the car to shakily survey the damage. His right fender was crumpled beyond repair. Its headlight had gone out, leaving the single right-hand low beam to throw its pale light across the floor. Something under the hood was hissing. Metal ticked to a stop. Without daring to see how much damage he had done, Packham banged the hood flat and jumped back into the driver's seat. Squealing the car into reverse and then punching it forward around the wreck, he could feel the twisted front fender dragging and tearing at his left tire. Ahead, the single beam of the Oldsmobile illuminated a barely legible sign, EXIT LEFT, with its inevitable entrance to a downward ramp. As the car scraped into the passageway, the hissing under the hood grew louder until something split with a bang and the engine ceased to turn.

With mounting horror, Packham realized that the scraping noise around him was caused by the walls of the ramp, which were now touching both sides of the car as it coasted downward under the pull of its own weight. He hammered at the wheel now, praying that the car would not hit an obstacle and stop. The car was surrounded by crushing hot blackness as its single beam picked out the way ahead. The ramp was longer than any previous, and steeper. By the angle of the car, Packham could tell that the incline of the ramp was growing instead of lessening.

Now there was a new scraping sound, from above. The roof was low here, so low that in places it touched the top of the car. As the scraping increased in volume, Packham knew that the tunnel was so cramped and narrow now that any second the car would slow down and stop, unable to move any farther.

The next instant he felt his stomach turn sourly over as the scraping ended and the car ground to a complete standstill. Tearing at the handle, Packham flung his full weight at the door, with no effect. Sheer panic overwhelmed him as he slammed his elbow at the side window, finally shattering it and sending spears of glass into the tendons of his arm. Beyond the window, less than two or three inches away, was the streaked gray concrete of the all-enclosing ramp wall. Suddenly aware of the searing pain in his right arm, Packham slumped over the wheel and cried.

Time passed until Packham was snapped back into panicky attention by the flickering of his remaining headlight. He raised his head from the steering wheel and stared out of the windshield. Ahead, pressed against the crumpled hood of the car, was the sheer concrete wall of a dead end. The headlight flickered off, then on again. Packham craned his head up at the far edge of the light pool, where something glittered. It was the reflective lettering of yet another EXIT sign. As the light began to fade from the headlamp and blackness shrank the circle of dimming brightness, Packham strained to read the words sprayed below the sign in crimson paint, a final message. It said simply:

ON THE LEFT HAND OF GOD SITS SATAN.

With a ping, the headlight and instrument panel lights went out. In the silence and the darkness, Packham heard a new noise.

A Legend of Sonora

Hildegarde Hawthorne

Two persons, a man and a woman, faced each other under a clump of live-oaks. Hard by were visible the walls of an adobe house crumbling with age. The sun was setting; a slight breeze stirred in the dark branches of the trees, which all through the hot Mexican day had been motionless. The woman was dark and small with large eyes and a graceful body; the man, a swarthy vaquero, in serape and sombrero.

"And you heard him say—that?" said she.

"Yes, señorita. He said, 'I love you! I love you!' twice, like that. And then he kissed her."

"Ah! he kissed her. Anything else?"

"This!" He handed her a slip of folded paper. It contained a woman's name, a few words of passion, and a signature. As the señorita's eyes perused it, they contracted, and she drew in a long breath. The vaquero watched her keenly. "I found it in the arbor after they had gone," said he.

She looked away dreamily. "Thank you, thank you, Mazeppa," she muttered. "It is late. I must go in now. Adios, Mazeppa!" She turned, and, moving slowly, vanished behind a corner of the adobe house.

The vaquero remained motionless until she was out of sight. Then he pressed his hands to his lips, and flung them out towards her with a passionate gesture. The next moment he had mounted his horse and was gone.

An hour passed. Again the sound of hoofs. A handsome young señor, jauntily attired, galloped up to the door of the house, and springing from the saddle, hitched his rein over a large hook projecting from the wall. "Hola! Maria, little one!" he called out, in a rich, joyous voice. "Where is my little Maria?"

The señorita appeared, smiling. She was in white, with a reboso drawn around her delicate face. She bore a two-handled silver cup, curiously chased. "See," she said, "I have brought you some wine. Such a long ride, just to see me!" She was holding out the cup towards him; but, as he was about to receive it, she drew it back suddenly. She was pale; her eyes glittered. "I too am thirsty," she said. She lifted the cup to her lips and took a deep draught. "Now, you shall finish it," she added, handing it to him.

He nodded to her laughingly. "To our love!" he said, and drained it. "But how strangely you look at me, little one!" he exclaimed, as he set the cup down and caught his breath. "Is anything wrong?"

"All is well," she answered. "I am happy. Are you happy?"

"I? I am with you, am I not?"

She put her hand in his. "Let us never be parted any more," she said. "Come; we'll walk to the hill-top and see the moon rise."

Hand in hand, they sauntered along the path up the bare hill-side. On and on they walked, slowly, slowly. Maria gave a little gasp, and glanced with dilated eyes at her lover. He smiled faintly, and tried to draw her towards him, but, somehow, did not; and still they moved slowly on their way. The hill-top seemed strangely far off. Maria pressed forward, grasping her lover's hand. What made the distance seem so long? Surely it was but a stroll of ten minutes; yet it was as though they had been walking an hour—a year—many years!

Down the hill-side path came a horseman, riding quietly and humming a love song. He was close upon the two figures before he appeared to be aware of them. They half stopped, as if to speak to him. The horse shivered and plunged. The rider stared at the couple but an instant, then, driving home his spurs, sprang past them.

"Mother of God!" he faltered, crossing himself as he threw a backward glance up the path, on which nothing was now visible, "the ghosts! The little girl who, they say down below, poisoned herself and her lover fifty years ago!"

276

Lemon Drops

Donald Burleson

Standing in the clubhouse door with Mom yelling "Supper!" to me across the way, I watch Lenny lick his grinning lips over the last summer-sticky lemon drop, and once more I wonder: how long can this go on?

Funny, the hold he has over me, now more than ever, it seems. I mean, listen, I'm thirteen just like him and I've got my own mind. Kids don't bully me. But somehow it has always been this way with Lenny. When he wants something and he turns those odd eyes on you and works his mouth up firm-looking like that, well, that's not bullying. It's—I really don't know what it is. I just get him what he wants.

What he wants? Always the same thing.

There has to be something wrong with a kid who would probably be willing to kill, to rob, to sell his mother into slavery, to do anything, for a big bag of lemon drops. Sure, they're good, I like them myself (or I used to, anyway)—but I think Lenny would go into withdrawal pains without them, like a heroin addict. It's really not healthy to like one thing *that* much.

But then nobody ever accused Lenny of being healthy or normal. Certainly not my folks. To me he's never been a *bad* kid, really—more like your Huckleberry Finn sort of character, not into drugs or anything like that, just into skipping school and pulling pranks and taking crazy chances and laughing at his own dirty jokes and hiding up in the woods and smoking a big black cigar and puking. What's wrong with that?

But the way my dad carried on when he first got wind of some of Lenny's antics, you'd think the kid was Jack the Ripper or something. I can hear Dad now: "Do you think I make the kind of mortgage payments I make and pay the kind of taxes I pay to live in this neighborhood so that you can run around with some lowlife little creep like that? From all the way over on Carter Street, for Christ's sake? It's practically a slum over there. I can just imagine what kind of family he comes from. And you've got your own friends around here, Tom. I don't want to see you hanging around with that kid." And so on. Parents.

But of course I went ahead then on the sly and played with Lenny anyway, and the rest of the guys did too, in spite of what *their* parents said. You couldn't just drop Lenny because your folks didn't like how he acted. He'd always had too strong a will for that. There he'd be, standing under a streetlamp with that peculiar grin and that kind of disgusting

277

way he had of licking his lips, popping one lemon drop after another into his mouth, and maybe you'd say, "Hey, Lenny, listen. My dad doesn't want me to—" And grinning all the time he'd punch you in the arm and say, "Hey." That would be the end of the discussion, and you'd be off on some weird romp with him after all, hoping to God your parents didn't find out. When Lenny looked at you hard and said let's go, you went.

I haven't ever had much of anything in common with Lenny, actually. I'm in Honors English at school, and Advanced Math; I'm no bookworm, but I know what I have to do and I do it. But Lenny—I don't think Lenny ever cracked a book open in his life. He and I have never been like two peas in a pod, for sure. But I've spent a lot of time with him, and we even let him into the club just before school was out for the summer. Maybe opposites do attract, or maybe it's just that way he has about him, of getting what he wants without quite seeming to push you.

Funny, but from the beginning this thing about lemon drops was something you just didn't talk about. One day one of the guys—who was it? Joel, I guess—made some crack to Lenny about renaming him "Lemmy." Well, all Lenny did was just look at him, kind of blank-like, not mean or anything. Just looked at him with those eyes. Joel sort of coughed and changed the subject, and nobody ever brought it up to Lenny again. *He* might bring it up: "Get me another bag of lemon drops." You went and got it, maybe with your lunch money.

One thing that struck you just about from the first time you met Lenny was that in his own strange way he always went further with things than anybody else would. Maybe the lemon drops are a symbol of that—I mean, a normal person might eat half a bag of them, sometimes, at the outside; I've seen Lenny put down two large bags and still be looking around for more. If you x-rayed his teeth they'd probably look like the inside of an anthill. But it wasn't just that, it was always everything that he did—always a stronger will, always one step further. That, of course, has had him in trouble more than once, and that stunt he pulled when I was with him that night on the railroad trestle a month ago was a perfect example.

Everybody talked about that for a long time. You'd think my folks would have felt a little sorry for him after what happened, but no—what did Dad say? "Well, I'm not surprised. It was his own stupid fault. I *told* you what to expect from his kind. I've seen that kind of kid before, all my life, and I wouldn't give you a nickel for a dozen of them. Maybe someday you'll learn, Tom, that your mother and I are better judges of character than you seem to think." And so forth and so on. All pure compassion, right?

Well, anyway, they'd die if they knew Lenny was back in the clubhouse. I can't even let the guys know that he's in here, because I'm not all that sure they could be trusted now to keep their mouths shut, the way things have turned out. So if I have Lenny hidden in here when one of them comes over, I always have to get him out of sight in a hurry.

Mom is calling "Supper!" and I have to go. Like I said, I don't know how long this can go on. It's getting hard to keep Lenny supplied with lemon drops, but he presses those lips into a thin line like that and I still can't say no to him. I hate feeding them to him, and more and more I hate coming in here at all, with that sickening strong lemon smell and that—*other* smell. That sticky yellow pool of lemon goo just about covers the whole top of the card table now. And every time I see that head sitting in the middle of it, grinning and licking those lips and looking at me with those eyes and leaking yellow at the neck and still asking for more, I wish I'd left the damn thing under the railroad trestle where I found it.

A Man of Discretion
(A Tale of *Gai Paris*)

Richard L. Tierney

C rime," said the man who called himself Shubik, "is a thing with as many definitions as there are people. And yet, most people know nothing of true crime. To them, a crime is an act which happens to offend them personally, usually at the expense of their pocketbooks or their superficial moral sensitivities. Yet, as I say, most of them have never experienced, or even witnessed, a true crime."

"I'm afraid I don't quite follow you," I prompted him.

"I'll put it this way," continued Shubik, leaning forward with his thin hands on the arms of his straight-backed chair: "true evil is a thing man has always had trouble seeing, and as a result society has never taken it seriously into account when making its laws. Much of our legal system concerns itself with acts which influence our ability to live together as a mass, and this is true even in a democracy. Obviously men cannot live together if one is going to steal from another, or seduce another's wife, or inflict violence and even death on every occasion when anger gets the better of good sense. Consequently our laws are drawn up to deal with these acts. And yet I maintain that the greatest crimes of all go unpunished, and even unnoticed, by society. Yes, and often it is society itself which perpetrates and encourages these crimes, simply because they do not hinder us from living together like a herd of cows."

"I am still in the dark," I confessed. "Perhaps you could cite an example."

Shubik frowned, and his lean face narrowed still more in a thoughtful scowl. Presently he rose and said: "Let's go out for a walk."

I followed him down the long, creaking stairs from his dusty garret room, and we emerged into the streets of Paris. It was good to get out of that high, stuffy chamber. Dusk was settling over the city, and the air was cool and fresh, and somehow suggestive of strange, enchanting things. The sky was clear, a few stars were twinkling out, and the merest crescent of a moon showed above the dark roofs of peaked, ancient houses. We made our way in silence down the narrow streets, meeting few people; and I said nothing, knowing that Shubik would continue when he felt so inclined.

"After all," he went on finally, "it isn't the masses who suffer most from these crimes. It is the most sensitive, the most intelligent, who are forced to experience them. An individual's perceptivity makes him all the more aware of the attacks of society, and causes him to retire still more into a defensive shell—and this in turn incites society to isolate him still more. It's what you'd call a 'vicious cycle,' I suppose."

"Do you mean the way in which society has neglected and abused so many of its great artists?" I ventured.

"Not exactly, although some of these men are cases in point. But the crimes to which I refer may happen—and *are* happening—to many other kinds of people. Moreover, it is always a result of environment or heredity rather than any evil intent on the individual's part."

"For God's sake, get to the point!" I remonstrated. "You've kept me on the string for half an hour. What crime could possibly be so awful as the one you suggest?"

"Murder is a terrible thing," said Shubik, "but how much more terrible must it be to take away a man's life without killing him, so that he can see and feel and think about what he is being denied! Consider, for instance, how a man would feel if he were to be denied all food and drink and yet could be kept alive somehow for the entirety of his potential life-span; kept alive, so that he would continually suffer from thirst and hunger. I tell you, it would be a foretaste of Hell itself!"

"I fail to see your point," I said. "Such a crime would certainly be objectionable to society, not to say impossible."

Shubik hesitated for a moment. Then he said: "There are other instincts just as natural as eating and drinking but not as fatal to thwart. You are married, Gaston, are you not?"

"I am," I replied, surprised at the trend his thoughts were taking.

280

"You have a charming wife, and two fine children."

"Quite so."

"Then consider: suppose this wonderful family had been denied you; that the instincts and desires which prompted you to marry and raise such fine children had been thwarted at the very beginning, by conditions outside your control and through no fault of your own, so that you had always been denied the pleasures you now experience. Would it not be most terrible indeed to know that no matter what you did you could never overcome the barrier keeping you from your greatest desires?"

"Perhaps," I acknowledged. "And yet, there are many who live such lives voluntarily—priests, for example, and others who take holy orders."

"But this is of their own choice, and they are fortunate in possessing a desire to please God which renders all other desires secondary. No, I speak of those more normal people whose natural impulses are blocked by the sneering conventions of a society whose standards they can never accept or fit into. I see you do not understand me. Well, then, have you ever been in the middle of a large gathering and felt more isolated than if you were on the moon? Have you ever been attracted by a woman's charms and then repelled and disgusted by her laughing, taunting ways? Have you felt yourself continually sneered down upon and laughed at for no real reason except that you were somehow inadequate to face any social situation? Yes, I am speaking of myself, as you have already guessed, but I make no apologies. Surely you must know why I walk the streets at night, and why I try to bury myself in the study of music, and why I roam the world from city to city in search of something I never find. It's because there has never been anything within my experience I can call true happiness. You are fortunate, Gaston: there is nothing I want more than a wife and a family and a home. But most women ignore me because I am ugly, and because I am ill at ease in their presence. A few laugh and joke at me, and that is painful; and then there are some who act polite and considerate, and they are the worst of all. I wish I could tell you what true crime really is, Gaston, and what it means to experience it—but I see that you understand less the more I try to tell you."

"I think I understand you quite well," I assured him, "and I have thoroughly enjoyed our evening together. But as it's getting late and I have to work tomorrow, I really must be getting on home. Perhaps we can continue this discussion another night."

So saying, I bid Shubik a very good evening and took my leave. The truth is I was becoming a bit irritated at his insistence about what he called "true crime." I have always been annoyed by people who set themselves up as martyrs or anything of the sort; but Shubik did not

seem offended. If anything, he acted as though he was somewhat relieved at my departure, and I went away hoping that it had done him
good to get a few things off his chest.

The eveing had only begun, and as I actually had no intention of
returning home so early I wandered to one of my favorite haunts near
the Boulevard Montparnasse. Here I joined several of my more congenial companions, with whom I spent the evening in pleasant debate over
several bottles of fine cognac. As a result, it was at a later hour than
usual that I returned to my home.

As I made my way down the dark streets I reflected a great deal on
my friend Shubik and the strange things he had said earlier that evening.
It occurred to me how much of a mystery the man was. I had met him at
a concert nearly a month before, and our mutual interest in music had
caused a spontaneous friendship between us. He seemed a very pleasant
fellow, and an interesting conversationalist; and it was not until later that
I began to notice any peculiarities about him. His physical characteristics
were rather striking, though certainly not of a sort to make him the
grotesque caricature he so often described himself to be. He was of
moderate height and very lean, both in face and form, and his complexion was very light, indeed almost pallid. Moreover he had a head of the
most brilliant red hair, which he kept trimmed short in the manner of a
bristle-brush, and his face was almost entirely covered with enormous
freckles, so that from a distance he seemed to have a rash. These characteristics, of which he was well aware, played constantly on his sensitive
mind, and he always referred to himself as "ugly" or "freakish" in an
apologetic sort of way. This attitude of his was so strong that he hated to
mingle with people in any great numbers, and under no circumstances
could he be induced to associate with women, as he always feared they
were laughing at him secretly. While I knew him, he lived the life of a
recluse in the garret of an ancient rooming house near the Latin Quarter.
There he would dwell all day, sleeping most of the time, or occasionally
listening to classical music played on an old hand-cranked phonograph.
In the evenings he would come out and wander through the dark streets,
playing strange music on a clarinet, and the donations which passers-by
would give him served to sustain him in his meagre existence.

What he did during the rest of the night I do not know, as he had no
friends. For a while I thought he might be a drug-addict, as I noticed
during one visit that he kept a small hypodermic syringe hidden in the
back of his record cabinet, together with several powerful narcotic capsules. But there were never any tell-tale marks on any visible part of his
body, nor did I ever find him in a condition that would suggest such an
indulgence. Indeed he was very temperate and frugal even in the matter
of alcoholic beverages, so that I was quite curious as to why he kept such

things about. Only once did I gain a clue, when one evening a man came up to Shubik's garret when I happened to be there; a tall, evil-looking man with a black cloak and thick, dark-rimmed spectacles. Shubik took him aside, and I noticed that the stranger slipped him a box similar to the one hidden in his record cabinet. When I questioned Shubik about it later, he explained that the capsules were medicine for his ulcers, and that the stranger was a pharmacist called Tièrno who lived on the Rue d'Auseil. At the time I had been satisfied with this explanation.

All these things kept turning over in my mind as I made my way homeward. Eventually I arrived at my door, and here I discovered that I had lost my keys. As it was after midnight I did not wish to rouse my neighbors to ask their help, which would have been a useless procedure in any case; and, as my wife had gone to Chartièrs to visit relatives over the weekend, I was left entirely without a means of ingress. Realizing that I must have left my keys in Shubik's garret room, I set out for his house immediately, considerably irritated, and wondering whether I would get any sleep that night.

Now it happened that my route took me through the wealthy residential district of Beaupaix; and as I was passing along the dark street opposite the splendid mansion of Don Ramòn Mières, the rich Spaniard, I suddenly glimpsed a black shadow darting across the spacious lawn. Curious, I stood still beneath a leafy tree and watched this dark form, which seemed to be that of a man shrouded in a great black cloak. Then my amazement redoubled as I saw the man stop beneath one of the ground-floor windows and quickly push it open, after which he clambered inside with the utmost agility. The whole drama had not taken quite a minute, and I was so astonished that I could hardly believe that it had taken place. Everything was silent, and unchanged save for the black opening of the gaping window.

Immediately I realized that the man must be a thief, and for several moments I watched to see if he would reappear. I had just decided to go and summon a gendarme, when I saw a movement in the window, and I stood still and waited to see what would next take place.

The dark figure descended from the window and moved quietly across the lawn, and it seemed to me that he was now encumbered with something heavy. As he approached I saw that he was carrying a large black bundle across his shoulders. For a moment he stood motionless between the trees bordering the edge of the lawn, as if watching to see that no one approached; then, stepping cautiously out onto the walk, he began to hurry across the street toward me. I was ready to step forth and accost him, but at that instant the dim light from the corner lamp illuminated his face briefly, and I shrank back startled. For the face I had glimpsed was that of my aquaintance, Ronald Shubik!

I do not know what kept me from crying out and revealing my presence, unless perhaps it was the strange mad gleam I saw flash briefly in the man's narrowed eyes. I did not move, and he passed by within a few feet of my shadowy hiding place without seeing me. Instantly I determined to follow him, wondering what he was carrying in that shapeless black bundle. He hurried down the street and turned into a narrow, stonewalled alley, while I followed some distance behind. Before long he arrived at a small German car, and I watched him place the bundle in the back seat, after which he climbed in and drove away.

For a time I scarcely knew what to do. Was this how Shubik spent his nightly hours—as a common thief? But no, certainly not as a *common* thief, for he could hardly have picked a richer man in all Paris to rob than Don Ramòn Mières. If my suspicions were correct, surely it was my duty to report Shubik to the gendarmes as speedily as possible; and yet, I could not do it without first making sure that I was right. Perhaps it was not Shubik I had seen after all, for my mind had been dwelling on him at the time, and in that brief and feeble light I might have mistaken another's features for his own.

So I set out walking rapidly toward the Latin Quarter, and eventually arrived in that decadent neighborhood where Shubik roomed. As I approached his house I spied the small German car parked around by the side, and in the same instant I saw a light blink on in the high garret room. Evidently Shubik had just preceded me. I entered the old, peak-roofed house, quickly climbed the four stories to his room, and knocked loudly at his door.

"It is I—Gaston," I announced. "Let me in."

For a moment there was silence. Then a bolt was drawn, the door opened, and Shubik stood before me. His appearance was more startling than ever, for his eyes were wide and staring and his face was dreadfully pale. When he had scrutinized me closely for a moment as if to assure himself that it was only me, he seemed slightly relieved.

"What do you want?" he demanded.

"My keys," I replied. "I believe I left them here by accident."

"Stay right where you are—I'll get them," he said, and he hurried back into the room. As soon as he had ceased to bar my way I stepped inside and closed the door. There on the musty, iron-frame bed that rested in the far corner lay an object that confirmed my dreadful suspicions—a large, oblong object wrapped loosely in the folds of a black cloak.

"What is that?" I asked bluntly.

Shubik was trembling as he looked at me, and his eyes were strangely bright. Yet he attempted to be nonchalant as he replied:

284

"Nothing—nothing that would interest you, Gaston—just some old blankets I picked up at an auction."

"It is hardly likely," I remarked, "that Don Ramòn Mières would hold an auction at his home in the middle of the night."

At this the poor fellow almost collapsed. Convinced of his guilt, I pushed him aside and strode over to the bed, determined to discover what sort of booty he had appropriated from the Mières residence. Quickly I grasped the edge of the cloak and flung it back.

But nothing had prepared me for what I saw. I had expected to find gold or perhaps valuable antiques; instead, I beheld the face and shoulders of a young woman who lay wrapped in the folds of the cloak! Her eyes were closed, and her face suggested the most peaceful and profound slumber. The skin of her neck and shoulders was as smooth and pale as ivory, and seemed even more deathly white in contrast with the black fabric on which the girl lay like a pearl set against black satin. Her dark hair was cut short in the Parisian manner, and her red lips were parted slightly in a delicate, expressionless languor. I do not remember ever seeing a woman look more exquisitely lovely than did this unconscious girl in that strange garret room.

But my shock was intensified when I *recognized* her—when I realized that she was the young Doña Mières, newly betrothed to the Austrian Duke, Gottfried von Hoffenstein, one of the richest men in all of Europe.

"Shubik!" I gasped, whirling about. "What have you done to her?"

"She is not dead," replied Shubik, his voice now quite calm. "I have merely given her a drug that will cause her to sleep soundly for several hours."

I could only gape at him stupidly. He noticed my confusion, and grinned at me nastily.

"You have spoiled everything, Gaston," he continued. "I worked a long time to achieve this, and now you've blundered in and upset it all. I took such pains, Gaston—you have no idea! I have watched the Mières household every night for five weeks, learning their habits, their hours, the number of their servants and when they came and went. I plotted every room in the house from my observations, and I acted out a thousand plans on paper before I decided which one was the best.

"You should have seen me, Gaston—I was so careful! I always knew what would be useful when the time came. I knew which hall window was always left open a crack, and even the way her bed faced, so that I would know just where to place the chloroform in the dark. The car and the cloak and the alley—all were chosen carefully for my plan. I chose the hour—yes, even the very minute—and it came off perfectly. But chance has upset all my planning, for now you have come and ruined everything!"

"This is horrible!" I exclaimed. "What made you do such a thing?"

"Fool, that you have not guessed!" cried Shubik, his eyes agleam. "The world has tried to deny me that which is rightfully mine, but it has not succeeded. I have thwarted society a dozen times, and never has a soul known that I slipped past its barriers. Ah, you are startled; but what I say is the truth. Tonight this girl would have been mine; and when I had done with her as I pleased, who would ever have been the wiser? She would have wakened in her own house, in her own bed, and what followed would have been considered the natural fruits of her marriage—but you have spoiled all that.

"Why do you look so shocked? You think I'm mad, but I tell you that whereas I've failed this once, *I've succeeded a dozen times before!* My blood runs in the veins of the world's greatest nobility. Why should I be denied the fundamental right of procreation when thousands of my inferiors continue to spawn indiscriminately? I was born in poverty, but my children shall be born into the best families of the world. If society won't let me raise my children, then I'll force society to raise them for me, in the best environments it has to offer. Why do you think I roam the world from place to place, living now in one country and now in another? You fool! You call me mad, but if you knew the wealth of my sons and daughters are due to inherit, it would stagger your mind!"

"Wretch!" I cried. "You are insane! I have never heard of anything so monstrous!"

"But where is the crime?" he shrieked. "I do no one any harm, and in the end no one is any the wiser. Only you stand in my way, Gaston, but I shall attend to that—*now*!"

He sprang at me, and I saw the hypodermic glittering in his hand. Before I could twist aside I felt the needle lance painfully into the muscle of my arm. I yelled and struck out, and my fist smashed against his hateful face and sent him sprawling back over the rickety furniture. He did not rise, but lay glaring malevolently up at me from the floor. My arm felt numb. I tried to move my fingers but could not, and when I took a step my brain began to whirl dizzily. I tried to cry out, but my tongue and throat were already numb and cottony, and would not function properly. Then Shubik rose and leered at me horribly; and the last thing I heard as I reeled and crashed to the floor was his grating laugh ringing madly in my ears . . .

And that is the end of all I know concerning the man called Shubik. When I regained consciousness I found myself shackled and surrounded by gendarmes who immediately began to interrogate me. They said they had found me unconscious in the garret room just after dawn, together with a frightened girl who could not remember how she had come there. They found the hypodermic and some capsules, too, and now they have taken me away to Belle-Santé and have locked me in this room with padded walls. They accuse me of monstrous practices, and the scandal is so great that even my wife will not come to see me. So that is why I have written this; for I must convince the police that it was Shubik, and not I, who did this thing. They will not believe that such a person exists, for it seems all his belongings have vanished with him; and no one can vouch for the fight we had in the garret room, as the landlord is evidently blind and deaf and there are no other roomers in that horrible place. Nor can the police find a man called Tièrno who sells drugs, nor even a street called the Rue d'Auseil. But they must believe me; for if they do not, who is going to stop Shubik from continuing his evil practice of polluting the world with his uncounted, illicit progeny . . . ?

The Man Who Made Friends with Electricity

Fritz Leiber

When Mr. Scott showed Peak House to Mr. Leverett, he hoped he wouldn't notice the high-tension pole outside the bedroom window, because it had twice before queered promising rentals—so many elderly people were foolishly nervous about electricity. There was nothing to be done about the pole except try to draw prospective tenants' attention away from it—electricity follows the hilltops and these lines supplied more than half of the juice used in Pacific Knolls.

But Mr. Scott's prayers and suave misdirections were in vain—Mr. Leverett's sharp eyes lit on the "negative feature" the instant they stepped out on the patio. The old New Englander studied the short thick wooden column, the 18-inch ridged glass insulators, the black transformer box that stepped down voltage for this house and a few others lower on the slope. His gaze next followed the heavy wires swinging off rhythmically four abreast across the empty gray-green hills. Then he cocked his head as his ears caught the low but steady frying sound, varying from a crackle to a buzz, of electrons leaking off the wires through the air.

"Listen to that!" Mr. Leverett said, his dry voice betraying excitement for the first time in the tour. "Fifty thousand volts if there's five! A power of power!"

"Must be unusual atmospheric conditions today—normally you can't hear a thing," Mr. Scott responded lightly, twisting the truth a little.

"You don't say?" Mr. Leverett commented, his voice dry again, but Mr. Scott knew better than to encourage conversation about a negative feature. "I want you to notice this lawn," he launched out heartily. "When the Pacific Knolls Golf Course was subdivided, the original owner of Peak House bought the entire eighteenth green and—"

For the rest of the tour Mr. Scott did his state-certified real estate broker's best, which in Southern California is no mean performance, but Mr. Leverett seemed a shade perfunctory in the attention he accorded it. Inwardly Mr. Scott chalked up another defeat by the damn pole.

On the quick retrace, however, Mr. Leverett insisted on their lingering on the patio. "Still holding out," he remarked about the buzz with an odd satisfaction. "You know, Mr. Scott, that's a restful sound to me. Like wind or a brook or the sea. I hate the clatter of machinery—that's the *other* reason I left New England—but this is like a sound of nature. Downright soothing. But you say it comes seldom?"

Mr. Scott was flexible—it was one of his great virtues as a salesman.

"Mr. Leverett," he confessed simply, "I've never stood on this patio when I didn't hear that sound. Sometimes it's softer, sometimes louder, but it's always there. I play it down, though, because most people don't care for it."

"Don't blame you," Mr. Leverett said. "Most people are a pack of fools or worse. Mr. Scott, are any of the people in the neighboring houses Communists to your knowledge?"

"No, sir!" Mr. Scott responded without an instant's hesitation. "There's not a Communist in Pacific Knolls. And that's something, believe me, I'd never shade the truth on."

"Believe you," Mr. Leverett said. "The east's packed with Communists. Seem scarcer out here. Mr. Scott, you've made yourself a deal. I'm taking a year's lease on Peak House as furnished and at the figure we last mentioned."

"Shake on it!" Mr. Scott boomed. "Mr. Leverett, you're the kind of person Pacific Knolls wants."

They shook. Mr. Leverett rocked on his heels, smiling up at the softly crackling wires with a satisfaction that was already a shade possessive.

"Fascinating thing, electricity," he said. "No end to the tricks it can do or you can do with it. For instance, if a man wanted to take off for elsewhere in an elegant flash, he'd only have to wet down the lawn good and take twenty-five foot of heavy copper wire in his two bare hands and whip the other end of it over those lines. Whang! Every bit as good as Sing Sing and a lot more satisfying to a man's inner needs."

Mr. Scott experienced a severe though momentary sinking of heart and even for one wildly frivolous moment considered welshing on the verbal agreement he'd just made. He remembered the red-haired lady who'd rented an apartment from him solely to have a quiet place in which to take an overdose of barbiturates. Then he reminded himself that Southern California is, according to a wise old saw, the home (actual or aimed-at) of the peach, the nut and the prune; and while he'd had few dealings with real or would-be starlets, he'd had enough of crackpots and retired grouches. Even if you piled fanciful death wishes and a passion for electricity atop rabid anti-communist and anti-machine manias, Mr. Leverett's personality was no more than par for the S. Cal., course.

Mr. Leverett said shrewdly, "You're worrying now, aren't you, I might be a suicider? Don't. Just like to think my thoughts. Speak them out too, however peculiar."

Mr. Scott's last fears melted and he became once more his pushingly congenial self as he invited Mr. Leverett down to the office to sign the papers.

Three days later he dropped by to see how the new tenant was making out and found him in the patio ensconced under the buzzing pole in an old rocker.

"Take a chair and sit," Mr. Leverett said, indicating one of the tubular modern pieces. "Mr. Scott, I want to tell you I'm finding Peak House every bit as restful as I hoped. I listen to the electricity and let my thoughts roam. Sometimes I hear voices in the electricity—the wires talking, as they say. You've heard of people who hear voices in the wind?"

"Yes, I have," Mr. Scott admitted a bit uncomfortably and then, recalling that Mr. Leverett's check for the first quarter's rent was safely cleared, was emboldened to speak his own thoughts. "But wind is a sound that varies a lot. That buzz is pretty monotonous to hear voices in."

"Pshaw," Mr. Leverett said with a little grin that made it impossible to tell how seriously he meant to be taken. "Bees are highly intelligent insects, entomologists say they even have a language, yet they do nothing but buzz. I hear voices in the electricity."

He rocked silently for a while after that and Mr. Scott sat.

"Yep, I hear voices in the electricity," Mr. Leverett said dreamily. "Electricity tells me how it roams the forty-eight states—even the forty-ninth by way of Canadian power lines. Electricity goes everywhere today—into our homes, every room of them, into our offices, into government buildings and military posts. And what it doesn't learn that way it overhears by the trace of it that trickles through our phone lines and over our air waves. Phone electricity's the little sister of power electricity, you might say, and little pitchers have big ears. Yep, electricity knows everything about us, our every last secret. Only it wouldn't think of telling most people what it knows, because they believe electricity is a cold mechanical force. It isn't—it's warm and pulsing and sensitive and friendly underneath, like any other live thing."

Mr. Scott, feeling a bit dreamy himself now, thought what good advertising copy that would make—imaginative stuff, folksy but poetic.

"*And* electricity's got a mite of viciousness too," Mr. Leverett continued. "You got to tame it. Know its ways, speak it fair, show no fear, make friends with it. Well now, Mr. Scott," he said in a brisker voice, standing up, "I know you've come here to check up on how I'm caring for Peak House. So let me give *you* the tour."

And in spite of Mr. Scott's protests that he had no such inquisitive intention, Mr. Leverett did just that.

Once he paused for an explanation: "I've put away the electric blanket and the toaster. Don't feel right about using electricity for menial jobs."

As far as Mr. Scott could see, he had added nothing to the furnishings of Peak House beyond the rocking chair and a large collection of Indian arrow heads.

Mr. Scott must have talked about the latter when he got home, for a week later his nine-year-old son said to him, "Hey, Dad, you know that old guy you unloaded Peak House onto?"

"Rented is the only proper expression, Bobby."

"Well, I went up to see his arrow heads. Dad, it turns out he's a snake-charmer!"

Dear God, thought Mr. Scott, *I knew there was going to be something really impossible about Leverett. Probably likes hilltops because they draw snakes in hot weather.*

"He didn't charm a real snake, though, Dad, just an old extension cord. He squatted down on the floor—this was after he showed me those crumby arrow heads—and waved his hands back and forth over it and pretty soon the end with the little box on it started to move around on the floor and all of a sudden it lifted up, like a cobra out of a basket. It was real spooky!"

"I've seen that sort of trick," Mr. Scott told Bobby. "There's a fine thread attached to the end of the wire pulling it up."

"I'd have seen a thread, Dad."

"Not if it were the same color as the background," Mr. Scott explained. Then he had a thought. "By the way, Bobby, was the other end of the cord plugged in?"

"Oh it was, Dad! He said he couldn't work the trick unless there was electricity in the cord. Because you see, Dad, he's really an electricity-charmer. I just said snake-charmer to make it more exciting. Afterwards we went outside and he charmed electricity down out of the wires and made it crawl all over his body. You could see it crawl from part to part."

"But how could you see that?" Mr. Scott demanded, struggling to keep his voice casual. He had a vision of Mr. Leverett standing dry and sedate, entwined by glimmering blue serpents with flashing diamond eyes and fangs that sparked.

"By the way it would make his hair stand on end, Dad. First on one side of his head, then on the other. Then he said, 'Electricity, crawl down my chest,' and a silk handkerchief hanging out of his top pocket stood out stiff and sharp. Dad, it was almost as good as the Museum of Science and Industry!"

Next day Mr. Scott dropped by Peak House, but he got no chance to ask his carefully thought-out questions, for Mr. Leverett greeted him with, "Reckon your boy told you about the little magic show I put on for him yesterday. I like children, Mr. Scott. Good Republican children like yours, that is."

"Why yes, he did," Mr. Scott admitted, disarmed and a bit flustered by the other's openness.

"I only showed him the simplest tricks, of course. Kid stuff."

"Of course," Mr. Scott echoed. "I guessed you must have used a fine thread to make the extension cord dance."

"Reckon you know all the answers, Mr. Scott," the other said, his eyes flashing. "But come across to the patio and sit for a while."

The buzzing was quite loud that day, yet after a bit Mr. Scott had to admit to himself that it *was* a restful sound. And it had more variety than he'd realized—mounting crackles, fading sizzles, hisses, hums, clicks, sighs. If you listened to it long enough, you probably would begin to hear voices.

Mr. Leverett, silently rocking, said, "Electricity tells me about all the work it does and all the fun it has—dances, singing, big crackling band concerts, trips to the stars, foot races that make rockets seem like snails. Worries, too. You know that electric breakdown they had in New York? Electricity told me why. Some of its folks went crazy—overwork, I guess—and just froze. It was a while before they could send others in from outside New York and heal the crazy ones and start them moving again through the big copper web. Electricity tells me it's fearful the same thing's going to happen in Chicago and San Francisco. Too much pressure.

"Electricity doesn't *mind* working for us. It's generous-hearted and it loves its job. But it would be grateful for a little more consideration—a little more recognition of its special problems.

"It's got its savage brothers to contend with, you see—the wild electricity that rages in storms and haunts the mountaintops and comes down to hunt and kill. Not civilized like the electricity in the wires, though it will be some day.

"For civilized electricity's a great teacher. Shows us how to live clean and in unity and brother-love. Power fails one place, electricity's rushing in from everywhere to fill the gap. Serves Georgia same as Vermont, Los Angeles same as Boston. Patriotic too—only revealed its greatest secrets to true-blue Americans like Edison and Franklin. Did you know it killed a Swede when he tried that kite trick? Yep, electricity's the greatest power for good in all the U.S.A."

Mr. Scott thought sleepily of what a neat little electricity cult Mr. Leverett could set up, every bit as good as Science of Mind or Krishna Venta or the Rosicrucians. He could imagine the patio full of earnest seekers while Krishna Leverett—or maybe High Electro Leverett—dispensed wisdom from his rocker, interpreting the words of the humming wires. Better not suggest it, though—in Southern California such things had a way of coming true.

Mr. Scott felt quite easy at heart as he went down the hill, though he did make a point of telling Bobby not to bother Mr. Leverett anymore.

But the prohibition didn't apply to himself. During the next months Mr. Scott made a point of dropping in at Peak House from time to time for a dose of "electric wisdom." He came to look forward to these restful, amusingly screwy breaks in the hectic round. Mr. Leverett appeared to do nothing whatever except sit in his rocker in the patio, yet stayed happy and serene. There was a lesson for anybody in that, if you thought about it.

Occasionally Mr. Scott spotted amusing side effects of Mr. Leverett's eccentricity. For instance, although he sometimes let the gas and water bills go, he always paid up phone and electricity on the dot.

And the newspapers eventually did report short but severe electric breakdowns in Chicago and San Francisco. Smiling a little frowningly at the coincidences, Mr. Scott decided he could add fortune-telling to the electricity cult he'd imagined for Mr. Leverett. "Your life's story foretold in the wires!"—more novel, anyway, than crystal balls or Talking with God.

Only once did the touch of the gruesome, that had troubled Mr. Scott in his first conversation with Mr. Leverett, come briefly back, when the old man chuckled and observed, "Recall what I told you about whipping a copper wire up there? I've thought of a simpler way, just squirt the hose at those H-T lines in a hard stream, gripping the metal nozzle. Might be best to use the hot water and throw a box of salt in the heater first." When Mr. Scott heard that he was glad that he'd warned Bobby against coming around.

But for the most part Mr. Leverett maintained his mood of happy serenity.

When the break in that mood came, it did so suddenly, though afterwards Mr. Scott realized there had been one warning note sounded when Mr. Leverett had added onto a rambling discourse, "By the way, I've learned that power electricity goes all over the world, just like the ghost electricity in radios and phones. It travels to foreign shores in batteries and condensers. Roams the lines in Europe and Asia. Some of it even slips over into Soviet territory. Wants to keep tabs on the Communists, I guess. Electric freedom-fighters."

On his next visit Mr. Scott found a great change. Mr. Leverett had deserted his rocking chair to pace the patio on the side away from the pole, though every now and then he would give a quick funny look up over his shoulder at the dark muttering wires.

"Glad to see you, Mr. Scott. I'm real shook up. Reckon I better tell someone about it so if something happens to me they'll be able to tell the FBI. Though I don't know what *they*'ll be able to do.

"Electricity just told me this morning it's got a world government—it had the nerve to call it that—and that it doesn't care a snap for either us *or* the Soviets and that there's Russian electricity in our wires and American electricity in theirs—it shifts back and forth with never a quiver of shame.

"When I heard that you could have knocked me down with a paper dart.

"What's more, electricity's determined to stop any big war that may come, no matter how rightful that war be or how much in defense of America. If the buttons are pushed for the atomic missiles, electricity's going to freeze and refuse to budge. And it'll flash out and kill anybody who tries to set them off another way.

"I pleaded with electricity, I told it I'd always thought of it as American and true—reminded it of Franklin and Edison—finally I commanded it to change its ways and behave decent, but it just chuckled at me with never a spark of love or loyalty.

"Then it threatened me back! It told me if I tried to stop it, if I revealed its plans it would summon down its savage brothers from the mountains and with their help it would seek me out and kill me! Mr. Scott, I'm all alone up here with electricity on my window sill. What am I going to do?"

Mr. Scott had considerable difficulty soothing Mr. Leverett enough to make his escape. In the end he had to promise to come back in the morning bright and early—silently vowing to himself that he'd be damned if he would.

His task was not made easier when the electricity overhead, which had been especially noisy this day, rose in a growl and Mr. Leverett turned and said harshly, "Yes, I hear!"

That night the Los Angeles area had one of its very rare thunderstorms, accompanied by gales of wind and torrents of rain. Palms and pines and eucalyptus were torn down, earth cliffs crumbled and sloshed, and the great square concrete spillways ran brimful from the hills to the sea.

The lightning was especially fierce. Several score Angelinos, to whom such a display was a novelty, phoned civil defense numbers to report or inquire fearfully about atomic attack.

Numerous freak accidents occurred. To the scene of one of these Mr. Scott was summoned next morning bright and early by the police — because it had occurred on a property he rented and because he was the only person known to be acquainted with the deceased.

The previous night Mr. Scott had awakened at the height of the storm when the lightning had been blinding as a photoflash and the thunder had cracked like a mile-long whip just above the roof. At that time he had remembered vividly what Mr. Leverett had said about electricity threatening to summon its wild giant brothers from the hills. But now, in the bright morning, he decided not to tell the police about that or say anything to them at all about Mr. Leverett's electricity mania—it would only complicate things to no purpose and perhaps make the fear at his heart more crazily real.

Mr. Scott saw the scene of the freak accident before anything was moved, even the body—except there was now, of course, no power in the heavy corroded wire wrapped tight as a bullwhip around the skinny shanks with only the browned and blackened fabric of cotton pyjamas between.

The police and the power-and-light men reconstructed the accident this way: At the height of the storm one of the high-tension lines had snapped a hundred feet away from the house and the end, whipped by the wind and its own tension, had struck back freakishly through the open bedroom window of Peak House and curled once around the legs of Mr. Leverett, who had likely been on his feet at the time, killing him instantly.

One had to strain that reconstruction, though, to explain the additional freakish elements in the accident—the facts that the high-tension wire had struck not only through the bedroom window, but then through the bedroom door to catch the old man in the hall, and that the black shiny cord of the phone was wrapped like a vine twice around the old man's right arm, as if to hold him back from escaping until the big wire had struck.

294

The Man with the Roller

E. G. Swain

On the edge of that vast tract of East Anglia, which retains its ancient name of the Fens, there may be found, by those who know where to seek it, a certain village called Stoneground. It was once a picturesque village. Today it is not to be called either a village, or picturesque. Man dwells not in one 'house of clay,' but in two, and the material of the second is drawn from the earth upon which this and the neighbouring villages stood. The unlovely signs of the industry have changed the place alike in aspect and in population. Many who have seen the fossil skeletons of great saurians brought out of the clay in which they have lain from prehistoric times, have thought that the inhabitants of the place have not since changed for the better. The chief habitations, however, have their foundations not upon clay, but upon a bed of gravel which anciently gave to the place its name, and upon the highest part of this gravel stands, and has stood for many centuries, the Parish Church, dominating the landscape for miles around.

Stoneground, however, is no longer the inaccessible village, which in the middle ages stood out above a waste of waters. Occasional floods serve to indicate what was once its ordinary outlook, but in more recent times the construction of roads and railways, and the drainage of the Fens, have given it freedom of communication with the world from which it was formerly isolated.

The Vicarage of Stoneground stands hard by the Church, and is renowned for its spacious garden, part of which, and that (as might be expected) the part nearest the house, is of ancient date. To the original plot successive Vicars have added adjacent lands, so that the garden has gradually acquired the state in which it now appears.

The Vicars have been many in number. Since Henry de Greville was instituted in the year 1140 there have been 30, all of whom have lived, and most of whom have died, in successive vicarage houses upon the present site.

The present incumbent, Mr Batchel, is a solitary man of somewhat studious habits, but is not too much enamoured of his solitude to receive visits, from time to time, from schoolboys and such. In the summer of the year 1906 he entertained two, who are the occasion of this narrative, though still unconscious of their part in it, for one of the two, celebrating his fifteenth birthday during his visit to Stoneground, was presented by

Mr Batchel with a new camera, with which he proceeded to photograph, with considerable skill, the surroundings of the house.

One of these photographs Mr Batchel thought particularly pleasing. It was a view of the house with the lawn in the foreground. A few small copies, such as the boy's camera was capable of producing, were sent to him by his young friend, some weeks after the visit, and again Mr Batchel was so much pleased with the picture, that he begged for the negative, with the intention of having the view enlarged.

The boy met the request with what seemed a needlessly modest plea. There were two negatives, he replied, but each of them had, in the same part of the picture, a small blur for which there was no accounting otherwise than by carelessness. His desire, therefore, was to discard these films, and to produce something more worthy of enlargement, upon a subsequent visit.

Mr Batchel, however, persisted in his request, and upon receipt of the negative, examined it with a lens. He was just able to detect the blur alluded to; an examination under a powerful glass, in fact, revealed something more than he had at first detected. The blur was like the nucleus of a comet as one sees it represented in pictures, and seemed to be connected with a faint streak which extended across the negative. It was, however, so inconsiderable a defect that Mr Batchel resolved to disregard it. He had a neighbour whose favourite pastime was photography, one who was notably skilled in everything that pertained to the art, and to him he sent the negative, with the request for an enlargement, reminding him of a long-standing promise to do any such service, when as had now happened, his friend might see fit to ask it.

This neighbour who had acquired such skill in photography was one Mr Groves, a young clergyman, residing in the Precincts of the Minster near at hand, which was visible from Mr Batchel's garden. He lodged with a Mrs Rumney, a superannuated servant of the Palace, and a strong-minded vigorous woman still, exactly such a one as Mr Groves needed to have about him. For he was a constant trial to Mrs Rumney, and but for the wholesome fear she begot in him, would have converted his rooms into a mere den. Her carpets and tablecloths were continually bespattered with chemicals; her chimney-piece ornaments had been unceremoniously stowed away and replaced by labelled bottles; even the bed of Mr Groves was, by day, strewn with drying films and mounts, and her old and favourite cat had a bald patch on his flank, the result of a mishap with the pyrogallic acid.

Mrs Rumney's lodger, however, was a great favourite with her, as such helpless men are apt to be with motherly women, and she took no small pride in his work. A life-size portrait of herself, originally a peace-offering, hung in her parlour, and had long excited the envy of every friend who took tea with her.

'Mr Groves,' she was wont to say, 'is a nice gentleman, *and* a gentleman; and chemical though he may be, I'd rather wait on him for nothing than what I would on anyone else for twice the money.'

Every new piece of photographic work was of interest to Mrs Rumney, and she expected to be allowed both to admire and to criticize. The view of Stoneground Vicarage, therefore, was shewn to her upon its arrival. 'Well may it want enlarging,' she remarked, 'and it no bigger than a postage stamp; it looks more like a doll's house than a vicarage,' and with this she went about her work, while Mr Groves retired to his darkroom with the film, to see what he could make of the task assigned to him.

Two days later, after repeated visits to his darkroom, he had made something considerable; and when Mrs Rumney brought him his chop for luncheon, she was lost in admiration. A large but unfinished print stood upon his easel, and such a picture of Stoneground Vicarage was in the making as was calculated to delight both the young photographer and the Vicar.

Mr Groves spent only his mornings, as a rule, in photography. His afternoons he gave to pastoral work, and the work upon this enlargement was over for the day. It required little more than 'touching up,' but it was this 'touching up' which made the difference between the enlargements of Mr Groves and those of the other men. The print, therefore, was to be left upon the easel until the morrow, when it was to be finished. Mrs Rumney and he, together, gave it an admiring inspection as she was carrying away the tray, and what they agreed in admiring most particularly was the smooth and open stretch of lawn, which made so excellent a foreground for the picture. 'It looks,' said Mrs Rumney, who had once been young, 'as if it was waiting for someone to come and dance on it.'

Mr Groves left his lodgings—we must now be particular about the hours—at half-past two, with the intention of returning, as usual, at five. 'As reg'lar as a clock,' Mrs Rumney was wont to say, 'and a sight more reg'lar than some clocks I knows of.'

Upon this day he was, nevertheless, somewhat late, some visit had detained him, unexpectedly, and it was a quarter-past five when he inserted his latch-key in Mrs Rumney's door.

Hardly had he entered, when his landlady, obviously awaiting him, appeared in the passage: her face, usually florid, was of the colour of parchment, and, breathing hurriedly and shortly, she pointed at the door of Mr Groves' room.

In some alarm at her condition, Mr Groves hastily questioned her; all she could say was: 'The photograph! The photograph!' Mr Groves could only suppose that his enlargement had met with some mishap for which Mrs Rumney was responsible. Perhaps she had allowed it to flutter into the fire. He turned towards his room in order to discover the worst, but at this Mrs Rumney laid a trembling hand upon his arm, and held him back. 'Don't go in,' she said, 'have your tea in the parlour.'

'Nonsense,' said Mr Groves, 'if that is gone we can easily do another.'

'Gone,' said his landlady, 'I wish to Heaven it was.'

The ensuing conversation shall not detain us. It will suffice to say that after a considerable time Mr Groves succeeded in quieting his landlady, so much so that she consented, still trembling violently, to enter the room with him. To speak truth, she was as much concerned for him as for herself, and she was not by nature a timid woman.

The room, so far from disclosing to Mr Groves any cause for excitement, appeared wholly unchanged. In its usual place stood every article of his stained and ill-used furniture, on the easel stood the photograph, precisely where he had left it; and except that his tea was not upon the table, everything was in its usual state and place.

But Mrs Rumney again became excited and tremulous. 'It's there,' she cried. 'Look at the lawn.'

Mr Groves stepped quickly forward and looked at the photograph. Then he turned as pale as Mrs Rumney herself.

There was a man, a man with an indescribably horrible suffering face, rolling the lawn with a large roller.

Mr Groves retreated in amazement to where Mrs Rumney had remained standing. 'Has anyone been in here?' he asked.

'Not a soul,' was the reply. 'I came in to make up the fire, and turned to have another look at the picture, when I saw that dead-alive face at the edge. It gave me the creeps,' she said, 'particularly from not having noticed it before. If that's anyone in Stoneground, I said to myself, I wonder the Vicar has him in the garden with that awful face. It took that hold of me I thought I must come and look at it again, and at five o'clock I brought your tea in. And then I saw him move along right in front, with a roller dragging behind him, like you see.'

Mr Groves was greatly puzzled. Mrs Rumney's story, of course, was incredible, but this strange evil-faced man had appeared in the photograph somehow. That he had not been there when the print was made was quite certain.

The problem soon ceased to alarm Mr Groves; in his mind it was investing itself with a scientific interest. He began to think of suspended chemical action, and other possible avenues of investigation. At Mrs Rumney's urgent entreaty, however, he turned the photograph upon the easel, and with only its white back presented to the room, he sat down and ordered tea to be brought in.

He did not look again at the picture. The face of the man had about it something unnaturally painful: he could remember, and still see, as it were, the drawn features, and the look of the man had unaccountably distressed him.

He finished his slight meal, and having lit a pipe, began to brood over the scientific possibilities of the problem. Had any other photograph upon the original film become involved in the one he had enlarged? Had the image of any other face, distorted by the enlarging lens, become a part of this picture? For the space of two hours he debated this possibility, and that, only to reject them all. His optical knowledge told him that no conceivable accident could have brought into his picture a man with a roller. No negative of his had ever contained such a man; if it had, no natural causes would suffice to leave him, as it were, hovering about the apparatus.

His repugnance to the actual thing had by this time lost its freshness, and he determined to end his scientific musings with another inspection of the object. So he approached the easel and turned the photograph round again. His horror returned, and with good cause. The man with the roller had now advanced to the middle of the lawn. The face was stricken still with the same indescribable look of suffering. The man seemed to be appealing to the spectator for some kind of help. Almost, he spoke.

Mr Groves was naturally reduced to a condition of extreme nervous excitement. Although not by nature what is called a nervous man, he trembled from head to foot. With a sudden effort, he turned away his head, took hold of the picture with his outstretched hand, and opening a drawer in his sideboard, thrust the thing underneath a folded tablecloth which was lying there. Then he closed the drawer and took up an entertaining book to distract his thoughts from the whole matter.

In this he succeeded very ill. Yet somehow the rest of the evening passed, and as it wore away, he lost something of his alarm. At ten o'clock, Mrs Rumney, knocking and receiving answer twice, lest by any chance she should find herself alone in the room, brought in the cocoa usually taken by her lodger at that hour. A hasty glance at the easel showed her that it stood empty, and her face betrayed her relief. She made no comment, and Mr Groves invited none.

The latter, however, could not make up his mind to go to bed. The face he had seen was taking firm hold upon his imagination, and seemed to fascinate him and repel him at the same time. Before long, he found himself wholly unable to resist the impulse to look at it once more. He took it again, with some indecision, from the drawer and laid it under the lamp.

The man with the roller had now passed completely over the lawn, and was near the left of the picture.

The shock to Mr Groves was again considerable. He stood facing the fire, trembling with excitement which refused to be suppressed. In this state his eye lighted upon the calendar hanging before him, and it furnished him with some distraction. The next day was his mother's birthday. Never did he omit to write a letter which should lie upon her breakfast-table, and the preoccupation of this evening had made him wholly forgetful of the matter. There was a collection of letters, however, from the pillar-box near at hand, at a quarter before midnight, so he turned to his desk, wrote a letter which would at least serve to convey his affectionate greetings, and having written it, went out into the night and posted it.

The clocks were striking midnight as he returned to his room. We may be sure that he did not resist the desire to glance at the photograph he had left on his table. But the results of that glance, he, at any rate, had not anticipated. The man with the roller had disappeared. The lawn lay as smooth and clear as at first, 'looking,' as Mrs Rumney had said, 'as if it was waiting for someone to come and dance on it.'

The photograph, after this, remained a photograph and nothing more. Mr Groves would have liked to persuade himself that it had never undergone these changes which he had witnessed, and which we have endeavoured to describe, but his sense of their reality was too insistent. He kept the print lying for a week upon his easel. Mrs Rumney, although she had ceased to dread it, was obviously relieved at its disappearance, when it was carried to Stoneground to be delivered to Mr Batchel. Mr Groves said nothing of the man with the roller, but gave the enlargement, without comment, into his friend's hands. The work of enlargement had been skilfully done, and was deservedly praised.

Mr Groves, making some modest disclaimer, observed that the view, with its spacious foreground of lawn, was such as could not have failed to enlarge well. And this lawn, he added, as they sat looking out of the Vicar's study, looks as well from within your house as from without. It must give you a sense of responsibility, he added, reflectively, to be sitting where your predecessors have sat for so many centuries and to be continuing their peaceful work. The mere presence before your window, of the turf upon which good men have walked, is an inspiration.

The Vicar made no reply to these somewhat sententious remarks. For a moment he seemed as if he would speak some words of conventional assent. Then he abruptly left the room, to return in a few minutes with a parchment book.

300

'Your remarks, Groves,' he said, as he seated himself again, 'recalled to me a curious bit of history: I went up to the old library to get the book. This is the journal of William Longue who was Vicar here up to the year 1602. What you said about the lawn will give you an interest in a certain portion of the journal. I will read it.'

Aug. 1, 1600—I am now returned in haste from a journey to Brightelmstone whither I had gone with full intention to remain about the space of two months. Master Josiah Wilburton, of my dear College of Emmanuel, having consented to assume the charge of my parish of Stoneground in the meantime. But I had intelligence, after 12 days' absence, by a messenger from the Churchwardens, that Master Wilburton had disappeared last Monday sennight, and had been no more seen. So here I am again in my study to the entire frustration of my plans, and can do nothing in my perplexity but sit and look out from my window, before which Andrew Birch rolleth the grass with much persistence. Andrew passeth so many times over the same place with his roller that I have just now stepped without to demand why he so wasteth his labour, and upon this he hath pointed out a place which is not levelled, and hath continued his rolling.

Aug. 2—There is a change in Andrew Birch since my absence, who hath indeed the aspect of one in great depression, which is noteworthy of so chearful a man. He haply shares our common trouble in respect of Master Wilburton, of whom we remain without tidings. Having made part of a sermon upon the seventh chapter of the former Epistle of St Paul to the Corinthians and the 27th verse, I found Andrew again at his task, and bade him desist and saddle my horse, being minded to ride forth and take counsel with my good friend John Palmer at the Deanery, who bore Master Wilburton great affection.

Aug. 2 continued—Dire news awaiteth me upon my return. The Sheriff's men have disinterred the body of poor Master W. from beneath the grass Andrew was rolling, and have arrested him on the charge of being his cause of death.

Aug. 10—Alas! Andrew Birch has been hanged, the Justice having mercifully ordered that he should hang by the neck until he should be dead, and not sooner molested. May the Lord have mercy on his soul. He made full confession before me, that he had slain Master Wilburton in heat upon his threatening to make me privy to certain peculation of which I should not have suspected so old a servant. The poor man bemoaned his evil temper in great contrition, and beat his breast, saying that he knew himself doomed for ever to roll the grass in the place where he had tried to conceal his wicked fact.

'Thank you,' said Mr Groves. 'Has that little negative got the date upon it?' Yes, replied Mr Batchel, as he examined it with his glass. The boy has marked it August 10. The Vicar seemed not to remark the coincidence with the date of Birch's execution. Needless to say that it did not escape Mr Groves. But he kept silence about the man with the roller, who has been no more seen to this day.

Doubtless there is more in our photography than we yet know of. The camera sees more than the eye, and chemicals in a freshly prepared and active state, have a power which they afterwards lose. Our units of time, adopted for the convenience of persons dealing with the ordinary movements of material objects, are of course conventional. Those who turn the instruments of science upon nature will always be in danger of seeing more than they looked for. There is such a disaster as that of knowing too much, and at some time or another it may overtake each of us. May we then be as wise as Mr Groves in our reticence, if our turn should come.

A Maniac

Maurice Level

He was neither malicious nor blood-thirsty. It was only that he had conceived a very special idea of the pleasures of existence. Perhaps it was that, having tried them all, he no longer found the thrill of the unexpected in any of them.

He went to the theater, not to follow the piece, or to look through his opera-glasses at the spectators, but because he hoped that some day a fire might break out. At the fair of Neuilly he visited the various menageries in anticipation of a catastrophe: the tamer attacked by the beasts. He had tried bullfights, but soon tired of them; the slaughter appeared too well-regulated, too natural, and it disgusted him to watch suffering.

What he was always looking for was the quick and keen anguish caused by some unexpected disaster, some new kind of accident; so much so that, having been at the Opera Comique on the night of the great fire, from which he escaped unhurt; that, having been a couple of steps from the cage the day the celebrated Fred was devoured by his lions, he lost almost all interest in theaters and menageries. To those who were astonished at this apparent change in his tastes, he replied:

"But there's nothing more to see there. They don't give me the slightest sensation. All that I care for is the effect produced on others and on me."

When he was deprived of these two favorite pleasures — it had taken him ten years to get what he wanted from them — he fell into a state of mental and physical depression, and for some months rarely left his house.

Then came a morning when the walls of Paris were covered with multi-colored posters that showed, on an azure background, a curious inclined track which came down, wound round, and fell like a ribbon. Up at the top, little bigger than a dot, a cyclist seemed to be waiting for a signal to rush down the giddy descent. At the same time the newspapers gave accounts of an extraordinary feat that explained the meaning of this weird picture.

It seemed that the cyclist dashed down the narrow path at full speed, went up round the loop, then down to the bottom. For a second during this fantastic performance he was head downwards, his feet up in the air.

The acrobat invited the press to come and examine the track and the machine so that they might see there was no trickery about it, and he explained that his ability to perform the feat was due to calculations of extreme precision, and that so long as he kept his nerve nothing could prevent its accomplishment.

Now it is certain that when the life of a man hangs on keeping his nerve, it hangs on a very insecure peg!

Since the appearance of the advertisement, our maniac had recovered some of his good humor. He went to the private demonstration, and becoming convinced that a new sensation awaited him, was in a seat on the first night to watch closely this looping the loop.

He had taken a box that faced the end of the track, and he sat there alone, not wishing to have near him any one who might distract his close attention.

The whole thing was over in a few minutes. He had just time to see the black speck appear on the end of the track, a formidable spurt, a plunge, a gigantic bound, and that was all. It gave him a thrill, swift and vivid as lightning.

But as he went out with the crowd, he reflected that though he might feel this sensation twice or thrice, it must eventually fail, as all the others had done. He had not found what he was looking for. Then came the thought that a man's nerve has limitations, that the strength of a bicycle is, after all, only relative, and that there is no track of the kind, however secure it may seem, that may not some time give way. And he arrived at the conclusion that it was inevitable that some day an accident must occur.

From this to deciding to watch for that accident was a very small step.

"I will go to see this looping of the loop every night," he decided. "I will go till I see that man break his head. If it doesn't happen during this three months in Paris, I will follow him elsewhere till it does."

For two months, every evening at the same time, he went to the same box and in the same seat. The management had grown to know him. He had taken the box for the whole period of the turn, and they wondered vainly what could account for this costly whim.

One evening when the acrobat had gone through his performance earlier than usual, he saw him in a corridor and went up to him. There was no need for an introduction.

"I know you already," said the bicyclist. "You are always at the hall. You come every night."

Surprised, he asked:

"It is true I am deeply interested in your performance. But who has told you so?"

The man smiled:

"No one. I see you."

"That is very surprising. At such a height . . . at such a moment . . . your mind is sufficiently free to pick out the spectators down below?"

"Certainly not. I don't see the spectators down below. It would be extremely dangerous for me to pay any attention to a crowd that moves and chatters. In all matters connected with my profession, in addition to the turn itself, its theory and practice, there is something else, a kind of trick . . ."

He started.

"A trick?"

"Don't misunderstand me. I don't mean trickery. I mean something of which the public has no suspicion, something that is perhaps the most delicate part of the whole performance. Shall I explain? Well, I accept it as a fact that it is not possible to empty the brain till it contains but one idea, impossible to keep the mind fixed on any one thought. As complete concentration is necessary, I choose in the hall some one object on which I fix my eyes. I see nothing but that object. From the second I have my gaze on it, nothing else exists. I get on the saddle. My hands gripping the bars, I think of nothing; neither of my balance, nor my direction. I am sure of my muscles; they are as firm as steel. There is only one part of me I am afraid of: my eyes. But once I have fixed them on something, I am sure of them as well. Now, the first night I performed here, it happened that my eyes fell on your box. I saw you. I saw nothing but you. Without knowing it, you caught and held my eyes . . . You became the point, the object of which I have told you. The second day I looked for you at the same place. The following days it was the same. And so it happens that now, as soon as I appear, by instinct my eyes turn to you. You help me; you are the precious aid indispensable to my performance. Now do you understand why I know you?"

Next day the maniac was in his usual seat. In the hall there were the usual movements and murmurs of keen anticipation. Suddenly a dense silence fell; that profound silence when you feel that an audience is holding its breath. The acrobat was on his machine, which was held by two men, waiting for the signal to set off. He was balanced to perfection, his hands grasping the bar, his head up, his gaze fixed straight ahead.

He cried "Hop!" and the men pushed him off.

Just at that moment, in the most natural way possible, the maniac rose, pushed back his seat, and went to one at the other side of the box. Then a terrible thing happened. The cyclist was thrown violently up in the air. His machine rushed forwards, flew up, and lurching out into the midst of the shrieks of terror that filled the hall, fell among the crowd.

With a methodical gesture the maniac put on his overcoat, smoothed his hat on the cuff of his sleeve, and went out.

Midnight House

William Fryer Harvey

I had often seen the name on the ordnance map, and had as often wondered what sort of a house it was.

If I had had the placing, it should have been among pine woods in some deep, waterless valley, or else in the Fens by a sluggish tidal river, with aspens whispering in a garden half choked by poisonous evergreens.

I might have placed it in a cathedral city, in a sunless alley overlooking the narrow strip of graveyard of a church no longer used; a house so surrounded by steeple and belfry that every sleeper in it would wake at midnight, aroused by the clamorous insistence of the chimes.

But the Midnight House of cold reality, that I had found by chance on the map when planning a walking tour that never came into being, was none of these. I saw no more than an inn on an old coaching road that crossed the moors as straight as an arrow, keeping to the hill-tops, so that I guessed it to be Roman.

Men have a certain way of living in accordance with their name that one often looks for in vain with places. The Pogsons will never produce a poet, whatever may be the fame they may achieve as lawyers, journalists, or sanitary engineers; but Monckton-in-the-Forest, through which I passed last week, is a railway junction and nothing more, in the middle of a bare plain; not a stone remains of the once famous priory that gave to the place its name.

I expected then to be disappointed, but for some reason or other I made a resolve, if ever chance should leave me within twenty miles of the inn, to spend a night in Midnight House.

I could not have chosen a better day. It was late in November and warm—too warm I had found for the last five-mile tramp across the heather. I had seen no one since noon, when a keeper on the distant skyline had tried in vain to make me understand that I was trespassing; and now at dusk I stood again on the high road with Midnight House below me in the hollow.

It would be hard to picture a more desolate scene—bare hills rising on every side to the dull, lead sky above; at one's feet heather, burnt black after last spring's firing, broken in places by patches of vivid emerald that marked the bogs.

The building of stone, roofed with heavy, lichen-covered flags, formed three sides of a square, the centre of which was evidently used as a farm-yard.

Nowhere was there sign of life; half the windows were shuttered, and, though the dim light of afternoon was fast waning, I saw no lamp in the tap-room, by the door which overlooked the road.

I knocked, but no one answered; and, growing impatient at the delay, walked round to the back of the house, only to be greeted by the savage barking of a collie, that tugged frantically at the chain which fastened it to the empty barrel that served it as kennel. The noise was at any rate sufficient to bring out the woman of the house, who listened stolidly to my request for a night's lodging, and then to my surprise refused me.

They were busy, she said, and had no time to look after visitors. I was not prepared for this. I knew that there were beds at the inn; it was used at least once a year by the men who rented the shooting, and I had not the slightest inclination for another ten-mile tramp along roads I did not know. A drop of rain on my cheek clenched the matter; grudgingly the woman saw reason in my arguments and finally consented to take me in. She showed me into the dining-room, lit the fire, and left me with the welcome news that the ham and eggs would be ready in half an hour's time.

The room in which I found myself was of some size, panelled half-way up to the ceiling, though the natural beauty of the wood had been recently spoiled by a coat of drab-coloured paint.

The windows were, as usual, firmly shut; and from the musty smell I gathered that it was little used. Half a dozen sporting prints hung on the walls; over the mantelpiece was a cheap German engraving representing the death of Isaac; on the sideboard were two glass cases, containing a heron and two pied blackbirds, both atrociously stuffed; while above that piece of hideous Victorian furniture, two highly coloured portraits of the Duke and Duchess of York gazed smilingly upon the patriarch.

Altogether the room was not a cheerful one, and I was relieved to find a copy of *East Lynne* lying on the horsehair sofa. Most inns contain the book; the fourteen chapters which I have read represent as many evenings spent alone in wayside hostelries.

Just before six the woman came in to lay the table. From my chair in the shadow by the fireside I watched her unobserved. She moved slowly; the simplest action was performed with a strange deliberation, as if her mind, half bent upon something else, found novelty in what before was commonplace. The expression of her face gave no clue to her thoughts. I saw only that her features were strong and hard.

As soon as the meal was upon the table she left the room, without having exchanged a word; and feeling unusually lonely, I sat down to make the best of the ham and eggs and the fifteenth chapter of *East Lynne*.

The food was good enough, better than I had expected; but for some reason or other my spirits were no lighter when, the table having been cleared, I drew up my chair to the fire and filled my pipe.

'If this house is not already haunted,' I said to myself, 'it is certainly time it were so,' and I began to pass in review a whole procession of ghosts without finding one that seemed really suited to the place.

At half-past nine, and the hour was none too soon, the woman reappeared with a candle, and intimated gruffly that she would show me my room. She stopped opposite a door at the end of a corridor to the left of the stair head. 'You had better wedge the windows, if you want to sleep with them open; people complain a deal about their rattling.' I thanked her and bade her good night.

I was spared at least the horror of a four-poster, though the crimson-canopied erection, which occupied at least a quarter of the room, seemed at first sight to be little better. There was no wardrobe, but in its place a door, papered over with the same material as the walls and, at first sight, indistinguishable from them, opened into a closet, empty save for a row of hooks and lighted by a single window.

I noticed that neither of the doors had keys, and that a red velvet bell-pull by the bed was no longer fastened to its wire, but hung useless from a nail driven into one of the beams of the ceiling.

I am in the habit of securely bolting my door whenever I spend a night away from home, a piece of common prudence which nothing less than an awful fright from a sleep-walker taught me twenty years ago.

To do so was on this occasion impossible, but I dragged a heavy chest across the door which led into the passage, placing the water-jug against the inner one, in case the wind should blow it open in the night: then, after wedging the window with my pocket-knife, I got into bed, but not to sleep. Twice I heard the clock outside strike the hour, twice the half-hour, yet, late as it was, the house seemed still awake. Distant footsteps echoed down the stone passages; once I caught the crash of broken crockery—never the sound of a voice. At length I fell asleep, with the same feeling of unaccountable depression that had dogged me since sundown still upon me.

I had in truth walked far too far that day to receive the inestimable boon of the weary, a dim consciousness of annihilation. Instead I tramped again over dream moors with a Baedeker in my hand, trying in vain to find the valley of the shadow.

I came at last to a mountain tarn, filled with brown peat water; on the marge a huge ferry-boat was drawn up, on which crowds of men, women, and children were embarking. The boat at last was full and we were putting off, the heavy sails filling before a wind which never ruffled the surface of the water, when someone cried that there was still another to come, pointing as he spoke to an old man who stood on the shore madly gesticulating. An argument followed, some in the boat saying that it was too late to put back, others that the man would perish with cold if we left him there on the shelterless moor. But we were too eager to see the valley of the shadow, and the steersman held on his course. As we left him, a sudden change came across the old man's features; the mask of benevolence vanished; we saw only a face of such utter malignancy that the children in fright ran whimpering to their mothers.

In the boat they whispered his name, how he was a man for ever seeking to gain entrance to the ferry, that he might accomplish some awful purpose, and in joy at our escape a strange song was raised, which rose and fell like the music of a running stream.

I was awakened by the sound of rain upon the window; the water in the brook outside had already risen and was making itself heard, but with a sound so soothingly monotonous that I was soon asleep again.

Again I dreamed. This time I was a citizen of a great leaguered city. The once fertile plain that stretched from the walls to the dim horizon lay ravaged by the armies that had swept over it. The sun was sinking as a crowd of half-starved wretches came to the western gate, clamouring to come in. They were the peasants, caught between the besieging hosts and the frowning barriers of the city that had no food for mouths other than its own. As I stood at the postern to the right of the main gate with a little knot of companions, a man approached who at once attracted our attention. He was a huge fellow, in the prime of life, straight as a tree, and strong enough to carry an ox. He came up to our leader and asked to be let in. 'I have travelled day and night for twelve months,' he said, 'that I might fight by your side.' The last sally had cost us dear and we were short of men such as he. 'Come in and welcome,' said the captain of the guard at last. He had already taken a key from his breast and was unlocking the postern, when I cried out. Something in the man's face I had recognized; it was that of the old man who had tried to get into the ferry. 'He's a spy!' I shouted. 'Lock the gates, for God's sake! Shut the window, or he'll climb in!'

I jumped out of bed with my own words ringing in my ears. Some window at any rate required shutting; it was the one in the cupboard opening out of my room. Wind had come with the rain and the sash had been loosened. The air was no longer close and the clouds were lifting, scudding over the moon. I craned out my neck, drinking in the cool night air. As I did so, I noticed an oblong patch of light on the roadway; it came from an upper window at the opposite end of the building; now and then the patch was crossed by a shadow. The people of the inn kept strangely late hours.

I did not at once go back to bed, but, stiff and sore, drew up a chair to the window with pillows and a couple of blankets, and there I sat for fully half an hour, listening to the howling of the dog, a wail of utter weariness far too dismal for the moon alone to have awakened. Then it suddenly turned into an angry growl, and I caught the sound of distant hoofs upon the road. At the same time the shadow reappeared upon the blind, the window was pulled up, and the hard, sour face of my landlady peered out into the darkness.

Evidently she was expecting someone. A minute later a horse, that had been hard ridden, drew up steaming before the door; its rider dismounted.

'Leave the beast to me,' said the woman from the window, in a voice hardly raised above a whisper. 'I'll see that it's made all right in the stable. Come straight upstairs; it's the third room on the right.'

The man took up what seemed to be a heavy bag and, leaving his horse, passed on up the stair. I heard him stumble at the step on the landing and swear beneath his breath. Just then the clock struck three. I began to wonder if any mischief were brewing in Midnight House.

I have only the vaguest recollection of what happened between then and dawn. My attempts to obtain sleep were not as great as the struggles I made to free myself from the awful nightmares that took possession of me as soon as I began to lose consciousness. All I knew was that there was a spirit of evil abroad, an ugly, horrible spirit, that was trying to enter the house; and that every one seemed to be blind to its true nature, seemed to be helping it to gain its end. That was the lurid background of my dreams. One thing alone I remember clearly, a long-drawn-out cry, real and no wild fantasy, that came out of the night to die away into nothingness.

When I got up in the morning soon after nine, I had a splitting headache that made me resolve to be less ready in future to sample strange beds and stranger inns.

I entered the dining-room to find myself no longer alone. A tall, middle-aged man, with a look about him as if he had passed anything but a restful night, was seated at the table. He had just finished breakfast, and rose to go as I took my place. He wished me a curt good morning and left the room. I hurried over my meal, paid my bill to the same impassive-faced woman, the only occupant of the house I had seen, and shouldering my rucksack, set out along the road. I walked on for two miles, until I had nearly reached the summit of a steep incline, and was hesitating over which of three roads to take, when, turning round, I saw the stranger approaching.

As soon as his horse had overtaken me I asked him the way.

'By the by,' I said, 'can you tell me anything about that inn? It's the gloomiest house I ever slept in. Is it haunted?'

'Not that I know of. How can a house be haunted when there are no such things as ghosts?'

Something in the ill-concealed superiority of the tone in which he replied made me look at him more closely. He seemed to read my thoughts. 'Yes, I'm the doctor,' he said, 'and precious little I get out of the business, I can tell you. You are not looking out for a quiet country practice yourself, I suppose? I don't think a night's work like this last's would tempt you.'

'I don't know what it was,' I said, 'but, if I was to hazard a guess, I should say some singularly wicked man must have died in the inn last night.'

He laughed out loud. 'You're rather wide of the mark, for the fact is I have been helping to usher into the world another pretty innocent. As things turned out, the child did not live above half an hour, not altogether to the mother's sorrow, I should judge. People talk pretty freely in the country. There's nothing else to do; and we all know each other's affairs. It might have come into the world in better circumstances, certainly; but after all is said and done, we shan't have much to complain of if we can keep the birth-rate from falling any lower. What was it last year? Some appallingly low figure, but I can't remember the actual one. Yes, I've always been interested in statistics. They can explain nearly everything.'

I was not quite so sure.

Midnight Promises

Richard T. Chizmar

She peeks around the edge of the door. Tiptoes inside the room and kisses him good morning. A soft peck on the cheek.

He doesn't stir.

She walks over to the window and pulls open the curtains. It's June and the sky is rainbow blue with lazy white clouds swimming by. The view is a pretty one—distant trees swaying in the breeze, a bed of flowers blooming in the foreground—and she wishes, as she does every morning, that she could open the window just a crack.

She places her bag at the foot of the bed, takes off her windbreaker and sits down in the chair. She gently takes his right hand and begins stroking each of his fingers.

Later, when he wakes up, she'll move over to his left side so that he'll be able to see outside the window.

But for now she sits with her back bathed in golden sunlight.

The cancer is taking him away—inch by inch.

Every day, a little more of him disappears.

And she sits and watches.

Always she watches.

She leaves at night now but only because they make her.

"You need your rest, Mrs. Collins."

"We'll take good care of him."

"I promise that we'll call if your husband needs you for anything."

"You remember what happened last time, Mrs. Collins. We don't want a repeat of that, now do we?"

So now she goes home each night. Precisely at ten o'clock with the other visitors.

A silent elevator ride to the lobby. A slow walk to the parking lot. And the lonely drive home.

Home . . . where there is nothing left for her.

Just a quiet, cold house. A mug of hot cocoa in the dark kitchen. The day's mail. And an empty bed.

Home is like a stranger to her now. Or perhaps *she* is the stranger. She can remember a time when this house smiled at her each time she walked through the door. Whispered in her ear as she crossed the foyer that everything was safe and sound and wonderful.

Now there is only silence.

Not even a whisper of life there: no lights or television or radio. No laughter or idle conversation. Nothing.

Just the same damn thing, night after night after night.

Hot cocoa. Mail. Bed.

And, of course, the nightmares.

They come more often now.

Sometimes—very, very rarely—she dreams happy thoughts: *A close-up of his smile. The sound of his laughter. The feel of his lips on her mouth. The touch of his hand as they walk barefoot on a moonlit beach.*

But most nights she dreams darker thoughts: *an x-ray view of his torso . . . showing nothing. Absolutely nothing inside—just a hollowed-out husk of a man. Surviving on nothing but air.*

Or her standing alone in a cold, driving rain. Standing above his open grave. Dropping a single red rose onto the shiny black casket . . .

Or the apple dream. This one is the worst of all—sheer terror. *She sees the two of them sitting in front of a large desk of dark, polished wood. Holding hands. Listening to a doctor. The doctor's face is grim. His lip is trembling. He tells them that the first reports were wrong, that the cancer has spread and he holds up an x-ray . . . and the image is that of an apple tree. Tumors everywhere, hanging there like fat, ripe apples. Dozens of them. Dark and moist and plump. Waiting to be picked . . .*

Thank God, this dream doesn't come very often.

Because when it does, she almost always wakes up screaming.

It's lunchtime and the hallway is buzzing with activity.

She gets up and closes the door.

He's sleeping again, but she isn't worried about the noise disturbing him. It's the smell—he can't stand the smell of the hospital food. It makes him nauseous.

312

A lot of things do that to him. Food. Flowers. Perfume. Even some liquids. They all smell funny now. One of the drugs is responsible, but she can't remember which one.

He doesn't eat the food, anyway. Not anymore. They use a tube for that now. A shiny, little clear thing that snakes right into his stomach.

She remembers that as a particularly bad time—the week he stopped eating.

But even worse was when he stopped talking.

It's been thirteen days now. And barely a whisper in all that time. Too weak, the doctors explain. Too many drugs.

So, most days, they just sit there and hold hands and stare into each other's eyes. Sometimes they smile and make silly faces, sometimes they just sit there and cry.

With the door closed, the room is very quiet except for the constant beeping of the I.V. She turns the volume down a notch—she knows the machines as well as any nurse on the floor—and starts to read again from a letter she'd written him just before they were married. Her voice cracks several times and there are tears in her eyes, but still she keeps reading. She has a stack of letters in her bag, tightly-bound with a thick rubber band, and she is determined to get through them all.

The mornings are no kinder than the nights. Same routine every day— up by six-thirty, out the door by seven-thirty.

She starts each morning with a long, hot shower and she always tries her hardest to think of something nice, something cheerful to start the day with. But she never can.

She forces herself to eat a good breakfast most of the time. Toast. Fruit. Juice. For energy. She knows this was the reason she'd gotten sick last month and needed to see the doctor—not because she was sleeping in his hospital room every night! Not because she was overtired, for goodness' sake!

She had simply forgotten to eat. For three or four days. She can't remember which.

So now she takes the time to eat most mornings. And when she's done, she washes the dishes and wipes down the countertop. Then she grabs her keys from the foyer and locks the door behind her. She gets into her car and pulls away from the curb. And never once looks back.

Dinner is served at quarter to six.

She closes the door as soon as she hears the familiar squeaking of the tray-cart working its way down the hallway.

He's awake now and they are looking at photos.

High school. College. Summers at the beach. Even pictures of the wedding. She brought them all.

He smiles at most of the pictures. Points and grins and raises what's left of his eyebrows. It's the most animated—and alert—he's been in weeks, and it does her heart wonders to see him this way.

When she gets to one particular photo, he really surprises her. His face lights up like a child's and he takes it from her with trembling fingers.

It's an old photo. From the very first summer they spent together. A narrow strip of three small black-and-whites from one of those cheap, little booths you sit inside. In the first two, their faces are pressed together cheek-to-cheek and they're grinning like goofy kids. In the last one, they're kissing.

He lifts the photo to his face and tries to kiss it. But the tubes get in the way.

So she takes it from him and kisses it herself, then lays it on the sheet atop his chest.

He smiles at her and closes his eyes.

She does the same and moments later when she hears the whisper— *"thank you"*—she thinks she must be dreaming . . .

Until she opens her eyes and sees his stare and the tears streaming down his cheeks.

And at that exact moment, she knows with complete certainty that she is doing the right thing—the letters, the photos . . .

In her heart, she knows . . .

Just after eight o'clock, he falls asleep again and she returns the photos to her bag. Except for his favorite one—she leaves that right where it is.

She holds his hand and watches him sleep until ten. Just like so many times before.

Then she kisses him goodnight and heads for the elevator.

Sometimes, when she's away from the hospital, she tries to convince herself that he's improving. That he's looking better. And that she'll walk through the door the next morning and he'll be sitting up and talking and maybe eating some scrambled eggs. And she'll bounce over to the bed and say, "Hey, kiddo, I *thought* you had some color in those cheeks last night—"

But she knows none of this is true. She knows what's really happening.

Fourteen hours a day is enough to convince anyone.

He'd lost his hair during the second cycle of chemo.

By the end of the third, he was thirty pounds lighter.

A month later—halfway into the final cycle—they knew it wasn't working.

So they'd switched to different drugs and a different program.

And it had worked for a while, too. For a few weeks, at least, he seemed to stabilize. His energy crept up a few notches, his weight maintained.

But then, as if the whole thing was just some sort of cruel joke, it all went downhill and fast.

He stopped eating.

His skin turned a sick combination of yellow and green.

He started to sweat so much and the smell . . . oh God the smell . . .

And then, almost overnight, the pain doubled. Then tripled.

And then it got so bad that he started to cry—something she had never seen before. Not when his mother died, not when they first learned about the cancer. Never.

So the doctors had immediately injected him with the heavy stuff . . .

. . . and most of the pain had gone away . . .

. . . almost overnight, just as fast as it had come, it had gone away . . .

. . . and her husband had gone away with it.

Now he sleeps most of the time.

And when he *is* awake—well, it isn't much different than when he's still sleeping. Or at least it seems that way to her. His eyes are so milky and unfocused, he barely moves a finger, he doesn't talk . . .

She feels miserably guilty for thinking this way. Of course, she's glad he no longer feels the pain. Of course, she's grateful to the doctors for making him so much more comfortable.

But God, she can't help it—she misses his voice, his laugh, his charm; she misses the way he once looked at her.

Without those things, she is not only afraid, she is all alone.

She slides the ring onto his finger and closes his hand into a fist. His fingers are skinny and gnarled—like an old man's—and she's worried that the ring will fall off. Tumble down to the floor and no one will find it.

She lets go of his hand and stares at it for a long moment, then walks over to the window.

It's almost midnight and a full moon is shining far away in the distance, coating the trees with a silver luster, making everything look wet and slick like just after a rainfall.

She parts the curtains slightly and a sliver of moonbeam enters the room.

She looks at her bag on the floor. Thinks about the letters and the photos inside. Wonders why she didn't leave the bag back in the car.

She knows she's stalling, but she can't help it.

She turns and looks into the shadows: at the blinking machines and the tangle of tubes and the clear, dripping bag with the big red sticker that reads: *CHEMO: Do Not Handle Without Protective Gloves.*

She stares at the man she loves so dearly, the only man she has *ever* loved.

Thirty-four years of life and he's been there over half of them, she thinks.

Just you and me against the world, kiddo . . .

She puts her hand inside her jacket pocket.

Walks to his bedside and leans over.

Kisses his sweaty forehead.

Closes her eyes and whispers: "I'll forever love you, my darling."

And her words will live in this room forever.

She places the gun to his forehead and makes good on her promise.

There's a sudden explosion of sound and light and she falls hard to the floor.

She looks up involuntarily and shudders.

And then, for the first time in all their years together, she breaks her word to him. She opens her mouth wide, slides the cold barrel inside and pulls the trigger.

A promise kept.

A promise broken.

And the unending silence of night.

Misadventures in the
Skin Trade

Don D'Ammassa

Someone stole my skin the other day. I know how that must sound, but it's the simple truth. They were clever though, replacing it with a substitute that was so close it fooled me for a while. But not for long. I mean, how much more intimately can you know anything than your very own skin? It's not like clothing, for Christ's sake!

Sorry. I didn't mean to lose control there, but you have to admit, it's an unsettling thing to discover, that your body is covered with something foreign, a synthetic of some kind, perhaps, or in this case a stranger's skin. How's that for a disgusting thought? Would you want something like that wrapped tightly around your flesh? No, I didn't think so. So maybe you can understand how I feel about it.

I have to concede I was fooled for a while, even though I noticed some inconsistencies first thing that morning. It's not the kind of conclusion you accept readily, though, and I made excuses. Perhaps I had just never noticed the small blemish on the right thigh, and that fresh scratch on my side . . . I could have done that with a fingernail in my sleep.

There were other clues that I chose not to recognize. When Marie walked out, years ago now, she complained that I thought more of my own body than I did of hers. It did no good to point out that unless she began to take adequate care of herself, she would never regain the firm muscle tone, proper ratio of weight to height, or that wonderfully clear complexion which had attracted me to her in the first place. I myself had not varied more than a few pounds from my base weight in over a decade, and I examined my body constantly for signs of imperfection.

But on that late summer morning following the theft of my skin, there was a thin but unmistakable finger's width of loose flesh around my waist.

Still I failed to recognize the implications, assuming instead that I had been lax in my exercises, or perhaps had slipped into unhealthy eating habits. This latter explanation seemed even more credible when I discovered a cluster of small dark spots on my nose, infected pores, and by the time I had thoroughly cleaned them and applied a disinfectant, my nose was as red as a drunkard's and as painful as a prizefighter's. Resolving to ruthlessly re-examine both my diet and my training routine that evening,

I set off to work mildly concerned but not yet aware of the true nature of my condition.

The feeling that something was subtly wrong persisted all day. I've worked the same position on the assembly line for four years now, and I've trained my body to work as a piece of the machinery. The rhythms are a part of me as I am a part of them, and every flexing muscle, every twist of elbow and wrist, each individual stretch of skin over flesh is predictable and familiar. But not that morning.

I couldn't quite put my finger on it at first. I had fallen into the routine as always, three connections on the left, three on the right, rotate the unit, check the solder joint, rotate again, fasten the clip, arms back while the unit shifted to the next station and a new one offered itself. More than a thousand times I had merged with the operation smoothly, without a moment's hesitation. But that morning, it felt wrong, the kinesthetics were different, not enough to interfere with my performance of the work required, but enough to put my nerves on edge. I've always been proud of my self discipline, the way I've trained my body to respond instantly to everything I ask of it. If we aren't captains of our own bodies, how can we expect to control the world around us?

I was troubled throughout the day and distracted on the drive home. My work clothes went into the hamper; I never wore the same set more than once without washing them. Then my usual thorough shower, starting with my hair, which had grown to be nearly an inch long. Time for a trim. Three applications of shampoo and a rinse, then a thorough scrubbing with a stiff spined brush, followed by a final shampoo. Then my face, concentrating on my nose this time. I had installed a mirror on the shower wall years before, but it rarely proved effective, the image obscured by rising steam as quickly as I could clear it away. But I used it this time, concentrating to make certain there'd been no recurrence of the invading blackheads I'd discovered that morning.

Other than that, I kept to my routine, ears, back of the neck, then throat and chin. I scrubbed myself until the flesh was warm and glowing and the sense of wrongness started to recede. Chest and armpits and navel, shoulders and back and waist. The superfluous flesh at my midriff was still there and still worrisome, but I was confident that I could work it off in a few days.

I was tempted as always to quickly pass over my genitals, the weakest and least perfect part of the male body, but as usual I forced myself to overcompensate and lather them thoroughly, scrubbing vigorously enough that my breath became sharp and ragged. I shaved myself once a week to facilitate this process, but there were so many folds of flesh that might conceal infections or other unpleasantness, I was never completely satisfied that my efforts were complete.

318

Just below my left knee, I discovered a tiny, tear-shaped scar. I almost passed it by. It was faint, an absence of feature rather than a blatant disfigurement. It wasn't fresh, had in fact entirely healed. But I had never seen it before, never once in the forty years I had lived in this body.

I forced myself to eat, carefully measuring the portions, even though I had little appetite. Dressed in loose-fitting pants and sleeveless shirt, I cleared away the dishes and walked thoughtfully down to the exercise room in the basement, spent the next two hours following my established pattern, pushing each group of muscles to their limit, then slightly beyond. The routine helped to suppress the growing sense of uneasiness, shift it temporarily into some recess of my mind where I could pretend that everything was normal.

Of course you know I was fooling myself, but it's easy to judge things like this from the outside, a lot more difficult to accept that someone has violated the sanctity of your most precious possession, your body itself.

I would normally have showered again, just a warm rinse this time, but as soon as I stopped, those nagging doubts returned. So I chose instead to jog for a while, even though it was already dark outside. There's a heavily wooded area threaded with paths just a block from my house, not the safest place even in the daylight, but I wasn't afraid of being attacked. There were far easier victims available and I'd never had any trouble with the scruffy punks who frequented the area.

Moving at a carefully regulated pace, I ran north until I reached the housing project, then looped back on a narrower path, one so nearly overgrown that I was forced to use my bare arms to fend off stray branches. When the parkway lights were visible to the west, I changed routes again, angling southward, knowing I would eventually cross the paved footpath that led fairly directly back toward my house. I'd never run out here in the dark before and found it somewhat disorienting, but the forested area wasn't so extensive that there was any real chance I might lose my way.

Back home, I stripped and showered, was toweling myself dry when I found the rash. It wasn't much of one, just a thin streak of red spots along my right forearm, almost certainly an allergic reaction to something I had brushed away from my face. The only problem with that was, I had never suffered from any allergies in the past. My skin was tough and resilient and resistant to irritation, just like the rest of my body.

That's when I realized I was wearing someone else's skin.

You might expect that I would have become frantic when faced with the truth, but actually I grew quite calm. Now that I had an explanation for the bizarre inconsistencies that had been showing up all day, knew that they were not signs of my own weakness, the loss of tight body control, but actually the result of a hostile act, I felt a sense of relief and prepared to deal with the situation.

Naturally my first thought was to wonder who was responsible, and why. I didn't have any real enemies, at least not since Marie walked out on me, so it wasn't malice. That left envy. Perfectly understandable, of course; everyone who knew me envied my body, the men anyway. Women admired it as well, but they just wanted to use it for their own pleasure, in ways that would weaken me. Marie had been different, at least when we first married; it was only later that she began making irrational demands, insisting that there was something wrong with using our bodies only for healthy, life affirming purposes.

I was actually quite relieved when she finally left.

But once the motive was understood, the number of potential thieves became bewilderingly high. There was no one I knew whose body could even begin to approach my own hard won near perfection, and frankly I doubted that any of them would be able to substantially improve their situation just by draping themselves in my skin. But jealousy is an irrational emotion, independent of logic.

Using a yellow lined pad, I quickly made a list of every male I could think of. It had to be a man, of course. Then I put check marks next to the ones who were closest to me in size, although I made the marks darker for those who bulked a bit more than me, mindful of the misfit at my waist. There were a half dozen prime candidates and I copied those names onto a second sheet, arranged in order of probability, based on my intuition. One of these men was almost certainly responsible, although there were a few others on my original list whom I could not completely rule out. The thought that it might be a complete stranger, someone who had watched me secretly and waited for a chance to strike, was disturbing, and I decided that if that unlikely explanation was the correct one, there was little I could do about it. It was far more likely that the man responsible was known to me, though, and I proceeded on that assumption.

Although I was impatient to act, it was impractical until the next day, a Friday. Two of my top candidates worked at Eblis, though not in my department. I would need to be circumspect. It was necessary to identify the guilty party without letting on that I knew of the switch.

I was able to eliminate Ned Sanders before the shift started, disappointing since I'd placed him at the top of my list. He was having a cigarette in the cafeteria, in violation of the posted rules, and I regretted the necessity of approaching closely enough that I would have to breathe that polluted air. Sanders was almost exactly my size, but soft, unseasoned. He was shop steward and the company always managed to find a

320

way to assign him the less strenuous jobs, spot inspection, cycle counting, things like that. He saw me coming, half turned in my direction.

"Morning, Dougherty. How're they hanging?"

I was inured to Sanders' language, which was so peppered with obscenities that he has twice been reported to the shift supervisor by women working the line. Although I really hoped that he was the one I was after, I realized the impossibility of that when he raised his arm to wave at me. Sanders had a vulture tattooed on the inside of his left forearm.

Eric Nicholson was my third choice, and he worked the day shift here at Eblis, so I went looking for him at lunch time. He's kind of young, but the right size, even keeps himself in pretty good shape although his posture is bad and I've heard that he drinks. It was hot in the cafeteria and a lot of people took their lunch outside, ate it sitting on the grassy slope that faced the cemetery.

He was there all right, lying off by himself in a patch of sunlight with his shirt off. I couldn't have asked for a better chance. With one arm across his eyes to shut out the light, he didn't even see me standing there, staring down at him.

What I could see of his skin was tanned, smooth, and firm, and I experienced a sense of familiarity. There were some minor inconsistencies, but I figured whatever process had allowed him to switch his skin for mine couldn't have been absolutely perfect. Perhaps it dried out a little while in transit. The skeleton and muscles underneath had to be at least slightly different in configuration, and that would change the distribution of tautness and wrinkles, at least until the skin had a chance to adjust to its new platform. No scars, no tattoos, and the small scrape mark on his elbow was fresh, might have been done since the transfer.

I couldn't be certain, but it seemed likely Nicholson was responsible. Now all I had to do was recover my property.

Nicholson lived alone, a small rundown house in one of the older sections of Managansett. I'd driven him to work a time or two when his car was in for repairs and although I didn't remember the exact address, when I drove through the neighborhood after work that afternoon, I identified it easily. It was set all by itself at the rear of a lot cluttered with untrimmed shrubs, mock orange, rosebushes, lilacs, and forsythia. There'd be no difficulty approaching the house unseen once darkness fell.

I drove home thoughtfully, planning my attack.

For the most part, everything went quite well. I returned after midnight, parking several blocks away, then reached Nicholson's back yard by a roundabout route, easily avoiding the widely spaced streetlights that futilely attempted to bring a sense of security to the neighborhood. His doors were locked but almost all of the ground floor windows were open to the night air. I slipped inside so quietly I wondered if I had missed my calling in not taking up burglary.

The penlight in my pocket was unnecessary. A lamp was still glowing in the front room, a short neon tube buzzed over the kitchen sink. There were two bedrooms, both with their doors open, one piled high with junk, tools, furniture, boxes filled with off season clothing, even some canned goods. Nicholson was asleep in the other, sprawling naked on his stomach diagonally across the bed.

Almost as if he knew I'd be coming and wanted to make it easier for me.

I regretted the necessity to damage my stolen skin but by using the wrench to crush the top of his skull, I figured most of the incidental damage would be concealed under my hair. I might have to let it grow longer in the future, but I'd just increase the number of times I shampooed it to compensate. When I was quite sure that he had stopped breathing, I turned on the bedroom lights.

Obviously Nicholson had used some more subtle technique, since he had managed his theft without assaulting me. He'd have been wiser to finish me off, but I imagine he was smugly convinced that I'd never notice the difference, or if I did, that I'd be unable to figure out the identity of the guilty party.

I went outside and retrieved the ice chest I'd left below the window. Nicholson's methods were clearly more efficient than mine, but I didn't have time to try to figure out how he'd done it. The longer my skin spent on his body, the less likely I was to retrieve it before serious damage had been done. It was a futile effort on his part, when you think about it. Sure, for the time being he'd reap the benefits of my years of discipline and conditioning, but unless he gave up his own lax ways and poor habits, deterioration would be inevitable and he'd be no better off than before. Then I realized that logically he would strike again, find a new skin to replace the old, had perhaps already gone through this same routine in the past. I had not felt any remorse when I killed him. I mean, considering the depraved nature of his crime against me, he deserved no better. But add to that the possibility . . . no, the probability that I was saving many others from a similar fate. Why, in a sense, I was serving the community as well as myself, destroying a monstrous wolf lurking unsuspected among the sheep.

His skin came off quite readily under the flensing knife. I took this as further proof of his guilt; the tissues had not completely reknitted themselves. After washing it off in the shower stall, I carefully folded my skin, wrapped it in cellophane, and buried it in the shaved ice, now rapidly melting into a chilly slush. It will probably involve some experimentation to put things right, so I have returned to my own place where I can work undisturbed.

I'm writing this all down in case anything goes wrong, so that there will be a record, a warning, something to alert the rest of you to the danger. I can't believe Nicholson was an isolated case; there must be others like him preying on the innocent. Those facelifts that actors and politicians have, the ones that are so unbelievably effective—at least some of those are probably excuses to cover up what has really happened.

There's no doubt in my mind that I will be able to reattach my skin. I took measurements to be certain, but there wasn't really time for it to shrink or stretch unnaturally, though I suppose it might be uncomfortable at first. Marie left behind her sewing basket, so I have needles and plenty of thread to close the seams. No, I don't expect to have any great difficulty with that part.

It's cutting Nicholson's alien skin off my body beforehand that poses the challenge.

Missed Connection

Ramsey Campbell

Outside the train the night rocked like a sea. Distant lights bobbed up and sailed away, waves of earth surged up violently and sank. The hurtling train swayed wildly. In the aisle crowds collided; people grabbed one another, clutching for support; their noise was deafening. But Ted had reached the door, and was wrenching it open.

"Oh no you don't," a voice said.

He woke. Was he home at last, and in bed? But already the jumble of sound had rushed into his ears: the harsh clicking repetitions of the tracks, the ebb and flow of tangled voices. He was still on the train.

He opened his eyes to glance at this watch. God, time seemed to have waited for him while he'd slept. Across the aisle the compulsive talker never faltered. "They're not what they used to be," he was saying. "Nothing is these days." Hadn't he said that before? No, Ted silenced himself: no déjà vu, thank you. He'd had enough philosophy of time this term to last him the rest of his life.

The train hadn't even left the city yet. Perhaps it had halted while Ted was asleep. He shifted so that he could look out of the window, trying to be stealthy: whenever he moved, the fat woman next to him encroached further. Specks of a new rain glittered on the windows. Beneath street-lamps, gleams of orange light drifted across the mirrors of streets drawn by the movement of the train. At the end of a street, another train passed.

No, it couldn't have been. What, then? Momentarily he'd seen windows passing beyond a street, a glimpse of moving frames like a strip of film pulled through a gate. An unlit bus, probably. It had seemed to pace the train, but the far ends of streets were deserted now. Someone trod on his toe.

Jesus, it was the whining child. He'd stood up to rummage another toy out of the suitcase. "Watch the man's feet," his mother shouted. "Just you sit down and shut up or I'll belt you one." "Aw, I wanna get something else," the child whined. "I wanna play." God, Ted hoped they weren't going to keep up their double act for the rest of the journey. How much longer? He bared his watch. It had stopped.

Well, that was great. Just fantastic. Now he couldn't tell how long he had still to suffer; he hadn't been home by this route before. All he needed now was for the train to stall. Anything might happen on the railway; the train wouldn't have been so crowded if there hadn't been some foul-up elsewhere; the public address system had mumbled an explanation. How long would he have to be stifled by this crowd?

He glanced warily at them. The child toyed with a gadget; his face grew petulant, preparing to whine. The mother ignored him ostenta-tiously and pored over a love story. The fat woman settled herself again; her lapful of carriers crackled and rustled. The sounds were close, flat-tened; all sounds were—a perpetual coughing, the stream of logorrhea across the aisle, the loud underlying tangle of conversations, mixed blur-rily with the rush of the train. People spilled from the corridors into the aisle, swaying expressionlessly as wax. Stale smoke drifted in, to hang in the trapped June heat. Ted pressed himself closer to the window, trying to make even the tiniest gap between himself and the fat woman. He couldn't stand much more of this.

He must be overtired; he felt on edge, somehow vulnerable. The university term had been taxing. Still, he needn't be neurotic. The jour-ney wouldn't last forever. He turned to the window, drawing into him-self, itching with sweat.

The city was petering out. Jagged icicles of streetlamps hung beneath shades, houses gaped. A distant train crossed a vague street. Again? It had seemed to pass through a derelict alley. Perhaps a terrace walling off the end of a street had looked like a carriage. Or perhaps it had been the train on which he was trapped, reflected somehow. The night was seeping into the city; it swept away the last walls, and filled the windows of the train.

It made them into mirrors. The reflected carriage closed him in. The fat woman sat forward; her lap rustled loudly. Her reflection appeared, multiplied by the double glazing: her two noses overlapped, her four lips opened moistly. All the faces became explosions of flesh, far too much of it, surrounding him wherever he looked, hot and oily and luxuriantly featured. His own face had exploded too. He must distract himself. He dragged Robbe-Grillet from his pocket.

The child whined, the man talked, talked; the tracks chattered rapidly. Ted read the same words over and over, but they became increasingly meaningless; Ted read the same words over and over, but they became increasingly meaningless. He found himself hoping to find they had changed. He stared glumly through the window, which was thickly veined with rain. Then he peered closer. This time there certainly was a train out there.

It was perhaps two hundred yards away, and racing neck and neck with his own train. It squirmed a little, distorted by the watery veins. He strained to see more clearly. There was something odd about the train. The dimness of its windows could be an effect of the downpour. But why were the windows flickering, appearing and vanishing, like an incompetently projected film? Of course—the train was passing through a forest.

He gazed fascinated. The image seemed hypnotic; it drew him. He grew unaware of the stifling carriage, the rush of noise. The dim rectangular will-o'-the-wisps swayed jerkily between the glistening pillars of the trees. The forest was thinning. As a child might, he looked forward to the sight of the unobscured train. The trees fell back, giving way to a field. But nothing at all emerged.

He gasped, and craned back to peer at the swiftly dwindling forest, as though the train might be lurking in there like an animal. But there was only the long edge of the forest, fleeing backwards. The bare fields spread around him, soaked and glittering.

He wished he could ask someone whether they had seen it too. But when he'd gasped, the mother and child had gaped only at him. Again he felt nervously vulnerable: as though his skin were drawn too tight, and thinning. Around him they coughed, whined, shouted, chattered incessantly; tracks clattered. Now he felt more than stifled by the crowd, he felt alienated. Hadn't he felt so earlier, before he'd had the dream? He couldn't talk to anyone; he was trapped in his own mind. The crowd was a huge muddled entity, hemming him in with flesh and noise.

He wanted a sandwich. He wanted to use the toilet. In fact he simply wanted to prove somehow that he wasn't helpless: even lean out of a window for a while. "Will you keep my seat?" he asked the fat woman, but she was asleep, jaw dangling. "Will you keep my seat?" he asked the mother, but she only murmured vaguely, shrugging. The child gaped at him. When Ted stood up anyway, the nearest of the standing passengers gazed speculatively at his place. He sat down again, muttering.

The fat woman snorted deep in her throat, as though choking rhythmically; she rolled against him. God! He shoved her away, but she rolled closer. He thrust his shoulder against hers and braced his feet. The mother and child stared at him. He gazed from the window, to ignore them.

The rain was thinning. Beside the train the ground soared abruptly; an embankment glistened with dim grass and flowers, skimming by. It pressed reflections closer to him; the faces overgrown with flesh became more solid. Surely he must be nearly home. Shouldn't the train reach a station soon? The embankment sank; wind cleared rain from the glass. The ground flattened and became fields, and a train matched the speed of his own.

It wasn't the same train, not the one from the trees. Its lights were dim, but why not? Of course, he thought gladly: it was being shunted into a siding. No doubt they shunted many trains at night, that was why the other train had vanished. But this train was closer, hardly a hundred yards away; and it was not empty. Dim faces rode in the dim carriages, bobbing slightly.

Perhaps the train was a reflection, on rain or mist. On bare fields? Sweat crept over him, making his skin uneasy; he felt a vague panic. It couldn't be a reflection, for the seat opposite him on the other train was empty. There was something wrong with the faces. Ahead the ground swooped up, carrying a road over a bridge. He heard his own train plunge into a short tunnel. But there wasn't a bridge for the other train, it was heading straight for— The bridge swept over him, shouting; then fields sailed by. They were deserted. There was no second train.

Oh God, he was hallucinating. He hadn't taken many drugs in his time, surely too few to cause a flashback. Was he having a breakdown? For a moment he was unsure which train he was riding. Sweat stifled him; the noise of the carriage enclosed him, impalpable and roaring.

Oh come on, one needn't be mad to hallucinate. He'd decided earlier that he was overtired. Didn't tiredness sometimes force dreams into one's waking life? In any case, the train need not have been a hallucination. Its track must have curved beside the road, the bridge had prevented him from seeing where it had gone. The explanations soothed him, but still unease was planted deep in him. A thought lurked, something that had happened before, that he'd forgotten. It didn't matter. He must be near the end of the journey.

The crowd shifted restlessly, rocking; voices jumbled. Drifts of smoke sank through the ponderous heat, the cougher persisted harshly. The child banged his feet repetitively beneath his seat, the mother stared emptily away, the talker rattled on. Soon be home now, soon.

Outside the ground was rising. The luxuriant faces stared back from the window with their overlapping eyes. It's all right, nothing's wrong. But as the ground walled off the landscape, Ted felt panic growing. The embankment rushed by. He was waiting for it to sink, so that he could see what lay beyond. There was nothing, nothing lying in wait; why should there be? The embankment began to descend. Wind tugged the last lines of rain from the window. The embankment sped away behind, into the dark. At once its place was taken by a train.

It was much closer: less than fifty yards away. And it looked disturbingly similar to the last train. Though the dim carriages were crowded, their aisles clogged with people, the seat opposite Ted's was empty.

Panic threaded him like wire; his body felt unstable. There was something very odd about that train. Dim and vague though they were, the faces of its passengers looked even more abnormal than his own train's exploded reflections. Some were very pale, others looked vividly stained. The shapes of all of them were wrong.

His panic blazed up. He hardly knew where he was. He swayed, borne helplessly over clattering tracks; he was on one of the trains. He saw faces, flesh exploding beyond glass; they might be reflections, or— The fat woman sagged against him, snatching him back to himself for a moment. He was trapped in the hot suffocating carriage. A train, dim and flickering as though full of candlelight, was keeping pace with him. Within its windows, all the vague deformed faces were staring straight at him.

He struggled to rise. He had to get away. Where? If he found a guard, perhaps— He must get away from the window, from the staring vaguenesses. He fought to thrust back the fat woman; she was pinning him to the seat. Sweat clothed him. He was still struggling to free himself when he saw that the two trains were converging. They were going to collide.

"Ay, well," the talkative man said. "Not long now. We're nearly there."

He'd said that before: just before Ted had fallen asleep. Everything was wrong; there was no reality to hold the nightmare back. "Christ!" Ted screamed. One or two people stared at him, someone laughed; their eyes had gone dead.

He wrenched himself free. The fat woman toppled toward the window, snoring convulsively. He staggered down the aisle, hurled against seats and people by the swaying of the carriage. He glanced fearfully toward the window, and his mind grew numb. Perhaps it already was, for he thought that the ground had fallen away, leaving the other train still racing alongside, and closing.

He shouldered wildly through the crowd. People muttered resentfully. They moved aside sluggishly; some stood in his path, staring at him. The trains were almost touching now. A maze of hot moist flesh hindered him, choking the aisle, swaying repeatedly into his path. He clawed through. Behind him the muttering grew, resentful, furious; a hand grabbed him. But he'd reached the end of the carriage.

Outside the door a dim distorted face lolled toward him, staring. He hurled himself toward the far door, against the swaying. He must throw himself clear. Any injury would be preferable to meeting his vague mounting dread. He wrenched at the handle.

"Oh no you don't," a voice said, and the trains collided.

There was no sound, and immediately no light. The trains seemed less to collide than to merge. In the absolute darkness, an image lit up in Ted's mind: a wrecked train lying beside a track, and himself crawling away from an open door. At once the image began to dwindle. He tried to hold on to it, but he was being borne away into the darkness. He wasn't the lone survivor, after all. They had come back to take him with them, they resented his escape. The image fled, was a point of light, went out.

He was lying back in his seat. He felt the carriage swaying, amid total silence. He kept his eyes closed as long as he could. When he opened them at last, he tried to scream; but as he saw more, he tried to stay absolutely quiet, still, invisible. Perhaps that would make it all go away.

But the fat woman slumped against him. Without looking, he could make out that she had lost part of her face. The aisles were still crowded; objects swayed there. Outside the windows was nothing but darkness. Opposite him the mother's jaw hung far too wide. But despite their appearance his companions were moving, though slowly as clockwork on the point of running down, in the dim unsteady light. The child's body moved jerkily, and in the object dangling on its neck, a mouth began to whine.

Missing

Poppy Z. Brite

It was high summer and the breeze coming over the levee from the river carried a hint of cleanly rotting fish, a phantom of oyster shell still slick with silver glue. There was another smell on the breeze, something browner, from a deeper part of the river, a smell that might make night strollers quicken their step and look away from the middle of the darkly shining water.

"Someone drowned a week ago," said Andrew, and Lucian answered, "Bullshit—it's sewage."

But it was the smell, along with the heat like a dirty, oily blanket, that drove them out of the nightclub. Notes descending on a saxophone followed them into the street like a string of colored beads. In the street the smell was still noticeable, but it mingled with the grease-dripping odor of frying oysters, the sharp scent of oil paints and turpentine left behind by the street artists who had all gone home hours ago. Jackson Square brooded behind dark curlicues of iron. Within, pigeons might roost, a needle might roll from one unhappy hand to another.

Lucian pressed his face briefly against the railing. It was cool against his smooth pale cheek, but when he turned back to Andrew, a dirty stripe bisected his nose and forehead.

Andrew spit on a handkerchief and dabbed at Lucian's face. "For God's sake don't lick your lips now. A thousand diseases on that railing." Lucian twisted half-heartedly away from the sticky handkerchief, smiling.

Although they had left their nightclub, the club at which they listened to whatever might be new and sometimes played their own music, their night's drinking was far from over. On their way to Lucian's room they passed a lone, shabby man bent over backwards pointing a wailing saxophone at the sky. A crack somewhere deep inside the instrument made the notes rattle like bones, but Andrew dug out a quarter and aimed it at the shoe box by the man's feet. The quarter bounced out and rolled across the sidewalk, but the man didn't stop playing.

They passed a pizza parlor that reeked of tomatoes stewed in oregano and a foreign grocery which, though closed, wafted out a thousand mysterious, delicious smells, the smells of a kitchen in the Great Pyramid. Under it all they could still sense the wet brown river scent. Lucian's narrow nostrils widened imperceptibly.

They passed along the streets in silence, two white non-jazz musicians stirring up air in the French Quarter. The buildings they passed grew darker, more broken. Feet padded along behind them for two blocks, then, deterred by Andrew's wide-shouldered bulk, disappeared down a side street that led toward the river.

A few minutes later Lucian passed a broken street light, turned down an alley, and nudged a heavy door open with his shoulder. They ducked under a flapping black curtain, sending down a rain of dust, and emerged in a dark little shop lit by two kerosene lamps. Orange shadows licked at the walls of the shop, which were lined with shelves of tiny bottles and boxes. The bottles were queerly shaped, long-necked, made of thick ancient glass colored blue and amber, with stoppers instead of screw-on caps. Most of their contents were murky and indecipherable. The boxes gave off an odor of moldy cardboard. It was easy to imagine clicking, roiling nests of insects in the dark corners of the shelves.

Lucian stood slightly stiff-necked, embarrassed, staring at a spot somewhere to the left of the woman who sat in a corner of the shop.

"Good evening, Mrs. Carstairs. How's business?"

"As always. No one comes. No one wants magic anymore." The woman pulled a gray blanket more snugly around her shoulders. At her feet sat a bowl of colorless mush, perhaps oatmeal, in which a bent spoon was buried at an angle.

"Sorry to hear it. We'll just go on upstairs, then." Lucian ducked through another curtain at the back of the shop. Andrew heard him clattering up a flight of stairs. He looked back at Lucian's landlady, who didn't appear to have noticed him. She was busily scratching herself under the gray blanket. His knee banged the corner of a long wooden box. He stiffened but couldn't keep from glancing down.

Under the glass top the thin little figure reclined, grinning up at him. It should have been a skeleton, but a thin layer of iridescent parchment still stretched over its face and the ratty framework of its hands, and he thought there were small, opaque marbles left deep in its eyesockets—he had never let himself look closely enough to be sure. A few dry strands of bone-colored hair twisted across a rotten silk pillow.

"It isn't so hard to do," said Mrs. Carstairs, "if you love them enough."

Andrew stared back at her. She made no acknowledgement of what she had said, turned her nodding head not an inch in his direction, but only huddled serenely, surrounded by vials of powdered bat's tongue, boxes which contained fragments of the bones of saints and murdered men. And at her feet sat a bowl that might be oatmeal. Andrew swallowed the sour spit in his mouth and hurried up the stairs after Lucian.

Lucian had rummaged in his failing little refrigerator and found a bottle of beer for Andrew. For himself he had pulled out a Donald Duck orange juice bottle half full of a violet sludge. It was vodka mixed nearly half-and-half with a cheap Japanese plum wine that seemed to have about the same consistency as ketchup. It was vile, and it filled the tiny room with a rotten fruity smell that stayed in Lucian's clothes. Lucian claimed the concoction could get him drunk faster than anything else on earth.

He sloshed some of it into a jelly jar that still had gray-white label scrapings on its side. At the first sip, his long eyelashes lowered in contentment; this was the taste he knew like the inside of a lover's mouth, the taste of his world. He took another gulp and lay back on his unmade bed, gazing past Andrew at the window. The moon's weak glow was diluted and made greasy by the dirty glass.

Andrew watched him. Lucian was languid now. In the street there was always a certain tension to his shoulders and slender neck, because Lucian was slight and exquisite-looking and wore silky little scarves and long black jackets that made him look rich even though he wasn't. When he wasn't being prodded for money he didn't have, he was being harassed for the European fineness of his face, and on the darkest, narrowest streets his eyes took on a watchful look. Andrew, who was large and Aryanly handsome, usually walked home with his friend on late nights, not minding the long, lonely walk back to his own apartment.

Lucian nudged his shoes off. He wasn't wearing any socks. He shook a few strands of feathery hair, dark auburn delicately frosted with silver-blond, out of his eyes and smiled at Andrew over the rim of his jelly jar. Andrew stood up, stretching, nearly knocking over his rickety chair. The ceiling of this room was unusually low. It was all right for Lucian, but Andrew, who was half a foot taller, felt clumsy and claustrophobic here. "Do you mind if I open a window?"

"By all means, open a window—any window will do." Lucian's voice was heavy with plum wine and sarcasm; there was only one tiny window in the room. Andrew shoved at its smeary glass until it slid up. He hadn't heard Lucian move, but when he turned back to the room, Lucian was holding out a fresh beer. Their fingers kissed briefly and sweat-stickily as Andrew took the bottle.

Lucian's fingers were longer than the palms they stemmed from, very slim and clean, slightly flattened at the tips. The tips had been splayed and pressed out by Lucian's Juno, the only expensive thing in the room. It stood on four stilt legs in a corner behind Andrew, its black and white keys gleaming opaquely in the half-light from the window. Lucian's fingertips hid a crystalline magic, a sense of tone and pressure that could milk every spangle, every drop of color from a piece of music. He stayed in his room during the day, sleeping naked and innocent through the hottest part of the afternoon, then playing till nightfall, pulling spills and showers of notes from the battered little Juno to float out the window, to drift downstairs and be smothered among Mrs. Carstairs' bottles and packets. Once every month a check arrived from a faceless, sexless relative in Baton Rouge. For a few days Lucian and Andrew would eat in prettily decorated restaurants, drink in well-lit, airy bars outside the French Quarter. Then it was back to dark clubs and sludgy plum wine until the next check came. Andrew could sing; the lyrics he wrote were attempts to capture in words the shimmering transparency of Lucian's music, and he could barely play guitar. They tried to expand the boundaries of all the music they had ever heard, composing intricate symphonies together whenever Mrs. Carstairs was too caught up in her rituals to bang on her ceiling with a broom handle.

Lucian stretched out his feet, flexing his toes comfortably. His toenails were the color of pearls, faintly shiny. He slurped down the last drops of violet sludge and filled the jelly jar again. "That skeleton—" Andrew began.

"What skeleton?"

"The one downstairs."

"Oh, Mrs. Carstairs' corpse. Very charming."

"Why do you suppose she keeps it? Is it some kind of weird advertisement?"

"It's her husband. Was."

"No!"

"Something like that. It's too small to be a man's body, isn't it? Her child, then. She told me about it at great length once. If I'd been sober it would have shocked me."

"The skeleton of her child? In a glass box?"

"It died a long time ago. Her one and only, I guess. She couldn't stand to bury it and let it rot. She's a witch, you know, or calls herself one. She knew how to make it dry up. Mummify it."

"Didn't she have to take the insides out?"

"I suppose so. God, Andrew, forget it."

Andrew stopped talking about it but did not forget it. His eyes drifted and came to rest on Lucian's midsection. Lucian had unbuttoned his shirt, and the hollows in his slatted ribcage were full of silver shadow. Andrew watched the narrow chest expand and collapse again and again. His mind slipped back to the little body downstairs. Mrs. Carstairs would have gone to bed by now, so it was alone down there, keeping company with the dusty bottles and nests of roaches. Perhaps a faint phosphorescence lit the spaces between its bones.

Mrs. Carstairs had been unable to let go of the child completely; she had clung to the only part of it left to her, and perhaps if she pressed her forehead to the glass she could catch its sleeping thoughts. She had preserved the essence of the child, the cleanest part. She had seen parts of its body no one had been meant to see, but those parts were gone now. He imagined its chest cavity stuffed with fragrant linen, its skull scoured with dry spices. It was an ivory being, a husk.

Lucian pressed his lips together, stifling a yawn. It overcame him and his jaws gaped. Andrew glimpsed two rows of even teeth, a soft little tongue stained purple. "It's late," Lucian said. "I want to go to bed."

"Play for me first."

"It's too late."

"Please. Just a little."

Lucian's eyes flicked heavenward, but he was smiling. "Five minutes. No more."

He positioned himself behind the Juno, pressed buttons, twisted the volume knob nearly to zero. His eyelashes, black in the murky light, swept his pale cheeks. His hands moved and a flood of notes erupted, pouring away, cutting through the damp, heavy air in the room.

Andrew leaned forward, lips slightly parted. The music swelled and shattered. Each shard was a fragment of colored glass, a particle of spice. He closed his eyes and watched the music weave a tapestry across the insides of his eyelids. Its colors were streaky and bright, glittering.

When he realized that he was hearing nothing, he opened his eyes. Lucian had stopped playing and was sniffing the air. The tip of his straight nose twitched.

"There's that damn rotten smell again."

Andrew pulled in a noseful of air. The full, wet smell was there again, under the fruity odor of the wine and the tangy, private scent of their sweat. Andrew nodded. Lucian shrugged. "I can't do anything about it. It's too hot to close the window." He grew brisk. "There. You've had your music. It's late; go home. I'll see you tomorrow night." He pushed Andrew toward the door.

Andrew knew Lucian would undress and lie in bed with the orange juice bottle next to him, drinking until the needling heat became a far-away thing, beneath notice, and sleep was possible. At the door Andrew turned back, not sure why he was doing such an unfamiliar and faintly embarrassing thing, and put his arms around Lucian. Lucian stiffened, surprised; then he decided to go along with it and slipped his arms awkwardly around Andrew's neck. It was a brief, clumsy hug, but when it was over, Andrew felt obscurely better. "I'll see you tomorrow, then."

"Don't you always?"

A car ground by outside and in its shifting light a band of shadow slid across Lucian's eyes. Lucian's lips curved in a forlorn smile.

Andrew picked his way down the stairs. Lucian held the door open to give Andrew whatever light could be had; as he ducked under the curtain Andrew heard the door click shut. He stood in the dark shop for a moment, letting his eyes adjust to the light filtered and masked by Mrs. Carstairs' heavy black draperies. When he took a step forward, his shoe struck the corner of the long wooden box. The glass shivered. He sensed something shifting inside, settling. If he pulled aside the draperies, let in the hazy moonlight, he would see—

He didn't want to. He headed for where he knew the door was, and had one bad moment when his hand found instead the thick, moist velvet of the draperies; then he was outside looking up at Lucian's window, which was as dark as any other window in the sprawling block of buildings.

Back in his clean studio apartment, with a fan whirring at the foot of his bed and a street light glowing comfortably outside his window, Andrew brought his cassette player to bed with him and was lulled to sleep by a cascade of shimmering notes, the one tape Lucian had allowed him to make of their music. The notes swirled around Andrew's room looking for a crack, a hole, a route of escape. Eventually they slipped under the door and floated away on an eddy of wind toward the river.

The next day was hotter and more humid; people gasped in the streets like swimmers, and flies swarmed in glistening blue-green clouds above piles of garbage. The day smelled of coconut suntan lotion and seafood being deepfried in hot oil. As the shadows in the streets lengthened and the colors of the day deepened into smudgy blues and violets, Andrew made his way back to Lucian's room. The brown river smell had begun to creep back into the air. As Andrew nudged through the empty shop and climbed the stairs, the smell deepened and grew soft around the edges.

Lucian was still in bed. A sheet was twisted between his legs and pulled up across his body. Its corner touched one of his pale pink nipples.

Andrew knelt beside the bed. A warm dampness soaked through the knees of his pants, thick and sticky. He was kneeling in a puddle of vodka and plum wine. The fruity odor had grown sour in the heat. Lucian's long eyelashes were poised just above his cheeks, ready to sweep down. Andrew touched Lucian's hand. The fingers were stiff; he heard the clean sharp nails scratching delicately against the sheet under the pressure of his own hand. A bright cardboard package lay on the floor next to the bed: DozEze. Sleeping pills. Only two were gone. Lucian had not meant it, then.

Andrew buried his face in the sheet, smelling cotton, a ghost of detergent, old sweat, all edged with the brown smell of the river. Neon patterns that swelled and burst behind his eyelids, resolved themselves into Lucian's face. The silky dark lashes, the dulling white glimmer behind the lowered lids, the parted pink lips were too lovely, too alone.

334

Andrew squeezed his eyes more tightly shut. How could he leave this room now? How could he give the proper authorities the signal to descend on this lonely little body with scalpels and death certificates and jars of formaldehyde?

After a few minutes he gently pushed Lucian to one side and lay down next to him.

This was a warm night, but they were beginning to cool off; there would be no more sweltering sheetless midnights, no more parched red days. Andrew rubbed at the smeary glass of the window and peered out. The man with the saxophone was still there, bending and writhing under the broken street light. Stupid place for a street musician. No one ever passed by here. Andrew had shut the window so he wouldn't have to hear the dying-cat wailing.

He switched on the Juno and poked tentatively at a few keys. The sounds they made were pretty, but there was no crystalline waterfall of notes, no undercurrent of magic dust. Still, he was getting better, already was better on the keyboard than he had ever been on the guitar.

He crossed the room and sat on the floor at the foot of the bed, resting his forehead on the corner of the long wooden box he had constructed. The edge of the glass top dug into his eyebrow.

Andrew didn't have to remember to breathe shallowly any more; he did it without thinking about it. He had none of the secrets of the woman downstairs, the witch, and the smell up here was very brown, very wet. That would pass in time. Lucian would be clean again; at last he would achieve a primal state of purity. Andrew thought of sticks of ivory, of dry perfumed husks.

He raised his head and looked into the box.

Mistress Marian's Light

Gertrude Morton

Far down the Maine coast, in one of the many harbors of that good old State, is a picturesque little island inhabited by simple fisher folk. Generation after generation has been born, lived, and died in this same island village, yet all the people seem to retain the customs and quaint ways of fifty years ago; from the old, weather-worn sailor, to the youngest child among them, they seem, to an unusual degree, guileless and simple and kindly, while to the stranger within their gates their goodness is unlimited. It is like a reminiscence of bygone days to partake of their generous hospitality.

At a late hour one soft, sweet night in early summer, while sojourning for a time among these people, I noticed, far down on a point of land, that rocky and wave-worn, makes out into the sea, a strange light, that seemed to be suspended a few feet from the earth. Soft and wavering it was, sometimes dim; but so unmistakably a light, that I was somewhat perplexed, and the next morning I asked my hostess the cause of the strange phenomenon.

The woman's countenance changed in an instant, and she assumed a sympathetic, pitying look as she replied, with a wise, uncanny shake of her head, "Why, that is Mistress Marian's light." And so she went on and told me this story.

Away down on the point, where the brown soil of the interior of the island begins to mingle with the white sand along the sea, there was, many years ago, a small cottage, built by a seafaring man, who, with his family, occupied it for a short time. They then removed to a neighboring shore, and the house remained untenanted many months.

In the course of time two strangers came to the island—an old man and his little daughter. Venerable indeed was the father, and with his snow-white hair and beard, and his dignified, scholarly bearing, he might have been a king among men. No one seemed to know just when or how they came; they appeared suddenly and unexpectedly, and seemed to find relief in the quietness of the place. As a wandering meteor, travelling through limitless space, finds rest somewhere in God's great universe, so did these two strangers find a dwelling-place in this secluded spot.

To the little uninhabited cottage on the point they went, and the simple life of the islanders became their life. They became a part, and still not a part, of the fisher folk. The dignified old man was so unlike any one whom they had ever seen before that they were shy of him; and long though he lived among them, quietly assisting the needy, and lending a helping hand to all, they were never quite at ease with him, though they worshipped him from afar. It was as though he breathed a rarer atmosphere than they, and dwelt above them; and they were content to accept his kindness and to marvel at his greatness.

Not so the child, with her soft brown eyes and her gentle, winning manner. "A lady born and bred, she is," the good dames said, one to another, many times. But she was a child, strangely alone, so the motherly arms were opened to her, and the children made this little Marian their playmate.

They seemed to be people of means—this father and daughter. The cottage was furnished comfortably, even luxuriously, and many books, some of them in quaint and curious bindings, were about. On the low walls hung several pictures, the like of which the islanders had never seen before; rich rugs covered the bare floors; a piece of rare Eastern embroidery was flung over a low couch; upon an oddly carved shelf were some bits of china, delicate and fragile, as though fashioned from rose leaves; while everywhere in the tiny house were evidences of refinement. From what faraway land the strangers came, or why they sought refuge on the little island, they themselves never said, nor were they ever questioned. The people, with their simple faith and childlike credulity, accepted the fact of their coming as they did all the good things that befell them—thankful, asking naught.

So these two lived on in an alien land, their lives replete with the satisfaction that comes from helping others, their desire to do good satisfied by the appreciation with which their efforts were met. Thus the little girl, the dainty Marian, grew to maidenhood, learning much from her father and his books, but more from Nature: of the sea with its wonderful treasures; of the rocks that she loved, gaunt and gray though they were; of flowers and fishes and birds. She learned, too, much of human nature—the kindly side—from the people about her; and their interests she made hers. Every mother on the island felt a deep affection for her, and her young mates were proud to be called her friends. She was a constant surprise to them. The dainty gowns that she fashioned for herself, out of strange fabrics, were marvels; even her language seemed somehow different from theirs; and when a stranger chanced to visit the little building where they gathered on Sundays for worship, "our young lady," brown-eyed "Mistress Marian," was always pointed out with secret pride. So she grew to pure and noble womanhood, winning respect and admiration from all.

The lads of the village were filled with unspeakable delight when she spoke to them in her sweet, low voice. Not one of them but that would have risked his limbs, almost his life, for anything that she wanted—a wildflower, a stone, or a bright bit of seaweed. Yet for none of them had she more than a word or a smile, except for tall, manly Phil Anderson. From her childhood she had seemed to set him apart from all others as a hero; and when he came to her out on the rocks one sweet summer night, when the moon was softly shining and the sea was bright with the phosphorescent gleam, and told her of his love for her, she accepted it quietly and trustfully.

It was a happy summer for the two, passing all too quickly. When autumn came, Phil was to sail with his father on one more voyage—to make his fortune, he said; then he was coming back to marry Marian and to take her away into the great world of which they were never tired of talking.

So the weeks slipped by. October came. The trees donned their gayest colors; each bush took its own particular, matchless tint, and the breakers dashed high in the cool breeze, as though to speed the parting, which was even then at hand. One bright, cool morning Phil went down to the little house to say good-by. Tremblingly the old man bade the brave young sailor farewell, then sent him out to the rocks—the place of their betrothal—where Marian was waiting. Silently he took her in his strong arms, kissed her soft hair, her forehead and her sweet red lips, then turned and strode quickly away, as though he could not trust his courage longer.

A year passed, bringing two letters to Marian from her lover, telling her of such success as even his fondest hopes had failed to picture. At the end of the third year, just after another letter had come, telling her that the *Watersprite* was homeward bound, and happiness seemed in store for her, her father died. For months the old man had been slowly failing, living only in his daughter's happiness. Now that she did not need him longer, he seemed to lose all power of holding on to his life, and one evening passed quietly away with the setting of the sun.

The grief of the young girl was well-nigh unbearable. The only bright thing that life seemed to hold for her was the fact that her lover was on his way to her. So she waited anxiously, longingly, expecting tidings every day. But after the third letter no news came.

As the days lengthened to weeks, and the weeks to months, the islanders were filled with apprehension and forebodings. A gloom settled over the people, which even the lingering Indian summer failed to brighten; and when, one bleak November day, beneath a darkening sky, a strange vessel came into the harbor with tidings that the gallant *Watersprite* had sunk and every soul on board had perished, it was almost a relief to the anxious watchers. Certainty, though hard to bear, was better than hope deferred.

Gently did sympathetic friends tell the mournful news to the lonely girl at the point; but dazed and bewildered, she did not seem to comprehend their meaning. For days she lay in a kind of stupor, unheeding everything, even the presence of the kind old dame who watched by her side night and day with tear-dimmed eyes. Only when the waves dashed loudest would the girl stir uneasily, raising her head as though listening for some one's command.

At last she awoke from her long sleep, coming back once more to life and to her senses; but the beautiful hair was as white as the foam that dashed against the rocks she used to love, and the dark eyes looked large and mournful beneath the snowy wealth. As strength slowly came back to her, so also came the firm conviction that her lover was not dead, but would one day return to her. So firm was her faith that she grew cheerful, almost happy. Once more she assumed her duties—clothing little children, ministering to the sick and aged, helping weary housewives. There was not a person on the island who had not at one time or another felt her kindly influence or her strong, stimulating presence.

Every night at dusk, after her day's work was done, she would place a large bright light in the window of the little sitting-room that looked toward the harbor, leaving the curtain drawn aside, so that should he for whom she watched come at night, he would find her still waiting for him. Not a night did she fail in this most important of all her duties. Her light was a bright beacon. Sailors soon learned to know it and look for it, and they never looked in vain; it was always there, steady, clear, unwavering.

Thus passed several years, when suddenly, mysteriously, without a shadow of warning, Mistress Marian disappeared. As silently as years ago she had entered the life of the fisher folk, so now did she leave it; and as they knew not then whence she came, neither did they know now whither she went.

There were many conjectures as to her strange disappearance. One old sailor affirmed that one night when he was out fishing he saw a little boat come from the point, bearing a solitary passenger with snow-white hair, who rowed out toward a large ship that could be dimly seen, as through a fog, and was taken on board; then the huge ship quickly vanished. But as this old man was well known to take his black bottle with him on his fishing expeditions, and as no other person could be found who saw the wonderful ship, his story did not gain the credence that its ingenuity deserved. The most of the people inclined to the belief that she had gone back to her father's relatives; but how, when, or where, not even the old woman who lived with her could tell.

A decade or two passed, and the old house in its exposed locality grew more and more weatherworn and dilapidated; and finally, one winter, doubtless feeling that its time of usefulness had passed, it succumbed to fate and, during a heavy gale, fell to the ground. Some of the timbers were washed away, others were used for fire-wood by campers and fishermen; so that after a time nothing remained to mark the spot where the cottage had been, save a few damp, moss-covered logs.

But still in this same place on quiet summer nights during the hot sultry time of July and August—the time when the *Watersprite* was said to have perished—this weird, white, uncertain, trembling light, a few feet from the ground, is at times plainly seen. Not all the scientific explanations of wiser heads can convince the simple villagers that this strange light is any other than Marian's beacon for her sailor lover, or shake their faith in the plausibility of a story handed down from successive generations.

The merriest sailing party, rounding the point of a sweet summer night, will become subdued at the sight of the light, while the timid maiden will nestle closer to the skipper at the helm, as she says in awe-struck tones, "See! Mistress Marian's light is still burning."

Mrs Vail

Kim Newman

Y ou have asked me for a story to add to your collection. A *ghost* story. I confess that I am unsure whether the following—shall we say, *anecdote*—qualifies as such. You must make up your minds as to whether the case of Martin Vail is fit to referral to Mr Carnacki of Cheyne Walk or to Dr Freud of Vienna.

Martin Vail has not lately been much in our society, but you must all have cause to remember him. It is scarcely a secret that Mrs Twemlow, celebrated authoress of *Love's Sundered Shadows* and other popular fictions, drew heavily upon Martin Vail in creating the character of Lord Rurik Davenant, the degenerate who is much given to importuning the heroine of her currently notorious volume, *Perfume and Poison.*

Since his marriage, Martin has lived a somewhat reclusive life. Certainly in comparison with his former habits. The reasons for this withdrawal from his old circles will, I hope, become evident. Uniquely among our crowd, I have had some acquaintance with Mrs Martin Vail, the former Miss Louisa Sorrell. A deaf mute since childhood, Mrs Vail is nevertheless one of the most charming and pleasant ladies of my acquaintance. I shall brook no unkind remarks to the effect that Mrs Vail's pre-eminence among her sex is a result of her inability to talk.

Some days ago, I had cause to be in the vicinity of the Vail residence on business—something tedious about an old lady's much-altered will, with which I have no intention of burdening you. Naturally, I took the opportunity to call on Martin. I have to admit that I found him in a sorry state. Unshaven, ill-dressed, pale of complexion, nervous of manner. The transformation was complete.

'You must forgive my appearance,' Martin beseeched me. 'Three weeks ago, I found it necessary to put an end to my marriage . . .'

I made as if to protest. Mrs Vail had herself ushered me, with every courtesy, into her husband's study. Within the bounds of her infirmities, she seemed in the best of health, and in no way betrayed any breach in the household.

'I have killed my poor Louisa, and now she haunts me night and day. Her ghost walks the house. See . . .'

At this point, Mrs Vail did indeed enter the room. However, far from appearing as a discarnate spirit she displayed a most pleasing physical form, and was carrying with her a much appreciated tray of tea things.

'Look,' whispered Martin in a dreadful tone, 'the tray. See how it floats as if supported by untenanted air. It is she, Louisa, invisibly reproaching me for my crimes.'

Mrs Vail smiled prettily at me, indicating no more than a mild social embarrassment. She placed the tray on a low table between her husband and myself.

'See, the teapot rises as if on phantom wings. Behold, it pours . . .'

Mrs Vail poured out two cups of excellent Darjeeling. I quite enjoyed mine, while Martin's, I fear, went icy cold from neglect. He quaked in his armchair, paralysed by inexplicable horrors, while his wife performed the niceties. Then, as she withdrew from the room, Martin stared in her direction, but his eyes seeming not to focus.

'She's there. There, I tell you.'

'Quite,' I responded. 'I can see for myself. I must compliment your wife on her complexion. The married life obviously suits her. Now what is all this nonsense about a murder?'

'I drowned her in the bath, and cast her corpse weighted into the Serpentine. The body is irretrievably lost, but her spirit haunts me perpetually.'

My humour was, as you may suppose, wearing thin. 'Surely,' I said, determined to take a sarcastic view, 'the usual arrangement is that the ghost of the murdered wife is visible *only* to the guilty husband. Here, the situation seems to be the reverse.'

'That's it,' he cried, 'that's it exactly. You have no conception of the torments I suffer. Objects carried as if by transparent hands move through the corridors of my own house. Food and drink disappear into an absolute vacuum at my table. And—I hardly dare tell—in my conjugal bed there is a displacement of the clothes, as if heaped over a form that simply isn't there.'

Mrs Vail returned, bearing a plateful of scones, buttered and augmented with strawberry jam. Martin cringed, and waved a ragged hand in vain. I ate most of the scones. They were delicious, and, I assure you, bore no trace of any supernatural agency. Evidently, Mrs Vail had become accustomed to her husband's monomania. While he cried out in terror and writhed in a fashion that would do Henry Irving in the last act of *The Bells* credit, she serenely doled out her fine scones and shrugged in knowing tolerance at his antics.

'I killed her,' he said when she had departed again with the empty plate, 'I killed her because—you must believe me—because she *talked*. Not with her lips, but with some strange power that enabled her to talk inside my head. Incessantly, in a meaningless babble, a language without order. Since our wedding night, she has plagued me with this infernal chatter and now, past her death, her unnatural voice is with me still . . .'

No amount of scones would persuade me to endure much longer this sort of rot. I made my excuses and left, bidding a polite farewell to Martin and a sympathetic one to his wife.

'Louisa,' I addressed her as she handed me my hat, 'as you know, I am of the legal profession. It is clear to me that this is a troubled household. I believe I could, without blame being attached to your person, secure an annulment of your marriage. Take my card and please, I beg you, consider my services . . .'

Mrs Vail smiled sweetly at me and, after the merest glance at my card, returned it. She shook her head gently, the very image of the angel in the home.

'Ma'am,' I told her, 'I admire you greatly.'

With that, I left the house. At the end of the street, I happened to turn and look back. Mrs Vail was upon her doorstep still, taking delivery of a package from the butcher's boy. Plainly, the lad had no more difficulty than I in telling Louisa Vail from a ghost. I waved, and my wave was cheerfully returned.

I thought then, as to some extent I do now, that Martin Vail had gone quite mad. Of course, that was before this morning.

You must all know the story of the actress who misplaced her valuable necklace while boating in Hyde Park with a certain royal personage. And you must also know what came to light when she arranged for the Serpentine to be dragged . . .

The Mystics of Muelenburg

Tom Ligotti

If things are not what they seem—and we are forever reminded that this is the case—then it must also be observed that enough of us ignore this truth to keep the world from collapsing. Though never exact, always shifting somewhat, the *proportion* is crucial. For a certain number of minds are fated to depart for realms of delusion, as if in accordance with some hideous timetable, and many will never be returning to us. Even among those who remain, how difficult it can be to hold the focus sharp, to keep the picture of the world from fading, from blurring in selected zones and, on occasion, from sustaining epic deformations over the entire visible scene.

I one knew a man who claimed that, overnight, all the solid shapes of existence had been replaced by cheap substitutes: trees made of flimsy posterboard, houses built of colored foam, whole landscapes composed of hair-clippings. His own flesh, he said, was now just so much putty. Needless to add, this acquaintance had deserted the cause of appearances and could no longer be depended on to stick to the common story. Alone he had wandered into a tale of another sort altogether; for him, all things now participated in this nightmare of nonsense. But although his revelations conflicted with the lesser forms of truth, nonetheless he did live in the light of a greater truth: that all is unreal. Within him this knowledge was vividly present down to his very bones, which had been newly simulated by a compound of mud and dust and ashes.

In my own case, I must confess that the myth of a natural universe—that is, one that adheres to certain continuities whether we wish them or not—was losing its grip on me and was gradually being supplanted by a hallucinatory view of creation. Forms, having nothing to offer except a mere suggestion of firmness, declined in importance; fantasy, that misty domain of pure meaning, gained in power and influence. This was in the days when esoteric wisdom seemed to count for something in my mind, and I would willingly have sacrificed a great deal in its pursuit. Hence, my interest in the man who called himself Klaus Klingman; hence, too, that brief yet profitable association between us, which came about through channels too twisted to recall.

Without a doubt, Klingman was one of the illuminati and proved this many times over in various psychic experiments, particularly those of the séance type. For those outside scientific circles, I need only mention the man who was severally known as Nemo the Necromancer, Marlowe the Magus, and Master Marinetti, each of whom was none other than Klaus Klingman himself. But Klingman's highest achievement was not a matter of public spectacle and consisted entirely of this private triumph: that he had attained, by laborious effort, an unwavering acceptance of the spectral nature of things, which to him were neither what they seemed to be nor were they quite anything at all.

Klingman lived in the enormous upper story of a warehouse that had been part of his family's legacy to him, and there I often found him wandering amidst a few pieces of furniture and the cavernous wasteland of dim and empty storage space. Collapsing into an ancient armchair, reposing far beneath crumbling rafters, he would gaze beyond the physical body of his visitor, his eyes surveying remote worlds and his facial expression badly disorganized by dreams and large quantities of alcohol. "Fluidity, always fluidity," he shouted out, his voice carrying through the expansive haze around us, which muted daylight into dusk. The embodiment of his mystic precepts, he appeared at any given moment to be on the verge of an amazing disintegration, his particular complex of atoms ready to go shooting off into the great void like a burst of fireworks.

We discussed the dangers—for me and for the world—of adopting a visionary program of existence. "The chemistry of things is so delicate," he warned. "And this word chemistry, what does it mean but a mingling, a mixing, a gushing together? Things that people fear." Indeed, I had already suspected the hazards of his company, and, as the sun was setting over the city beyond the great windows of the warehouse, I became afraid. With an uncanny perception of my feelings, Klingman pointed at me and bellowed:

"The worst fear of the race—yes, the world suddenly transformed into a senseless nightmare, horrible disolution of things. Nothing compares, even oblivion is a sweet dream. You understand why, of course. Why this peculiar threat. These brooding psyches, all the busy minds everywhere. I hear them buzzing like flies in the blackness. I see them as glow worms flitting in the blackness. They are struggling, straining every second to keep the sky above them, to keep the sun in the sky, to keep the dead in the earth—to keep all things, so to speak, *where they belong*. What an undertaking! What a crushing task! Is it any wonder that they are all tempted by a universal vice, that in some dark street of the mind a single voice whispers to one and all, softly hissing, and says: 'Lay down your burden.' Then thoughts begin to drift, a mystical magnetism pulls them this way and that, faces start to change, shadows speak . . . sooner or later the sky comes down, melting like wax. But as you know, everything has not yet been lost: absolute terror has proved its security against this fate. Is it any wonder that these beings carry on the struggle at whatever cost?"

"And you?" I asked.

"I?"

"Yes, don't you shoulder the universe in your own way?"

"Not at all," he replied, smiling and sitting up in his chair as on a throne. "I am a lucky one, parasite of chaos, maggot of vice. Where I live is nightmare, thus a certain nonchalance. In a previous life, you know, I may actually have been at Muelenburg before it was lost in the delirium of history. Who can say? Smothered by centuries now. But *there* was an opportunity, a moment of distraction in which so much was nearly lost forever, so many lost in that medieval gloom, catastrophe of dreams. How their minds wandered in the shadows even as their bodies were seemingly bound to narrow rutted streets and apparently safeguarded by the spired cathedral which was erected between 1365 and 1399. A rare and fortuitous juncture when the burden of the heavens was heaviest — so much to keep in it's place — and the psyche so ill-developed, so easily taxed and tempted away from its labors. But they knew nothing about that, and never could. They only knew the prospect of absolute terror."

"In Muelenburg," I said, hoping to draw his conversation outward before it twisted further into itself. "You said the cathedral."

"I *see* the cathedral, the colossal vault above, the central aisle stretching out before us. The woodcarvings leer down from dark corners, animals and freaks, men in the mouths of demons. Are you taking notes again? Fine, then take notes. Who knows what you will remember of all this? Or will memory help you at all? In any case we are already there, sitting among the smothered sounds of the cathedral. Beyond the jeweled windows is the town in twilight."

Twilight, as Klingman explained and I must paraphrase, had come upon Muelenburg somewhat prematurely on a certain day deep into the autumn season. Early that afternoon, clouds had spread themselves evenly above the region surrounding the town, withholding heaven's light and giving a dull appearance to the landscape of forests, thatched farmhouses, and windmills standing still against the horizon. Within the high stone walls of Muelenburg itself, no one seemed particularly troubled that the narrow streets — normally so cluttered with the pointed shadows of peaked roofs and jutting gables at this time of day — were still immersed in a lukewarm dimness which turned merchants' brightly colored signs into faded artifacts of a dead town and which made faces look as if they were fashioned in pale clay. And in the central square — where the shadow from the clock-tower of the town hall at times overlapped those cast by the twin spires of the cathedral on the one hand, or the ones from high castle turrets looming at the border of the town on the other—there was only grayness undisturbed.

Where were the minds of the townspeople? How had they ceased paying homage to the ancient order of things? And when had the severing taken place that sent their world drifting on strange waters?

For some time they remained innocent of the disaster, going about their ways as the ashen twilight lingered far too long, as it encroached upon the hours that belonged to evening and suspended the town between day and night. Everywhere windows began to glow with the yellow light of lamps, creating the illusion that darkness was imminent. Any moment, it seemed, the natural cycle would relieve the town of the prolonged dusk it had suffered that autumn day. How well-received the blackness would have been by those who waited silently in sumptuous chambers or humble rooms, for no one could bear the sight of Muelenburg's twisting streets in that eerie, overstaying twilight. Even the nightwatchman shirked his nocturnal routine. And when the bells of the abbey sounded for the monks' prayers, each toll spread like an alarm throughout the town still held in the strange luminousness of the gloaming.

Exhausted by fear, many shuttered their windows, extinguished lamps, and retired to their beds, hoping that all would be made right in the interval. Others sat up with a candle, enjoying the lost luxury of shadows. A few, who were not fixed to the life of the town, broke through the unwatched gate and took to the roads, all the while gazing at the pale sky and wondering where they would go.

But whether they kept the hours in their dreams or in sleepless vigils, all were disturbed by something in the spaces around them, as if some strangeness had seeped into the atmosphere of their town, their homes, and perhaps their souls. The air seemed heavier somehow, resisting them slightly, and also seemed to be flowing with things that could not be perceived except as swift, shadowlike movement escaping all sensible recognition, transparent flight which barely caressed one's vision.

When the clock high in the tower of the town hall proved that a nightful of hours had passed, some opened their shutters, even ventured into the streets. But the sky still hovered over them like an infinite vault of glowing dust. Here and there throughout the town the people began to gather in whispering groups. Appeals were soon made at the castle and the cathedral, and speculations were offered to calm the crowd. There was a struggle in heaven, some had reasoned, which had influenced the gross reality of the visible world. Others proposed a deception by demons or an ingenious punishment from on high. A few, who met secretly in well-hidden chambers, spoke in stricken voices of old deities formerly driven from the earth who were now monstrously groping their way back. And all of these explications of the mystery were true in their own way, though none could abate the dread which had settled upon the town of Muelenburg.

Submerged in unvarying grayness, distracted and confused by phantasmal intrusions about them, the people of the town felt their world dissolving. Even the clock in the town hall tower failed to keep their moments from wandering strangely. Within such disorder were bred curious thoughts and actions. Thus, in the garden of the abbey an ancient tree was shunned and rumours spread concerning some change in its twisted silhouette, something flaccid and ropelike about its branches, until finally the monks dowsed it with oil and set it aflame, their circle of squinting faces bathing in the glare. Likewise, a fountain standing in one of the castle's most secluded courtyards became notorious when its waters appeared to suggest fabulous depths far beyond the natural dimensions of its shell-shaped basin. The cathedral itself had deteriorated into a hollow sanctuary where prayers were mocked by queer movements among the carved figures in cornices and by shadows streaming horribly in the twitching light of a thousand candles.

Throughout the town, all places and things bore evidence to striking revisions in the base realm of matter: precisely sculptured stone began to loosen and lump, an abandoned cart melded with the sucking mud of the street, and objects in desolate rooms lost themselves in the surfaces they pressed upon, making metal tongs mix with brick hearth, prismatic jewels with lavish velvet, a corpse with the wood of its coffin. At last the faces of Muelenburg became subject to changing expressions which at first were quite subtle, though later these divergences were so exaggerated that it was no longer possible to recapture original forms. It followed that the townspeople could no more recognize themselves than they could one another. All were carried off in the great torrent of their dreams, all spinning in that grayish whirlpool of indefinite twilight, all churning and in the end merging into utter blackness.

It was within this blackness that the souls of Muelenburg struggled and labored and ultimately awoke. The stars and high moon now lit up the night, and it seemed that their town had been returned to them. And so terrible had been their recent ordeal that of its beginning, its progress, and its termination, they could remember . . . nothing.

"Nothing?" I echoed.

"Of course," Klingman answered. "All of those terrible memories were left behind in the blackness. How could they bear to bring them back?"

"But your story," I protested. "These notes I've taken tonight."

"Privileged information, far off the main roads of historical record.

You know that sooner or later each of them recollected the episode in detail. It was all waiting for them in the place where they had left it—the blackness which is the domain of death. Or, if you wish, that blackness of the old alchemists' magic powder."

I remembered the necromantic learning that Klingman had both professed and proven, but still I observed: "Then nothing can be verified, nothing established as fact."

"Nothing at all," he agreed, "except the fact that I am one with the dead of Muelenburg and with all who have known the great dream in all its true liquescence. They have spoken to me as I am speaking to you. Many reminiscences imparted by those old dreamers, many drunken dialogues I have held with them."

"Like the drunkenness of this dialogue tonight," I said, openly disdaining his narrative.

"Perhaps, only much more vivid, more real. But the yarn which you suppose I alone have spun has served its purpose. To cure you of doubt, you first had to be made a doubter. Until now, pardon my saying so, you have shown no talent in that direction. You believed every wild thing that came along, provided it had the least evidence whatever. Unparalleled credulity. But tonight you have doubted and thus you are ready to be cured of this doubt. And didn't I mention time and again the dangers? Unfortunately, you cannot count yourself among those forgetful souls of Muelenburg. You even have your mnemonic notes, as if anyone will credit them when this night is over. The time is right again, and it has happened more than once, for the grip to go slack and for the return of fluidity in the world. And later so much will have to be washed away, assuming a renascence of things. Fluidity, always fluidity."

When I left his company that night, abandoning the dead and shapeless hours I had spent in that warehouse, Klingman was laughing like a madman. I remember him sloched in that threadbare throne, his face all flushed and contorted, his twisted mouth wailing at some hilarious arcana known only to himself, the sardonic laughter reverberating in the great spaces of the night. To all appearances, some ultimate phase of dissipation had seized his soul.

Nevertheless, that I had underrated or misunderstood the powers of Klaus Klingman was soon demonstrated to me, and to others. But no one else remembers that time when the night would not leave and no dawn appeared to be forthcoming. During the early part of the crisis there were sensible, rather than apocalyptic, explanations proffered everywhere: blackout, bizarre meteorological phenomena, an eclipse of sorts. Later, these myths became useless and ultimately unnecessary.

For no one else recalls the hysteria that prevailed when the stars and the moon seemed to become swollen in the blackness and to cast a lurid illumination upon the world. How many horrors await in that blackness to be restored to the memories of the dead. For no one else living remembers when everything began to change, no one else with the possible exception of Klaus Klingman.

In the red dawn following that gruesomely protracted night, I went to the warehouse. Unfortunately the place was untenanted, save by its spare furnishings and a few empty bottles. Klingman had disappeared, perhaps into that same blackness for which he seemed to have an incredible nostalgia. I, of course, make no appeals for belief. There can be no belief where there is no doubt. There cannot be something where there is no nothing. This is far from secret knowledge, as if such knowledge could change anything. This is only how it seems, and seeming is everything.

The Night Gil Rhys First Met His Love

Alan Rodgers

At the age of twenty-three, convulsing with the need for heroin on the sidewalk of a wide, dirty street, Gilman Rhys was a virgin. The fact bothered and distracted him.

It was three in the morning and he wasn't ready for the fit at all—he thought he'd been through the last of that weeks ago—and the neighborhood was hard and nasty. It wasn't the worst place (that was over in the projects where everyone had been hungry for a long time); thirty years ago this had been a shopping district, and while there were homes on the side streets, no one lived here—most of the houses were deserted or condemned. After seven p.m. most of the nasties went home and left the street to the bums and winos. But even if he had been squirming his way through a fit in the middle of the projects, he wouldn't have been scared. Gil had torn a *mean* monkey off his back, and he'd been desperate enough for long enough that being scared wasn't possible. It would be a while before anything ordinary would scare him.

Besides, if worse came to worst he had his pig-sticker—a beautiful switch-blade stiletto he'd scrounged off the body of a Latino after a gang war—in his back pocket. He'd had to use it before. No one sensible ever robs street people—they don't have much and what they do have smells bad—but more than once he'd had to cope with kids from the high school when they came cruising around looking for fun. Fearless or not, though, Gil didn't want any trouble. He'd got himself in a deep pit with junk, and he'd spent a lot of time and heart crawling out of it. He'd done lots of things that he was lots less than proud of, but what he'd done was done with, now, and all he wanted out of life was the chance to make something out of it he could live with.

The woman passed him on her way from the parking lot to the all-night diner. She was dressed like she had money—not an awful lot of money, not like she'd got it all from her folks, but more like the kind of money you have to make yourself. "Are you all right?" she asked. Her voice was neutral, not frightened or concerned.

He lied to her automatically: "I'll be okay. I fell. I'll get up in a minute," he said. He looked up to see her, wary of her, and he saw that her eyes were turquoise, alive with light and color. A long sensuous chill crawled up his backbone, raising hairs and goose-down on his forearms and the sides of his face. Some queer denizen of his id, set loose by the chaos in his forebrain, recognized her. It told him so.

That's her, it said. *She's the one.*

Gil shook his head, not understanding the voice or its genesis at all, and his ears began to ring.

You'll know her if you'll think of it for just a moment. She's yours.

"What?" he asked, thinking she had spoken. But she had already gone.

After a few moments, he got up, brushed himself off (which didn't do much good), and followed her into the diner.

When he got there he saw her sitting in a booth by one of the diner's big plate-glass windows, so he sat at the counter not far from her. The thing in his id was still shouting at him, but it had given up on words. It was stomping around on his heart and his gut like a child making a racket, trying to get its mother's attention by pounding on the walls with blocks. It made him afraid (the nasty, jittery kind of fear that turns mean and violent at any provocation), it exhilarated him, made him desire, made him lonely. None of it made any sense. Gil shifted in his seat uncomfortably.

The waitress looked at him from where she stood, further down the counter, and raised an eyebrow at him. "Coffee?" she asked.

He nodded.

She walked to the urn, poured a cup, and brought it to him. When she was done (just from seeing him she knew him well enough not to offer him a menu) he turned back toward the woman with the blue-blue eyes. He wanted to speak to her, to ask her what she'd said to him out there. But he was shy of her. Women frightened him in a way that thugs and

350

nasties and even high school ruffians didn't. He thought that was funny, sometimes: him, a mean, nasty, grimy junkie, afraid of women. But thinking it was funny didn't change it any.

She saw him looking at her, and her face jumped like suddenly she'd recognized him. But she didn't say anything. She looked away from him very pointedly, and she lit a cigarette. The index finger of her left hand — the one nearest him — drummed on the scratched formica table top.

Then the man in the kitchen set her ham and eggs and potatoes and toast on the stainless-steel shelf in the window between the kitchen and the counter, and the waitress went to get it, and for a moment the whole agenda of the diner changed. Gil was thinking he was hungry, and he had money, because he'd been to work at Manpower every day for at least a couple of weeks now, but he was way out of habit of spending money on food, and it was hard to do. Gil couldn't see into the kitchen because of the angle from where he was sitting, but he could smell things cooking, and he was tempted. Then the waitress was setting the plate in front of that strange woman, and Gil saw her staring at him, not straight on, but at his reflection in the plate-glass window. That spooked him, because her eyes were even bluer and ghostlier in *her* reflection than they were that first time he saw them, out on the street. And Gil forgot all about food.

The waitress started wiping the counter, down at the far end. After a few strokes she didn't look too happy about it at all, and she turned to Gil, not looking like business, the way waitresses usually do, but looking like she just wanted to talk to somebody. Gil wasn't in the mood for that, not at all. He was still trying to screw up his courage to talk to the girl. There was something important there, and it needed attending to.

"More coffee?" the waitress asked.

Gil's right hand was fiddling around with the spoon, trying to stir up the sugar even though it was already dissolved. He turned away from the girl's reflection to answer the waitress, swiveled his seat so he could sit in a more ordinary position.

"Pardon?"

"I asked if you wanted more coffee."

"Oh, no" — he gestured with the cup — "thanks. Still almost full."

But the waitress wouldn't go away. And what could Gil do? So, after a while, just to be polite, he said, "Nice weather, huh?"

The waitress nodded. (The weather had been horrible, actually — too humid, too hot, too many clouds.)

He sipped from his coffee cup. His seat felt uncomfortable.

"It's been slow tonight," the waitress told him.

He nodded.

She began to tell him about the night's trade. She was the sort of woman, Gil thought, who'd take hold of his ear and never relinquish it. After just a little while he found himself wondering if she could go on forever, and then he began to think that she could. He didn't want to listen; everything inside him shouted and shoved at him, trying to get him to *do* something, to get him *away* from the woman. But something about her pinned him where he sat, left him unable to do anything but nod and smile in response. He turned to look at the woman with the strange eyes . . .

. . . and she was sipping the last of her coffee, dabbing the corners of her mouth with a napkin, fussing with her purse, and getting up to pay her check. She stood at the register for a long while, waiting for the waitress to finish with Gil and take her money. Gil watched her, awed by her for reasons he didn't understand. She looked back at him as though she knew him very well.

Then the waitress finally made her way to the register, and the strange woman paid, and she left.

Gil wanted to leave right then, he wanted to follow her to wherever she was going and . . . he didn't know what. But he didn't dare. He knew that. He had to be careful; a junkie couldn't just go following strange women out of restaurants. It wasn't wise.

So he set his teeth and resigned himself to sit on the stool and wait out five or ten minutes of listening to the waitress, or staring into the distance, or *whatever* happened next. Maybe then, he thought, he'd try to find the woman. He had to talk to her. He had to . . . something. He didn't know what. He really didn't know. But whatever it was, he couldn't just run after her, screaming and shaking and acting like a lunatic.

At least that's what Gil was telling himself when the waitress got back from the register and put her hand on top of his, all warm and moist, and looked deep and soulfully into his eyes. She smiled at him dirty-like and the hackles went up on the back of his neck and he wanted to scream.

"There's nobody here," she said, "but you and me and the cook. And he's half deaf, or deafer. We could lock the place up, and—"

Gil didn't hear any more than that. He couldn't stand to listen. He got off his stool and bolted. He had to run, to get the hell *away* from that woman. He was at the door when he realized that he hadn't paid, so he took a dollar bill out of his shirt pocket (he liked to keep a little folding money where it was real handy so no one could see his wallet) he took a bill out of his pocket and threw it at the register.

He only ran a few yards after he'd got out of the place. The waitress wasn't going to follow him; he knew that as soon as he calmed down for a minute.

Before he even realized what he was doing, he found himself looking for the woman with the turquoise eyes, but she was nowhere in sight, in either direction. Gil even walked up the block to see if she had taken the side street, then walked back past the diner to check the major cross street at the block's other end. He didn't see her, though. He didn't see anyone at all.

He spent the whole night looking for her. Not looking in the sort of places where you'd expect a well-dressed white woman to go; Gil didn't even know those well enough to look in them. But he went to all the places *he* knew—the ones that he could picture her in, anyway. Gas stations, all-night newspaper stands, the twenty-four-hour grocery down at Kennedy and Rome. Places like that.

It didn't surprise him that she wasn't in any of them. Not *really*. But he'd hoped, he'd really hoped. . . .

When he was too tired to look anymore, when he was too tired to even *think* about looking anymore, it was quarter till five in the morning, and his boarding house had closed up tight as a clam at nine thirty. He went down to the park by the river, planning to stake out a bench and try to get at least a couple of hours' worth of sleep before the morning-shift cops came to shoo him away.

Maybe it was just pure chance that she was there, in the park, almost looking like she was waiting for him. But he never thought so. Not then or even later.

She was sitting on just the bench where he'd planned to sleep, which was way out of the way, in this really narrow little finger of the park (with the river on one side and the base-wall of the expressway on the other) that was shielded from the rest of it by a bushy-thick clump of pine trees.

"Hello," he said. He sat down on the bench beside her, but not close. Not close at all. She turned to look at him, and the words he was going to say, whatever they were, got confused and stumbled all over each other. After a while he said, "You're beautiful." But she didn't say anything, not for a long time.

She looked frightened, uneasy, and somehow at the same time not afraid of him at all. "Why do you say that?" she asked, finally. Her smile was gracious and flattered and a little coy. "Even if it is true, it's not the sort of thing strangers often come up to me and say."

"I . . ." He didn't have an answer for her. His face had fixed itself into an awkward, uncomfortable position. Everything was jumbled up, and he suspected she'd had a mindful hand in the jumbling. He found himself being more honest than he meant to be, more honest than was sensible. "I'm alone, I guess. Because I'm lonely."

She was quiet for a long while after he said that, and he really thought he'd said quite enough, thank you. "It's horrible to feel lonely, isn't it? I suppose that that is what I was feeling, too. Would you like to talk? Isn't the river beautiful this time of day?"

"That's deep and meaningful," he sneered—then brought himself up short: *What do I have to be hostile about . . . ?* And even more, *Why would I want to alienate her . . . ?* He didn't understand any of it, least of all himself. "I'm sorry. I shouldn't say things like that." He teased the roots of the grass with the toe of his work boot. "You're right. The river is beautiful."

"It's all right," she said. "Don't worry about it." She was staring at the dawn-lit corner of the sky. The sun had begun to edge its way onto the horizon. "You were in the diner. And on the street before that."

He blushed.

"You were staring at me."

"No . . . !" His throat choked on itself; he couldn't say anything else. But he wanted to deny it, loud and long, even if it meant she'd know he was lying. That thing in the back of his head was screaming again, *You too, you were staring too.* But Gil knew that wasn't the thing to say. Oh no.

"Let's walk," she said. Her voice sounded somehow compassionate, almost as though she thought she was offering him a mercy.

What could he do? His ears were ringing with a tone so high he could barely hear it, and he could feel his blood pounding in the back of his skull like it was all about to break open. He got up and followed her, trying to look as cool and nonchalant as he possibly could.

"I feel as though I've always known you," she said after they'd taken a few steps. *Dumb*, was the first thing he thought. Then, a moment later, *Ludicrous . . . !* He could feel the jumpy id-thing in the back of his head stretching to find the word; it'd been a long time since any part of him had had to use words like that.

But what she said settled in after a minute or two, and eventually he realized that she was right, that recognition was exactly what he was feeling.

"Yes," he said, agreeing with her. It was hard to say; he was still uneasy, his throat and his vocal cords still constricted and tense. "Maybe that's what it is."

She let that ride for a while, and they walked without talking until they were over by the pine trees.

"Do you come here often?" she asked.

He shrugged. "No, not often. Just when I need to."

"It's a good spot for sunrises," she said, and she pointed. Prosaically enough, the sun was rising over the river in all its gold and crimson glory. Gil had never really looked at it from here before; that really wasn't his sort of thing. If he was here and it was dawn, it was pretty certain he'd be sleeping, or trying to.

But he still looked when she pointed, and he saw the sun's disk three-quarters risen over the horizon, and he even reveled in the glory and the overstatement of it. He saw a pattern in the wondrously golden-backlit clouds.

"Can you see that?" he asked. "Over there, to the left of the sun?"

She shook her head. "It looks like a cloud to me."

Gil felt silly, but he didn't let that stop him. "Can't you see the big golden dragon? And that ray of sunlight is the dragon breathing fire. That's the head, there's the tail, and those over there are the arms and legs. The big cloud over there is a wing; the other one's behind it."

She smiled again. "Do you always notice that sort of thing?"

"I don't know," he said. He kneeled down, looking at something in the grass. "I guess not." He wanted to tell her a lie, to tell her that he always did, but he couldn't think fast enough, and he told her the truth by accident, before he'd even had the chance to tell his voice not to. Part of him was trembling, anxious, scared, but the part of him that was talking and moving and doing, that was cool and calm as he ever was, just like nothing at all was happening. Being calm like that scared Gil probably more than anything else.

He stood up, and he was holding a flower: a tiny yellow buttercup.

She looked at it. "For me?" she asked.

"Yes." He reached over and held it under her chin. "What is it they say you are if it shows yellow underneath you?"

"I don't know."

He threaded the flower into her hair.

"Well?" she asked, and when he didn't answer she asked again. "What did you see?"

"I couldn't tell," he said. "I can't see from here."

As he moved his hand away she caught it. She kissed him, softly and gently, on the lips. She *touched* him. "Love me." she said.

And—

Again . . .

—just like the other times, he felt it reaching up from deep inside him, twisting him, making him. . . .

Again . . . *!*

. . . want to *do* things, cruel, violent things, and suddenly like a daydream the world was made of blood, red, red, red, and he knew he had—

Again!

—to run or else he'd be doing something he could never undo, and he tried to break away from her but she had her arms around him *tight* and he couldn't get loose, and she was loving him, and *God* it was fine, and he had to get away but he couldn't even make himself try anymore, and—

—and—

—and suddenly he had the pig-sticker, the beautiful switch-blade, in his hand, and when he pushed its button he almost came, and it was all much, much too late. He drove the knife into her back and into her neck, and her belly, and her sides, and in his mind's eye the world was made of redness. And even though his eyes were closed because he couldn't bear to see what he was doing he was coming, and again, and again.

And then he was drowsy and weak in the knees with the satiation of a lifetime's unfulfilled lust. He fell to the ground, and his eyes opened, and he almost shrieked from fear of seeing what he'd done. . . .

. . . but he didn't, he gasped instead, because she was smiling at him, and there was nothing wrong with her at all.

Where he'd cut her there was mist wisping out of gloriously gaping holes, and when relex curiosity made him reach out and touch her he realized that she wasn't made of flesh and blood at all, but ghost; her arm was cool and powdery in his fingers for a moment, and then it was not there to touch at all. He saw it pass through his hand just the way one dim reflection supersedes another on a window.

But when she reached out to take the knife from him her touch was as real and cold as anything he'd ever felt and her smile was as lazy-lusty as any he'd ever imagined, and when she spoke to him her voice was as real as it had ever been.

"Your turn." She said it just like when the girl is going to give the guy a back rub in the movies. Her voice was just exactly the lover's coo he'd always dreamed.

A Night in Possum Holler

Ardath Mayhar

It took eight years to pay off all our debts. It took another seven to save enough for a down payment on the house we'd wanted for years. And then inflation took a hand, and we realized that we were like the frog in the well—crawl up two feet and fall back three. That's when we decided that instead of doing the sensible thing and holding on to our jobs in Houston we were going to take that sum and buy us a place up in Poor Man's Country, which is the accurate name of East Texas, when folks are feeling honest.

We knew we'd be broke and stay that way, but what the hell . . . it was better than knocking ourselves out playing Russian roulette with Houston traffic every morning and evening, breathing carbon monoxide and the effluents from the petroleum plants in Pasadena, as well as things less easily identified. We'd been poor before. There wasn't any great trick to that, and we'd learned all the dodges by the time we were weaned.

We spent a spring traveling up into the woodsy hills and poking around both with and without real estate agents. We wanted a bit of ground, which came well within the capabilities of the cash we had. Land in East Texas costs a fraction of what it costs in Houston, believe me. A house we could fix up would suit us very well. We found, once we got to looking hard, that we could pay *cash* for a place that our little hoard wouldn't even make a down payment on where we were.

Maudie almost laughed herself sick when she saw the name on the road sign the first time we went into Possum Holler. But she quit laughing when she was looking at the place we went to see. It was a little gem . . . to us, at least. Ten acres on a hill slope, with an all-season creek branch running across the low end. Lots of big hickories and a few oaks and a ring of huge pines circling the knoll where the house stood. And the house was nice. Shabby, yes. Rundown for years without paint, but the tin roof had saved it from leaks.

It was an old dog-run house—the kind that was two halves separated by a wide hallway running from front to back, open to the air. But that had been enclosed some time in the past, a kitchen built across the rear of it, and a nice screened porch across the front. The rooms had ten-foot ceilings and were big and square and solid. The thing was built of cypress, and there's just no decay in that stuff.

Because it was old-fashioned and would take a lot of work or money or both to get into shape, we bought it for a pittance. Also because it was in Possum Holler, which was a bit behind the back of beyond. Also for other reasons, but we didn't know about them at the time and it's too late to worry about them now.

We moved up in a borrowed camping trailer and set it up down by the road. There wasn't a really flat spot to put it anywhere else, and that was handy for getting in and out as we had to run into the Holler for nails and barbed wire and all the things it was so easy to forget when you do things like fixing up a place that's been neglected for twenty years. Then we rolled up our sleeves and went at it.

Maudie and I both grew up on shirttail farms. We knew how to work, and we made the fur fly. I rented a tractor, first off, and cut all the weeds and persimmon sprouts and sassafras clumps that had been making free with the pastureland for umpteen years. Maudie scrubbed woodwork and slapped on paint and put up new screen wire on the windows and around the porch. By the time I had fences mended and the land in shape she was ready for some help fixing the roof. Some of the tin was loose, and all of it needed a good thick coat of aluminum paint. Maudie's a willing old gal, but she had trick knees like you wouldn't believe, which made getting up on roofs nervous work for her.

We were getting pretty tired of that camp trailer by the time things were so that we could move into the house. Our stuff came out of storage on a Friday morning, and we hauled it out in four loads of a U-Haul trailer and parked it on the front porch. Arranging it took most of Saturday. Sunday morning we headed back for Houston to return the trailer, Maudie following me in our '78 Ford station wagon. We got back to the Holler about eight in the evening.

It took us most of the summer to do all that fixing up, and it was late September. An early norther was blowing through the woods, and we were glad to get back home. Maudie had a fire all set in the living room fireplace, and we looked forward to lighting that and sitting in our own, by God, house by our own fire and owing no man a thin dime.

We ate sandwiches by firelight and made coffee in an ancient granite pot we'd found at the General Merchandise store in the Holler. Pushed it right up into the coals, and it turned out the best cup of coffee I ever swallowed in my life. Then we just sat there, almost purring with satisfaction and smugness.

What did the Greeks call that? Hubris? The kind of pride that goeth before a fall . . .

And we got worse. All through September and October we kept working—there's always more to do when you take on a project like that. The tacky little job I got fifteen miles away at Nichols was a snap, and while I was working at it I was thinking about all the things I was going to do when I got home. Maudie was worse. She put an ad in a writer's magazine to do typing, and that let her stay at home all day. She'd type awhile and work awhile, and when I got home she'd be full of satisfaction.

You wouldn't think there'd be anything about that to bring a Wrath down on anybody, now would you? But what else could it be . . . Well.

Anyway, the fall wore itself out, and winter came on stronger than usual in that part of the world. Northers chased each other through the pine country, one right after the other, and we were mighty glad of our fireplace and the big woodpile that I'd accumulated while trimming and cleaning up our woodlot. Those thick cypress planks were good insulation by themselves, and we'd gone inside the floors and the walls and blown in more insulation, too. We were snug as bugs in a rug.

Other critters liked the setup, too. At night we'd hear scrufflings and gruntings under the house. Armadillos, the neighbors told us. And probably skunks. Mort Feldon gave us a pointer pup he said would be good at scaring away varmints, and we fixed him up a burrow under the porch. Then we stopped up all around the foundation . . . but those noises kept right on. Digging sounds. Grunting and snuffling sounds.

"You think there's a bear wintering under there?" Maudie asked, one night when things were unusually noisy.

"There's no bears left closer than the river," I said. "And precious few there. No, it's some tiny little old animal that can slip through the chinks. You can bet on that."

Funny thing, though. Pat, the pointer, didn't say a word, no matter how loud the critter got. He'd look up at me if I'd go out to check on him, and something in his eyes told me he knew exactly what that was digging away down there, and he hadn't the faintest intention of meddling with it.

We finally went to see Mr. Heaton at the store and laid our problem before him. He turned away and scrabbled among the packages of rat poison for a box of stuff that he said would kill anything up to a rhinoceros. But I noticed all the time we were talking that he looked a little funny and shaky. He came out onto the porch of the store when we drove off. Waved good-bye, as if he didn't expect to see us again. Of course, I didn't put it together and realize that until later . . .

We followed directions to the dot, put out old tuna fish cans of the stuff mixed with everything from cornmeal to hamburger, all under the house as far as we could push it with poles. Then we tied Pat up short, so he couldn't get any of it. And then we waited to see what would happen next.

Nothing did. The noise went on exactly as it had before, night after night. When a month went by without any results I went under and took out all that stuff and buried it deep and put a big flat rock over the hole so Pat couldn't dig it up.

Just after Christmas the hearth started to buckle. Did I tell you the house had two fireplaces? One for each of the original halves of the house, you see. One was in our living room, and that was the one we used. The other was in the room we took for our bedroom. When it was particularly cold we'd build a smudge in the fireplace to take the chill off the room, but we never had roaring fires there as we had on the other side of the house.

Maudie noticed the way the bricks were out of line one night when she was about to lay a fire there. When I came to her call, I could see that something had dug out under the hearth, so all the thicknesses of brick had sagged down into the hole. That was the only thing that could cause something like that—the hearth was a good three feet thick from top to bottom.

We knew that for certain, since we'd been so happy that someone had redone both fireplaces, filling in new brick from top to bottom beneath the firebox. It seemed as if whatever was giving us all the trouble at night had done it before now, digging out under fireplaces. Who knew how many times? And who could tell what it might be?

Well, there was nothing to be done that night. We didn't light a fire, for fear it might find a way to get a spark out through one of the cracks and into the old cypress of the walls. We just went to bed and snuggled close together until we warmed up some. Then we slept.

I woke with a jerk. Something had sounded—a sharp crack of noise. I reached to switch on the light, just as Maudie said, "Unh? Unh! Whasamatta?" in her usual sleep-drugged way.

Then it was on us.

The lamp was a little night-light affair, but even it was enough to show what came surging out of the hearth in a shower of mortar and bits of brick. It looked a little like a bear, at that. But it had no fur, and it had no face, and it was slimy as a snail. I tried to roll out from under as it came down on the bed, but it was no use. I stuck to it like a fly to flypaper, and I knew Maudie was in the same fix.

I could barely breathe, and that only because I had turned my face to one side. If I'd been facing up like Maudie was . . . maybe I'd have been luckier. She must have suffocated pretty quickly. She was gone when the thing lifted itself off of us.

It must have been hungry. It might have been hibernating, or whatever it did, for the whole twenty years the house hadn't been lived in. It ate Maudie almost entirely, right then and there. I could hear it chomping her bones and grinding and slobbering away over on that side of the bed.

Why didn't I run for it while the thing was busy? There's a good reason for that. While it was on top of me it glued me to the bed with that gunk that covered it. From the middle of my chest downward I seemed to be a part of the mattress. Nothing but my right arm and my left hand could move at all. It's a good thing I kept this pad beside the bed for making notes on supplies when I woke in the night and thought of them. At least I can keep my mind off what's happening.

Because when it finished Maudie it started in on me. But it's not as hungry now. It's been four days, and it's not much farther up than my knees. I figure tonight it'll get my right thigh, and tomorrow night the left one. It'd be better if I could bleed to death, but that slimy stuff seems to seal off the blood vessels, so that doesn't work.

If I can hang on without going stark crazy, in three more nights it'll get to a point where it will chomp up something I can't live without. That'll be damn good. I'm almost out of tablet, now. Maybe I will go off my rocker—that would make it easier. Some. I hope.

God, when we moved here I thought the Holler part of the name meant Hollow. Now I know it doesn't. It means Holler. Like scream, you know?

I do a lot of that.

The Night Is Freezing Fast

Thomas F. Monteleone

I t started with a curse—albeit a mild one.

"Oh *damn!*" cried Grandma from the kitchen. When ten-year-old Alan heard her cursing, he knew she was serious.

Grandpa eased the Dubuque newspaper down from his face, and spoke to her. "What's the matter?"

"I ran out of shortnin' for this cake . . . and if you want a nice dessert for Christmas dinner, you'll get yourself into town and get me some more."

"But it's a *blizzard* goin' on out there!" said Grandpa.

Grandma said nothing. Grandpa just sighed as he dropped his paper, shuffled across the room to the foyer closet.

Alan watched him open the door and pull out snow-boots, a beat-up corduroy hat, and a Mackinaw jacket of red and black plaid. He turned and looked wistfully at Alan, who was sitting in on the floor half-watching a football game.

"Want to take a ride, Alan?"

"Into town?"

"Yep. Fraid so."

"In the blizzard?"

Grandpa sighed, stole a look toward the kitchen. "Yep."

"Yeah! That'll be *great* fun," he said.

Alan ran to the closet and pulled on the heavy, rubber-coated boots, a knit watch-cap, and scarf. Then he shook into the goose down parka his mom had ordered from the L. L. Bean mail-order place. It was so *different* out here in Iowa.

"Forty-two years with that woman and I don't know how she figures she can . . ."

Grandpa had just closed the door to the mud-porch behind them. He was muttering as he faced into the stinging slap of the December wind, the bite of the ice-hard snowflakes attacking his cheeks. Alan heard on the radio that there would be roof-high drifts by morning if it kept up like this.

Grandpa stepped down to the path shovelled toward the garage. It was already starting to fill in and would need some new digging out pretty soon.

The hypnotic effect of the snow fascinated Alan. "Do you get storms like this all the time, Grandpa?"

" 'Bout once a month this bad." Grandpa reached the garage door, threw it up along its spring-loaded tracks. He shook his head and shivered from the wind-chill. "I don't know about you, but *I'd* rather be with your mom and dad, takin' that cruise right about now."

"No way! This is going to be the first *real* Christmas I ever had!"

"Why? Because it's a *white* one?" Grandpa chuckled as he opened the door of the 4-wheel-drive Scout, climbed in.

"Sure," said Alan. "Haven't you ever heard that song?"

Grandpa smiled. "Oh, I think I've heard it a time or two . . ."

"Well, that's what I mean. It *never* seems like Christmas in L.A.—even when it *is* Christmas!" Alan jumped into the Scout and slammed the door. The blizzard awaited them.

Grandpa eased the Scout from the driveway to Route 14A. Alan looked out across the flat landscape of the other farms in the distance, and felt disoriented. He could not tell where the snowy land stopped and the white of the sky began. When the Scout lurched forward out onto the main road it looked like they were constantly driving smack into a white sheet of paper, a white nothingness.

It was scary, thought Alan. Just as scary as driving into a pitch-black night.

"Oh, she picked a fine time to run out of something for that danged cake! Look at it, Alan. It's goin' to be a regular *white-out*, is what it is."

Alan nodded. "How do you know where you're going, Grandpa?"

Grandpa harrumphed. "Been on this road a million times, boy. Lived here all my life! I'm not about to get lost. But my God, it's *cold* out here! Hope this heater gets going pretty soon . . ."

They drove on in silence except for the skrunch of the tires on the packed snow and *thunk-thunk* of the wiper blades trying to move off the hard new flakes that pelted the glass. The heater still pumped chilly air into the cab and Alan's breath was almost freezing as it came out of his mouth.

He imagined that they were explorers on a far-away planet—an alien world of ice and eternally freezing winds. It was an instantaneous, catapulting adventure of the type only possible in the minds of imaginative ten-year-olds. There were creatures out in the blizzard—great white hulking things. Pale, reptilian, evil-eyed things. Alan squinted through the windshield, ready in his gun-turret if one turned on them. He would blast it with his laser-cannons . . .

"What in *heck*?" muttered Grandpa.

Abruptly, Alan was out of his fantasy-world as he stared past the flicking windshield wipers. There was a dark shape standing in the center of the white nothingness. As the Scout advanced along the invisible road, drawing closer to the contrasted object, it became clearer, more distinct.

It was a man. He was standing by what must be the roadside, waving a gloved hand at Grandpa.

Braking easily, Grandpa stopped the Scout and reached across to unlock the door. The blizzard rushed in ahead of the stranger, slicing through Alan's clothes like a cold knife. "Where you headed?!" cried Grandpa over the wind. "I'm going as far as town . . ."

"That'll do," said the stranger.

Alan caught a glimpse of him as he pushed into the back seat. He was wearing a thin coat that seemed to hang on him like a scarecrow's rags. He had a black scarf wrapped tight around his neck and a dark blue ski mask that covered his face under a floppy-brimmed old hat. Alan didn't like that—not being able to see the stranger's face.

"Cold as hell out there!" said the man as he smacked his gloved hands together. He laughed to himself, then: "Now there's a funny expression for you, ain't it? 'Cold as hell.' Don't make much sense, does it? But people still say it, don't they?"

"I guess they do," said Grandpa as he slipped the Scout into gear and started off again. Alan looked at the old man, who looked like an older version of his father, and thought he saw an expression of concern, if not apprehension, forming on the lined face.

"It's not so funny, though . . ." said the stranger, his voice lowering a bit. "Everybody figures hell to be this *hot* place, but it don't *have* to be, you know?"

"Never really thought about it much," said Grandpa, jiggling with the heater controls. It was so cold, thought Alan. It just didn't seem to want to work.

Alan shivered, uncertain whether or not it was from the lack of heat, or the words, the voice of the stranger.

"Matter of fact, it makes more sense to think of hell as full of all kinds of *different* pain. I mean, fire is so unimaginative, don't you think? Now, *cold* . . . something as cold as that wind out there could be just as bad, right?" The man in the back seat chuckled softly beneath the cover of the ski mask. Alan didn't like that sound.

Grandpa cleared his throat and faked a cough. "I don't think I've really thought much about that either," he said as he appeared to be concentrating on the snow-covered road ahead. Alan looked at his grandfather's face and could see the unsteadiness in the old man's eyes. It was the look of fear, slowly building.

"Maybe you should . . ." said the stranger.

"Why?" said Alan. "What do you mean?"

"It stands to reason that a demon would be comfortable in any kind of element—as long as it's harsh, as long as it's cruel."

Alan tried to clear his throat and failed. Something was stuck down there, even when he swallowed.

The stranger chuckled again. "Course, I'm getting off the track . . . we were talking about figures of speech, weren't we?"

"You're the one doing all the talking, mister," said Grandpa.

The stranger nodded. "Actually, a more appropriate expression would be 'cold as the *grave*' . . ."

"It's not *this* cold under the ground," said Alan defensively.

"Now, how would *you* know?" asked the stranger slowly. "You've never been in the grave . . . not *yet*, anyway."

"That's enough of that silly talk, mister!" said Grandpa. His voice was hard-sounding, but Alan detected fear beneath the thin layer of his words.

Alan looked from his grandfather to the stranger. As his eyes locked in with those behind the ski mask, Alan felt an ice-pick touch the tip of his spine. There was something about the stranger's eyes, something dark which seemed to lurch and caper violently behind them.

A dark chuckle came from the back seat.

"Silly talk? *Silly?*" asked the stranger. "Now what's silly and what's serious in the world today? Who can *tell* anymore?! Missiles and summit conferences! Vampires and garlic! Famine and epidemics! Full moons and maniacs!"

The words rattled out of the dark man and chilled Alan more deeply than the cold blast of the heater fan. He looked away and tried to stop the shiver which raced up and down his back-bone.

"Where'd you say you was goin', Mister?" asked Grandpa as he slowly eased off the gas-pedal.

"I didn't say."

"Well, how about sayin'—right now."

"Do I detect hostility in your voice, sir? Or is it something else?" Again came the deep-throated, whispery chuckle.

Alan kept his gaze upon the white-on-white panorama ahead. But he was listening to every word being exchanged between the dark stranger and his grandfather, who was suddenly assuming the proportions of a champion. He listened but he could not turn around, he could not look back. There was a fear gripping him now. It was a gnarled spindly claw reaching up for him, out of the darkness of his mind, closing in on him with a terrible certainty.

Grandpa hit the brakes a little too hard, and even the 4-wheel-drive of the Scout couldn't keep it from sliding off to the right to gently slap a bank of plowed snow. Alan watched his grandfather as he turned and stared at the stranger.

"Listen, Mister, I don't know what your game is, but I don't find it very amusin' like you seem to . . . And I don't appreciate the way you've dealt with our hospitality."

Grandpa glared at the man in the back seat, and Alan could feel the courage burning behind the old man's eyes. Just the sight of it gave Alan the strength to turn and face the stranger.

"Just trying to make conversation," said the man in a velvety-soft voice. It seemed to Alan that the stranger's voice could change any time he wanted it to, could sound any way at all. The man in the mask was like a ventriloquist or a magician, maybe . . .

"Well, to be truthful with you, Mister," Grandpa was saying. "I'm kinda tired of your 'conversation,' so why don't you climb out right here?"

The eyes behind the mask flitted between Grandpa and Alan once, twice. "I see . . ." said the voice. "No more silly stuff, eh?"

The stranger leaned forward, putting a gloved hand on the back of Alan's seat. The hand almost touched Alan's parka and he pulled away. He knew he didn't want the stranger touching him. Acid churned in his stomach.

"Very well," said the dark man. "I'll be leaving you for now . . . but one last thought, all right?"

"I'd rather not," said Grandpa, as the man squeezed out the open passenger's door.

"But you will . . ." Another soft laugh as the stranger stood in the drifted snow alongside the road. The eyes behind the mask darted from Grandpa to Alan and back again. "You see, it's just a short ride we're all taking . . . and the night is freezing fast."

Grandpa's eyes widened a bit as the words drifted slowly into the cab, cutting through the swirling, whipping-cold wind. Then he gunned the gas-pedal. "Good-bye, Mister . . ."

The Scout suddenly leaped forward in the snow with such force that Alan didn't have to pull the door closed—it slammed shut from the force of the acceleration.

Looking back, Alan could see the stranger quickly dwindle to nothing more than a black speck on the white wall behind them.

"Of all the people to be helpful to, and I have to pick a danged nut!" Grandpa forced a smile to his face. He looked at Alan and tapped his arm playfully. "Nothin' to worry about now, boy. He's behind us and gone."

"Who you figure he was?"

"Oh, just a nut, son. A kook. When you get older you'll realize that there's lots of 'funny' people in the world."

"You think he'll still be out on the road when we go back?"

Grandpa looked at Alan and tried to smile. It was an effort and it didn't look anything at all like a real smile.

"You were afraid of him, weren't you, boy?"

Alan nodded. "Weren't *you*?"

Grandpa didn't answer for an instant. He certainly *looked* scared. Then: "Well, kinda, I guess. But I've known about his type. Everybody runs into 'im . . . sooner or later, I guess."

"Really?" Alan didn't understand what the old man meant.

Grandpa looked ahead. "Well, here's the store . . ."

After parking, Grandpa ran into the Food-A-Rama for a pound of butter while Alan remained in the cab with the engine running, the heater fan wailing, and the doors locked. Looking out into the swirling snow, Alan could barely pick out single flakes anymore. Everything was blending into a furiously thick, white mist. The windows of the Scout were blank sheets of paper, he could see *nothing* beyond the glass.

Suddenly there was a dark shape at the driver's side, and the latch rattled on the door handle. The lock flipped up and Grandpa appeared with a small brown paper bag in his hand. "Boy, it's blowin' up terrible out here! What a time that woman has to send us out!"

"It looks worse," said Alan.

"Well, maybe not," said Grandpa, slipping the vehicle into gear. "Night's coming on. When it gets darker, the white-out won't be as bad."

They drove home along Route 28, which would eventually curve down and cross 14A. Alan fidgeted with the heater fan and the cab was finally starting to warm up a little bit. He felt better, but he couldn't get the stranger's voice out of his mind.

"Grandpa, what did that man mean about 'a short ride' we're all taking? And about the night freezing fast?"

"I don't rightly know what he meant, Alan. He was a kook, remember? He probably don't know himself what he meant by it . . ."

"Well, he sure did make it sound creepy, didn't he?"

"Yes, I guess he did," said Grandpa as he turned the wheel onto a crossing road. "Here we go, here's 14A. Almost home, boy! I hope your grandmother's got that fireplace hot!"

The Scout trundled along the snowed-up road until they reached a bright orange mailbox that marked the entrance to Grandpa's farm. Alan exhaled slowly, and felt the relief spreading into his bones. He hadn't wanted to say anything, but the white-white of the storm and the seeping cold had been bothering him, making him get a terrible headache, probably from squinting so much.

"*What* in—?" Grandpa eased off the accelerator as he saw the tall, thin figure standing in the snow-filled rut of the driveway.

"It's *him*, Grandpa . . ." said Alan in a whisper.

The dark man stepped aside as the Scout eased up to him. Angrily, Grandpa wound down the window, and let the storm rush into the cab. He shouted past the wind at the stranger. "You've got a lot of nerve comin' up to my house!"

The eyes behind the ski mask seemed to grow darker, unblinking. "Didn't have much choice," said the chameleon-voice.

Grandpa unlocked the door, and stepped out to face the man. "What do you mean by that?"

Soft laughter cut through the howl of the wind. "Come now! You *know* who I am . . . and *why* I'm here."

The words seemed to stop Grandpa in his tracks. Alan watched the old man's face flash suddenly pale. Grandpa nodded. "Maybe," he said, "but I never knew it to be like this . . ."

"There are countless ways," said the stranger. "Now excuse me, and step aside . . ."

"What?!" Grandpa sounded shocked.

Alan had climbed down from the Scout, standing behind the two men. He could hear naked terror couched in the back of his grandfather's throat, the trembling fear in his voice. Without realizing it, Alan was backing away from the Scout. His head was pounding like a jackhammer.

"Is it the *woman*?!" Grandpa was asking in a whisper.

The dark man shook his head.

Grandpa moaned loudly, letting it turn into words. "No! Not *him*! No, you can't mean it!"

"Aneurysm . . ." said the terribly soft voice behind the mask.

Suddenly Grandpa grabbed the stranger by the shoulder, and spun him around, facing him squarely. "No!" he shouted, his face twisted and ugly. "Me! Take me!"

"Can't do it," said the man.

367

"Grandpa, what's the matter?!" Alan started to feel dizzy. The pounding in his head had become a raging fire. It hurt so bad he wanted to scream.

"Yes you can!" yelled Grandpa. "I *know* you can!"

Alan watched as Grandpa reached out and grabbed at the tall thin man's ski mask. It seemed to come apart as he touched it, and fell away from beneath the droopy brimmed hat. For an instant, Alan could see— or at least he *thought* he saw—*nothing* beneath the mask. It was like staring into a night sky and suddenly realizing the *endlessness*, the eternity of it all. To Alan, it was just an eye-blink of time, and then he saw, for another instant, white, angular lines, dark hollows of empty sockets.

But the snow was swirling and whipping, and Grandpa was suddenly wrestling with the man, and the ache in his head was almost blinding him now. Alan screamed as the man wrapped his long thin arms around his grandfather and they seemed to dance briefly around in the snow.

"Run, boy!" screamed Grandpa.

Alan turned toward the house, then looked back and he saw Grandpa collapsing into the snow. The tall, dark man was gone.

"Grandpa!" Alan ran to the old man's side as he lay face up, his glazed eyes staring into the storm.

"Get your grandmother . . . quick," said the old man. "It's my heart."

"Don't die, Grandpa . . . not now!" Alan was frantic and didn't know what to do. He wanted to get help, but he didn't want to leave his grandfather in the storm like this.

"No choice in it," he said. "A deal's a deal."

Alan looked at his grandfather, suddenly puzzled. "What?"

Grandpa winced as new pain lanced his chest. "Don't matter now . . ." The old man closed his eyes and wheezed out a final breath.

Snowflakes danced across his face, and Alan noticed that his headache, like the dark man, had vanished.

No Need for Words

R. Chetwynd-Hayes

Neil was running through the woods. Slim branches whipped his face and hands, brambles tried to trip him; a protruding tree root did. Although he knew he could not go on much further, fear still drove him forward, reinforced his waning strength, made him see hope where none existed. He kept telling himself that the road lay beyond the ridge, but reason told him it could be miles away, for he had not planned his escape. He just removed the loose bar, slid through the aperture—and ran.

They must be on his trail now. Gliding round bushes, taking advantage of every shadow; moving quietly but quickly, experienced hunters who never failed to catch their quarry. He ran up an incline, then sank down exhausted beneath a tree.

Through a gap in the overhead leaves, he could see the full moon. The cold, silver light was like an arc lamp, and he edged round the tree, knowing he was a perfect target for anyone who might be lurking in the nearby bushes. He closed his eyes and listened to the thumping of his heart. How much longer would it be permitted to beat? How had such a nightmare shattered his peaceful life into splinters of horror?

His heart slowed down, his lungs ceased their frantic demand for air, and his limbs relaxed as a beautiful lassitude spread over his entire body. His memory conjured up a vivid moving picture, so real that the murmur of the night breeze was blotted out and for a while he forgot the dreaded hunters.

They came at sunset, the soft thud of their horses' hoofs echoing through the wide glades of the forest like the approach of muffled drums. Barbara and he had seen them through the cottage window, and knew at last, that the rumours were based on fact, that the danger which had been so exciting to talk about, was now approaching their front door.

He had locked that door; reinforced it with piled up furniture, but of course his efforts were futile. They had smashed in a window, torn the casement from its frame, then climbed in with swift, graceful movements. Dressed in black—all save the Scarlet Leader—even their faces were hidden under their black shapeless hoods from which lust-bright eyes glittered, like those of maundering cats in moonlight. In fact, that was how he thought of them. Black, lean cats, descending upon a pair of terrified mice. They worked—if that was the right word—in complete silence, perhaps so that their voices should not be recognized, guarding against the remote possibility that their prey might escape and live to bring testimony against them.

In a matter of seconds he and Barbara were gagged, their arms bound with thick cord, then carried out to the waiting horses.

It was as though he were a disinterested spectator, for now it seemed he was watching the horsemen riding down a broad avenue, with two struggling bundles on the leading horses. The rays of the dying sun made a pattern of phantom leaves on the riders, while their own shadows formed, then disappeared, as though they, too, were trying to escape.

They came at last to the great house; a sullen pile of grey, stone blocks, where glittering windows glared like so many red-tinted eyes out across the murmuring trees. The gates were open, but closed when the last rider had ridden through, while the ghosts of the long dead wailed in forgotten places.

He was now back across a saddle, looking down at the golden gravel, jolting up and down, hearing the crunching clip-clop of the pounding hoofs and the jingling rattle of harness. Shock had numbed his senses, so that terror had been subdued to a dull, nagging worry. Hope had sunk to a tiny, but not yet extinguished spark. Perhaps they meant no harm. This might only be a boisterous prank; a diversion to amuse the bored young bloods, and presently he and Barbara would be allowed to go home — and who knows — perhaps enriched by a gold coin for their inconvenience.

But the black riders did not laugh or behave in any way to suggest this was a harmless escapade. Not a word was exchanged; they might have been automatons, trained to obey a rigid code of instructions. When Neil struggled, an arm struck him soundly across the shoulders, but not he felt in anger, only as a reflex his movement had triggered into action.

Presently they stopped. The gravel path was a rough, rusty carpet that bordered an uncut lawn; a large, dull-black boot swung down and landed with a crunching thud. Hands grabbed his ankles and he was pulled backwards to go sprawling face uppermost across the path, where he could look up at the sun-flecked sky.

Then he saw Barbara's slim body slung over a brawny black shoulder and glimpsed her white, terrified face. He struggled up on to his knees, then like a fallen horse, scrambled wildly, until at last, he was up on his feet. The Scarlet Leader was standing nearby, and for the first time made a sound that approached speech. A growl — perhaps a low laugh — but it was so brief and so low, he might have supposed it had never happened. Then a red arm came up and pointed towards a flight of steps leading up to an open doorway.

370

They took him into a large, gloomy hall, then down more steps to lock him into a large room. It was lit only by a barred window, set up high near the ceiling. Here they left him alone.

The sun died. The darkness of night merged with the shadows, so that he could no longer see. But his ears waited for footsteps, plumbed the depths of silence for the tiniest sound. After some hours, he head a dog howl; a mournful cry that rang out over the dark reaches of night and made him shiver with fearful anticipation. Then, when dawn had painted her first grey streaks across the far wall, he heard the sound for which he had subconsciously been waiting. The scream of a woman who was either in the throes of intense agony or unendurable terror. He rushed to the door and began to hammer it with his clenched fists, while his shriek of protest raced round the room as a series of mounting echoes.

The dog howled again, then another added its lament and yet another, until the world was a place of fearful sounds that made Neil's brain reel so that he sank to the floor and covered his ears with trembling hands. The howling ceased and a thick blanket of silence once again descended upon the house.

It was not until the infant day had put out its pale fingers of yellow light, that the first thoughts of escape crept across his brain. The room was unfurnished, but there was a stout wooden box, a relic possibly of the days when the place had been a cellar. When he stood on this he was able to reach the window and examine the rusty, iron bars. Fortune—if she ever entered that house—smiled upon him. One bar was loose. He worked on it at irregular intervals all day. He stopped when they fed him for the second time, silently watching while he gobbled hot stew from a wooden bowl. Afterwards they locked the door and their echoing footsteps receded up the stairs. He removed the loosened bar, climbed through the narrow aperture, dropped to the ground and ran . . . and ran . . .

Neil opened his eyes and sat up. The forest was still quiet. The tree trunks gleamed softly and were in places splashed with moonlight. High up a faint mist crept slowly through the upper branches like the fluid shapes of unformed ghosts, but the scene was not frightening, although it might have been were it not for a more terrible and persistent dread. A sound had disturbed him and he waited for it to be repeated. He was not disappointed. From far away came the sound of a baying hound.

The rest had given him back a small measure of strength and he ran swiftly; with bowed head and lowered shoulders, keeping well within the shadows, pausing once in a while to regain his breath, then pressing on to the next tree, the next ridge, always hoping to find the road.

But they were gaining on him. From somewhere not far off came a chorus of yelping barks. Sometimes he fancied he heard the sound of running feet. The sharp spurs of fear made him draw upon his last reserves of strength; his body was a robot, driven by a terror-enslaved brain. Then he stumbled into a clearing. His eyes saw the lighted window and he was drawn towards it like a pin to a magnet. Through a red mist the light grew clearer—he saw the outline of a green door with an inverted horse-shoe set above it. Then he was there, banging on the door, whimpering like a hunted animal, before the red mist closed in and he was lost in a roaring inferno.

Neil was seated on a chair. A tall, bearded man and a little woman with the wizened skin of a russet apple, were looking down at him. He would have spoken, but the man laid a finger on his lips and jerked his head towards the door. He could smell their fear and hear its cause.

From beyond the door came a snuffling, whimpering sound, and the thud of many feet. The window trembled and the woman screamed when a hideous dog-face looked in. It was pressed right up against the glass, which the creature's hot breath was causing to steam over. The awful face was gradually becoming indistinct, like a picture when the light is turned down. The door trembled under a single, demanding blow.

Whatever pity might have lurked in the bearded man's eyes, it was now wiped away by an expression of abject terror. He raised his arm and pointed to the door, and when Neil cringed back, emphasized his unspoken order by a fierce jerk of his head. Again the door shuddered, and now there was a cowled head looking in through the window, the unblinking eyes staring straight at the young man on the chair. The woman groaned and clasped trembling hands to her mouth as the man reached out and gripped Neil by his shirt front, then twisted him round.

He looked up at the bearded face, seeing the fear from which cruelty is born; heard the woman go scurrying by, then felt the cold breeze on his back when the door was pulled open. The eyes glaring over his head, widened when they saw what stood beyond the open door, then the arm muscles contracted and Neil was being pushed backwards—back—back—then hurled out into the night, where a ring of masked faces were waiting.

Wrists tied behind his back . . . struggling forward . . . sometimes stumbling . . . black horsemen behind . . . Scarlet Leader in front . . . an owl hoots . . . a rabbit runs across the path . . . a man comes out of the woods . . . two dead pheasants slung over his shoulder . . . he sees the black riders . . . is gone . . . his footsteps can be heard crashing through the woods . . .

The rattle of harness . . . the plod of hoofs . . . a horse snorts . . .

but They are silent . . . perhaps . . . perhaps . . . do not look to the side . . . do not turn your head . . . look to your front where He is riding . . . See! . . . He is tall; the shoulders are broad, the back tapers down to a narrow waist . . . but what is this? . . . a strand of real hair has escaped from under the red hood . . . can it be that He is human after all? . . .

There was the house, bleak and forbidding . . . bathed in moonlight . . . although even the moon could not kill the shadows that lurk in windows and doorways . . .

Words tumbled across his brain . . . jumping, leaping, remembering an old rhyming jingle that lay hidden in childhood. The wind stirred among the trees and turned the leaves into green tongues.

> *Walk by day and run by night,*
> *But go not abroad when the moon is bright,*
> *For 'tis then they ride in black gown and hood,*
> *And bind fast the wanderer who sleeps in the wood.*

> *If you should lay eyes on He who wears red,*
> *Then hasten you home with fear and dread,*
> *Bolt fast the door, shut out the night,*
> *And say your prayers by candlelight.*

The wind went home, the trees slept, and Neil again passed through the open gateway, and up to the great house.

He was not taken back to the little room in the cellar, but through the house and out into what had once been the garden. This was a space of some hundred square feet, completely enclosed by a high brick wall. At the far end stood a structure that could have been an altar, or merely a place of confinement. Three stone steps led up to a broad platform, flanked on either side by two stone pillars.

At regular intervals along the walls were flaming torches set in sconces, and the flickering light lanced back and forth across the stone-paved ground. Neil watched the cowled figures take up positions round the walls, then he was led forward until he and his escort stood a few feet from the pillared altar.

From somewhere in his rear a drum began to beat in a slow, pulsating rhythm that seemed to be keeping time with the dancing shadows. The black figures began to move rhythmically from side to side in a barely perceptible swaying; they made a low growling sound, a grotesque form of chanting.

Footsteps were marching from the house: footsteps that kept in time with the beating drum; each foot raised and brought down with a resounding thud, like that of a drill-sergeant in a ceremonial parade. Neil jerked his head round, then cried out.

The Scarlet Leader was marching in front, and behind him, each arm held firmly by a black rider, was a naked woman. Her form was familiar but her head was covered by a black hood. Neil began to struggle but his guards tightened their grip and one black-gloved hand was thrust over his mouth.

They led her up to the altar, then chained each wrist to a post, so that she hung there with outstretched arms and black-covered head. The Scarlet Leader walked round the altar, then turned to face the pinioned victim. The drums ceased to beat, the black figures became silent and still; the night seemed to hold its breath, as though waiting for the ultimate. Then the Scarlet One—He who knew—raised his arms and—howled.

The hideous sound ran round the walls and was taken up by each motionless figure. It leapt from mouth to mouth until there was only one great bestial cry rising up to the silver sky. The drum took up its rhythmic beat, now louder and faster, and the black riders left the walls and began to leap and prance like hungry dogs that have smelt meat.

The Scarlet Leader leaped up on to the altar and, raising the lower part of his cowl, gently nipped the girl's white shoulder. The act was done quickly, almost gently, but it seemed to have some symbolic significance to the prancing crowd, for they renewed their cries, only now with an element of triumph.

Neil's escort were not exempt from the general air of rejoicing. They too began to hop from one foot to another, and give vent to an occasional howl. Gradually the iron grips were relaxed, so that presently he was able to pull himself free and go running up the steps to the altar. He pushed the Scarlet One aside and tore frantically at the black hood that hid Barbara's face. But his trembling fingers were awkward and her head kept threshing from side to side. At last he saw a thin tape that was tied in a neat bow beneath her chin. This he undid with two quick jerks of his hand.

The hood hung limp, a loose black bag, a crumpled crown to the slender white body, with a trickle of blood running down one shoulder. Before he could remove it, the Scarlet Leader eased him gently away, then gave one shrill cry, that must have been a signal, for the faceless revellers suddenly froze into black, silent statues. The red hands came out and gently gripped the hood between long, slender fingers. The unveiling, the peeling of a forbidden fruit, the denuding of a cabbage. The similies slashed through Neil's brain as the hand slowly lifted—then with a flourish whipped away the black hood, and Barbara's face was revealed.

A cascade of dark auburn hair still hung down to her white shoulders. She was as she always had been, save for one important change. Her face was that of a pink and white dog. The blue eyes were hers, but they were encased in loose pouches of skin. Her nose was a round blob of wet blackness; her cheeks and chin were covered with long, straggling hair. The thin grey lips were dimpled by protruding eyeteeth and short tapering ears grew out from either side of the sloping head. They twitched, then flattened, as though in alarm. When Neil screamed, she growled; when he shrank back, she bared pointed teeth; when he vomited, she howled.

Now they all removed their hoods. A sea of dog faces. Grey, red, black—some with tapering snouts; others, flattened features. Some resembled an overbred Pekinese; still others favoured the dignified lineaments of a lordly St Bernard. The Scarlet Leader himself bore more than a passing likeness to a red setter. In a strange way he was beautiful. The glorious burnt-gold hair covered his head and face, and his red tongue licked drooling chops in a most friendly fashion. Had he been gifted with a tail, he would have doubtlessly have wagged it.

He reached up and the chains snapped open, so that Barbara was free to go bounding down from the altar and seek refuge among the pack. One handed her a black robe and she slipped into it with all the grace of a greyhound taking on a second skin.

Neil did not struggle when they chained him to the altar, neither did he speak or make the slightest sound. After all, the world was but a piece of rotting rock, circling a third-rate sun, and all its creatures merely lice, that must sooner or later, take on many weird shapes.

When the Scarlet Leader bit his shoulder, the black pack howled and performed their ritual dance. There was pain while his face reformed and his vocal cords changed but this was only a passing phase.

Presently, he too went down among the pack and danced in torchlight, howling his defiance at the full moon.

Oasis

Brian Hodge

Things at Tri-Lakes started to turn sour in the early part of July, a July that'll always be the apex of the worst summer of my life . . .

It was a July night, unseasonably cool for a summer night in Southern Illinois. Upper sixties. Not that I was complaining. After a string of days around 100, the night felt like a preview of fall. And there was nothing I liked better than drinking beer under the open sky on a fall night with my friends.

"Times like this make me glad this place flopped." It was Phil; he was leaning back on his car's windshield, his legs stretched over the hood, one foot swaying to the sounds of Black Sabbath coming from inside.

"Sort of restores your faith in nature, doesn't it?" Rick said. He was sitting on one fender while I sat on the other.

"Nature had nothing to do with it. Just nobody wanted to build a house out here in the middle of nowhere. That's all."

"Oh, come on, where's your imagination? I like to think that nature triumphed out here. One little spot in the world that couldn't be civilized."

"Couldn't be civilized, hell. What do you think we're parked on? Asphalt doesn't grow wild, you know."

"Yeah, yeah. But they couldn't take it any farther. It's as if the ground and the water and the trees rejected everything else. Mother nature allowed the road so we could get here, but nothing more. Don't you see?"

Phil was shaking his head and smiling to himself. "Listen to Joyce Kilmer here," he said to me.

"Phillip, you got no soul," Rick accused.

Phil belched.

I eased off the fender and leaned into the car. I crushed my empty beer can (with aluminum anybody can be macho), dropped it into our empties sack, and fished out a new one from the cooler. After I sat back on the fender, I popped off the tab.

"Well, Chris," Phil said, "that's the first sound we've heard out of you in a half hour."

"Sorry. Just off in Chris's little world over here."

"Join the rest of us."

"In some silly argument over why this place flopped? The answer's clear to *me*." I walked around the car and put an arm around Rick's shoulder. "Twang's right." We called him Twang because he played the guitar. "This place wouldn't have it any other way."

"Then you're full of shit, too," Phil laughed.

"Is it so unbelievable that this land, this oasis, is so idyllic that it has its own spirit?" Occasionally I was possessed by fits of eloquence. The guys were usually mildly entertained. I wandered on down a little incline until I stood by the pond we were parked by. "I tell you, this land has its own soul, something that reaches out and touches others, something that protects it against intruders that don't show proper respect. For those that *do*, it nurtures them and gives them a haven, a sanctuary. Gentlemen . . . I give you Paradise." I ended the soliloquy by taking a leak into the pond.

The guys offered a round of mild applause.

"I swear," Phil said, "we're gonna have to keep you away from beer. It warps your little mind."

I smiled and we went on to new topics. But as it turned out, Rick and I were a lot closer to the truth than either of us would have believed.

We called the place Tri-Lakes. It was a housing subdivision that didn't go over, and all that was there was a narrow ribbon of road winding here and there to different stretches of lots. No houses, no foundations, not even any construction equipment anymore. I later heard stories about how the developers had trouble keeping a work crew out there: a couple of guys turned up missing, others found excuses to take jobs elsewhere and moved away, and so on. I suppose it just turned into one gigantic financial drain and the project was scrapped as a tax write-off.

I found the place a couple of summers before it went bad on us. One night I was out with this girl and we were driving around in the country north of town. I'd just gotten my license the week before, so driving around was a pretty big deal. She was fifteen, so dating someone who could drive was also a big deal. Anyway, I turned off the main road, drove a little bit along this new road, and found a turn-off. A big gaudy sign stood at the entrance, painted green and yellow and brown (nature colors, I guess) with white lettering. It read: PLEASANT HILLS. CHOICE LOTS NOW AVAILABLE! 3 STOCKED LAKES. COMING SOON—TENNIS COURTS.

AND SOMETHING INSIDE ME SAID, *Drive on. Go find a nice cemetery or something.*

But the girl put her hand on my knee and said, "Let's check it out."

It was mainly just woodland, with plenty of lot space. We saw two ponds ("lake" was an exaggeration), but couldn't find the third. It seemed safe enough. I was only too willing to credit my initial fear to a dying twinge of conscience at the prospect of ravaging the girl next to me.

By the time I left that night, I was feeling very good indeed about Pleasant Hills. I brought Phil and Rick out the next night; they liked it too. I was the first to call it Tri-Lakes (even though we never found the third one), and the name stuck. Our favorite spot was this cul-de-sac at the end of one branch of the drive. We'd park by the bigger pond, where a big grove of trees rested just ahead. The sky was huge and open, sharing stars like you never saw in town.

Tri-Lakes gave us a place to go when we couldn't find a party, or didn't feel like cruising. We'd sit and drink and listen to the stereo. It was like the place was for us alone.

It was a great place to take girls, too. It had everything needed to kindle romance — solitude, moonlight, water. Tri-Lakes became a pretty lucky spot for me. I even managed to talk a couple of girls into skinny-dipping out there. No minor feat. I didn't hear the stories of the developer's problems until months later. I guess I should've associated them with that little twinge of fear at first finding the place. But I didn't. I was just having too much fun.

The next weekend (after our debate over Nature Triumphant) we were back into the scorchers. The days were up around 100 again, and the humidity was just as wicked. If we'd had any brains, we would've been tucked away in the car with the air-conditioner cranked to the max.

"I got my housing assignment in the mail," Phil said.

"Really?"

"Yeah. I got the hall I wanted, too. My roommate's name is Ashley Hopkins." He laughed softly. "Ashley. What kind of a name is that? He'll probably wear eye shadow."

"To Ashley," I said, and raised my beer in a toast. "Long may he swish."

We laughed and drank and looked at Rick. He was sitting down by the pond, tossing pebbles into the water. Little plinking noises drifted up through the still air.

I couldn't believe how uncomfortable it was. The air was damp and heavy, the humidity hanging in the air like a thin fog. The only thing that could've made it worse was mosquitoes. I wondered where they were, why they weren't out in force. It didn't seem right.

"Ever wish we hadn't graduated?"

"That'd just be putting off the inevitable," I said absently. "Besides, things won't be much different for me and Rick. We'll just be going to junior college. You, though. Three hundred miles away."

"Gonna miss me, dear?"

378

I nodded, meaning it. "Yeah."

"Maybe you'll join me next year."

"Maybe."

Rick came up then, a little wobbly. He was smaller than Phil and me, got drunk easier. His long hair made him look younger, too, like an innocent little kid. "What's going on?"

"Phil's got a faggot for a roommate."

"Coming out of the closet at last, huh, Phil?"

"His name's Ashley," Phil said, then took a thoughtful sip of beer. "Yeah, he'll probably be a scrawny little fellow, with long hair, and he'll play guitar."

"All right, asshole, you're just jealous 'cause I'm gonna be the greatest thing since Eddie Van Halen."

"You?" Phil laughed. "C'mon, Twang, time to be realistic."

They loved to fight, to argue, more in fun than out of spite. It was a little like watching Spock and McCoy go at it on the reruns of *Star Trek*.

I emptied a beer, crushed the can, and tossed it toward the sack. Two points.

It was so quiet. The silence caught my ear more than their talking. Silence wasn't right. There weren't any bugs buzzing or chirruping away in the weeds. But there were *always* bugs, raising nine kinds of hell. But now . . . no sound at all. Except from that grove of trees ahead of us. It wasn't wind, exactly—

"*Chris!*"

"Huh?"

Phil laughed. "I called you three times, old boy. What's your problem? You going catatonic on us?"

"Listen."

They settled down for a moment. "I don't hear anything."

"That's just it. Where are all the bugs? And listen to that grove of trees."

"That's just . . . just wind." But Phil didn't sound quite so sure.

"I don't think so."

"It sounds like a giant breathing," Rick said.

He was right. It was a deep sound that came and went, like huge bellows. Drawing in, letting out, in, out . . .

"I don't like this at all," Rick said.

"Yeah, let's get out of here."

We scrambled for the car. I fell in behind the wheel and fired it up. Rick stopped to scoop up our sack of empties from the asphalt.

"Forget that!" Phil yelled.

Rick heaved the sack toward the trees, a gesture that looked comically defiant. I saw the empty cans fly out and catch the moonlight before falling from sight. Then I was peeling away. We all glanced back at the grove of trees, half-expecting to see something huge and terrible come charging out after us. But nothing did.

We were going to feel pretty silly about the whole thing.

Eventually.

A couple of days later I was invited to a barbecue that Phil's older brother was popping for. He lived just beyond the north edge of town. I drove out toward the house, but when it came time to make the turn, I shot on past.

I suppose it was curiosity more than anything that made me head out to Tri-Lakes again. By this time I was feeling a little sheepish about the way I'd panicked; even though none of us had since mentioned it.

There was still plenty of daylight when I parked. Everything seemed normal enough, with an army of bugs buzzing away, birds chirping, and the wind whispering through the grove of trees. I even went so far as to step into the grove. I stopped in front of the largest tree. It was a big mother, maybe four feet thick at the base. Huge limbs branched off like dozens of powerful arms.

And that was all.

My faith restored, I started to leave, only half-realizing that the sack of cans Rick had thrown had since disappeared.

The next Friday turned out like so many others . . . we picked up a case of beer and hit the road, eventually winding up at Tri-Lakes. We didn't feel like driving. Cruising was a festive event. Stopping was more for the brooding occasions. And Rick was definitely in a brooding frame of mind. Thursday morning he had slammed a car door on his left hand, cancelling a weekend gig he'd been counting on.

"Why now?" He sounded close to crying. "Why not my right hand? At least I could've played."

"Look on the bright side," Phil said. "With those plastic splints, you've got a good bottleneck slide." It was cruel humor at best.

"Yeah, sure."

"Listen," I told him, handing him a beer. "Maybe you can use the time to write some new songs, some really good ones."

"Yeah, maybe I will." He held the can clumsily in his left hand, prying at the tab with his right fingers. "Oww! Shit!"

"What'd you do?"

"Bent back my fingernail! Son of a bitch!" He wound up and hurled the unopened can into the grove. I heard it smack off a tree.

"Hey, steady," Phil said, and we both moved closer to Rick. He had his head lowered, rubbing his eyes. I hadn't realized just how much this gig had meant to him.

"I'm sorry," he moaned. "This has just been a lousy couple of days."

Phil touched his shoulder. "There'll be other chances. You're talented enough to make the best of them."

"I guess." Rick sniffed. He started over toward the grove.

"Hey, don't worry about the beer. We got plenty, jeeze."

He mumbled something back that I couldn't quite understand, it probably had something to do with my proverb that it's a mortal sin to waste good beer. But I didn't give my real reason for wanting him to stay out of the grove. When I saw *Star Wars*, I thought it was a little hokey the way Obi-Wan Kenobi felt "a disturbance in the Force" when the planet Alderan was blown up. But when I heard the beer can bounce off that tree, I suddenly knew what that feeling was like. The whole mood of the place just shifted, like something huge was mighty pissed indeed. I watched almost breathless as Rick disappeared into the grove.

"I really feel sorry for him," Phil said quietly.

"Yeah, me too."

"I wish I hadn't made that crack about slide guitar. Man, that was so stupid."

"Forget it. Rick will."

And then Rick screamed. Short but loud. I couldn't be sure, but I thought I heard the rustle of brush at the same time.

"What the hell?" Phil grabbed me by the arm. "Rick?"

No answer. That scared me, because I didn't think Rick was in a joking mood. All at once, old memories rushed at me. My initial reaction to the place, the stories about the developers . . .

Phil ran over to his car and hit the headlights. They glared into the grove, illuminating the foremost trees, emphasizing the shadows in the background. It was a stage of green and black. With no sign of Rick.

The bugs were quiet, too.

Phil was leaning into his trunk. Then he came running over to me, carrying a jack and a tire iron. He gave me the iron; the punier one. "Well?" He glanced my way, fear in his eyes.

I sighed. "Let's go."

We walked side by side into the grove, so close our shoulders pressed tightly the whole way. We kept the weapons ready to swing, and our heads swiveled back and forth nonstop. Our feet crunched on sticks and dead leaves, and I winced at every little sound, sure that each one was going to bring something out of the shadows to drag me off.

The only thing we found was the beer can, split open at the seam and resting in a big foamy splash. But there was no Rick, no blood, no scrap of clothing. Nothing. We must have looked around for a half hour or more.

On the way back into town, Phil and I didn't say a word. I don't know about him, but I was still shaking. I guess we were both wondering what we were going to tell the police, our parents, and our friends.

But mostly, I guess we were still trying to figure out what to tell ourselves.

All that happened over three years ago.

I spent a semester at junior college, and then left town to go to school up north with Phil. I didn't come home very often, and neither did he. For us, not only Tri-Lakes had lost its innocence, but the whole town had as well. It had a shadow hanging over it, one that wouldn't go away for a long, long time. Maybe never.

And so far, I've never gotten over missing Rick. There's an ache inside because I know I'll never see him again. The dreams of his that will never be realized will always frustrate me.

This past week I've been home for Thanksgiving. It's been cool but sunny and dry, the perfect Thanksgiving weather as far as I'm concerned. Yesterday, we had a houseful of relatives and other guests. Some of them were here just for the day; others stayed on to visit a little longer. Most of them were content to stay stuffed and lounge around the house.

I'm not fond of big crowds, so by this morning I was ready to get out of the house for a while. There wasn't anyplace to go, really, so I just drove. North. And yes, I ended up at Tri-Lakes for the first time in more than three years.

It looked about the same. The leaves left on the trees were bright shades of yellow and orange and red, and the water reflected a vivid blue sky. Still lovely after the years. Unspoiled . . . even in late fall, it looked more alive than ever.

I was feeling a mixture of relief and apprehension as I parked in our old spot. When I stepped from the car, I noticed that the asphalt was starting to crack and crumble, with grass and weeds sprouting up across its surface. Then I walked toward the grove, holding my vest shut against the wind.

The biggest tree looked bigger than ever. I think I stared at it for a full minute or more before I saw what was bothering me about it.

There's a shape in the trunk, a few feet off the ground, a shape that bulges slightly from the main structure of the bark. Like so many optical illusions, you have to look hard to see it, but once you know it's there, you can't miss it. The shape has its own trunk, and two legs and two arms and a head. There's a slight indentation where the mouth would be, as if gaping in a scream.

382

I had an idea. I pulled out my pocket knife and used the thickest blade to dig into the bark, right where the left hand is. Just as I thought. You see, it takes plastic forever to decompose; there's nothing organic about it, like there is in flesh and bone and cotton clothes.

There, embedded in the bark, is a plastic splint.

Old Mrs Cartwright

Basil Copper

I

Old Mrs Cartwright hobbled down the path of the Zoological Gardens in the gathering dusk in a state of apprehension verging on panic. Her figure was grotesque, even pathetic in the twilight; her black, flapping clothing hanging round her body awkwardly, her shadow stencilled on to the dust of the white concrete path like one of those Gillray-style passe-partout silhouette pictures of her youth.

She regretted, even as she panted past the antelope enclosure, that she had ever promised her sister she would look after the boy for the day. Lionel didn't like her, that was the truth; there was always trouble when he was about. And the Zoological Gardens idea had been a mistake from the start. Mrs Cartwright had to admit to herself that she disliked the child even as much as he appeared to dislike her.

It was a terrible thing to say, even in the privacy of one's own thoughts, but there was the truth of it. Lionel was an odd child. His heavy-lidded, yellow eyes were more like an animal's than a human being and he had a disconcerting way of standing quite still and staring at her that she found unnerving; there was something of the animal too in his attitude, which he could keep up for minutes on end without seeming to tire. To be fair to the boy, most thirteen-year-olds had queer ways, old Mrs Cartwright had to admit, though her experience of children was limited.

Her own husband had been killed in the first World War and she had been left a young widow, like so many thousands of others. She had never married again. Her sister Sylvia was much younger than her, in fact something like eighteen years separated them, and her only child, Lionel, had been born late in life. Though Mrs Cartwright hadn't liked to mention this to her sister, Lionel's attitude towards his own mother seemed little better to her than the one he adopted to his aunt. But Sylvia didn't seem to notice; she doted on the boy, even though he was big for his age and quite grown-up in his attitude to adults.

There was something else old Mrs Cartwright felt to be peculiar to Lionel, but for the moment it eluded her. It was something she could never quite pinpoint, but it stemmed from the uncanny way Lionel had of appearing and disappearing suddenly, usually at the most awkward moments. He seemed to walk so lightly on the balls of his feet, that he could appear right beside a person with no audible indication of his presence. That too was unnatural, the old woman thought, as she slackened her pace for a moment and peered about her in the dusk.

Sometimes the boy would sit in a curious, hunched-up posture as though listening for something, and then his yellow eyes would glow and his immobile figure and tense, cat-like face would seem to contain such pent-up fury that old Mrs Cartwright felt almost afraid. It was ridiculous, she would tell herself, but even though she repeated this a hundred times, she was always left with the same conclusion. There was something queer about the child and all Sylvia's praising of Lionel's virtues could not erase this impression from her mind.

Lionel had been more difficult than ever today. Sylvia had gone up to see relatives in Mitcham and the boy must go to the Zoo. He had already been up twice with school parties this year, so the request was a surprising one to old Mrs Cartwright. But Sylvia merely laughed with that maddeningly obtuse attitude she had to what her sister called "situations" and had said it would do them both good. It had been a trying day. It had begun when Lionel had half-frightened to death another boy on the bus with something he had said or done. Whatever it was, the child had to be taken off by its parents, half-hysterical, and there was a nasty atmosphere for the rest of the journey.

The conductor kept giving Lionel dark looks and had muttered something to Mrs Cartwright about reporting the matter. And then when they got off there was a tremendous hullabaloo, with the conductor shouting that something had bit him. Everyone on the lower deck got up and hunted about for a dog and the conductor kept shouting and holding his leg. Old Mrs Cartwright had to admit there was a tear in his trousers and what looked like a nasty gash beneath. The conductor looked around for Lionel but the boy was nowhere to be seen. He rang the bell with ill grace and as the bus went up the hill Mrs Cartwright was left with the image of him binding up his leg with his handkerchief.

She retained a bad impression of the entire incident for the rest of the afternoon, an impression which was not improved by the spectacle of

384

Lionel hiding in a gateway until the bus had passed out of sight. His deep yellow eyes glowed with pleasure and he was smiling quietly to himself as they walked the rest of the way to the Zoo.

Once in the Zoo it had been an enervating atmosphere for the old lady. The day was hot and the paddocks and enclosures were crowded; Mrs Cartwright thought the monkeys with their red behinds were vulgar and disgusting and some of the manners of the visitors seemed little improvement on those of the animals. No, she said to herself, she was past enjoying these sort of places and in the company of such a boy the day was one in which enjoyment was hardly likely to figure.

She was getting old, she told herself; her heart was not what it was and the noise of the animals, the pressure of the crowds round the cages, and the heat had fatigued her greatly by early afternoon. But Lionel's interest in the animals was insatiable; it was his intention, no less, to see every single creature the Zoo contained, and he had mapped out an itinerary which would enable them to carry out this exhausting programme.

Old Mrs Cartwright was more than glad when lunch-time came; though the restaurant was crowded, the breeze from the fans, the pleasant view from the open window, the comfortable chair, the cheerfulness of the waitress and, above all, the scalding hot coffee with which they finished the salad and ice-cream meal, more than compensated for the tiresomeness of the morning and the presence of her nephew.

Lionel had been a little less trouble than usual. He ate his food with his usual unsmiling stolidity, answered his aunt's occasional comments in monosyllables and spent much time in consulting the elaborate chart of the Zoo enclosures he had drawn up. The only blot on the meal-time was the curious attitude of the waitress, who seemed to regard Lionel with considerable caution. Twice during the meal she asked if old Mrs Cartwright had brought a dog in with her and though she was assured that this was not so, she continued to look under the table whenever she passed, with a worried expression on her pale, oval face.

It was when she got up to pay the check that Mrs Cartwright heard the muffled clatter of dishes on the thick carpet; she found the waitress surrounded by a small crowd of diners. Her face was paler than ever and tears trembled on her eyelids.

"There was a dog under the table!" she said furiously.

She indicated her torn and laddered stocking; the skin of her leg was punctured and a thin trickle of blood ran down.

"It flew out when I was clearing away," she said, as someone helped her to a chair.

Mrs Cartwright paid her bill and went out with a strange feeling of foreboding. Lionel was nowhere about. Fortunately, he had already left the restaurant before the affair with the dog. Mrs Cartwright found him a moment or two later leaning up against the railings surrounding the bear-pit; she was glad that he had lost the sullen look. He was quite attractive when he smiled, though she did not much care for the way the edges of his mouth curled, which took away much of the attraction of the smile.

It was already getting late when old Mrs Cartwright and Lionel entered the Lion House. She hated big cats but the boy was fascinated by them and if there had been no regulation closing times in the Gardens, he might well have spent the night there. The house was half empty and the cats were quiet after having been fed. Old Mrs Cartwright sank on a bench with relief. With a little luck she could count on at least twenty minutes of freedom from anxiety and exertion. Lionel was already making a tour of the cages. A deep-throated roar throbbed through the Lion House and she heard with alarm a big body crash against the bars at the far end of the large Victorian structure. She was about to call out when the beast's roaring changed to deep purrs of contentment and she saw Lionel, his yellow eyes fixed on the lion's, as the two faced each other through the bars.

There were still several people in the Lion House and there was no further noise from the cages, so old Mrs Cartwright dozed off for a few minutes, mentally and physically exhausted by the exertions of the day. She slept longer than she intended and when she awoke saw with a start of alarm that it was already getting dark outside; the Lion House was quite deserted and the slanting red rays of the declining sun sent feeble beams through the oval windows. The yellow eyes of the cats blinked eerily at her from the dusk of the cages as she hurried past, and she thought once again uneasily of her nephew.

There was no sign of Lionel; and what was more the entire Gardens seemed to be deserted. Was it possible that they had already closed and her presence in the Lion House had somehow been overlooked? Mrs Cartwright plodded grimly on down the never-ending paths; leaves rustled in the light wind which had sprung up and strange animal noises, like the sounds of the jungle, came across the park on the night air.

Old Mrs Cartwright's heart was full of anger and irritation against the boy; it was just like Lionel to go off and leave her in this way. To tell the truth she hated most animals and the atmosphere of these nasty gardens at dusk was not at all to her taste. She had left her umbrella somewhere, her feet ached and on top of it all she could not seem to find her way out. She had been making for the northern entrance, but here she was once again back near the bear-pits.

She moved on down the paths, a forlorn figure, her black, old-fashioned coat flapping in the breeze. A deep, belling vibration sounded from ahead; it made a mournful echo in the carmine dusk of the vast gardens. The cougar called again, twice more, each time a rasping weight on old Mrs Cartwright's heart, and then was silent.

She could feel her breath hissing in her throat as she came out at the junction of four concrete paths she had not noticed before. She stepped to the left along a paddock in which antlered forms moved mysteriously in the warm darkness. She walked away, out into the middle of the path, calling Lionel anxiously by name.

There was no reply, only a brittle echo, and the rustling of great wings from the aviary beyond. A bird called solemnly from one of the houses and the slow chorus was taken up by a dozen others. Old Mrs Cartwright stood hesitant for a moment, wondering which path to take. The attenuated form of a crane was like a sinister pink question mark in the dusk.

Then she set off again, her pace slower now, tottering a little from the weight of the bag she carried, her heart thudding with frightening loudness.

She was passing along a narrow path fringed with bushes when she heard the rustling. At first she thought it came from the cages beyond, and increased her pace a little. But it seemed to keep in step with her, just beyond the bushes to the left hand side. Old Mrs Cartwright stopped and found that the noise had stopped also. She did not like this. The darkness had by now almost descended, there was no-one at all in the Zoological Gardens, and she still seemed no nearer to finding her way out.

Her heart beat like a great bell in her throat. The rustling began again.

"Lionel, is that you?" she called in a tremulous voice. "Be a good boy and don't play games."

But there came no answer, only the vibrating echo of her own faltering tones. The lion roared again, from a long way across the park, and this was followed by myriad other noises. The animals seemed restless and uneasy. Mrs Cartwright was glad they were in their cages; the cries were unnerving at this time of night.

The crackling in the bushes crept closer. She seemed unable to move. She could see the edges of the bushes quivering in the faint light that still came from the sky. She dropped the bag as something came at her throat out of the tunnel of boughs. Shriek after shriek left her and as life faded she was left with only the impression of the animal's burning yellow eyes.

II

The affair made a great scandal at the Zoo, whose authorities were, of course, aghast at any suggestion that one of their animals could have been responsible. A thorough check was made but every beast was accounted for and all the cages and enclosures were intact. The Medical Officer had a difficult passage explaining things to the Coroner when the time came.

Old Mrs Cartwright had died of a heart attack, of course. But not before her tongue had been torn out of her mouth. Shock and loss of blood had been contributory factors. But some wild beast had been responsible and there was talk of rats or other nocturnal creatures from the park outside the Zoo walls. Another curious feature to the doctor's mind was the flesh found beneath the dead woman's fingernails. Although covered with black hairs, it was definitely human.

Old Mrs Cartwright had been found only a hundred yards from one of the Zoo's main entrances where at least two of the keepers were still on duty. The boy Lionel had reported himself at the gate some while after. The doctor had felt it best not to distress the lad with his aunt's death and after taking Lionel's address had given him his bus fare home. Although Lionel's demeanour was normal and he told Doctor Swanson he had not been worried at being locked in after dark, the doctor had his own misgivings. His own private view was that the boy had been terrified. His face and forehead were covered with cuts and scratches, evidently caused by his hurried flight through the bushes. In fact the cuts were so bad that the doctor felt it necessary to give the boy treatment before sending him home.

Lionel's face was almost ecstatic and his yellow eyes glowed with pale fire as he let himself into the house with his own key.

"Did you have a nice time with Auntie, dear?" said his mother from her accustomed place in front of the television.

"Yes, Mummy," said Lionel. "I had a lovely day at the zoo."

The Overcoat

Steve Rasnic Tem

When I first saw the overcoat I thought it was a man slumped there, in the alley between Ellison's Deli and the Apex Pool Hall. A warmly dressed, elderly man, the collar and shoulders of the gray and black tweed coat pushed up over his neck and half-concealing his small, white head. The angle and the lighting had deceived me—the coat was neckless and headless. Yet it seemed to be propped up there, sitting in an unnatural way.

It was an elegant coat for all its age and wear. A subtle blending of black and gray weaves, with here and there a touch of white. The seams and shoulders had maintained their positions well. The buttons were large, black, old-fashioned; they appeared to be wooden, and each bore an ornate cross, like something from a crusader's armor, the crosses highlighted in silver in the dim morning light that spilled over the high walls of the alley. The lapels were wide, as were the shoulders; the coat would have come down to about mid-thigh if I had tried it on. All in all, it was the kind of garment I could really become attached to.

Actually, I had once had a coat very much like it, passed down to me from my father, who had worn it almost every day for the last years of his life. Even during the summers, much to my mother's annoyance.

But now I couldn't bring myself to touch it.

I never saw my father touch my mother. I never heard him say more than commonplaces to her. But he loved that coat. It kept him warm, however shabby he and it might have become together.

"A good coat is all a man needs, really," he'd say. "Hell, get a big coat, I always say, big a one as you can find. My daddy had one that'd sleep a family of four pretty comfortable." Then he'd horse-laugh. It was my father's favorite joke, and he repeated it often.

"A man's inners get soft and raw as he gets older." That was another of my father's theories. "A good coat protects 'em, keeps your guts from sloshing around, hanging all out if you know what I mean." I didn't, but it would have been foolish to say so. I used to wonder how my father came to be convinced of such craziness. That particular theory gave me nightmares. I'd dream of my father standing in the doorway all bundled up in his old coat. Then he opened it. Each time in the dream I'd want to believe he had brought home something from the butcher's—they just hadn't bothered to wrap it. But then the raw red and gray lumps started

389

to fall, and my father was screaming soundlessly, like a fish. There were bleeding horrors beneath that old coat.

My father died of consumption, but by that time he was eaten up by cancer and other nameless ills. Too much drinking, smoking and carousing, the doctor said. That and passing out in the street and having to sleep there all night. No help for someone like that, the doctor said. Just another drunk. Just another bum. No help for those kind. Nothing you could ever do for them would save them. Everything you did for them became a dangerous drain on your own life. They were determined to crap out on you.

I never got to say goodbye to my father. But I got his coat "for my protection." Just like it had protected my father. My mother said it was the only thing he ever wrote down by way of a will.

When I put that big old coat on I'd find myself unbuttoning it every few minutes to see what I looked like beneath it. Or I'd run a finger under the front of it, then check my finger.

I had my father's coat for a year before I met the tramp in the diner. He wore a baseball cap and a light-weight summer shirt, even though it was late fall. The cheap radio he carried—held closely to the ear because, he said, he'd lost the earphones, or they'd been stolen but he didn't want to accuse anyone—had British flag decals pasted all over it. "The British Invasion!" "The British Are Coming!" He was probably fifty years old, maybe fifty-five. His hair was extremely short and missing in spots, as if he'd had scabies that had had to be cut out.

He sat down across from me, our knees touching under the cracked formica table. "Nice coat," he said.

"Thank you." I felt incongruously formal. I noticed the liver spots like birthmarks on his hands.

"The British are coming," he said, pointing to his radio with a knowing look.

"I see." I smiled, feeling ridiculous.

"My name's Frank," he said. And smiled back.

"Steve," I said. And smiled again. But then his liver-spotted hand reached out and touched me under the table.

I reached down and removed his hand then, just as I had scolded my own father many times during his last years, when he'd been childish or mean with my mother. I held the tramp in my eyes. "You shouldn't do things like that, Frank. Someone else might have really hurt you bad for doing a thing like that."

Frank looked down, ashamed. "I'm sorry. I'm *bad* sometimes."

Again surprising myself, I reached over and touched his sleeve. "It's all right, Frank. Just be careful about that sort of thing."

He looked up at me, and then I knew he thought of himself as the consummate con-artist. And maybe some days he actually was. "I'm awfully cold. No place to go. Could I have that coat?"

Part con-artist and part child. I've never quite understood my actions that night. I gave him my father's coat. Maybe it would protect him, keep his raw "inners" safe. It was much too big for him. Walking away, he looked like a clown. He stuck the radio inside, and said out loud that it tickled, singing into his chest. I was cold walking home.

This coat propped up in the alley was very like that one. But I couldn't touch it, couldn't try it on.

The next day the coat was still there. The garbage around it had a slightly different arrangement, and for some reason that bothered me. Partially opened cans lay around the coat, but they certainly hadn't been touched by your standard electric can opener. They were bent lopsided, the tops twisted as if they'd been punched, crushed, chewed, the contents sucked out. I picked up a can; blood spotted the bent lid.

I stared at the coat. Blood dotted the cuff of the right sleeve. At least I was pretty sure it was blood. I was also pretty sure that it hadn't been there yesterday. In all my admiration for that overcoat, I would have noticed.

I looked at the bulges in the cloth about where a stomach and chest would be. They weren't very large, and about what you'd expect in a coat left bent that way, stiffened with age or filth, and beginning to lose some of its shape. There was a mild breeze in the alley, no doubt concentrated because of the high walls and the ever-so-slight slope of the building that dead-ended the alley. That, I was sure, was what made the bulges seem to stir, to breathe as I stared at them.

I turned to leave. I was feeling sad, and frightened, and something else not quite explainable.

Nor can I explain what I did next. I reached into my jacket pocket — I'd bought it at Sears, a short corduroy jacket with what I hoped was a reassuringly dull history — and pulled out the chocolate bar I was carrying there. I dropped it behind me, by the overcoat. Then I walked out of the alley without looking back. Perhaps I do too many things I can't explain.

I lived then in a poor, run-down section of the city, the kind of neighborhood I'd always gravitated to. Old tenements with architectural character crumbling to plasterdust in the corners, peeling off the walls. Plumbing and electricity working haphazardly in buildings not designed for them originally. Cheap, roomy apartments, and frequently someone passed out on the steps in front of the building, or on the hall steps inside. You stepped over them, or picked them up and carried them if you knew them a bit and they lived there. Dogs and derelicts would come in to relieve themselves, sometimes together. It made my few friends crazy, but none of it ever bothered me.

There was something about those people. Their needs were naked; there was little point hiding them. It made me wonder if I would become that way if I lost the little I had. A child again, with no need to pretend, asking without hesitation. Whether deserved or not, those people let you love them. They couldn't help letting you love them. In that regard they were quite different from my father. Maybe I could do something, and maybe my effort wasn't wasted. I wasn't a saint, but I carried them to their rooms. I wasn't even a very nice person at that time—I was much too full of myself—and yet I bought them meals, gave them rides in my car. I had no illusions—they didn't give a damn about me—but they let me love them.

The ones who actually lived in the streets, who had no homes nor even an occasional rented room, were nearly invisible most of the time. When the weather got cold—when you began seeing the large boxes erected over gratings, the sections of plywood and sheet metal and plastic dragged into dark backalleys, the spaces under the overpasses turned into rough-made caves—you realized how many of them there were. A city within the city seeking its own kind of shelter. It made you wonder where they had all come from, and I was convinced I didn't see most of them during the course of a normal day, even if we lived on the same block. I began to wonder if there might be some you never saw at all, who didn't want to be seen, ever, except by their own kind.

I wasn't a saint. And I wasn't their own kind, although sometimes I dreamed I was.

In ancient times, the unwanted were cast out to die from exposure, without modern miracle of the cardboard box or the plastic grocery bag.

Each day I left a few more groceries in the alley, an offering to the overcoat. Which altered itself slightly each day, lost more of its shape, as if it were shrinking from within. Starving itself no matter how much I fed it. Its lack of progress frustrated me. Malnutrition is a terrible thing; the coat's persistent ill health enraged me. I wasn't their kind, never would be. Each day the food I had left the day before had been ripped from its packages and devoured.

A pack of dogs could have done such a thing, but they would have disturbed the coat as well. And although the coat was collapsing a bit, it still retained its luster, and any movement of the overcoat was no more than that a body might make after being forced to sit in one place for too long a time.

❊ ❊ ❊

People screamed, hit each other, abused each other all the time. Sometimes in the streets, to a stranger, but most of the time it would be a couple, or someone and their kid, screaming and pounding and snapping and slapping right on the other side of that rotting panel of plaster, only a few feet from your nose. It was always a question of when to call the cops. Most of the time you didn't, else you'd be calling them ten times a night. Usually if there was a gun shot, or if the context of the screams indicated there might be a knife or club involved, then you called. Lots of people got badly hurt, but what were you supposed to do? Even the cops couldn't tell you when you should call. You shut your door and turned up the TV. Pretty soon it was just white noise. I wasn't a saint.

An old man sprawled on the sidewalk near the opening of the alley, sobbing and spitting up into a metal can, a crumpled bit of paper in his hand. He said somebody went and tore up his million dollar lottery ticket, now how was he going to get right?

The coat was quite sunken now, but still splendid, a beautiful piece of goods. I still secretly wanted to slip it under my arm, take it home and maybe even wear it, protect myself from the cold for a change. The jacket from Sears always seemed too thin for the city winds; the high buildings and narrow street-canyons resulted in a "wind tunnel" effect. I really needed a heavier, old-fashioned coat. But I was still afraid, wondering if the wrong person might see me, and if there was a wrong person to see me.

Some of the groceries from last time were untouched, unopened. I gazed at the coat, now looking slumped in defeat. It seemed much thinner than I remembered, more like an autumn jacket, as if some of the lining had been eaten out. What had I been thinking of? There was nothing here but an old coat, and groceries a fool had left for the dogs and cats and rats to rummage through. I kicked at one of the unmolested cans.

It thumped and clacked against pavement, a harsh metallic sound, coming to rest against one sleeve of the coat.

A long, wormlike finger, followed by something like an eye, webbed skin shrouding something unrecognizable, darted out and snagged the can. Sucked it back so quickly the sleeve looked empty again, like after an amputation.

The coat began to dance, a waltz and then a jitterbug.

There was the sound of metal warping, then a moist sound.

I don't understand why I didn't run then. But I'm not the only one who's ever missed a chance to escape.

More pale worm-ends shot out of sleeves, collar, and open waist, unrecognizable pink and gray flesh. In the flurry the can was ejected, empty.

And in the flurry I saw my father open his old, bloody coat, and his pink and gray entrails falling loose. Disease-ridden, worthless, and all because he was careless, irresponsible, depending on an old coat to protect him from everything. Dying and leaving us alone. Didn't even get to say goodbye. And then he leaves me that goddamned coat. As if that's what's going to protect me, keep me safe and sane as I grow older.

And now here's this thing, itself so much like a mass of diseased entrails, some new mutated breed of homeless derelict in the city. But it's no better than any of the rest of them. It pretends to be helpless, and then it rips cans apart. It lets me give it food, but gives me nothing in return, not even its improved health. There's no helping them. They'll drain you if you let them, and then they won't even let you say goodbye. They'll leave you a filthy old coat, good for nothing but to hide the disease, letting it eat you to raw hamburger if you don't open the coat and look in time.

I turned and left there. But slowly.

Somehow my neighbors knew a truce had been broken. Somehow they knew I was on to their manipulations.

During the next two weeks someone stole two books of checks out of my apartment. The police found the kids who did it; their father, a fellow tenant, had ordered them to climb over the transom. The police stopped me for urinating in public. I hadn't done it—a man was sick and I had turned my back on the street and gone over to the corner to see if I could help. He ran away. The police let me go with a warning. Someone drew a nail down the length of my car; someone else—or maybe it was the same person—slashed the left front tire. The hotel where I lived was noisy all the time; there were parties, fights, and party/fights late every night.

Someone groped me in the hall. Someone spat on me. Someone whispered endearments I couldn't begin to understand. Before, they had always let me love them. I had needed them to let me love them.

When I went back to the overcoat the material was nearly flat. Just in case, I had brought a loaf of bread and a can of peas. I scattered the slices of bread all around. Like leaves over a drunkard sleeping under a tree. There was no response. I threw the can into the middle of the black and gray folds. Nothing. I kicked at the beautiful overcoat.

The coat turned on its side. Something long, pink, and gray drifted out of one sleeve. It stirred ever so slightly.

I picked up a brick at the side of the alley and dropped it on the pink and gray thing. The coat spasmed, but only minutely. I picked up more bricks and dropped them over various parts of the coat. I emptied a barrel of trash and rolled the barrel up and down the length of the coat, pressing it flat. I did a silly dance on it. If I'd had a match I would have set the whole thing on fire, like a schoolboy dumb to evil with a stray cat.

I turned and left the alley. Again, I did not run.

I gave away all the things I didn't need. The other tenants were overly thankful. I gave away my food too, and some of my clothes, to the mission down the street. But no jackets, no coats.

When I moved back into my mother's house for the first time since my father had died, she was very happy to see me, but also very surprised.

My friends were pleased that I lived at last in a respectable place, but I think their sudden victory caught them unaware, and they didn't enjoy it as much for that.

Some people said I was a really good person to have helped the poor the way I did. I cut those people off rudely, sometimes saying the worst things I could think of to get them to leave me alone. I couldn't stand to hear anyone compliment me. "I was never one of them," I'd say sometimes. "Do I *look* like one of them? You can't do anything for people like that. I didn't even say goodbye."

And even more than before, I dream about an overcoat, opening slowly, like bat wings, showing off the bloody mysteries inside.

Playing for Keeps

Lawrence Watt-Evans

Carefully, Jason leaned out the open window and peered about. The moon was half full, providing him with plenty of light to see that the side lawn was smooth and empty, the hedge dark and unbroken. Nothing moved, nothing was out of place.

He pulled his head back in and listened for a moment. He heard nothing but crickets and his own breathing; his parents and his kid sister were, he was sure, sound asleep.

The coast was clear.

Cautiously, he climbed headfirst out the window onto the porch roof, then pulled himself down the sloping asphalt shingles on his belly. At the edge he reached down and grasped the corner pillar, then gradually worked his feet around, crab-fashion, until he was able to swing his left leg down onto a foothold in the gingerbread.

From there it was easy; he slid the other leg around and shinnied quickly down the pole to the railing, and dropped from there down behind the bushes.

The bushes rustled more than he liked, and he froze for a moment, staring out at the vacant lawn gleaming silver in the moonlight.

The way was still clear. He was out of the house, free to roam. He could slip down to the pond and catch himself a frog without his parents knowing a thing about it.

He gazed critically at the wide back yard, and decided that it was too open, too visible. He would find another route, rather than cutting straight across all that lawn.

The hedge that ran along the boundary with the MacPhersons' yard would provide cover. He could follow it to the back corner, then make a short dash to the trees, and from there to the pond it was all woods.

A dash across the side yard, the long creep down the hedge, another dash, and the woods. It would be easy. It would be fun, too, as if he were a soldier dodging bullets or something. He crept out from behind the bush, looked quickly to either side, and ran.

A dozen steps and he was across the lawn, diving for the shelter of the hedge's shadow. He landed on his knees and elbows with his nose inches from the leaves, leaves that looked dead black in the pale light.

He glanced back at the lawn just in time to see the shadow stretch out across the grass.

Horrified, he looked up.

A figure loomed over him, shadowy black, tall, taller than seemed possible, its head bloated and misshapen. He gaped up in surprise. He fought down the urge to cry or scream as a gaunt hand reached down toward him.

The hand grabbed him by the back of his collar and hauled him upright, then yanked him clean off his feet. He dangled helplessly.

"Guess what, kid," a deep, deep voice said, "I'm the boogey man."

He wanted to say something smart, something scathing, in reply to this terrifying stranger, but all he could manage was, "No, you're not; there isn't any boogey man."

Teeth glinted as his captor smiled. "Maybe you're right, boy; maybe I'm not. But I might as well be. Now, you must be Jason Price; why don't we go see what your parents think about you being out at this hour?" He casually lifted the struggling boy over the hedge and marched up toward the street, Jason still dangling from his hand.

From his altered angle Jason could see his foe more clearly; he was no longer a mass of empty shadow. The weird bloating of the head was really just a battered, wide-brimmed felt hat; the teeth were flat, human teeth, the eyes dark and smiling, the hands large, but just hands, with only five fingers apiece. He was just a man, whoever he was.

396

They reached the street and turned left, toward Jason's house, and Jason demanded, "Put me down; I'll walk from here."

"I don't think so," the other replied; he marched on.

"You're ruining my shirt," Jason complained.

His captor shrugged. "That's too bad."

He turned and marched up the front walk, strode smoothly up the porch steps, and with the boy still dangling from his right hand, rang the bell with his left.

There was a long moment's wait, and Jason heard banging and voices within. The porch light flashed on and his father opened the door, wearing his old bathrobe.

"What is it?" he asked, blinking.

"Mr. Price?" the self-proclaimed boogey man said, "I believe this belongs to you." He held Jason up to the light.

"Jason?" Price gaped, then remembered himself. "Oh, of course. Thank you, Mr. Crowley. Where'd you catch him?"

"Oh, I happened to be behind the hedge next door when he climbed down the porch."

"Oh. Well, thank you; put him down, I'll take care of him now."

"All right." Crowley lowered Jason roughly, not quite dropping him. "He's all yours for now, Mr. Price."

"Thank you, Mr. Crowley."

"Just remember," Crowley said with a broad smile, "the third time I keep him."

Price managed a feeble reflection of the other's grin. "Of course." He grabbed Jason's arm and hauled him into the house. "Good night, Mr. Crowley; thanks again."

Crowley tipped his hat and stood, smiling, as Price closed the door.

As soon as the latch clicked into place, Jason demanded, "Who's that guy? What was he doin' back there?"

"Never mind who that is, Jason; what the Hell were you doing outside at this hour?"

"Aw, Jesus, Dad, I just wanted to go down to the pond and catch some frogs when there wasn't anybody else around to scare 'em off!"

"Well, you'll have to find some better time to do it than the middle of the night! Don't you know it's dangerous running around in the dark? You could get arrested, or attacked. You're lucky it was Mr. Crowley who found you, and not some pervert!"

"How do you know *Crowley's* not a pervert?" Jason countered.

"Well, if you must know, he's the new security patrolman for the block; the Neighborhood Council hired him last month."

"So what business is it of his if I go catch frogs?"

"That's one of the things we're paying him for, to make sure you kids don't go running around at all hours, so we don't have teenagers screwing in the woods back there."

"What's that got to do with me? I'm only eleven!"

"And that's too damn young to be running around at two in the morning!" Price bellowed.

Jason sensed that he wasn't going to get anywhere by arguing his right to roam free at night. "I still think Crowley's a pervert!" he said, trying a different tack.

"We checked him out, boy, don't you think we didn't—and if he *is* a pervert, that's all the more reason for you to stay in at night the way you're supposed to, so he won't catch you again!"

Jason couldn't think of an answer to that; he shut up and stared at his father in silent defiance.

He wasn't actually punished, just sent back to bed. He watched his father close and lock the window, then stamp out and close the door. He sat in bed, thinking, and it was a long hour before he finally slid down and fell asleep.

The following night he stayed inside, but spent two hours crouched at the window, watching the yard, watching the MacPhersons' yard, studying every detail of the hedge in between, leaning over to stare at the woods far off to the right.

He saw no sign of Crowley, but he didn't risk climbing out; he had seen no sign of Crowley before he was caught, either.

The next day, at school, one of the kids mentioned "the boogey man," and Jason was surprised to hear that half a dozen of his friends knew about Crowley's presence. In fact, some knew considerably more than he did.

"He's six foot five, my dad says," Bill Jenkins told him. "Six foot five, and he weighs a hunnerd and sixty-five pounds, but he's strong enough to pick a kid up and carry him like he weighs nuthin'."

Jason nodded agreement. "He's strong, all right."

"He lives in the top floor apartment at that place on Elm, the one with that tower on the corner, and he sleeps all day and only comes out at night. He was like that anyway, that's why they hired him."

"Maybe there's something wrong with him, so he can't stand the sun," Sam Hessen suggested.

"Maybe he's really the boogey man, like he says," Jim Fairleigh said.

"There ain't any boogey man!" Jason said.

"How d'you know?" Jim countered.

"There just ain't," Jason insisted. "He's like Santa Claus or the Easter Bunny, something the grown-ups use to get kids to behave."

"Well, this Crowley guy sure is strange, whether he's the boogey man or not," Bill said. "He *tells* everybody he's the boogey man."

"I think he's a pervert," Jason said.

"Naw," Bill said. "They wouldn't hire a perv!"

"How would they know?"

"Well, he ain't never been arrested, I heard my dad tell my mom that. Clean record, he says."

"If he's really the boogey man they wouldn't have caught him," Jim pointed out.

"There ain't any boogey man," Jason insisted.

"Where'd they find him?" Sam asked.

"*I* don't know," Bill replied. Nobody else volunteered any more information.

Jason mulled it all over, and after he had given it sufficient thought, he announced to his friends, "I'm not gonna take it."

"What aren't you gonna take?" Sam asked.

"I'm not gonna take this Crowley character or any of his boogey man crap. It's a free country, ain't it? Who's he to tell me I can't take a walk in the middle of the night if I want?"

"He's just doin' what our parents want, that's all," Joe Kimball said. "I don't think it's his idea. I kinda think he likes kids, from what I seen; he's always makin' jokes and smilin', talkin' about how he'd like to keep 'em."

"Well, I'm not gonna take it," Jason insisted.

"Suit yourself," Bill said with a shrug, "but *I'm* not gonna argue with him."

The bell rang, putting an end to the conversation.

That night Jason watched out his window again, very carefully, starting the moment his bedroom door was closed. He saw no sign of Crowley anywhere. He waited and watched.

The moon was two-thirds full, the sky was clear, and Jason saw no sign of Crowley. He heard the crickets chirping, an occasional frog calling faintly to him from the pond.

Finally, at half past two, he slid out the window onto the porch roof and made his way to the ground.

From the bushes by the porch he stared critically at the hedge. That had been his mistake, he decided, going to the hedge. Crowley might be lurking there right now, and even if he weren't he could sneak along the other side and Jason wouldn't be able to spot him.

If he were to go straight across the back lawn, though, Crowley wouldn't have anywhere to hide, and Jason didn't think he was the sort who would chase a kid halfway across town. No, Jason told himself, Crowley was an ambusher; it went with the calm smiling style.

With that in mind, he slipped out from behind the bushes and headed straight back toward the trees, across the open expanse of lawn.

As he passed the back corner of the house something grabbed the back of his shirt, and he was snatched up into the air.

"Guess what, Jason," that deep voice said. "It's the boogey man, and I've got you again."

Jason was furious; how could he have been caught so easily? He thrashed, kicking, and tried to drive his elbow back into Crowley's chest.

Crowley did not bother with subtlety; his left hand flashed out as his right twisted, and his long bony fingers clamped around Jason's throat.

"Stop it, boy," he said.

Jason struggled for another few seconds, then stopped as his air supply ran out. The grip loosened.

"Listen to me, Jason," Crowley said. "I don't want any of this from you. I caught you where you had no business being, outside at this hour; now you behave yourself, or you'll get a lot worse than anything you've got from me yet."

The voice was flat and deadly, and Jason believed it completely. He put up no further resistance as the rest of the scene was acted out much as before. He was carried helplessly to his front porch, the doorbell brought his father, and Price and Crowley exchanged polite words, Crowley smiling all the time. He was then left in his father's custody.

This time he didn't talk back or argue; the memory of that grip on his throat was too fresh. He nodded quietly and went back to bed when his father had finished yelling.

The next day, however, the pain and fright had faded, and his indignation had begun to mount. How had Crowley dared to treat him like that? He was an innocent child, not some kind of axe-murderer trying to escape. His parents were paying their fake boogey man to protect them, not to manhandle their children. What if his larynx had collapsed? He'd seen that happen on a doctor show on TV, and the person had almost died, and they had had to cut her throat open and stick tubes in.

He told himself that he should have complained, should have said something to his father. Why hadn't he?

Well, he decided, it wasn't Dad's business; this was between him and Crowley. He'd handle it on his own. He was almost twelve now, old enough to take care of himself.

Besides, he wasn't sure that his father would believe him. A glance in the mirror showed no bruises or other marks on his neck.

He thought about it for the rest of the day, making plans, and that afternoon, while he was at Sam's house and Sam was in the bathroom, he snuck into Sam's older brother Al's room. He knew that Al had what he wanted; he'd seen him show it off once, and had seen where he put it afterward.

400

It was right where he had seen it before. He stuck it in his pocket and hurried back out of the room before he was caught.

That night it rained, and Jason stayed inside. He woke up briefly around three and glanced out the window, and thought he saw something tall and dark moving across the lawn. Before he could focus on it it was gone; he stared futilely for a few minutes, then went back to bed.

The rain lingered through the following day and night, but the day after that was sunny and warm, a lovely spring day.

Night arrived, and Jason watched television disinterestedly as he pretended to do his math homework. Finally, at ten-thirty, his mother turned off the set and shooed him upstairs.

He lay awake in bed waiting.

At one, he rose and dressed silently, then fished his stolen prize from its hiding place in his bureau drawer. With it safe in his pocket he crossed to the window and opened it.

The night air was cool and fresh, the singing of the crickets soothing, but Jason wasn't concerned with that. He stared out at the lawn, studied every foot of the hedge, peered at the back corner of the house.

He didn't see Crowley, but he had no doubt that the tall dark man was out there, waiting.

He hoped he was out there. He intended to show this Mr. Crowley that Jason Price wasn't just a rag doll you could throw around as you pleased.

He climbed out onto the porch roof, made his way to the ground, and without preamble marched boldly out across the lawn.

Crowley reared up from behind the hedge, his shadow falling across Jason so suddenly that the boy started. Jason's hand dove into his pocket.

Crowley stepped through the hedge with a hissing of branches against cloth, and strode purposefully toward Jason.

"Not this time, Mr. Boogey Man!" Jason said as he whipped out the switchblade and pressed the button.

Crowley didn't say a word; he just kept coming, one slow deliberate step at a time.

That wasn't in the plan; Jason had thought that Crowley would stop at the sight of the knife shining silver in the moonlight, would stand back frightened, and Jason had planned out a little speech, telling him that he couldn't bully Jason Price. But Crowley wasn't stopping.

He finally came to a halt one step away from Jason, staring down at the boy from the black shadows of his decrepit hat.

"Get away from me!" Jason said, brandishing the knife.

Crowley reached out with both hands, reached out and hooked his fingers into the front of Jason's shirt. He hooked his fingers into the

401

fabric and clenched them into fists, and started to pick Jason up off the ground.

"No!" Jason shouted; he stabbed wildly.

Crowley gave a little grunt as the knife was jammed into his belly, and the world froze for the two of them.

Jason stared in utter horror at his hand, at the short little slit he had cut in Crowley's flannel shirt, and at the gleaming steel blade that joined the two, the blade that was sunk three inches into Crowley's flesh.

He hadn't meant for this to happen. He had just committed murder. He had stabbed a human being, stuck a knife into a man.

All he had wanted to do was scare the man, the way the man had scared him. He hadn't meant to hurt anyone. He was a good boy, not a trouble-maker or a delinquent.

He was going to jail, and the other prisoners, the *real* murderers, would beat him and do whatever the terrible things were that men did to each other, and he might be stabbed himself, might feel the steel biting into him and his blood spilling out hot and red. He stared in fascinated revulsion at the knife, at the gleaming steel blade embedded in Mr. Crowley's belly.

He realized, at last, that the blade was clean. There was no blood.

The hands tightened on his shirt and yanked upward, and the moment of frozen time was broken and gone. The knife pulled out of the flesh, and still no blood flowed. Instead Jason smelled burning, hot and metallic, and saw a wisp of black smoke curling up. The tip of the switchblade was black where it had gone in.

His eyes moved up across Crowley's chest to his face, a face that was somehow changed from what it had been, as if a mask had come off. The tall figure grinned, and a dusky red glow showed between jagged teeth. His eyes gleamed dark green around slit pupils.

"Guess what, Jason," that deep and terrible voice said. "I really *am* the boogey man." The grin widened, the red glow brightened.

"And the third time, I keep you."

Proxy

John Metcalfe

I

He woke up from the dream, panting, dry-lipped, with miserable eyes. As yet he was but half awake, and his mind was still steeped in all the sweet entrancement of the night. He could see a face, vague now and shadowy, yet clear, too, through that glamorous haze of sleep with the terrible clearness of the remote and the illusory.

Before he woke he would try to work back to that place where he had met her, would try to snatch a few moments of queer, shimmering heaven from the hard and worthless day that threatened. Let him get her clear before him again in all the passionate intimacy of dream. Oh, if he could but do it!

It had not been so much her face that had bewitched him. Nothing so definite as a face, perhaps, could make one cry and cry in ecstasy of longing. It was some strange enchantment that vanished in the daylight and could not be recalled. Those dream moments pulsed with a desolating sweetness—poignant, heart-breaking, ineffable.

Yet let him get some poor idea of what she had been like, let him but see her just that once again!

So, feverishly, half awake, he battled, crying to see her just that once again.

A woman with the knowledge of good and evil, who understood him, looking at him calmly with deep, clear eyes. A broad forehead—he thought it serene and noble as a goddess's—and above it, golden-bronze wisps of hair that trembled in the breeze and light. They had kissed secretly, and some faint suggestion of sweet guilt and a smothered laugh breaking from her lips made a great, hot wave of passion overwhelm him. Something in her smiling, sun-browned face, with those curls of burnished bronze and the wet, alluring scarlet of the mouth, seemed half mocking, half compassionate. Dimly he seemed able to remember whole days of dalliance where she had been kind, viewing his mad desire with an easy tolerance, almost a maternal pity. It was not that he wanted! Anything but that!

He was more than half awake now, and the vision was slipping from him; quickly he became conscious of the details of the furniture of his bedroom, of the unwelcome light streaming in through the windows, of, yes, of someone knocking to rouse him. He sat up.

He dressed absent-mindedly, neglecting such things as the set of his tie and the grooming of his hair. Not that that was unusual. Failing any special stimulus, he was prone to avoid even very slight exertion; it was an ingrained habit now, bred perhaps of a morbid, energy-destroying introspection; perhaps, too, of a real monotony in his life.

People called him a slacker, and his doctor, who visited him once a week, seemed to find him interesting but contemptible. Brisk young men with forceful, clear-cut faces, very modern and very confident, saw worthlessness written all over him. Supersensitive, he felt their reproach, and, pitifully, acquiesced in it. He felt himself degenerate. Little things showed which way the mind blew—a general lassitude always enveloping him, premature baldness, and a disposition in his wrists to become suddenly damp and clammy when he walked uphill.

Now as he had his breakfast he answered his sister's remarks with more than his usual preoccupation. The exotic glamour of his dreams still held his mind and still he was thinking, thinking fixedly of the dim, twilight country of the night, and of the strangely smiling face that he had seen. It was, above all, the necessity of expression that tortured him. He was panting under the longing to conserve this experience that had come to him, to perform the first duty of the artistic soul.

Throughout the day it was the same. He used to spend his time partly in long and lonely walks, partly in his work of illustrating magazines. In this latter employment he had gained some considerable success, sufficient, indeed, with a patrimony of a hundred a year to keep his sister and himself quite comfortably in a cottage near the Downs. Now he was sitting, pencil in hand, striving to catch the elusive charm before it vanished.

His sister Amabel came in.

"How goes it, Claudie?" she asked brightly with a sympathetic glance at the bowed figure. He grunted.

"As usual. Here's the last hour's work." He made a motion towards the virgin sheets before him.

Often and often had she seen him sit like this, pursuing shadows, gazing sullenly at the wall or out of the window, with the paper white and blank upon the board. Then, indeed, he wrestled, but often to no purpose. Excusing him, she would remind herself that the effort of self-expression, when it is sincere, is the hardest, the most strenuous toil in which man can engage. When it is sincere!

They had tea together, and then Claude went alone for a walk along the Downs. Still the face haunted him. With the artist's instinct—or infirmity—he posed the woman of his dreams in the setting of the scenery around him. Just where he was walking, indeed, the view was none too romantic. He was ascending a path leading past an old fever hospital and the corporation waterworks to a stretch of waste land that gave place later to some private gallops, the property of the Lord of the Manor. He was deeply preoccupied, and hardly paid attention to the direction in which he was walking, yet his steps followed one another with the steady, sure succession of one pursuing a well-known course. When, presently, he came to a turning, he took the path to the right without a moment's hesitation.

Now the path became a rough, chalky track that wound gently aslant the sloping side of a rolling down. In the valley below was a sheepfold, tightly packed. Up from it, in the clear air of evening, rose the dreamy, multitudinous tinkle of the bells.

Presently the track ended in a cul-de-sac. The place where it disappeared was a somewhat evil locality, where rank bramble hemmed in a little depression in the down, and flies buzzed heavily about the lush grass. On a hot afternoon the air would be stifling as the breath of a laundry, and the land would seem to gasp, feverish and impure.

Claude paused and looked curiously about him. "Whatever did I come here for?" he was saying to himself, when, suddenly, something seemed to strike upon his brain. What was it? A momentary loosening of what had once been tense, an instantaneous resolution of what had been obscure. Something like a flash of strangely wakened memory. He turned aside and looked up the path in the direction from which he had come. The figure of the dream woman was becoming plainer in his mind. Yes. But how changed! He gasped. The evanescent glamour of dream had disappeared and left—a woman indeed, and pretty, but a woman with the coarse prettiness of a stained and cheapened soul. It might well have been one of the village girls, of whose debased loves this place was like as not the witness.

Again he gazed around him, and a feeling of nausea overcame him. The obscene little valley, full of gross suggestion, revolted him. He turned his back on it, and walked quickly up the path.

He soon gained the top of the down, and after a moment's hesitation decided to return home by the way he had come. The change from the still oppression of the valley to the fine, vigorous air of the hill was delightful. Striding rapidly along, he felt his whole being become cleansed and vivified, and an unaccustomed elation seemed for the instant to add spring and rhythm to his steps.

Coming back he was overtaken by his doctor, who came out of the gates of the fever hospital in his car. Claude accepted the little man's offer of a lift, and they were soon spinning smoothly and silently along.

"You're looking better to-day," said the doctor in a tone of brisk professionalism. "Exercise is the thing. I see you've been having some lately. Now you were really seedy the last time I gave you a lift down this way."

Claude made no reply. In the fading light he had the fleeting impression that the doctor was looking at him sideways from the corner of an alert and curious eye. As he got out of the car and said good-night he asked himself, "Now when did the little crank give me a lift before? — I half remember . . ."

II

That first night on which he saw the dream-woman and tried to make paper and pencil record something of her fascination hung for some time in his mind as an uneasy memory. Fresh air and exercise did something to lift him out of morbid introspection, but there were still bad times when cold baths and long tramps lost their saving power, and all the good work seemed to be undone.

In the evening an unhealthy exaltation would sometimes come upon him, and he would grow excited, flushed and feverish. Or in the morning, languorous, enervating visions would float luxuriously before him, and he would give himself up to them, half gladly, half ashamedly, as to some illicit joy. Strangely enough he connected these bad times with the haunting woman of his dreams.

It was about a fortnight later that he saw her again. He awoke in the morning with the same face, beautiful and mocking, set before him. There as he looked at it, it seemed to be steeped in pensive light, and the bronze gold of its clustering curls moved gently in the breeze. A peculiar sadness, almost a reproach, dwelt in the eyes. Once the lips moved, talking. . . .

Again Claude, wrestling and battling with himself, sat in his workroom after breakfast, striving to portray the face that haunted him. A poet would have sought to envisage the ineffable in verse, a composer might have agonised his passion into terms of sound, the artist was driven as surely to the one mode of expression that lay open.

This time he felt the task come easier. The face that had so baffled all his efforts at the first attempt now seemed a little less vague and impossible of transcription. Claude wondered whether this were due merely to a lessening of the ideal. He opened a drawer, and, taking from it his previous trials, compared them with what he had just drawn. Both were infinitely disappointing, yet of the two the later drawn was certainly the clearer.

A curious feeling came upon him, and a perplexed expression passed over his face. Turning his eyes away from the drawings he looked out of the window, his brows knit in mental effort. It was no doubt a passing fancy, but for a moment he could almost swear that the faces on the paper were somehow linked up with a forgotten previous experience. He had the baffling sense of strain and tension that sometimes accompanies a supreme attempt at recollection.

He turned to the drawing again, and, taking up his pencil, began somewhat idly to sketch new lines into the shadowy background. Once more he wondered why this face took such hold upon his imagination. He had seen it but twice or thrice in his dreams, yet even now, in a relatively calm and sober moment, his whole being thrilled in ecstasy before it. Dreamily he asked himself what it was in the flowing, somewhat sensuous lines of the face that appealed to him with such overwhelming power. It was a pity he was so dead tired that morning—with a little more energy he might have finished the thing, but he had risen as little refreshed as if he had not slept. Yes . . .

A peculiar thing was happening. As he was thus drowsily puzzling, his pencil was mechanically passing over the paper before him. Presently the preoccupied artist awoke from his reverie and looked down. A startled exclamation escaped him. The background which before had been vague and nebulous was now filled in with some clearness. What was more, it seemed strongly to suggest some place that he had seen. On the left sloping lines indicated a hillside, and beyond was the white, winding ribbon of a descending path.

Claude looked wonderingly at the drawing. He had heard of reporters who had taken down lengthy speeches verbatim whilst they themselves were talking or half asleep, but this was the first time he had had a like experience. It was even a little eerie. He was certain he knew this place that he had drawn. To be sure, a hillside slope with a winding path was no uncommon conjunction, but there was still the peculiar feeling of instant recognition to be accounted for. Now where had he seen this place before? He cast his mind back over the walks of the last week, but could find no satisfactory answer.

He tried then to get the face clear before him just as it had appeared to him in his dreams. One thing was immediately apparent—the *macabre* scenery of the drawing had attached itself to the face. The artist laughed. "This," he thought, "would interest the little doctor who's always psychology mad—" Then suddenly his laughter died away. A queer thought had come to him.

It presented itself something like this. What if this woman is something more than a mere dream, what if, somewhere back in my experience, I have actually met her, what if, in some place that I half remember, she is really living now?

The idea was startling. It took strong hold upon him, and he considered it carefully in all its bearings. He had, indeed, an undercurrent of sceptical thought, but the notion was so interesting that he would continue at least to play with it. All that morning he wondered over it, even going to the trouble, though smilingly, of looking through an old album of family photographs. At the end of his otherwise fruitless endeavours one thing at least appeared certain — somewhere he had really seen that hillside slope and the descending path.

III

When he was roused the next morning, he knew that he had had the dream again. He was dog tired, and his whole body ached from top to toe. The August morning light that filtered through the Venetian blinds seemed to his mind to discover frowse and a squalid disorder in his bedroom. His clothes were strewn riotously about the room, and, lying in different corners, were his boots, thickly stained with chalk. Petulantly he noticed, too, that he had left his door open, so that through it now ascended the sound of wakeful bustle in the kitchen. His throat was sore and parched and his temples throbbed.

That morning he could do no work. In the afternoon he went for his usual walk over the Downs, and once again upon the lonely hills he pondered the problem of the dream.

Half unconsciously he turned his steps in the direction of a western spur lying some two miles from the town. It was not one of his favourite walks, but he lacked energy for a climb into the lonelier and more beautiful uplands, and pursued indolently what for some reason proved to be the path of least resistance. Here the backs of mean cottages gave on to the sinuous track, and some miserable fowls scuttled before him, raising clouds of dust; farther on and to the right larger buildings threatened — an isolation hospital and the straddling ugliness of a waterworks.

Suddenly he remembered where he was. In a flash the sordid prospect about him became familiar. This was where he had walked two weeks or more ago, and straight before him waited the evil little valley. In another moment a further connection had made itself apparent — later on where the path dipped into the depression in the down the view was exactly that of his later dreams. In the sudden shock of discovery Claude found himself trembling with a strange excitement.

He went on, walking rapidly. It was still hot, and he mopped his face with his handkerchief. In his rear, following more slowly at a distance of several hundred yards, came slouching a farm hand, and at his heels a dog.

408

Claude soon reached the parting in the ways where the lower track skirted the sloping ground that rose to the upland gallops on the left. It was here that the country of his dreams was set; there he saw the sombre hillside and there the white path dipping downwards to the valley bottom. Without stopping he walked on quickly, and began with hurrying pulses to descend the track. Behind him, coming at more moderate pace, lurched the labourer and his dog.

Presently, on turning a sharpish bend, he saw below him the little hollow, pent in by the sides of the hill and circled by a coarse and ragged growth of bramble. With the sight there came a vision hanging in his eyes of something foul and violent. Something quick and furtive done hurriedly in an evil moment amid the crowding obscenities of twilight, something that had happened and he could half remember. A feeling of misgiving rose strong within him and a perspiration broke out on his face and round his wrists.

In the valley, partly covered by a tangle of gross plants, lay a rotting log, and behind it, screened by the rank weeds, and bordered by the rude hedge of brambles, stretched a ditch. Here the coarse vegetation was bruised and dashed, and the smell of trampled nettles still hung heavy in the air.

Sick with nameless fear, Claude stopped in front of the spot and looked, fascinated. Under the odorous litter of dying weed the ground seemed to be scraped together in a heap, and here and there in the soil about the log were long, curving marks such as might be made by writhing feet. A horrid suspicion gained possession of his mind; he hesitated, trembling, half inclined to leave the place before the entry of the oncoming labourer.

While he vacillated, the dog, now some little distance ahead of its master, came sniffing curiously along the ditch. In another moment it had reached the heap and stopped. Then, suddenly plunging down its head, the creature started scratching.

It had come! First a shoe and then a foot, and next the torn edges of a skirt appeared. Quickly now the animal in its excitement turned to the other end of the huddled mass, and dragged away a heap of crumpled weed that hid what lay beneath.

The afternoon sun, beating strongly down upon that evil scene, fell aslant the face of the labourer stricken into bucolic terror by what he saw. It shone too into the staring eyes of Claude, pale blue marbles that fixed themselves in horror upon the sight of violence. He, the poor, nerve-racked Multiple, was looking with all the curious, almost detached intentness of a struck mind at what he had half expected to see—the face of the victim of his loving and homicidal other self—the woman he had murdered in his dreams.

Drowsily the flies were buzzing.

The Rose of Knock

Alan Ryan

My job be keeping the dirt.

I've done it for years now, and my father done it afore me and his father afore him and so on and so on. It's good work, keeping the dirt, healthy and clean, you know, and outdoors. There's much to be said for outdoors work. Much indeed.

And good dirt it is too, and never mind what some be saying. They be making jokes about Mayo—"Mayo, God help us!" they be saying and laughing fit to burst—but Mayo is fine country, the best, God's own country, and the dirt be the finest in all Ireland. And it be my job to be keeping it. And so I does.

The best Mayo land of all, for my money, is the land hereabouts, all the lovely rolling hills round about the shrine at Knock. Oh, it's fine, it truly is, this land of ours. And well it might be, as if Our Lady and her suffering Son had planned it all that way from the beginning, as no doubt, come to think, they did. Me, I'd take it for a fact. No better place could Our Blessed Mother have come by for a visit than the hills of Knock, County Mayo, and the shrine sits today in the very place she touched.

And the flowers. I keeps the flowers too, of course, the roses, oh, the roses, and every other kind of flower a soul could be wanting. But the roses is best, full and strong, scented enough to make you dizzy, they are, and the color as rich as a strong man's blood. The thorns, of course, is wicked, and that's only as it should be. A thing as lovely and sacred as the roses has the right to be protecting itself, no argument about that. There's some that say it's the thorns as does it, pricking at prying, thieving fingers and drawing blood from them and so feeding the blood to the flowers and that's where they get their color. But, me, I'm keeping my own counsel on that one for now. All I does is keep the dirt, and my lips is sealed for the rest of it.

Well, the story I'm telling you is about the shrine itself, the shrine of Our Lady, and it starts at the time the Pope himself come for a visit. It

410

was a grand time, it was, that time, what with the crowds and the holidays and Himself up there on that big altar built special for the occasion. A fine Mass it was, and a fine talk he give, and everyone there said they'd never seen a finer. Of course, the ground took something of a beating and a wearing down, thousands of feet tramping all over the hills, but it was a fine time and it's not every day in the year that the Pope himself comes by for to say the Mass. When it was all said and done, and the Pope gone on from here to America, I got the dirt back into shape very smart, and there was no lack of willing hands to help with the work.

So the Pope says his Mass and moves on. But before he goes, he tells the local bigwigs and the priests at the shrine how much he loves the people of Ireland. And he gives over a token for all to remember him by and, don't you know, it's a rose, this lovely rose, full the size of our own here at Knock, and it's gold, or gold-covered or whatever the term they use. A golden rose, same as our own right here, right down to the wicked thorns and all. And so of course they be telling him how they'll treasure it and all of us in Knock and Mayo and how we'll be making a special place for to be showing it off proper the way it deserves. And so they done it, built this special little shrine sort-of thing, with a special glass case inside for the rose and hours posted when you could come inside to see it and the tour buses with the Americans is coming thick and fast ever since, I can tell you that for sure.

And the rose sits there, all shiny and grand behind the glass in its case, and a few years go by, the way they will, day in, day out, nothing much changing. And then along comes some thieving good-for-nothings and steals it, steals it right out of the shrine.

It hardly needs saying that the first thought everyone had was that it was the dirty Protestants from the north that done it. They'll steal anything, was the general thought, spoil anything, kill anything, and you'd best be locking your doors of a night and not be answering to strangers. Why, the rose'd be the perfect target, don't you see, for them to be stealing, who do they hate more than the Pope, and wasn't it the Pope himself that give us the rose! Many's the argument and the anger that foamed higher than the froth on a good-sized pint in the locals for weeks after the affair.

But it wasn't the Protestants that done it, though, truth to tell, I wouldn't put it past them. Oh, no. It weren't them at all.

I know.

I know who done it.

I seen them with my own two eyes when they first come to the shrine. I seen them when they was hanging about, looking things over, so to say, and planning out how they'd do it. And I seen them when they done it and, God knows, I seen them after.

411

They were two young fellows, nothing special to notice about them at all, and they come driving into the village one afternoon as easy as you please. There I am, working the dirt, as usual, by the side of the road just on the way into Knock and they bring the car over beside me and come to a stop. It's an old car, nothing much to be remembering about it, but I see that they've come onto the grass by the road, and the ground being still soft and wet from the morning's rain, them tires is going to be leaving terrible deep tracks in the dirt. But they're strangers and maybe don't know any better, so I says nothing and the two of them get out and come walking towards me.

They're pleasant-looking fellows, I'll give them that, and they're clean-shaven and dressed a cut above the average. They could be university fellows, I says to myself, not thinking much of anything. So I straighten up from the dirt where I'm working and lay the tools down and push back my cap and straighten my jacket and the two of them come on walking towards me.

"Morning," says the one.

By which I knew they weren't country boys and had been sleeping in late half the day.

"Afternoon," I says.

The two of them smiled, as nice as you please.

"Is this the road for Knock?" says the one that spoke before.

"You're in it," says I.

"Well, then," says the one that does the talking, only now he doesn't know what to be saying. The other one hangs back a little and keeps looking off across the field.

"Well, then," the talker says again. "Could you recommend a decent place for us to be staying the night? We've been driving all day and we're looking to rest now."

Which I knew already was not the truth, but of course I says nothing. So I told them to look in on Mrs. Boyle, in Church Street, who has rooms to let for bed-and-breakfast, nothing fancy but it's clean and quiet, and right across the way from her was Billy O'Mara's Greentree where they could get a pint and a bite to eat if they were minded. So they said they'd do it and thanked me very polite and still smiling and then turned and went back to the car and in a minute were on their way. I could see in the dirt where the tires had left tracks as deep as your hand and no hope of mending it.

There's roses all around the shrine, great bushes and trellises and the stone walls covered with them, and more flowers lining the pathways and usually, when the weather's fine, I end the day by tending to them. So there I am, coming on to dinnertime, looking over the roses and

412

improving them where they'd let a hand get at them through the thorns, and here's these same two fellows strolling in with the last few stragglers of the day to visit the shrine and see the golden rose from the Pope.

They never seen none of me that time for I didn't like the look of them, putting on airs with their clothes and their smiles, and sleeping half the day and speaking other than the truth, so I stayed hid behind the bushes and just watched them going in. They kept with the bunch they went in with, tourists and all, never separating nor drawing attention to themselves, and then come out the other door with the same group. Me, I'm still hid in the bushes, because now my curiosity's aroused.

Well, the two come out and start walking along the path back to the car park, but then they begin to drop back a little behind the others, who of course are the last ones, and me following along on the other side of the bushes where the roses keep me safe but I can see the two of them plain as day.

They're talking quiet to each other and laughing. Then the one I called the talker says something very clever and reaches out to the bushes to pluck a rose. He gets the rose all right, because he went at it pretty bold, but the rose got him too. That is to say, the thorns stuck him hard and made a good job of it.

"Christ!" he says and snatches his hand back quick, and if I was inclined to smile at the likes of them, I would have.

But the other is laughing his head off. The talker, he just keeps shaking his hand to kill the pain and then he sees the blood welling up from the fingers where the thorns went into him and he starts in to swearing all over again, which of course only made the other one laugh all the harder. They went on like that for a minute, then the talker flings the rose away on the ground and the two of them goes off, and the last I hear or see of them, the talker is saying, "Ah, stuff it, will ya?" and the other be laughing still.

Once they're gone, I come out from the bushes through a little space known to none but me and stand in the path. The two of them are gone and good riddance to them. The only sign of their coming is the rose torn from the bush and lying now in the path.

I picked it up and held it for a minute, thinking about the work of idle hands that destroy the good things of God's earth. But it was dinnertime already and I could feel the rumblings, so I went off quick and done what I had to do.

If anyone was watching, which no one was, they might have thought the thorns would get me too. But the plain fact is, the thorns have never touched me. Nor did they ever touch my father afore me. That's the way of it with the roses.

I took this one, which had a couple of branches still attached and a couple of buds that would never see the light of day now they were picked, and went around to the place I use behind the shrine. I dug a little shallow pit with my bare hands, never using tools when I have to do this so as to keep the dirt and roses pure, and lay the rose in it and covered it up and smoothed the place good. Burying the dead roses returns them quicker to the dirt. My father taught me that.

I always bury the roses.

And the thorns have never touched me.

I seen them later at the Greentree and Billy O'Mara himself putting their dinner in front of them. I kept to myself, just talking to the regulars, at the other end of the place, but sort of keeping an eye on the two of them. Still, there was nothing to see, of course, excepting the way the talker kept looking hard at Billy's girl, Noreen, who was bringing out food for some of the others. Now, it's a known fact that Billy's Noreen is not above flinging an eye at a stranger, but it's all in good fun, so to say, and no one really thinks nothing ill of it. But there was Billy himself carrying the food instead of her and I figured he must have sensed something irregular about these two or else he would have let Noreen do the carrying same as always. But they just eat their dinner, nothing fancy, and paid and left a few coins on the bar for Billy and went on their way.

Mostly I give it no thought after that for the rest of the evening, except of course to think about the rose.

Two days went by and I sees nor hide nor hair of them. It happened then that a little errand brought me round to Mrs. Boyle's and I stopped, as a body would, just to pay my respects and take a cup of tea and a slice of bread, and it turns out that the two stayed but the one night and paid up fair and square and went on their way in the morning after breakfast and not a bit of the silverware missing.

It was a week later when they come back.

This time, though, it's not by daylight they come, but in the dark of night. It was only the purest happanstance that I was there to see them at it, as if it were the will of God, though of course it made no difference, me not being one to take on two young fellows by myself, not being as dumb as all that. But it did happen that I'd left a pair of gloves outside, near the roses, when I was working at the end of the day, and then forgot them when a call of nature summoned me off. Later, in the Greentree, I remembered them and, since it was a fine clear night, with the moon shining bright on the hills, I thought to take a stroll, easy like and peaceful, back out to the shrine and retrieve the gloves or they'd be spoiled with the damp from the night. And the long and the short is, I'm making my way along the row of rosebushes toward the rear of the holy

414

shrine itself, and there right ahead of me I hear the voices whispering in the night and of course I know it's them and of course I know what they're after.

Well, I creep up very quiet as close as I can get, with only the roses betwixt me and them, and of course they're planning what I thought. Tools they have, I see, but so cocksure are they of getting away with it easy that they haven't even bothered themselves with masks. It's them, the same two, no mistaking it, and not a bit surprised I am, neither.

Then the next thing I know, they're working on the lock of the door. They must have already disconnected the alarms before I got there, because nary a sound is there to hear except a little scraping of metal and tools at the lock and the rustling of the roses before me. So upset I was, I could have sworn I heard the thorns almost rubbing and clicking together with anguish.

And then they're inside, the thieves, and the door closed tight behind them.

So I wait, crouching behind the rosebushes and listening to the queer little sounds of the night and the shifting of the branches and the leaves. There was nothing for it. If they were set on stealing the Pope's golden rose, then steal it they would and be damned. So I waited right there, feeling the dampness seeping into my bones but waiting it out till the end.

And finally they come out and I see the one, the talker, smiling in the moonlight and the other, looking more solemn and serious, following close behind on his heels, like he was wanting to start running but hadn't got up the nerve in front of his friend. The talker has the rose in his hand, so they must have broken or cut the glass of the case to get it out and now they're on their way, just as easy as you please. Almost on their way, that is, for they haven't got off yet with their little prize. I can see it, shining in the moonlight, that golden rose come all the way from Rome, Italy, and the Pope's own gift to Knock. There it is, shining and glowing like a thing alive, looking almost to tremble with anger in the thieving hand that held it. And of course, it wasn't enough to be stealing it, no, they has to stand there in the moonlight and be gloating over it, proud like and pleased with themselves and holding the thing up and looking at it all around. Even the nervous one was getting into the spirit of the thing and starting in to smile just a bit around the edges, like now he thought maybe they had actually pulled it off and were getting away with it after all.

But it almost hardly needs saying, that was not to be.

So finally they're done looking at the rose and congratulating themselves with their wit and cleverness. The talker, the one that's holding it, goes to stick it inside his coat and the thorns on the thing cut into him and he yelps like a dog with its tail trod on and drops it in the path. He stands there cursing and nursing at his hand and sucking at the blood on his finger and the other one, the jumpy one, is looking every which way up and down and not knowing what to do. It takes them a minute or two to sort themselves out, with the rose lying there on the ground between them and the both of them leery to touch it. Then the talker bends over and picks it up by the bottom of the stem, very gingerly like, and holds it just with the tips of his fingers, and they start off.

But they're spooked now, see, and eager to be off the pathways, which is, for one thing, lighted up bright by the moon and for another walled in by the rosebushes.

"Here," says the second one all of a sudden and heads towards where I'm crouching, for he thinks he sees an opening, which indeed he does, through the bushes to the other side, desperation being good for the eyesight.

It'll come as no surprise that, the very instant he puts out a cautious arm to widen the opening just enough to slip through, he stumbles on a branch or a root or maybe just on his own fear and worry and lurches backwards and tumbles right into the other fellow, who swears all over again as the rose he's carrying catches at his hand and draws blood anew and then he stumbles forward into the other fellow and it's a pure circus to see the two of them thrashing and crashing about in the rosebushes with the thorns snatching and tearing at their clothes and their faces and hands. It could have played on any music hall stage in the civilized world and brought down the house every time.

Me, I never said nary a word, just waited till it was over, and over I knew it soon would be.

You'd scarce think it could happen, but I've seen it once or twice before this, and my father and grandfather seen it too in their times and I know it myself for a fact. There was the two of them, lying still at last, and the branches of the rosebushes wrapped tight around them, all about their arms which was pinned to their sides and about their throats which was dark with blood and about their faces which was darker. Them thorns was sticking right into them, like they was meaning to burrow inside if they could, buried deep as a sturdy nail in a slab of wood.

I let them lie there for a bit, all tangled in the bushes, giving them time to let the thorns drink deep, as you might say, and slake the thirst that was on them. They don't drink often but they drink full deep when they do. And the dirt, of course, my own precious dirt, was getting its own too, just sopping up what was spilled.

When I thought it was near enough time, and it's a thing to be patient about too, I went off to the place behind the shrine and started in digging. It was a hard job I had of it, what with using my bare hands to get a hole big enough, and it took the wind out of me, I can say that. But it wasn't as hard as you might think, neither, for the earth, rich and thick as it is, come away fair easy for all that. Eager and willing, you might almost say.

When I had the hole dug deep enough, back I went to the bushes and began extricating the two fellows from where they lay tangled. They might have wished for the same ease with the bushes as I had, for the flowers brushed soft against my hands and the scent was rich and sweet in my nose and the thorns, not a one of them, ever touched my skin, no more than they might have touched my father's. All in all, I made a fast job of it and had them out of there quick and dragged them in, the earth not being particular about gracefulness and all such under the circumstances, and scooping the dirt back on top of them, which likewise went real easy and natural and lay flat like it had been to start with.

And of course the rose of Knock lay with them, buried in the earth to return all the quicker to the dirt. It's where it belongs, seeing as how it was picked, so to put it, at least for a while, until it renews itself and grows again and is ready to return, like the other roses of Knock and hereabouts.

That's the way of it. What's taken from the earth goes back to the earth, at least for a time. The roses have their way and their rights and likewise too the dirt itself, and even the thorns, and wasn't it thorns, remember, that drew the blood of Christ Himself. They protect their own, they do, keep themselves whole and safe and in the end they come back even stronger.

One day, when enough time has gone by, I'll dig around among the bones of those thieving fellows and take out the golden rose and put it back in the shrine, and I have no doubt it'll be taken for a miracle. That's none of my concern, though. It's just God's simple work I be doing here and not for me to question: tending the roses, feeding the thorns, keeping the dirt.

Sandprint

Norman Partridge

Ben Winslow couldn't understand how someone who didn't exist could have accumulated so much junk.

Irene Benjamin's possessions were piled in little islands on the sea-blue carpet. Book awards, reviews, first editions, and yes—Ben forced a smile—even rejection slips.

Ben chugged rum from a heavy tumbler. He thumbed through a stack of rejections, glancing at the coldly rational notes his wife had written on each. Irene had always handled the rejections, always protected his ego. And now, without Irene and Irene Benjamin, without both of them . . .

"I'm lost," Ben whispered.

Ben tossed the rejections into a cardboard box and finished his drink. Outside, waves surged against the beach. A muggy wind whipped through the doorway, rustling the paper islands. Kona wind, heavy with the perfume of the night, heavy with the threat of a storm.

Ben leaned against the sliding-glass door and listened to the sea whisper over the sand. In California, wet sand was like concrete, the waves like thunderous slaps. But here in Hawaii the sand was soft, forgiving . . .

Somewhere in the past, Irene Kaneholani had taught him about the sand. "Ben, this scene with the sailor and the ghost is great, but the description of Infinity Beach is all wrong," she had insisted. "The sand there isn't gray, like this gritty California stuff. It's golden, Ben, *golden* and *soft*."

"Give me a break," he'd protested. "I'm a starving college student. I've never traveled, except via bad Elvis Presley movies. Why'd I let you pick Hawaii, anyway? I can't write about things I—"

"—don't know." Irene giggled. "C'mon, Ben, that's why we're working together. Two heads *are* better than one. And when we hit the best-seller list with this little opus we'll quit Berkeley and move to Kauai. I've had my eye on the perfect spot for the ultimate beach house ever since I was a little girl. We'll have lots of golden children, I'll get fat, and before you know it you'll be a regular *kamaaina* . . ."

Smiling, Ben had eyed the battered typewriter and shrugged.

She'd kissed him then. "Okay. Now that I've lifted your big bad depression, you're gonna suffer for that Elvis Presley crack."

Ben closed the glass door and thumbed the lock. The Elvis record she'd tortured him with so long ago sat on the turntable. How many times had he listened to it in the last month? Had he listened to anything else?

Ben cued the needle onto worn vinyl. Elvis sang. *"Night and you . . . and blue Hawaii . . ."*

Ben walked to the kitchen and poured himself another rum. The plastic bottle slipped from his fingers, bounced once, and rolled toward the living room, sloshing golden liquor over blue tile. Then the bottle reversed direction and returned to him.

"Ghosts," he whispered.

No. Not in the real world.

In the real world, it's like this: if you build a house on stilts, in sand, there's simply no way that it will stay perfectly level, even if it's the ultimate beach house that you've been dreaming about since you were a kid. At least that's what Ben had told Irene. But Irene Kaneholani hadn't liked his explanation. She'd wanted Irene Benjamin's home to be perfect.

"She's real, Ben. She's us."

"Irene, you're getting weird about this. Irene Benjamin isn't real. She's just a publisher's gimmick, someone the editors invented to appeal to the romance fans."

"No, Ben. She's much more than that."

The idea seemed ridiculous to Ben, but he couldn't say that. He couldn't tell Irene that he was truly worried about her, about *them*. He couldn't say, *When you put on those fancy suits, those silk blouses, I wonder what happened to that college girl who used to live in one pair of jeans. These days you buy shoes so expensive that they'd make Imelda Marcos blush, and the salesgirls at Liberty House positively salivate when you visit the perfume counter. And when you put on those clothes and spray yourself with those scents, it's like you're a different person, like you're not the girl I fell in love with anymore.*

No. He couldn't say that. He couldn't hurt her that way. So he tried to make light of it. "It's a con, honey. Irene Benjamin—psychic chronicler of ghostly romance. It's just a name that looks good on glossy book jackets." He grinned. "There's a reason they didn't put our names together and come up with Winslow Kaneholani, you know."

Laughter. The last laughter heard in Irene Benjamin's house.

Ben drank. It wasn't right that he wouldn't hear his wife's laughter anymore.

"Night and you . . . night and you . . . and blue . . ."

It wasn't fair.

Drink in hand, Ben entered the bedroom. On the hibiscus-print spread were three boxes addressed to Irene's family on Maui. Mostly fancy clothes and perfumes, stuff Irene's sisters would want.

Ben knifed open the middle box, telling himself, "Just one more look."

He dug through a layer of silk blouses, past a bag filled with turquoise jewelry, and found a pancake-sized hunk of plaster stamped with a child's hand-print. Irene's Hawaiian name was printed underneath. *AILINA* .

The plaster was cold. Ben traced the tiny lifeline, ran his fingers over the name.

Irene, Ailina, and Irene. All of them gone.

It wasn't fair.

It had been a mistake. The moonlight swim. The Kona wind. The wave that took them away and never returned. The wave that left him behind.

"Night and you . . . night and you . . . night and you . . ."

Ben gripped the plaster hand-print. Ailina had been real, as real as Irene Kaneholani.

Maybe, in her own way, Irene Benjamin had been real, too.

Everything was on the beach.

A receding wave foamed around the first box, tugging it into the surf. Ben grabbed a book award, wound up like a discus thrower, and sent the bronze plate flying into the night.

"You took them all," he shouted. "You took too much. You owe me."

A warm wave surged around his ankles; soft sand tickled his feet as the water receded. Boxes and manuscripts drifted out to sea like toy boats; Ben threw a dry, dusty protea arrangement after them and shouted a hearty *bon voyage.*

Ben tumbled another box and threw clothes, perfume bottles, and jewelry into the sea. Everything had to go. Only then would the sea understand that when it took Ben's love, it took three people. It wasn't right, taking all of them, and leaving him with nothing at all.

Sweaty and exhilarated, Ben reached for more.

In the sand, next to the empty box, he found the plaster hand-print.

Ailina. The sea seemed to whisper the name. Ben shuddered, gripping the plaster disc tightly, his big fingers overflowing the tiny furrows made by a child's fingers so long ago, and suddenly he saw Ailina for the first time, a poor girl who dreamed of wearing elegant clothes and perfumes that were advertised in slick magazines. A sweet, serious little girl who dreamed of living in the ultimate beach house on a perfect piece of land in Hawaii. He saw that little girl, and he remembered how hard she'd worked for her dreams as she grew older, and he remembered all the struggles he'd shared with her.

Ben and his wife. The two of them. And Irene Benjamin, and Ailina. The four of them.

Berkeley. Rejects. Agents. Publishers. Together, they'd shared it all, along with the eventual success. In some ways, for both of them, for all four of them, success had been the greatest struggle of all.

The clothes, the perfumes, the jewelry . . . even the beach house. They were her things, after all. They belonged to a child named Ailina, and to a woman named Irene Kaneholani. They belonged to Irene Benjamin, as well.

And to a man named Benjamin Winslow.

He remembered his wife's words *(She's real, Ben. She's us.)*, and now he understood them.

Not three, not even four, but one.

And, realizing that for the first time, one was more than Ben Winslow could stand to lose.

A wave crashed behind him. He whirled. Warm water closed around his legs—pushing, then pulling, pulling—drawing him off balance. A protea stem scratched his ankle. Wet clothes slithered across the slick sand like heavy slugs. Perfume bottles bobbed in the surf. Ben splashed after them. He caught them up and wrapped them in a cotton dress, smelling a dozen scents that spoke his wife's name.

He recovered what he could. Then, exhausted, he dumped his bundle at water's edge.

A spent wave lapped at his ankles, and he stepped on something hard—the plaster hand-print, half buried in the wet sand. Gingerly, he pulled it up, saw the tiny golden hand printed in the sand, the name printed backward beneath it.

Ben's fingers slipped between the soft, sandy fingers. Interlocked.

"Ailina."

The Kona wind rippled over the waves. Muggy breath warmed Ben's neck.

Between his fingers, the sand grew warm.

Wriggled.

Ben's lips brushed the sand and found her golden lips waiting there, open to his kiss. And then there was only the soft, warm sand, and the Kona wind, and the wave closing over them.

Seasons of Belief

Michael Bishop

In the dead of winter, in a high-ceilinged room in a drafty, many-gabled house, a family had gathered to pass the twilight hour after supper. Father was reading a book, Mother was busy with thimble and needle at her quilting frame, and the children were stretched out in front of the room's copper-colored space heater with their crayons and several big yellow-gray sheets of newsprint.

It was not long before their bedtime. The silence in the room had grown as thick and muffling as the coverlets of snow on the house's gables and windowsills. In everyone's mind was the half-formed thought that the first word spoken into this stillness would seem as loud and unexpected as a Fourth of July firecracker.

In everyone's mind, that is, except Stefa's. Stefa was five. She had suddenly grown tired of drawing trees across her paper and of worrying about explaining to everyone else what her fine, treelike trees were *really* supposed to be. Father would mistake them for people, Mother for tornadoes or big green bananas, and Jimbo, willfully, for scribbles. Stefa was also tired of sharing the crayons, even though the box contained at least a hundred of them. Only a few were good honest colors like red, yellow, blue, green, and orange. All the rest were impostors like burnt sienna, aquamarine, raw umber, goldenrod, or colors equally shady; and what, exactly, were they *good* for?

Stefa threw her good honest green crayon on the floor and watched it roll under the space heater. "Tell us a story," she demanded.

Her brother, Jimbo, who was seven, jumped as if a Fourth of July firecracker had just exploded. But after looking disapprovingly at Stefa, he turned to his parents and repeated his sister's request: "Yes, tell us a story. We're tired of drawing."

"Your turn," said Mother, looking directly at her husband. "Last night I told them about rollerskating to the circus."

The children hurried across the room and crumpled the pages of Father's book climbing into his lap. When they were finally settled on either side of him in the big green chair, Stefa said:

"A scary story, please."

"All right," Father told them, finally adjusted to their presence. "This is a story about the grither—because Stefa wants a scary story."

"What's a grither?" Jimbo asked.

"A grither is a creature," began the children's father, "who lives in the wreck of an ancient packet ship in the ice floes of the Arctic Circle. There is only one grither in the entire world, and each time he hears his name spoken aloud by any member of the human population, he sets off to find that impertinent person and make sure that he never says his name again. He has very, very good ears, the grither does, and he cannot tolerate being the object of anyone's gossip."

"Don't tell *this* story," Stefa cautioned her father, "I don't want you to tell it."

Mother looked up from her quilting frame. "It may be too late to stop him, Stefa. Your father has already mentioned the grither's name, and the creature is probably on his way to our house right this very moment."

"He's only just started," the father said. "It'll take him a while to get here, of course, and if I'm careful to keep this story short, the grither may not be able to reach our house before I've finished. He depends on hearing his name several times to get to where he needs to go."

"Don't tell it," Stefa pleaded, hoping that her father would go on to the last possible moment before their safety was irrevocably compromised and the grither sprang into the room to devour them.

"Do you know why the grither is called a grither?" Father asked, looking first at Stefa and then at Jimbo.

"Why?" the children asked together.

"Because the grither has fists as big as basketballs and arms as long as boa constrictors. When he finally locates the human busybodies who have been tossing his lovely name around, he opens up his fists, reaches out his arms, and—*grithers 'em in!* Just like that, Stefa and Jimbo, just as if he were hugging his cousins at a family reunion—he *grithers 'em in!*"

Jimbo and Stefa shuddered and pressed themselves more tightly against their father.

"Is the grither a bigfoot?" the boy asked.

"No," Father responded. "The grither isn't a bigfoot, or an abominable snowman, or any of those other doubtful monsters that people sometimes think they've seen. The grither has never been seen by *anyone*—except, of course, by the people whom he grithers in and gobbles up. And those unfortunate folks are no longer around to tell us what he looks like."

"What does he look like?" asked Jimbo.

"Well, besides his basketball fists and boa-constrictor arms, the grither has a body as tall and supple as a poplar tree. You can see right through him, though, as if he were made of melting, colorless gelatin. He looks a little bit like a plastic road map because inside his legs and arms and chest and face you can see the tiny red and blue veins that twist through his body and help to hold him together. The blue's for fear, the red's for rage, and these feelings, flowing through his veins, help to keep him warm, too. As you may imagine, it's very chilly in the hold of a packet ship stuck in the pack ice—much chillier, my children, than it ever gets here."

"Then why doesn't he leave?" Stefa objected.

"He does," Father said. "Every time he hears anyone speaking his name aloud. When I first started telling this story, the grither snaked his way out of that shipwrecked vessel's hold, slithered over the gunwales, and began loping across the blue-white Arctic deserts toward the sound of our voices. He doesn't like gossip, as I've already told you, but he's always glad for the chance to go somewhere to stifle it. He's coming now. Listen."

"No!" shrieked Stefa, covering her ears and shutting her eyes. But even so she could hear the sighing of the wind in the naked oaks—a sound as sinister as a siren at midnight.

"Where is he now?" Jimbo asked. The boy peered at the room's solitary, icy window, sneaked a look at the door, and glanced suspiciously at the innocent ceiling.

"That's hard to say," Father replied. "But as he comes to get whoever's gossiping about him, he always sings this song." And, narrowing his eyes and doing something strange to his voice, Father showed them how the song was sung:

> *I am the grither, gruesome and hungry.*
> *Here I come, folks,*
> *All the while grimacing.*
> *You cannot escape me—it's simply impossible.*
> *Don't even try.*
> *I am the grither, crude and most grum.*
> *Pleading is useless.*
> *So are your prayers—also your rabbit's feet.*
> *The grither is greedy*
> *For only one thing:*
> *To silence your gossip, folks.*
> *That's why this song says*
> *Your moments are numbered.*
> *I'm quite sorry for you.*
> *I'm quite sorry for you.*
> *So please do accept*
> *My most heartfelt apologies.*

Scandalized, Stefa protested, "That doesn't even *rhyme*! There aren't no sound-alikes!"

424

" 'Any,' " Mother interjected.

"There aren't *any* sound-alikes," Stefa corrected herself.

"That's true," Father admitted. "And the grither doesn't sing very well, either."

"But where is he now?" Jimbo asked.

Father tilted his head and listened to the sound of the grither's song as it was apparently borne to him on the sighing winter wind. "Maine," he said. "The grither's in Maine—but he's heading relentlessly south and taking all the shortcuts he knows."

"Stop!" cried Stefa. "Don't tell any more!"

"It's cheating," said Father, "if you don't finish the story. You just have to be sure to finish it before the grither arrives—that's the main thing. Now that the grither's on his way, it would be terribly unfair to leave him stranded in Bangor. He doesn't like short trips, you know."

"It isn't fair to the people in Maine, either," Mother pointed out. "He's always traipsing back and forth through their state, and we can't allow that revengeful critter to impose on their hospitality any more than he already manages to."

"No, we can't," Father agreed.

"Well, then," said Stefa impatiently, "please hurry up and finish telling the story."

"Yes," said Jimbo. "Maybe you can leave him stranded in New Jersey or Virginia. Virginia's a pretty state."

"That's an idea," said Father, contemplating this notion. "All right, then. I'll go on with my story. You may be wondering where the grither came from in the first place. Well, the fact is—"

Just then the telephone—which hung from a wall in the kitchen, right next to the pantry door—began to ring. Stefa thought that the burring noise it emitted was exactly the sort of sound you could expect a statue in the park to make, if only statues could come alive in the cold to shiver and suffer.

"Would you mind getting that?" Mother asked Father. "I've almost finished quilting this square."

"Oh no!" cried Jimbo and Stefa in unison.

Father shrugged amiably, eased himself out of the big green chair, and disappeared into the kitchen to make the phone stop ringing. He caught it on the sixth or seventh burr.

Stefa and Jimbo, with a warm dent between them in the cushion, looked at each other and made worried faces. They lived in the South, but not *that* far south, and the grither was descending upon them like a ravenous avalanche. Stefa could not understand her parents' lack of concern—they were usually very sensible people.

"Where is he now?" she moaned. "Where is he now?"

425

"Boston, maybe," Mother said, without looking up from the quilting frame. "Or Philadelphia, if he's flying."

"Flying?" said Jimbo. "How?"

"Well," said Mother, briefly pursing her lips as she forced the needle through two layers of cloth and the cotton batting between them, "the grither's ears—which are invisibly small to start with—get bigger and bigger each time his name is spoken. By the time it's been spoken ten or twelve times, they're big enough to carry him wherever he's going; a pair of miraculous, transparent wings." Mother took off her thimble, kissed her thumb, and tugged thoughtfully at her ear lobe. "I'd imagine our grither's over Philadelphia, or maybe Baltimore, by now. He ought to have an extremely nice pair of ear-wings—we've been gossiping about him for quite some time."

"Daddy!" Stefa screamed at the kitchen. *Daddy!*

Father came strolling back into the living room with his hands in his pockets. "Here I am," he said. He sat down between the children.

"Hurry," Stefa advised him. "Finish telling the story."

"Who was that?" Mother asked, nodding her head toward the kitchen and the telephone.

"I don't know," Father responded mysteriously. (Stefa was not sure if he had winked at Mother or not.) "Someone who knows who we are and who wondered if we were home. I said we were, of course."

"Was it the grither?" Jimbo asked, his face betraying both excitement and alarm.

"I don't know that, either. You see, Jimbo, the caller didn't say who he was and I've never heard the grither speak before. How do you suppose I ought to be able to recognize his voice?"

"You sang his silly song," Stefa reminded him.

"Right," Father said. "But that was from memory."

Neither Stefa nor Jimbo understood the precise meaning of this explanation, but it kept them from asking any more questions about the grither's voice. It didn't, however, keep them from worrying about the telephone call.

Pounding her kneecaps, Stefa urged Father to finish the story.

"Washington, D.C.," Mother noncommittally informed her family. "I believe he's over Washington."

"Please," said Stefa.

"Well," said Father, trying to take up where the telephone call had interrupted him, "the grither came into existence when a royal packet ship steaming between Boston, Massachusetts, and Portsmouth, England, was blown ridiculously off course by a storm and driven up Baffin Bay toward the Pole. Not a soul aboard that ship survived—but before they all drowned or froze to death, they lifted their voices into the storm

426

to remind the heavens that they were under the King's protection. The grither was born from the fear, rage, and disappointment of those who died. And it has ever since been merciless to those who speak its name because the storm was merciless to those who had to die to give the grither life."

"Is that all?" asked Stefa.

"Richmond, Virginia," said Mother. "He's soaring over Richmond— on his way to Winston-Salem."

"No," said Father, looking at his little girl. "Not quite all. The story goes that the grither won't cease to exist until—"

There was a knock on the door. Mother looked at Father. Stefa and Jimbo looked at each other. The wind, as it curled around the gables of the house, set the walls and floorboards a-creaking. The light bulb hanging from its cord in the center of the room began to bob and dance.

And a voice beyond the door was singing:

The grither is greedy
For only one thing:
To silence your gossip, folks.
That's why this song says
Your moments are numbered.
I'm quite sorry for you.
So please do accept
My most heartfelt apologies.

When the singing was finished, the knocking on the door grew louder and louder.

"Who's going to answer it?" asked Father.

Stefa and Jimbo shrank back against the big green chair's bolster cushion and gave their father disbelieving looks. When Mother saw their fear, she in turn gave Father a look of reproach and warning.

"I'm sorry," Father began contritely. "It's really just—"

But the door banged open with a crash, a huge furry figure leapt through the opening with a roar of Arctic air, and the double row of tiny blue flames in the space heater rippled and guttered as the same voice that had been singing the grither's song cried out in malevolent glee:

"Gotcha!"

The entire family gasped as a single person. Father, indeed, jumped out of his chair.

Then they all saw that the figure who had sprung through the door was Stefa and Jimbo's grandfather, dressed for the season in a raccoon coat and a Russian hat. Coming into the high-ceilinged room behind him,

Grandmother had the practicality and presence of mind to close the wide-thrown door.

"Grandfather sometimes gets carried away," she apologized.

"I telephoned to say we were coming," said Grandfather unrepentantly, winking at Mother. "Didn't this husband of yours tell the children?"

Father's mouth was still open. He had neither the practicality nor the presence of mind to close it.

"I've finished with this," said Mother, rising from her quilting frame. "Let's go into the kitchen for coffee and doughnuts." She led Grandmother and Grandfather, scolding each other and laughing, out of the dim and drafty living room to the comfort of the kitchen table.

"Where's the grither?" Stefa demanded of her father, wiping tears of fright from her eyes. "Where's the *real* grither?"

"Yes," said Jimbo. "What about the rest of the story?"

Father closed his mouth and put his hands in his pockets. Then he opened his mouth and said very slowly:

"I hope neither of you really believes in the grither. You don't, do you?"

"No-o-ohh," the children managed.

"Good," boomed Father jovially. "Because if you don't believe in what isn't, it can't do you any harm. Can it?"

Stefa and Jimbo looked at each other. In unison, each prompted by the other, they doubtfully shook their heads.

"It's almost bedtime. Come into the kitchen for milk and doughnuts, and then we'll go up to bed." Father paused before leaving and looked at the floor. "But first pick up your crayons, please."

Alone in the high-ceilinged living room, Stefa and Jimbo got down in front of the space heater to pick up their scattered crayons—the aquamarines and goldenrods as well as the reds and blues.

"Winston-Salem isn't too far from here," Jimbo said as they gathered up the crayons. "I've seen it on a map at school."

And Stefa whispered miserably, "I wonder where the grither is right now." For Stefa believed in the grither, and what she believed in could certainly do her harm, couldn't it?

"Look," said Jimbo, and he pointed at the rime-coated window across the room. In the final moments of dusk, with the electric glare of the light bulb glinting off the glass, the window was veined with slender threads of red and blue, and the glass itself seemed to be melting—just like leftover Jell-O when no one has put it back in the refrigerator.

But because they weren't a bit surprised, Stefa and Jimbo didn't even scream. . . .

428

The Shaggy House

Joe R. Lansdale

For William F. Nolan

The old Ford moved silently through the night, cruised down the street slowly. The driver, an elderly white-haired man, had his window down and he was paying more attention to looking out of it, studying the houses, than he was to his driving. The car bumped the curb. The old man cursed softly, whipped it back into the dark, silent street.

Beaumont Street came to a dead end. The old man turned around, drove back up. This was his third trip tonight, up and down the short street, and for the third time he was certain. The houses on Beaumont Street were dying, turning gray, growing ugly, looking dreadfully sick, and it all seemed to have happened overnight.

His own house was the sickest looking among them. The paint was peeling—he'd just had it painted last year!—the window panes looked like the bottom of a lover's leap for flies—yet there were no fly bodies—and there was a general sagginess about the place, as if it were old like himself and the spirit had gone out of its lumber bones.

The other houses on the block were not much better. A certain degree of that was to be expected. The houses were old, and the inhabitants of the houses, in many cases, were older. The entire block consisted of retired couples and singles, the youngest of which was a man in his late sixties. But still, the block had always taken pride in their houses, managed somehow to mow the lawns and get the painting done, and then one day it all goes to rot.

And it had happened the moment that creepy house had appeared in the neighborhood, had literally sprung up overnight on the vacant lot across from his house. A gothic-hideous house, as brown and dead looking as the late Fall grass.

Craziest thing, however, was the fact that no one had seen or heard it being built. Just one day the block had gone to bed and the next morning they had awakened to find the nasty old thing sitting over there, crouched like a big hungry toad, the two upper story windows looking like cold, calculating eyes.

Who the hell ever heard of putting up a house overnight? For that matter, who ever heard of prefab, weathered gothics? And last, but not least, why had they not seen anyone come out of or go into the house? It had been there a week, and so far no one had moved in, and there were no rent ads in the paper for it. He had checked.

Of course, a certain amount of the mystery might be explained if his wife were correct.

"Why you old fool, they moved that house in there. And for that matter, Harry, they just might have moved it in while we were sitting on the front porch watching. We're so old we don't notice what goes on anymore."

Harry gnashed his false teeth together so hard he ground powder out of the bicuspids. "Well," he said to the interior of the car, "you may be old, Edith, but I'm not."

No, he wasn't so old that he hadn't noticed the change in the neighborhood, the way the houses seemed to be infected with that old ruin's disease. And he knew that old house was somehow responsible for the damage, and he intended to get to the bottom of it.

A shape loomed in the headlights. Harry slammed his foot on the brakes and screeched the tires sharply.

An elderly, balding man ambled around to Harry's side of the car and stuck his face through the open window.

"Lem!" Harry said. "You trying to commit suicide?"

"No, I was fixing to go over there and burn that damned house down."

"You too, Lem?"

"Me too. Saw you cruising around looking. Figured you'd figured what I'd figured."

Harry looked at Lem cautiously. "And what have we figured?"

"That damned old house isn't up to any good, and that something's got to be done about it before the whole neighborhood turns to ruins."

"You've noticed how the houses look?"

"Any fool with eyes in his head and a pair of glasses can see what's going on."

"But why?"

"Who gives a damn why, let's just do something. I got some matches here, and a can of lighter fluid in my coat pocket—"

"Lem, we can't just commit arson. Look, get in. I don't like sitting here in the street."

Lem turned to look at the house. They were almost even with it. "Neither do I. That thing gives me the creeps."

Lem went around and got in. Harry drove up the block, parked at the far end where the street intersected another. Lem got out his pipe and packed it, filled the Ford with the smell of cinnamon.

"You're gonna get cancer yet," Harry said.

"Being as I'm ninety, it'll have to work fast."

Harry gnashed his bicuspids again. There was a certain logic in that, and just a month ago Edith had talked him into giving up his cigars for health reasons.

After a moment Lem produced a flask from his coat pocket, unscrewed the lid and removed the pipe from his mouth. "Cheers."

Harry sniffed. "Is that whiskey?"

"Prune juice." Lem smiled slyly.

"I bet."

Lem tossed a shot down his throat. "Wheee," he said, lifting the bottle away from his face. "That'll put lead in your pencil!"

"Let me have a snort of that."

Harry drank, gave the flask back to Lem who capped it, returned it to his pocket and put his pipe back into his face.

Unconsciously, they had both turned in their seats to look out the back window of the Ford, so they could see the house. Harry thought that the high-peaked roof looked a lot like a witch's hat there in the moonlight.

"Bright night," Lem said. "Holy Christ, Harry."

"I see it, I see it."

The old house trembled, moved.

It turned its head. No other image could possibly come to mind. The house was flexible, and now its two upstairs windows were no longer facing across the street, they were looking down the street, toward Harry and Lem. Then the head turned again, looked in the other direction, like a cautious pedestrian about to step out into a traffic zone. The turning of its head sounded like the creaking of an old tree in a high wind.

"God," Harry said.

The house stood, revealed thick, peasant girl legs and feet beneath its firm, wooden skirt, and then it stepped from the lot and began crossing the street. As it went, a window on either side of the house went up, and two spindly arms appeared as if suddenly poked through short shirt sleeves. The arms and hands were not as thick as the legs and feet; the hands were nearly flat, the fingers like gnarled oak branches.

"It's heading for my house," Harry said.

"Shut up!" Lem said. "You're talking too loud."

"Edith!"

"Edith's all right," Lem said. "Betcha a dog to a doughnut it's the house it wants. Watch!"

The house's rubbery front porch lips curled back and the front door opened to reveal rows of long, hollow, wood-screw teeth. With a creak it bent to nestle its mouth against the apex of Harry's roof, to latch its teeth there like a leech attaching itself to a swimmer's leg. And then came the low, soft sucking sounds, like gentle winds moaning against your roof at night; a sound you hear in your dreams and you almost wake, but from the back of your head comes a little hypnotic voice saying: "Sleep. It's only the wind crying, touching your roof, passing on," and so you sleep.

A shingle fell from Harry's house, caught a breeze and glided into the street. The front porch sagged ever so slightly. There was the soft sound of snapping wood from somewhere deep within. The windows grew darker and the glass rattled frightened in its frames.

After what seemed an eternity, but could only have been moments, the thing lifted its grotesque head and something dark and fluid dripped from its mouth, dribbled down the roof of Harry's house and splashed in the yard. Then there was a sound from the gothic beast, a sound like a rattlesnake clacking, a sort of contented laughter from deep in its chest.

The house turned on its silly feet, crept and creaked, arms swinging, back across the street, turned to face Harry's house, then like a tired man home from work, it settled sighing into its place once more. The two upper story windows grew dark, as if thick lids had closed over them. The front porch lips smacked once, then there was silence and no movement.

Harry turned to Lem, who had replaced the pipe with the whiskey flask. The whiskey gurgled loudly in the cool Fall night.

"Did you see . . . ?"

"Of course I did," Lem said, lowering the flask, wiping a sleeve across his mouth.

"Can't be."

"Somehow it is."

"But how?"

Lem shook his head. "Maybe it's like those science fiction books I read, like something out of them, an alien, or worse yet, something that has always been among us but has gone undetected for the most part.

"Say it's some kind of great space beast that landed here on Earth, a kind of chameleon that can camouflage itself by looking like a house. Perhaps it's some kind of vampire. Only it isn't blood it wants, but the energy out of houses." Lem tipped up his flask again.

"Houses haven't got energy."

Lem lowered the flask. "They've got their own special kind of energy. Listen: houses are built for the most part—least these houses were—by people who love them, people who wanted good solid homes. They were built before those soulless glass and plastic turd mounds that dot the skyline, before contractors were throwing dirt into the foundation instead of gravel, before they were pocketing the money that should have gone on good studs, two-by-fours and two-by-sixes. And these houses, the ones built with hope and love, absorbed these sensations, and what is hope and love but a kind of energy? You with me, Harry?"

"I guess, but . . . oh, rave on."

"So the walls of these houses took in that love and held it, and maybe that love, that energy, became the pulse, the heartbeat of the house. See what I'm getting at, Harry?

"Who appreciates and loves their homes more than folks our age, people who were alive when folks cared about what they built, people, who in their old age, find themselves more home-ridden, more dependent upon those four walls, more grateful of anything that keeps out the craziness of this newer world, keeps out the wind and the rain and the sun and those who would do us harm?

"This thing, maybe it can smell out, sense the houses that hold the most energy, and along it comes in the dead of night and it settles in and starts to draw the life out of them, like a vampire sucking out a victim's blood, and where the vampire's victims get weak and sag and grow pale, our houses do much the same. Because, you see, Harry, they have become living things. Not living in the way we normally think of it, but in a sort of silent, watchful way."

Harry blinked several times. "But why did it take the form of a gothic type house, why not a simple frame?"

"Maybe the last houses it was among looked a lot like that, and when it finished it came here. And to it these houses look basically the same as all the others. You see, Harry, it's not impersonating *our* houses, it's impersonating *a* house."

"That's wild, Lem."

"And the more I drink from this flask, the wilder I'll get. Take this for instance: it could look like anything. Consider all the ghettos in the world, the slums, the places that no amount of Federal Aid, money and repair seem to fix. Perhaps these chameleons, or whatever you want to call them, live there as well—because despair fills walls as much as love—and they become the top floors of rundown tenement houses, the shanties alongside other shanties on Louisiana rivers—"

"And they feed on this love or despair, this energy?"

"Exactly, and when it's sucked out, the houses die and the creatures move on."

"What are we going to do about it?"

Lem turned up the flask and swigged. When he lowered it, he said, "*Something*, that's for sure."

They left the car, cat-pawed across the street, crept through backyards toward the sleeping house. When they were almost to the lot where the house squatted, they stopped beneath a sycamore tree and wore its shadow. They passed the flask back and forth.

Way out beyond the suburbs, in the brain of the city, they could hear traffic sounds. And much closer, from the ship channel, came the forlorn hoot of a plodding tug.

"Now what?" Harry asked.

"We sneak up on it from the rear, around by the back door—"

"Back door! If the front door is its mouth, Lem, the back door must be its—"

"We're not going inside, we're going to snoop, stupid, then we're going to do something."

"Like what?"

"We'll cross that blazing tightwire when we get to it. Now move!"

They moved, came to the back door. Lem reached out to touch the doorknob. "How about this?" he whispered. "No knob, just a black spot that looks like one. From a distance—hell, up close—you couldn't tell it was a fake without touching. Come on, let's look in the windows."

"Windows?" Harry said, but Lem had already moved around the edge of the house, and when Harry caught up with him, he was stooping at one of the windows, looking in.

"This is crazy," Lem said. "There's a stairway and furniture and cobwebs even . . . No, wait a minute. Feel!"

Harry crept up beside him, reluctantly touched the window. It was most certainly not glass, and it was not transparent either. It was cold and hard like the scale of a fish.

"It's just an illusion, like the doorknob," Harry said.

"Only a more complicated type of illusion, something it does with its mind probably. There's no furniture, no stairs, no nothing inside there but some kind of guts, I guess, the juice of our houses."

The house shivered, sent vibrations up Harry's palm. Harry remembered those long arms that had come out of the side windows earlier. He envisioned one popping out now, plucking him up.

The house burped, loudly.

Suddenly Lem was wearing Harry for a hat.

"Get down off me," Lem said, "or you're going to wake up with a tube up your nose."

Harry climbed down. "It's too much for us, Lem. In the movies they'd bring in the army, use nukes."

Lem took the can of lighter fluid out of his coat pocket. It was the large economy size.

"Sssssshhhh," Lem said. He brought out his pocket knife and a book of matches.

"You're going to blow us up!"

Lem tore the lining out of one of his coat pockets, squirted lighter fluid on it, poked one end of the lining into the fluid can with the point of his knife. He put the rag-stuffed can on the ground, the matches beside it. Then he took his knife, stuck it quickly into the house's side, ripped down.

Something black and odorous oozed out. The house trembled.

"That's like a mosquito bite to this thing," Lem said. "Give me that can and matches."

"I don't like this," Harry said, but he handed the can and matches to Lem. Lem stuck the can halfway into the wound, let the rag dangle.

"Now run like hell," Lem said, and struck a match.

Harry started running toward the street as fast as his arthritic legs would carry him.

Lem lit the pocket lining. The fluid-soaked cloth jumped to bright life.

Lem turned to run. He hadn't gone three steps when the can blew. The heat slapped his back and the explosion thundered inside his head. He reached the street, looked back.

The house opened its front door and howled like a sixty-mile-an-hour tornado. The upstairs front window shades went up, eyes glinted savagely in the moonlight. A spear of flame spurted out of the house's side.

Harry was crossing the street, running for his house when he looked back. The creature howled again. Arms came out of its sides. All around windows went up and wings sprouted out of them.

"Jesus," Harry said, and he turned away from his house so as not to lead it to Edith. He started up the street toward his car.

Lem came up behind him laughing. "Ha! Ha! Flame on!"

Harry glanced back.

The explosion had ignited internal gases and the thing was howling flames now. Its tongue flapped out and slapped the street. Its wings fluttered and it rose up into the sky.

Doors opened all down the block.

Windows went up.

Edith's head poked out of one of the windows. "Harry?"

"Be back, be back, be back," Harry said, and ran on.

Behind him Lem said, "Pacemaker, don't fail me now."

They reached the car wheezing.

"There . . . she . . . goes," Lem panted. "After it!"

A bright orange-red mass darted shrieking across the night sky, moved toward the ship channel, losing altitude.

The Ford coughed to life, hit the street. They went left, driving fast. Lem hung out of the window, pointing up, saying, "There it goes! Turn left. No, now over there. Turn right!"

"The ship channel!" Harry yelled. "It's almost to the ship channel."

"Falling, falling," Lem said.

It was.

They drove up the ship channel bridge. The house-thing blazed above them, moaned loud enough to shake the windows in the Ford. The sky was full of smoke.

Harry pulled over to the bridge railing, parked, jumped out with Lem. Other cars had pulled over. Women, men and children burst out of them, ran to the railing, looked and pointed up.

The great flaming beast howled once more, loudly, then fell, hit the water with a thunderous splash.

"Ah, ha!" Harry yelled. "Dammit, Lem, we've done it, the block is free. Tomorrow we break out the paint, buy new windows, get some shingles . . ."

The last of the thing slipped under the waves with a hiss. A black cloud hung over the water for a moment, thinned to gray. There was a brief glow beneath the expanding ripples, then darkness.

Lem lifted his flask in toast. "Ha! Ha! Flame out!"

Silted In

Karl Edward Wagner

The pain in his chest was back again. Perhaps it was worse this time, but he couldn't remember.

He leaned against the sink, trying to belch. The kitchen counter was stacked high with dishes: to his right dirty ones; to his left clean ones, waiting to dry themselves. He rinsed the suds from his hands, staring at them as the suds peeled away. Were the wrinkles from the dishwater, or had he grown that much older?

He sat down heavily at the kitchen table, remembered his cup of coffee. It had grown cold, but he sipped it without tasting. That was enough of the dishes for today; tomorrow he'd make a fresh start.

He hated the dishes. Each one was a memory. This was *her* coffee cup. This was her favorite glass. They drank together from these wine glasses. They'd picked out this china pattern together. This casserole dish was a wedding present. This skillet was the one she used to make her special omelets. This was the ashtray she always kept beside her favorite chair.

Her chair. He shuffled into the living room, collapsed across the swaybacked couch. Her chair waited there for her, just as she had left it. He wouldn't sit in it. A guest might, but he never had guests now.

A broken spring pressed into his consciousness, and he shifted his weight. Not much weight now. Once he had enjoyed cooking for her. Now every meal he fixed reminded him of her. He left his food untasted. When he cleaned out the freezer, her dog had grown plump on roasts and steaks and chops, stews and soups and etouffées, fried chicken and roast goose and curried duck. After her dog died, he simply scraped the untouched food into the dog's old bowl, left it on the back porch for whatever might be hungry. When his stomach gave him too much pain, he made a sandwich of something, sometimes ate it.

The mail truck was honking beside his mailbox, and he remembered that he hadn't checked his mail all week. Once he had waited impatiently each day for the mail to come. Now it was only bills, duns, letters from angry publishers, some misdirected letters for her, a few magazines whose subscriptions still ran.

He was out of breath when he climbed back up the steps from the street. He stared at his reflection in the hallway mirror without recognition, then dumped the armload of unopened mail onto the pile that sprawled across the coffee table.

The phone started to ring, but his answering machine silently took charge. He never played back the messages, used the phone only now and again to order a pizza. No one comes up into the hills at night.

"Why don't you answer it?" Bogey asked him. He was working his way through a bottle, waiting for Ingrid to show up.

"Might be my agent. He's been stalling my publishers as long as he can. Now I owe him money, too."

"Maybe it's her."

He ignored the poster and found the bathroom. He took a long piss, a decidedly realistic touch which was the trendiest verism in horror fiction this season. So inspired, he groped his way into his study, dropped into the leather swivel chair she had bought him for his last birthday. He supposed it was a gift.

He brought up the IBM word processor and hit the command for global search and replace, instructed it to replace the phrase "make love" with "piss on" throughout the novel. Yes, go ahead and replace without asking.

While the computer sorted that out, he fumbled with the bank of stereo equipment, tried to focus his eyes on the spines of a thousand record albums. He reached out to touch several favorites, pulled his hand away reluctantly each time. Every album was a memory. The Blues Project album he'd played while they made love for the first time. The Jefferson Airplane album she loved to dance to: Don't you need somebody to love? And not the Grateful Dead—too many stoned nights of sitting on the floor under the black lights, passing the pipe around. Hendrix? No, too many acid-trip memories.

"You're burning out, man," Jimi told him.

"Better to burn out than to fade away," he answered. "You should know."

Jimi shrugged and went back to tuning his Fender Stratocaster.

He left the stereo on, still without making a selection. Sometimes a beer helped him get started.

The dishes were still waiting in the sink, and Jim Morrison was looking in the refrigerator. He reached an arm in past Jimbo and snagged the last beer. He'd have to remember to go to the store soon.

"Fucking self-indulgent," Jim said.

"What was? Oh, here." He offered Jimbo the beer can.

Jim shook his head. "No. I meant changing 'fuck' to 'piss on' in the novel."

"It's the same thing. And anyway, it's so New Wave."

"How would you know? You're past forty."

"I was New Wave back in the sixties."

"And you're still stuck in the sixties."

"And so are you."

"Maybe so. But I *know* that I'm dead."

"You and all my heroes."

Back in his study he sipped his beer and considered his old Royal portable. Maybe that was the trouble. He'd never really made the shift to high-tech creativity. Stick with the manual typewriter. Maybe go back to the roots: a quill pen, or even clay tablets.

He rolled in a sheet of paper, typed *1* at the top of the page. He sipped the rest of his beer and stared at the blank page. After a while he noticed that the beer can was empty.

The battery in his car was dead, but there was a 7-11 just down the hill. His chest was aching again by the time he got back. He chugged a fresh brew while he put away the rest of the six-pack, a Redi-Maid cheese sandwich, a jar of instant coffee and a pack of cigarettes. The long belch made him feel better.

James Dean was browsing along his bookshelves when he returned to the living room. He was looking at a copy of *Electric Visions*. "I always wondered why you dedicated this book to me," he said.

"It was my first book. You were my first hero—even before Elvis. I grew up in the fifties wanting to be like you."

James read from the copyright page: "1966." He nodded toward the rest of the top shelf. "You write these others, too?"

"Fourteen hardcovers in ten years. I lived up to your image. Check

438

out some of the reviews I stuck inside the books: The New Wave's brightest New Star. Sci-fi's rebellious new talent. The angriest and most original writer in decades. Great jacket blurbs."

James Dean helped himself to a cigarette. "I don't notice any reviews more recent than 1978."

"Saving reviews is the mark of a beginner." There hadn't been many since 1978, and those had been less than kind. The last had pronounced sentence: Tired rehash of traditional themes by one of the genre's Old Hands. He hadn't finished a book since then.

James French-inhaled. "Don't see many books since 1978 here either."

"Whole next shelf."

"Looks like reprints mostly."

"My books are considered classics. They're kept in print."

"What a load of bull."

"Why don't you go take a spin in your Porsche?"

The remark was in poor taste, and he decided to play his tape of *Rebel Without a Cause* by way of apology. And then he remembered how she had cried when the cops gunned down Sal Mineo. Maybe he should get some work done instead.

The stereo and the word processor were both still on when he returned to his study, and there was a sheet of paper in his typewriter with *1* typed across the top. He studied all of this in some confusion. He cut power switches, cranked out the blank sheet of paper, carefully placed it in a clean manila folder and dated the tab.

He sat down. Maybe he should listen to a tape. Something that wouldn't remind him of her. He turned his stereo back on. The tapes were buried under a heap of unanswered correspondence, unread magazines, unfinished manuscripts on the spare bed. He sat back down.

It might be best to make a fresh start by tackling an unfinished manuscript. There were a few, several, maybe a dozen, or more. They were all somewhere on the spare bed, hidden beneath one overturned stack or another. He'd paid fifteen bucks for the brass bed when he'd moved in, twenty years ago. Spent two days stripping the multilayered paint, polishing with Brass-O. Five bucks to Goodwill for the stained mattress and box springs. They'd slept together on it their first year together, until he pulled down a big enough advance to convert his former housemate's room into their bedroom, pay for a proper double bed. He'd always meant to sell the single brass bed, put in proper shelves instead.

He never slept in their bedroom now. It held her clothes, her pictures, her scent, her memories.

It would be an all-day chore to sort through all the mess to find just the right manuscript whose moment had come. Best to tackle that tomorrow.

He pulled out an abused legal pad, wrote *I* across the first yellow page.

His stomach was hurting now. That made it hard to choose which pen to write with. He thought there might still be some milk left.

He drank a glass of milk and then a cup of coffee and smoked three Winstons, while he waited for his muse to awaken. The living room walls were hung with the same black-light posters they had put there when they'd first moved in together, back in the late sixties. He supposed that the black lights still worked, although it had been years since he had switched them on. About all that had changed over the years were occasional new bookshelves, growing against the walls like awkward shelf-fungus. They were triple-stacked with books he really meant to read, although he hadn't been able to finish reading a book in years.

I can't see you because of your books, she had warned him on occasion, from her chair across the room from his. And then he would stick together another shelf, try to clear away the confusion of books and magazines piled in the middle of the living room, try to explain the necessity of keeping copies of *Locus* from 1969. In another year the pile would grow back.

My books are my life, he would tell her. Now that she was gone, he had grown to hate them almost as much as he had grown to hate himself. They were memories, and he clung to them while hating them, for memories were all he had left of his life.

It was getting dark. He glanced toward the front door, thinking it was about time for the cat to show up to be fed. He remembered that he hadn't seen the cat in weeks.

Time to get back to work. He would write all night.

The cigarettes started him coughing again. She had nagged him to see a doctor about that cough. He treasured the cough for that memory of her concern.

He drank a glass of water from the tap, then remembered that her plants needed watering. She had left him with her plants, and he tried to keep them watered. He was crying again by the time he completed his rounds with the watering can. That made the cough worse. His chest ached.

"What you need is to stop feeling sorry for yourself," Elvis advised him. "Stop moping around this dump. Go out and get yourself a new woman."

"Too old for chasing tail at the singles bars," he protested, reaching around Elvis to select some pills from the medicine cabinet. Shitty street-

440

speed they sold now only made him long for the good old days of dex and Ritalin and black beauties.

"Never too old to make a comeback," The King said.

"Who says I need to make a comeback?"

"Shit. Look at yourself."

"You look at yourself, dammit! You've got an extra chin and sleeping bags under your eyes. Try to squeeze that stomach into one of those black leather jackets you slouched in back when I was trying to grow sideburns like yours."

"But I'm not getting any older now."

"And I won't grow up either."

"It's not the same thing."

Street-speed always made him hungry. He ate half of the cheese sandwich, felt vaguely nauseated, and had a swallow of Maalox for dessert. His head was starting to ache, so he chased the Maalox with several aspirin.

He really ought to take a break before getting back to work. There was nothing on television that interested him at all, and he wondered again why he paid for all the cable channels that were offered. Still, best to have access; there might be something that would inspire him—or at least fill the empty hours of pain.

He could watch a tape. The trouble was that the tapes were unsorted and unlabeled, stuffed away into boxes and piled together with all the other debris of his life. He could dig through it all, but then he would run the risk of pulling out a cassette of a film that was special to her. He would never watch *To Have and Have Not* again. Best just to turn on Cable News and let it run.

He put the rest of the cheese sandwich out for the cat, in case he came back during the night. His stomach was hurting too much to finish eating. Despite the Maalox, he felt like vomiting. Somehow he knew that once he started vomiting, he would never stop—not until all that he spewed out was bright blood, and then not until he had no more blood to offer. A toilet bowl for a sacrificial altar.

There was inspiration at last. Vomiting was back in vogue now— proof that great concepts never die.

While the fire was in him, he brought up the IBM, instructed global search to replace "kiss" with "vomit on."

That was more than enough creativity for one day. He felt drained. It was time to relax with a cold beer. Maybe he could play a record. He wondered if she had left him a little pot, maybe hidden away in a plastic film canister.

But film canisters reminded him of all the photographs they had taken together, frozen memories of the two of them in love, enjoying their life together. He was too depressed to listen to a record now. Best just to sit in the darkness and sip his beer.

Janis Joplin was trying to plug in one of the black lights, but she needed an extension cord. Giving it up, she plopped down onto the couch and grinned at him. She was wearing lots of beads and a shapeless paisley blouse over patched and faded bell-bottoms. From somewhere she produced a pint of Southern Comfort, took a pull, offered the bottle to him.

"Good for that cough," she urged in her semi-hoarse voice.

"Thanks," he said. "I got a beer."

Janis shook back her loose waves of hair, looked around the room. "Place hasn't changed."

"It never does."

"You're stuck in the past, man."

"Maybe. It sure beats living in the future."

"Oh wow." Janis was searching for something in her beaded handbag. "You're buried alive, man."

"Beats just being buried."

"Shit, man. You're lost among your artifacts, man. I mean, like you've stored up memories like quicksand and jumped right in."

"Maybe I'm an artifact myself. Just like you."

Janis laughed her gravelly cackle. "Shit, man. You're all left alone with the pieces of your life, and all the time life is passing you by. Buried alive in the blues, man."

"Since she left me, all I have left to look forward to is my past."

"Hey, man. You got to let it go. You got to let *her* go. You know how that old song goes."

Janis began to sing in her voice that reminded him of cream sherry stirred into cracked ice:

> *Look up and down that long lonesome road,*
> *Where all of our friends have gone, my love,*
> *And you and I must go.*
> *They say all good friends must part someday,*
> *So why not you and I, my love,*
> *Why not you and I?*

"Guess I'm just not ready to let it all go," he said finally. But now he was alone in the darkness, his chest hurt, and his beer was empty.

She shouldn't have left him.

He tossed the beer can into the trash, turned off the kitchen light. One thing to do before sprawling out across the couch to try to sleep.

442

He opened the upright freezer. It had only been a matter of removing the shelves.

"Goodnight, my love," he whispered to her.

Sitting in the Corner, Whimpering Quietly

Dennis Etchison

It was one of those bright places you never expect to find in the middle of the night, a place of porcelain and neon lighting and whitewashed walls. I walked in with my old army bag stuffed full of a month's dirty clothes and swung it on top of one of the long line of waiting, open washing machines.

A quarter to three in the morning.

And nobody in sight for miles and miles.

I let out a sigh, which not surprisingly turned into a yawn, and felt for the change in my pocket.

I didn't see her at first. That is to say, I knew she was there without turning around. I think it was the cigarette smoke. It cut a sharp edge through the hot, stifling, humid dryer air that hung so thick in the laundromat you felt you could stick out your finger and jab a hole in it.

"Well, he finally got what he wanted."

I moved along the wall to the corner detergent dispenser. It was very late and I couldn't sleep and I had come here to be alone, just to have something to do and to be left alone to do it, and I was in no mood to try my hand at winning friends and influencing people.

I heard water running in the sink next to me.

"That's what he thought, all right." Her voice came very close to me now, going on as if picking up a running conversation we might have been having.

I turned my head just long enough for a quick glance at her.

She was young but not too, twenty-nine going on forty, and pretty, too, but not really very. She had long hair hanging down to the middle of her thin back, with blond streaks bleached in, *tres chic,* you know, and one of her phony eyelashes was coming unglued in the warm, wet air.

"A house in the Valley, two cars—no, three—paid vacation in the Virgin Islands, and a son, yeah, a little Vladimir Jr. to carry on his

443

glorious family name. Just like he always wanted. But that was *all* he wanted—that's the part they never tell you in front."

She dropped the butt of her Pall Mall and lit another at once, pulling long, hard drags down into her lungs.

"Last week the kid took the gun from the closet and walked up to me in the kitchen," she continued, starting to hand-wash a sheet in the sink. "Pointed it right at my head and said, 'Bang, you're dead, Mommy.' 'Well,' I said, 'are you gonna do it or not? Don't ever point one of those things at someone unless you're gonna use it.'

"So he did. The kid pulled the trigger. I didn't think he had the guts. 'Course it wasn't loaded. That *really* pissed me off. It was just like Vladimir, not teaching him what it means to be a—but what would his dad know about that? About what it takes to be a man."

She scrubbed at the soiled sheet, pausing to jerk a wet hand up to move a strand of hair away from her face. I couldn't help taking a better look at her face then. It was like the rest of her, young and yet old, drawn and tight, made up expensively even now, in the middle of the night, though obviously in haste, and tired, and blank. For a second then, overpoweringly, I had the belief that she was the same young/old woman I had seen seated in the window of a beauty salon in Beverly Hills once; and later, in a cocktail lounge with another girl, waiting, with long, sharp fingernails the color of blood. French-inhaling a Marlboro and with a look on her face that told you she had a hundred dollar bill in her purse. And that she was waiting. Just waiting.

She picked up her Pall Mall with a wet thumb and first finger, drawing hard.

I noticed the clock on the wall: three o'clock.

"That was when I got it. All these years, trying to figure a way to teach him and that God damned kid of his something."

I fed a couple of nickels into the detergent machine.

She paused long enough to take a couple of more lengthy hits from her Pall Mall. It was so quiet you could hear the sound of the smoke blowing out into the white light.

"So tonight he comes home and makes the pitcher of martinis, as usual, and goes into his room and closes the door. I go to the door and ask him what the hell's wrong *this* time. He says he doesn't know. He just wants me to leave him alone."

She laughed startlingly, hoarsely.

"Okay, hot shot, I'll leave you the hell alone, I think. You wanna come home from your fucking office looking like a corpse again tonight and lay around until you fall asleep for the zillionth time? All right, I'll let you!

"We'll find out if that's what you really want.

"Only first you and that little pussy of a son of yours are gonna get a lesson you'll never forget."

She turned on the water full force. It gushed out, flooding the basin faster than it could empty.

"Who ever said if you wash it in cold water it'll come out. *Damn.* Why the hell did I have to give him the striped sheets, anyway?

"So I wake the kid up. It doesn't matter—he's awake, and the bed's all wet as usual. I ask him if he remembers what I taught him.

"It takes a minute or two, but he finally catches on, the dumb little bastard.

"So I go get the bullets down and tell him to go in there and prove to me that he remembers what it was I beat the shit out of him for last week. . . ."

I started to dump my stuff into a machine at the far end of the room. Then, all of a sudden, the thread of what she had been saying got through to me.

I turned back to look at her.

She was grinding a bar of soap into the sheet now. At the edges the spot was a thick brown, almost black, but at the heart I noticed it was still a deep, gummy shade close to the color of her nails as her fingers flashed violently around the material. The steam was rising up from the basin to surround her.

I closed my eyes fast.

Outside, a car came suddenly from nowhere and passed hurriedly by, swishing away down the empty boulevard.

She finished the story. I didn't want to hear it, tried to block it out of my ears but she told it through to the finish. It didn't matter to her. She had never been talking to me anyway.

My eyes jammed shut, harder and harder, until I saw gray shapes that seemed to move in front of me. Never before in my life up to that moment could I remember feeling so detached, so out of it. I leaned the heels of my hands against the washer. The quarter slipped from my fingers, clanked against the enamel and hit the cold, cracked cement floor.

The last thing I heard her saying was:

". . . So afterward I tell the kid to go back to bed, to go to sleep, just to go the hell to sleep, but he can't. Or won't. He just sits there on the floor in the corner, the gun still in his lap, whimpering quietly. That was how I left him, the little sissy. . . ."

Disgusted—tired and sick and disgusted out of all memory and beyond all hope—I forced my things back into the bag and stumbled out of the laundromat. She said something after me but I didn't want to hear what it was.

I pulled my coat up around my ears. I was starting to shiver. I snorted, at no one in particular, at the night and all the people in it, everywhere, the stupid, unthinking people who don't know enough to leave a man alone, just to leave you the hell alone the times when you need it most. There was no place left for me to go, no place at all anywhere in the city. And so, breathing steam, I made it away from there as fast as I could, heading off down the street in the same direction as the car and blinking fast, being careful not to step on any cracks, all the way back to my room. My quiet room.

Sneakers

Marc Laidlaw

What are you dreaming, kid?
    Oh, don't squeeze your eyes, you can't shut me out. Rolling over won't help—not that blanket either. It might protect you from monsters but not from me.

Let me show you something. Got it right here. . . .

Well look at that. Is it your mom? Can't you see her plain as day? Yeah, well try moonlight. Cold and white, not like the sun, all washed out; a five-hundred-thousandth of daylight. It can't protect you.

She doesn't look healthy, kid. Her eyes are yellow, soft as cobwebs— touch them and they'll tear. Her skin is like that too, isn't it? No, Mom's not doing so good. Hair all falling out. Her teeth are swollen, black, and charred.

Yeah, something's wrong.

You don't look so good yourself, kiddo—

"Mom . . . ?"

What if she doesn't answer?

Louder this time: "Mom!"

Brent sat up, wide-awake now, sensing the shadows on the walls taking off like owls in flight. And that voice. He could still hear it. Were those rubber footsteps running away down the alley, a nightmare in tennis shoes taking off before it was caught? He could still see his mother's face, peeling, rotten, dead.

Why wouldn't she answer?

He knew it was only a dream, she just hadn't heard him calling, tied up in her own dreams. A dream like any other. Like last night, when he had seen his father burning up in an auto wreck, broken bones coming through the ends of his chopped-off arms; and the night before that, an old memory of torturing a puppy, leaving it in the street where it got hit and squashed and spilled. And the night before? Something bad, he knew, though he couldn't quite capture it.

Every night he had come awake at the worst moments. Alone, frightened of the dream's reality, of the hold it had on the dark corners of his waking world. If that voice had whispered when he was awake, he knew the walls might melt and bulge, breathing, as the blankets crawled up his face and snaked down his throat, suffocating him. That voice knew all his secrets, it whispered from a mouth filled with maggots, fanged with steel pins, a slashed and twisting tongue.

How did it know him?

Brent lay back and watched the dark ceiling until it began to spin, and he felt himself drifting back to sleep. Everything would be safe now, the voice had run away, he would have okay dreams. At least until tomorrow night.

It was not fear, the next night, that kept him from sleeping. Curiosity. He stuffed pillows beneath his covers to create an elongated shape, then he sat on the floor inside his closet with a flashlight. He had drunk a cup of instant coffee after dinner, to help him stay awake.

He heard the clock downstairs chiming eleven; sometime later the television went off and the shower splashed briefly in his parents' bathroom. Midnight passed. A car went through the alley, though its headlights could not reach him in the closet.

At one o'clock, a cat's meow.

The sneakers came at two. Footsteps in the alley.

Brent nudged the door ajar and looked out at the pane of his window. He could see windows in the opposite house, a drooping net of telephone wires, the eye of a distant streetlight.

Footsteps coming closer. It could be just anyone. He thought he heard the squeak of rubber; it was such a real sound. This couldn't be the whisperer.

Then they stopped outside, just below his window. Not a sound did they make, for five minutes, ten, until he knew that he had fallen asleep and dreamed their approach, was dreaming even now, listening to his heart beating and a dog barking far away, and then the voice said, You're awake.

Brent pressed back into the closet, holding his flashlight as if it were a crucifix or a stake in a vampire movie. He didn't have a hammer, though.

Why don't you come out of there?

He shook his head, wishing that he were sound asleep now, where these whispers could only touch his dreams, could only make him see things. Not awake, like this, where if he took that talk too seriously, he knew the walls could melt.

I'm still here, kiddo. What did you wait up for?

Holding his flashlight clenched.

A walk, maybe?

He opened the closet door and crept out, first toward the bed, then toward the door of his room. Into the hall.

That's right.

Was he really doing this? No. It was a dream after all, because the hall was different, it wasn't the hall in his house: the paintings were of places that didn't exist, changing color, blobs of grey and blue shifting as if worms had been mashed on the canvases, were still alive. That wasn't his parents' door swinging wide, with something coming to look out. He mustn't look. There was a cage across the door so he was safe, but he mustn't look.

Downstairs, though, it was his living room. Dreams were like that. Completely real one minute, nonsense the next.

Like Alice in Wonderland. Like the Brothers Grimm or *Time Bandits*.

Who's real, kid? Not me. Not you. I promise.

Don't wake the Red King.

Don't pinch yourself unless you want to know who's dreaming.

Don't open the back door and look into the alley, because here I am.

He turned on his flashlight.

Right behind you.

The black bag—if it was a bag—came down fast over Brent's eyes and whipped shut around his neck, smothering. He got lifted up and thrown across a bony shoulder. The sneakers started squeaking as he heard the alley gravel scatter.

Say bye-bye to Mommy and Daddy.

He was dreaming, this wasn't real.

There, that's what I meant, whispered the voice.

Someone to Dump On

Terry Lamsley

For days Jean Feltham had been in need of something to aim her anger at. Her frustration at no longer being fully in charge, at having (as she saw it) her role as a mother usurped and her authority in the family questioned, had reached danger point. She needed someone to dump on. Neville provided the perfect target, and she went for him at once.

She did it in a round-about way, through Robert, her husband.

'How could you have invited him?' she demanded. 'You *know* I can't stand him. He may be your cousin, but you admit he gives even you the creeps. What the hell have you asked him down for? God!' She drew her fingertips down the bridge of her nose in an angry gesture peculiar to herself, and stared at him impatiently.

'I didn't,' said Robert. 'I just mentioned, months ago, that we'd all be here for a week, and I'd get in touch. He must have misunderstood me.'

'He's good at that: getting the wrong end of the stick.'

'I thought I might go and see him one day, perhaps take the kids, to give you a day off. You know he likes to see them.'

'That's just one of the things I hate about him: his obsession with the children. It's not natural. He hangs about and watches them, and tries to join in their games.'

'It's only his way. He's terribly lonely. And he's a child himself.'

'A clumsy, stupid, middle-aged, sinister one. I don't want him around. I've got enough to put up with. I won't speak to the little sod.'

'You're being a bit hard,' said Robert. 'He's the family albatross, hanging around all our necks. It's only fair to take a turn to look after him every now and then. His mother's an old woman. He's put a terrible strain on her over the years; the suicide attempts, and the trouble with the neighbours. If he's here for a few days it'll give her a break.'

'I wish one of his attempts to top himself had been successful,' said Jean bitterly. 'This is our holiday, for Christ's sake. *My* holiday. And what's it been like so far? A bloody mess. And now *he* turns up! The moment we arrive! In fact, he must have been waiting for us to get here: he was here before we were. I tell you, Rob, I've had it up to here.' She held her hand high above her head. 'Get rid of him. Either he goes, or I do.'

Robert frowned, trying to contain his own anger, aware that there was justice in his wife's complaint. From her point of view their summer vacation, a three week tour through the south of France, had been worse than no holiday at all. She had hated it. Their mistake had been in going with the other families: four adults and seven children, who they hardly knew, in two big camper-vans. If they had just taken their own three kids, Tina, Nina and Gavin, and travelled in their own car, there would have been no problem; they would have been under no pressure.

But Jean, a serious, solitary soul, could not function as a member of any group outside her own family. Also, socially and morally, she felt herself to be a thousand miles away from the other two couples and their children. Her ways were not theirs. She was interested in gardens, museums, architecture: culture, which she wanted her children to see and share. The others, who liked to call themselves 'The Band of Gypsies,' were only interested in good times, getting drunk, and topless sun-bathing. They left their children to do what they liked most of the time, so long as they, the adults, were able to indulge themselves without interruption.

It was not so much the boozing and lounging about that Jean objected to. She and Rob were, of course, free to go their own way while the others got drunk (Rob did not join in the orgies, though Jean knew he would like to have done; another source of tension and resentment), and the two of them frequently went for walks while the rest of the party caroused. Even so, their conversations during these expeditions were mostly about the slack, irresponsible behaviour of their companions, and were thus repetitive and depressing.

Jean could have coped with that, and with the second-rate compromise of a holiday, if her own children had not been so adversely affected; if they had not, all three of them, sunk in just twenty-two days into a state of anarchy that brought to her mind disturbing scenes from *Lord of the Flies*. The trouble was that all the children had chosen to wander about together in a rowdy, disorganised, disaffected gang, completely independent of their parents and creating their own kind of small-scale havoc, perhaps in unconscious protest at what they perceived to be parental negligence. Jean was not surprised to find this reaction exhibited by the other children, and even sympathised with them to some extent, but she was aghast to find her own children copying their behaviour so enthusiastically.

Tina, Nina and Gavin had always been as good as gold. They had kept aloof from the kind of cynical contempt for adults so many young people seemed to affect these days. But recently, all of a sudden, they had succumbed, and had (or so it seemed to Jean) thrown in their lot with the enemy.

She had no idea what to do about it. They were out of her control, and everything she did to attempt to re-establish her authority only made

450

things worse. She felt incompetent as a mother, and feared that she was becoming a figure of fun. She was sure that the rest of the group, with the exception of Rob, were all laughing at her and enjoying her embarrassment.

As for Rob, she was not quite sure about him: he seemed half-hearted in his condemnation of the others, and reluctant to come down completely on her side or discipline his children. But she was used to that from him: he could always see two or more sides to every question, and rarely provided the support she needed when she was really up against it. She could handle that. It was part of the pattern; it was the story of her married life. What she couldn't handle was the realisation that for some reason her own children found the disruptive, rebellious antics of the other seven attractive, seductive and exciting.

That was what really rankled: that her children preferred the company of infant outlaws to that of their own parents, and took every opportunity they could to get away and play wild, dangerous, even destructive games with the others. They didn't seem to give a jot about her and Rob any more. This too-sudden rejection was more than Jean could take on board. It stunned her, and she was temporarily overcome, trapped in a mesh of negative, helpless feelings.

And she and Rob were stranded. They had to stand and take it. They had to put up with the situation, at least on the surface, because they were in the minority, and the vehicles they were travelling in belonged to the other two couples, who were having the time of their lives.

But now the three weeks were up at last. They were back in England: they were, all sixteen of them, on a camping site on the side of a dale in deepest Derbyshire, less than two hours' drive from home, and Jean was in a mood to assert herself and get back on top.

The group had originally planned to spend one more week together, and she and Rob had decided to give it a go. It would be easy enough to sneak away from the others if they felt the need to, if things got worse. But she was not prepared to take any bullshit from anyone. Particularly not from a pathetic creepy-crawly like Rob's cousin Neville, the Feltham family curse. If Rob didn't get rid of him pronto—today—she would rent a car and take the kids home in the morning. Rob could stay and piss the week away with the others if he wanted to, and she had a feeling that he probably would. Well, it might be good for him, and for her, if he did!

She waited for him to respond to her challenge.

'Don't paint yourself into a corner over this, Jean,' Rob said, with a grim yet reasonable, even reassuring, smile. 'After all, we don't know if he intends to stay. I doubt if he does. He's brought nothing with him, as far as I can see: no rucksack or tent, so he can't be expecting to sleep here with us.'

'God forbid. Just let him try. I expect his mother got him into a bed and breakfast place somewhere in the village. He's done that before, hasn't he? Dropped in on us out of the blue, and hovered about in the background, like he's doing now. Has he spoken to you yet? Has he even explained what the hell he's here for?'

'No,' Robert said lamely, 'he hasn't. I don't know what's the matter with him. He's keeping his distance: he seems to be avoiding me.'

'He's pally enough with Tina and Gavin. He's got plenty to say to them. Look at him. He's all over them.'

'Hm,' said Robert, following her gaze towards the trio, who were standing some distance away. 'They don't seem to mind. They used to say they couldn't stand him.'

'That's because the other kids accepted him as soon as they saw him. He's just the sort of person *they'd* like. He could almost *be* one of them, a member of the gang.'

'He looks the part, as though he's been sleeping in a hedge,' agreed Rob. 'He's really let himself go. I hope he's okay: I don't like the look of him at all.'

'Me neither. But that's standard. He looks his usual shifty, scruffy, nasty little self to me. I expect he's had another of his "relapses," as his mother calls them, and got himself into trouble; in which case he'll be on those long-term drugs that turn him into an even more boring little crawler than he normally is. I can't stand it, Rob: I mean it. He has to go.'

'You're right. I'll speak to him,' Robert said, sounding not quite as enthusiastic as she would have liked, and he wandered off towards his cousin.

As he did so, the seven children from the other two families, moving together in a herd, swept out from somewhere and surrounded Neville, Tina and Gavin in a tumultuous, bickering circle. They started tugging at Neville's jacket and bouncing up and down around him. Even from a distance it was obvious that he was enjoying himself. He was waving his bent arms about level with his shoulders, as though aping the actions of a bird, dancing on his toes, and giggling in the unguarded, abandoned way that Jean had always found so disgusting. Suddenly the group of children ran away, drawing Neville with them. He stumbled along a few steps behind them, flapping his arms like a demented, out-of-condition turkey. The whole party vanished through a gate and down the sloping field beyond.

Robert, who had only gone a few steps, stopped.

452

'I'm not chasing after him now,' he said. 'I don't think he can come to any harm. I'll talk to him later.'

'If you don't, I will,' said Jean, using her most dangerous voice.

Robert gave her a bleak look. 'No problem,' he said, 'just leave it to me. I'm going into the village now. You remember we arranged that your sister would send our mail to be collected at the post office. There'll probably be a few things from work that need my signature, and I'll have to get that sorted out. It shouldn't take long, though. I'll take Nina if she's feeling better.'

Their eldest daughter had been resting in a tent since they had arrived, hours earlier, and was still recovering from sea-sickness brought on by a choppy cross-Channel ferry trip. Jean nodded.

'It'll do her good. You can pick up some fresh milk while you're at it.'

The evening meal was cooking on the barbecue when Robert and Nina got back. Jean was looking after it, turning the chops and sausages with an absurdly clumsy pair of wooden tongs.

She looked cross.

The other adults were sitting at a rustic table, drinking Bulgarian Red out of half-pint glasses. One of them was playing a guitar. They were singing an obscene version (with words of their own composition) of 'Don't cry for me, Argentina,' a tune which had, for some inexplicable reason, become the theme song of their holiday. There was no sign of any of the children.

The day had been oppressively hot, but was no longer bright. The sun had turned sullen and moody, and slipped behind a veil of immobile, steamy cloud. Nina, drooping from the effort of even such a short walk, and still not quite well, returned to her tent. Robert stowed the milk in the shade under one of the vans and sat on a plastic chair close to the barbecue.

'I see it's your turn to be chef yet again,' he observed.

Jean made a disgusted sound.

'Why?' asked Robert.

'Because I'm bloody hungry,' she replied shortly.

Robert opened the big brown envelope he had collected and began sifting through the batch of letters it contained. He sighed heavily from time to time, or clicked his tongue. Twice he laughed sardonically, as though in quiet desperation.

'Anything interesting?' asked Jean.

'It's pretty much what I expected. Leave the staff to run the place for a few weeks, and everything starts to fall apart.'

'Nothing serious, though?' she said, smearing Taco sauce on chicken drumsticks.

453

'Nothing I can't handle.'

Robert went through all the business letters first, then started opening the private mail.

'Hey, Jean, guess what we've got here?'

'I'm not in a guessing mood. Tell me.'

'It's a letter from old Molly Feltham, Neville's mother. First time I've heard from her in years.'

'If she wants us to foster him she can piss off. What does she say?'

'It's hard to read. Her arthritis must be really bad.' Rob studied the letter for some moments, holding it close to his face. 'I think she must have finally gone nuts, or I'm reading this wrong.' he said finally. 'She seems to be telling us Neville's dead—or "gone beyond," as she puts it.'

'That's wishful thinking, on either her part or yours,' observed Jean.

'It's not, though. I'm right. Look here: she says the funeral was on the seventeenth. That's eight days ago.' He handed her the letter, pointing with his finger to the bottom of the first page.

Jean read through the section twice, carefully. 'That's the message I get,' she said, with a flippancy that sounded slightly false. 'What's going on?'

'I've no idea. It can't be a joke: old Molly hasn't laughed at anything since Neville was born, forty-five years ago.'

'Then she must be crazy.'

'Hm,' said Rob, and looked up at her uneasily. Jean busied herself with the drumsticks, spreading them out on the metal grill, concentrating harder than was necessary.

'Well, we know he's not dead, there's no doubt about that,' said Rob. 'We saw him this afternoon.'

'We did. Unfortunately,' Jean agreed, avoiding his eyes.

'Where *is* the old bugger?' Rob said, and coughed. 'Is he about?'

'I haven't seen him since he went off with the kids, before you went into the village. He's not been back, and neither have they.'

'None of them?'

'Not one.'

'Christ.' Rob got up and began looking around. 'I'd better go and find them.'

'You had. The meal is almost ready.'

Robert noticed that her voice had changed in the last few minutes. It had gone low and lifeless again, as it had been a lot of the time during their holiday.

He was stepping across to the rustic table to enlist the assistance of the other parents when he heard the sound of children's voices. Then he saw small figures running up the hill towards him. He stared at them anxiously. They were the other families' kids: he could see no sign of Tina, Gavin or Neville among them.

The little gang came tearing up to their parents, then ran across to Jean, the barbecue, and the smell of cooking. They were obviously ravenous. Robert asked one of them where the missing trio was. The little boy seemed not to understand, and Robert took him gently by the shoulders and hunkered down in front of him.

'I'm worried about Tina and Gavin,' he said slowly, grimly. 'Do you know where they are?'

'They went off with the man,' the boy said.

'I know. But when did you last see them?'

'Ages ago.'

'How long?'

'When did we last see Tina and Gavin?' the boy shouted to the other children, who were grabbing plate-loads of sausages, chops and buns.

'*Ages* ago,' they chorused.

'See? I told you,' said the boy.

Robert let him go. Jean came and stood next to him. 'What shall we do?' she asked. He thought she was almost in tears.

The other adults had thrown themselves on the food and were opening more bottles of wine. 'We'll get no help from them,' said Robert. 'We'll just have to search around.'

'Yes, but where do we start?'

'Bloody hell, I don't know. Anywhere but here.'

They were interrupted by one of the children, who stopped eating long enough to shout 'Here they come, Mr Feltham.' He pointed down the hill to where an evening mist was beginning to form in the bottom of the dale. Three figures, two small and one quite large, were walking towards them out of the haze.

Behind them walked three other people, all men, one of them in a dark uniform. They moved slowly and deliberately, as if they were in no great hurry to reach their destination. The three familiar figures in front seemed to increase their pace, however, and began to draw away from the men.

Neville looked, even from a distance, idiotically happy. He seemed to be skipping with delight; or perhaps he was merely tripping on the uneven ground. Jean took hold of her husband's left arm with both hands.

'Oh, Rob, thank God. I was getting really worried, and thinking the most dreadful, silly things.'

'Me too,' said Rob, and licked his dry lips.

'I'm even glad to see Neville,' continued Jean.

'I'm going to have to give him hell, though, for going off with them like that.'

'And I won't stop you,' Jean said. 'Look, the old fool's even waving at us. Wave back.'

They both waved. Tina and Gavin waved. They all waved at each other. Strangely, for no reason in particular, Robert remembered the last occasion before this present visit that he had seen Neville. Robert had driven him to the railway station, bought him a ticket, and seen him on the train. Neville had hung out of the carriage window until the train pulled out, his big white head bouncing slowly like a balloon in a draught, and had stuck his arm right out as the train left the station, giving an exaggerated, childish wave of goodbye. Then, abruptly, he had disappeared. Remembering the incident, Robert felt a momentary flutter of panic.

He must have shuddered. Jean felt it, in his arm.

'What's wrong?' she asked.

'Nothing.'

'No.' She shook her head. 'Something's wrong. I don't feel right.'

Nevertheless, they both continued to wave. Only Neville was waving back now; Neville and one of the three men at the rear, who was moving a hand about in the air above his head in an uncertain gesture, as though not quite sure what was going on.

'I wonder who they are, the people behind?' asked Jean.

'No idea.'

'They seem to be coming our way. I think one of them is a policeman or something like that.'

'Christ,' Robert groaned. 'I hope Neville hasn't done something stupid.'

The pair watched in silence as the two small groups drew nearer. At one point the advancing parties dropped down into a hollow and disappeared from view. Moments later, to Jean and Robert's surprise, the heads of the three men reappeared over the crest of the dip. There was no sign of Neville or the children.

They waited as the men, who somehow seemed to be holding back, got slowly nearer. Robert thought that everything had gone very quiet. Behind him, not far away, his fellow holiday-makers were enjoying their wine and half-burnt meal, but he could barely hear them. Their voices were no more intrusive than insects murmuring in the distance. Also, he noticed how huge the landscape around him had suddenly become. The fields seemed to stretch away into infinity.

'I think those men want to talk to us,' said Jean.

'You may be right. Let's go and see what they've got to say.'

456

'Where do you think Neville and the children have got to?' Jean whispered, as they walked forward together.

Robert shook his head in obvious distress. 'No idea,' he managed to say, and gulped for air.

The three men finally reached them. The one in uniform spoke first.

'I'm looking for a Mr and Mrs Feltham. We were told at the site office that they're camping out here somewhere.'

'That's us,' Jean managed to say.

The man's face fell. He suddenly seemed too upset to speak. At last he blurted out, 'I'm sorry. I've got some . . .' He fell silent, and looked embarrassed.

Jean nodded, and finished the sentence for him. 'Bad news,' she said.

Something More

Gordon Van Gelder

I got my first hamster when I was in sixth grade. For my twelfth birthday I received a little plastic Habitrail cage and an adorable yellow and white rodent. I named her Fidget. I kept the cage by my desk, and I remember watching her scurry from corner to corner, run on the wheel, hold her food between her little paws, push on the roof of her sky den, and I kept thinking about her life and wondering if there was anything more to it. When Fidget died two years later, in a bigger cage, I asked myself the same question.

My name is Alan. I have been alive for twenty-two years. I work as an editorial assistant for a scientific book publisher. I have a degree from the University of Pennsylvania in mathematics, and I believe I have excellent opportunities for advancement at work. I live alone in my parents' old house.

I gave up on hamsters in high school, preoccupied with other things, learning how to be myself. I bought Heisenberg in a pet store when my roommate withdrew freshman year, so that I wouldn't feel stupid talking to myself in the little dorm room. Heisenberg lived in an aquarium and ran through cardboard tubes I took from the bathroom. I used to joke that she was the ideal college roommate, since she did nothing more than eat and sleep, and never said stupid things to me. She chewed through her plastic wheel. I also joked about using the pick-up line, "Want to come up to my room and see my warm furry thing?" There actually was an instance when I lured a date up to my room in order to see the golden teddy-bear hamster; it surprised me terribly when my date didn't laugh at the pass I made.

Heisenberg lasted only a year—in spite of all the suggestions I received for a "proper burial," I threw her corpse into a big green dumpster—and then I got long-haired Descartes. Descartes was fat and lazy and never once ran on the wheel I bought for her. I came in one night and found her lying on her back; she'd fallen trying to climb out of the cage and bashed her head on the ceramic food bowl. After her, I wondered if there would be any more.

Working for a scientific publisher is good for me, since I love writing and I love mathematics. Mathematics creates an ideal world for me, a place where every piece fits together, a place without boundaries. Like putting one foot in front of the other, I know there is always one more number.

Since I graduated, I've done a lot of reading on my own time: I amassed scores of books during college that I'd never had time to read. Every work of fiction seems to be about a person whose state of contentment is suddenly disrupted, and then that person goes through experiences that bring him or her to a new home, a new state of contentment. The pattern is classic or trite, depending on whether you accept things as they are.

I used to write the same sort of stories—people who solve their problems, people who go on journeys. Now I write about people who have everything they want from life. It's not easy, even when I use myself as a model. I read a lot of science fiction because it pushes back the envelope of existence, it goes as far as it can. I read it even though it's usually as hackneyed as everything else I read. It's not as though I have a lot of options.

I think I know why I have a "thing" for rodents. When I was very young, my family visited some friends in New Hampshire. My brother was six, I was three—all my memories of it now are confused with the photos we've got, but I remember our friends had two guinea pigs and a huge front lawn. We let the guinea pigs run around on the lawn and chased them. I have a picture in my mind of my family playing on the green grass and everybody was happy. If that's not the first memory of my life, it's close enough.

I love this room. Even though I've got the whole house to myself, I still consider this room to be mine. It's full of books and records, and there are too many tiny mementoes of my life on the bookshelves for me ever to leave here. The bed was made for me in fourth grade, and even though it's very small, it's the most comfortable place in the world. The windows face south and east, and the most beautiful sun rays pass through them in the morning. The posters on the blue walls have been there since high school: a long psychedelic shot of a desolate sandscape with pyramids in the distance, and an aerial view of blue mountain ridges, one after another. In high school I used to stare dreamily at them and think about escape. Now I'm old and jaded and I know there's a solid wall behind them.

My latest hamster is Sartre; I bought him yesterday. He's a brooding little animal, given to sitting in the corner and staring through the glass. I put an empty tissue box into the cage, and he pushed litter into it and sleeps there, a little home within a home for him. I wonder how long he'll last. He climbs on top of the box and tries to escape.

My parents' marriage was never a happy one, and the fighting grew worse after I went to school. So did the substance abuse. I can imagine the whole scene in my mind, the insults hurled like breaking glasses, the shrieking, the first shove after the words ran out, the kitchen knife. I can even visualize which knife, the middle-sized of the set of five. I visited him in the cell, and I cried when I saw his filthy fingers, like he'd been trying to dig out of a corner of the cage. He said the hard part was over, he'd make it now. I'd still like to know why they left his belt with him.
    Male hamsters devour their young, if I remember correctly. I wouldn't know: I've never even had two hamsters in the same cage.

Sartre scurries around the cage, digs into the green chlorophyll litter, runs on the wheel. Around and around. He drinks from the water bottle, sits on his haunches and stares out the cage. At nothing.
    I've got fifty or sixty years left of my life, if all goes well. Time to fall in and out of love again, time to write something lasting, time to travel, time to pursue some quirks in the fabric of mathematics.
    Why do I feel the walls closing in on me?
    Sartre is soft and his nose wiggles as I hold him. Like most of the hamsters I've owned, he continually tries to elude my grasp. But I hold him tightly.
    I wish there were more to life than dying.
    Tighter.
    I feel like I'm on the verge of something momentous, but there's nothing there.
    Tighter.

I drop the rodent back into the cage, and as I wash my hands I wonder if I'll get another one. I wonder if I can deal with any more hamsters at all.

The Spider

Basil Copper

I

M. Pinet arrived at the small country hotel just as dusk was falling on a wet October day. All about him was the melancholy of autumn and the headlights of his car stencilled a pallid path across the glaucous surface of the soaking, leaf-scattered road.

M. Pinet was feeling pleased with himself. A representative of a large firm of Paris textile manufacturers, he had previously travelled the flat, monotonous areas of Northern France and had felt his mind becoming as rigid and unyielding as the poplar lined roads he had daily traversed.

But now, he had been given another district, from Lyons in the south to the Ile de France, with an increase in salary as well, and he greatly appreciated the change. The beauty of his new surroundings, moreover, the different atmosphere of a novel routine had released all his pent-up drive; his latest had been a very successful tour indeed and his wallet bulged with the notes and banker's orders of clients.

At present he was about fifty miles south of Paris and had decided that he was too tired to push on to his home in the suburb of Courbevoie. He had already driven all the way from Auxerre and hadn't started until the afternoon, but he had made good time nevertheless. His bags of samples and the long bolts of cloth in the back of his small shooting brake shifted from side to side as he turned on the bad surface of the second class road through the forest.

He was feeling more than usually tired and the traffic in the Paris direction had been even heavier than normal for the time of year. He had reached the outskirts of a small village that was unfamiliar to him and had then spotted the lights of a fair-sized auberge set back from the road, amid clean-smelling pine trees. The chairs and tables of summer were now stacked under canvas between the box hedges but there came a welcome glow of light from the hallway and as he ran his car in under the heavy shadow of the trees he could see a zinc-covered bar and a thousand reflections from bottles that looked as though they contained most warming liquids. There were no other vehicles parked in front of the inn, but that did not worry M. Pinet. He had no particular desire for company; uppermost in his mind was the thought of a half bottle of wine to chase away the dank chill of autumn, a good dinner and eight hours' refreshing sleep before pushing on to Paris in the morning.

He parked his car, securely locked it and a few moments later found himself in a delightful-looking hall, containing a bar, some leather stools and a profusion of late summer flowers. A cat lay stretched on the polished tile floor. There was no other sign of life, apart from a man dressed in city clothes who was drinking cognac. He went out a moment after M. Pinet came in, muttering a sotto voce good evening and a short time later M. Pinet saw a big blue Mercedes, which had evidently been parked lower down the road, go by the window.

In response to the sharp, insistent bell on the zinc counter there presently came the shuffling of slippers and the patron appeared. He was all bonhomie and effusive welcome; yes, of course monsieur could have a room and dinner if he desired. It was the end of the season and he would not find it very gay—there was no one else dining in, but the chef could make him anything within reason. He would have his baggage fetched, if he wished.

All this was very gratifying and as M. Pinet signed the register he should have been pleased. He had brought his solitary valise in with him and after an aperitif he began to forget the dreariness of the autumn evening and the mile after mile of sodden woods outside. He was agreeably surprised, too, at the sumptuous furnishings of the dining room, which could easily have seated over two hundred people; the patron explained that many visitors came out from Paris to dine during the season.

M. Pinet felt he was being unfair, but it was the character of the landlord which spoiled what otherwise would have been a delightful sojourn. He hadn't caught the man's name, but there was something about him which put M. Pinet off. He was an average sized man with a triangular yellow face, a bald head and unnaturally large ears. His little eyes sparkled meanly, redolent of greed and insincerity and his wide slit mouth, which often parted to reveal gold teeth, was the crowning glory of an exceedingly ugly visage.

To M. Pinet's discomfort this individual set out to make himself ingratiatingly helpful, and personally waited on him at dinner. Of other staff M. Pinet saw none, though there must have been people in the kitchen beyond as he frequently heard the low murmur of voices and once a

461

plump woman in a low-cut black frock, possibly the patron's wife, walked by in the distance, giving him a stiff nod.

But first M. Pinet wanted a wash and the landlord indicated the door of the toilet. It was down a short corridor off the dining room; he had to fumble for the light switch and he then saw to his disgust that there was a large brown spider on the floor of the cracked stone corridor.

It seemed to watch him with little metallic eyes and with a sense of bubbling horror, M. Pinet felt it crack beneath his foot as he ground it with his heel. He had an innate fear of spiders, almost pathological in its intensity, and the violent physical nausea stayed with him until dinner.

As he opened the door of the toilet and switched on the light there, M. Pinet could not repress a cry of panic. Faugh! There were two more of the monsters here, one on the wall near his head and the other on the floor near the toilet seat. M. Pinet fancied he could almost hear the low scratch of its legs, as it moved experimentally, its strange blue metallic eyes—the most curious he had ever seen in an insect—seeming to gaze at him with reproach. As it crunched beneath his almost hysterically wielded shoe, the eyes faded as the creature died. The other fled like lightning to a spot behind the lavatory cistern, wrenching another involuntary cry from M. Pinet's lips.

A moment later the landlord was at his side. He seemed amused and his small eyes were dancing.

"No, monsieur," he said. "Nothing to be alarmed about. The damp weather always brings them from the woods at this time of year. They will not harm you. They are my pets."

He made a sort of clucking noise with his mouth, which M. Pinet found hideously revolting and the great brown horror behind the cistern stirred. Before M. Pinet's disbelieving eyes it scuttled on to the landlord's open palm, where he stroked it and crooned to it in a thoroughly disgusting manner.

M. Pinet, pale and disconcerted, excused himself and made shift by washing his hands and face at the washbasin in the corridor. Back in the dining room he felt better and was relieved to see the partron first put the spider somewhere outside the back door. He was pleased too, to see this strange character wash his own hands before disappearing into the kitchen.

The dinner was an excellent one and as M. Pinet tipped his croutons into the soup, he felt his spirits revive; the landlord was undoubtedly a somewhat peculiar man but he certainly knew how to produce a fine meal. M. Pinet was by this time so far soothed by his surroundings that he invited the landlord to join him at the table for a drink after his dinner was over. Contrary to his expectations the landlord seemed to draw more out of him than the information he gained in return. In answer to

M. Pinet's point-blank question, as to whether he had been at the inn long, the patron replied, "No, not long. We move around quite a bit, my wife and I."

M. Pinet did not pursue the subject. He had decided to pay for his meal before going to bed and settle for his accommodation in the morning. He was a methodically-minded man and though it all came to the same thing in the end, he preferred to do it this way. He had stepped up to the desk in a corner of the dining room and the landlord's eyes glistened and narrowed in an unpleasant manner as he spotted the huge bundle of notes in M. Pinet's wallet. The latter realised this was a mistake and somewhat awkwardly tried to cover them over with a batch of letters he carried, but this only served to draw more attention by its obvious clumsiness.

The landlord stared at him unblinkingly, as he said, quite without emphasis, "You have had a successful season, monsieur." It was a statement, not a question and M. Pinet managed to turn the conversation quickly to the subject of his room. A few moments later he said goodnight and carried his own bag up to the chamber indicated on the first floor.

The well carpeted corridor had bowls of flowers on tables at intervals and bright lights were burning; there was an uneasy moment, however, as M. Pinet put his key in the lock of room No. 12. All the lights in the corridor suddenly went out, evidently controlled from downstairs and for a long minute M. Pinet was in total darkness. A faint scratching noise away to his left brought sweat to his forehead but a moment later he was inside his room and light flooded from the ceiling fixture. He locked the door and stood against it for a few seconds, taking in the contents of the room.

It was a prettily conceived chamber and any other time M. Pinet would have been taken with its heavily contrived charm; but tonight, with his nerves curiously shaken, he was in no mood for atmosphere. He merely undressed as quickly as he could, turned up his bed, got a novel from his valise and noisily cleaned his teeth in the basin in the corner. The mirror reflected back an image that was noticeably pale. Before getting into bed he heard the faint noise of footsteps outside and looking through the window was disconcerted to see the figure of the landlord, silhouetted against the light from an open door, furtively studying his car. A moment later he moved off and M. Pinet heard a door slam somewhere below him. He got into bed.

The novel was a bad one and M. Pinet was greatly tired but somehow he did not want to sleep. He kept his bedside lamp burning but despite this eventually drifted off into a doze. Some time later he was awakened by the noise of a car driving away from the inn. Even as he became fully

463

conscious he heard the faint sound of its engine die with a hum in the distance as the trees enveloped it.

For some reason M. Pinet's mind became agitated at this and he felt a great desire to look out of the window to see if his car was still in front of the hotel. Before he could move, however, he heard a faint scratching noise; his nerves strained as they were, he turned his head with infinite slowness in an effort to locate the sound. Eventually—a quick glance at his watch showed him that it was after two a.m.—he narrowed down the source of the sound as coming from the triangular area formed by the corner of the ceiling furthest from him.

It was in the gloomiest part of the chamber, for the light from the reading lamp extended only a yard or two; to switch on the main light M. Pinet would have to cross over to the door and he was loath to do this, particularly in his bare feet. He compromised by turning up the bedside lamp so that the light shone towards the far corner of the room. There was something there, but it was still so wrapped in shadow that he could not make out what it was.

He groped for his glasses on the table by the bed; to do this he had to lower the lamp to its usual position and while he was fumbling with this he heard his spectacle case fall with a soft thump on to the carpet at his bedside. He looked down; the spectacles were only about two feet from him but again, he had great reserve about stretching out his hand to the carpet. Dry-mouthed he turned, as the scratching noise came again and a cry was strangled in his throat as he saw the shadowy thing scuttle a little closer towards him across the ceiling; even without his glasses he did not need to be told what it was but his senses still refused to believe.

Something furry, like a tarantula, bigger than a soup-plate, round and with legs as thick as telephone cables. Its legs rustled together as it came across the ceiling with old-maidish deliberation and a thin purring noise came from it. As it edged forward into the brightness of the lamp M. Pinet saw with sick fear that it was covered with brown fur and had an obscene parody of a mouth.

He looked round desperately for a stick or any other weapon, but there was nothing; his tongue stuck to the roof of his mouth, denying him the shriek which would have saved him; his pyjamas streamed with perspiration and moisture dabbled his forehead. He closed his eyes once and opened them with an effort, hoping against hope that he was in the grip of a nightmare. But the obscene, sliding thing was nearer still and M. Pinet gave up hope. He saw now that the creature had metallic blue eyes, like the eyes of the insects he had crushed in the washroom and as they glared into his own with implacable hatred he noticed with a last shock of surprise that they were very like the landlord's.

The insect paused and then launched itself on a thick silken thread; a nauseous stench was in his nostrils, the great spider gave a sibilant rattle and then it was on his mouth, covering his face and eyes with its bloated, sticky carcase. M. Pinet gave shriek after shriek as consciousness mercifully died.

II

A most curious case," said the doctor, washing his hands in the washbasin of M. Pinet's room. "Heart sound as a bell, yet he must have died instantaneously from some great shock. Never come across anything like it. There'll have to be an inquiry, of course."

And the doctor, who was a matter-of-fact human being, gave a heavy sigh. The landlord's wife, who stood just inside the door of the death chamber, timidly assented.

Down below in the bar the landlord, who lived by the secret fears of his customers, smiled a curious smile. He fondled a thick bundle of notes under the counter.

In the room above, a tiny brown spider, not more than an eighth of an inch across, scuttled nervously across the dead man's forehead. The doctor brushed it impatiently away and it fell out of sight by the side of the bed.

Still Frame

Jack C. Haldeman II

The old man came slowly into focus. Diffused shades of gray gradually became sharp images on the ground-glass screen. Robert framed the picture as the man stared into the camera with dead eyes. The shutter snapped, capturing what was left of his soul on Kodak Tri-X film, ASA 400.

The photographer smiled. He knew a good shot when one fell into his lap.

Robert Whitten was sitting on top of the world. Barely twenty-five years old, he had it all and he knew it. He moved to his left to get a different angle and the old man, bored, looked away. Robert refocused and adjusted his exposure.

The man was sitting in a cane-backed chair and staring out the window of the nursing home where he'd lived for the past ten years. The white curtains shifted in the meager summer breeze. Robert held still for a moment, and as the old man's eyes started to close he pressed the shutter release and fired off three quick shots.

The man turned around sharply and started to say something, but stopped. Instead, he shook his head wearily and turned his face to the wall.

The session was over. Robert let his camera hang on its strap as he jotted a few notes in his worn notebook: the date, shutter speeds, f-stops; all technical information, cold hard numbers, nothing about the man. After all, he'd already picked up the release forms from the nursing home manager. He was legally cleared to photograph the old man. What else did he have to know? The man was old and photogenic. That was all that mattered.

Robert lit a cigarette as he walked out onto the broad front porch of the old wood frame house. A woman, fanning herself as she rocked back and forth, looked up at him and smiled. He looked away from the broken teeth and wrinkled skin and started down the steps to the gravel driveway.

As he reached his car, he noticed two women sitting together on a swing hanging from the far end of the porch. He removed the 50mm lens from his camera and slipped on the medium telephoto he carried in a case on his hip. He raised the camera and focused. It was as if he were standing beside them. He let his cigarette drop and ground it into the gravel with his heel.

The women wore faded white cotton dresses and they had a sameness about them that could have come from being sisters or it could have come with the equalizing effects of age. Gaunt and white-haired, they were having an animated discussion as the swing slowly moved back and forth. Robert framed them dispassionately as they laughed, concentrating on the shifting light and depth of field.

One woman leaned over and whispered something in the other's ear. They giggled and clapped their hands together like schoolgirls. The expressions on their faces were perfect. Except for the passing of eighty years they could have been children. The chain on the swing was rusted, the paint was cracked and peeling in places. The age splotches on their hands and faces stood out clearly. Liver spots.

Only their eyes held life. It somehow shined through the ruin of the years. Robert snapped the picture and knew he had another winner. He opened the car door and set the camera on the front seat.

As he started his Mercedes, he reached down and flipped on the air conditioner. The face of the woman fanning herself was still fresh in his mind. Slipping the car into gear, he drove down the driveway and turned left, scattering gravel as he spun his wheels getting away from the nursing home as rapidly as possible. Old people depressed him. He felt trapped by them.

It was ironic, of course, since old people had brought him everything he had.

Five years ago Robert had dropped out of college to try his luck at full-time photography. He loved animals and had always wanted to be a wildlife photographer. For several months he lived alone in a cabin deep in the mountains. His days were spent following deer, birds, and bears with his camera. He would stand for hours waiting for the sun to be *just* right, waiting for the perfect picture. His nights were spent working in a makeshift darkroom. When he came back to civilization, he carried a thick portfolio of excellent prints. None of them sold.

In order to support himself, Robert took a job as staff photographer for a small local paper. The rest had been mostly luck as far as he could tell. It started with a shot he'd taken early one morning of an old wino rummaging through a garbage can. The man looked up just as Robert snapped the shutter, and the hopelessness and longing in the man's eyes vaulted Robert to the front page of a hundred newspapers.

Everything had grown from that one photo. Everything.

His editor suggested that he try a feature on the elderly street people in town, and although he didn't think much of the idea, Robert went ahead and shot it. Every bag lady and bum that he encountered depressed him, yet he couldn't deny the appeal the photographs would have. He could see the pathos that other people would see in his pictures, but he couldn't feel it himself. It was as if something was missing deep inside him.

The feature was enlarged and ran every Sunday for a month. Many of the pictures were picked up by the wire services, and UPI ran the shot of two old men sleeping in a doorway in over two hundred papers around the world.

Time and *Newsweek* reprinted part of the series as did several foreign publications including *Paris Match* and *Le Monde*. *Esquire* ran a feature-length article on the young photographer just before his collection *Street People* was published by Doubleday in an oversized limited edition just in time for the Christmas trade.

The book sold well and the paperback edition did even better. Robert quit the newspaper, and with a healthy advance from Doubleday he began shooting the companion edition, *Ancient Eyes*. It was a natural follow-up with a built-in market and he hated every minute. He even hated it the instant he tripped the shutter capturing the old sharecropper leaning against the fence at twilight. That was the one that got him the

Pulitzer Prize. It also locked him into photographing old people, seemingly forever.

It was also the time the nightmares started. First came the troubled sleep, the endless series of bad dreams. Then it was little things he started seeing at the edge of his vision, little creepy things with no real shape or form.

The psychiatrists were no help. For two hundred dollars an hour they came up with lots of words and theories, but no cures. He felt trapped by the very things that had brought him success. That much was clear. If he had to live with nightmares in order to live with wealth, he figured he could handle it. Money was a great buffer, the best. It could solve all kinds of problems.

He pulled the Mercedes into the circular drive in front of the condominium he'd bought last year out of royalties from *Ancient Eyes*, leaving the car to be parked by the attendant who opened the door for him. He didn't relax until the elevator let him out in front of the door to his condo, ten floors above and light-years away from the world of the old people.

He threw his jacket over the back of the white sofa and flipped through his mail. Nothing there. His telephone-answering machine held nothing important. Kicking off his shoes, he went to the bar by the balcony and poured himself a drink.

Robert's walls were covered with prints of all sizes. Some were matted, some were framed and covered with glass. They were all photographs of birds and animals. A large color print of a bald eagle dominated one wall, surrounded by smaller prints of hawks in flight. A study of a family of raccoons lined the wall to the bedroom. There were no pictures of people.

He sat for a minute sipping scotch and remembered the old man. The film was in his camera bag and he opened it, taking out the three canisters that held what he'd shot earlier.

For a moment he rolled the film around on the coffee table in front of him, trying to decide if he wanted to work anymore today or not. He faced no deadlines, but a couple of the shots had looked pretty good and he was curious.

Robert took the film into the large darkroom he'd had built off the bathroom and loaded it into the developing tank. While the tank slowly rotated, Robert got down his trays and filled them with chemicals. He took the protective cover off the enlarger and cleaned the lens and negative carrier with a few sprays from a can of compressed air. After the negatives had finished their final rinse, Robert hung them in the drying closet. It would take a few minutes for the film to dry, so he left the darkroom, stripped, and stepped into the shower.

The water felt good, hot and steamy. As Robert soaped himself up, he relaxed and felt the weariness from the nursing home wash away. He closed his eyes and let the hot water rinse them off.

Stepping from the shower, he dried himself and did a few deep knee bends. His body was in good shape and he exercised regularly. No fat, no flab, not so much as a single gray hair. After a day of looking at wrinkled and ruined people, it was good to remind himself of his youth. He touched his toes twice and slipped into a robe.

Walking into the darkroom, Robert's curiosity got the better of him. Rather than taking the time to run contact sheets of the day's work, he went directly to the roll that had the shots of the old man. He held it up to the dim safety light and found his place. There were only ten negatives, but they all looked good. He slipped the first one into the enlarger and pulled out a sheet of 8 by 10 paper.

The exhaust fan whirred softly in the darkened room as he focused the enlarger, cropping the picture as he went along. Blurs of black and gray became sharp lines, defined images. This was the part of photography he liked best. Everything that went before only led up to this final step. The print was all that counted.

He studied the old man carefully, with an eye for detail. Only when preparing the print did he notice the small things: a scar on the man's forehead, a wisp of hair from a small mole on his cheek. All these details were what made the photograph successful, but he never noticed them until this stage, always taking for granted that they would be there and they always were. He estimated the correct exposure and flipped the red filter out of the enlarger.

For seven seconds the black-and-white image of the old man stared up at Robert from the easel under the enlarger. The man had an intensity in his eyes—a strange mixture of hate and despair—that Robert hadn't noticed when he'd taken the picture. It burned through the milky film of the old man's cataracts with a surprising fierceness.

The man also had a faint area of skin discoloration on the side of his face that had escaped Robert. If he didn't like the effect, Robert could always eliminate the discoloration by dodging it out in the final print. He rubbed the side of his face absently as he stood by the enlarger, staring down at the old man staring back at him from a small square of light in the darkness.

Seven seconds passed, ticked away precisely by the large timer over the enlarger. Robert flipped the red filter back into place and slid the paper into the developer.

Handling it only by the edges with a pair of plastic tongs, he moved the blank paper gently around in the shallow tray, touching it occasionally at the corners to keep it under the fluid. After a few seconds the latent image started to appear; slowly at first, with only the darkest parts of the photograph appearing as a ghostlike outline.

Gradually, the print gained substance, the blacks became a deeper, almost absolute black. The white areas stood out in sharp contrast as the shades of gray supplied the detail. Robert watched the old man's eyes carefully, judging the stage of development by the grain of the print.

When the print was fully developed, Robert transferred it to the stop bath for a few seconds and moved it into the fixer. He swirled the print around for a couple of minutes and dipped it into the running water in the washer. Impatient to get a good look at what he had, Robert took the print out of the water and stepped out of the darkroom into the well-lit bathroom to examine it.

He flattened the print against the large mirror over the double sink, sticking it beneath the strong light. He stepped back to get a general idea of how the cropping had worked. It looked good, and he leaned in close to check the focusing and detail. He still couldn't decide whether or not he should dodge out the man's skin discoloration.

Robert decided it could use a little longer exposure and smoothed down a corner of the print with his finger. As he did, he noticed some small brownish blotches on the back of his hand. They looked almost like developer stains, but that was hardly possible. He'd been in up to his elbows in developer for years and it had never happened before. He rubbed at them, but they didn't go away.

Turning on the water, he rinsed off his hands. It didn't help. He ran the water as hot as he could stand it and scrubbed with soap, but the spots wouldn't go away. Annoyed, he shut off the water angrily. The damn things would have to wear away.

Robert took the print off the mirror and stopped for a second. Was that a spot of gray hair at his temples? He looked closer, rubbing his hair with his fingers. No, it was nothing. He hated the idea of gray hair, the first sure sign of old age. Gray hair marked the beginning of that inescapable slide into the world of old people, the people he couldn't stand, the people he made both his reputation and living from.

He went back into the darkroom and dropped the photograph back into the print washer. Even though it was a test print, he knew there were people who would pay a lot for it.

He moved the strip of film to the next negative and cropped the picture almost automatically. The old man had been looking away from the camera, his gray hair backlighted by the light from the window.

It would make an effective print. Robert softened the light from the window just a little and brought out the highlights on the man's hair, improving on reality. As he finished moving the print through the trays, he considered making a large one later to display at his upcoming show. It would undoubtedly sell very well.

He took it out to the bathroom to look at it in the light. Details he had missed in the darkroom caught his eye. The man had a cracked thumbnail, an ugly wart half hidden behind his ear. While that only served to make the print more effective, it made Robert feel uncomfortable.

Satisfied with the photograph, he peeled it off the mirror, and as he did, he saw himself reflected in the still-wet glass. It was a distorted image, warped by the rivulets of water as they ran down the mirror. His features twisted as he stared, unable to take his eyes away. It was as if he were watching a wax figure melt in an impossibly hot room. The flesh slid off and was replaced by bone, a gleaming white skull mocking him with vacant eye sockets and a frozen grin.

He grabbed a towel and rubbed the mirror violently. It helped, but not much.

His reflection stared back at him with unbelieving eyes through the musty cloud of cataracts. His hair was solid gray. A patch of skin discoloration spread across his cheek. His hand rose to touch the side of his face and as it did, he looked down and saw the cracked fingernails, the swollen knuckles. He screamed, and it was a violent, hollow sound torn from the depths of his soul. It echoed against the walls of the bathroom and went no farther.

He opened his robe and his body was thin and wasted. His hips jutted out sharply and the flesh hung from his bones in useless folds of dead tissue.

Still clutching the print, he staggered out to the living room. Somehow he managed to punch the proper numbers on the telephone.

"Hillside Nursing Home," said a female voice on the other end.

"This is Robert Whitten," he gasped. "I need . . . I need some information on a patient." His voice was raspy and he couldn't control the tremors in his hands.

"Oh yes, Mr. Whitten. I'm a big fan of yours. We saw you around this afternoon taking pictures. What can I do for you? You'll have to speak up. We seem to have a bad connection."

"An old man. I was taking pictures of him today."

"Most of our clients are elderly, Mr. Whitten. Could you give me a better idea who it is that you're looking for?"

"Front room. Something wrong with his skin." Robert coughed and saw with horror that he was spitting up blood.

"That would be poor Mr. Freeman. It was so sudden."

"Sudden? What do you mean?"

"Just like that. Alive one minute and dead the next. Of course, that happens here. Like I say, many of our clients are elderly and you have to expect—"

Robert hung up the phone and wiped the blood from his mouth. He was slobbering now, a mixture of saliva and blood. His eyes wouldn't focus and his arms and legs shook uncontrollably.

Through his clouded vision, he thought the room was filling up with faces. It could have been his imagination; he could no longer tell. They were all old. They had come to collect what he owed them.

He took the still-wet print in his shaking hands and sat down to wait for the inevitable.

It didn't take long.

The Stranger

Ambrose Bierce

A man stepped out of the darkness into the little illuminated circle about our failing campfire and seated himself upon a rock.

"You are not the first to explore this region," he said, gravely.

Nobody controverted his statement; he was himself proof of its truth, for he was not of our party and must have been somewhere near when we camped. Moreover, he must have companions not far away; it was not a place where one would be living or traveling alone. For more than a week we had seen, besides ourselves and our animals, only such living things as rattlesnakes and horned toads. In an Arizona desert one does not long coexist with only such creatures as these: one must have pack animals, supplies, arms—"an outfit." And all these imply comrades. It was perhaps a doubt as to what manner of men this unceremonious stanger's comrades might be, together with something in his words interpretable as a challenge, that caused every man of our half-dozen "gentlemen adventurers" to rise to a sitting posture and lay his hand upon a weapon—an act signifying, in that time and place, a policy of expectation. The stranger gave the matter no attention and began again to speak in the same deliberate, uninflected monotone in which he had delivered his first sentence:

"Thirty years ago Ramon Gallegos, William Shaw, George W. Kent and Berry Davis, all of Tucson, crossed the Santa Catalina mountains and traveled due west, as nearly as the configuration of the country permitted. We were prospecting and it was our intention, if we found nothing, to push through to the Gila river at some point near Big Bend, where we understood there was a settlement. We had a good outfit but no guide—just Ramon Gallegos, William Shaw, George W. Kent and Berry Davis."

The man repeated the names slowly and distinctly, as if to fix them in the memories of his audience, every member of which was now attentively observing him, but with a slackened apprehension regarding his possible companions somewhere in the darkness that seemed to enclose us like a black wall; in the manner of this volunteer historian was no suggestion of an unfriendly purpose. His act was rather that of a harmless lunatic than an enemy. We were not so new to the country as not to know that the solitary life of many a plainsman had a tendency to develop eccentricities of conduct and character not always easily distinguishable from mental aberration. A man is like a tree: in a forest of his fellows he will grow as straight as his generic and individual nature permits; alone in the open, he yields to the deforming stresses and tortions that environ him. Some such thoughts were in my mind as I watched the man from the shadow of my hat, pulled low to shut out the firelight. A witless fellow, no doubt, but what could he be doing there in the heart of a desert?

Having undertaken to tell this story, I wish that I could describe the man's appearance; that would be a natural thing to do. Unfortunately, and somewhat strangely, I find myself unable to do so with any degree of confidence, for afterward no two of us agreed as to what he wore and how he looked; and when I try to set down my own impressions they elude me. Anyone can tell some kind of story; narration is one of the elemental powers of the race. But the talent for description is a gift.

Nobody having broken silence the visitor went on to say:

"This country was not then what it is now. There was not a ranch between the Gila and the Gulf. There was a little game here and there in the mountains, and near the infrequent water-holes grass enough to keep our animals from starvation. If we should be so fortunate as to encounter no Indians we might get through. But within a week the purpose of the expedition had altered from discovery of wealth to preservation of life. We had gone too far to go back, for what was ahead could be no worse than what was behind; so we pushed on, riding by night to avoid Indians and the intolerable heat, and concealing ourselves by day as best we could. Sometimes, having exhausted our supply of wild meat and emptied our casks, we were days without food or drink; then a water-hole or a shallow pool in the bottom of an *arroyo* so restored our strength and sanity that we were able to shoot some of the wild animals that sought it also. Sometimes it was a bear, sometimes an antelope, a coyote, a cougar—that was as God pleased; all were food.

"One morning as we skirted a mountain range, seeking a practicable pass, we were attacked by a band of Apaches who had followed our trail up a gulch—it is not far from here. Knowing that they outnumbered us ten to one, they took none of their usual cowardly precautions, but dashed upon us at a gallop, firing and yelling. Fighting was out of the question: we urged our feeble animals up the gulch as far as there was footing for a hoof, then threw ourselves out of our saddles and took to the *chaparral* on one of the slopes, abandoning our entire outfit to the enemy. But we retained our rifles, every man—Ramon Gallegos, William Shaw, George W. Kent and Berry Davis."

"Same old crowd," said the humorist of our party. He was an Eastern man, unfamiliar with the decent observances of social intercourse. A gesture of disapproval from our leader silenced him and the stranger proceeded with his tale:

"The savages dismounted also, and some of them ran up the gulch beyond the point at which we had left it, cutting off further retreat in that direction and forcing us on up the side. Unfortunately the *chaparral* extended only a short distance up the slope, and as we came into the open ground above we took the fire of a dozen rifles; but Apaches shoot badly when in a hurry, and God so willed it that none of us fell. Twenty yards up the slope, beyond the edge of the brush, were vertical cliffs, in which, directly in front of us, was a narrow opening. Into that we ran, finding ourselves in a cavern about as large as an ordinary room in a house. Here for a time we were safe: a single man with a repeating rifle could defend the entrance against all the Apaches in the land. But against hunger and thirst we had no defense. Courage we still had, but hope was a memory.

"Not one of those Indians did we afterward see, but by the smoke and glare of their fires in the gulch we knew that by day and by night they watched with ready rifles in the edge of the bush—knew that if we made a sortie not a man of us would live to take three steps into the open. For three days, watching in turn, we held out before our suffering became insupportable. Then—it was the morning of the fourth day—Ramon Gallegos said:

" 'Señores, I know not well of the good God and what please him. I have live without religion, and I am not acquaint with that of you. Pardon, señores, if I shock you, but for me the time is come to beat the game of the Apache.'

"He knelt upon the rock floor of the cave and pressed his pistol against his temple. 'Madre de Dios,' he said, 'comes now the soul of Ramon Gallegos.'

"And so he left us—William Shaw, George W. Kent and Berry Davis.

"I was the leader: it was for me to speak.

474

" 'He was a brave man,' I said—'he knew when to die, and how. It is foolish to go mad from thirst and fall by Apache bullets, or be skinned alive—it is in bad taste. Let us join Ramon Gallegos.'

" 'That is right,' said William Shaw.

" 'That is right,' said George W. Kent.

"I straightened the limbs of Ramon Gallegos and put a handkerchief over his face. Then William Shaw said: 'I should like to look like that—a little while.'

"And George W. Kent said that he felt that way, too.

" 'It shall be so,' I said: 'the red devils will wait a week. William Shaw and George W. Kent, draw and kneel.'

"They did so and I stood before them.

" 'Almighty God, our Father,' said I.

" 'Almighty God, our Father,' said William Shaw.

" 'Almighty God, our Father,' said George W. Kent.

" 'Forgive us our sins,' said I.

" 'Forgive us our sins,' said they.

" 'And receive our souls.'

" 'And receive our souls.'

" 'Amen!'

" 'Amen!'

"I laid them beside Ramon Gallegos and covered their faces."

There was a quick commotion on the opposite side of the campfire: one of our party had sprung to his feet, pistol in hand.

"And you!" he shouted—"*you* dared to escape?—you dare to be alive? You cowardly hound, I'll send you to join them if I hang for it!"

But with the leap of a panther the captain was upon him, grasping his wrist. "Hold it in, Sam Yountsey, hold it in!"

We were now all upon our feet—except the stranger, who sat motionless and apparently inattentive. Some one seized Yountsey's other arm.

"Captain," I said, "there is something wrong here. This fellow is either a lunatic or merely a liar—just a plain, every-day liar whom Yountsey had no call to kill. If this man was of that party it had five members, one of whom—probably himself—he has not named."

"Yes," said the captain, releasing the insurgent, who sat down, "there is something—unusual. Years ago four dead bodies of white men, scalped and shamefully mutilated, were found about the mouth of that cave. They are buried there; I have seen the graves—we shall all see them to-morrow."

The stranger rose, standing tall in the light of the expiring fire, which in our breathless attention to his story we had neglected to keep going.

"There were four," he said—"Ramon Gallegos, William Shaw, George W. Kent and Berry Davis."

With this reiterated roll-call of the dead he walked into the darkness and we saw him no more.

At that moment one of our party, who had been on guard, strode in among us, rifle in hand and somewhat excited.

"Captain," he said, "for the last half-hour three men have been standing out there on the *mesa*." He pointed in the direction taken by the stranger. "I could see them distinctly, for the moon is up, but as they had no guns and I had them covered with mine I thought it was their move. They have made none, but, damn it! they have got on to my nerves."

"Go back to your post, and stay till you see them again," said the captain. "The rest of you lie down again, or I'll kick you all into the fire."

The sentinel obediently withdrew, swearing, and did not return. As we were arranging our blankets the fiery Yountsey said: "I beg your pardon, Captain, but who the devil do you take them to be?"

"Ramon Gallegos, William Shaw and George W. Kent."

"But how about Berry Davis? I ought to have shot him."

"Quite needless; you couldn't have made him any deader. Go to sleep."

A Street Was Chosen

Ramsey Campbell

A street was chosen. Within its parameters, homes were randomly selected. Preliminary research yielded details of the occupants as follows:

A (husband, insurance salesman, 30; wife, 28; infant daughter, 18 months)

B (widow, 67)

C (husband, 73; wife, 75; son, library assistant, 38)

D (mother, bank clerk, 32; daughter, 3)

E (husband, social worker, 35; wife, social worker, 34)

F (electrician, male, 51; assistant, male, 25)

G (husband, 42; wife, industrial chemist, 38; son, 4; infant son, 2)

H (mother, 86; son, teacher, 44; son's wife, head-mistress, 41; granddaughter, 12; grandson, 11)

I (window-cleaner, male, 53)

J (tax officer, female, 55)

K (milkman, male, 39)

L (waiter, 43)

It was noted that subjects I–L occupied apartments in the same house. Further preliminary observation established that:

(a) Subject B wrote letters to newspapers

(b) The children of couples A and G visited each other's homes to play

(c) Granddaughter H sat with child D while mother D was elsewhere on an average of 1 evening per week

(d) Husband G experienced bouts of temporary impotence lasting between 6 and 8 days

(e) Elder F performed sexual acts with his partner in order to maintain the relationship

(f) Subject L had recently been released into the community after treatment for schizophrenia

It was decided that stimuli should be applied gradually and with caution. During an initial 8-night period, the following actions were taken:

(1,i) Each night a flower was uprooted from the garden of subject B, and all evidence of removal was erased

(1, ii) The lights in house H were caused to switch on at random intervals for periods of up to 5 minutes between the hours of 3 and 6 in the morning

(1, iii) On alternate nights, subject J was wakened shortly after entering deep sleep by telephone calls purporting to advertise life insurance

(1, iv) The tinfoil caps of milk-bottles delivered to subject D were removed after delivery, and feeding nipples substituted

At the end of 8 days, it was noted that subject B was less inclined than previously to engage her neighbours in conversation, and more prone to argue or to take offence. From the 7th day onwards she was seen to spend extended periods at the windows which overlooked her garden.

Subjects F were employed by couple H to trace the source of an apparent electrical malfunction. It was observed that mother H became increasingly hostile to her son's wife both during this process and after electricians F had failed to locate any fault in the wiring. Observations suggested that she blamed either her daughter-in-law or her grandchildren for tampering with the electricity in order to disturb her sleep.

Subject J was observed to approach subject A in order to obtain names and addresses of insurance companies which advertised by telephone. It was noted that when the list provided by A failed to yield the required explanation, A undertook to make further enquiries on J's behalf.

It was observed that subject D initially responded to the substitution of nipples as if it were a joke. After 2 days, however, she was seen to accuse subject K of the substitution. At the end of the 8-day period she cancelled the delivery and ordered milk from a rival company. It was decided to discontinue the substitution for an indefinite period.

After observations were completed, the following stimuli were applied during a period of 15 days:

(2, i) An anonymous letter based on a computer analysis of B's prose style was published in the free newspaper received by all subjects, objecting to the existence of househusbands and claiming that the writer was aware of two people who committed adultery while their children played together

(2, ii) Every third night as subject L walked home, he was approached by religious pamphleteers whose faces had been altered to resemble the other tenants of his building in the order I, K, J, I, K

(2, iii) The dustbin of subjects F was overturned, and pages from a magazine depicting naked prepubertal boys were scattered around it

(2, iv) The figure of subject I was projected on the bedroom window of subjects E and caused to appear to pass through it while husband E was alone in the room

(2, v) Brochures advertising old folks' homes were sent on alternate days to son C

(2, vi) Telephone calls using a simulation of the voice of subject J were made between 3 and 5 in the morning on 6 occasions to house A, complaining that J had just received another advertising call

At the end of the second period of stimuli, the following observations were made:

After the appearance of the letter in the newspaper, husband G was observed to suffer a bout of impotence lasting 11 days. It was also noted that subject D attempted to befriend wives A and G, who appeared to be suspicious of her motives. As a result of this encounter, increasing strain was recorded within couples A and G.

Subject L was seen to examine the mail addressed to subjects I, J, and K, and also to attempt to view the apartments of these subjects through the keyholes. Whenever any two of these subjects began a conversation while L was in the building, attempts by L to overhear were observed. Also noted was the growing tendency of L to scrutinise the faces of diners while he waited on them in the restaurant.

After the elder of subjects F discovered the pages which had apparently been hidden in the dustbin, several disagreements of increasing length and violence between subjects F were recorded, both subjects accusing the other of responsibility for the material. At the end of 11 days, the younger of the subjects was seen to take up residence beyond the parameters of the present experiment. It was further observed that mother G required her sons to promise to inform her or their father if they were approached in any way by subjects F.

It was noted that subject E did not mention the apparition of subject I to his wife.

After the first delivery of brochures to their son, parents C were observed to cease speaking to him, despite his denial of responsibility for the receipt of the material. It was noted that parents C opened and destroyed all brochures subsequently delivered. Hot meals prepared for son C were left on the table for him for up to 1 hour before his consumption of them.

Husband A was seen twice to request subject J not to telephone his house after 11 o'clock at night. When the calls continued, wife A was observed to threaten J with legal action, despite J's denial of all knowledge. During this confrontation, subject L was seen to accuse J of attempting to distress both himself and wife A. It was recorded that wife A advised him to take up the matter with the landlord of the apartments.

A decision was reached to increase the level of stimuli. The following actions were taken during a 6-day period:

(3, i) In the absence of subject B, all the furniture in her house was dismantled

(3, ii) Several brochures concerning euthanasia and the right to die were addressed to son C

(3, iii) Whenever husband G succeeded in achieving an erection, the car alarm of subjects A was made to sound

(3, iv) A box of fireworks labelled as a free sample was delivered to children H. Several fireworks were later removed and were exploded inside the house of subject F

(3, v) The face of subject B was made to appear above the beds of children G. When infant G fled, he was caused to fall downstairs. Snapping of the neck was observed to occur

(3, vi) Live insects were introduced into meals which subject L was about to serve to diners

(3, vii) The outer doors of apartments I and K were painted crimson overnight

During and after this period, the following observations were made:
After parents C were seen to examine the brochures addressed to their son, it was noted that they placed his belongings outside the house and employed a neighbour to change the external locks. It was observed that when on his return son C attempted to protest that he owned the house, he was refused any response. Later he was found to be sleeping in a public park. Information was received that when his workmates attempted to counsel him he quit his job. It was observed that although

mother C wished to take the son's belongings into the house, father C insisted on their remaining outside.

Grandmother H was seen to attack grandchildren H under the impression that they were responsible for the damage to house F, although the police had accepted evidence that the children could not have been involved. When mother H defended her children from their grandmother, it was noted that she was accused of having succeeded professionally at the expense of her husband. A protracted argument between all five subjects H was observed, after which increases in tension between all subjects were recorded, the greatest increase being between son and wife.

It was observed that when granddaughter H offered to sit with child D, mother D refused to employ her. Mother H was later seen to accuse mother D of attempting to befriend families in the hope of developing a sexual relationship with the father.

Husband G was observed to destroy the headlights of car A with a hammer. The ensuing altercation was seen to be terminated when wife G reported that infant G had been injured on the stairs. It was noted that infant G died en route to the nearest hospital.

It was recorded that subject L was unable to determine whether or not the insects placed in the meals he was about to serve were objectively real. It was noted that this confusion caused L to lose his job. Subsequently L was observed to attempt to persuade several of the other subjects that a pattern was discernible in the various recent events, without success. It was noted that L overheard subjects I and K suggesting that L had repainted their doors.

Surviving child G was seen to inform its parents that subject B had driven infant G out of the children's room. It was observed that when mother G confronted B with this, B accused G of having caused the apparition by experimenting on the children with drugs produced in the laboratory where G worked. It was further noted that subjects E attempted to intervene in the argument but were met with hostility bordering on accusation, both by B and G and by several bystanders. When subject I was attracted by the confrontation, husband E was observed to take refuge in house E.

It was noted that subject L approached his landlord and tried to persuade him that subjects I, J, and K were conspiring against L. It was further observed that when L was given notice to quit the apartment, L set fire to the building in the absence of the other tenants. Temperatures in excess of 450 degrees Celsius were recorded, and it was observed that L was trapped beneath a fallen lintel. Melting of the flesh was seen to precede loss of consciousness, and death was subsequently observed.

Husband E was seen to propose a separation from wife E while refusing to explain his motives. The separation was observed to take place and to become permanent.

Preparations for suicide by subject B were observed. It was noted that the previously dismantled chair used by B for support gave way as the subject was seen to decide against this course of action. Dislocation of the neck by hanging was recorded, and death from strangulation ensued after a period of 53 minutes 27 seconds. It was further observed that after 8 days subject F entered house B and discovered the corpse of subject B.

Because of the risk of discovery, it was decided to discontinue the experiment at this stage. Since the results were judged to be inconclusive, it is proposed that several further experiments on larger groups of subjects should be conducted simultaneously. Communities have been chosen at random, and within them a further random selection of streets has been made.

Surrogate

Janet Fox

Steve was repainting the walls of what had been the guest bedroom when he heard the doorbell. "Diane," he shouted, and certain that he'd done his duty, turned back to rolling a pale yellow swath onto the wall. The new crib, bureau and bassinet that Diane had bought lay under protecting sheets and there were several unopened boxes bearing a toystore logo. His own attitude was as chaotic and half-formed as this room. Earlier he'd given up all hope of being a father, and it took a certain effort of will to resurrect that hope. He was trying, mostly for Diane's sake, but turning this room into a nursery still seemed a kind of a fantasy.

The bell resounded through the house again, an impatient sound, and he shouted again, this time with less confidence. He put down the roller and listened but heard no footsteps. "Damn, she must have gone out." He wiped his hands and hurried toward the door just as the bell sounded again. Through the screen he saw a young woman very visibly pregnant under a cheap dress whose pink-and-yellow print was very nearly phosphorescent. Her eyelids drooped under a layer of blue eyeshadow, and lipstick more nearly black than red glistened on her lips. Her jaw worked a wad of gum.

"Mr. Winston?"

"Yes, I'm Steven Winston."

He felt a hand on his shoulder and realized that Diane was behind him.

"I'm Kelsy Adams," she said, thrusting out a small hand as several plastic bracelets clacked together on her wrist. Confusedly he clasped hands with her.

"I'm sorry—" he began.

She patted her stomach. "I'm your surrogate mother." He heard Diane's indrawn breath, felt her hand clutch his arm. The moment with its tension lengthened until it threatened to pull reality apart, yet here she was on their doorstep in a splash of sunlight. He'd never seen her before, yet it was his child she carried. Thrown badly off balance, he could feel only anger.

"You had no right to come here," he said. "According to the terms of our agreement—"

"Invite her in," whispered Diane.

"No. No, you'll have to go. This isn't right."

"The neighbors . . . invite her in."

Reluctantly he opened the screen. "All right, we'll talk," he said. "But only for a few minutes." Diane moved newspapers off the divan with a nervous motion. She wore what Steve called her white look—shocked but still functioning. It turned her normal fragile prettiness harsh somehow, masklike, hollow.

"Maybe I should've called," said Kelsy, settling herself on the cushions with the air of a cat getting comfortable.

"How did you find us? The terms of our contract stated that we were to have no contact."

"I got the information from a . . . friend who works in the office."

"Well, I'm calling Doctor Joshua," Steve said. "I think something is very wrong here."

As he moved toward the phone, a dribble of mascara melted down Kelsy's cheek. "I had to go somewhere, I got kicked out of my apartment. Those old biddies said I had . . . bad . . . morals." Diane moved to stand beside her, looking down helplessly. "I didn't know people would think I—" began Kelsy, the rest lost in the tissue that Diane handed her.

Diane made a warning gesture as Steve reached for the phone. "Calling the doctor isn't going to change the fact that she's here. She's not just on paper; she's real."

"But this isn't how it's supposed to be. It can cause terrible complications. It must nullify the agreement."

"I'm causing trouble. I'll go. I'll go and you'll never have to see me

483

again." Kelsy wiped her face, smudging streaks of blackness across her cheek, a strangely vulnerable gesture.

"How can anything be nullified?" Diane said. "Look at her. It's your—our baby. What does it matter about your agreements and pieces of paper?"

"I didn't mean to bother you; I just didn't know where else to go, but I see I can't stay here." For all of her protests Kelsy wasn't making any moves to leave the comfort of the cushions.

"Don't go. Not just yet. I'll fix us some coffee, no, some juice, that'd be better." A tentative smile appeared amid the ruined makeup. A simpleminded girl, Steve thought. That was all she was. This agreement might be the only stable relationship in her life. But even as he lectured himself, trying to find some compassion, he was wondering how a simpleminded girl could so easily break the security of a doctor's private files.

After Kelsy had downed her second glass of juice, Diane directed her to the bathroom so she could, as she put it, put on a new face. "I wonder if we shouldn't call the doctor," Steve said. "He shouldn't be so careless with confidential information."

"But what if he cancels the agreement? Did we wait this long for it to be like the other time, when I—" Her voice fell to a murmur. "Lost the baby." Her skin seemed translucent, stretched taut over the fine bones of her face, and he was afraid to say anything as if the sound of his voice would shatter her.

"Here I am, back to normal." The greasy layers of makeup had been replaced, making strangely harsh the youthful contours of her face. "And I'm ready to go. You've been really nice. I'm glad I could meet you even if it was only for a few minutes."

Steve followed her toward the door, amazed that this whole soap-opera episode was to be so easily concluded. "I'm glad I met you, too," said Diane. Kelsy was going out the door, smiling back toward Diane. Steve shouted a warning as he saw her foot in its flimsy high-heeled shoe miss the step. Too late to catch her; he caught Diane, who was screaming and bolting forward. Kelsy had fallen full length on the sidewalk and for the moment she hadn't moved. Diane knelt beside her to cradle her head. "Maybe we ought to get an ambulance," Steve said, but Kelsy was already stirring, trying to rise.

"No, she's all right, but we'd better get her inside." Steve helped her to stand but she didn't seem too steady on her feet, so he picked her up. She seemed small somehow, and lighter than she should have been. He put her on the couch.

Diane was carrying a cheap plastic suitcase. "This was left out by the curb. Her things must be in it."

484

"But she can't stay here."

"Only for the night. In the morning I'll see that she gets to the doctor's office for a checkup."

"This is crazy."

Diane came closer and put her arms around him. "It isn't crazy, is it, for me to want your baby—no matter how it comes about."

Still half-asleep, Steve lurched across the living room on his way to the kitchen to make coffee. On the couch, Kelsy, covered to the neck with a wrinkled sheet, looked like something in a cocoon. Her face devoid of the makeup was youthful. She could be hardly out of her teens, he supposed, and as he looked at her, he speculated on the kind of life that would make a woman agree to the surrogate arrangement. He supposed he should feel pity and responsibility, yet as he stood there he was feeling a kind of anxiety, the feeling that at any moment she would awaken and blink and stare at him with eyes gone ferally red in reflected light. Stupid. He turned away.

As he was drinking the coffee, Diane joined him, her slim elegance enveloped in one of his old blanket-cloth robes. "It's been over a week," he said in a tentative voice. "Don't you think it's time she left to get a place of her own?"

"I hate to think of her being alone."

"But this situation, it's impossible. I can just imagine what the Cartons—or the Pendletons—are thinking."

"I told Midge Pendleton that she's my baby sister," said Diane with a pleased, wicked grin that was uncharacteristic of her.

"But her clothes, her appearance—"

"I've been meaning to take her shopping—get her some nicer things. We can afford it."

"But what about the money, the fee she got for the baby?"

"I'm afraid she has no head for money, poor thing, and, well, who cares about that. It's not as if we ever thought we could buy a child."

He paused. He guessed he *had* thought so, when the agreement was made. It had all seemed so clear, so businesslike.

"Don't you feel the least bit responsible?"

"Of course I do," he said, "but there's something wrong about this. It's—" He couldn't explain. He could talk about the social and moral viewpoints, but that wouldn't begin to touch it. The wrongness was the kind that made hair bristle at the back of the neck and brought an undefined sound of warning up from the throat.

"What are you trying to pull?" He had burst into the living room, startling Kelsy, who was sitting on the floor putting together a jigsaw puzzle. "I happened to run into Doctor Joshua today," he said, feeling as if he were playing the part of an irate father in a play. Kelsy's condition wasn't nearly so noticeable in the simple cotton smocks that Diane had bought for her, and with the makeup toned down, she looked like a teenager. "He told me that our surrogate mother had missed her last two appointments and that he couldn't locate her at her old address."

"What are you shouting about?" Diane stood in the kitchen doorway.

"I thought the reason for her being here was to care for her health."

As jigsaw pieces scattered, Kelsy scrambled to her feet and hurried to stand beside Diane. He couldn't tell if he were imagining it but her stomach seemed smaller under the loose blouse. It *was* smaller. Or did it only seem so?

"He doesn't like me," said Kelsy.

"She's afraid of Doctor Joshua," explained Diane, putting an arm around Kelsy's shoulders. "We were going to find another doctor, one with more understanding, but we've been so busy shopping and—"

"We can't have her living here—sleeping on the couch, taking up all your time."

"The couch, I've been meaning to mention it to you. I think it'd be a good idea if we set the guest bed up again in the smaller bedroom."

"But that's the nursery. It's all fixed up."

"Of course it is—it will be. But it's important for Kelsy to be comfortable."

He felt that he stood at a crossroads of sorts, yet how could he be certain that the bulge under Kelsy's smock was really diminished? And if it was, how did one explain it without sprawling over into the kinds of ideas that only crazy people believed in? He only knew that under the murky surface of doing one's duty and living up to one's responsibility to one's fellow man, he hated her, with all the hatred of one species for another.

The nursery was a pale yellow with large decals of teddy bears in various costumes. Huddled in a shadowy corner was the baby furniture. A mobile of glittering plastic animals hung over the bed and Kelsy was reaching up to touch it with a languid motion. As it spun, a music box tinkled out a tinny melody. She sat against the pillow with knees up, the posture easy for her now that her stomach had flattened. The absorption had been a gradual process which Diane had never mentioned, but Steve had watched each change with fascination, feeling a vague sense of loss. The process had given Kelsy an additional layer of fat so that the drawn-up knees were dimpled and her breasts were scarcely noticeable under the pink shift with its print of clowns and balloons.

Her face had grown rounder, fuller, and there was never any makeup on it now. She was smiling an odd, secretive smile, thinking, he supposed, that she'd won. He stepped closer to the doorway; a board squeaked; she saw him.

"You scared me," she said with a little pout. He could almost be charmed by it; he could see how Diane might be.

"You scared *me*," he said with a smile that was only an ironic twist of the lips. "What are you, really?"

She looked at him out of large shining brown eyes and was silent. Maybe she didn't know herself. Maybe this usurpation was as natural to her as the cuckoo laying its eggs in another bird's nest.

It seemed equally instinctual when he reached for her, locking his hands around the chubby throat. There was a moment of self-loathing, of unreality before he began to squeeze.

He felt a blow from behind, at first unlocalized until a pain spread through his chest. He fell to the floor, his scrabbling hand confirming the double-looped shape of the handles of Diane's sewing shears. Warm liquid flooded into his nose and mouth and he felt that he was drowning in lukewarm water, but the substance that dribbled out over his hand was red. His fading consciousness supplied a kind of glowing haze to the figures seated on the bed. Diane's expression was both fierce and gentle at once as she looked down on Kelsy's tousled head cradled against her breast. Somewhere in the background the music box was endlessly droning its mechanical lullaby.

They're Coming for You

Les Daniels

Mr. Bliss came home from work early one Monday afternoon. It was a big mistake.

He'd had a headache, and his secretary, after offering him various patent medicines, complete with their manufacturers' slogans, had said, "Why don't you take the rest of the day off, Mr. Bliss."

Everyone called him Mr. Bliss. The others in the office were Dave or Dan or Charlie, but he was Mr. Bliss. He liked it that way. Sometimes he thought that even his wife should call him Mr. Bliss.

Instead, she was calling on God.

Her voice came from on high. From upstairs. In the bedroom. She didn't seem to be in pain, but Mr. Bliss could remedy that.

She wasn't alone; someone was grunting in harmony with her cries to the creator. Mr. Bliss was bitter about this.

Without even waiting to hang up his overcoat, he tiptoed into the kitchen and plucked from its magnetic rack one of the Japanese knives his wife had ordered after watching a television commercial. They were designed for cutting things into small pieces, and they were guaranteed for life, however long that happened to be. Mr. Bliss would see to it that his wife had no cause for complaint. He turned away from the rack, paused for a sigh, then went back and selected another knife. The first was for the one who wanted to meet God, and the second for the one who was making those animal noises.

After a moment's reflection he decided to use the back stairs. They were more secretive, somehow, and Mr. Bliss intended to have a big secret just as soon as he could get organized.

He had an erection for the first time in weeks, and his headache was gone.

He moved as quickly and carefully as he could, sliding across the checkerboard linoleum and taking the back stairs two at a time in slow, painful, thigh-straining stretches. He knew there was a step which creaked, couldn't recall which one it was, and knew he would step on it anyway.

That hardly mattered. The groans and wails were reaching a crescendo, and Mr. Bliss suspected that not even a brass band behind him could have distracted the people above him from their business. They were about to achieve something, and he wanted very much to be there before they did.

The bedroom took up the entire top floor of the house. It had been a whim of his to flatter his young bride with as spacious a spawning ground as his salary would allow; the tastefully carpeted stairs led up to it in front as inexorably as the shabby wooden stairs crept up the back.

Mr. Bliss creaked at the appointed spot, cursed quietly, and opened the door.

His wife's eyes, rolled back in her head, were like wet marble. Her lips fluttered as she blew damp hair from her face. The beautiful breasts that had persuaded him to marry her were covered with sweat, and not all of it was hers.

Mr. Bliss didn't even recognize the man; he was nobody, The milkman? A census taker? He was plump, and he needed a haircut. It was all very discouraging. Cuckolding by an Adonis would at least have been understandable, but this was a personal affront.

Mr. Bliss dropped one knife to the floor, grasped the other in both hands, and slammed its point into the pudgy interloper at the spot where spine meets skull.

It worked at once. The man gave one more grunt and toppled over backward, blade grinding against bone as head and handle hit the floor.

Mrs. Bliss was there, baffled and bedraggled, spread-eagled naked against sopping sheets.

Mr. Bliss picked up the other knife.

He pulled her up by the hair and stabbed her in the face. She blubbered blood. Madly but methodically, he shoved the sharp steel into every place where he thought she'd like it least.

Most of his experiments were successful.

She died unhappily.

The last expression she was able to muster was a mixture of pain, reproach, and resignation that thrilled him more than anything she'd shown him since their wedding night.

He wasn't done with her yet. She had never been so submissive.

It was late that night before he put down the knife and put on his clothes.

Mr. Bliss had made a terrible mess. Cleaning up was always a chore, as she had so frequently reminded him, but he was equal to the task. The worst part was that he had stabbed the water bed, but at least the flood had diluted some of the blood.

He buried them in separate sections of the flower garden and showed up late for work. This was an unprecedented event. The quizzical eyebrows of his colleagues got on his nerves.

For some reason he didn't feel like going home that night. He went to a motel instead. He watched television. He saw a movie about someone killing several other people, but it didn't amuse him as much as he'd hoped. He felt that it was in bad taste.

He left the "Do Not Disturb" sign on the doorknob of his room each day; he did not wish to be disturbed. Still, the unmade bed to which he returned each night began to bother him. It reminded him of home.

After a few days Mr. Bliss was ashamed to go to the office. He was still wearing the same clothes he'd left home in, and he was convinced that his colleagues could smell him. No one had ever longed for the weekend as passionately as he did.

Then he had two days of peace in his motel room, huddling under the covers in the dark and watching people kill each other in a phosphorescent glow, but on Sunday night he looked at his socks and knew he would have to go back to the house.

He wasn't happy about this.

When he opened the front door, it reminded him of his last entrance. He felt that the stage was set. Still, all he had to do was go upstairs and get some clothes. He could be gone in a matter of minutes. He knew where everything was.

489

He used the front stairs. The carpeting made them quieter, and somehow he felt the need for stealth. Anyway, he didn't like the ones in the back anymore.

Halfway up the stairs, he noticed two paintings of roses that his wife had put there. He took them down. This was his house now, and the pictures had always vaguely annoyed him. Unfortunately, the blank spaces he left on the wall bothered him, too.

He didn't know what to do with the paintings, so he carried them up into the bedroom. There seemed to be no way to get rid of them. He was afraid this might be an omen, and for a second considered the idea of burying them in the garden. This made him laugh, but he didn't like the sound. He decided not to do it again.

Mr. Bliss stood in the middle of the bedroom and looked around critically. He'd made quite a neat job of it. He was just opening a dresser drawer when he heard a thump from below. He stared at his underwear.

A scrape followed the thump, and then the sound of something bumping up the back stairs.

He didn't wonder what it was, not even for an instant. He closed his underwear drawer and turned around. His left eyelid twitched; he could feel it. He was walking without thinking toward the front stairs when he heard the door below them open. Just a little sound, a bolt slipping a latch. Suddenly the inside of his head felt as big as the bedroom.

He knew they were coming for him, one from each side. What could he do? He ran around the room, slamming into each wall and finding it solid. Then he took up a post beside the bed and put a hand over his mouth. A giggle spilled between his fingers, and it made him angry, for this was a proud moment.

They were coming for him.

Whatever became of him (no more job, no more television), he had inspired a miracle. The dead had come back to life to punish him. How many men could say as much? Come clump, come thump, come slithering sounds! This was a triumph.

He stepped back against the wall to get a better view. As both doors opened, his eyes flicked back and forth. His tongue followed, licking his lips. He experienced an ecstasy of terror.

The stranger, of course, had used the back stairs.

He had tried to forget what a mess he had made of them, especially his wife. And now they were even worse.

And yet, as she dragged herself across the floor, there was something in her pale flesh, spotted with purple where the blood had settled, and striped with rust where the blood had spilled, that called to him as it rarely had before. Her skin was clumped with rich brown earth. She needs a bath, he thought, and he began to snort with laughter that would soon be uncontrollable.

Her lover, approaching from the other side, was hardly marked. There had been no wish to punish him, only to make him stop. Still, the single blow of the TV knife had severed his spine, and his head lurched unpleasantly. The odd disappointment Mr. Bliss had felt in the man's flabbiness intensified. After six days in the ground what crawled toward him was positively puffy.

Mr. Bliss tried to choke back his chuckles till his eyes watered and snot shot from his nose. Even as his end approached, he saw their impossible lust for vengeance as his ultimate vindication.

Yet his feet were not as willing to die as he was; they backed over the carpet toward the closet door.

His wife looked up at him, as well as she could. The eyes in her sockets seemed shriveled, like inquisitive prunes. A part of her where he had cut too deeply and too often dropped quietly to the floor.

Her lover shuffled forward on hands and knees, leaving some sort of a trail behind him.

Mr. Bliss pulled the gleaming brass bed around to make a barricade. He stepped back into the closet. The smell of her perfume and of her sex enveloped him. He was buried in her gowns.

His wife reached the bed first and grasped the fresh linen with the few fingers she had left. She hauled herself up. Stains smeared the sheets. This was certainly the time to slam the closet door, but he wanted to watch. He was positively fascinated.

She squirmed on the pillows, arms flailing, then collapsed on her back. There were gurgles. Could she be really dead at last?

No.

It didn't matter. Her lover crawled over the counterpane. Mr. Bliss wanted to go to the bathroom, but the way was blocked.

He cringed when his wife's lover (who was this creeping corpse, anyway?) stretched out fat fingers, but instead of clawing for revenge, they fell on what had been the breasts of the body beneath him. They began to move gently.

Mr. Bliss blushed as the ritual began. He heard sounds that had embarrassed him even when the meat was live: liquid lurchings, ghastly groans, and supernatural screams.

He shut himself in the closet. What was at work on the bed did not even deign to notice him. He was buried in silk and polyester.

It was worse than he had feared. It was unbearable.

They hadn't come for him at all.

They had come for each other.

Thirst

Bill Pronzini

March said, "We're going to die out here, Flake."

"Don't talk like that."

"I don't want to die this way."

"You're not going to die."

"I don't want to die of thirst, Flake!"

"There are worse ways."

"No, no, there's no worse way."

"Quit thinking about it."

"How much water is left?"

"A couple of swallows apiece, that's all."

"Let me have my share. My throat's on fire!"

Flake stopped slogging forward and squinted at March for a few seconds. He took the last of the canteens from his shoulder, unscrewed the cap, and drank two mouthfuls to make sure he got them. Then he handed the canteen to March.

March took it with nerveless fingers. He sank to his knees in the reddish desert sand, his throat working spasmodically as he drank. When he had licked away the last drop he cradled the canteen to his chest and knelt there rocking with it.

Flake watched him dispassionately. "Come on, get up."

"What's the use? There's no more water. We're going to die of thirst."

"I told you to shut up about that."

March looked up at him with eyes like a wounded animal's. "You think he made it, Flake?"

"Who, Brennan?"

"Yes, Brennan."

"What do you want to think about him for?"

"He didn't take all the gasoline for the jeep."

"He had enough."

March whimpered, "Why, Flake? Why'd he do it?"

"Why the hell you think he did it?"

"Those deposits we found are rich, the ore samples proved that — sure. But there's more than enough for all of us."

"Brennan's got the fever. He wants it all."

"But he was our friend, our partner!"

"Forget about him," Flake said. "We'll worry about Brennan when we get out of this desert."

March began to laugh. "That's a good one, by God. That's rich."

"What's the matter with you?"

"*When* we get out of this desert, you said. *When.* Oh, that's a funny one—"

Flake slapped him. March grew silent, his dusty fingers moving like reddish spiders on the surface of the canteen. "You're around my neck like a goddamn albatross," Flake said. "You haven't let up for three days now. I don't know why I don't leave you and go on alone."

"No, Flake, please . . ."

"Get up, then."

"I can't. I can't move."

Flake caught March by the shoulders and lifted him to his feet. March stood there swaying. Flake began shuffling forward again, pulling March along by one arm. The reddish sand burned beneath their booted feet. Stillness, heat, nothing moving, hidden eyes watching them, waiting. Time passed, but they were in a state of timelessness.

"Flake."

"What is it now?"

"Can't we rest?"

Flake shaded his eyes to look skyward. The sun was falling now, shot through with blood-colored streaks; it had the look of a maniac's eye.

"It'll be dark in a few hours," he said. "We'll rest then."

To ease the pressure of its weight against his spine, Flake adjusted the canvas knapsack of dry foodstuffs. March seemed to want to cry, watching him, but there was no moisture left in him for tears. He stumbled after Flake.

They had covered another quarter of a mile when Flake came to a sudden standstill. "There's something out there," he said.

"I don't see anything."

"There," Flake said, pointing.

"What is it?"

"I don't know. We're too far away."

They moved closer, eyes straining against swollen, peeling lids. "Flake!" March cried. "Oh Jesus, Flake, it's the jeep!"

Flake began to run, stumbling, falling once in his haste. The jeep lay on its side near a shallow dry wash choked with mesquite and smoke trees. Three of its tires had blown out, the windshield was shattered and its body dented and scored in a dozen places.

Flake staggered up to it and looked inside, looked around it and down into the dry wash. There was no sign of Brennan, no sign of the four canteens Brennan had taken from their camp in the Red Hills.

March came lurching up. "Brennan?"

"Gone."

"On foot, like us?"

"Yeah."

"What happened? How'd he wreck the jeep?"

"Blowout, probably. He lost control and rolled it over."

"Can we fix it? Make it run?"

"No."

"Why not? Christ, Flake!"

"Radiator's busted, three tires blown, engine and steering probably bunged up too. How far you think we'd get if we could get it started?"

"Radiator," March said. "Flake, the *radiator* . . ."

"I already checked. If there was any water left after the smash-up, Brennan got it."

March made another whimpering sound. He sank to his knees, hugging himself, and began the rocking motion again.

"Get up," Flake said.

"It's no good, we're going to die of thirst—"

"You son of a bitch, get up! Brennan's out there somewhere with the canteens. Maybe we can find him."

"How? He could be anywhere . . ."

"Maybe he was bunged up in the crash, too. If he's hurt he couldn't have got far. We might still catch him."

"He's had three days on us, Flake. This must have happened the first day out."

Flake said nothing. He turned away from the jeep and followed the rim of the dry wash to the west. March remained kneeling on the ground, watching him, until Flake was almost out of sight; then he got to his feet and began to lurch spindle-legged after him.

It was almost dusk when Flake found the first canteen.

He had been following a trail that had become visible not far from the wrecked jeep. At that point there had been broken clumps of mesquite, other signs to indicate Brennan was hurt and crawling more than he was walking. The trail led through the arroyo where it hooked sharply to the south, then continued into the sun-baked wastes due west—toward the town of Sandoval, the starting point of their mining expedition two months before.

The canteen lay in the shadow of a clump of rabbit brush. Flake picked it up, shook it. Empty. He glanced over his shoulder, saw March a hundred yards away shambling like a drunk, and then struck out again at a quickened pace.

Five minutes later he found the second canteen, empty, and his urgency grew and soared. He summoned reserves of strength and plunged onward in a loose trot.

494

He had gone less then a hundred and fifty yards when he saw the third canteen—and then, some distance beyond it, the vulture. The bird had glided down through the graying sky, was about to settle near something in the shade of a natural stone bridge. Flake ran faster, waving his arms, shouting hoarsely in his burning throat. The vulture slapped the air with its heavy wings and lifted off again. But it stayed nearby, circling slowly, as Flake reached the motionless figure beneath the bridge and dropped down beside it.

Brennan was still alive, but by the look of him and by the faint irregularity of his pulse, he wouldn't be alive for long. His right leg was twisted at a grotesque angle. As badly hurt as he was, he had managed to crawl the better part of a mile in three days.

The fourth canteen was gripped in Brennan's fingers. Flake pried it loose, upended it over his mouth. Empty. He cast it away and shook Brennan savagely by the shoulders, but the bastard had already gone into a coma. Flake released him, worked the straps on the knapsack on Brennan's back. Inside were the ore samples and nothing else.

Flake struggled to his feet when he heard March approaching, but he didn't turn. He kept staring down at Brennan from between the blistered slits of his eyes.

"Flake! You found Brennan!"

"Yeah, I found him."

"Is he dead?"

"Almost."

"What about water? Is there—?"

"No. Not a drop."

"Oh, God, Flake!"

"Shut up and let me think."

"That's it, we're finished, there's no hope now . . ."

"Goddamn you, quit your whining."

"We're going to end up like him," March said. "We're going to die, Flake, die of thirst—"

Flake backhanded him viciously, knocked him to his knees. "No, we're not," he said. "Do you hear me? We're not."

"We are, we are, we are . . ."

"We're *not* going to die," Flake said.

They came out of the desert four days later—burnt, shriveled, caked head to foot with red dust like human figures molded from soft stone.

Their appearance and the subsequent story of their ordeal caused considerable excitement in Sandoval, much more so than the rich ore samples in Flake's knapsack. They received the best of care. They were celebrities as well as rich men; they had survived the plains of hell, and that set them apart, in the eyes of the people of Sandoval, from ordinary mortals.

It took more than a week before their burns and infirmities healed enough so that they could resume normal activity. In all that time March was strangely uncommunicative. At first the doctors had been afraid that he might have to be committed to an asylum; his eyes glittered in an unnatural way and he made sounds deep in his throat that were not human sounds. But then he began to get better, even if he still didn't have much to say. Flake thought that March would be his old self again in time. When you were a rich man, all your problems were solved in time.

Flake spent his first full day out of bed in renting them a fancy hacienda and organizing mining operations on their claim in the Red Hills. That night, when he returned to their temporary quarters, he found March sitting in the darkened kitchen. He told him all about the arrangements, but March didn't seem to be interested. Shrugging, Flake got down a bottle of tequila and poured himself a drink.

Behind him March said, "I've been thinking, Flake."

"Good for you. What about?"

"About Brennan."

Flake licked the back of his hand, salted it, licked off the salt, and drank the shot of tequila. "You'd better forget about Brennan," he said.

"I can't forget about him," March said. His eyes were bright. "What do you suppose people would say if we told them the whole story? Everything that happened out there in the desert."

"Don't be a damned fool."

March smiled. "We were thirsty, weren't we? So thirsty."

"That's right. And we did what we had to do to survive."

"Yes," March said. "We did what we had to do."

He stood up slowly and lifted a folded square of linen from the table. Under it was a long, thin carving knife. March picked up the knife and held it in his hand. Sweat shone on his skin; his eyes glittered now like bits of phosphorus. He took a step toward Flake.

Flake felt sudden fear. He opened his mouth to tell March to put the knife down, to ask him what the hell he thought he was doing. But the words caught in his throat.

"You know what we are, Flake? You know what we—what I—became out there the night we cut Brennan open and drained his blood into those four canteens?"

Flake knew, then, and he tried desperately to run—too late. March tripped him and knocked him down and straddled him, the knife held high.

"I'm still thirsty," March said.

To Receive Is Better

Michael Marshall Smith

I'd like to be going by car, but of course I don't know how to drive, and it would probably scare the shit out of me. A car would be much better, for lots of reasons. For a start, there's too many people out here. There's *so many* people. Wherever you turn there's more of them, looking tired, and rumpled, but whole. That's the strange thing. Everybody is whole.

A car would also be quicker. Sooner or later they're going to track me down, and I've got somewhere to go before they do. The public transport system sucks, incidentally. Long periods of being crowded into carriages that smell, interspersed with long waits for another line, and I don't have a lot of time. It's intimidating too. People stare. They just look and look, and they don't know the danger they're in. Because in a minute one of them is going to look just one second too long, and I'm going to pull his fucking face off, which will do neither of us any good.

So instead I turn and look out the window. There's nothing to see, because we're in a tunnel, and I have to shut my eye to stop myself from screaming. The carriage is like another tunnel, a tunnel with windows, and I feel like I've been buried far too deep. I grew up in tunnels, ones that had no windows. The people who made them didn't even bother to pretend that there was something to look out on, something to look for. Because there wasn't. Nothing's coming up, nothing that isn't going to involve some fucker coming at you with a knife. So they don't pretend. I'll say that for them, at least: they don't taunt you with false hopes.

Manny did, in a way, which is why I feel complicated about him. On the one hand, he was the best thing that ever happened to us. But look at it another way, and maybe we'd have been better off without him. I'm being unreasonable. Without Manny, the whole thing would have been worse, thirty years of utter fucking pointlessness. I wouldn't have known, of course, but I do now: and I'm glad it wasn't that way. Without Manny I wouldn't be where I am now. Standing in a subway carriage, running out of time.

People are giving me a wide berth, which I guess isn't so surprising. Partly it'll be my face, and my leg. People don't like that kind of thing. But probably it's mainly me. I know the way I am, can feel the fury I radiate. It's not a nice way to be, I know that, but then my life has not been nice. Maybe you should try it, and see how calm you stay.

The other reason I feel weird towards Manny is I don't know why he did it. Why he helped us. Sue 2 says it doesn't matter, but I think it does. If it was just an experiment, a hobby, then I think that makes a difference. I think I would have liked him less. As it happens, I don't think it was. I think it was probably just humanity, whatever the fuck that is. I think if it was an experiment, then what happened an hour ago would have panned out differently. For a start, he probably wouldn't be dead.

If everything's gone okay, then Sue 2 will be nearly where she's going by now, much closer than me. That's a habit I'm going to have to break, for a start. It's Sue now, just Sue. No numeral. And I'm just plain old Jack, or I will be if I get where I am going.

The first thing I can remember, the earliest glimpse of life, is the colour blue. I know now what I was seeing, but at the time I didn't know anything different, and I thought that blue was the only colour there was. A soft, hazy blue, a blue that had a soft hum in it and was always the same clammy temperature.

I have to get out of this subway very soon. I've taken an hour of it, and that's about as far as I can go. It's very noisy in here too, not a hum but a horrendous clattering. This is not the way I want to spend what may be the only time I have. People keep surging around me, and they've all got places to go. For the first time in my life, I'm surrounded by people who've actually got somewhere to go.

And the tunnel is the wrong colour. Blue is the colour of tunnels. I can't understand a tunnel unless it's blue. I spent the first four years of my life, as far as I can work out, in one of them. If it weren't for Manny, I'd be in one still. When he came to work at the Farm I could tell he was different straight away. I don't know how: I couldn't even think then, let alone speak. Maybe it was just he behaved differently when he was near us to the way the previous keeper had. I found out a lot later that Manny's wife had died having a dead baby, so maybe that was it.

What he did was take some of us, and let us live outside the tunnels. At first it was just a few, and then about half of the entire stock of spares. Some of the others never took to the world outside the tunnels, such as it was. They'd just come out every now and then, moving hopelessly around, mouths opening and shutting, and they always looked kind of blue somehow, as if the tunnel light had seeped into their skin. There were a few who never came out of the tunnels at all, but that was mainly because they'd been used too much already. Three years old and no arms. Tell me that's fucking reasonable.

Manny let us have the run of the facility, and sometimes let us go outside. He had to be careful, because there was a road a little too close to one side of the farm. People would have noticed a group of naked people stumbling around in the grass, and of course we were naked, because *they didn't give us any fucking clothes*. Right to the end we didn't have any clothes, and for years I thought it was always raining on the outside, because that's the only time he'd let us out.

I'm wearing one of Manny's suits now, and Sue's got some blue jeans and a shirt. The pants itch like hell, but I feel like a prince. Princes used to live in castles and fight monsters and sometimes they'd marry princesses and live happy ever after. I know about princes because I've been told.

Manny told us stuff, taught us. He tried to, anyway. With most of us it was too late. With *me* it was too late, probably. I can't write, and I can't read. I know there's big gaps in my head. Every now and then I can follow something through, and the way that makes me feel makes me realize that most of the time it doesn't happen. Things fall between the tracks. I can talk quite well, though. I was always one of Manny's favourites, and he used to talk to me a lot. I learnt from him. Part of what makes me so fucking angry is that I think I could have been clever. Manny said so. Sue says so. But it's too late now. It's far too fucking late.

I was ten when they first came for me. Manny got a phone call and suddenly he was in a panic. There were spares spread all over the facility and he had to run round, herding us all up. He got us into the tunnels just in time and we just sat in there, wondering what was going on.

In a while Manny came to the tunnel I was in, and he had this other guy with him who was big and nasty. They walked down the tunnel, the big guy kicking people out of the way. Everyone knew enough not to say anything: Manny had told us about that. Some of the people who never came out of the tunnels were crawling and shambling around, banging off the walls like they do, and the big guy just shoved them out of the way. They fell over like lumps of meat and then kept moving, making noises with their mouths.

Eventually Manny got to where I was and pointed me out. His hand was shaking and his face looked strange, like he was trying not to cry. The big guy grabbed me by the arm and took me out of the tunnel. He dragged me down to the operating room, where there were two more guys in white clothes and they put me on the table in there and cut off two of my fingers.

That's why I can't write. I'm right-handed, and they cut off my fucking fingers. Then they put a needle into my hand with see-through thread and sewed it up like they were in a hurry, and the big man took me back to the tunnel, opened the door and shoved me in. I didn't say anything. I didn't say anything the whole time.

Later Manny came and found me, and I shrank away from him, because I thought they were going to do something else. But he put his arms round me and I could tell the difference, and so I let him take me out into the main room. He put me in a chair and washed my hand which was all bloody, and then he sprayed it with some stuff that made it hurt a little less. Then he told me. He explained where I was, and why.

I was a spare, and I lived on a Farm. When people with money got pregnant, Manny said, doctors took a cell from the foetus and cloned another baby, so it had exactly the same cells as the baby that was going to be born. They grew the second baby until it could breathe, and then they sent it to a farm.

The spares live on the farm until something happens to the proper baby. If the proper baby damages a part of itself, then the doctors come to the farm and cut a bit off the spare and sew it onto the real baby, because it's easier that way because of cell rejection and stuff that I don't really understand. They sew the spare baby up again and push it back into the tunnels and the spare sits there until the real baby does something else to itself. And when it does, the doctors come back again.

Manny told me, and I told the others, and so we knew.

We were very, very lucky, and we knew it. There are farms dotted all over the place, and every one but ours was full of blue people that just crawled up and down the tunnels, sheets of paper with nothing written on them. Manny said that some keepers made extra money by letting real people in at night. Sometimes the real people would just drink beer and laugh at the spares, and sometimes they would fuck them. Nobody knows, and nobody cares. There's no point teaching spares, no point giving them a life. All that's going to happen is they're going to get whittled down.

On the other hand, maybe they have it easier. Because once you know how things stand, it becomes very difficult to take it. You just sit around, and wait, like all the others, but you *know* what you're waiting for. And you know who's to blame.

Like my brother Jack, for example. Jamming two fingers in a door when he was ten was only the start of it. When he was eighteen he rolled his expensive car and smashed up the bones in his leg. That's another of the reasons I don't want to be on this fucking subway: people notice when something like that's missing. Just like they notice that the left side of my face is raw, where they took a graft off when some woman threw scalding water at him. He's got most of my stomach, too. Stupid fucker ate too much spicy food, drank too much wine. Don't know what those kind of things are like, of course: but they can't have been that nice. They can't have been nice enough. And then last year he went to some party, got drunk, got into a fight and lost his right eye. And so, of course, I lost mine.

It's a laugh being in a farm. It's a real riot. People stump around, dripping fluids, clapping hands with no fingers together and shitting into colostomy bags. I don't know what was worse: the ones who knew what was going on and felt hate like a cancer, or those who just ricocheted slowly round the tunnels like grubs. Sometimes the tunnel people would stay still for days, sometimes they would move around. There was no telling what they'd do, because there was no-one inside their heads. That's what Manny did for us, in fact, for Sue and Jenny and me: he put people inside our heads. Sometimes we used to sit around and talk about the real people, imagine what they were doing, what it would be like to be them instead of us. Manny said that wasn't good for us, but we did it anyway. Even spares should be allowed to dream.

It could have gone on like that forever, or until the real people started to get old and fall apart. The end comes quickly then, I'm told. There's a limit to what you can cut off. Or at least there's supposed to be: but when you've seen blind spares with no arms and legs wriggling in dark corners, you wonder.

But then this afternoon the phone went, and we all dutifully stood up and limped into the tunnel. I went with Sue 2, and we sat next to each other. Manny used to say we loved each other, but how the fuck do I know. I feel happier when she's around, that's all I know. She doesn't have any teeth and her left arm's gone and they've taken both of her ovaries, but I like her. She makes me laugh.

Eventually Manny came in with the usual kind of heavy guy and I saw that this time Manny looked worse than ever. He took a long time walking around, until the guy with him started shouting, and then in the end he found Jenny 2, and pointed at her.

Jenny 2 was one of Manny's favourites. Her and Sue and me, we were the ones he could talk to. The man took Jenny out and Manny watched him go. When the door was shut he sat down and started to cry.

The real Jenny was in a hotel fire. All her skin was gone. Jenny 2 wasn't going to be coming back.

We sat with Manny, and waited, and then suddenly he stood up. He grabbed Sue by the hand and told me to follow and he took us to his quarters and gave me the clothes I'm wearing now. He gave us some money, and told us where to go. I think somehow he knew what was going to happen. Either that, or he just couldn't take it any more.

We'd hardly got our clothes on when all hell broke loose. We hid when the men came to find Manny, and we heard what happened.

Jenny 2 had spoken. They don't use drugs or anaesthetic, except when the shock of the operation will actually kill the spare. Obviously. Why bother? Jenny 2 was in a terminal operation, so she was awake. When the guy stood over her, smiling as he was about to take the first slice out of her face, she couldn't help herself, and I don't blame her.

"Please," she said. "Please don't."

Three words. It isn't much. It isn't so fucking much. But it was enough. She shouldn't have been able to say anything at all.

Manny got in the way as they tried to open the tunnels and so they shot him and went in anyway. We ran then, so I don't know what they did. I shouldn't think they killed them, because most had lots of parts left. Cut out bits of their brain, probably, to make sure they were all tunnel people.

We ran, and we walked and we finally made the city. I said goodbye to Sue at the subway, because she was going home on foot. I've got further to go, and they'll be looking for us, so we had to split up. We knew it made sense, and I don't know about love, but I'd lose both of my hands to have her with me now.

Time's running out for both of us, but I don't care. Manny got addresses for us, so we know where to go. Sue thinks we'll be able to take their places. I don't, but I couldn't tell her. We would give ourselves away too soon, because we just don't know enough. We wouldn't have a chance. It was always just a dream, really, something to talk about.

But one thing I am going to do. I'm going to meet him. I'm going to find Jack's house, and walk up to his door, and I'm going to look at him face to face.

And before they come and find me, I'm going to take a few things back.

Tomorrow Is Forever

Hugh B. Cave

The details of his departure from the front were still annoyingly vague, but that he had entered a new and unfamiliar region was now certain, and the strangeness of his surroundings disturbed him. On what mission had he been sent here? Where were his comrades?

He had walked at least a day and a night, yet there was no real day or night in this place by which to measure time. There was silence and a road—and there were dim shadow-shapes who plodded aimlessly on, like himself, to no apparent destination.

Were there no towns, no villages, in this shrouded valley? Must he trudge forever through a changeless twilight, along a road that led to nowhere?

He was tired and walked slowly. And hungry, too, though it was a kind of hunger, he sensed, that food and drink would not appease. "I would give the Iron Cross I won in Poland," he thought glumly, "to be back with Fedor and Karl and Fritz in the mud of the Caucasus. Is there no way *out* of this accursed place?"

Presently, hearing footsteps, he paused again, and out of the twilight another of the plodding people came toward him. This time it was one of his own kind. His hope came alive, and with an arm upflung in greeting he strode forward. "Wait!" he shouted. "I wish to talk!"

But the man was deaf and blind to him, and trudged past without recognition. The road was once more empty.

Shaking with anger, he resumed his journey. It did not occur to him to be afraid—he was a soldier, sheathed in an armor of arrogance through which fear had not yet found an opening. But beneath his anger lay bewilderment and a nagging sense of aloneness. Panic beat its dark wings more insistently, now, against the wall of his calm. What *was* this valley in which he wandered?

On he went, measuring time by his weariness and the sound of his boots, until at last, ahead, there were lights in the darkness.

It was not a large place—not important—but about it was something old and familiar that puzzled him anew. The shape of its twisting streets tugged at his memory, and a voice within him whispered a warning.

But here were people and houses, and the sound of voices bright against the night. He heard a child's laughter and the warm wonder of a woman singing. With a click of his heels and new stiffness in his shoulders, he confronted the first man who approached.

"What is this place?"

The man was old, with graying hair and a bent body. Beside him skipped a dark-haired child whose hand he clasped. They chatted gaily and laughed at some private joy they shared, and without a glance in his direction, went past.

Embittered, he sullenly watched them. "Because I'm alone," he thought, "they choose to be insulting. Very well, I *am* alone. But not for always. The day has come in hundreds of other miserable villages such as this, and will come here." They would regret their insolence, these people. He would learn the name of the place and report it.

But it was not easy to learn the name. Identifying signs had been removed, and though the pattern of its streets and the shape of its houses told him its nationality, he could not sort it from the scores of similar places he had seen. "They are all alike, these worthless towns," he reflected. "They were built to be destroyed."

His scorn was a good thing. Strengthening his pride, it held in check the beating wings of panic as, one after another, the people he accosted ignored him.

Were they imbeciles, these people? By the church he confronted a slender girl of twenty—"You! *Fraulein*! Tell me what place this is!"—and she turned instead, with her sweetest smile, to a young man who approached from the opposite direction.

In the square he spoke to children dancing—"Stop it! An end to this nonsense! I have questions to ask!"—and they romped away without hearing.

From street to street, his anger mounting, he sought information. None saw him. None heard. At last, his rage past holding, he rushed at a youth who would not listen, and swung his fist.

Feeling nothing, the youth walked on.

The beating wings broke down his barrier then, and drove him to flight. He wanted no more of this place that would have none of him! He ran back the way he had come, seeking the long road of shadows that had led him here.

But the way was changed. The streets formed and reformed before him, ever different. At every turn were more of the huddled houses, more lights, more people—and no end to his flight. The path of departure had disappeared.

He stopped at last. Running was futile. The wings were thunder-loud and louder. He turned once more to the people who passed—but now tears drenched his face and terror rode his voice. "Speak to me! Look at me! The way out of here—please!" But he was not there. They saw only one another.

As the lights dimmed and the streets emptied of life, he went on dragging feet from house to house, looking in. Who *were* these people, so warless in a world at war? In this house a golden-haired girl knelt before the fire to play with eager children. In this, four nodding elders ringed a table spread with food. In this, young couples danced to gay music, and a laughing lass lifted her lips for a lover's kiss. In all he found peace. But none found him.

"Are they deaf to the roar of the guns, also?" he wondered. "And the thunder of the bombs?"

On he went. The sound of his voice at their windows did not disturb them, nor the pounding of his fists.

At every door his voice grew shriller, and as the sound of his boots rang hollowly through street after street, terror supplanted his rage. The lights were dimming. Windows darkened one by one, and the sound of voices ceased as the village blinked its eyes for sleep.

At last he gave up. His rage was spent. The wings had beaten all pride from him. Only a great and lasting fear remained, and the thought that he was alone, quite alone, and might be alone forever. Crying, he crouched in a doorway.

The village slept. Through its steets, now, dim shadows moved, plodding aimlessly as he had plodded.

He watched them. Some he recognized. "This one I knew in Kharkov, before he perished from the cold. This one we left behind at Kiev." One by one they passed, without seeing him. Suddenly his hands clawed at the pavement and he was erect, shouting hoarsely in a last, hopeless struggle to be heard.

"Friedrich! Friedrich! In God's name, wait for me! It is Kropp, your friend!"

But the shadow passed. Not even Friedrich could hear. He sank again in the doorway, staring animal-eyed.

It *had* been Friedrich; he was certain. No mistake was possible. When you have marched with a man all those months, fought by his side, shared food and bedding with him . . .

"I was the first to reach him when he fell," he thought dazedly. "It was I who tore the bayonet from his heart and dug the grave in which we buried him. We marched together in Poland, and through half of Russia. We were together at Lidice . . ."

Lidice! His eyes grew large and, stumbling to his feet again, he stared anew at the shapes and shadows of the village—this village in which now, forever, he would walk unwanted. *Lidice!*

He knew then the name of the valley, and the meaning of the long, dark road along which he had come. He knew where he was.

Traps

F. Paul Wilson

Skippy Super Chunk peanut butter was the best bait.

Hank smeared it on the pedals of the four traps he'd bought. They were Victors. Something about the way the big red V in their logo formed itself around the shape of a mouse's head gave him a feeling that they knew what they were about.

Not that he took any pleasure in killing mice. He may not have had the bumper sticker, but he most certainly did brake for animals. He didn't like killing anything. Even ants. Live and let live was fine with him, but he drew the line at the threshold of his house. They could live long and prosper out *there*, he would live in *here*. When they came inside, it was war.

He'd had a few in the basement of their last house and caught them all with Skippy-baited Victors. But he always felt guilty when he found one of the little things dead in the trap, so frail and harmless-looking with its white underbelly and little pink feet and tail. The eyes were always the worst—shiny black and guileless, wide open and looking at him, almost saying, *Why? I don't eat much.*

Hank knew he could be a real sentimental jerk at times.

He consoled himself with the knowledge that the mouse didn't feel any pain in the trap. Better than those warfarin poisons where they crawl off to their nest and slowly bleed to death. With a trap, the instant the nibbling mouse disturbs the baited pedal, *wham*! the bow snaps down and breaks its neck. It's on its way to mouse heaven before it knows what hit it.

Hank was doing this on the sly. Gloria wouldn't be able to sleep a wink if she thought there were mice overhead in the ceiling. And the twins, God, they'd want to catch them and make them pets and give them names. With the trip to Disney World just three days off, all they could talk about was Mickey and Minnie. They'd never forgive him for killing a mouse. Best to set the traps before they came home in the afternoon and dispose of the little carcasses in the morning after everyone was gone. Luckily, this was his slack season and he had some time at home to take care of it.

He wondered how the mice were getting in. He knew they were up there because he'd heard them last night. Something had awakened him at about 2:30 this morning—a noise, a bad dream, he didn't remember what—and as he was lying there spooned against Gloria he heard little claws scraping on the other side of the ceiling. It sounded like two or three of them under the insulation, clawing on the plasterboard, making themselves a winter home. He was ticked. This was a brand-new two-story colonial, just built, barely lived in for six months, and already they had uninvited guests. And in the attic no less.

Well, they were in a woodsy area and it was fall, the time of year when woodsy things start looking for winter quarters. He wished them all a safe and warm winter. But not in this house.

Before setting the traps, he fitted a bolt on the attic door. The house had one of those swing-down attic doors in the hall ceiling right outside their bedroom. It had a pull cord on this side and a folding ladder on the upper side. The twins had been fascinated with it since they moved in. The attic had always been off-limits to them, but you never knew. He had visions of one of them pulling the ladder down, climbing up there,

506

and touching one of the traps. Instant broken finger. So he screwed a little sliding bolt in place to head off that trauma at the pass.

He took the four traps up to the attic and gingerly set the bows. As he stood on the ladder and spaced them out on the particleboard flooring around the opening, he noticed an odd odor. The few times he had been up here before, the attic had been filled with the clean smell of plywood and kiln-dried fir studs. Now there was a sour tint to the air. Vaguely unpleasant. Mouse B.O.? He didn't know. He just knew that something about it didn't set well with him.

He returned to the second floor, bolted the ceiling door closed, and hit the switch that turned off the attic light. Everything was set, and well before Gloria and the girls got home.

Kate crawled into Hank's lap as he leaned back in the recliner and watched the six o'clock *Eyewitness News.*

"Let's read Mickey's book," she said.

That was all Kim had to hear. She ran in from the kitchen like a shot. "Me too! Me too!"

"Just three days and we'll be in Disney World!" Hank said.

So with his two pale blond seven-year-old darlings snuggled up against him, Hank opened up "Mickey's book" for the nightly ritual of the past two weeks. Not a book actually, just a brochure touting all the park's attractions. But it had become a Holy Book of sorts for the twins and they never tired of paging through it. This had to be their twentieth guided tour in as many days and their blue eyes were just as wide and full of wonder this time as the first.

Hank had come to see Disney World as a religious experience for seven-year-olds. Moslems had Mecca, Catholics had the Vatican, Japanese had Mount Fuji. Kids had Disney World on the East Coast and Disneyland on the West. Katie and Kim would start out on their first pilgrimage Thanksgiving morning.

He hugged them closer, absorbing their excitement. This was what life was all about. And he was determined to show them the best time of their lives. The sky was the limit. Any ride, any attraction, he didn't care how many times they wanted to go on it, he'd take them. Four days of fantasy at Mickey's Place with no real-world intrusions. No *Time,* no *Daily News,* no Eyewitness Special Reports, no background noise about wars or floods or muggings or bombings or mousetraps.

Nothing about mousetraps.

The snap of the trap woke Hank with a start. It was faint, muffled by the intervening plasterboard and insulation. He must have been subconsciously attuned to it, because he heard it and Gloria didn't.

He checked the clock—12:42—and tried to go back to sleep. Hopefully, that was the end of that.

He was just dozing back off when a second trap sprang with a muffled snap. Two of them. Sounded like he had a popular attic.

He didn't know when he got to sleep again. It took a while.

When Hank had the house to himself again the next morning, he pulled down the ceiling door and unfolded the ladder. Halfway up, he hesitated. This wasn't going to be pleasant. He knew when he stuck his head up through that opening he'd be eye-level with the attic floor—and with the dead mice. Those shiny reproachful little black eyes . . .

He took a deep breath and stepped up a couple of rungs.

Yes, two of the traps had been sprung and two sets of little black eyes were staring at him. Eyes and little else. At first he thought it was a trick of the light, of the angle, but as he hurried the rest of the way up, he saw it was true.

The heads were still in the traps, but the bodies were gone. Little bits of gray fur were scattered here and there, but that was it. Sort of gave him the creeps. Something had eaten the dead mice. Something bigger than a mouse. A discomforting thought.

And that odor was worse. He still couldn't identify it, but it was taking on a stomach-turning quality.

He decided it was time for an inspection tour of the grounds. His home was being invaded. He wanted to know how.

He found the little buggers' route of invasion on the south side of the house. He had two heating-cooling zones inside, with one unit in the basement and one in the attic. The compressor blowers for both were outside on the south side. The hoses to the upstairs unit ran up the side of the house to the attic through an aluminum leader.

That was how they were getting in.

There wasn't much space in the leader, but a mouse can squeeze through the tiniest opening. The rule of thumb—as all mouse experts knew—was that if it can get its head through, the rest of the body can follow. They were crawling into the leader, climbing up along the hoses inside, and following them into the attic. Simple.

But what had eaten them?

Up above the spot where the hoses ran through the siding, he noticed the triangular gable vent hanging free on its right side. Something had pulled it loose. As he watched, a squirrel poked its head out, looked at him, then scurried up onto the roof. It ran a few feet along the edge, jumped onto an overhanging oak branch, and disappeared into the reddening leaves.

Great! He was collecting a regular menagerie up there!

So much for the joys of a wooded lot. Gloria and he had chosen this semi-rural development because they liked the seclusion of an acre lot and the safety for the twins of living on a cul-de-sac. They both had grown up in New Jersey, and Toms River seemed like as good a place as any to raise kids. The house was expensive but they were a two-income family—she a teacher and he a CPA—so they went for it.

So far, theirs was the only house completed in this section, although two new foundations had just started. It would be nice to have neighbors. Until recently, the only other building in sight had been a deserted stone church of unknown age and long-forgotten denomination a few hundred yards south of here. The belfry of that old building had concerned him for a while—bats, you know. Very high rabies rate. But he spoke to the workmen when they bulldozed it down last week to start another cul-de-sac, and they told him they hadn't seen a single bat. Lots of animal droppings up there, but no bats.

He wondered: Would a squirrel eat a couple of dead mice? He thought they only ate nuts and berries. Maybe this one was a carnivore. Didn't matter. One way or another, something had to be done about that gable vent. He went to get the ladder.

He had everything taken care of by the time Gloria and the girls got home from their respective schools.

He'd tacked the gable vent back into place. He couldn't see how that squirrel had pulled it free, but it wouldn't get it out now. He also plugged up the upper and lower ends of the hose leader with an aeresol foam insulation he picked up at Rickel's. It occurred to him as he watched the mustard-colored gunk harden into a solid Styrofoam plug that he was cutting off the mouse exit as well as the mouse entryway. Hopefully, they were all out for the day. When they came back they'd be locked out and would have to go somewhere else. And even more hopefully, the squirrel hadn't left a friend in the attic behind the resecured gable vent.

Hank hardly slept at all that night. He kept listening for the snap of a trap, hoping he wouldn't hear it, yet waiting for it. Hours passed. The last time he remembered on the clock radio LED was 3:34. He must have fallen asleep after that.

Dawn was just starting to bleach out the night when the snap came. He came wide awake with the sound. The clock said 5:10. But the noise didn't end with that single snap. Whatever was up there began to thrash. He could hear the wooden base of the trap slapping against the attic flooring. Something bigger than a mouse, maybe a squirrel, was caught but still alive. He heard another snap and a squeal of pain. God, it was alive and hurt! His stomach turned.

Gloria rolled over, a silhouette in the growing light.

"Djoo hear somin?" she mumbled, still nine-tenths asleep.

Suddenly the attic went still.

"Nothing," he said. "Some animals fighting outside. Go back to sleep."

She did. He couldn't.

He approached the attic door with dread. He did *not* want to go up there. What if it was still alive? What if it was weak and paralyzed but still breathing? He'd have to kill it. He didn't know if he could do that. But he'd have to. It would be the only humane thing to do. How? Drown it? Smother it in a plastic bag? He began to sweat.

This was crazy. He was wimping out over a rodent in his attic. Enough already! He flipped the attic light switch, slipped the bolt, and pulled on the cord. The door angled down on its hinges.

But it didn't come down alone. Something came with it, flying right at his face.

He yelled like a fool in a funhouse and batted it away. Then he saw what it was: one of the mousetraps. At first glance it looked empty, but when he went to pick it up, he saw what was in it and almost tossed his cookies.

A fury little forearm, no longer than the last two bones on his pinky finger, was caught under the bow. It looked like it once might have been attached to a squirrel, but now it ended in a ragged bloody stump where it had been chewed off just below the shoulder.

Where the hell was the rest of it?

Visions of the squirrel chewing off its own arm swam around him until he remembered that auto-amputation only occurred with arresting traps, the kind that were chained down. Animals had been known to chew off a limb to escape those. The squirrel could have dragged the mousetrap with it.

But it hadn't.

Hank stood at the halfway point on those steps a long while. He finally decided he had wasted enough time. He clenched his teeth, told himself it was dead, and poked his head up. He started and almost fell off the stairs when he turned his head and found the squirrel's tail only two inches from his nose. It was caught in the bow of another trap—the second snap he had heard this morning. But there was no body attached.

This was getting a bit gory. He couldn't buy a squirrel chewing off its arm and then its tail. If anything, it would drag the tail trap after it until it got stuck someplace.

Nope. Something had eaten it. Something that didn't smell too good, because the attic was really beginning to stink.

510

He ducked down the ladder, grabbed the flashlight he always kept in the night table, then hurried back up to the attic. The light from the single bulb over the opening in the floor didn't reach very far. And even with daylight filtering in through the gable vents, there were lots of dark spots. He wanted the flashlight so he could get a good look along the inside of the eaves and into all the corners.

He searched carefully, and as he moved through the attic he had a vague sense of another presence, a faint awareness of something else here, a tantalizing hint of furtive movement just out of his range of vision.

He shook it off. The closeness up here, the poor lighting, the missing animal carcasses—it had all set his imagination in motion. He gave the attic a thorough going over and found nothing but a few droppings. Big droppings. Bigger than something a mouse or squirrel would leave. Maybe possum-sized. Or raccoon-sized.

Was that the answer? A possum or a coon? He didn't know much about them, but he'd seen them around in the woods, and he knew every time he put turkey or chicken scraps in the garbage, something would get the lid off the trash can and tear the Hefty bag apart until every last piece of meat was gone. Raccoons were notorious for that. If they'd eat leftover chicken, why not dead mice and squirrels?

Made sense to him. But how was it getting in? A check of the gable vent he'd resecured yesterday gave him the answer. It had been pulled free again. Well, he'd fix that right now.

He went down to his workshop and got a hammer and some heavy nails. He felt pretty good as he pounded them into the edges of the vent, securing it from the *inside*. He knew what he was up against now and knew something that big would be easy to keep out. No raccoon or possum was going to pull this vent free again. And just to be sure, he went over to the north side and reinforced the gable vent there.

That was it. His house was his own again.

Wednesday night was chaotic. Excitement was at a fever pitch with the twins packing their own little suitcases full of stuffed animals and placing them by the front door so they'd be all set to go first thing in the morning.

Hank helped Gloria with the final packing of the big suitcases and they both fell into bed around midnight. He had little trouble getting off to sleep. There probably weren't any mice left, there weren't any squirrels, and he was sure no raccoon or possum was getting in tonight. So why stay awake listening?

The snap of a trap woke him around 3:30. No thrashing, no slapping, just the snap. Another mouse. A second trap went off ten minutes later.

Then a third. *Damn!* He waited. The fourth and final trap sprang at 4:00 A.M.

Hank lay tense and rigid in bed and wondered what to do. Everybody would be up at first light, just a couple of hours from now, getting ready for the drive to Newark Airport. He couldn't leave those mouse carcasses up there all the time they were away—they'd rot and the whole house would be stinking by the time they got back.

He slipped out of bed and grabbed the flashlight.

"What's wrong?" Gloria asked, awakened by the movement.

"Just getting some water," he whispered.

She rolled over and he closed the bedroom door behind him. He didn't waste any time. He had to get up there and get rid of the dead mice before the girls woke up. These damn animals were really getting on his nerves. He pulled the door down and hurried up.

Hank stood on the ladder and gaped at the traps. All four had been sprung but lay empty on the flooring around him, the peanut butter untouched. No mice heads, no bits of fur. What could have tripped them without getting caught? It was almost like a game.

He looked around warily. He was standing in a narrow cone of light. The rest of the attic was dark. Very dark. The sense of something else up here with him was very strong now. So was the odor. It was worse than ever.

Imagination again.

He waved the flashlight around quickly but saw no scurrying or lurking shapes along the eaves or in the corners. He made a second sweep, more slowly this time, more careful. He crouched and moved all along the edges, bumping his head now and again on a rafter, his flashlight held ahead of him like a gun.

Finally, when he was satisfied nothing of any size was lurking about, he checked the gable vent.

It had been yanked loose again. Some of the nails had pulled free, and those that hadn't had ripped through the vent's plastic edge.

He was uneasy now. No raccoon was strong enough to do this. He didn't know many *men* who could do it without a crowbar. This was getting out of hand. He suddenly wanted to get downstairs and bolt the attic door behind him. He'd call a professional exterminator as soon as they got back from Orlando.

He spun about, sure that something had moved behind him, but all was still, all was dark but for the pool of light under the bulb. Yet . . .

Quickly now, he headed back toward the light, toward the ladder, toward the empty traps. As he sidled along, he checked in the corners and along the eaves one last time, and wondered how and why the traps had been sprung. He saw nothing. Whatever it was, if it had come in, it

512

wasn't here anymore. Maybe the attic light had scared it off. If that was the case, he'd leave the light on all night. All *week*.

His big mistake was looking for it along the floor.

It got him as he came around the heating unit. He saw a flash movement as it swung down from the rafters—big as a rottweiler, brown scruffy fur, a face that was all mouth with huge countless teeth, four clawed arms extended toward him as it held on to the beams above with still two more limbs—and that was all. It engulfed his head and lifted him off the floor in one sweeping motion. For a few spasming seconds his fingers tore futilely at its matted fur and his legs kicked and writhed silently in the air. As life and consciousness fled that foul smothering unbearable agony, he sensed the bottomless pit of its hunger and thought helplessly of the open attic door, of the ladder going down, and of Gloria and the twins sleeping below.

The Traveller

R. H. *Benson*

'I am amazed, not that the Traveller returns from
that Bourne, but that he returns so seldom.'
The Pilgrims' Way

On one of these evenings as we sat together after dinner in front of the wide open fireplace in the central room of the house, we began to talk on that old subject—the relation of Science to Faith.

'It is no wonder,' said the priest, 'if their conclusions appear to differ, to shallow minds who think that the last words are being said on both sides; because their standpoints are so different. The scientific view is that you are not justified to committing yourself one inch ahead of your intellectual evidence: the religious view is that in order to find out anything worth knowing your faith must always be a little in advance of your evidence; you must advance *en échelon*. There is the principle of our Lord's promises. 'Act as if it were true, and light will be given.' The scientist on the other hand says, 'Do not presume to commit yourself until light is given.' The difference between the methods lies, of course, in the fact that Religion admits the heart and the whole man to the witness-box, while Science only admits the head—scarcely even the senses. Yet surely the evidence of experience is on the side of Religion. Every really great achievement is inspired by motives of the heart, and not of the head; by feeling and passion, not by a calculation of probabilities. And so are the mysteries of God unveiled by those who carry them first by assault; 'The Kingdom of Heaven suffereth violence; and the violent will take it by force.'

'For example,' he continued after a moment, 'the scientific view of haunted houses is that there is no evidence for them beyond that which may be accounted for by telepathy, a kind of thought-reading. Yet if you can penetrate that veneer of scientific thought that is so common now, you find that by far the larger part of mankind still believes in them. Practically, not one of us really accepts the scientific view as an adequate one.'

'Have you ever had an experience of that kind yourself?' I asked.

'Well,' said the priest, smiling, 'you are sure you will not laugh at it? There is nothing commoner than to think such things a subject for humour; and that I cannot bear. Each such story is sacred to one person at the very least, and therefore should be to all reverent people.'

I assured him that I would not treat his story with disrespect.

'Well,' he answered, 'I do not think you will, and I will tell you. It only happened a very few years ago. This was how it began:

'A friend of mine was, and is still, in charge of a church in Kent, which I will not name; but it is within twenty miles of Canterbury. The district fell into Catholic hands a good many years ago. I received a telegram, in this house, a day or two before Christmas, from my friend, saying that he had been suddenly seized with a very bad attack of influenza, which was devastating Kent at that time; and asking me to come down, if possible at once, and take his place over Christmas. I had only lately given up active work, owing to growing infirmity, but it was impossible to resist this appeal; so Parker packed my things and we went together by the next train.

'I found my friend really ill, and quite incapable of doing anything; so I assured him that I could manage perfectly, and that he need not be anxious.

'On the next day, a Wednesday, and Christmas Eve, I went down to the little church to hear confessions. It was a beautiful old church, though tiny, and full of interesting things: the old altar had been set up again; there was a rood-loft with a staircase leading on to it; and an awmbry on the north of the sanctuary had been fitted up as a receptacle for the Most Holy Sacrament, instead of the old hanging pyx. One of the most interesting discoveries made in the church was that of the old confessional. In the lower half of the rood-screen, on the south side, a square hole had been found, filled up with an insertion of oak; but an antiquarian of the Alcuin Club, whom my friend had asked to examine the church, declared that this without doubt was the place where in pre-Reformation times confessions were heard. So it had been restored, and put to its ancient use; and now on this Christmas Eve I sat within the chancel in the dim fragrant light, while penitents came and knelt outside the screen on the single step, and made their confessions through the old opening.

'I know this is a great platitude, but I never can look at a piece of old furniture without a curious thrill at a thing that has been so much saturated with human emotion; but, above all that I have ever seen, I think that this old confessional moved me. Through that little opening had come so many thousands of sins, great and little, weighted with sorrow; and back again, in Divine exchange for those burdens, had returned the balm of the Saviour's blood. "Behold! a door opened in heaven," through which that strange commerce of sin and grace may be carried on—grace pressed down and running over, given into the bosom in exchange for sin! *O bonum commercium!'*

The priest was silent for a moment, his eyes glowing. Then he went on.

'Well, Christmas Day and the three following festivals passed away very happily. On the Sunday night after service, as I came out of the vestry, I saw a child waiting. She told me, when I asked her if she wanted me, that her father and others of her family wished to make their confessions on the following evening about six o'clock. They had had influenza in the house, and had not been able to come out before; but the father was going to work next day, as he was so much better, and would come, if it pleased me, and some of his children to make their confessions in the evening and their communions the following morning.

'Monday dawned, and I offered the Holy Sacrifice as usual, and spent the morning chiefly with my friend, who was now able to sit up and talk a good deal, though he was not yet allowed to leave his bed.

'In the afternoon I went for a walk.

'All the morning there had rested a depression on my soul such as I have not often felt; it was of a peculiar quality. Every soul that tries, however poorly, to serve God, knows by experience those heavinesses by which our Lord tests and confirms His own; but it was not like that. An element of terror mingled with it, as of impending evil.

'As I started for my walk along the high road this depression deepened. There seemed no physical reason for it that I could perceive. I was well myself, and the weather was fair; yet air and exercise did not affect it. I turned at last, about half-past three o'clock, at a milestone that marked sixteen miles to Canterbury.

'I rested there for a moment, looking to the south-east, and saw that far on the horizon heavy clouds were gathering; and then I started homewards. As I went I heard a far-away boom, as of distant guns, and I thought at first that there was some sea-fort to the south where artillery practice was being held; but presently I noticed that it was too irregular and prolonged for the report of a gun; and then it was with a sense of relief that I came to the conclusion it was a far-away thunderstorm, for I felt that the state of the atmosphere might explain away this depression that so troubled me. The thunder seemed to come nearer, pealed more loudly three or four times and ceased.

'But I felt no relief. When I reached home a little after four Parker brought me in some tea, and I fell asleep afterwards in a chair before the fire. I was wakened after a troubled and unhappy dream by Parker bringing in my coat and telling me it was time to keep my appointment at the church. I could not remember what my dream was, but it was sinister and suggestive of evil, and, with the shreds of it still clinging to me, I looked at Parker with something of fear as he stood silently by my chair holding the coat.

'The church stood only a few steps away, for the garden and church-yard adjoined one another. As I went down carrying the lantern that Parker had lighted for me, I remember hearing far away to the south, beyond the village, the beat of a horse's hoofs. The horse seemed to be in a gallop, but presently the noise died away behind a ridge.

'When I entered the church I found that the sacristan had lighted a candle or two as I had asked him, and I could just make out the kneeling figures of three or four people in the north aisle.

'When I was ready I took my seat in the chair beyond the screen, at the place I have described; and then, one by one, the labourer and his children came up and made their confessions. I remember feeling again, as on Christmas Eve, the strange charm of this old place of penitence, so redolent of God and man, each in his tenderest character of Saviour and penitent; with the red light burning like a luminous flower in the dark before me, to remind me how God was indeed tabernacling with men, and was their God.

'Now I do not know how long I had been there, when again I heard the beat of a horse's hoofs, but this time in the village just below the churchyard; then again there fell a sudden silence. Then presently a gust of wind flung the door wide, and the candles began to gutter and flare in the draught. One of the girls went and closed the door.

'Presently the boy who was kneeling by me at that time finished his confession, received absolution and went down the church, and I waited for the next, not knowing how many there were.

'After waiting a minute or two I turned in my seat, and was about to get up, thinking there was no one else, when a voice whispered sharply through the hole a single sentence. I could not catch the words, but I supposed they were the usual formula for a blessing, so I gave the blessing and waited, a little astonished at not having heard the penitent come up.

'Then the voice began again.'

The priest stopped a moment and looked round, and I could see that he was trembling a little.

'Would you rather not go on?' I said. 'I think it disturbs you to tell me.'

'No, no,' he said; 'it is all right, but it was very dreadful—very dreadful.'

'Well, the voice began again in a loud quick whisper, but the odd thing was that I could hardly understand a word; there were just phrases here and there, like the name of God and of our Lady, that I could catch. Then there were a few old French words that I knew, "*le roy*" came over and over again. Just at first I thought it must be some extreme form of dialect unknown to me; then I thought it must be a very old man who was deaf, because when I tried, after a few sentences, to explain that I could not understand, the penitent paid no attention, but whispered on quickly without a pause. Presently I could percieve that he was in a terrible state of mind; the voice broke and sobbed, and then almost cried out, but still in this loud whisper; then on the other side of the screen I could hear fingers working and moving uneasily, as if entreating admittance at some barred door. Then at last there was silence for a moment, and then plainly some closing formula was repeated, which gradually grew lower and ceased. Then, as I rose, meaning to come round and explain that I had not been able to hear, a loud moan or two came from the penitent. I stood up quickly and looked through the upper part of the screen, and there was no one there.

'I can give you no idea of what a shock that was to me. I stood there glaring, I suppose, through the screen down at the empty step for a moment or two, and perhaps I said something aloud, for I heard a voice from the end of the church.

' "Did you call, sir?" And there stood the sacristan, with his keys and lantern, ready to lock up.

'I still stood without answering for a moment, and then I spoke; my voice sounded oddly in my ears.

' "Is there any one else, Williams? Are they all gone?" or something like that.

'Williams lifted his lantern and looked round the dusky church.

' "No, sir, there is no one."

'I crossed the chancel to go to the vestry, but as I was half-way,

517

suddenly again in the quiet village there broke out the desperate gallop of a horse.

' "There! there!" I cried, "do you hear that?"

'Williams came up the church towards me.

' "Are you ill, sir?" he said. "Shall I fetch your servant?"

'I made an effort and told him it was nothing; but he insisted on seeing me home: I did not like to ask him whether he had heard the gallop of the horse; for, after all, I thought, perhaps there was no connection between that and the voice that whispered.

'I felt very much shaken and disturbed; and after dinner, which I took alone of course, I thought I would go to bed very soon. On my way up, however, I looked into my friend's room for a few minutes. He seemed very bright and eager to talk, and I stayed very much longer than I had intended. I said nothing of what had happened in the church; but listened to him while he talked about the village and the neighbourhood. Finally, as I was on the point of bidding him good-night, he said something like this:

' "Well, I mustn't keep you, but I've been thinking while you've been in church of an old story that is told by antiquarians about this place. They say that one of St Thomas à Becket's murderers came here on the very evening of the murder. It is his day, today, you know, and that is what put me in mind of it, I suppose."

'While my friend said this, my old heart began to beat furiously; but with a strong effort of self-control, I told him I should like to hear the story.

' "Oh! there's nothing much to tell," said my friend; "and they don't know who it's supposed to have been; but it is said to have been either one of the four knights, or one of the men-at-arms."

' "But how did he come here?" I asked, "and what for?"

' "Oh! he's supposed to have been in terror of his soul, and that he rushed here to get absolution, which, of course, was impossible."

' "But tell me," I said. "Did he come here alone, or how?"

' "Well, you know, after the murder they ransacked the Archbishop's house and stables; and it is said that this man got one of the fastest horses and rode like a madman, not knowing where he was going; and that he dashed into the village, and into the church where the priest was: and then afterwards, mounted again and rode off. The priest, too, is buried in the chancel, somewhere, I believe. You see it's a very vague and improbable story. At the Gatehouse at Malling, too, you know, they say that one of the knights slept there the night after the murder."

'I said nothing more; but I suppose I looked strange, because my friend began to look at me with some anxiety, and then ordered me off to bed: so I took my candle and went.

518

'Now,' said the priest, turning to me, 'that is the story. I need not say that I have thought about it a great deal ever since: and there are only two theories which appear to me credible, and two others, which would no doubt be suggested, which appear to me incredible.

'First, you may say that I was obviously unwell: my previous depression and dreaming showed that, and therefore that I dreamt the whole thing. If you wish to think that—well, you must think it.

'Secondly, you may say, with the Psychical Research Society, that the whole thing was transmitted from my friend's brain to mine; that his was in an energetic, and mine in a passive state, or something of the kind.

'These two theories would be called "scientific," which term means that they are not a hair's-breadth in advance of the facts with which the intellect, a poor instrument at the best, is capable of dealing. And these two "scientific" theories create in their turn a new brood of insoluble difficulties.

'Or you may take your stand upon the spiritual world, and use the faculties which God has given you for dealing with it, and then you will no longer be helplessly puzzled, and your intellect will no longer overstrain itself at a task for which it was never made. And you may say, I think, that you prefer one of two theories.

'First, that human emotion has a power of influencing or saturating inanimate nature. Of course this is only the old familiar sacramental principle of all creation. The expressions of your face, for instance, caused by the shifting of the chemical particles of which it is composed, vary with your varying emotions. Thus we might say that the violent passions of hatred, anger, terror, remorse, of this poor murderer, seven hundred years ago, combined to make a potent spiritual fluid that bit so deep into the very place where it was all poured out, that under certain circumstances it is reproduced. A phonograph, for example, is a very coarse parallel, in which the vibrations of sound translate themselves first into terms of wax, and then re-emerge again as vibrations when certain conditions are fulfilled.

'Or, secondly, you may be old-fashioned and simple, and say that by some law, vast and inexorable, beyond our perception, the personal spirit of the very man is chained to the place, and forced to expiate his sin again and again, year by year, by attempting to express his grief and to seek forgiveness, without the possibility of receiving it. Of course we do not know who he was; whether one of the knights who afterwards did receive absolution, which possibly was not ratified by God; or one of the men-at-arms who assisted, and who, as an anonymous chronicle says "*sine confessione et viatico subito rapti sunt.*"

'There is nothing materialistic, I think, in believing that spiritual beings may be bound to express themselves within limits of time and space;

and that inanimate nature, as well as animate, may be the vehicles of the unseen. Arguments against such possibilities have surely, once for all, been silenced, for Christians at any rate, by the Incarnation and the Sacramental system, of which the whole principle is that the Infinite and Eternal did once, and does still, express Itself under forms of inanimate nature, in terms of time and space.

'With regard to another point, perhaps I need not remind you that a thunderstorm broke over Canterbury on the day and hour of the actual murder of the Archbishop.'

The Tuckahoe

Nancy Etchemendy

It's getting on toward dark, and I keep hoping maybe I've caught a fever and I'm out of my head. Maybe there isn't anything waiting under the house to get me as soon as I step outside. Maybe Pa and Lemmy are just playing a trick on me, and they'll come strutting through the front door any minute now, smug as a couple of tom turkeys. Oh, how I'd like that. Pa, he'd laugh at me, because that's his way, to make a joke out of Ruben, who'll never be a man. And Lemmy would probably hook his thumbs in his belt and call me his sissy little brother, seeing me wrapped up in Momma's quilt like this, shaking, and nothing sticking out except my nose and the barrel of Grampa's Colt pistol. But I wouldn't mind. It would be all right, just this once. If they come in here alive and whole, if they could prove tuckahoe is just tuckahoe, and that empty thing on the porch isn't really what's left of Momma. Then they could laugh all they want, and it would be all right. Just this once.

The rain started in again a couple hours ago, just like last night. Makes my heart crawl up into my throat and lie there twitching like a half-dead frog. I lit all the lamps and tried to make a fire in the fireplace. But the fire, it don't seem to burn right. It looks just the way I feel, puny and wavery, like it might not be here in the morning. I tried to give myself a good talking-to, just like Momma would if she saw me now. "Ruben," she'd say, "the Lord helps them that helps themselves." But I don't think the Lord had much to do with this rain, nor with the thing that ate Momma.

Last night, when the storm first started, I had a feeling this wasn't any regular rain. Didn't seem natural the way it poured out of the sky. It came down in long, wavy curtains, like somebody'd emptied a bunch of big tin washtubs all at one time. There weren't any drops at all except from the splashes when it hit the ground. And the lightning felt wrong too. I've never seen such lightning before. Why, it lit up the sky blue and white all night long, one bolt right after another. Early on in the evening, it hit the two big poplars down by the road, both at the same time. Before the rain put the fire out, they were burnt to pure cinders, and there was nothing left this morning except black poles.

The thing that made my skin creep worst of all, though, was the smell. I usually like the smell of rain, especially this time of year, when the tree sap is running and the ground is already a little damp. But this smelled funny, kind of like that oily stuff Pa sprays on the crops sometimes to kill the bugs. I told Pa that. I said the rain smelled real bad, like oil or something. I even went out on the porch and got a little on my fingers so he could smell it for himself.

But Pa, he has a stubborn streak, and most of the time he doesn't pay attention till something turns around and bites him right on the toe. He looked at me kind of sideways, scratching his beard, and he said, "Ruben, I don't smell a blame thing. Quit acting like an old woman." And Lemmy made it worse by laughing outright.

I saw right then I might as well not waste any more breath on those two, so I just shut my mouth and went over to the table to watch Momma kneading bread. I like to watch her when she has her sleeves rolled up and her hands all covered with flour. Sometimes a lock of fine, brown hair falls down in her eyes, and she asks me if I'll tuck it back for her. Last night, when I tucked her hair back in, she whispered, "The rain don't smell right to me, neither, if you want to know the truth." Remembering that now makes me feel like crying.

After a while, I lay down by the fire and tried to read in one of my schoolbooks about this fellow who'd discovered the South Pole, but it wasn't any use. I kept getting this stickery feeling all up and down my back. Made me think Lemmy or somebody had sneaked up behind me and was trying to scare me. But every time I twisted around to look, there was nobody there at all, just the front window lit up all cold and blue, and the curtains of rain outside, and the roar of thunder. The more I stared at that book, the more I thought about the window, and the queerer I felt about what I might see through it if I turned around again. The hairs on my arms and the back of my neck stood up, and pretty soon a cold sweat broke out on my lip, right where I'm starting to get a few little mustache hairs. I made up my mind the only way to get myself over being afraid was to go take a good long look through the window to prove there was nothing peering in, fearsome or otherwise.

I put my book down on the rug where I'd been lying, and I got up and walked to the window, which was misted over a little on account of its being warmer inside than out. I spit on my sleeve and rubbed a little place in the glass. I couldn't see really good, because the rain and lightning made everything look so different. The straw grass on the front acre might have been a stranger's pond, and Momma's chicken coop loomed up in the night like one of those dinosaurs I've seen in books. I squinted for a long time, and finally after I had things figured out a little, I saw the chickens were all riled up, flapping around in the rain. That struck me as just plain unnatural, for chickens are pretty much like people when it comes to staying indoors on a wet night.

Then I saw the other thing, and it gave me a chill so deep I felt like I'd been dropped down a well. Through that little place in the glass, I made out something creeping towards the root cellar. I stood still as a lump of salt to get a better look, though my blood was hammering inside my veins, and my knees felt like cheese. The next bolt of lightning lit up everything almost as clear as day, and just for a second, even with the rain, I got a perfect sight of the thing.

There's a funny kind of toadstool that grows down in the dimmest part of the woods. Tuckahoe, Pa calls them, but Momma says they aren't like any tuckahoe she's ever seen, and we aren't to eat them under any circumstances. I wouldn't want to anyway, for the sight of them makes my stomach turn somersaults. You never find just one or two, coming up separately around dead wood like regular mushrooms. These tuckahoe like to grow from the heart of a living tree, a hundred or more together in a slippery, gray clump, like overgrown frogs' eggs. No single one of them is bigger than a man's thumb, but I've seen nests two feet around stuck onto unlucky maples and dogwoods. Lemmy, he gets bored sometimes and knocks the clumps down and hacks them up with a stick for fun. But me, I'd rather stay as far away from them as I can.

Tuckahoe. That's what I thought of as I watched that thing crawl across our front acre in the stinking rain. I felt the sweat gathering into little streams on my forehead while I told myself to stop and think. It couldn't be tuckahoe, because it was too big, big as a man. Besides that, it was moving, and darn fast, too. Tuckahoe couldn't move by itself, not that I ever heard of anyway.

I could feel a howl building up in my throat, getting ready to come out whether I wanted it to or not, when all of a sudden there was a big crash from the back of the house and the whole place shook. I think I did let out a yell then, but nobody paid any attention, because they were all running to see what had caused the commotion. By the time I got my wits together enough to follow them, Pa and Lemmy were standing by the back door looking out into the storm. A good-sized limb from the old oak tree by the kitchen had broken loose in the wind and come down on the roof. Pa was growling and cursing, and Momma was out in the rain with a *Farm Journal* over her head, trying to see if the roof was all right.

All I could think of was that thing crawling around out there, and I said, "Get her back inside! Get her out of the rain!" My voice cracked, just like it always does when I most wish it wouldn't.

And Lemmy gave me one of those cockeyed half smiles of his and said, "For Pete's sake. You'd think she's made of sugar or something. The rain won't melt her, you know."

Then I hit Lemmy in the stomach, and he hit me in the nose. And the next thing I knew, Momma was standing over me with an ice pack, yelling a blue streak, and dripping rainwater all over the kitchen floor. I didn't care. I just closed my eyes and let her yell. As long as she was back inside, that's all that mattered to me.

I remember lying in bed this morning thinking the tuckahoe thing must have been nothing but a bad dream. I heard birds chirping outside the window, and I watched a little finger of sunlight move across a spiderweb in the corner. The rain had stopped, and the clouds were no more than a few raggedy strings way up high. I felt so good that I whistled while I put my pants on, and said good morning to Lemmy even though my nose was still pretty sore.

Momma was getting ready to go out and fetch the eggs from the chickens, like she does every morning. She had to pull on a pair of high rubber boots, because the front acre was ankle-deep in mud from the storm. I stood in the sunshine on the porch and watched her wade out towards the chicken coop. She had a basket hanging from one arm for the eggs. She got about ten or fifteen steps away, then stopped dead still with the basket swinging from her elbow. She turned around, and the look on her face made me swallow without meaning to.

"There's something kind of funny out here, Ruben," she said. "Better ask Pa to come and take a look."

I hollered for Pa, and he grumbled, for he hates to get up from his chair. But he lumbered out into the mud, and Lemmy and I rolled up our pants and followed him.

Momma had come across a patch of slimy stuff. It could have been egg whites maybe, except it was sort of milky, and where would egg whites come from anyway, when there were no yolks or shells lying around? Pa frowned at it, and he and Lemmy stuck their fingers in it. Then Pa said it wasn't anything to worry about, probably some new kind of bug left it, or it might be some kind of mildew, he didn't know.

All that time, I was standing on one foot and then the other, and my heart was ticking fast as a two-dollar watch. I had a pretty fair idea what had left that slime, and it didn't have anything to do with bugs. "Pa," I said, "I think you should know I saw some kind of strange thing crawling around out here last night, looked like one of those tuckahoe clumps, only almost as big as you are."

Lemmy rolled his eyes and spit in the mud right by my foot. Pa just looked mad and said, "Ruben, everybody knows you can't tell the difference between a tall tale and the truth. If you think I'm gonna swallow a story like that, you've got a brain about the size of a pea." Then he and Lemmy sloshed back to the house, talking and laughing. I stayed outside with Momma, because I felt like I was either going to throw things or cry, and I didn't want to give Pa the satisfaction of seeing it.

By and by, Momma and I went and took a look at the chicken coop. It turned out there were hardly any eggs in the boxes. That was spooky enough. But what we found just inside the chicken wire scared me a lot worse. I thought I saw two rags lying there on the ground, but when I looked closer, I saw it wasn't rags at all. It was two dead hens, just their feathers and skin, with nothing inside. I squinted and poked, but I couldn't find any rips or bites. It was like all the blood and meat and bones had been sucked right out of them, leaving them empty, without a single mark.

Momma turned all white when she saw those hens, and she told Pa about them as soon as we got back inside. But he treats her the same way he treats me, like she hasn't got the sense she was born with. He said to her, "What do you expect after a storm like that? If you were a chicken would you lay a lot of eggs with all that racket goin' on?" Then he said a coon must have gotten in and killed them.

I came pretty close to telling him right then and there that if he expected me to swallow a story like that, he must have a brain about the size of a pea. I know what a coon does to a chicken, and it doesn't look anything like that. But I never really said it. I just thought it. And now I'm glad, because all I want is just to see Pa alive, even if he's wrong sometimes.

Momma took her boots off and went into the kitchen and lit the fire in the gas range. She'd only gotten four eggs, and that was just two apiece for Pa and Lemmy, even if Momma and I went without. Pa was yelling about how he was half starved to death, and she couldn't very well expect him to haul an oak limb down off the roof with a half-empty stomach. He told her she'd better fry up a whole lot of spuds to make up the difference, and he snapped his suspenders, which Momma hates because it makes them wear out quicker.

Momma, she was busy with the griddle and slicing some bacon, and she said to me without looking, "Ruben, honey, will you go down to the root cellar and bring up some spuds?"

I just stood there. All of a sudden, it didn't matter how bright the sun was shining or how loud the birds were twittering. It might as well have been pitch dark and rain pouring down in buckets again as far as I was concerned. I was thinking about that slime on the front acre and those two empty chicken skins. And I could see the tuckahoe in my head, all smeary through that window in the glare of the lightning, headed straight for the root cellar.

Momma turned and frowned at me when I made no move for the door. Then the frown melted off into worry lines, and she said, "What's wrong, honey?"

"Momma, please don't make me go. There's something down there," I said. My throat was so dry I could hardly get the words out.

Then Pa, he jumped up out of his chair and grabbed me by the shirt and shook me. I saw the veins popping up on his big, thick neck, and his face was the color of a ripe tomato. I'd have shut my eyes, but I knew that would just make him madder, and I was scared that he'd backhand me or kick me like he sometimes does. Instead, he opened up his mouth so those ragged, yellow teeth of his showed like an animal's against the furry dark of his beard. I could feel his breath tickling my cheeks, hot and sharp from the hard cider he'd already drunk that morning. I wished he liked me better. Oh, how I wished it.

"You're a good-for-nothin' little momma's boy," he said, soft, almost a whisper. "There's nothin' down in that cellar but a few daddy long-legs and your own damn boogeymen. Now go get them spuds."

He let go of my shirt and shoved me backwards with his fist, and I stumbled like I always do, my feet being so darn big and my legs so stringy. I landed flat on the floor, and I hurt all over, inside and out. I was crying by then, which added even more to my shame. And I started thinking he was probably right. If I were any kind of a real man, I'd get up on my own two feet and go down there after those spuds, whether I was scared or not.

Lemmy stood up and started laughing and prancing around like a girl. "If it's gonna make you cry and all, honey," he said in a high, fake little voice, "*I'll* go get the dadblamed spuds."

Then I really got mad, because there aren't very many worse things in the world than to have somebody like Lemmy poking fun at you. I don't think I would have done it if I hadn't been so mad, and if I hadn't wanted so much to prove that I wasn't a sissy. Anyway, I got up and grabbed the basket and started wading through the mud to the root cellar.

There I was, out in the sun again, blue sky above, and trees aglitter with dew, just like any other spring morning. Made me feel like I could face almost anything. For a minute or two the world seemed so familiar that I began to whistle and enjoy the feel of the cool mud between my toes. Then, about a stone's throw from the cellar door, I came across another patch of slime, the same as we'd found by the chicken coop.

I squatted down beside it, nearly deaf from the noise of my heart. This slime seemed fresher than the other, and a smell came up from it like from the mouth of a cave that's too dark to see inside of. I stood up slowly, trying not to breathe too fast. My spine felt like ants were marching up it in a long, thick line. Still, I had it in my mind that a man wouldn't run. A man would stay and face whatever came his way.

That's when I heard the sound. It made me think of bees when they swarm in a tree, a thousand little voices raised together to make a single huge and angry one. I looked at the cellar door, and I saw it sort of moving, like there was something big leaning on it, trying to get out all at once. There's a crack between the door and the ground, a couple inches maybe. And through that crack came a mess of gray, wet-looking tucka-hoe.

Part of me was still trying to act brave, and it said to me, "Ruben, my boy, you must've eaten something that didn't agree with you, for you are seeing things."

But the rest of me, which was the bigger part, said, "If a fellow can't trust his own eyes, just what *can* he trust?" That bigger part of me didn't give a darn about whether I was brave or a man or not. It just believed what I was seeing and hearing. That's when I dropped the basket and hightailed it for the house.

By the time I came through the front door, I couldn't even talk. I just stood there shaking and sweating, with my mouth going open and shut. I was peeing my pants. I could feel it washing the mud off my feet onto Momma's clean floor, and I didn't even care. She let out a little cry. Pa got up and stared at me. I don't know what he saw in my face but it must have convinced him of something, because I've never seen him look like that before. He was scared, and I know it isn't right, but for just one second I was glad.

Pa grabbed his shotgun from the corner, and he said, "All right, Lemmy. We're gonna go find out what the hell is down there." Then he and Lemmy took off for the root cellar.

Momma got her quilt and she wrapped me up in it and made me sit down on the bench by the fire. She sat beside me, and rocked me and sang to me like she used to do before I got so big. That's all I wanted, just to bury my face in the good clean smells of Momma, and forget there was ever anything else.

We sat like that for a long time, waiting for Pa and Lemmy to come back, watching the sun creep past noon into afternoon and the clouds begin to sweep across the sky again. But Pa and Lemmy never came. And we never heard anything for sure, no roar of the shotgun going off, no terrible screams or cries for help. Once, I fancied I heard a kind of long moan, way off across the straw grass. It could have been the wind, or an owl. But somehow, it made me wonder what we'd do if we had to get away. The only gun in the house besides Pa's ten-gauge was Grampa's Colt pistol, which Pa always kept locked in his trunk. I was pretty sure I could break that lock with a hammer. I was pretty sure I could do a lot of things if it came to saving Momma.

After a time, Momma fell asleep, and I did too, still thinking about that lock. I was just too bone-weary to hold my eyes open anymore. I had a dream, a fine warm dream about fishing down by the river on a summer's day, and when I woke up it took me a minute to remember where I was.

The first thing I noticed was that Momma had left the bench. She was standing beside the front door with a butcher knife in her hands, whispering over and over again, "The Lord helps them that helps themselves. The Lord helps them that helps themselves." All at once, it came to me that there was a funny noise outside, like bees swarming in a tree.

I jumped up, tipping over the bench, and yelled, "Momma! Don't, Momma!"

She turned around and there was a crazy look in her eyes, like I saw once in the eyes of a neighbor woman who stood in the road and watched her house burn down. Momma's face was all shiny with sweat, and that lock of hair had come loose. Oh, how I wanted to tuck it back, and make everything all right. "I won't let it in here, Ruben," she said. "I swear I won't." Before I could get to her, she held up the knife and opened the door.

I stood at the window and screamed. I screamed for a long, long time, even after there was nothing left of Momma but skin and clothes and the butcher knife. No matter how she struck and slashed, the tuckahoe got her anyway. And when it was done, it disappeared under the porch, leaving patches of slime on the wood.

Twilight fell before I came to myself enough to get up and light the lamps. I went in and broke Pa's trunk to pieces with Momma's kitchen hatchet, and got out the Colt and figured out how to load it.

I've been waiting for Pa and Lemmy to come and tell me it was just a mean trick. But now the rain has started in again.

Uneasy Lie the Drowned

Donald Wandrei

He watched the graying sky anxiously, but without fear, and kept his ears attuned to the gusts of wind that pulled the waves higher. He had made many direct crossings of lakes in the past, alone, both in high riding and heavily laden canoes. This lake was new to him. It was miles across. He did not know its depths and shallows, its lily clusters, beds of weeds, or the way it responded to squalls.

The sky had been clear when he started out. A deep, rhythmic stroke of the paddle, and a twist of the blade. Out and forward. Down and back again. Each time that he brought the paddle astern, an expert drag on the blade kept the canoe on its straight course. It was a simple trick. He could go on for hours, stroking steadily on the right, but midway to his goal, and still unwearied, he switched over to the left.

As often happened in fall along the border lakes, a squall was brewing. A mass of slate-black clouds bloomed out of Canada and swallowed the setting sun. He changed his pace, increased the power of his thrust and pull, sent the canoe skimming more swiftly across the waters.

The lake, hitherto calm, began to spawn groups of nervously racing ripples. The wind chased them in all directions over the surface. They vanished, and left a deceptive tranquillity, until more of the uneasy whirls and lines skittered along. A swell gradually made its presence, in slow undulations, then in an occasional small wave that broke, and always higher swells, and more strongly marked crests.

The water itself, leaf-green at mid-afternoon, darkened as the sun disappeared. The green turned to a sodden blue, and went down to a dull black. And far under that black, four hundred feet and more, lay the solid rock that formed the deep-gouged bed of all these northern lakes. Rock, and the sediment of centuries, saturated logs, perhaps the wrecks of sunken boats and bodies of the drowned for the pike and the muskellunge to forget.

Even the stillness had given way to disturbing sound. The constant, quiet slur of waters divided by the canoe became a slap, at irregular intervals, and with mounting force. The canoe, no longer gliding at even balance, began to rise a little, dip a little, and the lake smacked the fore keel. From the far distance came the advance echo of a mighty rushing howl. The dark mass of pine and spruce that lined the shore, now less than two miles ahead, stirred with a mournful unrest. The air grew colder.

During all the summers that Morse Calkins had spent canoeing and hunting, camping and fishing through the lakes and forests of northern Minnesota, he had not until now experienced a doubt in his mastery. His alarm crept up from his heart to his brain because he could not account for the apprehension. He had been lost in the woods, had rescued himself from a capsized canoe, outdistanced forest fires, escaped the charge of a full-grown moose. He had survived many a squall. Yet the germ of an obscure panic haunted him. Less than two miles, a mile and a half, to the camp where the three companions of this expedition awaited his arrival.

There came a lull.

As though a gigantic, invisible hand closed over the canoe, it lost momentum.

Instantly aware of the drag, he could not understand it. None of the possible causes that he was familiar with seemed adequate reason. A bed of weeds—there was no shallow here, only bottom hundreds of feet down. An added weight—he had not yet shipped water. The pressure of wind—the wind blew fitfully, not steadily, not enough to retard him. A drift of current—perhaps, but currents were more common to rivers than lakes.

The canoe lagged further. His senses, alert to every mood of the craft, warned him of pressure astern. For some strange, incomprehensible motive, he kept his eyes glued on the dark forest and the black mountains of clouds ahead. The prow of the canoe tilted upward higher than it should rise to crest a wave.

He stroked suddenly, deeply, the muscles knotting at his shoulders, and the veins rising on his arms, while his knuckles stood out in naked, bony lumps.

The canoe slowed to a standstill. The bow rode still higher. All his strength and power, his hardest paddling, could not move the canoe. He saw the sweat seep from wrinkles at his wrist, but the swart hairs were half-erect. Odd. Hot and cold—he couldn't be both.

Morse turned and glared all at once, as if expecting to find someone else in the canoe, someone to curse.

There was no one else in the canoe—yet.

But there was a hand clutching the stern, and the fingers of another hand crawled into sight, sliding over the rim. Morse watched them with an expression of detachment. It was almost a silly expression, for the anesthetic of shock had paralyzed him in one instantaneous flood.

A pair of hands—well, why not? A swimmer whom he hadn't noticed—or the exhausted survivor from a boat that had foundered—but the hands wouldn't have inched their way up with so stealthy an approach. These thoughts floated vaguely somewhere in back of his reeling consciousness. No swimmer, no living human being, ever possessed hands of such soapy fatness.

They slid along the side, those plump, bloated fingers, and found a grip. He couldn't make out a trace of knuckles or joints or veins. The nails were entirely missing. Only thick coils remained, like enormously pudgy, gray-white worms.

Above the stern rose a tangle of hair. It was wet, matted. Then the forehead and eyes and face, except that of these there existed only a swollen, fissured blob, the features of one drowned and immersed for months.

To Morse, it seemed that his arms and legs would never carry out his command, that his body drifted through lazy gestures akin to a slow-motion picture. Yet he found himself bringing the oar blade down again and again on those horrific hands. He was not aware of having made a mad lunge forward that almost capsized his craft, or of whirling around and lifting the oar above his head. Only his hammering upon the fingers and head of the corpse, there in all that tumult of wind and waters, formed a positive reality.

He could not pound or pry them loose.

The lips curled around the distended, protruding tongue—an illusion bred of darkness and terror. It couldn't be. Nor the gasped whistle of an inarticulate attempt at speech, like the hiss of steam escaping. He didn't hear it. He couldn't hear it above the rumble and boom of thunder.

Thunder—of course. In the old days, cannon had been fired to roil quiet waters and bring to the surface bodies of the drowned. The thunder, the roaring, reverberating claps and wild wind over the lake had raised this dead thing from its lodging. The rest was imagination. Mustn't let his nerves go.

He heard a husky, gurgling rattle. Once he had listened to a dying soldier whose message bubbled away upon the bullets that had punctured his lungs. This was a sound more appalling, because of its deliberation, and the words choked on the wind, "Don't, Morse. I came up to see you. I had to see you. I was Pete LaRoy."

Morse didn't know that he shouted. There was frenzy in his voice. It rode the storm. "Go back where you came from! I don't care who you are! I've got to make camp—a storm's coming up—get away from here, damn you! Why don't you go back?" The oar thudded, slipped off those fat fingers. Morse wondered what insane impulse drove him to talk aloud. You can't talk to the drowned.

"I can't go back, Morse. I've got to know you. I've got to talk to you. I had to come up. You see, my canoe sank and I drowned—"

"No! No! Go down where you belong!" Was that crazed babble his? What made him answer ghost-words that he dreamed?

"I will. But not yet. I drowned by accident, Morse. It shouldn't have happened. I wasn't prepared. I hadn't lived as long as I was supposed to. I ought to have gone on living. If I had, I'd have met you. I'd have become a friend of yours. We would have made plans together. We would have seen a lot of each other."

The thick, blurry speech submerged the gusts that now began to lash the rising waters. Morse wished that the gale would scream down a million-fold louder and blast into oblivion those corrupt words and that hoarse voice.

Morse panted—and he himself found time to doubt if he made such soft, persuasive answer—"I don't want to know you, whatever you are."

"But I want to know you, Morse Calkins. You see, if I hadn't drowned months ago—was it months? I don't remember. Time doesn't mean anything to me now. If I hadn't drowned, if I had managed to get across the lake safely, I'd have known you well by now. So when I felt you pass over me, something tugged me. You pulled me up where I could see you—"

"No! No! I didn't have anything to do with it! Get the hell back!"

"Oh yes, you did, Morse. You compelled me to come up. Pete LaRoy—you never heard the name before, did you?"

"I don't want to hear it again. Let me go. I've got to reach camp before the storm breaks at its worst. Why don't you just let go and drop back?"

"I will. But not yet. I have something to do that I didn't have time to do when I was Pete LaRoy and living. I'm dead now. Maybe I'm not Pete LaRoy. But the part of me that remembers Pete LaRoy knows what he would have done if he'd kept on living. That part of me felt you coming over the surface of the lake. I had to rise up. I had to come as I am, and I'm here as I am, because there's a mission I've got to carry out. It's the same mission that I couldn't carry out when I drowned, but that I must have carried out if I'd gone on living."

Morse was hitting, slashing, jabbing again with the oar. The flat of the blade struck the monstrous head with sickening, mushy thuds. He pried at the rotten fingers, but they slid along the side and clung as though glued to the withes. He was breathing harshly. The spray that had begun to blow made his own hands slippery, and glistened wetly on the gray-white thing at the stern.

"Please," Morse said thickly, and again, "go away, go down," and then suddenly his voice went screeching up a high, thin crescendo, "let go, God damn you! You're dead and drowned! Get the hell down and rot where you belong!"

The fingers, bashed into loathsome pulp by the blows from the oar, curled over like talons. What was left of Pete LaRoy said in the same

531

guttural drawl as before, "Yes, Morse, I'll go when I've accomplished my mission. I've got to go down where I belong, then. I haven't told you why I came. Don't you want to know?"

"You said you had to see me. You've seen me. Isn't that enough? Are you going to hang on till doomsday?"

"Don't you know why I came? What my mission is?"

"For God's sake, let go!" Morse's voice was getting raw. His howl ended on a sort of piping whistle. His eyes were beginning to glare. He had forgotten the storm. He didn't realize how dark it had become, how blackness came rushing across the lake to merge with the rioting waters. His whole world had narrowed to those pulpy hands and the fat, featureless face that lay under the tangle of hair.

The horrible voice gurgled again, with a noise of drowning, a rattle of death. "It's a strange destiny that drives me, Morse. I don't understand it any more than you do. Sometimes I think I almost know. Then it slips away from me. In the life that I should have lived, I would be here now to kill you."

"To—to—kill—" Morse choked. There was a gagging in his throat that he couldn't gulp away.

"Yes, to kill you. You see, Morse, if I'd gone on living my natural life, I'd have got to know you. We'd have been friends for a while. And then we'd have quarreled and turned bitter enemies. We'd have hated each other as much as we liked each other before. But we'd have tried to suppress our hatred, because we'd have been on this long camping trip. And then today we'd have started across this lake, and our hatred would have flared into the open, and you'd have made a dive for me, and I'd have knocked you overboard and paddled away, leaving you to drown.

"It's _you_ who should have gone down, Morse Calkins, and _I_ who should have gone on living."

The slow, creepy speech died away. Morse saw tiny rivers running down the face and the hands from the torrents of rain that now deluged the lake. The wind had stormed up to a gale, and the waves had begun to crash in foaming white caps. Into the dips dropped the canoe, and slid up the six-foot crests, and shipped the breaking spume.

Morse lurched drunkenly. His eyes felt like flaming coals. His own hair was plastered to his scalp. Streams of rain trickled down his face, sloshed down his back, squished into his boots.

The gray-white visitor bobbed with the rise and fall of the canoe. The soft, fat hands did not relinquish their grip. The dead, decaying head stayed always at the stern.

With a cry that was more like a hoarse bleat, Morse dived for the fingers, yammering as he tried to pull them loose. Their touch was a dreadful sensation that made him gag in crazed horror. He beat and pounded them while the rain glistened like tears on his yellow face.

The double weight on the stern stood the canoe straight on end as it started to mount a roaring white-cap. It plunged beneath the surface. Morse pitched out. The pudgy hands, oddly, seemed to be clinging to his. And then they had somehow enfolded him and he was beating frenziedly at something that had long been pulp.

His last upward glance showed him only raging blackness and the drive of rain.

He was still fighting when the waters closed over his head.

The Village Bully

J. Sheridan Le Fanu

About thirty years ago there lived in the town of Chapelizod an ill-conditioned fellow of herculean strength, well known throughout the neighbourhood by the title of Bully Larkin. In addition to his remarkable physical superiority, this fellow had acquired a degree of skill as a pugilist which alone would have made him formidable. As it was, he was the autocrat of the village, and carried not the sceptre in vain. Conscious of his superiority, and perfectly secure of impunity, he lorded it over his fellows in a spirit of cowardly and brutal insolence, which made him hated even more profoundly than he was feared.

Upon more than one occasion he had deliberately forced quarrels upon men whom he had singled out for the exhibition of his savage prowess; and in every encounter his over-matched antagonist had received an amount of "punishment" which edified and appalled the spectators, and in some instances left ineffaceable scars and lasting injuries after it.

Bully Larkin's pluck had never been fairly tried. For, owing to his prodigious superiority in weight, strength, and skill, his victories had always been certain and easy; and in proportion to the facility with which he uniformly smashed an antagonist, his pugnacity and insolence were inflamed. He thus became an odious nuisance in the neighbourhood, and the terror of every mother who had a son, and of every wife who had a husband who possessed a spirit to resent insult, or the smallest confidence in his own pugilistic capabilities.

Now it happened that there was a young fellow named Ned Moran—better known by the soubriquet of "Long Ned," from his slender, lathy proportions—at that time living in the town. He was, in truth, a mere lad, nineteen years of age, and fully twelve years younger than the stalwart bully. This, however, as the reader will see, secured for him no exemption from the dastardly provocations of the ill-conditioned pugilist. Long Ned, in an evil hour, had thrown eyes of affection upon a certain buxom damsel, who notwithstanding Bully Larkin's amorous rivalry, inclined to reciprocate them.

I need not say how easily the spark of jealousy, once kindled, is blown into a flame, and how naturally, in a coarse and ungoverned nature, it explodes in acts of violence and outrage.

"The bully" watched his opportunity, and contrived to provoke Ned Moran, while drinking in a public-house with a party of friends, into an altercation, in the course of which he failed not to put such insults upon his rival as manhood could not tolerate. Long Ned, though a simple, good-natured sort of fellow, was by no means deficient in spirit, and retorted in a tone of defiance which edified the more timid, and gave his opponent the opportunity he secretly coveted.

Bully Larkin challenged the heroic youth, whose pretty face he had privately consigned to the mangling and bloody discipline he was himself so capable of administering. The quarrel, which he had himself contrived to get up, to a certain degree covered the ill blood and malignant premeditation which inspired his proceedings, and Long Ned, being full of generous ire and whiskey punch, accepted the gauge of battle on the instant. The whole party, accompanied by a mob of idle men and boys, and in short by all who could snatch a moment from the calls of business, proceeded in slow procession through the old gate into the Phoenix Park, and mounting the hill overlooking the town, selected near its summit a level spot on which to decide the quarrel.

The combatants stripped, and a child might have seen in the contrast presented by the slight, lank form and limbs of the lad, and the muscular and massive build of his veteran antagonist, how desperate was the chance of poor Ned Moran.

"Seconds" and "bottle-holders"—selected of course for their love of the game—were appointed, and "the fight" commenced.

I will not shock my readers with a description of the cool-blooded butchery that followed. The result of the combat was what anybody might have predicted. At the eleventh round, poor Ned refused to "give in"; the brawny pugilist, unhurt, in good wind, and pale with concentrated and as yet unslaked revenge, had the gratification of seeing his opponent seated upon his second's knee, unable to hold up his head, his left arm disabled; his face a bloody, swollen, and shapeless mass; his breast scarred and bloody, and his whole body panting and quivering with rage and exhaustion.

"Give in Ned, my boy," cried more than one of the bystanders.

"Never, never," shrieked he, with a voice hoarse and choking.

Time being "up," his second placed him on his feet again. Blinded with his own blood, panting and staggering, he presented but a helpless mark for the blows of his stalwart opponent. It was plain that a touch would have been sufficient to throw him to the earth. But Larkin had no notion of letting him off so easily. He closed with him without striking a blow (the effect of which, prematurely dealt, would have been to bring him at once to the ground, and so put an end to the combat), and getting his battered and almost senseless head under his arm, fast in that peculiar "fix" known to the fancy pleasantly by the name of "chancery," he held him firmly, while with monotonous and brutal strokes he beat his fist, as it seemed, almost into his face. A cry of "shame" broke from the crowd, for it was plain that the beaten man was now insensible, and supported only by the herculean arm of the bully. The round and the fight ended by his hurling him upon the ground, falling upon him at the same time with his knee upon his chest.

The bully rose, wiping the perspiration from his white face with his blood-stained hands, but Ned lay stretched and motionless upon the grass. It was impossible to get him upon his legs for another round. So he was carried down, just as he was, to the pond which then lay close to the old Park gate, and his head and body were washed beside it. Contrary to the belief of all he was not dead. He was carried home, and after some months to a certain extent recovered. But he never held up his head again, and before the year was over he had died of consumption. Nobody could doubt how the disease had been induced, but there was no actual proof to connect the cause and effect, and the ruffian Larkin escaped the vengeance of the law. A strange retribution, however, awaited him.

After the death of Long Ned, he became less quarrelsome than before, but more sullen and reserved. Some said "he took it to heart," and others, that his conscience was not at ease about it. Be this as it may, however, his health did not suffer by reason of his presumed agitations, nor was his worldly prosperity marred by the blasting curses with which poor Moran's enraged mother pursued him; on the contrary, he had rather risen in the world, and obtained regular and well-remunerated employment from the Chief Secretary's gardener, at the other side of the Park. He still lived in Chapelizod, whither, on the close of his day's work, he used to return across the Fifteen Acres.

It was about three years after the catastrophe we have mentioned, and late in the autumn, when, one night, contrary to his habit, he did not appear at the house where he lodged, neither had he been seen anywhere, during the evening, in the village. His hours of return had been so very regular, that his absence excited considerable surprise, though, of course, no actual alarm; and, at the usual hour, the house was closed for the night, and the absent lodger consigned to the mercy of the elements, and the care of his presiding star. Early in the morning, however, he was found lying in a state of utter helplessness upon the slope immediately overlooking the Chapelizod gate. He had been smitten with a paralytic stroke: his right side was dead; and it was many weeks before he had recovered his speech sufficiently to make himself at all understood.

He then made the following relation:—He had been detained, it appeared, later than usual, and darkness had closed before he commenced his homeward walk across the Park. It was a moonlit night, but masses of ragged clouds were slowly drifting across the heavens. He had not encountered a human figure, and no sounds but the softened rush of the wind sweeping through bushes and hollows met his ear. These wild and monotonous sounds, and the utter solitude which surrounded him, did not, however, excite any of those uneasy sensations which are ascribed to superstition, although he said he did feel depressed, or, in his own phraseology, "lonesome." Just as he crossed the brow of the hill which shelters the town of Chapelizod, the moon shone out for some moments with unclouded lustre, and his eye, which happened to wander by the shadowy enclosures which lay at the foot of the slope, was arrested by the sight of a human figure climbing, with all the haste of one pursued, over the churchyard wall, and running up the steep ascent directly towards him. Stories of "resurrectionists" crossed his recollection, as he observed this suspicious-looking figure. But he began, momentarily, to be aware with a sort of fearful instinct which he could not explain, that the running figure was directing his steps, with a sinister purpose, towards himself.

The form was that of a man with a loose coat about him, which, as he ran, he disengaged, and as well as Larkin could see, for the moon was again wading in clouds, threw from him. The figure thus advanced until within some two score yards of him, it arrested its speed, and approached with a loose, swaggering gait. The moon again shone out bright and clear, and, gracious God! what was the spectacle before him? He saw as distinctly as if he had been presented there in the flesh, Ned Moran, himself, stripped naked from the waist upward, as if for pugilistic combat, and drawing towards him in silence. Larkin would have shouted, prayed, cursed, fled across the Park, but he was absolutely powerless; the apparition stopped within a few steps, and leered on him with a ghastly mimicry of the defiant state with which pugilists strive to cow one another before combat. For a time, which he could not so much as conjecture, he was held in the fascination of that unearthly gaze, and at last the thing, whatever it was, on a sudden swaggered close up to him with extended palms. With an impulse of horror, Larkin put out his hand to keep the figure off, and their palms touched—at least, so he believed—for a thrill of unspeakable agony, running through his arm, pervaded his entire frame, and he fell senseless to the earth.

Though Larkin lived for many years after, his punishment was terrible. He was incurably maimed; and being unable to work, he was forced, for existence, to beg alms of those who had once feared and flattered him. He suffered, too, increasingly, under his own horrible interpretation of the preternatural encounter which was the beginning of all his miseries. It was vain to endeavour to shake his faith in the reality of the apparition, and equally vain, as some compassionately did, to try to persuade him that the greeting with which his vision closed was intended, while inflicting a temporary trial, to signify a compensating reconciliation.

"No, no," he used to say, "all won't do. I know the meaning of it well enough; it is a challenge to meet him in the other world—in Hell, where I am going—that's what it means, and nothing else."

And so, miserable and refusing comfort, he lived on for some years, and then died, and was buried in the same narrow churchyard which contains the remains of his victim.

I need hardly say, how absolute was the faith of the honest inhabitants, at the time when I heard the story, in the reality of the preternatural summons which, through the portals of terror, sickness, and misery, had summoned Bully Larkin to his long, last home, and that, too, upon the very ground on which he had signalised the guiltiest triumph of his violent and vindictive career.

The Visit

William F. Nolan

So . . ." he said. "You've been wanting to talk to me. I'm here. Let's talk."

"You're willing to be entirely open and frank?"

"Sure."

"You'll tell it to me straight? No evasions. No bullshit."

"You got it."

"You'll answer any question I ask?"

"I said so, didn't I. But keep your face close to the screen. That way the guard can't hear us."

"I'll be taking notes. For the book I'm doing."

"Shit, you're not going to use my real name, are you? I don't want my real name in some goddamn crime book."

"No, don't worry about that. I'll call you Dave. And I won't be using a last name. You'll be . . . a statistic."

"Great. I had a cousin named Dave. Real asshole."

"Shall we begin?"

"That's what I'm here for. Start your questions."

"How old were you when you killed for the first time?"

"Twelve. Like Billy the Kid. He knifed a guy when he was twelve, back in the Old West. I always felt close to the Kid. Wish I could have known him."

"Was it a man or a woman . . . the first one at twelve?"

"Neither. I snuffed a kid, same age as me. It was after he smart-mouthed me in class. I waited till he was walking home across the ravine, between the school and his house, and that's where I killed him, right there in the ravine."

"How?"

"With a stone. Crushed his skull. It broke open like an egg."

"Then what did you do?"

"Buried him. Ravine's a good place to bury people."

"Body ever found?"

"Nope. He just went to bone. His name was Bobby something. Big red-haired Irish kid. Had a real smart mouth on him."

"When was the next one?"

"When I was fifteen. After I ran away from home . . . that same summer."

"Man or woman?"

"Man. A bum. Railroad tramp. I was going West in this boxcar and he was in the same car, just the two of us. Had some food he didn't want to share so I wrung his skinny neck to get it. He was an old guy, so I had no trouble with him. But he *did* squawk like a chicken when you twist their heads off. Just like a damn chicken."

"Anyone find out? About the bum, I mean?"

"Christ, no. I pitched him out of the car when the train was crossing a river. Neat and easy. And the food made me sleepy. Had me a nice snooze."

"After these killings—the boy and the old man—did you have any remorse?"

"Me? Remorse? Hell, no. When you do somebody, it's like a high. You come down, but then you want another. Like with drugs."

538

"Ever use any?"

"Sure, I experimented some, but my real high was doing people. So I quit doing the drugs. To keep my head clear so I could enjoy myself. Didn't want anything getting in the way."

"You're what . . . how old now . . . thirty?"

"Thirty-two."

"So how many have you done since the first one at twelve?"

"I'm not like you. I don't make notes. Don't write things down on paper. That's why I don't have any exact figure to give you."

"Take a guess."

"Well . . . fifty or more. Maybe sixty. I just never kept count. But it's under a hundred for sure. I'd know if I did over a hundred. That'd be something to celebrate."

"What about mass killings? Ever been into those . . . or was it one at a time?"

"Hey, I've been into whatever comes up. Sure, I did some numbers once. In Frisco. In a big house near the Barbary Coast area. Big Victorian house."

"Tell me about it."

"It was at night, and this family came home before I expected them to. I was on the second floor, picking up whatever I could find, when the door slams downstairs and this guy and his wife and their two teenage daughters get home early from a play."

"Then you didn't go to the house planning to kill them?"

"No, it's like I said. I went there to pick up some money, jewels, whatever. Guy's gotta earn a living. I'd been staking out the place and earlier that evening I'd heard them through the screen, talking about going to this play, so I figured I'd have plenty of time to do a job on the place. But they left after the first act. Guess the play was lousy."

"So what happened after they came in?"

"I decided to do all four of them, just for the high. I'd never done four at once up to then."

"What were you carrying? What kind of weapon?"

"I had me a big belt knife and a sawed-off."

"Shotgun?"

"Yeah. It was a custom job. I'd trimmed the barrels. Turned it into a mean sonuvabitch."

"Shotguns make noise."

"I know—but I was careful about that. I've always been a real careful guy."

"Who'd you kill first?"

"The wife. She came upstairs to change her dress and I used the belt

539

knife on her. Got excited and near cut her head off. I was using one of those big Bowie type knives and I got a little carried away."

"Then what did you do?"

"Waited till the next one came upstairs. One of the daughters. She was about seventeen. Tall, with a nice ripe figure on her. I used one of her mother's stockings to do her. She was easy."

"In my research, I've found that most killers use the same method in all of their kills. You've been . . . unusual in this respect."

"Yeah, well, I'm an unusual type of guy. As to how I did them, I liked to improvise. Switch around, you know. Knife. Hammer. Rope. Stocking. Whatever. I got a different high each time. I get bored with the same routine, so I tried different things at different times. The police never could figure me out. I've always been ten steps ahead of them!"

"Did you use the shotgun in the house?"

"Sure did. I went downstairs after the stocking job and found the guy and his other daughter watching Cosby on TV. You ever watch Bill Cosby?"

"I've seen him."

"Funny, huh?"

"He can be funny, sure. What did you do downstairs when you found them watching television?"

"I tied them both on the couch and then used big sofa pillows to muffle the sawed-off. A barrel for each one. It really wasn't noisy at all. Got some blood and stuff on my shirt, but the noise was no problem."

"How'd you feel then . . . after eliminating the whole family?"

"Felt great. All charged up. I mean, doing four in one night. It was special."

"Sexually, how did it affect you?"

"Sexually?"

"Were you aroused? You used the word 'excited' earlier."

"I don't like to talk about sex. It's personal."

"You told me you'd answer any question I asked you with no bull-shit."

"Okay, all right . . . sure, I had a hard-on if that's what you want to know. The daughter did it. But I beat off before leaving the house and that took care of it."

"Have you ever had intercourse with any of your victims? Either during or after killing them?"

"Jesus, no! I don't fuck corpses if that's what you mean."

"It's not uncommon."

"It is with me. That's not my trip."

"Are you bisexual?"

"Look," he said, "let's skip all this sex shit, okay? I'm a normal guy when it comes to gash. I screw *women*. Period. Can we get off this?"

"Fine. Uh . . . have you ever collected body parts? Like, souvenirs of your kills?"

"This is sick."

"You didn't answer the question."

"The answer is—shit, no, I don't collect body parts. And I don't stuff people either. Didn't that guy in the *Psycho* movie stuff people?"

"I don't think so. I think it was birds. But he kept his mother's corpse in the basement. In a rocking chair. What about *your* mother? Were you close to her?"

"Let's keep my parents out of this. I'll answer any question about myself, but I'm not going to get into anything about my folks."

"All right, then . . . tell me about the most bizarre killing you've ever done. The weirdest one."

"That guard's giving us the eye. Maybe we'd better save it for the next visit."

"I guess we'd better."

"Time's up," said the guard. "Look, it's none of my business, mister, but I gotta wonder just why you'd wanta waste your time talkin' with 'The Butcher.' Even his own family stays away from him."

"I have my reasons."

"Yeah, I guess you do," said the guard.

And he led me back to my cell.

A Week in the Unlife

David J. Schow

I

When you stake a bloodsucker, the heartblood pumps out thick and black, the consistency of honey. I saw it make bubbles as it glurped out. The creature thrashed and squirmed and tried to pull out the stake—they always do, if you leave on their arms for the kill—but by the third whack it was, as Stoker might say, dispatched well and duly.

I lost count a long time ago. Doesn't matter. I no longer think of them as being even *former* human beings, and feel no anthropomorphic sympathy. In their eyes I see no tragedy, no romance, no seductive pulp appeal. Merely lust, rage at being outfoxed, and debased appetite, focused and sanguine.

People usually commit journals as legacy. So be it. Call me sentry, vigilante if you like. When they sleep their comatose sleep, I stalk and terminate them. When they walk, I hide. Better than they do.

They're really not as smart as popular fiction and films would lead you to believe. They do have cunning, an animalistic savvy. But I'm an experienced tracker; I know their spoor, the traces they leave, the way their presence charges the air. Things invisible or ephemeral to ordinary citizens, blackly obvious to me.

The journal is so you'll know, just in case my luck runs out.

Sundown. Nap time.

II

Naturally the police think of me as some sort of homicidal crackpot. That's a given; always has been for my predecessors. More watchers to evade. Caution comes reflexively to me these days. Police are slow and rational; they deal in the minutiae of a day-to-day world, deadly enough without the inclusion of bloodsuckers.

The police love to stop and search people. Fortunately for me, mallets and stakes and crosses and such are not yet illegal in this country. Lots of raised eyebrows and jokes and nudging but no actual arrests. When the time comes for them to recognize the plague that has descended upon their city, they will remember me, perhaps with grace.

My lot is friendless, solo. I know and expect such. It's okay.

City by city. I'm good at ferreting out the nests. To me, their kill-patterns are like a flashing red light. The police only see presumed loonies, draw no linkages; they bust and imprison mortals and never see the light.

I am not foolhardy enough to leave bloodsuckers lying. Even though the mean corpus usually dissolves, the stakes might be discovered. Sometimes there is other residue. City dumpsters and sewers provide adequate and fitting disposal for the leftovers of my mission.

The enemy casualties.

I wish I could advise the authorities, work hand-in-hand with them. Too complicated. Too many variables. Not a good control situation. Bloodsuckers have a maddening knack for vanishing into crevices, even hairline splits in logic.

Rule: Trust no one.

III

A female one, today. Funny. There aren't as many of them as you might suppose.

She had courted a human lover, so she claimed, like Romeo and Juliet—she could only visit him at night, and only after feeding, because bloodsuckers too can get carried away by passion.

I think she was intimating that she was a physical lover of other-worldly skill; I think she was fighting hard to tempt me not to eliminate her by saying so.

She did not use her mouth to seduce mortal men. I drove the stake into her brain, through the mouth. She was of recent vintage and did not melt or vaporize. When I fucked her remains, I was surprised to find her warm inside, not cold, like a cadaver. Warm.

With some of them, the human warmth is longer in leaving. But it always goes.

IV

I never met one before that gave up its existence without a struggle, but today I did, one that acted like he had been expecting me to wander along and relieve him of the burden of unlife. He did not deny what he was, nor attempt to trick me. He asked if he could talk a bit, before.

In a third-floor loft, the windows of which had been spray-painted flat black, he talked. Said he had always hated the taste of blood; said he preferred pineapple juice, or even coffee. He actually brewed a pot of coffee while we talked.

I allowed him to finish his cup before I put the ashwood length to his chest and drove deep and let his blackness gush. It dribbled, thinned by the coffee he had consumed.

V

Was thinking this afternoon perhaps I should start packing a Polar-oid or somesuch, to keep a visual body count, just in case this journal becomes public record someday. It'd be good to have illustra-tions, proof. I was thinking of that line you hear overused in the movies. I'm sure you know it: *"But there's no such THING as a vampire!"* What a howler; ranks right up there alongside *"It's crazy—but it just might work!"* and *"We can't stop now for a lot of silly native superstitions!"*

Right; shoot cozy little memory snaps, in case they whizz to mist or drop apart to smoking goo. That bull about how you're not supposed to be able to record their images is from the movies, too. There's so much misleading information running loose that the bloodsuckers—the real ones—have no trouble at all moving through any urban center, *with impunity,* as they say on cop shows.

Maybe it would be a good idea to tape record the sounds they make when they die. Videotape them begging not to be exterminated. That would bug the eyes of all those monster movie fans, you bet.

VI

So many of them beleaguering this city, it's easy to feel outnumbered. Like I said, I've lost count.

Tonight might be a good window for moving on. Like them, I become vulnerable if I remain too long, and it's prudent operating procedure not to leave patterns or become predictable.

It's easy. I don't own much. Most of what I carry, I carry inside.

VII

They pulled me over on Highway Ten, outbound, for a broken left tail light. A datafax photo of me was clipped to the visor in the Highway Patrol car. The journal book itself has been taken as evidence, so for now it's a felt-tip and high school notebook paper, which notes I hope to append to the journal proper later.

I have a cell with four bunks all to myself. The door is solid gray, with a food slot, unlike the barred cage of the bullpen. On the way back I noticed they had caught themselves a bloodsucker. Probably an accident; they probably don't even know what they have. There is no sunrise or sunset in the block, so if he gets out at night, they'll never know what happened. But I already know. Right now I will not say anything. I am exposed and at a disadvantage. The one I let slip today I can eliminate tenfold, next week.

VIII

New week. And I am vindicated at last.

I relaxed as soon as they showed me the photographs. How they managed the documentation on the last few bloodsuckers I trapped, I have no idea. But I was relieved. Now I don't have to explain this journal—which, as you can see, they returned to me immediately. They had thousands of questions. They needed to know about the mallets, the stakes, the preferred method of killstrike. I cautioned them not to attempt a sweep and clear at night, when the enemy is stronger.

They paid serious attention this time, which made me feel much better. Now the fight can be mounted en masse.

They also let me know I wouldn't have to stay in the cell. Just some paperwork to clear, and I'm out among them again. One of the officials—not a cop, but a doctor—congratulated me on a stout job well done. He shook my hand, on behalf of all of them, he said, and mentioned writing a book on my work. This is exciting!

As per my request, the bloodsucker in the adjacent solitary cell was moved. I told them that to be really sure, they should use one of my stakes. It was simple vanity, really, on my part. I turn my stakes out of ashwood on a lathe. I made sure they knew I'd permit my stakes to be used as working models for the proper manufacture of all they would soon need.

When the guards come back I really must ask how they managed such crisp 8x10s of so many bloodsuckers. All those names and dates. First class documentation.

I'm afraid I may be a bit envious.

When the Door Is Shut

D. N. J.

When the houses in Magdalene Street, beyond the Old Lodge, were recently being demolished, the clearing away of some flimsy lath-and-plaster accretions revealed a large solid chimney-stack of brick, of Tudor workmanship, with some pleasantly designed buttressing and chamfering, indicating that it was a portion of a substantial mansion. It stood a little way North of the new building, a few yards inside the wall. Beyond the chimney-stack, up the slope towards St Giles' Church, a fragment of ancient wall was discernible, with the base of a mullioned window, and further North still an old doorway. These were undoubtedly the remains of Copped Hall, a house of some size, which stood detached in a little close, called The Green Peele, with an avenue of lime-trees running East towards the Pond-yard, now the

Fellows' Garden. The houses on the Chesterton road abutted on the close and overlooked it. It was the property of the College, was partially demolished at the end of the eighteenth century, and became merged in the street. I have no doubt in my own mind that the doorway was the scene of two tragedies which took place in the eighteenth century.

The first incident is purely traditional, but there is an unmistakable allusion to the second event in that curious book, *Things Fleshly and Ghostly*, by Thomas Peck, in the chapter entitled "Of Foul and Lubberly Insecution." The incident is clumsily and obscurely hinted at, and Peck evidently took pains to avoid identification. But there is a singular entry in one of the College record books, which makes the story somewhat plainer. This entry is entitled "Concerning the death of Mr Richard Mauleverer," and contains a few facts, leanly told, with notes of a conversation. The record is written in the first person, and is signed "Jno Bellamy, Fellow of Magdalene College"; it seems to have been inscribed in the book on the day of Mr Mauleverer's funeral. Out of these two records I have pieced together the story as far as I can, just bridging one or two gaps by supplying obvious inferences, and I will tell it as a connected narrative, without undue citation.

Mr Richard Mauleverer came of a good Worcestershire family and was born in 1705. He entered Magdalene in 1723, as a commoner, where he did not waste much time in study; in 1726, by private influence, he was elected a Bye Fellow on the Spendluffe foundation, on taking his degree. He did not reside very long, and soon after, succeeded to some landed property; nothing is known of his movements until 1756, when he reappeared at Cambridge, and took a lease of Copped Hall; he was then a man of means and kept riding-horses. He was a bachelor, and lived at Copped Hall with a manservant and an old housekeeper. He was cordially received by the Fellows, the Master, Thomas Chapman, being apparently a distant connection; his chief crony, however, was John Bellamy, Wray Fellow, who had been a contemporary of Mauleverer's, and was a man of convivial habits. If Mr Bellamy had never been seen drunk, it was equally certain that he had seldom been seen what is ordinarily called sober; but he was a civil, witty man, given to harmless expletives, a good raconteur, and excellent company when he was free of the gout, to which he was a martyr. Mauleverer usually dined in hall at two o'clock dinner, after his morning ride, and spent the afternoon in the combination room. He was a strong and hearty man, of scanty discourse, good humoured enough, but very stubborn when he had once made up his mind.

The front door of Copped Hall was in the street, and admitted you to a small paved hall lighted by two slits of windows on either side of the door. To left and right were two parlours running through the house;

behind the hall, entered by a door opposite the front door, was a small study, where Mr Mauleverer mostly sat. The room had two windows, with a considerable space between them, looking out on the lime avenue. The fireplace was on the right, and to the left was a door which communicated with the garden by a short passage, which seemed to have been taken out of the room. If you went out into the avenue and looked back at the house, you saw the two windows of the study, with a bedroom above it with three windows; between the two windows of the study, and under the centre window of the bedroom, was a curious projection of brick like a large flat buttress.

Mr Mauleverer found the room dark when the summer foliage was out; he got into his head that a window had been stopped up in the centre, and on tapping about the panelling of the room he found that the space between the windows sounded hollow. So he had the panelling removed. In the space an archway appeared, with a strong nail-studded oak door, which had been very elaborately fastened up; the interstices had been plastered; but what at once attracted Mr Mauleverer's attention were two broad strips of lead, one nailed from the top of the door to the bottom, and one across the door halfway up, on which were traced some curious geometrical figures. Mr Mauleverer had the external buttress taken down, and the outer side of the door appeared, with similar strips of lead affixed. He decided to have the door reopened, and the lead was torn away.

It seems that the same day on which this was done, Mr Mauleverer received a note from an old Fellow of Jesus, Mr Hinde. He went to see him, but soon afterwards returned, asked for the strips of lead, and took them away with him, after which they were never seen again intact. He came back apparently rather troubled; and it seems that the same evening he told Mr Bellamy a confused story, related to him by Mr Hinde, of a murder that had been done at Copped Hall some seventy years before. The circumstances were obscure. But it is clear that a woman living at Copped Hall with her husband, a drunken brute, had been attacked by him in the garden, had fled to the house, and had endeavoured to close the door; the ruffian had burst it open, and killed her with an axe, for which he was very properly hanged at Huntingdon. Mr Hinde, he said, had urgently advised him to have the door closed up again, but that he said he would not do, for it was a convenience.

The first day that the door was opened a curious event happened; a bird flew in at the open door, as if chased by a hawk, with a loud out-cry, and was killed against a mirror in the room, making an ugly splash of blood on the glass, and cracking the mirror; a week later a very inexplicable thing occurred. Mr Mauleverer opening the door one evening saw something looking round one of the jambs, and perceived that it was a little ape, with white teeth and large eyes; it looked wickedly at him, and tried to dodge into the house; but Mr Mauleverer was too quick for it, and straddled across the threshold; the little creature ran quickly to the nearest lime-tree, climbed up the trunk, and Mr Mauleverer could not discover where it was, though he heard it hiss and chatter in the branches. It was thought that it was one of a pair of apes kept by Dr Long, Master of Pembroke Hall. Mr Mauleverer went across to Pembroke to see if it was so, but saw the two apes snug enough, and found little comfort in the sight.

A week later Mr Mauleverer had a strange conversation with Mr Bellamy in the latter's room. He told Mr Bellamy that he had awaked at night, and had heard something moving about in the room below, the dining parlour. He had gone down, and he had there seen and smelt something "which sickened him." "What was that?" said Mr Bellamy. "I do not know," said Mr Mauleverer. Then, after a pause, he said, "I do not know, but I reckon it must have been a bear!" "God-a-mercy!" said Mr Bellamy, putting down a tankard which he was raising to his lips, "Why a bear?" "Well," said Mr Mauleverer, slowly and painfully, "it was about that bigness, and very heavy; it shuffled to and fro; it put its foot softly and lumberingly to the ground, and then there fell a little clattering of claws upon the boards, as it pushed forwards." "God-a-mercy!" said Mr Bellamy again. "Yes, and worse than that," said Mr Mauleverer, as though finding some relief in the telling, "it smelt strong and rank like some great hairy beast, and when I came near it puffed its hot breath upon me—Faugh!" said Mr Mauleverer, with a kind of sickness upon him, and he took up his tankard and drank. Mr Bellamy sat musing, and then said, "I have heard of a man—indeed he was own uncle to myself—who saw snakes when no snakes were there; but that was under—under somewhat different circumstances; and I do not think he smelled them!" "I have had enough of it," said Mr Mauleverer suddenly, in a fury; "I will not have quadrupeds, with birds and feathered fowl, to make free of my house and garden. By God, I will not!" "I would not!" said Mr Bellamy, "but how did the matter end?" "The beast shuffled away," said Mr Mauleverer, "through the hall, into the study, and was hidden from my sight; the door stood open into the garden, though I am sure I closed it overnight." "I think I would tell the Mayor," said Mr Bellamy soothingly; and here the notes come to an end.

A week later—it was always on Saturday nights that the events had occurred—Mr Mauleverer did not dine in hall, but was busy all day in his study, the door being bolted. He had seen Mr Hinde again in the morning. The manservant was puzzled, because there came a smell from the study of something boiling. Mr Mauleverer ate a poor meal in haste, and went back to his study at nightfall, and the servant said that his hands were dirty and discoloured.

Late that night the servant was awaked by a sudden outcry in the garden. It was a moonlight night; he got hastily up and went to the window. He saw Mr Mauleverer flying, as for his life, into the house, screaming horribly aloud. After him ran something big and dusky. Mr Mauleverer got to the door, slipped in, closed it, and there was a silence of a minute or two while the creature sniffed about the door. Then came a great crash; the servant fled downstairs, and came into the study in great haste. He saw that the door was wide open, and a table had been overset. He made a light, and found Mr Mauleverer lying, his feet to the door, with a great gash on his forehead, quite dead. There was nothing else inside the room. When the body was examined, the inside of the hands were found all white, as if with chalk; and a lump of chalk was found broken on the carpet. In the orchard was found a little firebucket lying in the grass in the avenue, which seemed to have been bitten and spurned; there were some cinders hereabouts, and some lumps of what appeared to have been molten lead.

The only other thing of note in the room was that on the inner side of the door was found scrawled very hurriedly in chalk some words in Greek which appeared to be:

$$\text{ῥῦσαι ἡμᾶζ ἀπὸ τοῦ} \ . \ . \ .$$

But at the end of the last letter there was a great line, as if the door had been dashed in on the hand of the writer.

Mr Hinde died on the following day in his rooms at Jesus, of a stroke of palsy. He had been heavily affected by the news of the death, and it was thought to have hastened his end.

There was an inquest held, and the verdict given was that Mr Mauleverer died of a fall, occasioned by a sudden stroke of apoplexy. I daresay he did! After the apoplexy, the fall. But what did the apoplexy follow after? I hope with all my heart that Mr Mauleverer was knocked senseless by the blow, when the door was stove in.

Where Does Watson Road Go?

William Relling, Jr.

There are places, not always far from the city, where the dark can come and not be bothered by streetlights, and there aren't any people or cars around to cover the noises that come with the night time. Deserted roads and woods and old houses—places that are far away from what's familiar and comfortable, places where it's very easy for things that you normally wouldn't give a second thought, if you were in your own house or your own neighborhood, to make your skin tingle and your ears and eyes open wide when you're out there.

Those places have been on my mind lately, at least when I'm able to keep my thoughts together long enough to try and make some sense of what happened. It's not really very hard to find a place that has a reputation for bad happenings. It's not hard, if you're not afraid to look.

Our place was the quarry at the end of Watson Road.

Washington Boulevard was a big street that began downtown and ran east and west. It was a one-way street in the city until it crossed Tenth Avenue, and it was one of the major arteries for city traffic because it bisected the business district and ran directly into the suburbs. When it crossed the invisible line that separated the city from the suburbs, Washington Boulevard became Watson Road.

Watson Road wound westward another fifteen miles or so, through the suburbs and out into the boonies—through miles and miles of farmlands and woods that wouldn't be around for too many more years. The boonies started right after Watson Road crossed the interstate highway that circumscribed the western edge of town. That was where Watson Road completely changed its personality from a six-lane, violet-lit, concrete-curbed thoroughfare to a winding, twisting, no-shouldered, dark country road. You had to take it easy when you were driving on Watson Road, especially at night. There were always accidents.

Though once it crossed the interstate, Watson Road only ran for another six miles or so before it connected with old Highway 66, and that was the end of it. Six miles of farms and cornfields and oak trees and birch woods.

And the quarry.

It had been closed down years ago, long before I was born. The access road to the quarry was hard to find because it ran at a forty-five degree angle to Watson Road on the left hand side as you travelled west. You could really only see it if you drove the last half mile to the junction of Watson Road and Highway 66, then turned around and slid down the quarry road as you came back east. There were tall, overhanging trees that made it look like you were going into some kind of spooky tunnel, and on either side of the entrance were posts where a chain used to hang across the top of the road to keep people away from the old quarry.

We'd named the access drive to the quarry "Zombie Road," and no matter how scary the rest of Watson Road may have seemed, it had nothing on Zombie Road. All of the frightening things about Watson Road were crammed into a tiny, dirt-and-gravel drive that wound down into the heart of the woods for a mile and a quarter, where it ended abruptly at an ancient wooden gate that marked the entrance to the old quarry itself.

Zombie Road wound through scores of bent trees and piles of trash and the shells of dead automobiles. Many of the trees had faces painted on them in fluorescent reds and greens and yellows, in outlines of death's heads and screaming masks and monsters. Mostly they had been painted by younger kids who would only go down there during the day, because they'd be too afraid to go down there when it was dark.

The older kids went down at night, though, of course, nobody would ever think of taking a date to the quarry just to park and mess around. And nobody would think about snitching some beer or going down the road to smoke a little pot or anything like that. That wasn't what Zombie Road was for. The place didn't make you feel very romantic, or like you wanted to party.

But if you wanted to *scare* somebody . . .

Zombie Road had a reputation. I grew up hearing a lot of stories about missing persons—and one time they did find the body of a woman who had been murdered by her own husband. He dumped her where he thought nobody would ever find her, in the woods a half mile up from the quarry about ten yards from the edge of the road. Later on the guy told the police that he had stuffed his wife in a laundry bag and carried her down Zombie Road at night, all by himself. He had meant to take her farther into the woods, but something had spooked him. He must not have gotten in as far as he thought, though, because some kids found her *right alongside the road* a couple of nights later. My father told me that another funny thing about the story was that the police didn't find much left of the woman. Her husband swore that all he did was strangle her and bag her up. He had no idea what happened to the rest, to her head and all.

There were lots of other stories like that, and each of them only served to make Zombie Road more attractive to us kids. We went down Zombie Road dozens of times, usually whenever we had somebody along who had never been there before. It was always better if we could manage to set them up for a really good fright and send another guy on ahead who'd park on the road and wait for the rest of us to come along. Then he'd pop out and chase us—or whatever.

That was what was supposed to happen on the night we graduated from high school.

Denny Leeper's parents owned one of the farms off Watson Road, about two miles west of the interstate. In March, Denny had asked his father if he would let us have a graduation party outside in their back yard, where they had about two-thirds of an acre of land. It wasn't very hard for Denny to talk his dad into the idea. Mr. Leeper was a good guy.

Denny invited our whole graduating class to the party, some two hundred kids. Tim Gillette, another friend of ours, volunteered his rock 'n' roll band for no charge, so long as they didn't have another job that night—which as it turned out, they didn't. Anybody who was going to the party had to chip in for food and soda, and Brian Fisher—my friend Mike Fisher's older brother who was home from college for the summer—brought a trunkload of beer.

Our graduation ceremony that night was over at eight-thirty, and people began showing up at Denny's by nine. They were all ready for a good time.

Marcia and I got there about ten. We could hear the band and the people all the way up Watson Road, long before we turned onto the drive that led to Denny's house. There was no place for us to park on the drive, and it looked like there were at least a hundred cars lined along both sides of Watson Road.

I pulled up behind Mike Fisher's Pinto in time to see the driver's side door open and Mike pour himself out of his car. He rolled on the ground giggling while Marcia and I stood over him. We couldn't help laughing at him—Mike was wearing the brand new suit that his mom had bought for him, and the yellow tassel from his graduation cap dangled from his ear. He opened one eye, looked up at us upside-down, and burped: "H'lo, kids."

Marcia and I hoisted him up and steered him as best we could down the Leepers' driveway. Mike sang our school fight song all the way, even though he could only remember one verse.

Everybody at the party was doing just fine. Marcia and I went over to a table where Mrs. Leeper had set out sandwiches, and we said hello to Mr. Leeper—who was looking just as happy about the party as any of the kids there. He pointed toward Denny's sister, Debbie, who was a year younger than Denny and was dancing about five feet in front of where Tim Gillette was playing guitar. Mr. Leeper grinned at us and shouted over the music, "I think I might end up doing this all over again next year!"

Marcia and I mingled for a while, and both of us were hugged and kissed and congratulated by dozens of people—a lot of them we didn't even know. Brian Fisher personally brought us some beer, and we settled down under an old tree with Mike and Sherry Gabriel, who was Tim Gillette's girlfriend. Now and then somebody would cruise by us and tell us how great everybody was or what an outstanding party Denny had put together. We were having a fine time.

The Leepers' nearest neighbors lived at least a quarter of a mile away, but the music and the cars and the kids must have finally gotten to be too much for even them. Around midnight everyone at the party could hear a *chop-chop-chopping* overhead. A huge searchlight swept over the back yard, lighting up the people who were dancing or snuggling on the lawn or by the trees. A red light was spinning somewhere in front of the house, its reflection glancing off the sides of the house and into the back yard. The band stopped playing, and all of the kids started to move off.

Mr. Leeper came up to us and said, "Sorry, folks."

There was no trouble, and the police didn't stay for very long. The band packed up and the crowd peeled off, and after a while Tim came over and fell on the ground next to Sherry.

We waited until everybody else had cleared out, then went to help Denny and his folks pick up. Marcia invited everybody to her house for breakfast, but her mom didn't want us till 6 AM, so we had some time to kill.

It was after two, and we were sitting in the Leepers' living room. Mrs. Leeper was in the kitchen with Denny's girlfriend Jan and my girlfriend Marcia. Mike was curled up in a big leather recliner and was snoring very softly. Mr. Leeper was sitting next to Tim and Sherry on the couch.

Mr. Leeper was the first one to say anything about Zombie Road.

Sherry Gabriel didn't live near any of the rest of us. "What's Zombie Road?" she asked.

As I listened to their conversation I was looking through the Leepers' front window. The night was quiet and clear and the sky was full of bright stars. A glowing crescent moon hung above the horizon.

Brian Fisher was lying on the floor next to me, and he nudged me in the ribs with an elbow. I looked over at him, and he flashed me a crooked smile.

Mr. Leeper was telling Sherry stories about Zombie Road. I saw Mike in the recliner open his eyes slightly, though he kept on snoring, playing possum.

Sherry was listening to Mr. Leeper with her mouth hanging open. Tim Gillette had an arm around her shoulder, and he was grinning at her behind her back.

"Is it far away?" Sherry asked excitedly.

She didn't notice Mr. Leeper's wink to Tim. "Not very," he said. "But *I* wouldn't go down there. Nobody knows what lives down in that quarry. Nobody's ever been too anxious to find out."

Sherry shivered.

Brian eased himself from the floor and walked into the kitchen. I could hear him in there talking to Mrs. Leeper and the girls.

Sherry punched Tim playfully on the thigh. "How come you never told me about Zombie Road before?" she asked him.

Tim smiled. "I didn't want you to get scared."

Sherry pressed her lips together, pretending to pout. "Ooh, you," she squealed. She punched Tim again.

"We've been down there a hundred times," said Denny. Then he dropped his voice and said quietly: "Only it's a lot different at night than it is in the daytime."

I heard a door closing in the back of the house, then I tried to force myself to look serious as I said, "Sherry, if you really want to, we can take a run out and show you Zombie Road." I imitated Denny, lowering my voice like he'd done, and added: "But only if you want to."

Sherry squealed with delight.

Mike took Sherry and Tim in the Pinto—after making Tim *plead* with him to go, which was as fine an act as I'd ever seen Mike perform. I took Marcia and Denny and Jan with me.

We followed a few hundred yards behind the Pinto, and Mike—as usual—drove like a madman. I was sure that Mike and Tim were building Sherry up and keeping her distracted. Denny said that he didn't think Sherry was dumb—or at least not dumb enough to notice that Brian had somehow disappeared and hadn't come with us.

As we got closer to the quarry turnoff, we could see that every once in a while Mike would switch off his lights and drive in pitch darkness. Marcia snorted. "That's the same damn thing you guys did the first time you took me down," she said. "You'd think he'd come up with something new."

"Hey," I said, smiling. "It worked, didn't it?"

Marcia turned to look at Jan and Denny, who were in the back seat. "They scared the crap out of me," she said and all three of them laughed.

Mike was doing about sixty miles an hour when he came to Zombie Road, and he spun the Pinto into a 180 degree turn that spewed gravel and dirt a good ten feet in the air. "He's out of his mind," Denny said.

I slowed down to make the turn, and then I could see the Pinto's rear lights some two hundred yards ahead. The lights weren't moving. I braked my car to a stop behind the Pinto's rear bumper.

Mike was getting out of his car, and he walked back toward us. His feet crunched as he stepped up to my side, and he was chuckling as he folded his arms and rested them on the edge of my open window.

"It's great," he said. "Sherry is scared shitless. She white-knuckled Tim's arm all the way. I think she squeezed all the blood out of him."

"I didn't see Brian," I said.

"He's prob'ly down at the quarry already," Mike said. He leaned back and tapped a short tattoo on my car's roof. "Follow right behind me, okay? I'm not gonna use my lights, but keep yours on."

Mike's shadow glided in front of him as he walked back to the Pinto and slid into the driver's seat. The Pinto's headlights dimmed, and the car rolled forward in neutral.

I could hear Jan and Denny giggling over my shoulder as they moved closer together. I let my car coast out of gear and hung on the Pinto's rear end.

On either side of the road gnarled trees were dancing and weaving in the glare of my car's headlights. Occasionally the brightness would bounce back off of a rusted fender or broken shards of glass. Painted demon-faces and glowing monsters screamed at us silently from the trees as they were struck by the headlight beams.

All of a sudden Marcia gripped my right arm and held on tight. I turned around to look at her, but she wasn't looking at me. Instead she was staring straight ahead, and she had an odd, frightened look on her face.

"You okay?" I asked.

Marcia slowly shook her head no.

I smiled. "You scared?"

Her voice sounded very strange and far away. "Something's wrong," she whispered.

I hoped that Denny and Jan couldn't hear us. "What?" I whispered back.

Marcia still wouldn't look at me. I whispered again, more urgently, "What's the matter?"

Before she could answer me, the Pinto leaped forward. I dropped my car into gear just as Mike switched on his lights again and shot away. I accelerated hard, throwing Denny and Jan against the back seat. Denny *whooped* happily.

We cut a sharp left turn for the last eighth of a mile to the quarry gate, and on the right hand side of the road I caught a glimpse of Brian Fisher's car. It was pulled off the road just far enough so that it might be mistaken for a derelict—if you weren't looking for it.

555

The Pinto lurched to a stop with its front bumper not more than three or four feet from the quarry gate. I eased behind the Pinto, switched off my headlights, and pulled the key from the ignition.

Marcia was watching me. Her eyes got big and she breathed: "Noooo . . ."

Denny and Jan hadn't heard her because they had already gotten out of the car to walk over to Mike, who was pushing on the quarry gate. Tim and Sherry were still in the Pinto, and I could see that Tim was having a hard time coaxing Sherry out.

I tugged Marcia's arm gently and said, "Will you c'mon?"

She shook her head.

I felt myself starting to get mad and I snapped at her, "Look, Marcia—"

Then I caught myself. "Okay," I said—more softly, but still firm. "Stay here."

Tim had gotten Sherry out of the Pinto, and they joined the others by the quarry gate. Sherry was clutching Tim's arm. Mike was crawling around on the ground, trying to find a way to open the gate.

"What's with Marcia?" Tim asked me.

I shrugged. "I don't know. She got scared all of a sudden."

Sherry squeaked: "I don't blame her—"

She was cut off by a sound that all of us heard—an eerie wailing that came from somewhere behind the quarry gate. Sherry shrieked and pulled Tim close, and Mike fell flat on the ground, convulsed with laughter.

There came another wail, and Sherry broke from Tim's side. She ran back to the Pinto, yanked open the door, and curled up on the front seat, covering her eyes. She cried: "Timmmmmmmmmmm!"

Then we heard slow, shuffling footsteps moving toward us from the other side of the quarry gate. Tim clapped an arm around my shoulder.

Just as Mike screamed.

It all seemed to happen in incredibly fast motion, as if we were actors in an old silent movie that had been cranked up to run ten times its normal speed. Denny Leeper fell to his knees and he tried to pull Jan down with him—and all the while she was screaming and screaming. I turned around and saw Marcia through the windshield of my car. Her face was frozen in a mask of horror as she stared past me.

I could also see in the glass the reflection of what it was that terrified her.

I brought myself around slowly to face the awful, yellow-eyed, slobbering *nightmare* that stood on the other side of the quarry gate. With something that was not quite a hand, the thing was dragging an odd, lumpy sack that left a trail of sticky-looking, black wetness as it slid

556

along the ground behind the monster. It took an instant for me to recognize what the "sack" was.

It was Brian. With one claw the beast was dragging his limp body, and with the other it was holding his dismembered head by the hair. Brian's eyes were wide open.

The thing dropped Brian's head and body, and then it *shimmered*—seeming to dissolve right through the wooden gate without disturbing it. It was on us quickly—before I could run back to the car, before Jan could drag Denny up from the ground, before Mike could get out of its way. It was on us.

It saved me for last.

I have no idea how long ago that was. But it seems like a long time.

I don't know the reason why it chose that particular night to attack us, since we had all been down there so many times before. I don't know for certain what it did with what was left of the others, after it had eaten.

But I think I know what it's done to me.

When it attacked, it swept over me slowly and made itself a part of me. I could feel its own *sensations*, its own agony because *it became a part of me.* What it did to me was different from what it did to the others, because by the time it got around to me its hunger had already been satisfied. It didn't need to feed on me. It chose me for something else.

It swept over me, and then it disappeared.

Mr. Leeper came down Zombie Road by himself a few hours later, looking for us. It must have been when he didn't come back home that the police decided to close the road.

They looked for all of us. They searched the quarry and the woods. They found our cars, but that was all.

I'm sure they've closed Zombie Road, because nobody has been down here for such a long time. Not since Mr. Leeper, and he's the only one I've had.

And now I'm getting hungry.

Where Flies Are Born

Douglas Clegg

The train stopped suddenly, and Ellen sat there and watched her son fill in the coloring book with the three crayolas left to him: aquamarine, burnt sienna, and silver. She was doing this for him; she could put up with Frank and his tirades and possessiveness, but not when he tried to hurt Joey. No. She would make sure that Joey had a better life. Ellen turned to the crossword puzzle in the back of the magazine section to pass the time. She tried not to think of what they'd left behind. She was a patient woman, and so it didn't annoy her that it was another hour before anyone told the passengers that it would be a three hour stop, or more. *Or more,* translating into six hours. Then her patience wore thin and Joey was whining. The problem with the train, it soon became apparent, was one which would require disembarking. The town, if it could be called that, was a quarter mile ahead, and so they would be put up somewhere for the night. So this was to be their Great Escape. February third in a mountain town at thirty below. Frank would find them for sure; only a day's journey from Springfield. Frank would hunt them down, as he'd done last time, and bring them back to his little castle and she would make it okay for another five years before she went crazy again and had to run. *No.* She would make sure he wouldn't hurt Joey. She would kill him first. She would, with her bare hands, stop him from ever touching their son again.

Joey said, "Can't we just stay on the train? It's cold out there."

"You'll live," she said, bringing out the overnight case and following in a line with the other passengers out of the car. They trudged along the snowy tracks to the short strip of junction, where each was directed to a different motel or private house.

"I wanted a motel," she told the conductor. She and Joey were to be overnight guests of the Neesons', a farm family. "This isn't what I paid for," she said, "it's not what I expected at all."

"You can sleep in the station, you like," the man said, but she passed on that after looking around the filthy room with its greasy benches. "Anyway, the Neesons run a bed-and-breakfast, so you'll do fine there."

The Neesons arrived shortly in a four-wheel drive, looking all of fifty-three, tooth-rotted, with *country* indelibly sprayed across their grins and friendly winks. Mama Neeson, in her late fifties, spoke of the snow, of their warm house "where we'll all be safe as kittens in a minute," of the soup she'd been making. Papa Neeson was older (*old enough to be my father*, Ellen thought) and balder, eyes of a rodent, face of a baby-left-too-long-in-bathwater. Mama Neeson cooed over Joey, who was already asleep. *Damn you, Joey, for abandoning me to Neeson-talk.* Papa Neeson spoke of the snowfall and the roads. Ellen said very little, other than to thank them for putting her up.

"Our pleasure," Mama Neeson said, "the little ones will love the company."

"You have children?" Ellen winced at her inflection. She didn't *mean* it to sound as if Mama Neeson was too old to have what could be called "little ones."

"Adopted, you could say," Papa Neeson grumbled, "Mama, she loves kids, can't get enough of them, you get the instinct, you see, the sniffs for babies and you got to have them whether your body gives 'em up or not."

Ellen, embarrassed for his wife, shifted uncomfortably in the seat. What a rude man. This was what Frank would be like, under the skin, talking about women and their "sniffs," their "hankerings." Poor Mama Neeson, a houseful of babies and *this* man.

"I have three little ones," she said, "all under nine. How old's yours?"

"Six."

"He's an angel. Papa, ain't he just a little angel sent down from heaven?"

Papa Neeson glanced over to Joey, curled up in a ball against Ellen's side. "Don't say much, do he?"

The landscape was white and black; Ellen watched for ice patches in the road, but they went over it all smoothly. Woods rose up suddenly, parting for an empty flat stretch of land. They drove down a fenced road, snow piled all the way to the top of the fenceposts. Then, as they turned up another road, she saw the large white farmhouse, with a barn behind. *We better not be sleeping in the barn.*

Mama Neeson sighed. "Hope they're in bed. Put them to bed hours ago, but you know how they romp . . ."

"They love to romp," Papa Neeson said.

The bed was large and she and Joey sank into it as soon as they had the door closed behind them. Ellen was too tired to think, and Joey was still dreaming. Sleep came quickly, and was black and white, full of snowdrifts. She awoke, thirsty, before dawn. Ellen was half-asleep, but lifted her head towards the window: the sound of animals crunching in the snow outside. She looked out—had to open the window because of the frost on the pane. A hazy purple light brushed across the whiteness of the hills—the sun was somewhere rising beyond the treetops. A large brown bear sniffed along the porch rail. Bears should've frightened her, but this one seemed friendly and stupid, as it lumbered along in the tugging snow, nostrils wiggling. Sniffing the air; Mama Neeson would be up—four thirty—frying bacon, flipping hotcakes on the griddle, buttering toast. Country Mama. The little ones would rise from their quilts and trundle beds, ready to go out and milk cows or some such farm thing, and Papa Neeson would get out his shotgun to scare off the bear that came sniffing. She remembered Papa's phrase: "the sniffs for babies," and it gave her a discomforting thought about the bear.

She lay back on the bed, stroking Joey's fine hair, with this thought in her mind of the bear sniffing for the babies, when she saw a housefly circle above her head; then, another, coming from some corner of the room, joining its mate. Three more arrived. Finally, she was restless to swat them. She got out of bed and went to her overnight bag for hairspray. This was her favorite method of disposing of houseflies. She shook the can, and then sprayed in the direction of the (count them: nine) fat black houseflies. They buzzed in curves of infinity. In a minute, they began dropping, one by one, to the rug. Ellen enjoyed taking her boots and slapping each fly into the next life.

Her dry throat and heavy bladder sent her out to the hallway. Feeling along the wall for the light switch or the door to the bathroom—whichever came first. When she found the switch, she flicked it up, and a single unadorned bulb hummed into dull light.

A little girl stood at the end of the hall, too old for the diaper she wore; her stringy hair falling wildly almost to her feet; her skin bruised in several places—particularly around her mouth, which was swollen on the upper lip. In her small pudgy fingers was a length of thread. Ellen was so shocked by this sight that she could not say a word—the girl was only seven or so, and what her appearance indicated about the Neesons . . .

Papa Neeson was like Frank. Likes to beat people. Likes to beat children. Joey and his black eyes, this girl and her bruised face. I could kill them both.

The little girl's eyes crinkled up as if she were about to cry, wrinkled her forehead and nose, parted her swollen lips.

From the black and white canyon of her mouth: a fat green fly crawled the length of her lower lip, and then flew toward the light bulb above Ellen's head.

Later, when the sun was up, and the snow outside her window was blinding, Ellen knew she must've been half-dreaming, or perhaps it was a trick that the children played—for she'd seen all of them, the two-year-old, the five-year-old, and the girl. The boys had trooped out from the shadows of the hall. All wearing the filthy diapers, all bruised from beatings or worse. The only difference with the two younger boys was they had not yet torn the thread that had been used to sew their mouths and eyes and ears and nostrils closed. Such child abuse was beyond imagining. Ellen had seen them only briefly, and afterwards wondered if perhaps she hadn't *seen* wrong. But it was a dream, a very bad one, because the little girl had flicked the light off again. When Ellen reached to turn it back on, they had retreated into the shadows and the feeling of a surreal waking state came upon her. *The Neesons could not possibly be this evil.* With the light on, and her vision readjusting from the darkness, she saw only houseflies sweeping motes of dust through the heavy air.

At breakfast, Joey devoured his scrambled eggs like he hadn't eaten in days; Ellen had to admit they tasted better than she'd had before. "You live close to the earth," Papa Neeson said, "and it gives up its treasures."

Joey said, "Eggs come from chickens."

"Chickens come from eggs," Papa Neeson laughed, "and eggs are the beginning of all life. But we all gather our life from the earth, boy. You city folks don't feel it because you're removed. Out here, well, we get it under our fingernails, birth, death, and what comes in between."

"You're something of a philosopher," Ellen said, trying to hide her uneasiness. The image of the children still in her head, like a half-remembered dream. She was eager to get on her way, because that dream was beginning to seem more real. She had spent a half-hour in the shower trying to talk herself out of having seen the children and what had been done to them; then, ten minutes drying off, positive that she had seen what she'd seen. It was Frank's legacy: he had taught her to doubt what was right before her eyes. She wondered if Papa Neeson performed darker needlework on his babies.

"I'm a realist," Papa Neeson said. His eyes were bright and kind—it shocked her to look into them and think about what he might/might not have done.

Mama Neeson, sinking the last skillet into a washtub next to the stove, turned and said, "Papa just has a talent for making things work, Missus, for putting two and two together. That's how he grows, and that's how he gathers. Why if it weren't for him, where would my children be?"

"Where are they?" Joey asked.

Ellen, after her dream slash hallucination slash mind-your-own-business, was a bit apprehensive. She would be happy not to meet Mama Neeson's brood at all. "We have to get back to the train," she said. "They said by eleven."

Papa Neeson raised his eyebrows in an aside to his wife. "I saw some flies at the windows," he said. "They been bad again."

Mama Neeson shrugged her broad shoulders. "They got to let them out at times or they'd be bursting, now, wouldn't they. Must tickle something awful." She wiped her dripping hands on the flowerprint apron, back and forth like she could never get dry enough. Ellen saw a shining in the old woman's eyes like tears and hurt.

Joey clanked his fork on his plate; Ellen felt a lump in her throat, and imaginary spiders and flies crawling up the back of her neck. Something in the atmosphere had changed, and she didn't want to spend one more minute in this house with these people.

Joey clapped a fly between his hands, catching it mid-air.

"Mama's sorry you didn't see the kids," Papa Neeson said, steering over a slick patch on the newly plowed road.

"But you're not," Ellen said. She was feeling brave. She hated this man like she hated Frank. Maybe she'd report him to some child welfare agency when she got back to the train station. She could see herself killing this man.

"No," Papa Neeson nodded, "I'm not. Mama, she don't understand about other people, but I do."

"Well, I saw them. All three. What you do to them."

Papa Neeson sighed, pulling over and parking at the side of the road. "You don't understand. Don't know if I should waste my breath."

Joey was in the backseat, bundled up in blankets. He yawned. "Why we stopping?"

Ellen directed him to turn around and sit quietly. He was a good boy. "I have a husband who hits children, too."

Papa Neeson snapped, "I don't hit the kids, lady, and how dare you think I do, why you can just get out of my car right now if that's your attitude."

"I told you, I saw them," she said defiantly.

"You see the threads?"

Ellen could barely stand his smug attitude.

"You see 'em? You know *why* my kids look like that?"

Ellen reached for the door handle. She was going to get out. Fucking country people and their torture masked as discipline. Men, how she hated their power trips. Blood was boiling now; she was capable of anything, like two days ago when she took the baseball bat and slammed it against Frank's chest, hearing ribs cracking. She was not going to let a man hurt her child like that. Never again. The rage was rising up inside her the way it had only done twice in her life before, both times with Frank, both times protecting Joey.

Papa Neeson reached out and grabbed her wrist.

"Don't hold me like that," she snarled.

He let go.

Papa Neeson began crying, pressing his head into the steering wheel. "She just wanted them so bad, I had to go dig 'em up. I love her so much, and I didn't want her to die from hurting, so I just dig 'em up and I figured out what to do and did it."

When he calmed, he sat back up, looking straight ahead. "We better get to the junction. Train'll be ready. You got your life moving ahead with it, don't you?"

She said, "Tell me about your children. What's wrong with them?"

He looked her straight in the eyes, making her flinch because of his intensity. "Nothing, except they been dead for a good twenty to thirty years now, and my wife, she loves 'em like they're her own. I dig 'em up, see, I thought she was gonna die from grief not having none of her own, and I figured it out, you know, about the maggots and the flies, how they make things move if you put enough of 'em inside the bodies. I didn't count on 'em lasting this long, but what if they do? What if they *do*, lady? Mama, she loves those babies. We're only humans, lady, and humans need to hold babies, they need to love something other than themselves, don't they? Don't you? You got your boy, you know how much that's worth? Love beyond choosing, ain't it? Love that don't die. You know what it's like to hug a child when you never got to hug one before? So I figured and I figured some more, and I thought about what makes things live, how do we know something's alive, and I figured, when it moves it's alive, and when it don't move, it's dead. So Mama, I had her sew the flies in, but they keep laying eggs and more and more, and the kids, they got the minds of flies, and sometimes they rip out the threads, so sometimes flies get out, but it's a tiny price, ain't it, lady? When you need to love little ones, and you ain't got none, it's a tiny price, a day in hell's all, but then sunshine and children and love, lady, ain't it worth that?"

Ellen had a migraine by the time Papa Neeson dropped them off down at the junction. She barked at Joey. Apologized for it. Bought him a Pepsi from the machine by the restroom. People were boarding the train. She went to the restroom to wipe cold water across her face—made Joey promise to stand outside it and not go anywhere. The mirror in the bathroom was warped, and she thought she looked stunning: brown eyes circled with sleeplessness, the throbbing vein to the left side of her forehead, the dry, cracked lips. She thought of the threads, of the children tugging at them, popping them out to let the flies go. Ran a finger over her lips, imagining Mama Neeson taking her needle and thread, breaking the skin with tiny holes. Ears, nostrils, eyes, mouth, other openings, other places where flies could escape. Flies and life, sewn up into the bodies of dead children, buried by other grieving parents,

563

brought back by the country folks who ran the bed-and-breakfast, and who spoke of children that no one ever saw much of.

And when they did . . .

So here was Ellen's last happy image in the mountain town she and her son were briefly stranded in:

Mama Neeson kissing the bruised cheek of her little girl, tears in her squinty eyes, tears of joy for having children to love.

Behind her, someone opened the door.

Stood there.

Waiting for her to turn around.

"Look who I found," Frank said, dragging Joey behind him into the women's room.

Two weeks later, she was on the train again, with Joey, but it was better weather—snow was melting, the sun was exhaustingly bright, and she got off at the junction because she wanted to be there. *Frank is dead.* She could think it. She could remember the feel of the knife in her hands. No jury would convict her. She had been defending herself. Defending her son. Frank had come at Joey with his own toy dump truck. She had grabbed the carving knife—as she'd been planning to do since Frank had hauled them back to Springfield. She had gone with the knowledge of what she would have to do to keep Frank out of her little boy's life forever. Then, she had just waited for his temper to flare. She kept the knife with her, and when she saw him slamming the truck against Joey's scalp, she let the boiling blood and rage take her down with them. The blade went in hard, and she thought it would break when it hit bone. But she twisted it until Frank dropped the dump truck, and then she scraped it down like she was deboning a chicken.

All for Joey.

She lifted him in her arms as she stepped off the train, careful on the concrete because there was still some ice. Joey, wrapped in a blanket, sunglasses on his face, "sleeping," she told the nice lady who had been sitting across from them; Ellen, also wearing sunglasses and too much make-up, a scarf around her head, a heavy wool sweater around her shoulders, exhausted and determined.

Joey's not dead. Not really.

It hadn't been hard to track down the Neesons. She had called them before she got on the train, and they were not surprised to hear from her. "It happens this way," Mama Neeson told her, "our calling."

Ellen was not sure what to make of that comment, but she was so tired and confused that she let it go. Later, she might think that something of the Neesons' had perhaps rubbed off on her and her son. That, perhaps, just *meeting* them might be like inviting something into life that hadn't been considered before. *Something under your fingernails.*

She carried Joey to the payphone and dropped a quarter in. Joey was not waking up. She did not have to cry anymore. She told herself that, and was comforted. Things change, people move on, but some things could stay as they were. Good things.

"Mr. Neeson?"

"You're here already?" he asked. He sounded relieved.

"I took an early train."

"Mama's still asleep. She was up all night. Worries, you know. Upset for you."

"Well . . ."

"I'll be down there in a few minutes, then," he said, adding, "you're sure this is what you want?"

"Love beyond choosing," she reminded him. A spool of white thread fell out from Joey's curled hands, bouncing once, twice, on the ground, unraveling as it rolled.

Who Walks at Night

John Maclay

It was six months ago, about the time I turned forty, that I began to have the dreams.

I didn't really want them, or need them. You see, life had been pretty good to me, and I liked to think I'd already fulfilled a lot of the dreams I'd had when I started out. My own business, for example—I'd built it from a one-man operation to four locations and two dozen employees. A family—Mark and Judy were doing well in high school, and Ann was still the slim, attractive girl I'd married twenty years before. And the comforts—my big Colonial in a good suburb, my Mercedes, my country club.

All of this I had. But apparently, it wasn't enough. There was, I guess, some need in me that hadn't been met, some hidden, rebellious thing. Because . . .

The first dreams were innocent enough. In them, even though I'd spent a busy day before dropping off to sleep, I'd be working—back in the old times, when things weren't so sure. On the street, in my cheap suit, making deals, feeling great when I succeeded. Returning home to

Ann in the small apartment, and telling her about it. Then going out again the next morning, the whole world looking bright and free.

I was able to enjoy these dreams, to think of them as my mind's way of keeping things fresh for me, keeping the edge on. But about the next ones, I wasn't so sure. You see, Ann and I still had a great thing going, even in bed, and . . .

I'd be chasing nubile young women in my head, like Dagwood in the old cartoon strip. Or getting it on with girls I'd known years before, as I hadn't quite, not then. Or even meeting strange women under street-lights downtown, and going with them to cheap hotel rooms for nights of rough, coarse sex. And, though I'd apparently sleep peacefully through it — I'd ask Ann the next morning — it seemed so real.

So real — like the deal-making dreams, too, I was forced to admit — that I began to wonder if I wasn't losing my mind. That I even began to search my memory to try to find out if I had, recently, done some old-fashioned business, or taken up with some ladies of the night — and forgotten it; perhaps these were memories, instead of dreams.

Then one Saturday morning, after some particularly vivid ones, I laid it all out for Ann. Yet when I'd finished, she just gave me a big hug.

"You're all right, tiger," she said, nuzzling me. "You're just getting to be an *older*, furry tiger. Who wants to know he's still with it, in all departments. Well, let me tell you," she finished, holding me even tighter, "you are."

"I suppose you're right," I said. But I wasn't so sure.

And that night I had the first unsettling one.

. . . I was downtown again, but it was different. Where in the other dreams I'd been more or less myself, now I was something else. Rough clothes, a tough walk — but above all, a *feeling*, of being out, of being alienated from the tall glass buildings, the well-dressed people I passed. And yet, of being at home in this night-world, as they were not — and as such, drawing from it the primitive strength to fight back.

I went — in the dream — into a little, sleazy bar on a side street, and ordered a beer, reaching into my jeans to pull out a crumpled dollar bill and pay for it. Then, like the calculating animal I was, I looked around — and my eyes settled on *them*. The young couple, obviously slumming; the woman tall, winsome, the man orderly, well-dressed — as I'd been. I turned away, and for a long time, feigning disinterest, just sipped at my beer. But then it was time. Because — they were getting up to go.

Outside in the cool air I followed them, slipping in and out of door-ways with practiced skill. And when the right moment came — when there was no one else around and I was sure the young pair hadn't noticed me — I *sprang*.

"Gimme your money," I hissed, grabbing the woman around the

566

throat and laying the knife—where had it come from?—under her breast.

The man turned white, knees visibly buckling. "Yes . . . yes . . . don't . . . hurt!" he forced out, fumbling in his pocket and throwing his wallet down. But the woman, paralyzed by fear, still held on to her purse.

"Drop it!" I grunted into her ear, pulling her closer and poking her with the knife, feeling her firm behind against me. She let out a long sigh, and did.

Then it was time to *move*. Like a cat, I scrambled, scooping up their stuff from the sidewalk as I waved the knife in the air, then bounding off smoothly, noiselessly, always avoiding the light, seeking the shadows that were my home. And after only a few blocks I was already safe, the contents of their pocketbooks—the two hundred-odd dollars in cash, the salable credit cards—processed efficiently, as I ran, into my faded jacket, and the rest thrown away.

As I caught my breath in a doorway, I smiled—at how easy it had been; the man's weak cry of "Police!" a moment after I'd disappeared had seemed to hang, feeble and mocking, in the night air. And I also remembered—how the young woman's body had felt on mine. *If I'd tried,* I thought triumphantly—*he couldn't have done a goddam thing.*

. . . In the morning, Ann said I looked tired—as if I'd had a rough night. But though I may have been tired, I went through the whole day—the small administrative details of my business—easily and cheerfully. And with, I know, not a bit of embarrassment or shame—because, you see, I'd remembered the whole dream, its reality—but with *anticipation*. And that night . . . I went to bed early.

. . . It was continued, as I'd hoped it would be. The next night, too— but as my other self. As I walked through the city, I recalled with satisfaction the fencing of the stolen credit cards—*deals*, my "real" self reflected—and the two first-rate meals I'd had, with all the extra cash. The haircut and shave—and, as I looked down, the new shoes, with thick soles that would make my footsteps even more soundless. Also—it felt so good, so beautiful in my pocket—the *gun*.

Now I was entering the show bar, with its soft lights, its half-clad women on the stage. Flush, this time, with new-found wealth—no longer consigned to sit at the bar, nurse a beer, and fantasize, but able to walk right up to the tall, full-figured one I'd ached for, flash a fifty-dollar bill, and wait for her to come with me. To the cheap hotel room I'd rented— in which, after I'd enjoyed her body thoroughly, I collapsed into the best sleep I'd known in weeks.

. . . "Gee, tiger, you were restless!"—Anne's voice, the next morn- ing, after I'd risen, almost in a trance. I waited for her next words, half-fearing what they would be. "I even thought . . . you got up, walked around. Though you were still . . ." But as I dressed, and set off on my routine, waking day, her words strangely didn't bother me—because they were only a confirmation of what I'd begun to believe was true.

. . . The next night—when I *awoke*—it was twilight. I remember wondering about time frames—how it was always night, when I "slept," yet could be other times of day, in the "dreams." But it didn't really matter, because again I was there, I was *him*. Walking the downtown street, inconspicuous, unnoticed by the people going home from their office jobs. But with something, I quickly sensed, inside me—a thing planned out with animal cunning, a thing which accounted for the nervous anticipation, yet powerful exhilaration, I felt now. Something new, something *big*. And as I went, apparently, to my destination, any guilt, any repression I may have felt—*I* may have felt, my "other" self was able to reflect—was finally gone. Because I was ready for the win. The kill.

The plate-glass window, on the side street, said "LOANS"—I recognized it at once, as if I had passed it, even checked it out, the office inside, several times before. I would have, I knew. So now all I had to do was simple. Put my hand on the brass latch on the door, open it, go in. Turn the bolt with a flick of the wrist, lock the door behind me. Reach for the long cord, drop the venetian blind over the big window. Sealing myself—and *them*—inside my rampant ego, my wonderfully criminal mind.

Triumphantly, I pulled out the gun.

"Don't. Move." I said, as if I were in a gangster movie—but it was real. And I took a moment to look at them—as they stood frozen, trembling, blank expressions on their faces—the balding manager in a gray suit, the young accountant in shirtsleeves . . . and the girl, the young, slender thing in the soft, form-fitting dress.

And suddenly, diabolically, the dreams came together.

It was with a wonderful power that I walked around the counter and grabbed her—my arm around her breasts, the other hand poking the gun in her ribs—and made my ultimate deal.

"All the money," I ordered, "in a bag. Or else!"

The old and the young man complied, moving around the office shakily, stumbling over things in their terrified haste. But at length they had it ready.

"H-here," the manager gasped, handing it to me. "Now . . . please g-go!"

But it was then . . . that I smiled again. "Not yet," I said. "You see, I *lied*." And with the two men watching in horror, lifted the woman's dress, and—

. . . I was struggling to awake, in my own bed at home; struggling to escape, once and for all, this thing that had happened to me—and which had now assumed such devastating proportions, which I knew at last I didn't want. And finally, as I became conscious of myself—my real self, I hoped to God—lying there in a sweat, I made it back.

But the next morning, Ann looked at me strangely.

"Golly, honey!" she called from the bathroom as I dragged myself, physically and mentally exhausted, out of bed. "You did have a dream last night. And when I reached over to wake you—I thought . . . you were *gone*."

I tried to dismiss it; I really did. Went calmly out to work; got through my day with what, as I finally read about four o'clock in the eyes of my secretary, was an insane calm. One in which I was trying, and failing, to tell myself that I couldn't have lived my nightmare. Couldn't have really . . . moved outside my body . . . and done what I did. But I finally knew that it was all a pose—and so, with an unreal smile—a condemned man's smile, I thought sickly—I drove home.

Knowing—as I took one last look at the bright day, at sweet reality—exactly what I'd find.

There was only one police cruiser parked in front of the house—I'd expected more.

"Honey!" Ann said at the door, her face strained—and I eternally regretted that this thing, this anomaly, wherever in the world it had come from, had had to involve her. "These officers—they want to know—"

The policemen were young, crisply dressed, and obviously ill at ease at having had to come here, to this unlikely setting. But, to their credit, they had the facts.

"Descriptions," one of them mumbled, over the banal coffee Ann had apparently given them. "Must be some mistake, but—you'll have to come with us."

And in the line-up downtown, as I smiled my now-frozen smile, they faced me—the trendy couple from the bar, the ones from the loan office, the women . . . and a few more I hadn't even remembered.

Nodding in damning, righteous agreement.

"That's the man!"

The Winter Ghosts

Tanith Lee

Winter is a ghost that haunts the world. You know it by its grey transparencies, its crystalline white comings and goings.

It was early in the winter that I went to the town to see about some business for my Father, and was told I must call in on my Aunt. I resisted. "She has been good to you, young man," they said. She had paid for my education, and other things. My life was full of obligations, it seemed to me, and nowhere was I free to do what I wanted. I had been the slave of my school, and now was my Father's, working in his shop, where I did not want to be, and trapped in the village of my birth. I had seen and done nothing. But there again, what would I have chosen to do? I had no great driving talents. I liked to read and to lie a-bed, for either of which occupations there was now slight time. Every day I was up at dawn, for on Sunday I must go to church to show my respect to God. At night I ate my supper and fell between my sheets exhausted. What a life. The town and the prospect of visiting it had cheered me a little, despite the winter road and the stubborn old horse, the wayside packed by forest, starving beggars who seemed to signal from every glassy bush, according to rumour, and the first waves of wolves that I hated and feared along with everyone else. But now my sojourn in the town was to be divided between my Father's commission and my Aunt's fancy. It was decided; I was not to stay overnight at the inn, but at my Aunt's house. My heart sank into the floor, it stayed there, and I left it behind.

The ride was not too bad. A faint flurry of snow disturbed the horse, who for a mile kept stopping and shaking his head distractedly. I saw no beggars, and no wolves, though once I heard one howling. I arrived at the town gates before the sun set on a grey thick sky. I should proceed at once to the Aunt's, attending to my Father's wants in the morning.

I had not seen either the town or the Aunt since childhood. Both had been different then, more interesting to me. I had half anticipated some sense of purpose or festivity in the town, and there was none I could perceive, the shops blinkered, the populace running homeward before the cold. Hardly a soul on the streets. The inn looked welcoming with its gold and red sign, but now I was not going there.

What did I remember of the Aunt?

She had been slender and excitable, with a high hot colour in her cheeks. Her dark hair was drawn up with combs, and curled. She wore a dark red gown and was dancing, for it had been a festival—hence my anticipations—memories—of the town.

As a child I had liked her, but she had paid me very slight attention. Her own father was alive then, and had she not been engaged to be married? There was some tragedy or scandal never spoken of to me. Her money had come to her with the town house, at my Grandfather's death; my Father benefitted in other ways. My Aunt was then alone in the world. Having no one on whom to squander the excess of her small riches, she made provision for me and my two sisters. In me a less grateful wretch she could not have hoped to find. Far better I had liked the little drummer doll with his bells, the first gift she gave me indifferently at the festival. That was fifteen years ago. She would be old now, for she was not young then.

I reached her house, which stood to the side just off from the square. Ancient black trees, already edged with snow, occluded its walls. The shutters were fastened, and not a light showed. The house might have been deserted, the impression it gave. I dismounted, secured my horse, and tried the cumbersome knocker.

I had knocked some six or seven times before I got any answer. And then to my surprise it was the Aunt who had come to the door and opened it.

"Old Ermine died," said she, standing in the dim hall which just barely fluttered at her lamp. "Now I'm my own maid. My own housekeeper, too. You mustn't expect too much," she added, as if we had been speaking for an hour. It seemed she knew me, for who else but the looked-for nephew would call on her? Nevertheless I introduced myself politely, and then she extended her dry powdered cheek for my kiss. She was indeed as aged as I had feared, a skinny old woman in a wrinkled reddish dress, with eardrops of dull pearl which perhaps she had put on to honour my advent. She wore no rings, but her hands had been mutilated by rheumatism. She led me in.

It transpired there was still an antiquated man, Pers, she called him, who would see to my horse, as he saw to the fire in the parlour, and other manly work. I caught a glimpse of him, about a hundred he looked, but the horse was getting on too, they would be patient with each other.

The parlour was like home: crowded by slabs of the furniture which was all I knew, and that spelled affluence, and entrapment, had I given them names. Crystal and china, perhaps never used, bulged upon a wooden mountain, dully catching the firelight through their dust. The fire was a poor one—what else could you expect of Pers?

"Will you take some tea?"

I doubted there was a drop of spirit in the house, and felt a very real and unjust anger at her, my Aunt, forcing me here to this cage, uncomfortably not equipped to please me in the least.

We had tea, and some thin jam, and she told me I should not smoke, not in the rooms. I had guessed and not tried—truth to tell, I was not much of a smoker, though it was expected in a man, a sort of condoned vice.

By now it was night, these unshuttered back windows very black beyond the rusty curtains. In the town a few panes were alight, but they looked dim and parsimonious. My Aunt had lit two lamps, these windows of hers would have that look.

I forget properly what we spoke of. There were long silences; what could she expect? She asked me of my work, which I disliked, of my school, which she had provided and I hated. She asked of my uninteresting family, and my sisters one of whom was now married to a fat bumpkin very suitable to her.

Finally, in a sort of sneering pity, I said, "I remember you dancing in a red dress. You gave me a doll with bells. I was very young."

"Ah, that was another time." She added, obscurely, "Another woman."

Later we went into the dining room. And I had my first shock.

The long old table was hung with a lace cloth over mulberry velvet, and meticulously laid with china and a silver service. There were ten places, each fully set.

"I thought we dined alone, Aunt?"

"I never dine alone. But then again, you will see no one besides me. I, of course . . . I see them all. In my imagination, you understand."

Pers brought in the dishes, there were only three; they had come from an obliging cook shop, heated up in the kitchen below, but not sufficiently. Water was served with the meal. Very proper.

I was interested to see Pers pass every plate from the eight other settings. On to each was placed by my Aunt a tiny portion of the frugal meal. Pers filled each goblet from the water jug. I looked on, and tried to picture ghostly fingers raising the glasses, invisible hands plying the knives and forks. Pers left us.

"Who is here, Aunt? Won't you tell me?" I inquired, because I was so very bored, a leadenness had stayed with me compounded of snow, tiredness, inertia. Besides, how could her secret guests be a hidden matter when she paraded them?

But she was reticent.

"People of my past."

"Is Grandfather there?"

"Grandfather? Of course. It is a family table. He is at the table's head."

"Your fiancé, too?"

But she lowered her scaly eyes and would not answer. I had been indecorous, probably.

"Why did you never marry, Aunt?" I demanded brutally.

"It was a long time ago."

"I recall everything well. I recall the man—" I did not—"dancing with you downstairs."

"No, no," she said.

But I was irked enough that I did not allow her any rights to pain. She had interfered in my life, it seemed to me, and made things worse. She had forced me here when I might have drunk brandy at the inn. "Surely you can tell me? I've only heard stories of it—"

"What stories?"

"That he jilted you. Left you almost at the altar—"

"Oh the liars! Who said this?" She was inflamed now, surprising me a little.

"Servants—an old nurse I had—"

"None of it is true. He died. He wasn't young. His health wasn't good. The excitement . . . He took a chill and was dead in a week."

There was the longest silence yet.

"But you see him here tonight?" I even shocked myself at my grossness. Perhaps the water had made me drunk, I was used to a glass of wine at home.

At last she spoke to me. "Yes. I see them all. I invite them here. Why shouldn't you know? My father, my betrothed. My mother takes her place. And my mother's two sisters. Then there is my girlhood friend I see, there. She died so young. She is the youngest among us. And there is my tutor, whom I feared and loved, and who darts me terrible stern glances, because he thinks I have forgotten my lessons. And he's right in that, for I have. And old Ermine is with us too, now. I included her a month after her death, for she required her rest before that . . ."

A nasty but interesting idea came over me that I could see them after all. The Grandfather as I recalled him with his fob watch and high collar, the invented mother I had never myself witnessed and her aged crone sisters in their black and lace and old-fashioned hair. The young friend caught fast forever—perhaps she did not mind—I put her in an antique gown. The mature bridegroom, coughing a touch at his handkerchief. The elderly tutor. And old Ermine, that once or twice I had really seen, for she had been mercilessly sent to the village on my Aunt's errands when only a trace younger. I guessed Ermine was content, to sit at last at her mistress's table, even to the tepid meat and water.

"Pray don't let me prevent you," I said, "conversing with them all, if that's how you usually go on."

"You think me very eccentric," said my Aunt. "But those who are dear to me—those for whom I have a responsibility. What else should I do?"

As she had put me through the school, just so she kept these by her, these withered flowers, her ghostly dinner guests. Forever, or until her death, and—why not?—maybe beyond her death, they would sit nightly at this drab table, eat the unpalatable food—I was becoming as foolish as she.

"Well you must do as you think fit, Aunt. And now I thank you for this meal, but ask you to excuse me if I go presently to bed. The long ride tired me greatly, I'm up so early, and must be off early tomorrow, I fear, on my Father's commission."

She was startled a moment, then settled down. The old are early to bed also, she told me, she did not keep late hours. But I must take a cup of tea with her in the parlour, to cheer me for my couch. Out of the kindness of my unkind heart I consented. I spent one further hour with her before escaping to the dusty dark room aloft. There in the great bed, by the poor light of one thin candle, I had meant to read a smuggled book. But my own bane of tiredness came in on me. Soon the lines swam and I blew out the candle and yawned myself to oblivion.

There I dreamed of being a prisoner in my Aunt's house. I could not get out, and was in the act of bribing Pers to open a tiny door in the cellar for me—I think it did not in real life exist—when I woke. It was a milky dawn, and the fine snow blowing, and I had my Father's business to transact before I could start out on my ride home.

My Aunt was not yet risen, so I left my message of gratitude and farewell with Pers.

The business took up half the morning, and when it was done, I gathered myself to the inn and there on top of the bread and stale tea of my hasty breakfast, I put in three brandies against the rigours of the ride home, which truth to tell I was now dreading. I had a sort of presentiment of ill luck, which my drinking the brandy had, rather than dispelling it, brought closer.

Shortly after midday, though it looked more like dusk, I left the town, and the staid old horse and I went down the road, and in among the great stands of the forest.

The snow had stopped, and a freezing was coming on, you felt it approach like a stealthy noise. Now and then a branch cracked in the forest at the cold, but there was no other sound save for the plodding of the horse. A faint smoke hung once in the distance from some charcoal burners. Otherwise there was no hint of any human creature. I might have been alone in the woods at the world's edge out of a legend. And this thought oppressed me, even as I began to have a quite incompatible fear of robbers.

Robbers there were, but not of the mortal type. About an hour after I had got beyond the town, when my home in my Father's house, so despised, had begun to seem to me the dearest place on earth, a small pack of wolves started to follow me.

Despite all that is said, and agreed, on wolves, they are in fact not so much of a foe to a mounted man. But I feared them and disliked them in company with anyone I could think of. My childhood had been spiced by the tales of other children the wolves had carried off and eaten, and only a dead wolf was a pleasure to see, as occasionally I had.

Their eyes were the worst, for their shapes, loping along a few yards behind me, were almost lost in the trees. But out of the afternoon dusk now and then would come a green flash, or I would see an actual eye, fastened on me with a malevolent unique intensity.

I tried a sharp shout or two, which gave them doubts, but then on they loped again. I was the only moving thing of any size for miles. They were curious, and they were hungry.

How I longed for a joint of raw meat I might have brought to throw to them, how I longed to have drunk more, or less. Or that the old horse might have been pricked to a gallop. But my attempts to hurry him presently confused him—he did not like the wolves either, but was inclined more to congeal to stasis and shiver than to hasten off.

Perhaps they would get tired of me, and let me be.

They did not.

About midafternoon, when I had been followed a good hour, the old horse managed a brief canter, hit us into a low-slung bough that brought snow down on me, and stumbled. Between the bough and the stumble I went out of the saddle and slithered to the ground. As I lay there stunned, the horse, relieved of my slowing weight, gave me a bright whinny, and fled along the road.

I sat up before I was ready, and my head rang. Then I tried to get to my feet and slipped full length again. And then the wolves, there were five of them, came out of the trees and onto the road.

They stood looking at me, and vividly do I recollect their lean black shapes against the snow, each one exactly resembling the model of the others, as if all had been cast from a single mould of wickedness. Their eyes were like the eyes of cruel men, intent and hypnotic, yellow as flames. Was any one less than the others? An entity they were, one thing, and all gazing upon me. I despaired.

In that moment I imagined myself at the gate of death. And this is what I saw: First the terrible rending agony of being eaten alive, and then the mildewed pit of the dead, from which a faint drear voice was

575

calling me. "Come, dear nephew," it said, "sit down. I've laid a place for you."

And out of the teeth of wolves and shadows of the grave I emerged into that cold dining room with its table of mulberry and lace, and sat myself before a setting of dusty china and silver. To my right was an ugly young girl in an outdated gown, and to my left a balding scholar in a shabby coat. All around were old ladies with piled up fake curls, and a coughing man of sixty, and my Grandfather consulting his watch, for I had come late and kept them waiting. And there, opposite his place, sat my Aunt in her red dress and eardrops, nodding and smiling at me, as she helped me to a bobble of cold steamed food, and Pers filled my glass with water—

"No!" I cried, "you shan't!"

And I flung myself forward at the wolves. I was shouting and roaring, and out of my pocket I had taken my wooden matches, which I struck in panic and nearly set myself alight.

Perhaps it was these brief gusts of fire, or the awful noises I made, and which I myself heard as if from a great distance, but the foremost wolf backed off. As I rushed screaming down at them, all five turned sideways into the bushes, and bolted suddenly away from me between the trees.

They were gone.

For some minutes I remained, yelling and stamping, jumping up and down in the snow, while burnt matches stuck to my burnt fingers and the hole I had fired in my sleeve.

I recall I howled I would not go, I would not be caught forever, for eternity, in that smothering. No, not I.

When I came back to my wits, no hint of the wolves lingered. A vast emptiness was there, and I was blazing hot inside the great orb of the cold. I went down the road for something to do, and found the horse loitering at the wayside a quarter mile off.

I mounted him in silence, and he walked on.

Who would believe me? I have heard since of men frightening off wolf packs with loud cries and curious behaviour, but that was in other lands, and at another time. For then I knew only I had not been brave and had best keep quiet. More than their eyes and teeth I had feared the dinner table of my Aunt: I did not want to be another of her winter ghosts. It was that cowardice which made me turn against the wolves, and, seven months later, the same cowardice which made me run away for good to another less safe, stranger, and more ordinary life.

Wish Hound

Pat Murphy

Alice hugged Tommy at the bottom of the plane's ramp, but the boy did not set down the case he carried to return his mother's embrace. When she released him, the case shifted in his grasp as if something moved within, and Alice heard a muffled whimper through the cardboard.

Tommy, solid and self-assured even at age seven, watched her with steady blue eyes. "Dad gave me a dog," he said. "It's not a very big one."

Alice opened her mouth to speak, but stopped herself—the words she wanted to say were meant for Paul, her former husband, not for Tommy. Paul had taken the boy to his ranch for three weeks immediately following Alice's remarriage. He had promised to keep Tommy while Alice and her new husband, Joseph, traveled in England, a trip that they had been planning for almost a year. But when Paul was called away from the ranch on a business trip that would last several weeks, he had shipped the boy back to Alice.

Goddamn Paul, Alice thought with cold anger. He knows that I live in a city apartment, he knows that we are leaving for England soon—and not content with burdening me with a seven-year-old on my honeymoon, he tries to buy the kid's affections with a puppy. Goddamn him.

Alice waited until they got to the apartment, where Joseph was, before tackling the question of what would be done with the puppy. "We can't keep the puppy here, you understand that, don't you?" Alice held Tommy by the arm and tried to speak gently. The apartment seemed too full. With her and Joseph, it had been a comfortable size.

She had missed the boy when he left for his father's ranch, but at last she had had time for Joseph, a patient lover and now a husband. At last she had been able to sleep late with him on weekend mornings without being awakened by the sound of a knock at the door, to stay out late without worrying about the sitter, to putter about the kitchen, cooking dolmas, wonton soup, baklava, and other foods she had never tried to make before, wearing Joseph's robe because she liked its faint aroma of tobacco and aftershave until Joseph complained that it was starting to smell of her perfume.

Tommy looked at the small black dog that wiggled in his arms, trying to lick his face, and did not reply. The puppy whined, then twisted in his grasp, growled a tiny growl, and strove to attack Alice's hand with sharp new teeth.

"Your father should have known better than to give him to you," she said. "Joseph is allergic to animal hair." The boy shot Joseph a look of intense dislike, and Alice continued hurriedly. "Even if it weren't for that, we couldn't take him to England with us."

"I don't want to go to England," Tommy said. "I want to go back to the ranch. I hate England."

"That's silly. You haven't seen England yet. You might like it." Alice strove to be positive.

"I'll hate it." Tommy stood steadfast in the center of the room, puppy in his arms, his face set in a stubborn expression.

For the next week, Alice tried to give the puppy away—to friends, to relatives, to co-workers at the advertising agency where she was receptionist. No one wanted a puppy of uncertain breeding. And no one wanted to babysit a seven-year-old for a month. Tommy's aunt was planning on having house guests. His grandmother would be vacationing in Bermuda. The old lady who sat for Alice on weekends was leaving town.

"It's all right," Joseph said when she told him that Tommy would have to accompany them. "Tommy and I have to learn to get along sooner or later." Joseph was an accepting man; a history professor, he seemed to have adapted his spirit to the lessons of history. He was willing to compromise, to allow events to take their natural time.

Tommy was less accepting when she explained again why the dog had to go, why he could not keep it. He watched her with sullen eyes. Finally, on the last day before they were scheduled to leave, she asked Joseph to take the puppy to the pound while she fixed a bon-voyage dinner for the three of them.

The boy did not cry when Alice put the puppy in the carrying case and handed the case to Joseph to take to the pound. He set his jaw in a way that reminded her of Paul.

After Joseph left with the puppy, Alice stood in the doorway of the living room, where Tommy lay on his stomach, his head propped up on his hands, watching TV. The TV movie was an old Sherlock Holmes story—the *Hound of the Baskervilles*. On the screen, Basil Rathbone paced and smoked his pipe with enormous intensity, discussing the spectral hound with Watson.

"You want to go out to the park, Tommy?" Alice asked. "We could go to the playground."

Without looking around, Tommy shook his head in firm denial.

"We could go out and get some ice cream for dessert tonight. You can pick the flavor."

Again, a silent headshake. Alice retreated to the kitchen, unwilling to force Tommy to share his pain with her. While she chopped vegetables for dinner, she tried to ignore the baying of a hound on the TV.

That night, as she lay awake in bed, she told Joseph, "I'd feel so much better about all this if I thought Tommy understood that there's nothing we can do. He seems to blame you for dragging him away from his father's ranch and for this business about the dog. I just wish I could make him understand."

Joseph put his arm around her. "You're trying to treat him like a small adult and he's not. Kids aren't human. The way a kid feels about things doesn't necessarily make sense—it just is."

"I'm trying to be a good mother." She snuggled closer to him in bed. "You just don't understand him like I do, Joseph. He and I are alike in a lot of ways. But I just wish he could see that having to get rid of the puppy wasn't your fault. The whole thing was his father's fault."

"Well, it isn't really his fault either, is it?" Joseph asked. "He couldn't help having a business deal come up."

Alice kissed Joseph's cheek. "Don't waste your time trying to be fair to him, Joseph. You don't know him like I do. He always put his business before his family. Always."

A shadow of a frown, visible in the faint moonlight that shone through the window, crossed Joseph's face. "You really dislike him, don't you?"

"Hate is the word." Her voice was low but steady. "I save dislike for strangers. I only really hate people I used to love."

"Makes sense, I suppose." Joseph stroked her hair away from her eyes, then hesitated. "The kid's a lot like Paul, isn't he?"

"He's a lot like me, too." She used his shoulder as a pillow and settled down to sleep. "I'll try not to worry about Tommy. There's nothing to be done about it all anyway. And maybe he'll like England."

Tommy hated England. He hated London—complaining loudly in museums so that guards stared indignantly at the family, chasing pigeons in Trafalgar Square so that the old people who fed them scowled in annoyance. He got lost for three hours in Hyde Park and they finally found him talking to an organ grinder with a dancing poodle. He talked to people with dogs and to dogs themselves, but he did his best to ignore both Joseph and Alice except when he was complaining. He moped when they went to the theater without him, but complained that it was boring when they took him with them.

A guidebook to eastern England that Joseph purchased in a bookstore on Charing Cross (while Alice held the hand of an angry child to keep him from ransacking the shelves) suggested a small coastal resort community as an ideal vacation spot for families on tour. As a desperate move, they took the train from London to the coast, and found a bed-and-breakfast place in the little seaside town.

On the first day in the village, Joseph wanted to visit a small church on the edge of town that the guidebook had described. Under protest, Tommy accompanied them. He sulked on the walk through the village, kicking rocks into the gutter, stepping on and off the curb, dawdling at corners.

"Come on, Tommy, let's move it," Alice said, looking back at him.

"I don't want to see a stupid church," he complained. "I don't want to go at all."

"Come on, Tommy, don't make me angry." Alice turned back to Joseph frowning.

"Just keep walking," Joseph advised softly. "He'll realize that we're leaving him behind and he'll hurry to catch up." Joseph gently placed an arm around her shoulders. "And try to relax."

Alice smiled up at him. Having his arm around her reminded her of the idyllic time they had spent together. "You're so understanding," she murmured. "I'll try to relax. I just . . . I wish Tommy liked you better."

He shrugged. "We get along all right. Sure, it's a little tense, but that's only natural. He's a little jealous, that's all."

Alice looked back when they reached the end of the second block and Tommy was nowhere in sight. She shook her head in disgust. "Where could he have gone?"

They found him a block and a half back, a long enough distance for Alice to forget her resolve to be calm. Tommy was patting a Yorkshire terrier that he had found sleeping in the shade of a fish and chips stand. "He likes me," Tommy said, looking up at Alice. "But he's not as smart as my dog."

"You don't have a dog, Tommy," Alice snapped. "The puppy's at the pound. Now come on." She took the boy's hand and marched him along the village street toward the church. Joseph followed a step behind on the other side of the angry mother.

At the church, Tommy stopped at the door. "I want to go play over there," he said. "I don't want to go inside."

Alice fought the urge to hustle the boy inside as a punishment, guessing that it would be as much a punishment for her as for him. "Where do you want to play?" she asked sternly.

"Right over there." Tommy pointed over the low stone wall that separated the churchyard from the road. They had left the village behind, and the land sloped away from the road in pastureland, covered with clumps of scrubby grass and wildflowers. Beside the church, a wrought-iron fence overgrown with rose bushes divided an area of land from the rest of the pasture.

Alice nodded. "All right. Don't go any farther than that fence."

She released his hand with a feeling of relief and linked arms with Joseph once again. Inside the church, the air was cold and smelled faintly of damp stone and incense. Alice shivered and Joseph draped his jacket over her shoulders. Gratefully, she pulled it on, and smiled at him. "I've been wearing this as much as you have."

He grinned back. "It's the only thing that makes me indispensable. You'd freeze to death without me."

She took his hand. "Not the only thing."

As the guidebook had promised, the church was tiny, but the stained-glass windows were magnificent, far more elaborate than any they had seen in London's cathedrals. And for a change, no complaining child dragged on Alice's hand.

Joseph peered out through a low window that looked out onto the pastureland and reassured Alice that they could relax. "The kid looks happy enough. He's found himself a dog to play with."

Alice looked out. Tommy stood by the wrought-iron fence and as she watched, he hurled a stick high in the air. A black shadow, almost the size of the boy, bounded from the shade of the rose bushes and leaped after the stick. "Yeah, he looks happy."

So they took their time admiring the windows. Joseph read from the guidebook in the hushed tones that seemed appropriate for the quiet church, and they admired the carved pews, the altar stone, the crucifix from which Christ stared down with a sad expression. Even then, Alice lingered, reluctant to return to the outside world.

When at last they stepped back into the sunshine, Alice saw Tommy standing alone by the wrought-iron fence. "I guess the dog's master came and got it," Joseph remarked as they walked along the flagstones to the fenced-off area.

"Look, don't mention dogs around Tommy, will you?" she asked.

"Hey, take it easy." He put his arm around her, stopping her just before they reached the fence. "I won't mention the dog. You've been having a hard time of it, I know." He kissed her, in the sunshine by the fence where the smell of roses filled the air.

When Alice turned her head to lay it against his chest, she saw Tommy watching them, through the mesh of rose branches. Beneath his shock of hair, his blue eyes burned; his small face was distorted by a look of hatred.

"Tommy!" she said, startled by his expression. And the boy's face changed, assuming the sullen look that had become habitual to him. She hesitated, uncertain of what to say. Joseph had said that jealousy was natural, but she had not thought that the boy could hate the man so much. "How did you get in there?"

581

Tommy pointed to a gate in the fence a short distance from them.

"Hey, Tom, I bet you've found all kinds of things to show us," Joseph called. His attempt at joviality was met by a frown, but he led Alice to the gate and they entered the smaller yard. Tombstones—weathered so that names and dates were no longer legible—stood at drunken angles within the bounds of the fence. "It's the old graveyard that the guidebook mentione," Joseph said to Alice. "I'd guess there's a lot to see here."

Alice tried to join in Joseph's attempt to generate enthusiasm without much success. She peered at the headstones and wandered along the edge of the fence, kicking at rocks. In one corner of the fenced yard, she found a small grave, a quarter the size of the others, set apart from the rest by several feet. She pointed it out to Joseph. "Look. I guess it was a child—it's so small."

Joseph glanced inside the book and shook his head. "Nope, it's not a person at all. It's the first grave in the yard, though. Apparently, it's the guardian of the churchyard." He ran his finger down the page. "Says here that they figured that the first one to be buried in a new cemetery had to stand guard over it, so rather than burying a person, they buried ah . . . a dog." He looked at Alice half-apologetically.

"Yeah?" Tommy's face showed signs of interest. "What was the dog supposed to do?"

Joseph looked at Alice and she nodded. "Well, the spirit is called a church grim, and it's supposed to guard the cemetery against wickedness. It says here that the legend of the church grim may be related to the legends of the Wild Hunt—magical hounds that were supposed to roam the moors and chase people who were foolish enough to venture out after dark."

"They chase people like the hound of the Baskervilles did. What do they do if they catch them?" Tommy was still interested.

Joseph shrugged and closed the book. "It doesn't say."

"I'll bet they rip them up." The considering tone in the childish voice made Alice frown. She did not care for the turn the conversation had taken.

"That doesn't sound very nice, Tommy," she admonished him.

"It's okay if it's a wicked person," he argued. "Then it's okay."

Alice let the subject drop and they walked to the heart of the village in the growing twilight. Birds sang in the hedges and wildflowers grew by the side of the road. Tommy seemed happy for a change—he had picked up a stick and was using it to tap out a rhythm on the road as he walked a few paces behind Alice and Joseph. But when Alice looked back, she caught him watching them with a measuring look and she remembered his expression when he saw Joseph kiss her. She linked an arm with Joseph's protectively.

It was not until after they had gone out to dinner, returned to the bed-and-breakfast house, and Alice had put Tommy to bed, that she realized that the jacket she had worn was gone. She tried to remember whether she had worn it on her way back from the church, and she seemed to remember dropping it on a chair by the door in the entry hall of the house, but it was not there. Joseph shrugged when she mentioned it, saying, "If you left it in the churchyard, it'll still be there tomorrow."

"Maybe I dropped it in Tommy's room. I'll check." For some reason, the loss disturbed her.

Tommy's room was empty. His clothes were gone and his pajamas lay in an untidy heap on the floor. The full moon flooded the room with light and suddenly she felt cold. The only place the boy would have gone was back to the graveyard. She remembered the black beast that had leaped from the shadow of the fence and she shivered.

Joseph was already in bed when she returned to the room. She hesitated, then slipped on a sweater. He rolled over in bed to look at her. "Aren't you coming to bed?"

She paused. If he were to know where she was going, he would insist on accompanying her. She realized that it was foolish to worry about the jealousy of a seven-year-old, foolish to hear the wild baying of a hound in the back of her mind. But the jacket was gone and Tommy was gone. And Tommy hated Joseph.

"I'm still a little restless," she said. "I thought I'd go out for a walk before bed."

The crickets that chirped in the hedges lining the road fell silent when she passed. She walked quickly, clutching her sweater tightly around her against the chill night air.

Tommy was like her, she thought as she walked. He had the capacity to hate. Joseph did not understand that—he thought the child would learn to accept him. But Alice had seen the look in Tommy's eyes.

She reached the churchyard and paused by the stone wall. The scent of roses seemed stronger in the darkness than it had in the day. Over the sound of the crickets, she heard another sound—like the click of toenails on flagstones. A cloud had covered the moon and the church and grave-yard lay in darkness.

"Tommy!" Alice called over the wall. "It's time to come home." The crickets were silenced by her voice and she paused, listening to a hush that breathed. She stepped through the gap in the stone wall and fol-lowed the flagstones toward the iron fence. The scent of roses became almost overpowering.

A dark shadow separated itself from the darker shade by the fence, and she could dimly see a black beast with red-rimmed eyes, standing in her path. She froze in the darkness. Remembering advice that Paul had given her long ago, she spoke to the animal quietly and firmly. "I don't know what the hell you are—dog or guardian spirit, but you won't get my husband. I'll protect him."

The beast growled—a deep-throated sound that rose and fell, rose and fell. The animal stepped forward and still she stood frozen, confident that the animal would not attack. She had seen Tommy playing with it in the graveyard.

"I am your master's mother, dog. You are making a mistake."

Then another shadow stepped out from the shade of the fence as the moon came out from behind the cloud. Tommy held in his arms Joseph's jacket, which she had worn so often, the jacket that still carried the scent of her perfume. The moonlight shone on Tommy's eager eyes and she knew that it was no mistake.

The Wrong Way

Chet Williamson

Something was wrong. He thought about it while the announcer jabbered a commercial for aluminum siding and the car traveled another quarter mile down the expressway. And then he had it. The horse had been going in the opposite direction.

For eight years now he had driven this road to work in the morning, and nearly every day he saw that same craggy old man driving a sulky around the dirt track just twenty yards or so from the road. It always made him feel good. He'd heard how the old man had retired from farming, and had refused to sell his property for several hundred thousand dollars to a big corporation. *Good for you*, Trego would think. *They can't buy everything.* And he'd look at the horse and the sulky and the old man, and smile.

But today the horse and the man were going the other way around the track, counterclockwise. Trego couldn't remember a day when they'd done that. He wondered why, and for a minute he let the puzzle take the place of his brooding memory of breakfast, but his thoughts soon drifted back to Mona.

She'd been a bitch that morning—again. The eggs were cold, he'd found shell in one of them, the kid was yelping about something that had happened at kindergarten, and the 7:30 news blaring from the kitchen added nothing to brighten the morning. They'd fought about something, he couldn't remember what or even how it had turned out, so it couldn't have been very important.

The 8:30 news was almost over when he took his exit into town, and he had to listen to some feeble disco concoction as he joined the mob jerking spastically from one red light to the next. After fifteen more minutes, he pulled into the dark concrete hole that was the entrance to the parking garage. He plucked his ticket from the machine and accelerated down the enclosed slope, turning the wheel to the right when he reached the bottom.

Suddenly he slammed the brake pedal to the floor and lurched to a stop. A wall. There was a wall there, where there had always been a turn before. He looked behind him, shaken and confused, and saw the tunnel to the ramp he drove up every morning. But it was on the other side now. He had to take a left to go up it, not a right.

Horns honked impatiently and, grinding the gears, he threw the shift into a quick reverse. He backed up until he was once more parallel with the entry lane, and turned left up the ramp.

He felt totally disoriented. It was the same as it had always been, but the ramp, the spaces, the whole damned garage was going the wrong way, as if he were driving in a mirror image of what he knew to be real. Was it possible they could have rebuilt the whole thing over a weekend? He dismissed the idea as quickly as it had come. But what other explanation could there be?

He pulled into a parking space on the fifth level, grabbed his briefcase, opened the door and climbed out. As he held his thumb on the door button to lock it when it closed, he realized he was closing the right hand door. But he hadn't climbed over the gearshift and he hadn't crossed the passenger seat. He looked inside the car. There on the right side closest to him were the instrument panel and the steering wheel. He touched the wheel as if he didn't expect it to be there, but his fingers met the hard plastic and he knew that it was no dream, no phantom wheel. He pulled away from the car as if from a sleeping monster and pushed the door shut with his foot. Then he picked up the briefcase and went down the garage stairs to the walkway to his building.

It was all right now. The glass windows were on his left, as they should be, the courtyard on his right. There at the end of the pavement were the doors. It was all right, all was as it should be.

But the car, the garage, had he imagined it? He thought perhaps he'd been working too hard. That had to be it, that and his problems with Mona. *I must be more upset than I thought. Seeing things, that's all—maybe get away this weekend without her, that'll fix me up.* He pushed through the door,

585

readying his smile for the receptionist. He turned toward her station, but instead of the girl he saw a bank of five elevators. He stopped, his breath locked in his throat.

"Good morning, Mr. Trego." The voice came from his left, and he turned and looked. There she sat, on the left as he'd entered, the elevators on his right, the opposite of what he knew he'd seen every working day for eight years.

"It's not right . . ." he said softly, like a man in a dream.

"Sir?" She cocked her head and looked at him curiously. *What was wrong with him?* "Nothing . . . nothing." He fumbled inside his coat pocket for his wallet to show his company pass. It wasn't there. Panicked, he stabbed his hand to the other side of his chest.

There it lay in the left inside pocket, a small lump of leather over his heart.

"But I put it on the right . . . I *always* put it on the right."

"Mr. Trego?" Her voice purred soothingly, with studied concern. "Are you all right?"

He swallowed heavily and nodded, taking out the wallet and flipping it open automatically.

"I'll have to see your pass, Mr. Trego."

He looked at the wallet and saw his wife's picture. *No!* With trembling fingers he opened the other side of the three-fold. The pass was there. He showed it to the girl and stumbled unfamiliarly toward the bank of elevators.

Entering one, he pushed "4." The doors closed, but instead of the slight pressure on the soles of the feet that an ascending elevator causes, he felt a slight lift, a buoyant quality, as if he were descending. He looked at the floor lights, expecting to see "B" light up, but instead he saw "2," "3," and "4" blink in rapid succession.

His grip on the briefcase handle was turning his knuckles white as the door slid open. He stood in the car, not knowing whether to step off or to push "1," pray that the car took him to ground level, and run out into the hoped-for sanity of daylight.

But he saw the brushed chrome sign with the "4" on it, and he heard the soft babble of talk around the coffee machine. So he stepped into the hall and let the doors whisper shut behind him.

It was wrong. The coffee machine was to his left, not his right. The hall branched around to the right, not the left. It was all wrong, turned around as if in a funhouse mirror.

He staggered down the hall to his office and pushed open the door. The light was on, and a voice called cheerily, "Morrie! A little late today, aren't you? What's up?"

Al was sitting at Trego's desk. But it wasn't his desk. All of Al's things were on it, and pictures of Al's family were on the walls. Trego stared at the plate on the door. It read: A. M. Burrage. Trego turned slowly and looked at the door of the office across the hall.

It was there: M. L. Trego.

He managed a sick smile and turned back to Burrage, who lost his grin completely when he saw Trego's expression. "Hey, Morrie," he said, "you feel okay?"

Trego nodded, the set smile still in place on his pallid face.

Burrage shook his head. "Forgive me, but you look like hell. You oughta be home in bed, buddy."

"No, no . . ." Trego's voice was like the scraping of sandpaper. "I feel a little funny, but . . . but I'll be okay once I get going."

"Well, if you're sure. . . ." Burrage let himself be cut off by Trego's upraised palm. He sat looking after him as Trego shut the door, and waited until he heard the door of the office across the hall open and close softly. Then he rose, left his office, and walked down the hall to see Mr. Brian, the supervisor.

Five minutes later, Mr. Brian opened the door with Trego's name on it. Trego was sitting behind the desk, his overcoat still on, his face pale, staring dully at the telephone dial.

"Morrie?" Brian said.

Trego lifted his head slowly.

"Morrie? You okay?"

Trego didn't speak, didn't nod.

"Christ, you look awful, Morrie." Brian had his hand on Trego's shoulder. "Now you listen to me—you go home, you hear? We'll get along okay for a day or so without you."

Trego looked uncomprehendingly at Brian's round, concerned face.

"Can you drive all right? Maybe you should call Mona to pick you up." He shoved the phone in front of Trego, who looked at it again.

The numbers were still in reverse order.

"No!" he shouted, so loudly that Brian jumped. "I'll be all right! I can drive!"

"Sure," Brian said gently. "Sure you can. But you be careful. Traffic's still heavy."

"Yes," Trego said as he rose to his feet. "I'll be careful."

He shuffled out of the office and down the hall, leaving his briefcase behind him. Brian watched him leave, his look of concern deepening as he saw Trego pause at the end of the hall, as if uncertain of which way to go.

Twenty minutes later, a stocky man of medium height was ushered into Brian's office. He introduced himself as Lieutenant Hirsch from the city police department. His eyes looked tired.

"Mr. Brian," he began, "you have in your department an employee named Morris L. Trego."

It was a statement, not a question, so Brian merely nodded.

"Has he been in this morning, sir?"

"He has, yes."

"But he's not here now, is he?"

"No, he felt sick and I told him to go home. What's this all about, Lieutenant?"

"Just a few routine questions, sir."

"But why? What's wrong? Has something happened to Trego?"

"No, sir, not to Mr. Trego, no."

Brian's eyes narrowed. "What division or whatever are you with, Lieutenant?"

"I'm sorry, sir. I informed the receptionist and I thought she'd told you. Homicide."

Brian stared at the impassive eyes of the detective. "I think you'd better tell me what this is all about before I answer any more questions, Lieutenant."

Hirsch sighed noncommittally. "Mr. Trego is wanted for questioning in the death of his wife."

Brian suddenly felt dislocated, as if he were watching himself sitting across the desk from Hirsch. "Mona?"

"You knew her?"

"I've met her." Brian didn't know what to say, how to respond. "How—how did it happen? When?"

"This morning. I was just informed of it twenty minutes ago."

"But why do you suspect Trego?"

"The little girl. Their daughter. She's in shock, but she keeps saying her father killed her mother. Evidently the girl locked herself in the bathroom afterwards, stayed there for a while, and finally went across the street to a neighbor's house. The neighbor found Mrs. Trego and called the borough police. They got in touch with us."

Brian's secretary knocked on the door and opened it. "Lieutenant Hirsch? There's a call for you on line one." She closed the door.

Brian pushed a button on the console and handed Hirsch the receiver. Hirsch's end to the conversation was short, mostly grunts and murmurs of assent. He thanked the caller and hung up.

"Station," he told Brian. "Mr. Trego's been found. I'm afraid it's bad news. He's been killed in a traffic accident."

Brian grew pale, and he placed a hand to his forehead. "Goddammit,"

he said, "I shouldn't have let him drive in that condition. It's my fault."
He looked up at Hirsch. "How did it happen?"

"He hit a semi head-on. Killed instantly."

"Head-on?"

"He was heading north in the southbound lanes."

And while a work crew was prying what was left of Trego out of his crushed and splintered car, two policemen waited in the Trego kitchen for the county medical examiner, as did Mrs. Trego, her eyes and mouth agape, her neck bruised and clawed, her vertebrae snapped, and her head turned completely around on her shoulders.

Acknowledgments

Grateful acknowledgment is made to the following for permission to publish their copyrighted material.

"3.47 A.M." by David Langford. Copyright © 1983 by David Langford. Reprinted by permission of the author.

"Angry Man" by Darrell Schweitzer. Copyright © 1990 by FEAR Ltd. and John Gilbert. Reprinted by permission of the author.

"Another House, Another Home" by Bruce Boston. Copyright © 1987 by Bruce Boston. Reprinted by permission of the author.

"The Back of the Mirror" by Hugh B. Cave. Copyright © 1987 by Artimus Publications. Reprinted by permission of the author.

"Blood Ghost" by John Helfers. Copyright © 1996 by John Helfers. Reprinted by permission of the author.

"The Cage" by Ray Russell. Copyright © 1959 by Ray Russell. Reprinted by permission of the author.

"The Cat-Woman" by Mary Elizabeth Counselman. Copyright © 1933 by Popular Fiction Publication Company. Reprinted by permission of Weird Tales Ltd.

"The Champion" by Richard Laymon. Copyright © 1978 by Richard Laymon. Reprinted by permission of the author.

"The Clown" by Jessica Amanda Salmonsen. Copyright © 1977, 1986 by Jessica Amanda Salmonsen. Reprinted by permission of the author.

"The Cocomacaque" by Carl Jacobi. Copyright © 1970 by August Derleth; copyright © 1972 by Carl Jacobi. Reprinted by permission of the author and the author's agent, R. Dixon Smith.

594